The Last of Days

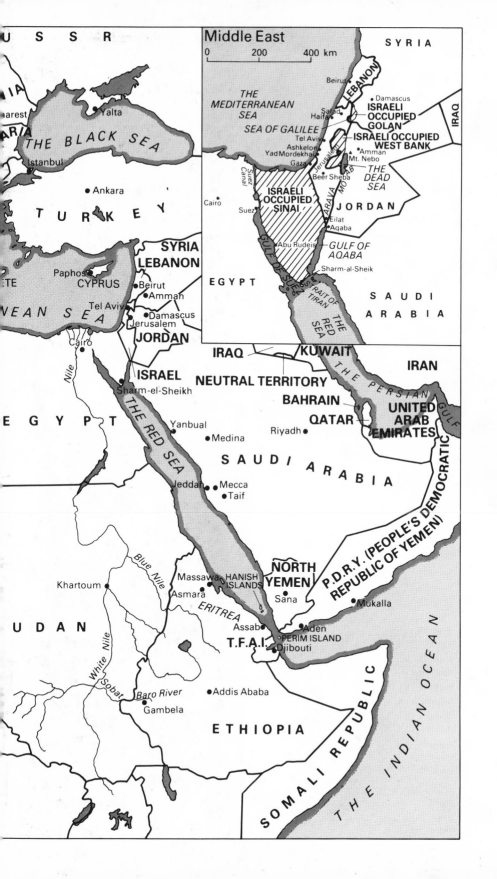

The Last of Days

Moris Farhi

CROWN PUBLISHERS, INC.   NEW YORK

This is a work of fiction. The characters, incidents, places, and dialogues
are products of the author's imagination and are not to be construed
as real. The author's use of names of actual persons, living or dead,
is incidental to the purposes of the plot and is not intended to change
the entirely fictional character of the work.

Permissions appear on page 539.

Published by Crown Publishers, Inc.,
One Park Avenue, New York, New York 10016
and simultaneously in Canada by General Publishing Company Limited
Manufactured in the United States of America
Library of Congress Cataloging in Publication Data
Farhi, Moris.
The last of days.
I. Title.
PR6056.A65L3   1983   823'.914   82-19803
ISBN: 0-517-54908-5
Book design by Camilla Filancia
10 9 8 7 6 5 4 3 2 1
First Edition

To my wife, NINA, *my blessing and hope—*
whose book this is also.

To my mother, PALOMBA —
who personifies love.
To my father, HAYIM DANIYEL —
humbly, with undying love, this offering at your resting place.
To my brother, CEKI —
always by my side, yesterday, today and tomorrow.
To my stepdaughter, RACHEL —
may you inherit the peaceful earth you so deserve.
To my GOULD *family, especially* ERIC *and* DANIELE —
gratefully for your love and support.
To ANTHEA, ASHER, BRENDA, IAN, RICHARD,
SELIM, TONY, TRICIA, VIVIANE —
for their faith.
And to DEBORAH, EMMANUEL, NATHANIEL,
REBECCA, SARAH —
in the hope that tomorrow might heal the wounds of today.

I should like to express my deepest gratitude
to those who helped me
throughout this work.
I wish especially to thank Victoria Pryor
for her unflagging faith and guidance;
Wing Commander J. Cartwright, O.B.E., R.A.F. (Ret'd),
for his insightful assistance, particularly on technical matters;
Barbara Grossman and Maureen Rissik for their editorial direction;
Sheila McIlwraith, Norman North and Caroline Dawnay
for their support and constructive criticisms;
Julian Lewis for his dedicated counsel;
Irene Way for her exhaustive work on draft after draft.

PRINCIPAL CHARACTERS

Abu Ismail   Arab mystic and politician; leader of the Warriors of Jihad (WOJ); self-declared Al-Mahdi, Savior of Islam

Idris Ali   Abu Ismail's chief of staff

Nazmi   Abu Ismail's bodyguard

Al-Munafiq   The Doubter, an imaginary being

Boaz Ben-Ya'ir   Colonel in the Israel Defense Forces

The Memouneh   Chief of Mossad; addressed mostly by his nickname, Zamora

Gad Kidan   High-ranking Mossad executive

Sanbat Abraham   An Israeli woman of Falasha origin; a Mossad operative specializing in ciphers

Osman Nusseibi   Colonel; chief of operations, Al-Moukhabarat al-Ammah (Jordanian Secret Service)

Samia Nusseibi   Osman's wife

Ivan Mikhailovich Volkov   KGB major-general, head of "wet affairs," Department Five

Kevork Dedeyan   Mossad's Armenian agent in the Horn of Africa

Tewodoros Wolde   Ethiopian officer; captain in the Imperial Paratroopers

Mussaddiq Hamdi   The Eritrean Liberation Front's Aden-based officer

Al Jameson   CIA station chief, Ethiopia

Getachew Iyessous   Major; executive in Ethiopia's Imperial Secret Service

Sigmund Schoenberg   Ex-Legionnaire; lieutenant in the French *Deuxième Bureau* in Djibouti, T.F. A.I.

Montblanc   Ex-Legionnaire; American CIA operative in Djibouti

Ischii Watanabe   Japanese terrorist, ex-*Rengo Sekigun* (Japanese Red Army)

Dr. Talat Fawzi   Lebanese physicist

Dr. Charles Quinn   CIA station chief, Lebanon

Yusuf   An Afar chieftain

Gentleman Jim   High-ranking CIA executive; Al Jameson's boss

ORGANIZATIONS
AND ACRONYMS

WOJ Warriors of Jihad

PFLP Popular Front for the Liberation of Palestine

PLO Palestine Liberation Organization

ELF Eritrean Liberation Front, a secessionist organization in Ethiopia

Rengo Sekigun Japanese Red Army, a terrorist organization

MPLA Popular Movement for the Liberation of Angola

Mossad Israeli Security Service

Al-Moukhabarat al-Ammah Jordanian Secret Service

CIA Central Intelligence Agency, USA

CIA-SO CIA-Special Operations

DIA Defense Intelligence Agency, USA

NSA National Security Agency, USA

KGB Committee of State Security, USSR

GRU Military Intelligence, USSR

ISS Imperial Secret Service, Ethiopia

DGS Directorate General of Security, Portugal

GID General Investigation Directorate, Libya

SDECE French Counter-Intelligence Service

SIS British Secret Intelligence Service

P.D.R.Y. People's Democratic Republic of Yemen (also known as South Yemen)

T.F.A.I. Territoire Français des Afars et des Issas; French colony that gained independence in 1977 as the Republic of Djibouti

UNRWA United Nations Relief and Works Agency

WHO World Health Organization (United Nations)

FAO Food and Agriculture Organization (United Nations)

IAEA International Atomic Energy Agency

OAU Organization of African Unity

USAID USA Aid Organization

RCC Libya's Revolutionary Command Council

Dergue Ethiopian armed forces junta

AWACS Airborne Warning and Control System

ELINT Electronic Intelligence

NBC suits Protective suits for Nuclear-Biological-Chemical warfare

". . . Gather yourselves together, that I may tell you
that which shall befall you in the last days . . ."

Genesis, 49:1

"But those of them that have deep learning
and those that truly believe in what has been revealed
to you and to other prophets before you: who
. . . have faith in Allah and the Last Day—these
shall be richly rewarded."

The Koran, Sura 4:160

"This know also, that in the last days perilous
times shall come."

2 Timothy, 3:1

I Am He Whom I Love;

and He Whom I Love Is I.

We Are Two Souls in One Body.

When You See Me, You See Him.

And When You See Him,

You See Us Both.

AL-HALLAJ

October 23, 1973

MT. NEBO, JORDAN

Abu Ismail reached the summit on angels' wings. He reclaimed his breath caressing the three talismans pinned to the underside of his aba: the blue Eye-of-the-Heart symbolizing the seat of Absolute Intellect warded off Evil; the bulb of garlic cocooned him with magic and the tiny horseshoe carved his soul's path.

He imbibed the setting sun. Ramadan was spinning out the Night of Decree.

Idris Ali, his chief of staff, and Nazmi, his bodyguard, concluded their search. Mount Nebo, where the Jew's prophet, Moses, had viewed Canaan and died, offered equal amenities to both mystic and assassin.

Idris Ali and Nazmi signaled safety. He blessed them with a smile. Idris Ali, the cornerstone of his fedayeen organization, the Warriors of Jihad, had become immaculate—a son, forged by his

1

spirit if not his flesh. Nazmi, formidable as a jinnee guarding a sacred pool, was his ever-present shield.

Idris Ali spread out the prayer mat to commandeer a corner of the earth for worship. Nazmi deposited next to it a container of salt which, in the hours to come, would increase thirst. As a supererogatory devotion on this extramundane night, Abu Ismail had decided to prolong his fast and intensify the ordeal of purification.

He waved dismissal. Idris Ali withdrew to a vantage point over the pomegranate orchards at the foot of the mountain; Nazmi down to the defile that stretched to the Jordan basin. They would keep watch during his communion. The enemy was close: his rivals in the Arab world, a breath away; the Jew, half a breath—perhaps even closer if, as Idris Ali suspected, they had infiltrated the ranks.

He sat, bending his arthritic limbs with difficulty. His eyes and mind stretched westward toward Jerusalem—Al-Quds, "The Sacred." In the days when the Jew had been stateless, sitting where he now sat, he had been able to see the milky valley of the River Jordan, green Jericho, and the Holy City all at the same time.

Now the ether billowed in a crimson haze. Al-Quds had disappeared from the horizon since that Hour of Catastrophe in June 1967 when she had fallen to the Jew.

He searched the crimson haze for Al-Munafiq—The Doubter, The Despoiler, the specter that penetrated the soul's innermost recesses, a greater curse than the Jew. An enemy who confronted the mystic in the hazardous plains of conscience and exposed his ineptitude at navigating the turbulent waters of worldliness that lay between the Soul and the True Faith.

Al-Munafiq, The Doubter, had been pursuing him throughout Ramadan. When, at the beginning of the fast, Abu Ismail had seen, while the world had stood blind, that Egypt and Syria were preparing for war against Israel, Al-Munafiq had tauntingly declared that history was disowning him. When, in the first days of the war, the Jew had staggered, almost broken, Al-Munafiq had persecuted him with the fear that the mantle of the designated Savior of Islam had been wrested from him. Only now, with the Jew poised over Egypt and Syria, had Al-Munafiq fallen silent. But the monster was still stalking, waiting for an opportunity to slaughter Allah's Shadow on Earth.

Abu Ismail redirected his mind toward Al-Quds. A glimpse of the center of the universe, from the very spot where the Jew had commenced desecrating history, would be an indication that the Last of Days were to be announced. Within Al-Quds's sanctuaries lay the tools for the Final Judgment. The golden-domed Mosque of Omar housed the Rock which would support the scales that would weigh the souls. From that Rock Mohammed had soared to Heaven. The silver-domed Al-Aqsa Mosque, revealed in the Koran as the Most Supreme, and therefore holier than the Ancient House of Mecca, held within its walls the Nineteen Nails driven in by the Prophet. These, by falling from their cavities one by one, timed the life of the world. When Abu Ismail had last prayed there, only three of the Nineteen Nails had remained. Now, the last had to fall.

The haze persisted. And Abu Ismail saw the Divine Purpose. Allah did not want the Faithful to witness Al-Quds's anguish. The crimson veil would be lifted when the Sacred City was reclaimed and reconsecrated. Until then, it would stand as harbinger of the blood and fire that would wash away Islam's shame.

Abu Ismail cleansed himself with sand, smoothed his sparse beard and performed the sunset prayer. When darkness fell, he entered the silence of Endlessness and ascended to the plane where Man and his Deity communed. An indefinable time later, he transmogrified, shed his mortal pains, and levitated.

He spread out his arms to display, perched on each, submission and aspiration, the twin weapons of a formidable spirit. He pierced his flesh with arrows of light to prove he was more than a mortal, created from superior blood.

The wind transmuted into a scimitar and rode the Dead Sea which had risen like a warrior's stallion. The ridges of Moab fell like infidel hordes cut down. The Fire of Hell, guarded by Nineteen Keepers, stoked the stars. The earth quickened for the seed of cataclysm.

"Allah, Lord of Creation, The Compassionate, The Merciful, King of the Last Judgment! Favor your humble servant! Command him to restore the True Religion!"

He became all-seeing, all-hearing, all-feeling. He sensed Jibril, through whom Allah revealed His Word, at his side. He whirled to hear and speak with the Angel who spoke and heard from all directions.

Jibril's voice reverberated with the light of Creation.

"Faithful, your soul is heavy."

"Look, Jibril! See! Around us cavort the mongrel Jordanian; across, the soul-snatching Jew propagates; to the north, the sewer-rat Syrian, and to the south, the aborted fetus of Cleopatra, the Egyptian, enjoy sodomy with the godless Russian; farther east and west and south and north, my Arab brothers hang the gold of oil on their beards and forelocks."

"Yes."

"This war with the Jew. My people are yet again humiliated. Soon the voice of anathema preaching that Arab and Jew should live side by side will be heard as regularly as the muezzin's call to prayers. Whither Islam then if it cannot seize the world for Allah? If it cannot establish the Theocracy of Al-Quds?"

"Faithful, what do you know of Al-Mahdi?"

"Al-Mahdi is the Caliph of Islam. He who will fulfill jihad in all four ways: by the heart, by the tongue, by the hand and by the sword. The Deliverer who will restore justice, equity and true religion to mankind."

"When is Al-Mahdi expected?"

"The sages say at the commencement of our fifteenth century. Six earthly years hence."

"The sages are correct, but not precise. When has Allah decreed the advent of Al-Mahdi?"

When there is nothing but oppression in the world, Nine Heavenly Years before the Day of Judgment."

"With the Jew in Al-Quds, there *is* nothing but oppression in the world! Therefore, the Nine Heavenly Years of Judgment have commenced."

"Then Al-Mahdi must be with us."

"You are Al-Mahdi, Faithful. Prepare to receive Divine Guidance."

Abu Ismail whirled while the light of purity, untouched by fire, bathed his face.

And the twin signs which would reveal Al-Mahdi to the Faithful erupted conjointly to confirm Jibril's annunciation. His teeth parted; his right cheek sank to form a crevice.

And Allah embraced him.

Later, during the postcoital repose of the Most Perfect Union, he received Divine Guidance.

Book One

PART I

Evil Enters Like a Needle, and Spreads Like an Oak Tree.

Ethiopian proverb

November 2, 1973

MASADA, ISRAEL

Boaz Ben-Ya'ir searched for a ripple on the water. Nature had partitioned the Dead Sea as precisely as the politicians' ruler, giving Jordan the eastern half, still branded by the sun, and Israel the western, already shadowed by the heights of the Judean Wilderness.

There were no ripples. Only a brave squall would venture into this lowest point on earth. "Dead" was an apt name for it. Its salt-bitter waters were barren, and it could not heave and spume like any other sea.

Boaz checked his watch: 5:28 P.M. He had lost the hour he had wanted for Masada.

On the airstrip, the Britten-Norman Islander opened up engines for takeoff. He caught a glimpse of the pilot. Still stunned by the task of transporting the war dead, the veteran had resented diverting to Suez to pick up Boaz, and had chosen to complete the run to Beersheba before dropping him at Masada.

The Islander took off.

Shlomo, odd-job man to Mossad, Israeli Intelligence, punched open the Ford's passenger door.

Boaz cast a final wistful look at Masada.

He knew the ancient fortress rock by rock. He had scaled its cliffs innumerable times as part of his training. He had helped with the excavations. And, to celebrate the ingathering of the tribes, he had Hebraized his surname, Franco, to that of Masada's last commander, Ben-Ya'ir. He had done so to invest himself with the

6

Zealot chieftain's fanaticism. Later, he had realized that he had resorted, like so many who had come to Zion, to the old Jewish custom of the sick man undergoing a change of name in order to regain health. Unperturbed by such occultism, he had accepted that the soul of a man, therefore his strength, resided in his name, and that the secret was to find one that was inviolable, as the angel had done for Jacob when he had renamed him Israel. Thus, he had also changed his first name, Rafael, to Boaz, which meant "in strength," and which had been the name of one of the two great bronze pillars at the entrance to Solomon's Temple.

He slid into Shlomo's car and glanced at the scuba equipment cocooned in bales of cotton. His stomach cramped with stress.

They entered the northbound lane. A signpost indicated sixteen kilometers to Ein Gedi, eighty-eight to Jerusalem.

Boaz handed Shlomo a stick of chewing gum, then unwrapped one for himself. "So, what's the latest?"

"Backup affirmative. A Sulubba clan. We've also pinpointed the cave where the tapes are. Aaron provided perfect bearings. We've drawn a map—it's with your kit."

Boaz, intent on immersing himself in the mission, chewed his gum assiduously.

Aaron Levi, Mossad's mole within the Warriors of Jihad (WOJ), had succeeded in recording, with miniaturized listening devices, Abu Ismail's communions with Allah during the WOJ leader's Ramadan retreat at Mount Nebo. One particular disputation, Aaron had alerted Mossad, outlined an operation that augured the long-threatened Second Holocaust. Unable to transmit details from the WOJ headquarters in Tripoli, Libya, where the contingent had returned, Aaron had backtracked to Jordan at the first opportunity to gather the tapes and bury them for collection by Mossad. Unfortunately, the move had blown his cover, and a platoon commanded by Idris Ali, the WOJ chief of staff, had set out in immediate pursuit. That the task of neutralizing Aaron should have been undertaken by Idris Ali himself had corroborated the portent of the tapes. For Idris Ali, mined from the quagmire of the Palestinian refugee camps, then smelted in the KGB's wet affairs (assassinations) department, had been honed, as Abu Ismail never ceased boasting, to become the deadliest sword in Islam. When, the previous night, Aaron's last signal had reported imminent capture, Mossad's duty officer had felt compelled to improvise a mission with the dual objective of collecting the tapes and rescuing Aaron. Boaz had been chosen as the spearhead.

He turned to Shlomo. "Anything new on Aaron?"

"We're almost sure they took him to Wahdat refugee camp.

That's always been the WOJ base in Jordan. The Sulubba were instructed to confirm. We're still waiting to hear from Gideon."

Boaz grunted. Both Gideon, Mossad's man in Amman, and the Sulubba nomads, recruited as backup, were astute ears. The fact that they had been unable to confirm suggested Idris Ali had sealed off Wahdat. That in itself was confirmation. "Return arrangements—as briefed?"

"Yes."

Boaz closed his eyes. He was finding it difficult to be consumed by the mission. The fact that the battles of the Yom Kippur War had exhausted him was part of the reason. The other part rested with the threat of the Second Holocaust. Irrespective of the outcome of this mission, Israel's—and his—Sisyphean task would continue. And the time for his burnt-out spirit to rekindle and view man and land in God's perspective would never come. "Right. Now drive gently. Get me to Ein Feshha by nightfall. Not before. Not after."

Shlomo nodded. He had learned long ago to humor the likes of Boaz. He had once told his wife that every naval commando behaved as if he were the Lord's anointed, and those attached to Sayeret Matkal, the crack unit from which the Israeli security branches drew their strike force, more so. But at that time Shlomo had only just joined the Security Services and was idealistic enough to moralize that it should be peopled with supermen of gentle manners. Not that the men of Sayeret Matkal, in ability at least, fell much short of supermanhood. They were the elite of Zahal—Israel Defense Forces. Officers of exceptional daring, ability and stamina, forever undergoing intensive training, they were always on combat alert, always selected for formidable missions. They were men with such a high ratio of success that their accomplishments were kept secret even from service records in case they became known to enemy agents. It had not taken Shlomo long to understand that men engaged in dangerous clandestine work were invariably whittled down to raw nerve ends.

Shlomo drove at a steady 50 kph to cover the forty-six kilometers to Ein Feshha by 6:30. To relieve the tedium, he studied his passenger.

Lieutenant Colonel Boaz Ben-Ya'ir was not tall; but framed with arms as thicks as legs, legs like a sumo wrestler's and a chest solid as a Centurion tank, he looked a colossus. The illusion was further enhanced by silvering close-cropped hair and a leathery face that converged in myriad scars at a broken nose. Those who claimed to have penetrated beyond Boaz's restless light brown eyes swore that here was a man who, even if skinned alive, could never disintegrate. Shlomo believed them. Though only forty years old, Boaz looked ageless.

He had distinguished himself both as a paratrooper and a naval commando. He had been awarded the Medal of Supreme Bravery during the paratroop action on Ammunition Hill in Jerusalem in the Six Day War. He had led the raid to Ras Ghareb, Egypt, that had airlifted the Soviet P12, 7-ton mobile search-radar on December 26, 1969, earning the Medal for Distinguished and Outstanding Service in Action. The latest citation from the Suez Canal bridgehead had recommended that he receive the Medal for Courage on the Field of Battle. When the recommendation was ratified, he would join the select few honored with the complete set of Zahal's decorations.

Shlomo lit a cigarette. His schoolboy adulation disturbed him. Seeing Boaz as the symbol of the true Israeli, the reborn spirit of Judah Maccabaeus, working miracles and shunning materialism, meant turning a blind eye to the other reality. Boaz was a killer. Very likely psychotic. Member of an anachronistic breed who vowed never to forgive the Arabs for killing Jews, or for transforming a nation of idealists into Arab-killers. That his perspective had changed with the Yom Kippur War was Shlomo's unpalatable proof that the gun, whether held or faced, dispensed with morality.

TEL AVIV, ISRAEL

At 5:38 P.M. the city seemed deserted. It was the first Friday in the wake of the war. The men were still at the front. The women, the elderly and the children had retreated into their homes, trying to find the will to celebrate the Sabbath. Those who had not lost relatives shared the grief of friends who had.

In the eastern quarter of the city known as Ha-Kiryah, "The Town," the air of reclusion was deceptive. For this suburb, which before the Six Day War had housed various Defense Ministry departments, had become in recent years the Israeli Security Services' nerve center. It accommodated headquarters for Mossad, as well as for Internal Security and for Military Intelligence. It also contained one of Israel's principal war rooms.

In the last, at sublevel 2, the activity, normally intense around the clock, had reached a peak. The Antennae, the team of radio operators who, a wit among them had claimed, could eavesdrop on Sadat's bowel movements, were completing final checks. They had been pulled out of their special units at the front to track Boaz —on this occasion commissioned to operate under electronic silence—by blanket monitoring of the frequencies for signals of alert from Jordanian, WOJ or any other source.

Prowling among them, Gad Kidan, duty officer, nursed his own anxieties. Gideon had finally signaled. The Sulubba had been unable to confirm that Aaron had been taken to Wahdat. Procedure prescribed that Kidan should scrap Aaron's rescue, and now, with the mission legitimate only for the collection of the.tapes, discharge Boaz and assign the task to a lesser agent.

Kidan was loath to do that.

Abu Ismail was Israel's Enemy Number One. Though most Mossad technocrats agreed with that premise, they could not see the ramifications. Bogged down by details of psychological evaluations and computerized predictions of strategy, they deluded themselves into thinking he was yet another terrorist leader seeking supremacy. Whereas Abu Ismail, leader of a secret religious brotherhood who had abandoned mysticism for the sword, had designated himself the Arabs' messiah. He had to be crushed.

Kidan shook his head despondently as he focused on Abu Ismail's most recent photograph, on permanent transmit on the monitor screens, to goad the radio crew to maximum effort. The photograph had been taken by Boaz on Friday, August 10, at Beirut airport VIP lounge. It showed Abu Ismail waiting to board a plane for Baghdad in the company of Dr. George Habash, leader of the Popular Front for the Liberation of Palestine (PFLP). Boaz had been poised to kill them both.

But the chief of Mossad, the Memouneh, "The Responsible," as he liked to be called, had ordered Boaz to hold fire and had reforged the operation to kidnap both terrorist leaders for an Eichmann-style trial. Inconceivably, he had almost succeeded; the Iraqi Caravelle bound for Baghdad had been duly intercepted by fighter-jets and diverted to Israel. The pandemonium following the futile search, and the recriminations over Boaz's bitter report from Beirut relating how Abu Ismail and Habash had switched planes at the last minute, had been worthy of the Wailing Wall.

Perversely, the farce had bolstered the Memouneh's image. This, despite a zealous campaign from a small minority led by Kidan that the Memouneh had now proved incompetent; that the misadventure was as serious a failure as the killing by an Israeli hit team in Lillehammer, Norway, on July 21, of one Ahmad Bouchiki, a waiter, mistakenly identified as Ali Hassan Salamah, Black September's planning chief. But the campaign had fallen on deaf ears.

The Memouneh belonged to the Establishment, that body of

founders who still dished out the *kreplach* soup. And that summed up Kidan's war.

Complacency had spread into the very marrow of the country. The Establishment, denying its senility, had undermined the country's strength like impotent fathers jealous of virile sons.

The Yom Kippur War served as proof. Days before it had broken out, reports from the CIA had urged concern both at the extent of the Egyptian army's autumn maneuvers on the west bank of Suez, and the redeployment of Syrian troops on the Golan. So had Israel's own electronic surveillance of the two fronts. But the old men and women had merely shaken limp heads.

Now they were crying over their dead.

And now was the time to proclaim that war was Israel's heritage. That never again would defiance be exchanged for appeasement. That any Arab success was a disaster of Biblical dimensions.

And if they refused to listen, they had to be put down. Kidan, and those like him, could not let them rule anymore.

That was why it was imperative that the present mission be carried out in its entirety. Boaz had to collect the tapes even if they did not prove momentous, as Aaron had claimed. Furthermore, Boaz had to proceed to Wahdat even if Aaron's rescue turned into a dead man's mission. Israel could afford to bleed—needed to bleed—because each bloodletting made her stronger.

To support his resolve, Kidan scanned the faces of the radio crew. Anxious—every one of them. Thinking Aaron was doomed; that Boaz might perish. The Jew's trepidation for his brother's fate. There had been some who, having survived the extermination camps, had committed suicide. The guilt of the living. Despair of the future. Historic plagues.

Kidan drank the last of his Turkish coffee. He was courting serious trouble. But there would be trouble anyway for commissioning Boaz without the Memouneh's authorization. Conversely, he could always count on Boaz to shield him. Like Isaiah's Suffering Servant, Boaz willingly bore the sins of others.

EIN FESHHA, ISRAELI OCCUPIED WEST BANK

Boaz zipped up his wet suit. The rocky beach was deserted. He glanced south along the coast toward the sound of outboard motors; the tiny Israeli naval post had pushed out its rubber dinghies. They would patrol routinely, close to the shore.

Behind Boaz, in the picnic grounds, Shlomo had established

radio contact with Control and was muttering codes. The only other sound came from a truck chugging northward, bearing dates from kibbutz Ein Gedi.

Boaz waded in, treading the soft salt on the seabed with distaste. When the water reached his chest, he bent his knees and let the buoyancy volley him up. Floating on his back, he put on his flippers. The tepid mineral-heavy water that clung like oil offended him. He commiserated with the rheumatics who bathed in these waters of Sodom for a miraculous cure. He had been wise to decide on a wet suit. It would impose the additional chore of hiding it, but at least he would not hoist himself onto enemy territory like a pillar of salt.

He tied the ropes of the three neoprene bags to his strap. The smallest contained his Bedouin clothes, the map pinpointing Aaron's cave, his 8-shot automatic, a silencer, spare magazines, a webbing belt of grenades, his commando knife, a small shovel and a torch. The other two contained the oxygen backpacks and the weight belts that would keep him submerged in the ultrabuoyant sea.

He pulled the air-intake stoppers of the inflatable collars around the bags, then backstroked in a circle. The bags, held up by their safety collars, skimmed over the water and aligned behind his flippers. Their weight had been worrying him, but now, even above water, they had neutral buoyancy. That reassured him: he should swim the fourteen kilometers in the estimated six hours.

He checked his watch: 6:52 P.M. Night had fallen; the stars, compensating for the weak moonlight, appeared to be very near. Across the water, the Jordanian shore stood as peaceful as on the seventh night of Creation.

According to Control, the Jordanian patrol boat had sailed from Suweima base, at the northern end of the Dead Sea, at 6:00 P.M. on a southwesterly course. She did not worry him. She was there merely to play at war. She set sail every night, always on a different bearing, to cruise up to the periphery of the sea line, there to maintain surveillance until dawn. Tonight, if she kept to her original direction, he would slip into Jordanian waters well beyond her vision, and dive as planned at the tenth kilometer, sometime after 11:00, and swim the remaining four kilometers underwater. If she changed to a course that might intersect his route, he would simply dive at the sea line and swim underwater the rest of the way.

It was unlikely the Jordanians would be on the lookout. They would not expect an enemy to come across the wider stretches of the Dead Sea when he had an equal chance of infiltration at its

narrowest, between the tonguelike Al Lisan peninsula and the
Israeli potash works, or through the various bridges over the River
Jordan that Israel had kept open to maintain some normality of
life for the occupied West Bank.

Shlomo, trousers rolled up to his knees, waded in with the
radio. "Kidan has no confirmation on Aaron, but Green is yours
—if you still insist on volunteering."

Boaz's rare smile flickered. Kidan was covering himself. "The
pathetic sod! Tell him I insist!"

Shlomo hurriedly waded back, reporting to Kidan conciliato-
rily, like a child between warring parents.

Boaz pulled out a flask of fresh water, took a few sips, and
washed his goggles. He put them on, checked that his eyes were
clear of salt, then put the flask back. From another pocket he took
out a filtered air-intake mouth-and-nose piece and strapped it on.

He paused for a moment to stare at the Judean Wilderness.
Nearby stood the Qumran caves where the Dead Sea Scrolls had
been found; not far south, the oasis of Ein Gedi, where Saul and
David had reclaimed each other, daubed the desert emerald. But
it was the air that had majesty. It carried the Scriptures to the
modern Jew, revived ancient history. Boaz was reminded of the
night when, as a newly commissioned officer, he had been taken
up in a plane with a group of fighter-pilot graduates and shown the
land of Israel being reclaimed while the lands of her neighbors
stretched in waste and neglect. Here he was, this time 396 meters
below sea level, and reclamation still permeated the air. Not only
of the land, but of its people.

He turned east, toward the Hills of Moab. He breaststroked
until the waterproof sacks ranged behind him. The drag was minimal. He changed his stroke, found his rhythm, then worked the
flippers. He drained his thoughts so that body would take over
mind for the next five hours, but held on to the image of his sister's
severed head.

JAFFA, ISRAEL

An hour into the mission, Gad Kidan parked his car near Jaffa's
Turkish Clock Tower. Residual guilt urged him to return to the
war room and sweat out the long wait. Defiantly he turned right
for the Artists' Quarter. Echoes from the mission, if any, would
not sound before Boaz reached Jordanian waters at about midnight.

He paused in front of the Franciscan Monastery of St. Peter
and bought some prickly pears from a stall. As the vendor peeled

them, he looked down at the houses overlooking Andromeda's
Rock. The woman was there, at the last house. He swallowed the
pears, seeds and all, and wondered whether he would have to
justify the mission to her.

Twenty minutes later, having breezed through the Artists'
Quarter—quiet and haunted like the rest of the country—he rang
her bell.

Sanbat Abraham, executive in Mossad Ciphers, opened the
door immediately, as if she had been expecting him. She was as
tense as when he had dismissed her that afternoon.

"*Sanbat Shalom*, Sanbat."

She led him in without acknowledging his greeting. She hated
his childish pun on her name. It was a sign of stress that indicated
either a setback or a troubled conscience. "What can I do for you,
Colonel?"

His hunger for her hurt him. He could trace his forebears to
the Court Jews of Central Europe, yet here he was lusting after
the ebony flesh of an African. "A coffee?"

She nodded and moved into the kitchen. He cast a quick look
at the room. Tidy. She had done her housework. She would soon
want to shower. In anticipation he stared at her buttocks. She
should have been called Shulamit after the bride of the *Song of
Songs*. *Sanbat*, in old Ethiopic, meant "sabbath." She had retained
it as her only link with her people, the Falashas, who worshiped
the Sabbath as the Savior of the Jews.

She brought the coffee. "Green, is it?"

"Yes."

"God be with him."

"First axiom for the high-ranking Mossadnik: don't fret over
every agent."

She sat at the table, wanting to kick him out. Instead she stared
at the photograph of her dead husband on the sideboard. Smiling
from the cockpit of his Mirage 111C, as if he had conquered the
world. Date: July 30, 1970. The day of the sole encounter between
Israeli and Russian pilots during the War of Attrition in Sinai. The
Russians had lost four MiG-21-Js in fifteen minutes and Uri, her
husband, had accounted for two of them. Three days later he had
fallen to a SAM-3. And she had been left to cope with loneliness
—to admit into her house a presence, any presence, even a rat like
Kidan. "You want me?"

He squirmed. If only she had not been so submissive. Why
could she not make a man lucky, not out of duty, but for pleasure?
But then would he have wanted her? "Plenty of time."

"We could get it over with."

Kidan smiled, then lit a cigarette and sipped his coffee.

She waited, staring into the void. She burned with widow's anger and stoked that with earlier angers. She wished for another life—one she could sail through easily.

Yet, she knew, compared with the norm in Israel, tarred by the night and fog of the Holocaust, her life had been relatively smooth. She had been separated from her Falasha tribe, barely six months old, in June 1941, at the tail end of the Abyssinian war when, despite the Italian surrender at Amba Alagi, pockets of the Colonial Infantry had continued fighting the allied forces. During one such skirmish, her parents, scrounging for food, had been caught in the crossfire. Her father had died instantly; her mother, wounded, had managed to drag her to the Allied lines. There fate had intervened. The soldiers had turned out to be a contingent of the Middle East Unit, and one among them, a Jew, told by her dying mother that they were Falashas, had taken charge of Sanbat. This man, whose identity Sanbat had never found out, had delivered her to Lieutenant Colonel Orde Wingate, commander of a native force of Ethiopians and Sudanese. Wingate who, during the troubled prewar days in Palestine, had created the Haganah's Special Night Squads, and whose passionate support of Zionism had earned him the title *Hayedid*, "The Friend," had proved true to his cognomen. Sanbat had been entrusted to the Mizrahis, an old Jewish-Italian couple in Asmara. Thereafter, until 1949, she had lived a blissful life. The Mizrahis, owners of a small hotel, had enjoyed both business with allied forces and the tolerance of the Ethiopians who had looked upon them as *insabbiati*, Italians caught in Ethiopian sands and assimilated. When in 1949 Mama Mizrahi had died, Papa Mizrahi had heard the call of Zion. Within a few months, they had traveled to Aden, there to join the multitude of Yemenite Jews airlifted to Eretz. A year later, Papa Mizrahi had died of old age.

Late childhood and early teens had been spent in the insularity of an orphanage in Rehovot. There she had undergone the processes of *giyur* for the symbolic conversion to Judaism according to Rabbinic law. At sixteen, she had moved to Tel Aviv to work as a shop assistant; at eighteen she had joined Zahal. Finding the army less prejudiced to the Oriental Jew, she had made it her career. At twenty-six she had met Uri, born Brian Abraham in Glasgow. Enchanted by her dusky skin and exotic origins, he had led her to the *chuppa* in the effervescent July after the Six Day War. Following his death, she had retreated into the sanctuary of the army, and had specialized in ciphers. Two years ago, she had been honorably discharged and transferred to Mossad. And there she still was.

"Boaz insisted on going after Aaron."

She looked up. Smug Kidan was blowing smoke circles. "And you couldn't dissuade him?"

"Don't worry about him, Sanbat."

"Why? Is he indestructible?"

"Practically."

"Why do you hate him?"

Kidan shook his head as if wrongly accused, rose and moved to the window. He stared at the old harbor. Back in 1948, during the War of Independence, he had stormed it with a company of the Irgun to wipe out the machine-gun nests. He had been a better man then. He had believed it was good to be a Jew. "Do you still love him?"

She glared at him, refusing to answer.

"He can't love—you know that."

"Aren't you trying to say he can't *make* love, Colonel?"

Kidan faced her. Her concern for him—that was what really hurt. And excited. "You tell me."

"His file says he's impotent."

"What do you say?"

Sanbat tried not to remember. Just before the war, on Rosh Hashanah, New Year's Eve, when Boaz had come to dinner. She had been happy—for the first time since her husband's death. She had not realized he had been pepped up with pills. Otherwise he would never have tried to touch her. And when he had left abruptly, she had finally reconciled herself to hopelessness. The week before she had accepted a post in Ethiopia which Mossad had urgently offered her. "Is that why you hate him, because he's impotent?"

"Is he?"

She screamed at him. "Yes! The death of his sister! The rape of her headless body! Don't you believe your psychiatrists' reports?"

He stubbed out his cigarette and grinned. That grin which counterpointed his touch, betrayed his prejudices and humiliated. "A girlfriend. A wife. A mistress. I could understand. But a sister . . . Isn't that incestuous?"

"A wife, a mistress, a girlfriend can always be replaced. A sister —never."

"Claptrap—pure Boaz. How can you still love him?"

She calmed down, smiled tauntingly. "Because of his soul."

Kidan, scowling, remembered the night two years ago when insomnia had driven him to the secluded beach of Caesarea where, to his irritation, he had stumbled upon Boaz, a cassette recorder in his hand, dancing the *zeybeki* in a trance. Neither computer nor psychiatrists had disinterred such a desperate quest for lost innocence. It was then Kidan had thought that perhaps he and Boaz were two halves of one personality; each, the other's shadow. If that were true, it explained his hunger for this black woman who despised him and loved Boaz. If he could accept that, he could also admit he had ordered Green in order to dispose of Boaz. "Don't you want to shower?"

"To make myself clean for you?"

"I'd like to watch. . . ."

She shook her head violently.

"Then let me watch you undress."

"Don't blink."

She turned her husband's photograph facedown, switched off the lights and undressed hurriedly, showing him nothing more than her shadow.

She lay down on the sofa and opened her legs. He climbed on her, shivering with excitement. He was hurting her because she was dry. But she did not mind. She was thinking of Boaz. If she could not have him inside her, she could at least share his mutilation.

November 3, 1973

THE MOAB WILDERNESS, JORDAN

Boaz surfaced and checked his watch: 12:53. He had swum across in six hours. He placed the oxygen backpack in its waterproof bag and let it sink.

He waded to an inlet concealed from the road that led north to Suweima and the Allenby Bridge.

Hé spent several minutes scanning the area. When certain it was deserted, he took off his wet suit, put on the Bedouin aba and strapped his gear beneath it. He buried the last waterproof bag, his wet suit and flippers. He threw his spade into the sea and wiped out his tracks with balls of thornbush.

Boaz scampered across the road, deep into the wadis. Running wherever possible, he proceeded toward Mount Nebo, fifteen kilometers to the northeast.

At 3:17 he reached a labyrinth of sandstone hillocks lying between Mount Nebo and Jureina. Ten minutes later, he found the cave where Aaron had hidden the tapes.

He examined the surroundings for signs of footprints. There were none.

He crawled in and sheltered against a wall. He listened for sounds. The cave was empty.

He lit his torch and surveyed the cave. Some rodent holes, layers of dust, a pile of gerbil bones. The last was Aaron's mark for the buried tapes.

He started digging.

About a meter down he found them, sealed in a plastic pouch. Cut to miniature strips, they had been stuck onto sheets of pressed apricot which, being a delicacy with the Bedouin, would attract little attention.

He covered the hole, wiped his tracks and left the cave.

At 4:28, six kilometers farther to the north, he reached the heights of the Husban canyon. From a vantage point, he scanned the wadis for the Sulubba encampment. Recruited as backup, they would smuggle Boaz into Wahdat refugee camp during the early-morning activity and cause a diversion while Boaz sought out Aaron. Then, when the rescue was accomplished, they would smuggle them out of the camp and escort them as far as the Madaba road.

It took him some time in the false dawn to spot the black goatskin tents. The location of the encampment beneath the rocky overhang of a deep wadi, half a kilometer away, surprised him. Normally, the Sulubba camped out in open land to claim the grazing grounds around them. Even more oddly, in a region abounding with wadis ideal for browsing goats, they had chosen one singularly barren and inaccessible and, in the process, had exposed themselves to the dangers of autumn rain torrents.

He pulled out his gun and slithered down to the wadi.

He progressed slowly, listening to the desert with apprehension. He had not sensed one watchman, nor heard a watchdog which, to a desert dweller, was as indispensable as his dagger.

He moved closer. The camels and goats lay tethered with their heads facing the open sides of the tents. That, at least, was normal.

He stared uneasily into the wadi. Betrayal was unnatural to the Bedouin in general, and unthinkable to the Sulubba. Though these nomads, as the descendants of the Crusaders' camp followers, were the outcasts of the desert, they were, nonetheless, by virtue of their skills as hunters, fighters, trackers, and diviners of waterholes, invariably allied to and protected by one tribe or another. Since these alliances were always bonded by their word, their survival depended on its inviolability.

He reached the fringe of the clearing. The Sulubba seemed to be asleep. With first light looming, they should have been brewing coffee. He edged nearer the animals and whistled sharply. They did not move.

He hurled himself into the first tent. Gerbils, foraging for food, scuttled away. He lifted the covers off the nearest pallet and stared at a boy's head smashed by a bullet. He felt his sandals stick in the blood-drenched sand. He pulled the covers off the other pallets. More bullet-torn bodies. He scrambled from tent to tent.

They had all been butchered. Camels, goats, dogs, men and boys. The women and girls had been carried away.

He leaned against the rock face. The Sulubba had abandoned their neutrality in the Arab-Israeli conflict in gratitude to the State of Israel for arresting a cholera epidemic. They had accepted the alliance as the Will of Allah who was known to use unorthodox methods to preserve the desert for its designated dwellers. Now, from beyond death, they would glimpse the real truth: the Sons of Isaac and Ishmael would destroy both the desert and its inhabitants before they destroyed each other.

First light slithered across the wadi. Soon vultures would crowd the sky and alert the border patrols.

He grappled with his fatigue and reexamined the carnage. Inconceivable as it seemed, the Sulubba seemed to have walked straight into an ambush. They had been killed by a coordinated burst. Probably from high terrain—while they had been on the move. Resistance had been impossible.

The abduction of the women and girls suggested the ambushers were not Bedouin raiders. The laws of the desert held women sacrosanct; carrying them off would stain the honor, name and ancestry of the raiders. Jordanian soldiers, mostly Bedouins themselves, adhered to the same code. Conversely, to have surprised the Sulubba, the ambushers must have been disciplined and highly trained. That indicated a commando unit. The histrionic arrangement of the corpses pointed to WOJ. Such mummery, WOJ believed, communicated to friend and foe the measure of their zeal.

Boaz considered aborting the rest of the mission. Without the Sulubba he could not create a diversion at the refugee camp. And since the Sulubba camels had been slaughtered, he had no chance of reaching the camp—still some twenty kilometers away—in time for the early-morning activity. Last, he had to deliver the tapes to Mossad.

But he could not bring himself to abandon Aaron. And the lightless eyes of the Sulubba boys begged for vengeance.

Screams shattered the desert's silence.

He climbed onto the overhang and crawled to where it met the sheer side of the hillock. Beyond lay a plateau which descended gently to another wadi through which the desert track snaked north toward Wahdat. The screams had come from the plateau. He edged his way around the hillock to the ledge on the other side. He saw them as he dropped for cover.

There were seventeen: nine women and eight girls. They had been stripped naked, and they had been lined up, side by side, in some perverse discipline, according to height. They were still screaming; and though, as Sulubba, they never veiled themselves, they were trying to cover their faces to maintain dignity in the presence of imminent rape. Six men, armed with submachine guns, shuffled about inspecting breasts, buttocks and genitals.

The men wore Jordanian uniforms. But their guns were Russian, and Russian weapons were not standard issue in the Jordanian army. They had to be members of Idris Ali's platoon.

A Land-Rover, bearing the emblem of the United Nations Relief and Works Agency (UNRWA), indicated that the unit had expropriated the vehicle from Wahdat.

Boaz screwed the silencer onto his gun, prepared spare magazines, and wiped his hands dry of sweat. The mission had been reprieved.

As the men dropped their guns to take off their trousers, he walked toward them, firing in rapid succession. The women and children stopped screaming and stared at the men falling as if struck down by Allah's wrath. Then the men started screaming.

Boaz watched them quiver in agony. He had disabled them, dispensing four bullets to each, at elbows and kneecaps.

The women and girls surrounded him, urging him to kill the men. He pushed aside a woman who was trying to wrench his gun from him to carry out the executions herself.

"Get dressed."

The women instantly acknowledged his authority, picked up their clothes and disappeared behind the rocks. Boaz slammed a new magazine into his gun and stared at the wounded. He always welcomed extremism. It clarified issues and enmities; left no room for partial right or wrong, hence no reason for hesitation. It was the constant negative that made him and WOJ the same; on contact they repelled each other predeterminedly.

Four of the men stared back with hatred and defiance. The eyes of the other two begged for mercy.

He was tempted to show them his circumcision, to declare his Jewishness, but they were Arabs, not Nazis; they would have been circumcised themselves. Instead he drew the Star of David on the sand. "Israeli."

The hatred in the eyes of the defiant four multiplied. One spat at him. He shot all four dead. To justify his madness, he reiterated to himself that they deserved their death, that rape warranted the heaviest punishment, that his sister had to be avenged yet again. And if the thousand eyes he had extinguished for those he had lost condemned him to a similar death, so be it. That also was part of the madness.

He turned to the two he had spared. One lay paralyzed with terror. He would be unable to answer questions. Boaz shot him, too. The other, though on the verge of hysteria, was still clinging to hope. Boaz squatted by him and addressed him in Arabic.

"Warriors of Jihad—are you?"

The man wailed pitifully.

Boaz prodded him with his gun. "What is it to be? This miserable world—or Paradise?"

"Mercy . . . Please. . . ."

"Answer then. What's your name?"

"Sharif."

"WOJ—are you?"

"Yes."

"Where are you camped?"

"Wahdat."

"What for?"

"Training."

"In organized killings of the Sulubba? And early-morning orgies with their women?"

"Just—training."

Boaz tapped the silencer on Sharif's shattered elbow. Sharif howled.

Boaz waited until the howl became a moan. "You can't be training, Sharif. Not with the Jordanians keeping a close watch!"

Sharif cast an agonized look at Boaz's gun, then mumbled, "We are . . . on a mission . . . with Idris Ali. . . ."

"Go on. . . ."

"We discovered . . . an Israeli spy. . . . We followed him."

"Did you catch him?"

Sharif paused.

Boaz waved his gun threateningly.

Sharif screeched. "Yes . . . Yes . . ."

"And?"

"We took him to the camp. Idris Ali wanted to know why he had returned to Mount Nebo . . . so soon after Abu Ismail's *ta-hannuth* . . . retreat."

"When did you leave camp?"

"Last evening."

"To ambush the Sulubba? Why?"

"They were asking questions. . . . Idris Ali knows the Sulubba. . . . Jew's mercenaries. . . . We were ordered to kill them before they informed on us. . . ."

"The Israeli spy—where's he being kept?"

"The UNRWA office. The blue house, near the gate."

"How many on guard duty?"

"None. Idris Ali didn't think it was necessary. . . ."

"When are you expected back?"

"We're not. We didn't know how long it would take to deal with the Sulubba. Our orders were to go straight to Amman—then fly to Tripoli."

Boaz checked his watch: 5:23. There was the UNWRA Land-Rover. He could reach Wahdat by 6:00—early enough to corner Idris Ali. He would have to take some of the women with him, but he could make use of them. They would be as loyal as their men, and their tales of atrocity about WOJ members posing as Jordanian soldiers would incense the troops stationed at the camp. That would provide him with the necessary diversion.

"One last question, Sharif. What was Abu Ismail doing at Mount Nebo?"

"He can see Al-Quds from there. That's where it had to happen. *Lailat al-qadr*—the Night of Decree."

"What?"

"The Divine Proclamation."

Boaz, perturbed, struck him.

Sharif, crossing the threshold of fear and pain, screamed his answer: "And it has been proclaimed. Abu Ismail is The Deliverer! Al-Mahdi! The Caliph of Islam who will execute Operation Dragons!"

Boaz felt panic rise within him. *Al-Mahdi* conjured visions of endless hordes on rampage. And "dragons" was the doom-ridden word of the Scriptures.

He stood up. The women had dressed and were squatting in a semicircle, waiting. Sharif was staring at him, suspended between apocalyptic hysteria and earthly pain.

Boaz pushed three of the oldest women and the youngest children toward the Land-Rover.

"Get in."

They did so without demur. He was about to tell the other women that they should wait, that he would send help from the camp, but they had anticipated him and were moving away. He watched them approach Sharif. He had intended to kill him also, but it was no longer necessary.

WAHDAT, JORDAN

At 6:11 A.M., Boaz abandoned the Land-Rover on the outskirts of Wahdat. He turned to the women.

"Take the children. Go into the village. Rouse the villagers and the troops! Don't say anything about me. Tell them you've escaped —and that your sisters are still captive."

The women nodded obediently.

"Now, go—give voice to your grief!"

The women ran toward the village.

Keeping directly in front of the morning sun, Boaz approached the camp. He reached the UNRWA parking compound without mishap. He paused to survey the camp.

It was as bleak as any in Arab lands. Wire barriers encircled the perimeter to meet at two oil drums that served as the main gate. The Arab observance of status divided the camp into three sections. The first, immediately behind the gate, consisted of a line of whitewashed brick houses on each side of a dirt track, the main thoroughfare by virtue of the drinking well situated in its middle. Beyond the houses stretched a conglomeration of mud and corrugated iron huts; and beyond those, extending into the desert, a patchwork of tents. The huts and tents were, respectively, the shelters of the refugees and their camp followers. The brick houses were for UNRWA personnel and families of repute.

Boaz concentrated on the UNRWA block. The first two houses served as school and infirmary. The third was the administration office, the blue house, so painted not because it was the UN color, but to ward off the evil eye.

That WOJ should have assistance from UNRWA did not surprise him. Staffed mainly by Palestinians, UNRWA had been notoriously active in preserving—and, at times, inflaming—the refugees' misery.

Boaz waited until Jordanian troops from the garrison, trailed by villagers and the wailing Sulubba women, appeared at the camp.

Within minutes, the soldiers had rounded up the UNRWA officials and refugee leaders. Boaz kept his eyes on the blue house. Idris Ali had not come out to investigate the commotion. Had

Sharif given him wrong information? Or had Idris Ali moved quarters? If so, he would have to scour the camp—a daunting task.

When the tumult in the compound reached the well, already crowded with people drawing water for morning chores, he sauntered toward the camp. Accusations and denials would prevail for a while.

He reached the UNRWA block and, seemingly bored by the commotion, sat by the school porch. Except for a little boy, no one paid him any attention. He waited until the boy reverted to watching the crowd, then slipped away from the porch and swiftly reached the back of the administration office. He took out his gun and screwed on the silencer.

There were two windows; one, wide enough for entry. He moved to it and listened for sounds. The house was silent. He looked in. The room was large. It had filing cabinets and a bed. The bed had not been used.

He forced the window open and slipped into the room. He tiptoed to the door and peered out.

The back room opened onto a narrow corridor; opposite, a door, left open, revealed an empty front room that had a desk and a typewriter. Down the corridor, there were two more doors, one on each side. Farther down, a small hall led to the entrance.

He ghosted down the corridor. He tried the door on the left. It was unlocked. He peered in. The kitchen, partitioned at one end to accommodate a toilet; both sides of the partition empty.

He moved to the door on the right. A cardboard sign pinned to it indicated it as the main office. Gently, he pushed the handle down. Also unlocked. He crouched down and swung the door open. He caught a glimpse of a large desk, a sophisticated tape recorder. The door hit an obstacle. He rolled into the room, his gun poised, seeking a target.

He identified the corpse instantly: Aaron. Purple-blue swollen face clotted with blood at the mouth. The eyes darkly reflecting horror.

A moment later, he heard footsteps at the front door.

He steadied his gun, dislodged a grenade from his belt, pulled the pin but kept the detonator down with his finger. He crouched low behind the door and gauged the footsteps. Two people: one man, one woman or child.

They stood, visible through the crack of the door as if wanting him to identify them. The man was tall and powerful. His hands were empty, though the bulge in his jacket indicated he was armed. The other was the boy who had been sitting opposite the school.

The man spoke, to Boaz's surprise, in Hebrew. "Please don't shoot. I am Osman Nusseibi."

Soft-spoken: by nature—not for effect. Boaz had not needed the formal introduction. There was a huge file at Mossad on Osman Nusseibi, colonel in Al-Moukhabarat al-Ammah, Jordanian Secret Service. A man renowned for diligent, often brilliant work. The wonder was that they had not crossed paths before.

"May I send the child away? So that we can talk?"

"Yes."

Osman Nusseibi patted the boy on the back. The boy ran off, very pleased with himself.

Osman walked into the room. Boaz kicked the door shut.

They stood at a distance, wary, sizing each other up.

"Whom do I have the pleasure of meeting?"

Boaz ignored the question. Osman, good-naturedly, did not press him. Boaz ran his eyes across the room. The window was open. If he threw the grenade, jumped out of the window, shot down those men of Osman's who would be outside, and ran to the UNRWA car compound. . . . A slim chance. He eased gently toward the window.

Osman pointed at Aaron. "Wouldn't you want him buried? A brave man. Killed himself."

Boaz edged closer to the window. "Tortured to death more likely."

"Tortured, yes. But not to death. He committed suicide. Choked himself."

Boaz glared at him. "That's new."

"If you bite hard on your tongue—cause enough bleeding— you can choke.—He knew any man can be made to talk, or write all he knows. . . ."

Boaz felt his scalp prickle. "Disappointing for you."

"I wasn't here. Rubbing shoulders with WOJ is not my line. Nor torture."

Boaz reached the window. His finger twitched to hurl the grenade.

Osman held out his hand appeasingly. "Don't try it, please."

"What else would you suggest?"

"The front door. Later. This way, you'll get killed. Oh, no doubt you'll kill me and my men in the process, but that would be a great pity."

"I could get away."

"Perhaps. Depends how many grenades you have, and whether you'd use them all against refugees."

"Grenades?"

"My dear friend, a man who keeps his hand in his aba is either playing with himself, or hiding an arsenal."

Boaz smiled grimly. "Ten grenades. One already primed. If it's my life against the refugees, it'll be the refugees."

Osman squatted down. "We're allies—I want you to believe that."

"That's original. Go on."

As if that were the cue he needed, Osman switched to Arabic and spoke with even greater confidence. "It's as important for Jordan as it is for Israel to stop Abu Ismail. In his vision of a theocracy, there's no room for the Jew or the Hashemite."

"Or the Christian—don't forget the Christian."

Osman rasped impatiently. "I am not being rhetorical. If we're to come to an agreement, we have to talk in earnest."

"Agreement?"

Osman took out a pack of cigarettes and offered it to Boaz. Boaz refused.

Osman lit one for himself. "There's a rumor going around that Abu Ismail has declared himself Al-Mahdi."

Boaz moved to the wall by the side of the window, out of range of possible snipers. "He's not the first. He won't be the last."

"Nonetheless, he's preparing something big. Code-name: Operation Dragons. Any idea what it can be?"

Boaz held his look. "No. You?"

Osman pointed to Aaron's corpse. "No . . . But he knew—Harun."

Boaz forced himself to look at Aaron. "Is that his name?"

"We both know who he is. And if Idris Ali had to deal with him personally—"

"Where is he—Idris Ali?"

"Gone. Back to Libya. Late last night."

"And you let him?"

Osman growled. "We can't hit WOJ when they're in the open. Our Arab brothers have little compassion for us—particularly after the troubles in 1970 with the Palestinians. You know that."

Boaz shrugged.

Osman inhaled deeply from his cigarette. "Perhaps the tapes can tell us what Operation Dragons is."

Boaz remained impassive. "What tapes?"

"Harun's. The ones you came to collect."

Boaz's hand tightened on the primed grenade.

Osman stubbed out his cigarette. "We intercepted his signal to Mossad. Decoded it. Tapes of Abu Ismail. Of utmost importance. Buried—for collection. Cover blown—come and get me. I was compelled to help. Not entirely on humanitarian grounds, I grant you. As I said, anything that concerns WOJ and is of utmost importance to Israel, is also of utmost importance to us. Alas, I got here too late. I had no option but to wait. Shitting myself, I don't mind admitting—in case Mossad couldn't mount a rescue. So—the tapes."

"If you decoded his signal, you must know where they are."

"Still playing games? Yes, we've got some coordinates. But they have Biblical references. Beyond our expertise, I regret to say."

Boaz pursed his lips in mock commiseration.

Osman pointed at the tape recorder on the desk. "I want copies of those tapes."

"Impossible."

"You don't seem to understand. You will keep the originals. That's imperative. I need to know what your evaluators make of them. Then, I hope, together we'll find ways of preempting Operation Dragons."

"How would we do that, Osman? Right now you're my prisoner. And I'm yours. What's likely to happen in the next minutes offers us little hope."

"My dear friend, nothing will happen."

"What about your men outside?"

"They'll carry Harun. We'll escort you back. South—the Arava valley. Safe from prying eyes."

"That would make history."

"Hardly. We've helped each other before. And we owe you a few. But for Mossad tipoffs, King Hussein would have been assassinated long ago. You can't dispute that, Boaz."

Boaz stared at him, disconcerted.

Osman chuckled and moved to the tape recorder. "That's right, Boaz. I know as much about you as you do of me. We've got a file on you—going almost as far back as your paratrooper days with Unit 202."

Boaz glowered. "I don't have the authority to make deals, Osman."

"Nor do I, if truth be known. But I'm making one. . . . Keep your grenade primed, if it'll make you feel safer."

THE ARAVA VALLEY, ISRAEL–JORDAN BORDER

Four of Osman's men laid out Aaron's body at the center of no-man's-land, then stood to attention. From the west, the military ambulance—summoned by Boaz with Osman's radio—streaked across the desert in a cloud of dust.

Boaz and Osman shook hands, longer than necessary, aware that the grip communicated more than an alliance of convenience.

The blast caught them in that position.

Boaz keeled over, pain searing across his back. When he managed to pull himself up on his arms, he saw Osman, blood-spattered, staggering in the direction of the blast, cursing in Arabic.

For long, interminable minutes, he stared at Osman's men, dead with gaping fissures in their bodies. There was no sign of Aaron's remains. Finally, he realized Aaron's corpse had been booby-trapped.

He managed to rise to his knees. He noted he was not too weak. He judged he had been hit by shrapnel—not very seriously.

He ran his hands over his chest to check his wounds. He felt a lump lodged in his palm. He stared at it. Part of a man's wrist, with the circular frame of a watch imbedded in the flesh. He started trembling. His hands continued searching. Other bits of flesh. Large and small splinters of bone. And finally, entwined in his hair, an ear. Quite intact.

He started screaming.

I Am Tired with My Own Life and the Lives of Those after Me.

T. S. ELIOT, A *Song for Simeon*

November 6, 1973

JERUSALEM, ISRAEL

From the Mossad office on the top floor, Gad Kidan watched the volatile crowd on Knesset Square. Some were carrying recriminations against the government's incompetence during the war; others were petitioning members of parliament for news of relatives presumed prisoners in Egypt or Syria. A third faction, gathered near the giant menorah, were demanding the continuation of the war until total victory and proclaiming that the seven-branched candelabrum, a gift from the British Parliament in the days when the West and not the oil sheikhs formulated foreign policy, now stood as a symbol of the West's betrayal. The zeal of this last group heartened Kidan. He could envisage rebuilding the nation on their shoulders.

He returned to the conference table and opened the folder containing the transcripts of Aaron's tapes.

They had been disappointing. Lengthy invocations from Abu Ismail to Allah on the evils of Israel and the decree for the jihad that would obliterate her. Nothing to constitute, as Aaron had claimed, intelligence of vital importance. Kidan had even wondered whether there had been other tapes that Boaz had failed to find, though the speculation, he suspected, stemmed from resentment. Boaz had not only had his citation ratified—thus achieving the distinction of a full set of decorations—but had also been promoted to full colonel—Kidan's own rank in the reserves.

Kidan wondered, as he always did in times of stress, why he tried so hard. His efforts always interacted with his loathing for

Boaz. Was it because Boaz symbolized Israel and he, Kidan, detested the Jewish state?

He was, after all, a European—born in Berlin. It had been his family, misguided intellectuals, who had dispatched him to Zion to work for the land and to partake in the purification of the Jew. He had found such aspirations degrading and had been grateful for the move only because it saved him from the concentration camps. The rest, particularly the steel he had acquired first in the ranks of the British army's Jewish Brigade, then in the Irgun, were his own achievements. Extraneous to Israel and the Jewish dream.

Thereafter, the more he had come into contact with his people, the less he had moderated his hatred for his Jewishness. Jews were relics of prehistory. Practitioners of a primitive religion, seekers of salvation as defined by hysterical prophets. Leeches clinging to time, with guile and pragmatism, awaiting the Messiah and the millennium, but knowing, deep in their hearts, that such insane notions were jokes in atrocious taste, typical of their spiteful God.

Thus, he remained a European. Forged by colonial history, initiated in the mysteries of power, member of a master pack.

His misfortune was that Europe had driven him to Israel. His fulfillment would lie in driving Israel into Europe.

That was why he sat on stools, tore his outer garments, prophesied doom. Why he fought the Establishment. And abhorred Boaz, the Jew.

The door opened. The Memouneh, chief of Mossad, compact, spring-heeled, walked in, solemnity accentuating the face Boaz had once compared to a Picasso portrait: the warrior Bar-Kokhba in profile, the scholar-martyr Akiba in full.

The Memouneh sat at the table without muttering the paternal greetings loved by his disciples. "Heard the news? We're near breakthrough at Kilometer 101. Looks like we'll sign a cease-fire with Egypt."

Kidan grunted. "And then what?"

"The POWs come home."

"And then?"

"We can try Syria."

"Step by step. One forward. Three backward."

"What do you want? A solution?"

"A once-and-for-all solution. Occupy Damascus, Cairo, Amman, Beirut—Riyadh, if necessary."

"And Moscow. Don't forget Moscow."

"I'm serious. We need to break their backs—for good."

"Children, Kidan. Have you buried children?"

"Time's not on our side—"

"Go forth—and multiply. Bring them up. Give them to the army—then talk about once-and-for-all solutions!"

Kidan, caution prevailing, smiled. "Let's agree to disagree, Zamora!"

The Memouneh grimaced at the name. Coined by a football-mad colleague, it implied that, like the legendary goalkeeper, he let few shots slip past him. Most of those who used it did so affectionately. Kidan never.

He placed a copy of the Scriptures before Kidan. "Read it."

Kidan glanced at the open page. A sentence was underlined:

Set Uriah in the forefront of the hottest battle, and withdraw from him, so that he may be hit, and die.

"Am I supposed to react?"

The Memouneh resonated each word. "If you ever again set up a mission behind my back, I'll skin you alive!"

Kidan tautened with anger. "The mission was imperative. How else could we have secured the tapes?"

"One of our ferrets in Jordan—"

"And Aaron? You expected me to abandon Aaron?"

The Memouneh growled. "I'd accept that if it were true. But I know you, Kidan! It was a dead man's mission!"

Kidan rose to ride his advantage. "I object to that, Zamora! Boaz came back. A little worse for wear, but only because he didn't have the wits to check for booby-traps!"

"Have you been to see him?"

Kidan forced a generous smile. "I thought I'd let him celebrate his promotion."

"Just pray he recovers!"

"Superficial wounds—why shouldn't he recover?"

"It's not the wounds. You pushed him too far! Sending him after weeks of fighting. Exhausted! And then the last straw. Splattered with a comrade's guts!"

Kidan fought down a surge of happiness. "Cracked up, has he? But—our best men don't crack up!"

The Memouneh's voice dropped menacingly low. "They do, Kidan. Because, unlike you, they are still human. Now sit down! Fortunately for you, every hand counts. I want to review the tapes."

Kidan sat down and resorted to a cigarette. The Memouneh, having recently given up smoking, watched him balefully, then continued. "It so happens, Kidan, you've stumbled on a hornet's nest."

"Ravings of a lunatic more likely. Dreams of unleashing global terror! Immolating Israel! Hot air!"

"I've run the transcript through the computer. There are key words repeated—again and again. Operation Dragons. Jihad. Jerusalem. Plane. Bomb. Firestorm. The Last of Days. The advent of Theocracy. Al-Mahdi."

"Vintage polemics. He's planning what every Palestinian terrorist group ends up planning. Convert a plane into a bomber, pass it off as a civilian airliner and send it on a kamikaze mission."

"The old standby? Last February we shot down a Libyan airliner in Sinai, killing one hundred six innocent people. And only a series of miracles prevented us from committing similar atrocities. Can't you see further than that?"

"Further where? That's the apogee. Remember the JAL 747 hijack from Amsterdam on July twentieth? They were going to crash it on Haifa if we hadn't threatened to blow them up in the air."

"That was Black September. We're talking about WOJ and Abu Ismail. Different leagues."

"Not so different."

"Come on, Kidan. Not every unshaven face is Yasir Arafat. Abu Ismail knows he can't penetrate our air defenses. If he stands a chance, it's by land or sea."

"All right—a series of fedayeen raids by land or sea. So what's new?"

"His target. The tapes suggest it's Jerusalem. Yet Jerusalem is more sacred to him than Mecca or Medina. According to his *War Rule*, Jerusalem will be the capital of his Islamic theocracy."

"Jerusalem is a red herring, Zamora."

"Firestorm—what does that conjure up for you?"

"Arab pyrotechnics, if you'll forgive the pun."

The Memouneh rose and started pacing. "What about Hiroshima?"

Kidan looked up sharply. "Hiroshima?"

"The A-bomb. *Firestorm* was how they described the blast."

"Are you suggesting Abu Ismail's going nuclear? That's preposterous!"

The Memouneh stopped pacing and looked out the window. The crowd in Knesset Square had increased, but it had quieted down. Mourning. Eighteen hundred fifty-four were known to be dead; there would be more from among the severely wounded and missing. About 2,500 before they stopped nailing down coffins. All those sons . . .

"And dragons, Kidan . . . Why dragons? Why something

Judeo-Christian? Why not some glorious reference from the Koran? Or a big emotional word like Revenge, Redemption, Retribution?"

"Really, Zamora—"

"Abu Ismail knows the Scriptures. There's a prophecy in Jeremiah: '*I will make Jerusalem heaps, and a den of dragons.*' "

"Don't you think you're projecting your worst fears?"

"Am I? I've just had a report from our cell in Libya. WOJ have a new slogan: *I will make Jerusalem heaps.*"

Kidan shook his head stubbornly. "But Jerusalem is sacred to him. You said so yourself. . . ."

"The Zealots of Masada held their wives and children sacred, too. Rather than surrender them to the Romans, they killed them."

"If we're looking for wild theories, why pick on a nuclear attack? Why not chemical warfare? Nerve gas? Or some biological agent? Deadly bacteria . . ."

"Why not indeed? It would be simpler. Except that Abu Ismail will want a big bang so that even Allah can hear him."

"Terrorists holding the world to ransom with a nuclear device. That's an old standby, too."

"Not just terrorists, Kidan. Terrorists backed by Libya!"

"Libya is not a nuclear power."

"Not for Qaddafi's lack of effort. He's tried everything to lay his hands on nuclear bombs."

"And he expects Abu Ismail to steal them for him?"

"Or the raw material."

"Impractical. Making nuclear bombs requires technology, personnel—"

"Hardly a problem with Libya's oil wealth. And if the raw material is plutonium instead of uranium, not all that difficult."

"There's a big flaw in that argument. If Abu Ismail got hold of a bomb, do you think he'd hand it over to Qaddafi?"

"That's the crux of it. Qaddafi, conceivably, might think twice before unleashing a nuclear holocaust. But Abu Ismail—as Al-Mahdi?"

Kidan waved agitated hands. "It's all conjecture. We have no proof."

The Memouneh sat down. His face, drained of color, looked embalmed. "Only because Abu Ismail hasn't said it in so many words. Or maybe Aaron couldn't record it—ran out of tape. Immaterial. Countermeasures against Operation Dragons are now priority."

Kidan shrugged, disinclined to argue further. What did it mat-

ter what Operation Dragons was? Abu Ismail had to be destroyed.
"Easier said than done. With Aaron dead we've lost our direct link
to WOJ. We're also desperately undermanned."

"Osman Nusseibi will help out—at least to keep tabs on WOJ."

Kidan looked shocked. "You've told him your evaluation?"

"No. But Abu Ismail as pretender to the throne of Islam's Savior—that's enough to give Osman nightmares."

"Countermeasures might run to a major offensive. We'll need
a commanding officer. . . ."

"That's decided. Boaz."

Kidan got up brusquely. Tormented by Furies—all bearing
Boaz's features. "Look, you may think Boaz is the noblest prick in
Israel."

He hesitated. "Why that reference to prick?"

"He's never failed a mission, Kidan."

"You don't send a tank after a snake."

"I'm an old-fashioned soldier. I'd send a tank after anything."

Kidan shook with fury. "He's not fit."

"We'll mend him."

"We're not here to provide psychotherapy—"

"Nor to flaunt jealousies!"

"Jealousies? For God's sake—he's cracked!"

"And you, Kidan. You think you're not—taking it out on a
woman who has eyes only for Boaz?"

Kidan flopped back in his chair, cursing humiliation for daring
to strike him down. "Shouldn't you get him out of hospital first?"

The Memouneh nodded. "I will. Somehow."

November 7, 1973

TEL AVIV, ISRAEL

FROM: OFFICE OF CENTRAL REFERENCE (MOSSAD)

Further to the Memouneh's directives for priority vigilance on WOJ's
Operation Dragons, the following summarized profile on Abu Ismail is
declassified for dissemination to rank and file and friendly intelligence
agencies.

SUBJECT: ABU ISMAIL, LEADER OF WARRIORS OF JIHAD (WOJ)

LIFE HISTORY

BORN AMIN TARIQ JAMAL, APRIL 24, 1920, IN HEBRON. PARENTS: DEVOUT
MUSLIMS (SUNNI). RELIGIOUS EDUCATION IN HEBRON MADRASA UNTIL MAY
17, 1939.

DURING WORLD WAR II, RECRUITED AS INTERPRETER BY BRITISH MILITARY AUTHORITIES.

AFTER THE WAR, CONVINCED THAT THE CREATION OF ISRAEL WAS MERELY A QUESTION OF TIME, JOINED THE ARAB OFFICE IN JERUSALEM, AND PLAYED A MAJOR ROLE IN DRAFTING THE ARAB CASE FOR PALESTINE: EVIDENCE SUBMITTED TO THE ANGLO-AMERICAN COMMITTEE OF INQUIRY (MARCH 1946).

UPON UN GENERAL ASSEMBLY PARTITION RESOLUTION OF 1947, JOINED TRANSJORDAN'S "ARAB LEGION" IN TIME FOR THE HOSTILITIES OF 1948.

PERFORMED BRILLIANTLY THROUGHOUT THE WAR OF INDEPENDENCE.

AFTER THE 1949 ARMISTICE, WHEN TRANSJORDAN ANNEXED THE WEST BANK (THUS BECOMING JORDAN), HE OPPOSED THE ANNEXATION AND SUPPORTED THE NOTORIOUS FORMER MUFTI OF JERUSALEM, HAJ AMIN AL-HUSAINI.

THE ALLIANCE WAS BRIEF.

THEREAFTER, SELF-ASCRIBED POLITICAL AND RELIGIOUS LEADER.

DECLARED HIMSELF MYSTIC WHILE IN EXILE IN BEIRUT (1950) AND INAUGURATED THE SECRET SOCIETY TARIQAT AL-QUDS, "BROTHERHOOD OF JERUSALEM," TO INSTRUCT INITIATES IN THE WILL OF ALLAH.

PLAYED A MAJOR PART IN PLOTTING THE ASSASSINATION OF KING ABDALLAH OF JORDAN (1951). HE IS KNOWN TO HAVE BEEN INVOLVED IN ASSASSINATION ATTEMPTS ON KING HUSSEIN.

NOTE: HE HAS REPEATEDLY DECLARED THAT "THE DUTY OF THE ARAB MASSES IS TO DESTROY BOTH ISRAEL AND JORDAN," THAT "THE HASHEMITES AND THE ZIONISTS LIVE ON THE DEBRIS OF ARAB SOULS."

THROUGHOUT THE FIFTIES AND SIXTIES, EXCOMMUNICATED FROM MAINSTREAM OF ARAB POLITICS, SPENT HIS TIME TRAVELING IN RUSSIA, CHINA, AFRICA, THE USA AND THOSE MUSLIM COUNTRIES OPEN TO HIM, TO ASSESS POLITICAL ASPIRATIONS.

AFTER TWENTY YEARS OF ISOLATION—DESCRIBED BY HIM AS "THE YEARS IN THE WILDERNESS THAT EVERY PROPHET MUST TREAD"—EMERGED AS THE MOST CHARISMATIC ARAB POLITICO-RELIGIOUS THINKER. (SEE "EVALUATION.")

DURING THAT TIME WROTE NUMEROUS PAMPHLETS, EACH ATTEMPTING TO ACCOMMODATE THE PERENNIAL DREAM OF PAN-ISLAMISM WITH EXTREMIST WESTERN IDEOLOGIES. THUS HIS PRESENT POLITICAL PHILOSOPHY, EXPOUNDED IN THE MANIFESTO THE DOCTRINE AND WAR RULE OF THE RADICAL THEOCRACY OF AL-QUDS (SEE SUBHEADING), INCORPORATES THE DOGMAS OF MACCHIAVELLI, JOHANN MOST, MARX, LENIN, MAO AND FRANZ FANON. THE INFLUENCES OF JOHANN MOST'S PHILOSOPHY OF TERROR AND FANON'S TENETS OF CONSERVATION OF ANCIENT CULTURES AS THE WEAPON AGAINST IMPERIALISM HAVE SANCTIONED HIS DETERMINATION TO CREATE A POWER BASE SIMILAR TO "THE ASSASSINS," THE ANCIENT ISMAILI SECT THAT PERPETRATED UNABATED VIOLENCE FOR RELIGIOUS–POLITICAL AIMS.

POPULARITY OF THE ABOVE-MENTIONED MANIFESTO RESULTED IN OFFI-CIAL INVESTITURE OF THE NAME ABU ISMAIL, "FATHER ISMAIL," HIS BROTH-ERHOOD NAME SINCE 1951.

OBTAINED SUPPORT FROM COLONEL QADDAFI OF LIBYA (1970).

REORGANIZED THE SECRET BROTHERHOOD, TARIQAT AL-QUDS, FIRST AS AL-FEDAYEEN AL-QUDS, THEN AS AL-FEDAYEEN AL-JIHAD, THE PRESENT WARRIORS OF JIHAD (WOJ) (1971).

SET UP HEADQUARTERS IN TRIPOLI, LIBYA (1971).

THE DOCTRINE AND WAR RULE OF THE RADICAL THEOCRACY OF AL-QUDS.

THIS DOCTRINE IS NOT AS CONFUSED AS THE TITLE SUGGESTS, BUT A SHREWD BLEND OF ALL MUSLIM ASPIRATIONS, INCLUDING SEEMINGLY CON-FLICTING ONES.

THE DOCTRINE PROPOSES A UTOPIAN SOCIALIST STATE, DIVESTED OF ALL LEADERSHIP SAVE THAT OF ALLAH, TO BE CREATED, FOLLOWING THE DIS-SOLUTION OF THE STATES OF ISRAEL AND JORDAN AND THE EXTERMINATION OF THE JEWISH PEOPLE, WITHIN "GREATER PALESTINE," WITH JERUSALEM AS ITS CAPITAL. IT ALSO PROPOSES THAT THIS STATE WILL BE THE FOUNDA-TION OF A GLOBAL ISLAMIC THEOCRACY.

IT FURTHER PROPOSES TO ESTABLISH THIS STATE BY STRICT ADHERENCE TO A WAR RULE.

THE DOCTRINE'S APPEAL LIES IN THE FOLLOWING FACTORS:

1. IT WILL DESTROY ISRAEL AND JORDAN AND THEIR PEOPLE.

2. IT WILL PROVIDE SOCIAL JUSTICE FOR THE OPPRESSED ARABS FOR WHOM POLITICS IS AN UNCHANGING LIFE OF MISERY UNDER A SUCCESSION OF TYRANTS.

3. IT WILL REESTABLISH THE ANCIENT WAY OF LIFE AS STIPULATED IN THE SHARI'A.

4. AS A THEOCRACY AND CALIPHATE, IT WILL ESTABLISH THE KINGDOM OF ALLAH.

5. BY ELEVATING JERUSALEM TO THE STATUS OF HOLY CITY, EVEN ABOVE MECCA AND MEDINA, IT WILL BREAK THE SPIRITUAL HOLD OF SAUDI ARABIA THAT MOST ARABS CONSIDER TOO PRO-WEST.

NOTE: THE DEMOTION OF MECCA AND MEDINA TO SECONDARY HOLINESS MAY SEEM AN IMPLAUSIBLE AIM, BUT IT MUST BE REMEMBERED THAT THE PROPHET MOHAMMED HAD INITIALLY URGED HIS FOLLOWERS TO PRAY IN THE DIRECTION OF JERUSALEM, AND THAT THE SUPREME MOSQUE, AL-MAS-JID AL-AQSA, WAS ERECTED, ACCORDING TO TRADITION, ON TEMPLE MOUNT.

6. AS A RELIGIOUS AND SPIRITUAL CENTER, THE THEOCRACY WILL CON-TROL ISLAM'S POLITICS AND WEALTH.

EVALUATION

ABU ISMAIL CONSIDERS HIMSELF CHOSEN BY ALLAH.

HE IS THE FIRST ARAB LEADER OF THE TWENTIETH CENTURY TO CREATE A MESSIANIC MOVEMENT.

HE IS AN ASTUTE POLITICIAN, READY TO EMBRACE ANY DOCTRINE THAT CAN SERVE HIS AIMS, AND IS OFTEN RUTHLESS AGAINST FELLOW ARABS. (ONE OF THE WAR RULES STIPULATES: "INTER-ARAB TERRORISM IS THE PRICE ARABS MUST PAY FOR THE ESTABLISHMENT OF THE THEOCRACY.")

HE IS A THEOCRAT WITH A DIFFERENCE: AN ECLECTIC WHO HAS WINNOWED THROUGH THE DOGMAS OF THE ISLAMIC SECTS AND RESTRUCTURED THEM INTO A RADICALLY REFORMIST ORDER.

THUS, WHILE HE UPHOLDS THE SUNNI TENET THAT THE FAITHFUL NEEDS NO INTERCESSOR BEFORE ALLAH, HE STIPULATES THE SHI'A TENET THAT THE FAITHFUL MUST HAVE A PIOUS IMAM, SUCH AS HE, TO MEDIATE HIS EARTHLY SOJOURN UNTIL THE ADVENT OF AL-MAHDI.

DESPITE SUCH LICENSE, OR BECAUSE OF IT, HE IS CONSIDERED AN ARIF, A MAN TO WHOM DIVINE WILL COMES IN THE VISION OF THE MYSTIC AS OPPOSED TO TRADITION OR REASON.

HE IS A FANATICAL ARABIST AND REFUSES TO ACCEPT THAT THE JEW, FOR CENTURIES, PERSECUTED AND MOCKED AS INFERIOR, SHOULD ACHIEVE EQUALITY WITH THE ARAB AND, IN THE CASE OF ISRAEL, PROVE SUPERIOR AT WARFARE.

SINCE 1951, HE HAS BEEN A TARGET NOT ONLY FOR OUR AGENTS, BUT ALSO FOR THOSE OF ARAB STATES. ARAB SATIRISTS MOCKINGLY ATTRIBUTE HIS SURVIVAL TO THE TRIPLE TALISMANS—BLUE-EYE, BULB OF GARLIC AND HORSESHOE—WHICH HE ALWAYS WEARS PINNED TO HIS CLOTHES. HIS FOLLOWERS BELIEVE HE HAS BEEN BESTOWED WITH BARAKA, THE PROTECTION OF THE PROPHET.

THIS CONVICTION IS FURTHER BROADENED BY HIS ASCETIC WAY OF LIFE, AND PARADOXICALLY BY THE NUMBER OF SONS HE HAS FATHERED THROUGH COUNTLESS WOMEN, SPREADING, AS IT WERE, THE DIVINE SEED.

HIS SEXUAL EXCESSES DO NOT CONTRADICT HIS ASCETICISM: HE USES WOMEN AS CHATTELS AND FOR PROPAGATION.

THIS ATTITUDE MAY BE PSYCHOLOGICALLY RELATED TO THE FACT THAT HE WAS BELIEVED TO HAVE MARRIED, IN 1938, A WOMAN CALLED RUQAYYA, THAT SHE BORE HIM A SON, BUT THAT BOTH MOTHER AND CHILD DIED WITHIN HOURS OF THE BIRTH. IT HAS BEEN IMPOSSIBLE TO VERIFY THE MARRIAGE AND THE DEATHS FOR LACK OF RECORDS.

November 9, 1973

TRIPOLI, LIBYA

In the command room, Abu Ismail completed the noon prayers, pulled himself up painfully and lingered at the window.

The palm-lined Shari'a Istiklâl skirted the bay toward the Marcus Aurelius triumphal arch. The sixteenth-century Spanish castle dominated the city, almost obliterating the octagonal minaret of the Karamanli mosque. And the Mediterranean lay open, beyond the Razel Sur breakwater, like the loins of a harlot. Throughout history, land and sea had consorted with pagans, Jews and Christians. It would be clear, to those who could see into the Divine Will, why Allah had summoned him to purify the world.

He caught sight of a limousine speeding toward the villa. Idris Ali was hurrying home to lay great deeds at his feet.

Controlling the joy of imminent reunion, he seated himself in the Louis XVI armchair and signaled Nazmi to open the drapes covering the side wall. The bodyguard revealed the plate glass that separated the command room from the mirrored harem.

Abu Ismail surveyed the naked bodies.

Before Qaddafi's revolution, the WOJ headquarters had been the pleasure palace of a Sanusi playboy diplomat. Although, upon receiving the mansion, Abu Ismail had duly exorcised it, he had done so, to the surprise of his followers, by word and not by deed. He had not destroyed the plethora of pornographic films, aids and costumes; the racks, whips, pulleys and chains of bondage; the wine cellars and the drug despository.

Since then, the appliances had helped loosen the tongues of many adversaries, as well as discipline the wayward warrior. The one-way mirror system had enabled him to spy on rebels and would-be deserters, and to video-record conferences with Qaddafi or members of the Revolutionary Command Council. The sexual aids, wines and drugs, liberally lavished on diplomats and intermediaries, had secured international support.

These successes had proved his contention that all—except he —had weak flesh and even weaker souls. They had also reconfirmed his faith in the methods of those martyrs of Islam, the *Hashishiyyin*—known to the West as "Assassins"—whose members, inducted with visions of Paradise during orgies of drugs and sex, had executed Allah's Will in blissful trance and without regard for personal safety.

Today, those undergoing indoctrination were the twenty technicians and the fifty virgins Idris Ali had dispatched a week earlier. The technicians, recruited from the oil industries of the Gulf, would form the labor for the bomb. The virgins, sturdy-bodied and politicized at Arab universities, would quench the task force's sexual and psychological needs by acting as houris, maidens of Paradise.

They were still asleep. They had been in the harem for three days and had been induced to copulate beyond exhaustion. Their faces reflected the peace that death, in the path of Allah, always provided.

Abu Ismail turned toward the television monitors, imbedded in the back wall. The screens showed two of his warriors, faces swathed in bandages, lying on adjacent beds. The WOJ team of surgeons and nurses stood in attendance.

One of the warriors, though deeply sedated, was moaning. His operation had necessitated extensive skin grafts. Abu Ismail felt pity stir within. But the warrior, chosen to be altered to the image of glory, would be redeemed.

He concentrated on the other. That one's bandages were being removed. When the new face appeared in close-up, Abu Ismail compared it with the photograph of a smiling man that had served as the model.

"Our physicist, Al-Mahdi?"

Abu Ismail surrendered to a smile, turned, and faced Idris Ali. For a moment, Savior and disciple imbibed each other's presence. Then Abu Ismail extended his right hand. Idris Ali kissed it and placed it on his forehead. Abu Ismail embraced him. "Are you well, my son?"

"I've traveled the world—struggled to be worthy of you. I've much to report."

Abu Ismail clasped him closer. "May your shadow never shrink. Shake off the dust of your travels first. Would you like a woman?"

Idris Ali fell to Abu Ismail's feet. "Just your blessing."

Abu Ismail caressed Idris Ali's hair. "You are my son. On you my favor rests."

✗

Later, as Nazmi served them both a narghile, Idris Ali presented his files.

"I'll accord my will to yours, Al-Mahdi, and start with thunder. Here—a comprehensive list of nuclear-material conveyances for the next six months. I found, as you predicted, the right man at the International Atomic Energy Agency in Vienna. Karl-Heinz Mueller—a lowly clerk, hungry for money, and an old Nazi. I pretended I was an Egyptian agent investigating possible collusion between Israel and an IAEA member. He procured the lists, without incurring suspicion, simply by photocopying them at source. His death, too, has caused no suspicion. I engorged him with wine, then suffocated him with his own vomit."

Abu Ismail ran his eyes over the photocopies. "I note you have singled out a target: Portuguese."

"My assignment was to find plutonium, Al-Mahdi. Enriched uranium, you informed me, requires complicated processes to extract weapons-grade material—processes too laborious for us, and likely to be detected by the enemy. That excludes all the uranium transports. The plutonium transports, all but one, are in the form of mixed fuel elements—again posing complex problems of extraction. The exception is the consignment from the Chinon Nuclear Power and Reprocessing Plant in France to the Sacavem Nuclear Power Station in Portugal. Fifteen kilos of plutonium dioxide— pure enough and very stable. A target that selects itself, I'm sure you'll agree."

Abu Ismail nodded. "So be it."

"We are fortunate in one aspect. The Sacavem cargo is the first of its kind between France and Portugal—a recent contract. Security would be untested."

Abu Ismail's eyes rippled with light. "Not fortunate, my son. That is how Allah supports a true jihad. Note further: the transportation is scheduled for the end of the Christian year. That coincides with the hajj. As I shall be seen to be in Mecca, the enemy will assume no water can run uphill. Moreover, my son, the early acquisition of the plutonium will enable us to attack on the date Allah favors most. April 25—the Jew's Independence Day. Now continue. . . ."

Idris Ali nodded solemnly. "I have here undertakings from twelve liberation groups to provide us with mercenaries. As you commissioned me when I reported from Aden, I have already engaged one: Musaddiq Hamdi of the Eritrean Liberation Front. Through him we have also secured a motor yacht, the *Succubus*, one of the fastest vessels in the Red Sea."

"Excellent. That completes our supply line. I have since requisitioned a DC-6B. We also have a submarine, the *Khanjar*. French built, class *Daphné*, modified to improve speed, range and firepower. I have instructed Qaddafi that she be seconded to the People's Democratic Republic of Yemen. Thus she will not appear to be ours. She is on her way now around the Cape. She should reach Aden in good time. Next?"

"Some of the other mercenaries will maintain surveillance on the Sacavem cargo, both at Chinon and Orly."

"And Lisbon? Do we have someone there to infiltrate the airport?"

"Portuguese airport employees are closely screened. But we should be able to subvert one. The Mozambique Front is shortlisting suitable candidates."

"Good."

"Last item on the mercenaries. I have a name for our high-explosives expert: Hiroshi Anami—a deserter from *Rengo Sekigun*,

the Japanese Red Army. He lives in obscurity—or so he believes
—in Hong Kong. He is equally proficient in electronics, which
should save us finding an expert in that field."

Abu Ismail shook his head in disapproval. "A deserter is brother
to the jackal."

"Al-Mahdi, to boil our water we need a vessel. *Rengo Sekigun*
normally execute deserters. They made an exception of him because he's the best in his field and might be needed again. It would
be hard to find another like him."

Abu Ismail smiled and nodded. "I accept your distinction."

Idris Ali, pleased, presented a box containing a mass of slides
and a manuscript. "Finally, our base. As you commanded me, I
tracked down the explorer, Jubal Wallace, to his retreat in the
northwest region of Australia. He was finishing his manuscript on
the Ethiopian Rift Valley. Here it is—with all his photographs."

Abu Ismail, allowing excitement to show for the first time,
leafed through the manuscript. "An inviolate wilderness—that was
how Jibril described it to me on the Night of Decree. You have
found such a place?"

"In the Danakil Alps. Uncharted, except by Wallace. There is
one site, a cluster of cliffs, which mirrors your revelation."

Abu Ismail closed his eyes with gratification. "Excellent. And
Wallace?"

"I killed him. Brutally. Also ransacked the place to conceal the
theft of the manuscript. They'll blame it on the local aborigines—
mostly degenerated by the settlers' alcohol."

"You have executed my commands perfectly, Idris Ali. You
will stand at my right hand forever."

"Command further tasks, Al-Mahdi."

Abu Ismail inclined his head and listened to the cosmic voice.
"Conduct a reconnaissance of the Danakil Alps. The base has to
be set up, supplied and made impregnable within six weeks. Scour
for a reserve base—also in Ethiopia, but as far from the Danakil
as possible. In relation to both, find a high-ranking Ethiopian—
preferably military—who will collaborate with us unquestioningly.
Whatever his price, I shall pay it. Perhaps your Russian, my son,
knows such a man. Go to him."

"How much shall I divulge?"

"Enough. Without him we cannot execute Operation Dragons.
But no details. We do not want him envious. Envy devours good
deeds."

"He hasn't agreed to join us yet."

"He will. If not now, when we get the plutonium. You must
understand, the issue is one nuclear blast. Similar to Nagasaki.

That will not seem the end of the world. There are few politicians —even in so-called democratic countries—who would hesitate to use such a bomb if they felt they could achieve their objectives without risking retaliation. I tell you, we could have found a hundred Americans or British or French instead of your Russian. The Infidel is interchangeable."

"I understand."

Abu Ismail opened his eyes and branded them on Idris Ali. "But beware of the Russian. He is after your soul."

"My soul is yours and Allah's, Al-Mahdi."

"Never forget that. I have made you my beloved son. There is no fury to equal the wrath of a forsaken father."

November 11, 1973

TEL HASHOMER, ISRAEL

Outside, disabled soldiers being transferred to rehabilitation centers were boarding ambulances and joking about the new careers open to them in sport and hedonism. The Memouneh dared not watch them.

Instead, he studied Sanbat Abraham, tightly holding the cake she had baked, still hopeful they might be permitted to see Boaz.

The senior medical officer had been discouraging. Boaz's wounds were healing, but his acute depression could deteriorate into depressive psychosis. Sleep therapy and mild chemotherapy had merely alleviated exhaustion; hypnosis therapy had failed for lack of cooperation—trite jargon for the soul's passage through its blackest midnight. Hope rested in the fact that lately Boaz had kept to his bed, fiercely demanding solitude. A man nurturing such fury had resources, either to destroy or to save himself.

The medical officer returned and handed the Memouneh the sealed Mossad file on Operation Dragons. "I'm sorry—he won't see anybody."

The Memouneh put the file in his briefcase.

The medical officer, under strain from shuttling between hospitals, sat down wearily. "We'll try drug-induced abreactions. If we can get him to reappraise his condition—"

"How soon?"

"You don't seem to understand. He may never recover."

"I want him out, Doctor. At the earliest. He's important."

The medical officer faced him angrily. "They're all important. Every poor shot-up boy here is important! A ruined life is a ruined life!"

The Memouneh drew in a heavy breath. "I didn't mean it that way."

"Is he your only fodder? Put him out to pasture. Let him fade. Give him the peace he wants."

The Memouneh stood up, somberly. How could he explain what Boaz represented in his vision of the future? If Boaz were permitted to fade away, it would mean the Arabs had succeeded in destroying Israel's purity. For Boaz's successors would be the Kidans. And these, fanatically worshiping profanity, in the manner of Israel's enemies, would contaminate the Jewish state and forfeit her right to existence.

"A few more days, Doctor. Then I want him out!"

"General, this is a hospital. You can't give orders here."

"I can, Doctor. And with due respect, I know Boaz. The longer he stays, the worse he'll get. Make him an outpatient—he has a chance. Just push him out!"

"Push him out where?"

"Anywhere he likes."

"And who'll watch over him? You?"

"If I have to."

The Memouneh nodded a salute and walked to the door.

Sanbat, flustered by the dispute, hurriedly rose from her chair and placed her cake on the desk. "If he doesn't want it, others might. . . ."

She rushed out without waiting for a response.

A few steps down the corridor, the Memouneh stopped and faced her. "You love Boaz, don't you?"

Sanbat, caught defenseless by the directness of the question, nodded. "But—he doesn't love me."

The Memouneh took her face between his hands. "He needs a crutch."

"I—I'm due to be posted to Ethiopia."

"Be his crutch, Sanbat."

November 12, 1973

SERPUKHOV, U.S.S.R.

The bucks had been battling for most of the afternoon. Now they struggled, not for supremacy, but to disentangle antlers. The does, over whom they had been fighting, had vanished. The bucks would die from starvation, interlocked.

The symbolism could not escape Idris Ali. This was how the

East and West struggled. It followed, therefore, that the outsider, Islam, should triumph.

"Idris Ali! Idris Ali!"

The voice cracked like a branch breaking under the weight of snow. The bucks, panicking, struggled desperately to separate; heaving antlers in opposite directions, they keeled over in an indistinguishable mass.

Idris Ali turned toward the voice. Ivan Mikhailovich Volkov, a spindly prototype of Russia's ageless and faceless new generation, was struggling through the trees. This was the KGB major general, head of wet affairs, Department Five, who held within his frail, sweaty hands such power that even birds feared loosing their droppings on him.

Volkov panted through a rib cage no thicker than a cat's cradle. "I've sent my colleagues packing. Now we can be alone."

Idris Ali allowed himself to be kissed and hugged, then, casually lifting his gun, aimed and fired twice. The bucks twitched into stillness.

✗

Idris Ali kept his eyes on the four girls serving supper. Earlier, when he had returned to Volkov's dacha, they had bathed and massaged him tantalizingly. He had had to admit that these swallows, as the KGB called them, had the edge over Abu Ismail's houris. But then, there was much in Russia to his liking.

"The new class, my dear comrade—does it shock you?"

Idris Ali turned to Volkov who sat unmoved by the girls' bouncing breasts, but tackled the vodka in the vivipotent manner of the Russian male, as if drink, like Fate, were a challenge he could never beat, and therefore irresistible.

"It's as it should be."

"Precisely. Philosophically speaking, an elite is an elite whatever the system. Islam included."

"Spoken like my mentor."

Volkov chuckled, then addressed the girls. "Leave us. Go bathe. Come back like roses."

The girls nodded deferentially and left.

Volkov filled up the glasses. "Well, my dear comrade. In the words of Lenin: Where to begin?"

"At the heart of the matter?"

"All right. You are here because you have perfected your plans for Operation Dragons. Now you want my commitment. Well, you have had my support ever since I plucked you from the Patrice

Lumumba Friendship University and reclaimed you through wet affairs."

"And Abu Ismail?"

Volkov scratched his bushy hair, the only youthful part of his fifty-year-old body. "What Abu Ismail is proposing is cataclysmic. . . . And, of course, I believe in cataclysms. It is the one aspect of evolution that produces better species. I also believe, at this juncture, we are the better species."

"But you have reservations . . . ?"

Volkov waved his arms. "You know the present situation in Russia. We are ruled by a gerontocracy still traumatized by Hitler's war. A wily, suspicious lot. There's need for caution."

"I also know you are strong, young and ready to push the old men into their graves. Caution would be the wrong policy."

"But there are a multitude of us young heads—all split into factions. From Western-style democrats to my cossacks. So I have bitter rivals. In particular those who pander to the old men. Termites dreaming of ruling the world after they've gnawed the foundations and brought the edifice down. Caution is imperative."

"Don't you trust WOJ, Ivan Mikhailovich?"

"Implicitly. But I'm merely the head of a very long tail. Since this tail stretches from the KGB to the GRU to the Red Army and right through the length and breadth of the Soviet Union, it is not easy to manipulate."

"But give your tail a body—that of a dragon—and there'd be no stopping it."

"Idris Ali, my dear comrade. I pray for such a transplant. But a dragon, unless it can spew fire, is a cumbersome animal."

"We shall have the fire . . . the plutonium."

Volkov chuckled and raised his glass. "Then you shall have me —head and tail. And that will be that—unless someone resurrects Saint George."

Idris Ali smiled and raised his glass, too. "So be it."

Volkov drank heartily. "Now, your little problem. The Ethiopian puppet. I have just the man: Captain Tewodoros Wolde of the Imperial Paratroopers. Headquartered in Massawa. A good soldier and ambitious. He has supplied intelligence to both the KGB and the GRU. Totally trustworthy, providing he believes the collaboration will further his lofty dreams. I'll fix a rendezvous. Take a box of chocolates. Latest infantry weapons is what he likes best."

Idris Ali nodded.

Volkov stretched, smiled, then refilled his glass. "I suggest we call back the girls, Idris Ali. Nothing like cracking a few hairy safes to seal an alliance."

November 14, 1973

ABDALLAH BRIDGE, ISRAELI OCCUPIED WEST BANK, ISRAEL— JORDAN BORDER

The Memouneh gathered his aba and sat down. This was not the first time he had posed as an Arab to meet one of their representatives. He remembered Golda Meir, in black veils, going secretly to Amman, in 1948, to dissuade King Abdallah from waging war on the Jewish state. King Abdallah, who had liked and admired the Jews, had proved powerless.

He looked up as Osman Nusseibi seated himself and felt a surge of hope. Osman was of the school of King Abdallah. Certainly not a Jew-hater. Moreover, as chief of operations of Al-Moukhabarat al-Ammah, he had enough evidence to know that Israel was, potentially, Jordan's best friend.

Osman smiled apologetically. "You will forgive me. It's modest fare. But I didn't want anyone to think I was receiving an important guest."

The Memouneh spread his eyes over the dilapidated desk: coffee and sugar in packets, a camp stove, a coffee pan, a jug of water, nuts, grapes, dates and preserved figs. "May your table always be so bountiful."

Osman, gratified, started brewing the coffee.

The Memouneh, always impresssed by a noble military gait and evident strength in a body even in repose, was reminded of Boaz. He did not think the association farfetched. Though Osman, tall, elegant, with mellow eyes, looked nothing like the stocky Boaz, he emanated the durability of a spiritual world. And the fresh scar on his neck, sustained from the explosives secreted in Aaron's disintegrating corpse, seemed like the manifestation of an inner wound.

The coffee boiled. Osman poured it into small cups.

The Memouneh sipped his coffee. "Before we start, I should tell you: I'm recording the conversation."

Osman chuckled and patted his jacket. "So am I. I hope it's only our memory we distrust."

The Memouneh smiled. "Excellent coffee."

"Try the figs. My wife preserved them."

The Memouneh took a spoonful of figs and washed them down with water. "Delicious. Health to your wife's hands."

"Thank you. I have two bits of information. One: WOJ have recruited virgins."

The Memouneh looked startled. "Virgins?"

"Fifty of them. From Beirut. Their virginity vouchsafed by Abu Ismail's doctor. That's firsthand from one of my agents—alas, not a virgin. They were taken to Tripoli."

"They'll probably be trained in smuggling arms. WOJ have used women before—"

"Before, yes. They don't have to anymore. Now they can smuggle arms anywhere—without risk—through Qaddafi's diplomatic bag."

The Memouneh conceded the point.

Osman helped himself to some nuts. "Do you like whores?"

"Pardon?"

"Would you, out of choice, go to a whore?"

"Not out of choice—no."

"Nor would true warriors."

"Meaning?"

"For the Muslim, virginity has special importance. I think Abu Ismail is providing his men with houris. Remember his *War Rule*, the influence of the sect of 'Assassins' . . ."

The Memouneh sipped his coffee and pondered.

Osman offered the plate of grapes. "Second. Even more disturbing—WOJ have also recruited technicians. Twenty of them."

The Memouneh looked up sharply. "What sort of technicians?"

"That's the interesting part. We've both had reports that WOJ have been negotiating with various terrorist and liberation groups. Most of them have an expert cadre, and WOJ could have had their pick. Instead, they've gone for civilians. To the Gulf. Oil industry."

"Oil industry uses every type of technician from explosives experts to geologists."

Osman pulled out a file from his briefcase. "These are mostly engineers. Two heavy mechanical; six light mechanical; two servomechanical; two electrical; one electronics; one metallurgical; two chemical. Also two with degrees in physics, and one medical doctor. I have their names and *curricula vitae*. All young—all exceptionally bright. Run them through your computer. You'll find there's a core capable of setting up a weapons-manufacturing plant. They can even go nuclear."

The Memouneh took the file. "That's a bit farfetched."

"A backyard bomb—not sophisticated? All they need is six kilos of plutonium. A mass the size of a tennis ball."

"All? Where would they get it?"

"You tell me. But isn't that what you believe Operation Dragons is about?"

The Memouneh savored a grape. "It's a possibility I've considered."

"Come, come, my friend. We've both evaluated the Mount Nebo tapes. We can both read between the lines. The Last of Days, and all that . . ."

The Memouneh nodded. "Anything else?"

Osman drained his coffee. "Just a query. How's Boaz Ben-Ya'ir?"

The Memouneh rose. "Coming along."

Osman rose too and scrutinized the Memouneh's face. "That sounds too casual to be convincing."

The Memouneh faced him. "He'll be all right. Why do you ask?"

"I can foresee desperate measures—probably jointly by us. If so, I'd like to team up with him."

"I'll convey the sentiment."

"I'm not being gracious. He's your best man."

"*One* of my best men."

"Your best. Look beyond his eyes. Beyond his strength."

The Memouneh stared at Osman, astounded. "You can say that—after meeting him once?"

"He's an open book."

"For those who can read suffering. I salute you."

November 15, 1973

MASSAWA, ETHIOPIA

Kevork Dedeyan scanned Massawa through infrared binoculars. The island farthest out, which gave its name to the town, accommodated the port and the old Moorish quarter. A causeway linked it to the second island, Taulud, which contained the Imperial Palace, the villas of the rich and the railway station. Another causeway linked Taulud with the peninsula, the domain of the poor, and carried the single-track railway and the Italian-built road toward the Rift Valley escarpment and Asmara.

At 3:00 A.M. Massawa was asleep—except for Captain Tewodoros Wolde and his paratroopers. The latter had been deployed in an unbroken line from the port to the peninsula, to enforce the curfew.

Dedeyan, perched in the bell tower of Taulud's Greco-Roman–

style church, resigned himself to the strains of immobility and sought comfort from the bell tower's cool masonry. He loved consecrated stones. They reimmersed him in the womb of the Armenian Apostolic Church, revealed visions of the True Cross, and made him feel a waterborn fighter in the mold of legendary heroes.

He redirected his attention toward Taulud's outermost villa. Captain Wolde and his faithful shadow, Sergeant Ketema, were still ramrod straight on the private beach. The motor yacht *Succubus*, with which they had exchanged signals, had cleared the breakwater and was on course for the villa's jetty.

Dedeyan exulted. The instinct that had smelled conspiracy in Wolde's peremptory curfew had borne fruit.

But then instinct had never failed him. Instinct, after all, was the Armenian's birthright—compensation for sharing with the Jew the bitter herbs of dispersion and genocide. Without it, the survivors of the 1916 Turkish deportation could not have evaporated into the wilderness of the Middle East, nor live invisibly in Istanbul, Damascus, Beirut, Amman, Cairo, Teheran, nor conspire, in exile, to topple the Soviet monolith that had pushed the Armenian state into the mud of history.

Moreover, instinct had revealed that rebirth of history—not only for the Jew, but for all the downtrodden—resided in Zionism; that when the Jew had consolidated the miracle of freedom and land, it would be the turn of the Armenian. Sentiment had complemented this peculiar logic. For centuries the wandering Jew and the wandering Armenian had practiced mutual aid, dispensing shelter, food and work as the pendulum of persecution swung from one to the other. Dedeyan himself had been reclaimed by a Jew from the slums of Alexandria after his widower father had fallen to a stray bullet during Egypt's anti-British disorders in 1946. He was prepared to swear that when the new strain of Armenian rose against the Kremlin, only the Jew would stand beside him. With that conviction, and with skills learned in protean lands where intrigue had been epidemic, he served Mossad zealously in the Horn of Africa.

He tightened his binoculars on the villa's beach. The *Succubus*'s arrival was intriguing. The craft, a 150-footer with twin diesel engines capable of a steady thirty knots, had been owned by Giovanni Varchi, an adventurer who had come to Ethiopia with Mussolini's army and stayed on to court danger in illicit trade. Varchi had unexpectedly died in Aden a couple of weeks ago, supposedly of a heart attack. Even more unexpectedly, the South Yemen authorities had impounded the *Succubus* forthwith and had auctioned her in compensation for vast debts allegedly incurred by

Varchi. Since the boat had been the envy of the Red Sea smugglers, the bidding, despite the short notice, had been fierce. To date, the new owner remained unknown.

The *Succubus* moored. Captain Wolde and Sergeant Ketema moved to the jetty. A few paratroopers boarded the boat. The skipper emerged and directed them to some crates on the deck.

Dedeyan studied the skipper in disbelief: Musaddiq Hamdi, Eritrean Liberation Front's Aden-based officer. Even more incredible was that Wolde, commander of martial law in Eritrea and ELF's scourge, was fraternizing with Hamdi.

The crates had been unloaded and opened. Wolde swaggered between RPG-7 grenade launchers, Sagger antitank missiles and Degtyarev RPD light machine guns. When he had completed his inspection, he nodded to Hamdi. The latter hurried to the cabin and returned, escorting another man.

As Wolde and the newcomer shook hands ceremoniously, Dedeyan froze. Having memorized countless photographs in Mossad files, he could not mistake Idris Ali.

Ten minutes later the night was handed back to the owls. Idris Ali, provided with a Land-Rover, had driven into the desert. Hamdi had sailed away, presumably back to Aden. Wolde and Sergeant Ketema had returned to barracks with the crates of arms.

Dedeyan settled down to sleep, frustrated that he could not tail Idris Ali. But he had seen enough to set Mossad buzzing. He also had a nugget of intelligence to goad Getachew Iyessous of the ISS, the Imperial Secret Service, and Al Jameson of the CIA into action. Both had proved good friends to Mossad in the past.

November 16, 1973

ASMARA, ETHIOPIA

The lease on Kagnew, the U.S. telecommunications base, was terminating; the transfer to the Imperial Army's Second Division had commenced.

In the officers' mess, Al Jameson, CIA station chief, saw himself as sitting in the clubroom of a once-mighty team no longer capable of winning a game. The men drank harder, the women organized functions with greater pretense, and the children cheered louder at their games.

Jameson turned to his visitor, Major Getachew Iyessous of the ISS. Getachew, at least, was a friend. An Ethiopian who still saw America as the sun that could melt the bitter ice of totalitarianism. "Dedeyan's obsessed with WOJ, Getachew. All Israeli agents are."

Getachew rummaged for his cigarettes. "He's never fed us false information."

"Just look at the evidence. A couple of infrared pics of some men unrecognizable even in blowup."

"One certainly looks like Wolde."

"Is he a traitor—that's the question."

Getachew fidgeted. He had posed the question to himself often enough. Wolde had gained popularity with young officers as a formidable soldier, a patriot and a radical. But Getachew suspected Wolde was a member of the armed forces junta which was plotting to overthrow the emperor and which called itself the *Dergue,* meaning "shadow," because its members had managed to remain unidentified. "Wolde makes me uneasy, Al."

Jameson stared into his beer. Wolde made him uneasy, too. One of those upstarts who had mushroomed during the Vietnam storms and grown big on the muck they had raked over the Stars and Stripes. "Assuming Dedeyan's right that Wolde's involved with Hamdi. He's obviously using Hamdi as his mole in the ELF. That's not treason. That's smart."

"Except that Hamdi has better patrons. Russians. South Yemenis. Libyans. He wouldn't jeopardize those connections. What can Wolde offer him?"

"His life—maybe."

"Hamdi's based in Aden—difficult to get at. Let me rephrase the question: What has Hamdi to offer Wolde? Why is he running guns to him? Who financed his purchase of the *Succubus?*"

"Are you suggesting an alliance between Wolde and ELF?"

"A triumvirate: Wolde–ELF–WOJ."

"For God's sake, Getachew! ELF hates Wolde! He's decimated them!"

"ELF's changed a lot since 1962 when a few chieftains took up arms against the emperor's annexation of the province. It's facing a takeover by Marxists. Hamdi's a Marxist—or he wouldn't be based and supported by South Yemen."

"So?"

"Times have changed for Ethiopia, too. Marxism again—hovering over the emperor's throne. I wouldn't be surprised if Wolde is one."

"You think Wolde's collaborating with the ELF to topple the emperor?"

"Possible—even if Wolde's not a Marxist. Revolutionaries aren't particular about their bedfellows, Al. A worsening of the Eritrean situation might help Wolde to launch a coup. The ELF would be only too happy to oblige. If the emperor is deposed, there'll be chaos. It would set the ELF on the road to independence."

"That might just make sense, old buddy. But what's WOJ got to do with either of them?"

"Maybe they've been contracted to arm Wolde. Maybe, at the same time, they're training the ELF for the glory of Islam."

"I'd buy that if Idris Ali was Robin Hood. He's not. He's Abu Ismail's right-hand man. And I can't see Abu Ismail crusading for ELF. Then again, Qaddafi holds the purse strings for both. If he's really keen to train the ELF, he can find better men. Any number of ex-officers from British, French and German armies itching to be his mercenaries. Also, whatever lip service Qaddafi and Abu Ismail might pay to Marxism, they puke at anything that smacks of red. False trail, Getachew."

Getachew fixed his languid eyes on Jameson. "Then why do you doubt your own words, Al?"

Jameson gulped down his beer. "Says who?"

"Al—if CIA's given up Ethiopia, say so. I'll understand. But don't put me off the scent."

Jameson accepted the rebuke. The trouble was not that the CIA had given up Ethiopia, but that a blight had hit America. The eagle that had guarded liberty, honesty and human rights—if not perfectly, certainly with greater conviction than the rest of its kin —had become the laughingstock of the vultures of tyranny. The free world that survived and prospered because of America now farted in Uncle Sam's face while one hand received his protection and the other masturbated perverts from the Kremlin to the Gulf. And, since the line of great presidents had dried up with Truman, there was no way to eradicate the blight. Thus, the youthful idealism of his generation to uphold morality and fight evil had withered and died. And so had the ultimate dream: glory and final rest in Arlington National Cemetery.

"Sorry, Getachew. What do you want me to do?"

"What I'm going to do. Ferret."

November 17, 1973

DJIBOUTI, T.F.A.I.

Sigmund Schoenberg lingered on avenue de Brazzaville. To the right the road stretched to the mosque; to the left it harbored an endless line of bars. Behind, the narrow streets converged toward place Menelik, the town center. Ahead flourished place Rimbaud with Moorish buildings of vaulted windows and delicate arcades.

Beyond, branching out like an estuary, lay the lanes of the old town—an inferno where even the goats pasted themselves against the walls to extract what little coolness there was in the shade.

Schoenberg had two masters: France and Israel; and Dedeyan's report on the recent activities of WOJ had plunged him into a dilemma.

Schoenberg, forty-five, was reckoned to be the oldest lieutenant in the *Troupes de Marine*—a maverick even to the crack overseas forces that had a tradition of eccentricity.

He was born in Alsace, branded a Jew. He was, in fact, of Huguenot descent. But in 1942, in the wake of the German occupation, the accusation of Jewish blood had dispatched the family for internment in Paris's Vel d'Hiv. Thence his parents had been shunted to Drancy for deportation to the concentration camps, and young Schoenberg, grouped with the children, had found himself in Pithiviers to await the decongestion of the transports. There, discovering fighting instincts, he had claimed his first life, a guard, and had escaped to the Vichy zone. Later, following the Allied invasion of North Africa, and anticipating the German occupation of Southern France, he had moved to Algeria. In the desert, he had conducted his own war, raiding villages and army camps for scraps.

At the end of the war, he had emerged in obsessive search of the Gestapo officer who had processed his parents. A Jewish investigator with the War Crimes Commission had directed him to the French Foreign Legion, and Schoenberg had duly enlisted at Sidi-bel-Abbès. After finding his Gestapo officer, dead at the hands of the Vietminh, he had adopted the Legion as his country. He had fought in every postwar campaign and had distinguished himself twice—in Dien Bien Phu and Jebel Beni Smir. In times of peace, he had excelled in field intelligence. In 1971, upon his honorable discharge, he had secured transfer to the regular army and had been posted with promotion to lieutenant to the *Deuxième Bureau*, Djibouti, in the Territoire Français des Afars et des Issas, T.F.A.I.

But Schoenberg had never regained his French identity—neither through the blood he had inherited nor, in Legionnaire terms, through the blood he had shed. Since his family had found existence only amid the condemned, he saw himself as a son of the Jew, albeit a stepson. In memory of their scattered ashes, he served Israel, imparting intelligence to Mossad, in full knowledge that the Israelis were using him as they would any Judeophile.

Some of his superiors, Schoenberg suspected, had gleaned his other allegiance, but had disregarded it on the grounds that he was a formidable soldier and an astute intelligence officer. Luckily, too, the French secret services were less infected by the misanthropy with which de Gaulle and his followers had ostracized Israel.

Lately, however, the situation had deteriorated. The French secret services had been forced to toe the official line as France, wooing Arab oil, had accepted terrorism against Israel as justifiable.

In terms of the T.F.A.I., a desert colony without resources, the situation had become even more disconcerting. The territory had lost its importance for France, and worse, had become an economic burden. Paris wished to grant it independence but, so far, plebiscites had rejected the offer. As opposed to the Afar and Issa nomads, numbers unknown, who had traditional links with Ethiopia and racial and religious ties with Somalia, the town dwellers wished to preserve their standard of living, incomparable with that of T.F.A.I.'s neighbors. Then again, both Ethiopia and Somalia had threatened to annex the territory in the wake of the French departure—if, that is, Russia did not pounce on Djibouti, so strategically placed on the Horn of Africa. In the hope that this stalemate could be broken with some mayhem, there were high-ranking officials in Paris who actually prayed for trouble. For these, WOJ presence in Ethiopia would be welcome. If WOJ were undertaking to help the ELF, they might conceivably extend services to the Afar Liberation Front, thus giving France the excuse to confer independence and decamp.

Schoenberg, anticipating a plethora of restrictions that would scuttle his efforts for Mossad, had decided that his only alternative rested in stirring the Americans.

Therein lay his dilemma. Whereas he could take orders from Mossad without qualms, he considered involvement with the CIA, without the blessing of his superiors, treasonable.

He took another look at place Rimbaud. There had been many places like it during his time in the Foreign Legion. In those days treason had been unthinkable. Allegiance was given to the Legion, and through it, to order. Straightforward. Good and bad—no shades in between. Biblical.

Sadly, but resolutely, he walked toward Bar Montblanc.

The name was Don Quixote Villon Beaumarchais de Vigny Combeau. The last was the surname; the preceding three the whim of his well-read Martinican father, and the first, the only literary name his Puerto Rican mother had been able to conjure. His nickname, Montblanc, though less illustrious, was evocative of his appearance: mountainous, muscle-bound, with crinkling, snow-white hair.

He was serving behind the bar.

"Welcome, pal. The first dozen are on the house."

Schoenberg smiled, disregarded the offered stool and waved a buff envelope. "I've got stamps to exchange."

Montblanc rubbed his hands gleefully. "Great, brother. Into the den. Be right with you."

Schoenberg walked through the beaded curtains into the bar's back room where Montblanc kept his radio set—legitimately, as a ham operator—and the valuable stamp collection which provided the excuse for meetings with informers and stringers.

Schoenberg sat in an armchair and ran his eyes around the room. It was covered with American bric-a-brac—in curious contrast to the Creole spirit that ruled Montblanc, and despite the fact that America had treated him indifferently.

Montblanc had had a troubled youth in New York after his family had settled there, and even more tumultuous times when increasing immigration from Puerto Rico had rekindled racial prejudice. In between, the U.S. Marine Corps had thrown him from one disastrous Korean front line to another.

Montblanc himself had often confessed that his making had been the Foreign Legion, which he had joined after Korea and which had honored him with the rank of sergeant, his nickname, several wounds, a citation and the right to live in French territory.

Yet, at the end of his contractual five years, he had spurned reenlistment—as had been expected of him—had criticized French abuse in Algeria, which had not been expected of him, and had promptly joined the CIA.

Schoenberg, who had served with him in Algeria, had taken a long time to understand the force that had kept Montblanc a die-hard American.

Stocktaking after Algeria, and finding the world—particularly Europe—slaves to Mammon, Montblanc had gone searching for a permanent set of values.

He had discovered these in the only charter that exalted the intellect: Jefferson's Declaration of Independence, and specifically the affirmation that life, liberty and the pursuit of happiness were every man's inalienable rights. It had not mattered that America had also enslaved herself to Mammon. She had at least preserved the Declaration so that some of her children, ingenuous like

Montblanc, could make it a reality. That objective had also served to compensate for the wife and children he had denied himself for fear that the future might mangle them.

"Right, pal." Montblanc shut the door, dropped a bottle of white rum on Schoenberg's lap, then sat opposite.

Schoenberg passed him the buff envelope. "I should warn you —I'm not here officially."

Montblanc studied Dedeyan's photographs. "You know me, Lieutenant. Quiet as the tomb."

"You could get your knuckles rapped."

Montblanc passed a humidor. "You watch yours. I'll watch mine."

Schoenberg picked up a cigar and lit it.

Montblanc waved the photographs. "Who are these guys?"

"According to my informer: Captain Tewodoros Wolde, martial law commander in Eritrea; and Musaddiq Hamdi, ELF's man in Aden. The third is Idris Ali of WOJ."

Montblanc whistled. "WOJ?"

Schoenberg relaxed. After the insouciance of Deuxième Bureau, Montblanc's interest was heartening. "WOJ, you may or may not know, is preparing something big. Operation Dragons . . ."

"Yeah, there's a Mossad report circulating."

"Well, Mossad have no leads. And they're desperate for one. Now, WOJ appears in Massawa, hobnobbing with the ELF and an up-and-coming Ethiopian officer. It all looks like local politics gone Machiavellian. But is it? That's what I think we should find out."

"For Mossad?"

Schoenberg shrugged uneasily. "Why not for ourselves? There shouldn't be any conflict of interest."

Montblanc flashed a smile. "I understand."

Schoenberg sipped some rum, discomforted by the fact that Montblanc had seen through him.

Montblanc rose and paced the room. "Actually, Lieutenant, the Company's having a rough ride. Tricky Dicky, and all that· . . . On the other hand, I'm my own man. That's the advantage coming from the wrong side of the tracks—I'm not expected to behave like an Ivy Leaguer or political hustler. So, you've got yourself an ally—if that's what you're asking."

"That's what I hoped."

Montblanc flashed another smile, then switched on a tape recorder. The room echoed with the vibrant voices of a male chorus singing a Legionnaire march.

" 'My regiment is my home; my mother I have never known. . . .' "

Schoenberg, startled, turned around sharply.

Montblanc chuckled. "Hell, Lieutenant. A little sentimentality goes a long way."

He started singing.

Unaccountably, Schoenberg joined in: " 'My father fell early in the field; I am alone in the world.' "

Then, emotionally, his voice broke.

Montblanc put an arm around Schoenberg's shoulders. "I guess we passed the test. Whatever's thrown us together—it'll hold."

November 21, 1973

YAD MORDECHAI, ISRAEL

It was not a long list. They were not Central European names, familiar to Germans, but Sephardic names like Eskenazi, Behar, Alchech, Franco. Names of Balkan Jews. Yet in each case the spelling was correct. There had been tens of thousands of such sheets, faultlessly prepared by Eichmann's Bureau IV, Section B-4, *Reichssicherheitshauptamt*.

Sanbat felt trapped in the kibbutz museum; every name shrieked at her in its death throes. She forced herself to concentrate on the one Boaz had caressed with trembling hands. Rachel Franco.

"Your mother?"

Boaz nodded.

"How do you know? It's not an uncommon name. . . ."

"The date."

Sanbat looked at the date: August 9, 1944. "But—it doesn't say it's from Greece. . . ."

Slowly, Boaz sank to his haunches and started crying.

The sight shocked her. She had forged herself into a true Israeli, had welcomed the new strain that had destroyed in the Jew the weaknesses of an enslaved past. Tears and feelings were not to be displayed. The nation was to be granite. That such a cult, so much part of the Israeli character, should be undermined in the toughest among them, was disorienting.

"Boaz . . . Don't cry. . . ."

He cried all the more—silently, immobile.

She became aware of other visitors: a group of Russian immigrants, brought by the Absorption Center for a glimpse of Israel's heroic beginnings. Panic-stricken that they would find a hero in tears, Sanbat nudged him.

"Boaz, please . . . People . . ."

He ignored her. Frozen in his agony, he looked like another exhibit.

An elderly woman, resembling an early settler from the Pale, approached. For some agonizing minutes she watched Boaz, then, herself in tears, started stroking his hair. She mumbled in hesitant Hebrew about relatives killed at Babi Yar; and praised the Lord that the listed people had found, for their names at least, refuge in Eretz Israel. Boaz's mouth quivered in acknowledgment, and his lips brushed her hand. Then the woman moved away, and Boaz reverted to his mourning. Sanbat could no longer control the compulsion to run out.

"I'll see you later. . . ."

He gave no indication of having heard her. As she reached the exit, she caught sight of the Russian woman. Still crying. Sanbat felt demeaned for having lost the knack. She left the museum, averting her eyes from the inscription at the entrance.

> *In this place*
> *Seek and look for what can be seen no more*
> *Hear voices that can be heard no more*
> *Understand—what is beyond all understanding*

She despaired of her mission. How could she make Boaz whole again?

She had posed the question repeatedly to the Memouneh. Each time he had given the same answer: she would find a way because she loved Boaz. When she had consented to try, he had pulled Boaz out of the hospital by forcing the doctors to demand his bed for a POW repatriated from Egypt. Boaz's unselfish assent, and his choice of Yad Mordechai, a kibbutz legendary for heroic resistance, as the place where he would continue his recovery, had only strengthened the Memouneh's argument that Boaz wanted to be reclaimed.

Sanbat stopped running. It was a beautiful day; the sun was still hot, and the breeze fragrant with the sea. Though the majority of the men were still at the front, the kibbutz was hard at work, leaving the historic sights to Sanbat and the group of Russian immigrants.

Foremost among these sights, the battlefield of May 1948 was one which, unlike the Holocaust-haunted museum, had often inspired Sanbat toward greater dedication to the Jewish state. There

141 kibbutzniks, with minimal arms and ammunition, had fought 2,000 Egyptians, armor, artillery and Spitfires, for six days, finally retreating with heavy casualties. Their stand had bought time for the Israeli forces to regroup and halt the Egyptian advance to Tel Aviv.

Yet on this occasion, Sanbat found the old slit trenches, the vast perimeter dotted with captured tanks and cardboard soldiers, strangely alienating. The heroism of 1948 did not relate to 1973. In 1948 there had been a messianic hope in the new nation, a positive idealism auguring a golden millennium once the guns had been silenced. Now, in the aftermath of the Yom Kippur War, the young nation still bled and despaired of the future because it could not see an end to the bleeding. Now there was a need to rethink everything.

She wandered around the swimming pool, back again, down to the palm-fringed rockery, up the stone steps to the shell-pocked ruins of the old water tower and the giant statue of Mordechai Anilewitz, the young commander of the Warsaw Ghetto uprising, in whose memory the kibbutz had been erected. And as she concentrated on the figure—dressed like a kibbutznik—standing vigil, grenade in hand, head looking over shoulder in search of the enemy, Sanbat felt a new perception. Boaz was a Mordechai Anilewitz, a martyr bringing light into darkness. The insight, if insight it was, comforted her, though it was unwise to draw comparisons between myth and reality. Yet myth and reality were the very essence of her Israel.

She sat at the foot of the statue and ventured toward her own reality.

She knew herself. She was a Daughter of the Book, a servant of the Lord. But shorn to that basic essence that could pass through the eye of a needle, she was a primitive. She was atavistic enough to sympathize with the starving Falashas of Ethiopia, her old people, but callous enough to withhold this sympathy from other starving masses. A member of a herd, more concerned with survival than her particular place in the Family of Man. Her loyalty to her country was unshakable, which made her a good Israeli; but she had never felt the urge to transcend the boundaries of self-preservation.

This disposition to survive was the harshest reality. It built too many defenses. It distanced events, distorted personal experiences as strange episodes. It prevented life from touching the nerves. Thus, her years with her late husband had been meaningless. Not because Uri had had to spend much of his time with his squadron. She herself had made the marriage an alliance of strangers. Uri had been a warrior-scholar, like the ancients. His interests had ranged from ichthyology to archaeology, from wine making to the cultivation of cacti. She could have delighted in him either as a paladin or an intellectual; she could have peeled him layer after bountiful layer and rejoiced in his completeness. Instead, fearful of the total union he had sought, she had restricted herself to the comfort of his physical presence.

Things might have been different had they had children. She had yearned for children—or so she believed. There were still stirrings in her that were undoubtedly protests of suppressed motherhood. Conversely, she had been relieved. In Israel, parents enjoyed their children for a short time. Only until manhood. Then the defense forces and war. Injury or death. At best, a succession of reprieves.

Nor had Uri wanted children. No doubt he had seen through her. A dutiful woman, but unable to live and breathe another person and therefore unsuited for motherhood.

And so it would continue. She would live from behind her barricades. Letting the Kidans provide a presence, yearning for the Boazes only because they were better men.

How then could she help Boaz? Could she leave the security of her defenses? Could she spread herself over his wounds?

✗

He turned up at the swimming pool, in a singlet bathing suit meant to hide his scars. His eyes were sunken, his mind still incarcerated in the museum where he had spent the morning.

She was wearing the tiniest bikini. He had not even looked at her. "I was thinking of going to the sea, Boaz. Want to join me?"

He seemed tempted, and looked northward toward Ashkelon. "Would you let me swim to Gibraltar?"

"Suicide? That's not you!"

"Always hide your shit—like a cat."

"Always leave a trace—like a man."

"Go home, Sanbat."

He dived into the pool.

When Sanbat left for the guest chalet an hour later, he was still swimming. He looked like a captive whale. She feared he would swim until his lungs burst.

✗

Sanbat spent the rest of the afternoon lying on her bed. Her body felt inanimate, though it was naked. But her mind steamed, seeking reawakening. She felt she might be brave enough to find it. Perhaps, then, body and mind would fuse.

She heard him come into the room next door and collapse on the bed.

She spurred her courage and shouted: "What do you want from life, Boaz? Besides death?"

To her surprise she received an answer, in a muffled voice. "Sanctity."

The concept, which she had never before contemplated as necessary for life, conjured a perfect calm. She sprang up and burst into his room. He lay on his bed, face buried in the pillow.

She realized she was still naked. That bolstered her courage. She moved nearer, until her pelvis stood close to his head. "Boaz . . ."

He jumped up and lifted her. She tried to wipe the tears from his face, but he would not let her touch him. He carried her back into her room, threw her on the bed and left. She heard him close his door; then realized he had handled her like an object.

Later, hearing him leave, she watched him from the window. Going back to the museum.

✗

That night she opened Boaz's psychiatric file. A note requested that consultants should closely study the appended abreactions. These, essays written by Boaz during sessions of psycholytic therapy conducted with low doses of LSD-25, provided the foundation for diagnosis and prognosis. Though Boaz had written the abreactions in no particular sequence, as would be expected from the variable effects of LSD-25, they had been compiled in chronological order.

She settled down to read the essays.

SALONIKA, GREECE: JUNE 11, 1939

Six candles, expired, on the plate that had held the biggest cake in all Greece. The party is over. But joy is still in the air. There is Olympian beauty on the hazy summit of Mount Khortiatis, and on the faces of Eli, eminent merchant, beloved father, and Rachel, beloved mother. Melancholy is in the air, too, since without it there can be no joy. The child feels like crying. He may be prescient. The house will crumble next year beneath the bombs of Fascist Italy. The following year, the jackboots of the Third Reich will establish a reign of terror in the land.

"Papa . . . ?"

"Yes, son?"

"Tell me about 1933. . . ."

"Nineteen thirty-three was the year when the world contracted cancer in the person of Adolf Hitler. It could have been an unforgivable year, but for one blessing. Your birth."

"Am I so important?"

"You will be a great man. You will be remembered on the Day of the Messiah."

"When will that day come, Papa?"

"After we return to our land."

"Is Greece not our land?"

"Greece is the land of a friend who loves us. But it is not the land God gave us."

"But we love Greece."

"Yes, my son. And if need be we must die for it. A good guest cherishes his host's house as much as his own."

The child turns to the mother. "Will I really be a great man, Mama?"

Rachel Franco sheds tears of joy. For her, the child is already a great man, because he loves them with the heart of Isaiah. Also, she has cause for happiness: her womb has flowered again, though the times are wrong for bearing fruit. Among the Jewesses of Europe, only the barren will die triumphantly. She speaks in Ladino. "Sí mi alma, sí mi corazón."

"Then you must both live to see it. I don't want to be great without you."

XANTHE, GREECE: AUGUST 5, 1944

The Rhodope mountains weep, pockmarked by artillery; vineyards lie ravaged; a flagpole bearing the swastika is imbedded in Xanthe's guts.

The boy stands before the corpses of the partisans. He recites the Kaddish, imploring God to overlook the absence of the ten good men who would have borne witness to Eli, honored father.

Suddenly he is surrounded. They are not in uniform, but they are not of his father's unit. They could be Gestapo. Or Communists, rival partisans. The leader pulls him up.

"The Jews—where are they?"

The boy points at his dead father, then at others.

"The women? The children?"

The boy points toward Xanthe.

"Taken away?"

The boy nods.

"How did you survive, boy?"

"I hid."

The man looks at the corpses.

The boy lowers his eyes. "I had to save my sister."

"Where's your sister?"

The boy stares at the man, defiant, hateful. "You won't find her."

"I am Nestor Papazogloû. . . . We came to help the Jews."

The boy spits. German words. He drops his trousers, points at his circumcision. "I'm a Jew! Kill me!"

"Pull up your trousers, boy."

"Kill me! Kill me!"

The man clasps him to his chest. "I've lost three sons, boy. Why should I kill a fourth?"

The boy clings to the man, weeps.

"Come, let's get your sister—and then to the mountains."

The boy looks toward Xanthe. "My mother . . ."

"There's nothing we can do."

The boy does not challenge his word. He kisses the dead partisans. He kisses the dead father. He turns to his rescuer. "Will you teach me to fight, sir?"

AUSCHWITZ, OCCUPIED POLAND, AUGUST 13, 1944–JANUARY 5, 1945
Another Eichmann transport stands on the platform. The new arrivals are herded for Selektion.

The Other-Self is a Capo and watches, inscrutable.

The elderly, the sick, the children and their mothers line up to the left—for the gas chambers. Men fit for work, women attractive enough for prostitution, children suitable for medical experiments line up to the right.

There is a commotion. The Other-Self notices Rachel Franco. She is refusing to join the labor queue. Wants to help the elderly, the sick. Walks to the death queue.

Dr. Josef Mengele, nicknamed the Angel of Death, mocks her. "*Quo vadis?*"

Mengele, patron of the medical experiments, is a cultured, witty superman. The Other-Self is familiar with the question. Mengele has posed it many times for the amusement of all. It refers to Saint Peter who, running away from Rome and persecution, meets Jesus on the Appian Way, walking toward Rome. "Master, where are you going?" asks Peter. "I am coming to Rome to be crucified again," replies Jesus. The answer shames the First Disciple, compels him to return to Rome, fulfil his destiny and attain martyrdom.

Rachel Franco answers, not without compassion. "*Venio Romam, iterum crucifigi.*"

Mengele, raging at her insolence, whips her. Drags her away from the gas queue. In Auschwitz, Zyklon B offers a relatively humane death. Hands her to the Other-Self for special duties.

The Other-Self renders her nameless with a number. "How can you know about Jesus—you, a Jew?"

"Jesus was one of our martyrs. Not the first. Nor the last."

The Other-Self tattoos her: NUR FUR OFFIZIERE. "Only for officers—that's privilege. You will be well treated in the brothel. It's your chance to live. There will be a better world—one day."

She tells him pitifully. "Nothing will change. Nothing ever does. Certainly not the world.

The Other-Self had not been watching her hands. She plunges the tattoo needles into her eyes. He stares, dumbfounded. Eyes like drains. Why doesn't she scream? "You fool!"

"There comes a time, my son, when you must be defiant. When you must liberate your soul from this world. Their world. When death becomes the only noble act."

But death is not hers for the asking. Despite her raddled sockets, her body is fresh, attractive. Countless pricks lance her. She is made pregnant. Aborted. Sterilized. Radiated. She is thrown at frozen men to revive them. She contracts pneumonia. Finally, she is dispatched for extermination.

By then she is famous. She has died and resurrected herself a million times. Without complaint, without ever screaming. The butchers believe she is amnesiac, or mute, or zombie. Some feel cheated because they have failed to humiliate her.

The Other-Self escorts her to her death.

She remembers his voice. Speaks for the first time since gouging her eyes. "Come with me, deserter."

He pretends he does not understand.

"Don't destroy your soul. Leave this world. Be a new man."

He pushes her into the gas chamber.

When her corpse is taken to the crematorium, her empty eyes, daubed with excreta, continue shouting.

"Be a new man!"

KAVALLA, GREECE: DECEMBER 8, 1946

The Communists have surrounded the farm. The wolves howl the news.

Nestor Papazogloû, second father, doctor, socialist, guerrilla leader, turns to the youth. "It is time. . . . A dying man should glorify life."

The youth protests. "You will not die. I won't let them. . . ."

"Come here, agorimou, let me hold you. . . ."

The youth runs to him.

Nestor Papazogloû clutches him to his bosom. "I am not a wise man. But I have learned one thing: a man ïs father to all. That's what makes us know God, even though it is women who experience the miracle of birth."

"I'll die with you!"

"Love the world—even the wayward children . . ."

The youth weeps.

Nestor pats him on the cheek. "Now, hide in the barn! When they take me away, run! East—to Turkey."

"No, I'll die with you."

"You have to take care of your sister. To Istanbul. To your uncle."

"Please, please—don't leave us."

Nestor Papazogloû kisses him, then tiny Perla. "I must, my son. Look after my little pearl."

The youth hangs on to his neck. "Why, Nestor? Why do they want you? You're one of them—you fought with them!"

"I fought because I love Greece. They fight because they love Russia —fairy tales."

Nestor Papazogloû gives the youth his gun, then runs out, holding arms high in surrender.

Later, from an olive grove, the youth watches the execution. He cries silently, while his sister, cradled in his arms, sleeps.

ISTANBUL, TURKEY: NOVEMBER 30, 1947

An Indian summer day. Beneath pencil-thin minarets, the Galata Bridge, like a sow, feeds the ferries.

In the old house overlooking the Golden Horn, the youth stares at his frail uncle's clotted blood. Photographs of Auschwitz litter the bathroom. The youth studies them. In one, a skeletal face is ringed. It does not look like Rachel Franco, but for two years his uncle had claimed it was. Last night, the gentle soul had cut his wrists.

The youth's friend Asher Baruh bursts in. "Did you hear? The United Nations voted for Partition in Palestine. Thirty-three to thirteen."

He had heard. Last night. With his uncle.

"Now we must go."

"When, Asher—when can we go?"

Asher smiles. "I can go tomorrow. Only good thing about being an orphan. I can do what I like."

"Tomorrow then. Let's die in the land of our forefathers."

Asher looks at him quizzically.

The youth reads him his uncle's suicide note.

" 'Forgive an old man who, even at this hour of triumph, despairs. Go to Eretz Israel. The Zionists will establish a house of prayer for all nations.' "

ASHDOD, PALESTINE: JANUARY 29, 1948

The Mediterranean rages. The Palmachniks pull on the ropes. The surf throws up illegal immigrants.

The cadavers of Europe, reincarnated, kiss the hands that helped them ashore. They do not feel the cold. Among them, he, Asher and tiny Perla stand bewildered. Is this the Promised Land?

Arc lights open up. Immigrants and Palmachniks scatter but the beach is surrounded. He drags Perla and Asher behind a dune.

The British order the immigrants into the trucks. The immigrants refuse: they will not be taken to detention camps in Cyprus; there will be a Jewish state soon. The British ignore them: until then, Union Jack rules. The immigrants bare chests. Singing the Hatikva, they dare the British to kill them. The British fire into the air. The Palmachniks tell the immigrants to surrender. They will be brought back after independence.

The youngsters remain hidden.

The immigrants march under escort, no longer singing.

The British search the beach.

The youngsters dart from dune to dune.

They run into a soldier.

Asher murmurs. "Please let us go. . . ."

The soldier mutters kindly. "I've got to turn you in. For your own good. They'll kill you all—them Arabs."

"Let them."

"God help me—don't you understand?"

"Please."

The soldier bites his lips. Looks away. "Go on, then. I ain't seen you. Go on! Quick!"

They run, and disappear into the night that is unlike any other night because it is the night of homecoming.

GONEN, ISRAEL: APRIL 16, 1953

The clouds rush over snowcapped Mount Hermon, bearing generous gifts of water. They have been warned about the storm, but they are young, and for the young spring is always summer. They put down tools, straggle back to the huts, drenched, full of laughter. They have been washed of dust, and with their clothes transparent, the young men and women stare at each other with unbridled desire. They joke: time to sow babies.

He pounds the watchtower, counts the kibbutzniks as they come in. Now and then he asks, "Have you seen Perla? Asher?" He is told his sister, Asher and six other kibbutzniks were grazing the cattle on the slopes. He scans the Golan Heights. The downpour has reduced visibility. He consoles himself: poor visibility afflicts the Syrian commando as much as the Israeli settler.

When night comes, he goes searching for the missing eight.

An hour after dawn, he finds a ring of cows. Behind them, on the defense, six kibbutzniks. He disbands them: so clustered they provide a perfect target for Syrian artillery. They laugh. They have been sitting targets for years in Gonen. He asks about Perla and Asher. They tell him they lost Perla during the storm. Asher is still searching for her.

He orders one of the kibbutzniks to take the cattle back. Recruits the others for the search. His body aches as if sharks are feasting on his innards.

At high noon he finds Asher. At a point on the slopes from where Gonen looks like the Biblical city of Golan, consecrated by Moses as a sanctuary, and not what it really is, a conglomerate of wood-and-corrugated-iron huts, perched on stony ground at the edge of the malaria-infested Hula swamps. The point is one where Perla, Asher and he had often paused to reassure each other that the land their sweat was reclaiming looked, most definitely, like a dream that might come true.

Asher is prostrate and bloodstained, but alive. He turns him over. An object rolls away from Asher's lap. He stares for long moments before he registers the open eyes which, while alive, had worshiped him for being brother and father. As his bowels loosen, as he retches, he tries to gouge his eyes with the barrel of his gun. But the kibbutzniks hold him fast. He protests their cruelty, begs them to spare him the sight of Perla, so ugly as a severed head. And knows, even as he screams, there is no blindness that can spare him the vision.

THE GOLAN HEIGHTS, SYRIA: APRIL 17, 1953

At night, he seeks out Druze shepherds. With a religion zealously kept secret, the Druze have been persecuted for a thousand years. The persecuted help one another. They tell him rumors about a decapitated corpse—in Banias, at the Syrian officers' club, by the spouting waters.

He steals into Banias. Incongruously, he remembers it started as a Greek city, consecrated to Pan; became Caesarea Philippi under the Romans. Not so incongruously he thinks about one Yeshua, later called Christ, who stood where he is standing and decided to go up to Jerusalem and the Cross. Jews seldom die in peace.

He storms the Syrian officers' club. Spews death at those unfortunate to be there. One who bemoans his fate confesses. The headless corpse is in the old Crusaders' fortress, Nimrod Castle. . . .

At Nimrod Castle, perched on a hill, he finds Perla's decapitated body, legs prized open.

He stares at what has become an obscene orifice, bruised and forced open by rifle barrels, drenched in semen.

The men scramble, shouting abuse. He hears shots. He prays they kill him. Only after he carries the little pearl's remains home does he realize he has killed her murderers.

"The day of death is better than the day of birth."

✗

Sanbat, trembling, her body glacial, stared at the pages. Then she forced herself to read the report analyzing the abreactions.

Common factors had been listed: remarkable clarity; impressionistic style; use of the third person; use of the present tense; historian's care for date and location; poet's eye for atmospheric detail.

Special attention was drawn to the Auschwitz essay. Boaz's service file specified that he had applied to Yad Vashem for information on his mother's fate and had been informed that she had been deported on the penultimate transport from Greece, had reached Auschwitz on August 13, 1944, and had been gassed on arrival. Thus, unlike the other abreactions recounting real events, his mother's ordeal and death were fantasized—transposed from the suffering of other inmates.

At one level this fiction reflected the guilt and grief of those Diaspora Jews who had escaped or survived the Holocaust. Compressing the horrors of the death camps, describing the agonies of anonymous millions through one identity, was the only way an outsider could imagine the unimaginable.

However, this abreaction, juxtaposed with Boaz's sister's death, revealed a greater disturbance—self-condemnation. Undeniably Boaz blamed himself for his sister's fate and extended this blame to the violent deaths of other loved ones: mother, father, Nestor Papazogloû, uncle—transferring a child's desolation toward parents who had abandoned him by dying, into culpability for their loss. Hence the stigma of *deserter* for the Other-Self used as the narrator in the Auschwitz abreaction.

More data were needed to determine the roots of Boaz's self-condemnation. It seemed probable that some of these lay in vestigial infantile incestuous fixations, compounded by the duality of love and death. The mother's imagined sexual defilement in Auschwitz was not dissimilar to the necrophilia wreaked on the sister. The mother's self-inflicted blindness—also imagined—was an act that Boaz had attempted on himself following his discovery of his sister's severed head. In both instances the Oedipal parallels were obvious. And, of course, the fact remained that since his sister's death Boaz had castigated himself with celibacy. Unable to separate sex and death, he had been reduced to impotence. The quotation from Ecclesiastes that ended the last abreaction suggested that Boaz saw his life as having ceased with his reprisal.

But, of course, it did not. It became a compensatory life dedicated to the Jewish state. In effect, Boaz endeavored to forge himself as the *new man* his mother/himself had urged him to be. A new man who had no weaknesses and was, therefore, incapable of deserting his charges.

The stresses of such an impossible goal within the harsh realities of service and combat inevitably assaulted the delicate balance of his tortured mind. A type of schizophrenia, defined as the Zionist syndrome for being peculiar to the Israelis, was the result. The' God-fearing idealist trapped by a colonial predicament; the plowman compelled to wield a gun; the pacifist forced to fulfill the expectations of generations of persecuted Jews by becoming hero and superman.

For Boaz there was no respite from the Zionist syndrome. Unlike the ordinary citizen conscript who could find some relief in family and civilian life, Boaz, always on active duty, had no such outlet. Nor, by virtue of his beliefs, could he transfer responsibility for his acts of violence, as most soldiers did, to the abstract figurehead of the State. Nor, it must be assumed, could he suppress fears of failure, doubt of competence, dread of pain—factors that once again might reduce him, in his own eyes, to the man who betrayed those dependent on him.

Boaz was now in the process of seeking his long-awaited deliverance. Since he would not consider a relationship, there were three courses open to him: to withdraw from sanity; to burden himself one last time with his people's passion and, in the manner of Isaiah's Suffering Servant, surrender to death; or to return, in terms of Gestalt therapy, to the unfinished business of life by assuming the mantle of Samson and bringing the temple down on both the enemy and himself. Each course required exceptional courage, and this he had. It was impossible to predict which he would choose.

✗

He came back shortly before midnight. Sanbat had been waiting in his room, wondering how she could show him that life must be reclaimed.

She faced him determinedly, but spoke in a torrent. "I must say this: I can put breath into you. Like God into Adam. You need never fear for me. You must decide. I've accepted a new assignment—but I can back out. . . ."

His eyes were the gentlest she had seen. "What assignment?"

"Ethiopia. We've had to recall most of our agents from Africa since they cut off diplomatic relations. I'm the obvious replacement. My background, the color of my skin, my proficiency in Amharic . . ."

"Sanbat, look . . ."

She took his hand. Thick, coarse, dry. Almost inanimate. "No, let me say it. If—if there's a chance we can . . ."

Gently, he pulled his hand away. "No chance, Sanbat. How can there be?"

Faced with defeat, her anger erupted. "Tell me one thing. What happened to Asher?"

He froze. "Who?"

"Asher. Your sister's boyfriend. Did he castrate himself? Does he punish himself as you do? What happened to him?"

He spoke after a long pause. "He found deliverance."

"How?"

"In Gonen we had a machine to pulp wood. The night after we buried my sister, Asher threw himself into it. We collected nearly a ton of wood chippings—every bit soaked with his blood."

Sanbat started wailing.

Boaz moved to the door, then paused. "Tell the Memouneh I've read the file on Operation Dragons. I want it—as my last mission."

PART III

The Dark Is So Many Corners.

E. E. CUMMINGS, *HIM: Three Plays and a Ballet*

November 23, 1973

MT. NEBO, JORDAN

Osman stood where he believed Abu Ismail had desecrated the Night of Decree. At the extremity of the horizon, the heights of Jerusalem were visible, ringed with mist.

Samia, his wife, held his hand. He had given her no reason for this sudden excursion. But she felt he sought on this desolate summit an answer to the anguish that had stricken him since the day, three weeks ago, he had returned home wounded, mourning four of his men.

She sensed there were terrible times ahead. She was tempted to transgress, for once, her acceptance of the secrecy of his work, and ask him to confide in her. But he would tell her nothing. The less she knew about his work, he had told her once, the safer she would be. It was the miracle of their love that amid this morass of subterfuge they lived, steadfastly, as a unit. She understood all that she could not know. He, so blessed, seldom buckled.

Occasionally, when his fears pushed him toward the abyss, he cried out for her; she, enveloping him, saved him.

She kissed his hand.

He spoke distractedly. "The Promised Land, Samia—as Moses saw it."

"Hardly as Moses saw it."

"Land, my Samia. Such a strange reality."

"And a dream . . ."

"Yes. People see with different eyes. Few of us Arabs ever see it as sanctified. We used to, in our Golden Age. Now, it's either someone's garden and we rage with envy. Or it's a patch we believe ought to be conquered. Not so the Jew, Samia. He sees land as a place to build. A mansion where he can receive the Almighty."

Samia sat on the earth. "Let's stay awhile. We don't often get the chance to be alone. Put your head on my lap."

Osman lay down, cushioning his head on her belly.

"Can you tell me what is making you so desperate, my Osman?"

"Losing you. And our daughters."

Samia caressed his face. Strong and yet fragile. "How do you expect to lose me?"

"There are madmen about."

"I don't look at other men—not even mad ones."

Osman guffawed.

Samia clasped him closer. "Who are these madmen, Osman?"

Osman ran his hands along her thighs. If he could bury himself in her—for good. . . . He had never wished for more. It had been the traditions of service, the codes of honor and duty that had harnessed him to his country and king. "I can't tell you."

He felt her shiver. He remembered how she used to shiver, in different ways, from arousal, pleasure, satiation, serenity. Now, she shivered with dread. And each year, more.

He wondered if her strength would stand against the threat of doom that Abu Ismail's tapes contained.

Had his cryptanalysts not been expert enough to break the Mossad code, had he not rushed to that cave before the Israelis had sent their man, he would have been blissfully ignorant of the looming cataclysm.

Instead, preening himself for having outplayed Mossad, he had listened to the tapes before replacing them. And, worse, feeding pride, he had confiscated the particular tape containing Abu Ismail's war plan so that none should ever hear it. He still kept it hidden, even from the king. The content of that one tape was so profane to Muslims that it had to be interred lest exposure fulfill its prophecy.

But how was he to generate the strength to carry the secret on his own?

"Osman, do you want to make love?"

"Here?"

"It would be delightful here."

Osman clung to her. Share his knowledge with whom? Samia? To threaten her sanity as his own stood threatened? The Israelis? How—without shaming his brethren, his Faith, and Allah, whose Will Abu Ismail claimed to interpret?

He turned to her to be saved.

November 26, 1973

HONG KONG, BRITISH CROWN COLONY

Ischii Watanabe computed his impressions. The harbor, congested with ships, ferries, junks. Small wallah wallahs, like the one taking him across to Kowloon, swarming the waters. A jumbo jet, almost within reach, swooping on Kai Tak airport. The skyscrapers of Hong Kong Island, pointing electric fingers at Victoria Peak; and, on the waterfront, sleazy Wan Chai, his sanctuary for years, misty with the sweat and fumes of prostitutes and bars. The rainbow fading fast?

"We're going to reclaim you."

Watanabe met the contemptuous look of the man sitting opposite. Idris Ali, WOJ. That had been the introduction as his thugs had waylaid him outside the Mah-Jongg parlor. Then the condemned man's walk through the narrow streets with stiletto knives pricking his skin.

"Look at you—living dead. Working like a dog, then burying yourself with gambling, drink and whores."

Watanabe shook his head, unable to accept that his life of exiled anonymity had become as fragile as the precision instruments he now designed for Lai Electronics. "I—I don't understand, sir. . . ."

"The bomb—still bothers you, does it?"

"What bomb?"

"Fifteen kilos of plastique, wired with the most ingenious trigger mechanism, fuses, booby-traps. Exploded in Ginza, Tokyo, November 30, 1969. *Rengo Sekigun*'s protest at the continuation of the Japan–U.S. security treaty. Ninety-five dead, one hundred seventy-eight wounded . . ."

Watanabe's cheeks caught fire. He recalled the carnage in a million gory details. For the past years, as he had expiated his past with a new life, applying his technological expertise to domestic gadgets, sharing his modest salary with various charities, giving blood regularly in the hope that each donation would return someone—though none of his victims—to life, the dead had abated their haunting. Now, here was this ice-shaman, telling him that retribution had finally arrived.

"The police are still looking for Hiroshi Anami. . . ."

The name chimed like a death knell, bringing back into focus the identity that had thrown him into *Rengo Sekigun*'s ranks. A *Burakumin*, one of Japan's untouchables, somehow gaining entry to university but despite his qualifications, drowning in the gutter of menial jobs.

"*Rengo Sekigun*—they're looking, too. They consider defection a capital crime."

The chimes pealed louder. Watanabe recalled the girl, name forgotten but a Burakumin like him, also seeking, as an urban guerrilla, to redress her low birth. For her, too, blood had proved too heavy. She had taken three days to die, bound, gagged and buried beneath floorboards on which her comrades had walked, talked, eaten, drunk and fornicated.

"You'll be safe with us. We'll even cure you of scruples."

Watanabe finally understood. He shook his head. "No more bombs! No—"

Idris Ali smiled, took out a photograph and dropped it on Watanabe's lap. "That's you, Ischii."

Watanabe stared at the picture of a corpse—headless, handless. "Me?"

"Well, the remains of a poor untouchable. We've had the body sent from Japan—refrigerated. Thawing now. Tomorrow he'll be found in an alley with your papers. No hands—so no fingerprints. No head—so no dental records."

Watanabe managed a croaked whisper. "And me?"

"First class and with a new identity on tonight's Pan-Am to Beirut. Then to Tripoli."

"If I refuse?"

Idris Ali laughed.

Watanabe began to weep.

November 29, 1973

SAFAD, ISRAEL

It felt good to be home again. The austere two rooms in an old house in the heart of the old sanctified city were his sole attachment. They offered a glorious view both of Mount Canaan to the east and of Mount Meiron to the west. A few alleyways from his home lay the ancient synagogue of Yitzhak Abuav with its three Arks where, occasionally, he attended the service.

Boaz had bought the apartment in preference to one in Haifa, suggested by Naval Command, seeking the pure mountain air imbued, in the words of the Cabalists, with knowledge and wisdom. Safad was the spiritual home of the Sephardic Jew—more so than Jerusalem. Whereas in Jerusalem the Jew could only worship with solemnity, in Safad he could also adorn himself with lyricism, maybe even heal wounds.

The apartment, overflowing with books on the historical Jesus and with Greek records—his main interests—was sparkling. His housekeeper, a Tunisian Jewess, kept it like a shrine.

There was no mail. His bank took care of his bills. Just two telegrams.

He placed a deck chair on the balcony facing Mount Meiron, where Rabbi Shimon Bar-Yohai, reputedly the author of *The Zohar*, was buried. He opened the telegrams.

Both were from the Memouneh. The first ordered him to meet Osman Nusseibi on December 5 at the Eilat–Aqaba border; the second contained a couplet:

> *The lamp has light before it is extinguished.*
> *Wounded lions still know how to roar.*

He felt at peace. He would have his last mission.

December 1, 1973

BEIRUT, LEBANON

Dr. Talat Fawzi, professor of physics at the American University of Beirut, ignored the black Chevrolet parked on the lay-by near his house. The site, situated at a sharp bend on the Ra's Beyrout, offered a dramatic view of St. George's Bay and was a favorite with courting couples.

He was preoccupied. He had been approached by the Massachusetts Institute of Technology to head their Physics Department and had until the end of the semester to decide.

The chair was exceptionally prestigious. Most physicists would have accepted it without deliberation. Moreover, in his case—if one agreed with the Arab press—it was an honor doubly unique because as a Muslim, and still not forty years old, he had proved himself more prodigious than Westerners and Jews.

He was hard put to analyze his reservations. Since receiving his doctorate at MIT, he had not ceased pining for its rarefied atmosphere. He also loved the Americans. It had been an American couple, the Andersons—she a fey, childless woman; he, a tough, voluble extrovert employed in the restorations of Ba'albek —who had adopted him some thirty years ago when, like so many other orphans in the highlands of Djebel Lounan, he had been awaiting death by starvation. It had been American love, charity and scholarships that had developed his formidable brain to its present eminence. The MIT chair would take him closer to the Andersons, now retired in Miami.

Yet a mass of intangibles anchored him to Lebanon. The land, having absorbed the blood of countless races, offered a meaningful past. In America there would only be a meaningless present. It was ironic that he, who might with one theory launch the world irretrievably into the future, should cling to the past; but in a world abandoned by God, spiraling toward destruction, the past provided the only perspective.

The last thought might have been prescience. Entering the house he was confronted by an evil apparition: Abu Ismail, sitting statuesquely before the panoramic window, head haloed by the sun, like his portrait in WOJ posters. He felt the first waves of fear.

"What are you doing here?"

"You know who I am?"

"Yes."

Abu Ismail introduced Idris Ali. "My chief of staff. Please sit down."

The solemn courtesy had an ominous edge and Fawzi sat.

Abu Ismail pointed at the coffee table where Fawzi's maid had set a bottle of arak, a bowl of ice cubes and plates of delicacies. "Eat if you wish."

Fawzi took arak and ice, and drank without waiting for it to chill. "What can I do for you?"

Abu Ismail smiled paternally. "You will help our cause."

Fawzi poured more arak. "I'm not a terrorist—I don't know one end of a gun from the other."

"You do not have to. I would like you to write a suicide note."

Cold sweat enveloped Fawzi. "What . . . ?"

"I shall dictate the text."

"I—I can't be of any help . . . if I'm dead. . . ."

"It is necessary to tie up loose ends."

Fawzi tried to extract some sense out of his crumbling world. "My work?"

"Your work is with us."

Fawzi poured himself a third drink. "I—I have no reason to . . . Nobody would believe . . ."

"There will be a corpse. Idris Ali—call him. . . ."

Idris Ali shouted toward the kitchen. "Talat!"

A sallow-skinned man, his face blotched by fading bruises, emerged. Fawzi experienced debilitating terror.

"Your double, Professor . . . He answers to your name."

"But who . . . ?"

"One of my warriors. He volunteered for special duties."

Fawzi stared at his "double." The man stood, casual and smiling, in a secret psychedelic world. "Where did you . . . find him?"

"We made him. Plastic surgery. The seams are just visible. Note the bruises on his face."

Fawzi felt the bile rise in him; with it his defiance found substance. "You must need me badly."

"We do."

"I—I—I won't cooperate! I despise everything you stand for. The killing, the terror . . ."

"A true Levantine. A crossbreed who dreams of a universal brotherhood where Christian, Jew and Arab cavort in the same bed."

Fawzi pulled himself up. "Get out!"

Abu Ismail pulled out a revolver. "Professor, watch carefully. I want to demonstrate what I can do. . . ." He turned to Fawzi's double. "Talat . . . Over here . . ."

Fawzi's double jumped to attention. "Command me, Al-Mahdi."

Fawzi stared aghast, shocked by the desecration of the hallowed name of the Hidden Imam.

Abu Ismail proffered the revolver to Fawzi's double. "Take the gun. Go out on the balcony. Breathe in the air. It will be for the last time."

"Yes, Al-Mahdi." The man took the revolver, opened the French windows and walked out onto the balcony.

Abu Ismail turned to Fawzi. "Now, the suicide note . . ."

"I won't write."

Idris Ali dug his fingers into Fawzi's neck. Fawzi tried to scream, but Idris Ali's other hand gagged his mouth. Abu Ismail handed him a pen and a sheet of Fawzi's personal stationery. "Now, write: 'A physicist has a brief creative life. When he burns out, he is of no further use. Alas, such is the case with me.' And sign it."

Fawzi marveled at Abu Ismail's insight. There had been times when he had contemplated suicide. How had Abu Ismail known about that innermost doubt?

The pain administered by Idris Ali's fingers became unbearable. He wrote the suicide note, through prisms of tears.

Idris Ali loosened his hold.

Abu Ismail turned to Fawzi's double who was watching, enchanted, the blood-orange sun poised on the rim of the sea. "Talat . . ."

"Yes, Al-Mahdi . . ."

"It is time to die for Allah's glory. Place the gun on your temple. Count to three. Then pull the trigger."

"Yes, Al-Mahdi."

Fawzi watched, horrified, as the man proceeded with Abu Is-mail's instructions. When the shot rang out, the disintegrating head, momentarily framed within the rubicund sun, struck him like an occult image—a glimpse of the abyss that was man's mind.

✗

The macabre suicide caused a furor. The news media ran the full spectrum of conflicting responses. Liberal sources reviewed the agonies of creative impotence, comparing the suicide with the seppuku of the Japanese author Yukio Mishima. Introverted intel-lectuals bemoaned that there would be no Arab renaissance be-cause the Arab genius was unable to live with itself. Extremists, casting doubts on the suicide, aired political motives ranging from social jealousy to assassination by Christian Arabs or Israelis, or both.

But the verdict of suicide remained. The body was buried with haste.

✗

On the night of the event, the CIA received warnings of possible enormity from its station chief in Lebanon, Dr. Charles Quinn, professor of mathematics at the American University of Beirut.

Quinn, in a disorderly report, contended that as Fawzi's inti-mate friend, he had reasons to doubt the authenticity of the sui-cide note. He argued, as a mathematician, that Fawzi, far from being burnt out, had been at the peak of his faculties. Then, in more hysterical terms, he postulated that, all his efforts at exam-ining his friend's corpse having failed, and that bribery of police inspectors, forensic pathologists and coroners being everyday oc-currences in a country where Muslim and Christian factions fought each other relentlessly, it had to be assumed that the sui-cide had been faked for purposes he dreaded to think.

The CIA, cognizant of Quinn's abnormal attachment to Fawzi, refrained from processing such an emotional report through the computer and filed it under "Misconnections."

December 5, 1973

EILAT-AQABA, ISRAEL—JORDAN BORDER

The nation was mourning David Ben-Gurion, the "Armed Prophet." As long as the old man had been alive, Israel, like the proverbial wife, had been clothed in dignity and power. Now, overnight, she looked frail, ancient as her history; and the Jew, suddenly orphaned, faced extinction in an indifferent world.

Boaz gazed at Eilat, a pointillist's blob where the pastel earth met the azure sea. There had to be hope for a people who had built a dynamic city on a desert coast where only twenty-five years ago there had been nothing but a few Egyptian army huts.

His sadness deepened. Eilat was delusory: here where the Jordanian resort Aqaba lay, a mere five kilometers along the shore, to all appearances a friendly neighbor, and beyond, where the Saudi Arabian coastline could be seen as a mellow landscape, it was easy to dream of continuity, easy to forget the hatred that permeated the region.

Osman's jeep stopped at the Jordanian border post. Boaz moved forward and met him in no-man's-land. They saluted ceremoniously, then cast parade looks at their soldiers on guard duty.

Boaz led Osman into the tent and extended his hand. Osman shook it warmly.

Boaz pointed at a chair, then at the tray of cold drinks.

Osman, despite the Muslim proscription, enjoyed alcohol and helped himself to a beer. "My condolences, Boaz. A great man—Ben-Gurion."

Boaz shot him a look.

Osman's eyes reflected sincerity. "It's a weakness in me to admire certain enemies."

Boaz nodded, sat down and switched on his tape recorder. Osman performed the same ritual.

They studied each other like old friends who had been parted too long and wondered how to rekindle the warmth.

"Your wounds, Boaz?"

"Healed."

Boaz, Osman noted, had changed. Nothing on the surface, except perhaps for the hair that seemed whiter. But inside, something had buckled. He looked like a degutted tank. "You look haunted, Boaz."

"I'm keeping sane."

Osman stared at him at length. "Is that it—your mind? It grieves me, Boaz. As your friend. It also heartens me. As your enemy."

"You should be preoccupied with other matters."

"To me you are the face of Israel. You reflect the good and the evil of your people. One warms to you as a friend because one finds compassion, humility, greatness and suffering. Equally, one hates you as an enemy because the arrogance, the syndrome of the Chosen People is also there. Or has been. The arrogance has disappeared. You don't look so invincible. That's what gives you the haunted look. And much as it saddens me to see you wilt, it gives me hope."

Boaz considered the remark, then pointedly pushed across another bottle of beer. "You've had our latest evaluation on Operation Dragons?"

"Target: Jerusalem? That's nonsense!"

Boaz stared thoughtfully at his companion. The "haunted look" seemed more applicable to Osman. The eyes had lost their fearlessness, and the geniality seemed to hang uncomfortably like clothes on a wasting man. "It's a sound evaluation, Osman. Jerusalem—the Holy City. Ours. Yours. And his. The unthinkable—that's Abu Ismail's trademark."

"That's not the unthinkable."

"What else?"

"His mind works on the grand scale, Boaz. He has no time for petty gestures. All or nothing!"

"Precisely. If he can't have Jerusalem, he wants it destroyed."

"That's settling for nothing. It would be true if he'd bid for all and lost. He hasn't—yet."

Boaz was surprised by Osman's vehemence. "What do you call 'all'?"

"The world—under his theocracy."

"That's the impossible."

Osman smiled bitterly. "There was a time when the Jewish state was an impossibility."

Boaz let the matter rest. "Jerusalem or the world—we have to get him. I believe you want us to team up. I have clearance."

"That's good to know."

The casual response irked Boaz. "Change of heart?"

Osman fidgeted. "You forget! We're still enemies! You still occupy the West Bank—our land. We still mourn men killed fighting you. We're still ostracized by our Arab brothers because we've resigned ourselves to having you as neighbors."

Boaz looked at Osman disconcertedly.

Osman stood up abruptly. "We're here to discuss the fishing rights in the Gulf. I suggest we get a move on."

Boaz nodded, aggrieved that the meeting had turned sour. Osman had stirred in him something akin to hope. "We're happy with the status quo."

"I'll reserve judgment until we've reviewed the limits. I've arranged for a boat."

✗

Osman had dismissed the crew of the Jordanian coast-guard dinghy on a point of protocol, and had steered a steady course straight down the sea line.

They had exchanged a few words, mainly to confirm coordinates. The rest of the time Osman had fixed melancholic eyes on Boaz.

Now, past Coral Island, Osman switched off the outboard motor, immersed his tape recorder's microphone in the sea, then gesticulated that Boaz should do the same. "Quite choppy today. Everything's getting soaked."

Boaz, puzzled, slipped his microphone into the water.

Osman brought out a flask. "I apologize for the cloak-and-dagger. But what I'm going to propose is unofficial. I also regret the harsh words—though the sentiments were genuine. Arak?"

Boaz took a sip, then, aware of the strain evident in Osman's prolixity, put a hand on Osman's shoulder. "Come on—get it off your chest."

Osman gulped down a mouthful. "All right. Brace yourself. A wild mission. So wild—I've sounded no one. Not even King Hussein. We assassinate Abu Ismail. You and I. No one else involved."

Boaz looked at Osman intently. "How? We can't get at him in Libya except by mounting a major raid. And we'd need a miracle to catch him on the hop."

"There's one place we can corner him."

"Where?"

Osman hesitated, then looking toward the Saudi Arabian coastline, spoke waveringly. "That's the wild part. Mecca. He's going on pilgrimage—the hajj."

Boaz gaped at him. "Mecca—?"

The secret shared, Osman felt drained of energy. He brought out his cigarettes and lit one. "Mecca."

"You think I can get into Mecca? Are you suggesting I convert?"

"You're circumcised. You speak perfect Turkish and Arabic. And you know a great deal about the Faith. You could pass as a Muslim."

"Assuming we get through, we can't kill him during the hajj."

"Why not? It's a tradition with us to assassinate our leaders at their devotions. That's how we lost King Abdallah."

"Osman, we're talking about Mecca! The sanctified city! Where you're not allowed to spill blood! Not even slaughter a chicken!"

"We'll respect that. We'll kill him just outside—in secular territory. I've spent a whole week working out a plan."

"You've wasted your time. It's a nonstarter."

"Afraid—are you?"

Boaz looked up sharply. "Afraid?"

"Of getting killed."

Boaz grinned, eyes blazing. "If you could guarantee that . . . and if you could also guarantee Abu Ismail's death . . . I'm your man! Whether it's Mecca, Samarkand or Xanadu!"

Osman took a sip of arak. "I guessed as much."

"Did you?"

"Death—that's your salvation."

"It's everyone's."

"Not mine. Grace comes from loved ones. I have my wife, my daughters."

"Then think about them!"

Osman growled. "You bastard! Doesn't it occur to you—what I have to bear? Coming to you for help . . ."

"I'm flattered."

"Damn your ego! I'm talking about my soul! I'm condemning myself to eternal damnation. Coming to you—an Infidel! Asking you, *colluding* with you to enter and desecrate Islam's holiest city! When I cross the bridge of Sir'at, it'll be the fires of Hell for me! That's the price I'm willing to pay."

"Why such a price, Osman?"

"Because I love my country."

"Your patriotism has never been in question. You certainly don't have to prove it by damning yourself. There must be another reason. . . ."

"You amaze me, Boaz. . . . One minute you're as thick as concrete—next minute you're playing with weights and scales."

"You haven't answered my question, Osman."

"I'd rather risk eternal damnation than let Abu Ismail outrage the Faith."

"Sounds impressive . . . but the real reason?"

Osman grimaced as he gulped down another mouthful. "All right. Much as I resist it, I fear your evaluation might be right. Operation Dragon's target might well be Jerusalem."

Boaz was not convinced. "Why me, Osman?"

"I can't do it on my own. Even the two of us is cutting it fine. I should also confess: I can't trust myself to do it alone."

"But why me—a Jew?"

Osman smiled wryly. "Can you see any of my people—any Muslim, in fact—who'd be willing to share my damnation?"

"If you explained . . ."

"Who knows what I know. And who'd believe me if I told them . . . ?"

"What do you know, Osman?"

"I told you: Abu Ismail is the enemy of the Faith. The appellation *Al-Mahdi* is not just artifice."

"You're holding something back."

"Yes—or no?"

Boaz searched Osman's eyes but failed to identify the secret. He nodded, stoically. "Yes—subject to the Memouneh's approval."

Osman snapped angrily. "Can't you be your own man?"

"If I were an Arab—or anybody else—I could be my own man. As an Israeli, I've got to think twice, and ask ten times, even to breathe—in case I offend the world. . . ."

Osman winced, then shrugged. "Very well. But make sure the Memouneh sits on it."

"Where do we go from here?"

"Hell. Where else?"

December 6, 1973

ATLIT, ISRAEL

The luxurious seaside bungalow, set apart from the naval compound, had been allocated as an exclusive holiday villa for Israel's small band of naval commandos. Despite its comforts and private beach, it had a sepulchral aura. It was, Boaz felt, an artificial shore where the country's most accomplished war-horses were asked to regale themselves while awaiting brutal death.

The Memouneh, whose suggestion it had been to discuss Osman's proposed mission at Atlit, had spent the afternoon brooding by the ruins of the nearby Pilgrims' Castle. The history of the Knights Templars, who had built it, was the Memouneh's pet subject. Parallels could be drawn between Israel and the religiomilitary order, both of whom had contested the Promised Land with Islam. The Memouneh did not want his young nation to make the same mistakes as the Crusaders.

In contrast, Boaz had dawdled by the sea, nursing the discomforting thought that his relationship with Fate being what it was, it would be earth and not water that would bury him.

The Memouneh rejoined him after sunset at the peak of his melancholy.

"It's sound, Boaz. Mecca's the ideal place. But not as a suicide mission."

Boaz stared at the stars. Did they ever listen to men talking by the sea and laugh? "You have my word."

"I'd accept it—any other time."

Boaz shrugged, squatted on his haunches, cupped his hands against the waves and let the water and sand trickle through.

"Boaz, listen. I'll give it top priority. Keep it between you, me and God—and maybe Golda. Back you and Osman every possible way. But only if I know you'll come back."

"I might fail. Get caught."

"That's not what I mean."

"We'll do our best to kill Abu Ismail. If we fail—that's our misfortune. If we succeed, that's all there is to it. It's not for me to tell you what to do, Zamora. But when the country's security is at stake, don't play the Good Samaritan."

The Memouneh picked up some seaweed, examined it a moment, smelled it, then placed it on the sand, carefully, as if it were a bunch of rare orchids. "You're right, of course."

Boaz stood up, letting the tension dissolve now that the decision had been taken.

"I often think about death, Boaz. In fact, I never stop thinking about it. Sometimes I even talk about it. . . ."

Boaz sank to his haunches again, let the spray hit him.

The Memouneh squatted too, alongside. "If I could attain an Eastern mysticism, see death as a phase in the wheel of life, a requisite for reincarnation, I'd go on my knees and beg for it. Alternatively, if I were a Christian or a Muslim, I could find hope and salvation in it. But I'm a Jew, and I know our history inside out. Death's never been gentlemanly with us. A sadist—every time. Take any Jew—and I'll swear he died debased. I know I'm not being fair. You could say the same of any man, but that would confuse the issue. . . ."

"The issue being—?"

"Anger. The Jews' revolt. I'd let rats eat my balls before I surrendered to Death."

"And if rats have already eaten your balls?"

"I'd grow new ones—of steel."

Boaz stood up and started walking toward the bungalow.

The Memouneh overtook him. "I've got one thing more to say."

Boaz stopped.

"You're an exceptional man, Boaz. You could have climbed any height—in Zahal or government. You could have had my job. But you chose isolation. That's being charitable. You chose live burial. Now, I'm asking you. Fulfill your potential. We need you!"

Boaz faced the Memouneh. He saw brotherly love. More than

that, he saw the eyes of his dead family, of Nestor Papazogloû, second father. The eyes begged. And he felt ashamed. "But you torment me. . . ."

The Memouneh remained impassive.

Boaz bellowed. "Ask me if *I* need *you!*"

The Memouneh walked to the bungalow, without answering.

December 9, 1973

LISBON, PORTUGAL

Gabriel Carvalho got out of his Volkswagen as the ferry crabbed away. He listened to the wind howling through Praça do Comércio, where Pombal's mellow-green colonnades watched over the Tagus. He shivered and cursed the night shift that played havoc with a man's metabolism.

Ten minutes to get across to Cacilhas, and another ten to drive home to Almada. In time to see his wife and daughter before they left for Mass.

He gazed at the Monument to the Discoveries showing Prince Henry the Navigator at the head of those who had explored the world; and beyond at the Manuelian monastery church, Mosteiro dos Jeronimos, built in white marble with the profits of the spice trade; and farther along, at the fortress of Belém. Lisbon, reputedly founded by Ulysses, emanated *saudades*, life's bittersweet essence.

Gabriel Carvalho loved his city almost as much as he loved his daughter and his wife. Collectively they had kept him sane during that terrible year in Mozambique fighting the Frelimo. He had had to journey, like Ulysses, to the nether regions to discover that a devoted wife, an angel of a child and a humble roof were preferable to all the golden calves in the world.

✗

He had not heard their laughter, and as he walked into the flat, the silence stunned him. He ran through the rooms: the beds had not been slept in.

He ran back to the front door to call on the neighbors. A man blocked his way. Before he could cry out, the man struck him.

When he regained consciousness, he became aware that he had been gagged and bound to a chair with ropes across his ankles and chest. He defecated in terror.

The man approached, holding a small parcel, blotched red. "You speak English, don't you, Carvalho?"

Carvalho nodded.

"I won't ungag you—not until you're over your next shock."

Carvalho watched him untie the small parcel. Incongruously, he thought about his plans for the afternoon. He was to take Maria and Isabel to Alfama, guide them through the old, shoulder-wide streets, and show them, at every corner, the Child Jesus in his mother-of-pearl crèche, ready to preside over Christmas. They were then to dine in a small restaurant where the *porco com amei-jōas* was the best, and where legends of ancient sailors and soldiers, gentlewomen and whores, poets and villains, Jews and Moors, the Inquisition and autos-da-fé still survived in local quatrains.

Having unwrapped the parcel, the man revealed a small amputated finger bearing a tiny pearl ring. He placed the finger on Carvalho's lap. Carvalho stared at it, trying to clear the disorder in his mind.

"Amputated fingers lose much of their beauty, but you should recognize the ring."

Carvalho shook his head, unseeing, uncomprehending.

"You bought it last year, for your little girl, Isabel." The man placed a Polaroid photograph on Carvalho's lap. "By way of proof, here's a photograph. It doesn't show Isabel at her best, but then amputation *is* painful."

Carvlaho's mind creased in on itself. But the respite he sought, the disintegration of his brain, did not materialize. He managed to vomit and, as bile flooded his mouth, he thought he might suffocate and happily die.

The man loosened the gag and forced open Carvalho's mouth. Carvalho wailed. . . . "*Māe de Deus, Māe de Deus, Māe de—*"

The man wiped off Carvalho's vomit with the tablecloth. He took his time so that Carvalho would conquer his hysteria. "I will ungag you. But you must not scream. Do you understand?"

Carvalho slumped back, exhausted and broken.

The man untied the gag and placed another Polaroid photograph on his lap. "One last proof: we have your wife, too."

"What will you do to them?"

"Hold them for a while."

"Isabel . . ."

"She'll be all right—minus a finger, of course. The amputation was carried out expertly—by our surgeon."

"But why—what do you want from them?"

"Nothing—from them. But a lot from you."

"I—I haven't got much money. I could raise some."

"We don't want money. Just your cooperation. . . ."

"I'll—I'll do anything."

"Good." The man picked up the finger and waved it savagely. "To make it absolutely clear. If you contact the police, we'll kill your wife and child. We have no pity."

"Please—I believe you!"

The man untied him, slowly, to increase Carvalho's anxiety.

Carvalho dragged himself up and edged away, embarrassed by the smell of his clothes. "I'm sorry—I'm all messy. I couldn't help it."

"It's a good sign. Shows you care. Make sure you bathe and clear up after I leave—in case you get visitors."

Carvalho nodded. "You said—my cooperation . . ."

The man sat down, ran his eyes around the room and smiled like a guest who has been made most welcome. "We've planned a hit. Lisbon airport."

Carvalho started to shake. "You want to hit troop transports—to Mozambique, Angola. . . . You're Frelimo or MPLA. . . ."

The man laughed. "Neither. Idris Ali. WOJ. Which means you won't be betraying your country. Just joining the fight against Israel."

Carvalho stared at him. "I—I'm only a cargo clerk. . . ."

"That's what we're going to hit—cargo!"

"What cargo?"

Idris Ali winked teasingly. "Jaffa oranges."

Carvalho barely registered the words.

"Now, a few details. Friends and relatives will inquire after your wife and daughter. You'll tell them they've gone away—holiday or on a visit. What would be best?"

"I . . . er . . . My wife has a rich uncle in Brazil. I can say he invited them."

"Good. Only make sure nobody gets suspicious. From tomorrow, you'll keep yourself to your office. Go on overtime. With your family away, it would look natural."

"Yes."

"You'll receive two daily calls. One from your wife—"

"You'll let me speak to her?"

"Briefly. The other—from me. You'll know I haven't forgotten you. And I'll know you're keeping your end of the bargain. Occasionally I may ask you to provide things. . . ."

"What things?"

"Plans, information, tools, odds and ends . . ."

"What if I can't get them?"

"Make sure you do. When we move for the hit, you'll help us get into the airport. Six hours later, your wife and daughter will be returned."

Carvalho bit his lips. "When will it be—the hit?"

"Soon." Idris Ali got up, moved to the door, then stopped, and smiled sweetly. "Don't look so despondent. Jews are your enemies, too—Christ-killers!"

December 11, 1973

ATHENS, GREECE

The music, Mikis Theodorakis's *Mauthausen*, was inspired. Boaz, hair and beard thickening, danced defiantly, like the last of the mastodons, a creature assured of extinction.

The proprietor of the taverna, a Mossad agent, had not objected to closing down for the night. But he had cautioned Boaz: though Papadopoulos had been overthrown, the oppressive regime continued to ban Theodorakis's works.

Boaz opened a new bottle of ouzo, then sensed a presence behind him. He spun around, holding the bottle like a weapon.

Osman moved toward him, genial smile on erect body. "You dance well."

"Never abuse a man's privacy, Osman."

"I have clearance from the Memouneh. Won't you offer me a drink?"

Boaz passed him the bottle and switched off the record player.

Osman drank a mouthful. "I have found an identity for you—for Mecca."

"I thought we agreed. I'll provide my own identity. My own passport. My own visa."

"This one's foolproof. Jordanian. Resident abroad."

"Can't be foolproof. Not in a small country like Jordan. People know people—whatever their residency." He sat down on the floor. "I'd rather be alone, Osman."

"To wallow in self-pity?"

"Self-pity?"

"What else? When you indulge in entrechats while the world disintegrates?"

Boaz growled. "I need time to prepare."

Osman shook his head sadly. "You came out of Greece thirty years ago. You've never dared return—not even for Mossad. Now you've found a dead man's mission—and you're here to prepare. Take my word for it, Boaz. Nothing prepares a man for death. Not visits to ancestral grounds! Nor the blessings of the dead."

Osman's last words came out muffled. Boaz had jumped up and grabbed him by his jacket.

"That's why you came—to lecture me!"

"Who do you think you are—a carefree pagan?"

Just as suddenly Boaz relaxed his grip. Osman had seen into him—but not to the very depths. True, he had come to Greece to take leave of the world ritualistically, to tie about his person ribbons of memories, and to leave behind tears as token remnants of his clay. He had believed that in so doing he could bestow sanctity on his last deed, and through it, his life. The irony was that he had not dared travel north to Salonika where the voices of his mother and father still inhabited the ether.

He felt his temples throb. The soul held its own measure of life. His could contain no more without dying. Therefore, to live, the soul had to sever itself from life. "But then . . . without weakness . . . ?"

"You face God with your wounds suppurating. You show Him how much you've loved Him."

Boaz howled with contemptuous laughter. "You're as pathetic as I am, Osman."

Osman ruffled Boaz's hair. "That must be the secret of our friendship. Let's go. I want to check every detail before I leave for Medina."

Boaz stared around him. He moved away from Osman, picked up the *Mauthausen* record, then smashed it.

December 13, 1973

ASMARA, ETHIOPIA

The moon that had crowned the Nile and the Sudanese wilderness surrendered to the false dawn. The Ethiopian Airlines Boeing 707 began its descent. Sanbat remained chained to her thoughts.

Her posting to Ethiopia, as safe-house keeper, was a provisional assignment until an adequate replacement could be trained, or until Israel and Ethiopia reestablished diplomatic relations. With the Arab oil blackmail even more effective in the Third World, the likelihood of the latter seemed remote. If she wished, she could make the appointment her own. Considering the overseas bonus, insurance and pension plans, she was to be envied. And yet . . .

She feared that the debilitating emptiness she had felt since leaving Israel was now perhaps permanent. But there would be some compensation. Having left Boaz behind, she would cease bleeding—just like a corpse.

✗

She disembarked at 6:00 A.M. at Yohannes IV airport. Despite the alpine morning, Asmara promised a stifling day. The burnt-wood smell of Africa, once associated with death, enveloped her. It confirmed the feeling that she had returned to the Diaspora for burial.

Coming through customs, she spotted Kevork Dedeyan and the stocky Ethiopian accompanying him.

Dedeyan greeted her warmly, then introduced his companion. "Major Getachew Iyessous . . . Imperial Air Force . . ."

Getachew Iyessous, openly admiring her gold-embroidered *shamma*, proffered a hand, and spoke in Amharic. "Now Imperial Security Service. Welcome home, Sanbat."

His direct approach—contrasting with the Israeli cult of secrecy—shocked and pleased her. "Thank you, Major Iyessous."

"Getachew. In Ethiopia we use the first name."

She had placed Getachew's accent as Tigrean. That complemented her favorable impression. In her youth, old-timers had recounted that the Tigreans were as noble as the Falashas because like the black Jews, they were proud highlanders who had accompanied the Queen of Sheba to Jerusalem, there to receive the seed of Solomon.

"Silly of me to forget, Getachew."

Getachew chuckled graciously, then took out bread rolls from a paper bag and passed them around. "Kevork's taking the first flight back to Massawa. So a stand-up breakfast. Fish sandwiches. Eat the lemon, too."

"Another tradition?"

"Insurance. In case the fish is bad."

She had been reticent toward Getachew. Now she understood why. He was uncannily like Boaz—but with an open smile and a sense of humor. She wondered if Getachew had any sexual problems. Then, resentfully, asked herself if Boaz, his face, his body, his problems, were going to be imprinted on all the men she met.

Dedeyan studied Sanbat and Getachew. Since the disruption of diplomatic relations, Arab pressure on Ethiopia had been so fierce that overnight, the large Mossad cell had been reduced to one agent in deep cover: himself. Fortunately, the reduction had proved as much of an inconvenience to the Ethiopians as to the Israelis. Ethiopia, as the only other non-Muslim state within the vast Arab domain that stretched from the Persian Gulf to the Atlantic, had, like Israel, daunting security problems. These centered on the subversive activities of the various secessionist groups, in particular the ELF, backed by both the Arabs and Russia. Already voices in the Arab League predicted that within a few years Eritrea would become an independent state, thus transforming the

Red Sea into a Muslim lake. Then, Ethiopia—and Israel—severed from vital supply routes, would suffocate and expire. Alarmed by such prophecies, the Ethiopians, who had been so dependent on Israeli proficiency, had asked the Jewish state, at clandestine meetings in the U.N., for a new team of experts. So far, Israel had been able to comply with one, Sanbat.

Sanbat and Getachew would be working closely; since both were first-class operators, the only doubt had centered on their compatibility. Having watched them exchange small-talk harmoniously in Amharic, Dedeyan felt as relieved as a successful marriage broker. "I have to go."

Sanbat faced him, instantly professional. "What about my briefing?"

"Getachew will see to that. You're on routine work for the moment. But brace yourself—we may be in for a storm."

✗

The safe house, an old Italian-built structure that had seen better days before its conversion, was situated on Queen Elizabeth II Avenue, close to Asmara's night-life center and main thoroughfare, Haile Selassie I Avenue.

The ground floor was occupied by a travel agency, Majestic Tours, which had been set up by the ISS to keep surveillance on undesirable tourists, and which had a large staff of "tour operators" covering every port, airport, hotel and visitworthy site.

Sanbat settled in and immediately began the laborious process of reorganizing communications and streamlining the input on all visitors to Ethiopia. If there was any substance to the WOJ–ELF connection, Mossad expected an influx of WOJ commandos.

✗

Later, Getachew went to Kagnew, the U.S. telecommunications base. Al Jameson had gone ferreting in Addis Ababa, but his staff were under orders to relay any pertinent intelligence. There was none.

He went to the officers' mess for a beer.

Getachew devoted his rare moments of solitude exclusively to thoughts of his country. In an empire torn by regional, tribal, racial and religious divisions, crippled by poverty, hunger and disease, retarded by a medieval feudal system, and at the opposite pole of a world basking in riches and technology, patriotism was the only way to generate hope.

Patriotism was also his heritage. He was the progeny of great warriors. His father had died fighting the Fascists in the Second

World War; his uncle Zewde had been decorated as an Abyssinian irregular. His great-grandfather had caused havoc among the Italians in the 1896 battle of Adua. Getachew himself, serving as a fighter pilot, had been cited for bravery on the Somalian front during the skirmishes of the sixties.

He was also a devout Christian and chose to believe that Solomon's seduction of Queen Sheba—so devilish—was as divinely ordained as Judas's betrayal of Jesus. He felt as much pride in the blood of the Hebrews that flowed in his veins as in the beatitude of the kingdom of Axum, which had been the first civilization to embrace Christianity.

Though so imbued with the glorious past, he was fully aware of Haile Selassie's sins. As a Tigrean, he was a member of the race most abused by the ruling Amharas and most justified in joining a dissident group. In fact, he had been approached on several occasions by the Tigrinya Liberation Front, created in the wake of the ELF. But much as he hated the emperor's tyrannical rule, much as he protested at the gross expenditure on numerous palaces while people died in their thousands from famine, he believed that only the Imperial Throne preserved Ethiopia's unity. Unless patriots like himself stamped out the secessionists and secured a liberal succession to the throne, the empire would fragment with the death of the old Lion of Judah. The land and its many peoples would be prey to radical Arabs, soulless Russians and cybernetic Chinese, all three already storming at the gates. And before long, Christianity would be wiped out in yet another corner of the world. It was ironic that while the Christian world washed its hands, the only helping hand to the African Jesus was extended by Israel, that other nation facing death but refusing to die.

December 15, 1973

ISTANBUL, TURKEY

The wind blowing from the Marmara Sea burst through Gülhane Park and exploded on Beyazıt Square. Those who braved the cold, hurried. Some cast cursory glances at Boaz, sitting beneath the giant oak tree of Istanbul's famous teahouse, and thought him eccentric.

Boaz observed each look for signs of threat while pretending to read the Fodor guidebook. He had chosen to stay outdoors, at the price of conspicuousness, so that he could observe his man as he arrived at Kapalı Çarşı, the enclosed bazaar, and ascertain whether he had drawn the attention of *Milli Istihbarat Teşkilatı*, the Turkish secret service. If so, he could bolt and lose himself within the bazaar's 4,000 shops. He had no reason to expect trouble, but prudence was a reflex.

There was also a sentimental reason for his interlude. In his early youth, he and his uncle, who had a stall in the bazaar, had often sat beneath the giant oak, known as the Tree of Idleness, watching Greek, Jewish, Armenian, Kurd and Laz merchants outwit each other while their Turkish counterparts nurtured their spirits by sipping tea between prayers. Boaz's love for the Turks, rooted in those years, had survived the alienation of his later incursions into Turkey on Mossad business.

He sat up as he spotted the swarthy Turk turn into Beyazıt Square. The man was one of that special breed known as *iş bitirici*, "job accomplisher," who could, at a price, procure anything from a new identity to oil-drilling rights in the Aegean. The *iş bitirici* walked past; he appeared, from his happy whistling, to have secured Boaz's requirements: a Turkish passport and the special visa issued for a round trip to Saudi Arabia for purposes of the hajj only.

Boaz waited, scanning the square carefully, until certain that the *iş bitirici* had not been followed. Then he hurried toward the bazaar.

He caught up with the man halfway through the vine-covered courtyard of the secondhand booksellers, still occupying the site of the Byzantian paper market, *Chartoprateia*. He slowed down and watched him enter a dusty bookshop. He walked past and saw İskender Ağa, the owner of the shop and Boaz's middleman, exchange greetings with the *iş bitirici*. He stopped near a barrow overladen with battered books.

He rummaged through them while the boy from the coffee stall rushed in three orders. That augured well. When the *iş bitirici* left, Boaz, still checking for possible tails, bought some paperbacks, then strolled to İskender Ağa's shop.

İskender Ağa, named after Alexander the Great, was a mountain of a man, past seventy, bald like an old wrestler, with mischievous blue eyes. "*Shalom, Yahudi.*"

The greeting did not offend Boaz. İskender Ağa loved the Jew —ever since that day in September 1918 when, fighting General Allenby's forces in Palestine, he had been left for dead during the retreat from Megiddo, and had been found and nursed back to health by some *chalutzim*. He had never forgotten that the pioneers, though having switched loyalties from Turkey to Britain in their aim to establish a Jewish state, had upheld zealously man's greatest virtue, mercy.

Boaz spoke to him in Turkish. *"Merhaba,* İskender Ağa."

"I see you haven't forgotten *mama-loshen.*"

Boaz chuckled. İskender Ağa's use of "mother tongue" in Yiddish for Turkish was a surrealistic touch typical of the old man.

"You like my joke, ah, Jew? Good. Never lose your sense of humor. Sit down. I have ordered coffee."

Boaz sat on a stool.

The boy from the coffee stall brought in two large cups, placed them on the counter, and rushed out.

"Big cups, Jew, because we are big men."

"Allah bless you, İskender."

"He does. Thanks be to Him."

Boaz sipped the coffee. The ritual as a prelude to business was an unwritten law. "You look well, İskender."

"I still jump on the old woman."

"May you always be so rampant."

"And may you turn your mind to Eve's daughters. I tell you, the tastiest apricot is between a woman's legs."

Boaz nodded. He had never understood how İskender Ağa had guessed at the deadness inside him; every time they met the old man repeated the same crass words. He finished his coffee.

"I see, Jew, you drink in a hurry."

"I don't want to impose on your time."

"Whenever I speak of apricots you want to run. One day you'll run to death without having tasted apricot—and that will be your greatest tragedy."

Boaz smiled obliquely.

İskender Ağa shook his head, then from behind the dusty books, produced a bedraggled *Nüfus Cüzdanı,* the Turkish identity card. "This has been forged to the specifications you gave me. The man named is now officially alive. The passport has been made for him."

Boaz looked through the identity card: 1932 issue, complete with entries such as ration stamps and military service history.

From behind another dusty pile İskender Ağa produced a Turkish passport. "One passport for Saudi Arabia. With hajj visa."

Boaz flipped through the passport; except for the official Turkish stamp and photograph it was ready for use. He compared the entries with those of the identity card. "Perfect."

İskender Ağa smiled and took out a rubber stamp from his pocket. "The stamp—fresh from Fourth Bureau, the passport office. Now give me the photographs."

Boaz handed him a dozen photographs.

İskender Ağa glanced at them, then paused ominously. "It's you, Jew."

Boaz kept silent.

"I thought the passport was for an important Israeli Arab because the Saudis won't admit Israeli Muslims. But you? Jews aren't allowed in Mecca. I won't permit the desecration of the Holy City."

"It is important I go, İskender."

"Important for the Jew?"

"For peace. Your brothers in faith need it as much as the Jew."

İskender Ağa paced up and down behind the counter, then lit a cigarette. "Listen, Jew—we have done business before. We have grown to respect—love—each other. . . ."

"Yes."

"I must know. Why do you want to go to Mecca?"

"I can't tell you."

"You don't trust me?"

"If I didn't, İskender, I wouldn't have brought my photographs. I could have asked for a blank passport."

"And what good would that have done? Unless there are corresponding photographs in the visa application forms you run a great risk. You need me to place them at the visa office. So tell me another lie. . . ."

"No lies, old man. It's best you don't know."

İskender Ağa resumed his pacing. "If I take the passport back . . . what will you do? Kill me? I am not afraid to die, Jew."

"A man who kills his father is damned for eternity, İskender. I've been damned enough in this life."

İskender Ağa sank down on a chair and stared at his cigarette smoke. This was the first time in his long years in the passport market that he had hesitated. "You say it is for peace, Jew?"

"I will say more—it is also for Allah!"

İskender Ağa glared at Boaz. The claim did not strike him as profane. He was wise and knew there had been times when man, even an Infidel, had been the Deity's savior. "Will you swear on your mother's soul?"

Boaz did not flinch. "And my father's. And my sister's."

İskender Ağa closed his eyes, sat immobile for a while, then spoke gravely. "Very well. No man whom I trust would swear such terrible oaths in vain."

Boaz relaxed.

İskender Ağa stuck one of Boaz's photographs in the passport, then carefully rubber-stamped it with the Turkish crescent and star. He handed the passport to Boaz, holding on to the remaining photographs. "These will be in Saudi records by tonight."

Boaz pocketed the passport and brought out an envelope containing seventy thousand Turkish liras. "You're a good man, İskender."

İskender Ağa slipped the money into a drawer. "Good men are in Paradise, Jew. One thing . . ."

"Yes?"

"Eternal damnation is also the lot of the father who kills a son. Have pity on me. If you return from Mecca with sins against Allah, I shall hear of it. And I will live long enough to avenge Him!"

Boaz nodded, then, impulsively, took İskender Ağa's hand and, in the traditional gesture of reverence, kissed it and placed it on his forehead.

December 17, 1973

BENGHAZI, LIBYA

Abu Ismail pulled his tormented body upright. The task force for Operations Dragons stood before him, naked, chanting and swaying to the wind. He tried to regulate his breath, to direct strength to his arthritic limbs.

Winter had invaded the Mediterranean. There was anguish in the ruins of the Ptolemaic city of Berenice; the rock-hewn tombs of those ancients the scimitar had conquered stood hollow-eyed as if on the wrong side of resurrection. Immediately to the southwest, Moor-white Benghazi folded her palm trees like a sinner cowering from the wrath of Allah. Abu Ismail recalled an old desert poem:

> As no one can escape, I, too, must take my cup
> and drink from death's dark pool.

The words were similar to those uttered by Jesus before his arrest and ensuing Passion. It was strange that he, Al-Mahdi, should muse in like vein. He was not a common prophet.

It was the pain. Or witchcraft from The Doubter. He clasped his talismans and reassured himself that his crumbling body would turn whole for the Last Judgment. He challenged The Doubter: *I am a man for whom death is as unreal as a universe without Allah.*

He turned to his warriors. Their bodies, strong and taut after intensive training, glistened with defiance. Their minds, harnessed in relentless sessions of indoctrination, shone like the burning mirror of a phalanx of shields.

Abu Ismail held up his hand. Instantly, the chanting stopped. Idris Ali inspected the men and women, correcting, where necessary, their rhythmic sway; when he nodded his satisfaction, Abu Ismail addressed them.

"My warriors. You stand before Allah without rank or privilege, without wordly goods, without thoughts of *Shaytan*. You stand naked, as He created you and as you will face Him for judgment. You are the most fortunate among the Faithful. Unlike others lost in the world's labyrinths and therefore damned, you stand before an arrow-straight path that leads to salvation. You have been chosen to know religion before death. Allah is nearer to you than your jugular vein. You need only triumph in your tasks and He will clutch you to His bosom."

He paused. Each warrior, each maiden, each technician glowed with the fluorescent eyes of the true mystic.

"Brand this oath onto your spirit: *'If I forget thee, O Al-Quds, let my right hand forget her cunning. If I do not remember thee, let my tongue cleave to the roof of my mouth.'* "

The timeless psalm, barely paraphrased to voice the anguish of the Faithful, created intense emotion among the warriors. Such was the power of words.

"My warriors! Next year in Al-Quds!"

Hidden loudspeakers drowned the ruins with the rousing music of paradise. The warriors whirled with increased vigor.

Abu Ismail floated toward the sea, disrobed and fell upon the waves like the hand of Creation. He drank greedily from the sandy waters. Then, on limbs fresh and miraculously healed, he ran to his warriors, to share with them the visions of Paradise. They had stopped whirling and now danced, closer and closer, to couple their bodies. Moments later, vibrant tongues like butterflies darted across his genitals as blessed maidens enveloped him within eager orifices fragrant with sandalwood.

Abu Ismail felt his seed rise and shouted once more: "Next year in Al-Quds!"

PART IV

Sow the Earth with the Dragon's Teeth.

EDITH HAMILTON, *Mythology*

December 22, 1973

TRIPOLI, LIBYA

From a stream of coded reports received by WOJ Signals, two were given priority.

The first, from the WOJ lookout in Chinon, France, informed headquarters that the plutonium cargo for Sacavem, Portugal, had left the Centrale Nucléaire d'Avoine-Chinon early that evening and that, taking into account its slow progress under heavy escort, its estimated time of arrival at Orly would be noon the next day.

The second, from the WOJ mercenary planted at Orly Airport, Paris, disclosed that the plutonium, specified as "ingots," had been allocated, according to the cargo computer, to flight AF 205 scheduled for Lisbon–Caracas–Bogotá–Quito–Lima–Santiago, departing on December 23 at 10:50 P.M.

December 23, 1973

ALMADA, PORTUGAL

At 4:50 P.M., Idris Ali, having alerted Gabriel Carvalho minutes earlier by telephone that the operation was on, parked his car near the cargo clerk's flat.

He settled down to wait until 8:30, the time he had said he would pick up Carvalho to run a final check. If Carvalho had unwisely alerted the police or the Directorate General of Security, he would be warned by the heavy traffic of personnel. Equally,

98

should the WOJ lookouts monitoring the security activity at the airport spot a general alarm, they would telephone Carvalho and tell him to collect the corpses of his wife and child. The news would propel Carvalho out of his flat, giving Idris Ali time both to dispose of the man and to regroup his task force for an alternative attack.

But Carvalho, Idris Ali was certain, would remain meek as long as his family stayed alive—albeit incarcerated under guard in a secluded suburban villa that WOJ used as a safe house. Carvalho's wife and daughter had been allowed to speak with him daily.

At 8:30 P.M. Idris Ali left his car. As he had expected, Carvalho had not contacted the police or the DGS.

During his vigil he had observed his airport task force drive north, in five cars, at ten-minute intervals, toward Lisbon—a remarkable feat of synchronization considering that the men had been lying low in as far-flung places as Setúbal, Marateca, Alcácer do Sal, Grândola and Santiago do Cacém. By 8:30 P.M., they had taken prearranged positions within striking distance of the airport. They would stay at those points, unless ordered to regroup for a change of plan, until zero hour.

✗

Idris Ali had not seen Carvalho since December 9. The robust thirty-five-year-old now looked a man of sixty. His hair, left unwashed and sticky white with dandruff, had thinned out severely. His emaciated face had the waxen sheen of a mummy. His hands shook uncontrollably; his legs barely supported him. Only his eyes, one moment blazing ferociously and the next dying like embers, showed he still retained some life-force.

Idris Ali was incensed. "You've neglected yourself."

"I'm all right."

"You were supposed to lead a normal life—not let go!"

Carvalho's voice expired in a screech. "I'm all right, I said!"

Idris Ali slapped him hard. "No hysterics!"

Carvalho pitched on his legs but somehow held his footing. "No . . . No . . . I promise . . ."

"Your colleagues—friends . . . What do they say?"

"They know nothing. They think I'm ill. I told them, an attack of malaria—which I'd contracted in Mozambique."

"They suggested you contact your wife?"

"I told them I didn't want to worry her."

Idris Ali, propitiated, sat down.

Carvalho, a lost soul in his own home, shuffled in search of sanctuary. He found a corner by the little altar of the Mother of

God; then, like an animal at bay, faced Idris Ali. "When will I speak to them?"

"Any minute now."

Carvalho tried to smile; failing, he turned back to the altar. He caressed the Virgin's statuette, checked the candles, replaced one that was sputtering. He felt calmer. "How are they?"

"Fine. They miss you, of course."

Carvalho bit his lips. "When—will you . . . When will I see them?"

"Six hours after the operation—as I promised . . . all being well."

"All will be well."

Idris Ali pressed the point. "Much depends on you."

"I won't fail them."

Idris Ali nodded.

For a while they stared at each other, Carvalho's eyes shuttling between hatred and compliance. Then he started talking as if Idris Ali were a confidant. His arms encompassed the spotlessly clean apartment, the Christmas decorations. "Look how their eyes will feast."

Idris Ali looked, feigning interest.

Carvalho pointed to a row of dried flowers above the sofa. "You see those carnations? Each is wrapped with a love poem. An old Portuguese custom for husband and wife to have over the bed."

"Very touching."

"We sleep here—Maria and I. My daughter—she has the only bedroom. The poems—I wrote them. One for every month of our marriage. And every month happy until . . ."

Idris Ali anticipated the tears. "This month can be happy too, Carvalho. The happiest ever. You don't appreciate happiness until you lose it. . . ."

Carvalho glared at him, surprised that he should possess insight and sickened by the way he had reduced it to banality.

Idris Ali tried a friendlier tone. "How many carnations?"

"Sixty-three."

The telephone rang, liberating Idris Ali from the sentimental intemperance. Carvalho grabbed the receiver, heard his wife on the line, and wailed hoarsely. "Maria . . . Maria . . . Maria . . . Maria . . ."

Idris Ali prodded him. "Make it short and happy. You'll see her very soon."

Carvalho acquiesced with his eyes.

Idris Ali went to the toilet to let Carvalho and his wife have their last words in peace. The Faith expected chivalry from its warriors.

LISBON, PORTUGAL

At 10:20 P.M., at a telephone booth on Avenida do Aeroporto, Idris Ali received confirmation from his safe house that AF 205, loaded with the Sacavem cargo, was boarding passengers and would depart on time from Orly.

At 10:50 P.M., AF 205's departure time, Idris Ali, disguised with a beard, a long wig and glasses, reached the six men sprawled on the grass verge of the Alvalade Park near the airport traffic circle. The six, disguised as airport porters, were seemingly engaged in a heated argument in Portuguese.

Abdallah, the leader of the six, turned up the volume of a portable tape recorder. An even more voluble debate on a football game filled the air. Idris Ali joined in the commandos' mime. A few passers-by, already in Christmas spirit, gave them encouraging shouts, finding it natural that football supporters should argue vehemently out in the open on a cold night.

Idris Ali leaned against a tree and let the adrenaline flow.

He had assembled five platoons for the airport and two to use against the Airport Emergency Force, each coded with the initial of its leader. The airport platoons comprised four men, except for Platoon A, which had six. The last, led by Abdallah, had been allocated the control tower. Platoon B, under the leadership of Badran, sat in a tractor-trailer on the Avenida Gomes da Costa, waiting to move to the cargo terminal. Platoon H, under Hafez, disguised as tourists, stood ready at the Lisbon-Sheraton Hotel. Platoon M, led by Mahmud, and Platoon Q, led by Qasim, were at assault positions, respectively at the northern and western boundary fences. The remaining two platoons, S and J, led by Suleiman and Jamal, comprising twenty men each, were in the vicinity of the *Regimento de Artilharia* 1 barracks, where the Lisbon Airport Emergency Force was billeted.

The platoons were manned by crack commandos recruited from various Arab liberation organizations. Since joining WOJ, they had undergone intensive training in Syria, Iraq and the U.S.S.R.; some had even been seconded to foreign revolutionary groups to gain proficiency in urban warfare.

Furthermore, as they did not have license to fail on this operation, they had been subjected to systematic attacks on their spiritual fortitude. Only when each person had thrown off man-made ideologies, and been reduced to the terrors of abandonment by Allah, had he been considered adequately programmed. In their theopathic state, they would brave any ordeal for their most coveted birthright, the fallen warrior's place in Paradise.

At 10:55 P.M., at a nearby telephone booth, Idris Ali received final confirmation from the safe house that AF 205 had left Paris on schedule.

He signaled attack.

Abdallah led Platoon A out of the park, in the direction of the airport.

In their wake, Idris Ali flashed a light down Avenida do Brasil to Carvalho's Volkswagen. When he saw Carvalho pull out from the curb, he, too, hurried toward the airport.

*

At 11:00 P.M., Carvalho stopped at the staff entrance barrier. The guard on duty was Torres, A dour man, invalided out from Mozambique with a punctured lung, Torres performed his duties strictly according to the book; but he had a soft spot for other veterans—in his view, unsung heroes all—and had been known to waive rules in their favor.

Carvalho showed his pass. "Evening, Torres."

"You're late."

"Don't I know it. . . . A whole hour . . ."

Torres looked into the empty car. "Nothing wrong, I hope."

Carvalho let his distraught face punctuate his words. "Plenty —goddamn malaria . . . But I count my blessings. Some never came back. . . ."

"Yeah . . . Some never even had a burial."

Torres opened the trunk, gave it a cursory glance, then banged it shut. He lifted the barrier and waved Carvalho on.

Carvalho laid limp hands on the steering wheel. He was sweating profusely as if in the grip of a real malarial attack. He could picture Idris Ali, hidden in the shadows behind, gun trained on Torres. And beyond Idris Ali, a whole army of them. If he failed, not only would Maria and Isabel die, but Torres too, and God knew how many more.

"Get going, friend."

Carvalho made his hand quiver on the gear lever. "I—I'm shaking all over. . . . Can you help me, Torres? Drive me to the parking lot—it's just ahead. . . ."

"You want me to lose my job?"

Carvalho felt sorry for him. But he would feel sorrier if Torres got killed. "I must punch in, don't you understand? I need the money. It'll pass . . . in a few minutes. . . ."

Torres, moved by a comrade's suffering, looked around helplessly. He could see the staff parking lot some fifty meters away. Most of the night shift had come in. The traffic at the barrier would be minimal. He decided the latecomers could wait a minute or so. He opened the door and pushed Carvalho aside. "To hell with it! If a man can't help his brother . . ."

Carvalho started to weep.

Torres, interpreting the tears as gratitude, ruffled Carvalho's hair. "Never abandon a fallen comrade—that's what the army taught me about life, Carvalho. Jesus couldn't have put it better. . . ."

Carvalho curled up in his seat.

Torres pressed on the accelerator. As he drove, he kept an eye on the mirror for any approaching car. He saw none.

In the process of parking the car and helping Carvalho out, Torres lost sight of the barrier for a few moments. But that did not worry him: any car stopping there would announce its presence by its headlights.

It took Idris Ali and Platoon A a few seconds to waft through. Platoon A dispersed to the vicinity of the control tower. Idris Ali made straight for Carvalho's office.

⚔

At 11:05 P.M., an unmarked tractor-trailer, bearing Oporto registration plates and loaded with barrels of port wine, stopped at the air cargo gate. The driver, Badran, leader of Platoon B, handed the necessary documents to the guard.

The latter, familiar with most drivers, gave him a quizzical look. "New driver?"

Badran smiled timidly. Though his Portuguese, learned in Mozambique, was fluent, he did not want to betray his accent. To keep the conversation simple, he gave the guard the respect due to a person of high authority. "Yes, sir."

The guard checked the papers, carefully examining Badran's impeccably forged driver's license and the tractor-trailer's documentation, provided by Carvalho and stating that the vehicle was leased to "Guilherme Trucking Company." He also inspected the bill of lading—authentic, having been procured from a reputable wholesaler—and the cargo agency pass, also provided by Carvalho.

He handed them back with a grunt and waved Badran on. "Better get a move on. There's a big transporter due any minute."

"Yes, sir."

Badran drove through, whistling the first few bars of "April in Portugal."

⚔

In the tractor-trailer, the other three members of Platoon B, cramped inside empty barrels, climbed out as soon as they felt the vehicle begin moving. They tore open specially marked barrels to assemble their arsenal. The weapons, the latest and most sophisticated from Russia, had been smuggled into Portugal by Frelimo. They had enough firepower to raze the airport to the ground and, if need be, fight off the Portuguese air force.

✗

Two minutes behind the tractor-trailer, the heavy-duty transporter assigned to the Sacavem plutonium arrived with its escort of twenty outriders from the public security police and three troop carriers, each with ten national republican guards.

✗

Abdallah surveyed his objective. Taking command of the control tower was the most crucial part of the operation. Ideally, it should have been the last phase, accomplished just before AF 205 entered her glide path, when the air traffic controllers would be too engrossed in their duties either to resist, set off an alert or advise the aircraft to overshoot and land elsewhere. Storming the tower so early on, occupying it for the next two hours and forcing it to function normally without alarming any of the departments that maintained communications with it, would require steel nerves, impeccable discipline and the utmost skill.

The irony was that the unorthodox course had been forced on WOJ by the sins of lesser guerrillas. In prehijack days, airport security had been mainly concerned with theft and smuggling, the inconsiderate but innocent intrusions of sightseers, and such ground incidents that might endanger air traffic. Now, it had to bolster itself against military activities. Consequently, most European airports, including Lisbon, had installed surface radar scanners that provided, even in zero-zero visibility, a precise picture of the airfield, and defined every movement on it, even that of an individual. It was imperative to neutralize this surface radar scanner.

Abdallah checked his watch: 11:10 P.M. He started walking toward the tower. Ahead of him, his men strolling in porters' uniforms, miming to the heated Portuguese from their hidden tape recorder, converged on the building. The two policemen stationed at the tower entrance deemed them unworthy of interest.

Abdallah reached the tower entrance seconds behind his men. As the latter disposed of the two policemen, he pulled out his silencer-fixed gun and rang for the elevator. He signaled three of his men up the stairs and watched as the other two dragged the policemen in. The elevator arrived, empty. Abdallah held the door open. His two men, having undressed the dead policemen, pushed them into the car. Abdallah let the doors shut, then jammed the control keys.

The two commandos put on the policemen's uniforms and took position at the entrance. They would remain there to deter unauthorized personnel from entering. Those authorized would become hostages. There would be no language problems. All the members of Platoon A had been chosen for their proficiency in Portuguese, which they had learned in Angola where they had undergone field training.

Abdallah climbed the stairs. On the first landing, the door to the air traffic controllers' rest room was open. One of his comrades held a gun on three terrified controllers; they would be brought up to the control room shortly. He scrambled up to the second landing. The fourth member of his platoon had already invaded the approach controllers' room and had killed one of the two men on duty. The surviving approach controller was pleading for his life with petrified eyes. Abdallah scrambled to the fourth floor. He found his fifth man crouched by the control room door.

Abdallah stormed in, closely followed by the last commando. "Stay where you are!"

There were four men manning radar screens. They stared back at him in shock. Abdallah's commando herded them and took charge of the telephones and radio consoles. One of the air traffic controllers, pricked into action by this rough treatment, tried to switch on an intercom. Abdallah shot him between the eyes. The man catapulted across the room. His colleagues shrank from the body.

"Any other heroes?"

The three controllers managed to shake their heads.

Abdallah pushed them into a corner. "Good. Sit there—and cooperate."

The controllers sat down. Abdallah picked up a telephone and dialed Carvalho's office. As it rang, he checked his watch: 11:14.

✗

Carvalho passed the telephone to Idris Ali, then continued staring at the Christmas presents piled in a corner. They were from colleagues, concerned about his health and spirits.

Idris Ali, now dressed in dungarees, mumbled his satisfaction, then slammed down the receiver. To curb his tension, he moved to the window and scanned the airport.

Lisbon Airport Authority, sensitive to the fact that the Portela de Sacavem Airport had the status of a natural bridge between Europe and other continents, had made it one of the least vulnerable in the world. The three runways, one short, one intermediary and one long, had been enclosed within a circular complex on the valid theory that a perimeter could be better patrolled or, if need be, sealed off. Irrespective of the ground radar scanner that maintained surveillance on the airfield, the compound had a protective fence running along its boundaries. The inner and outer roadways along the fence were constantly patrolled by mobile customs guards, guard dogs and security police, with electronic surveillance—wherever it did not interfere with the workings of the approach equipment and their associated communication systems—providing backup.

Yet, Lisbon Airport was not impregnable. Unless defended by a brigade group, no international airport could be protected from a coordinated attack. Idris Ali had spotted every chink through which his task force could infiltrate, every space where his warriors could take cover in the dark.

He checked his watch: 11:18 P.M. He turned to Carvalho and hauled him out of his chair. "Let's go."

✗

At 11:20 P.M., Platoon B's tractor-trailer ground to a halt some two hundred meters from the unloading bays. Badran jumped out, opened the hood, fiddled with the engine for a while, then shook his head dejectedly.

Moments later, four security police outriders from the Sacavem transporter escort surrounded the vehicle.

Their commanding officer, a national guard lieutenant, stormed out of the troop carrier and ran over to Badran. "What's going on?"

Badran gesticulated furiously. "Fucking carburetor—it's been acting up. . . ."

"You can't stop here! We have to get through. We'll push you over if we have to."

Badran feigned indignation. "You can't do that!"

"Can you roll it to the side?"

"I think so. . . ."

"Get on with it then!"

Badran, grumbling, jumped into the cab. He released the hand brake, and let the tractor-trailer freewheel to the edge of the road. The lieutenant shouted directions until satisfied there was enough

room for the transporter to pass, then sent the outriders back to
their positions.

The transporter squeezed through the gap and dragged its way
to its designated loading bay.

Badran, still playacting fury, walked toward the customs office.

✗

At 11:25 P.M. Carvalho and Idris Ali reached the mechanical transport duty room. Idris Ali pushed Carvalho in and stood by the
door, ready, if necessary, to intervene. He lit a cigarette and
smoked it surreptitiously, as if taking an unauthorized break.

With only one more flight scheduled for the night, the mechanical transport duty room was empty except for the duty officer, a fat man prone to dozing whatever the shift. "How goes it,
Carvalho?"

"All go. You'd think there'd be no cargo so near Christmas, but
no, we're up to our ears. I need a couple of cars. . . ."

The duty officer yawned, waited until Carvalho signed the
motor pool registry, then handed out two sets of keys.

Outside, Carvalho handed one set to Idris Ali and led him to
the car pool. They took two Land-Rovers and drove them to the
loading bays. They parked them on the grass next to B Platoon's
tractor-trailer, left the keys inside and walked back to the office
complex.

As they disappeared in the dark, Badran returned from the
customs office with orders to repair his tractor-trailer as soon as
possible, and notification that he had lost his place in line.

Badran set to repairing the carburetor. His most difficult task,
securing the tractor-trailer at a strategic location, had been accomplished without a hitch. Since the two Land-Rovers parked next to
the tractor-trailer indicated that Idris Ali had been equally successful, the omens were good.

✗

Once the control tower had been occupied and the threat of the
surface radar eliminated, Platoons M and Q had no difficulty in
penetrating the airport complex.

Platoon M scaled the northernmost fence by the long runway
at 11:22 P.M., completing the operation in less than two minutes,
thus giving itself a seven-minute margin between mobile patrols.

Platoon Q had an easier task. With only the Air France flight
due in, the intermediary runway had closed down and security
had been reduced accordingly. Platoon Q scaled the western fence

at 11:24 P.M., safe in the knowledge that they had over twenty minutes to evade the next patrol.

At 11:27 P.M., the two platoons met at the intersection of the long and intermediary runways, then dispersed to their final positions on either side of the long runway and set up cover with camouflage netting.

✗

At 11:40 P.M., Platoon H arrived from the Lisbon-Sheraton Hotel in a taxi. Wearing loose-fitting suits, they sauntered into the terminal building, seemingly in an alcoholic haze. They presented themselves at the Air France counter with return tickets purchased in Caracas by WOJ couriers and duly endorsed for AF 205 that morning. Pretending the need to sober up in the departures lounge until embarkation at 2:20 A.M., they checked in their travel-worn luggage, then passed through passport control with forged documents identifying them as oil engineers from Maracaibo, Venezuela, returning from their week's leave in Lisbon.

Once inside the Departures Lounge, as yet empty, and free of the usual surveillance, Platoon H straggled into the rest room. They came out, at brief intervals, dressed in white cleaners' overalls—procured for them by Carvalho—that they had worn beneath their suits. Now, to foil an alert through the discovery of discarded clothing, they wore their suits beneath their overalls.

Blending casually into the scenery, Platoon H slipped through various exit points onto the tarmac. At 11:53 P.M., having cleared without mishap the hangars that separated the passenger and cargo terminals, they regrouped by Platoon B's tractor-trailer.

At 11:50 P.M., both Platoons B and H, fully armed, moved out of the cargo area in the two Land-Rovers left there by Idris Ali and Carvalho.

December 24, 1973

LISBON, PORTUGAL

At 12:15 A.M., Platoon B parked its Land-Rover at the rear of the airport fire station to block its western exit. The warriors, armed with silencer-fitted guns, scrambled through the staff entrance into the locker room.

A minute later, Platoon H, equally armed and attacking from the front, jumped off its Land-Rover at the eastern exit. Hafez, the leader, drove on and screeched to a stop by the fire officer's desk.

Simultaneously, Platoons B and H spilled into the station and surrounded those on duty.

There were twelve firemen: two crews—one for each fire engine on standby—gathered at the mess table in the corner, playing cards, drinking coffee or reading the newspaper. The fire officer, whose duty was to man the telephone and coordinate routine or emergency procedures, had been engrossed in a crossword puzzle. They tried to make a stand. The men at the mess table sprang up; the fire officer reached for the telephone.

Hafez shot him at point-blank range; the warriors aimed their guns at the firemen. The latter backed away, offering no further resistance.

By 12:25 A.M., the firemen, bound and gagged with chloroform pads, had been piled unconscious in the staff locker room. Badran and Hafez had twenty minutes to familiarize themselves with the controls of the fire engine. They anticipated no problems. They had practiced extensively on identical ones during rehearsals in Libya.

✗

At 12:30 A.M., Platoons M and Q completed digging. They had toiled slowly and silently, taking breaks when security patrols had checked the runway. That they had remained undetected, perfectly camouflaging themselves and their weapons, was a tribute to their Russian instructors.

Now, ensconced beneath netting, well spread out on the grass facing both the runway and the main terminal building, with all weapons ready, including the two SAM-7 missiles, they were to all intents and purposes in control of the airport.

✗

At 12:38 A.M., Idris Ali received final signals from the fire station and the control tower. From the latter, Abdallah also confirmed the preparedness of Platoons M and Q.

Idris Ali turned to Carvalho. "Last task, Carvalho."

Carvalho dragged himself up. "Where to?"

"The men's room."

"What for?"

"To absolve you."

Carvalho followed Idris Ali, wondering in what ingenious way he could be exonerated from his collaboration.

The rest room was across the corridor. They went in casually, Carvalho first.

Idris Ali checked that the stalls were empty, then moved to the farthest from the door. He lowered the seat. "Drop your trousers down to your knees. And sit on the toilet."

Carvalho, distractedly, did as he was told.

"Roll up your sleeves. Give me your hands—palms upward."

Carvalho rolled up his sleeves and extended his arms, clinging to reason even in unreality. "Handcuffs?"

"Your wife and child are dead, Carvalho. Neater this way."

Carvalho's mind disintegrated. The sacred features of his family settled as dust in another realm.

Idris Ali's hand streaked past his palms. The steel blade caught the light. Having severed Carvalho's arteries, it still glittered, bloodless.

Carvalho sighed as his blood spurted. Warm. Soothing. Purifying. "Oh . . . Oh . . . Oh . . ."

He saw an object, identified it—perplexed—as a safety razor, watched it fall between his legs into the toilet bowl. He saw his palms, open in supplication, bearing stigmata. The hands had crossed the darkness; his body would follow. Ahead lay Resurrection, and the great white throne of the Alpha and the Omega. He exulted. " 'Worthy is the Lamb, that was slain . . .' "

"Keep it soft, Carvalho. Loud prayers offend the Heavens."

Carvalho smiled at the cherubic face and dropped his voice to a whisper. " 'The Lord is my shepherd; I shall not want . . .' "

He was happy, the happiest he had ever been. He felt the cherub push his arms into the tomb. He heard the dewdrops fall on peaceful waters—perhaps the baptismal waters of the Jordan. He could close his eyes. He had housed gentle Jesus in his heart more regally than any cathedral.

Idris Ali, having pushed Carvalho's hands into the toilet, stood back to look at him. With the stall door closed, and the gap at the bottom showing trousers down at his ankles, Carvalho would appear to be defecating. No one would disturb him in the next half hour. Later, when he was found, it would be assumed he had committed suicide.

The disappearance of his wife and daughter—now being buried in the grounds of the WOJ safe house—would be considered motive enough.

✗

At 12:51 A.M., Idris Ali entered the control tower. The controllers, gagged and bound, sat docilely in a corner. The surface radar screen showed Platoons M and Q entrenched by the long runway. Platoons B and H were standing ready at the fire station. There had been no false moves, no snags.

Flight AF 205 had already blipped its way onto the main radar screen. A floor below, the approach controller, grateful that his life had been spared, was guiding it in.

Idris Ali checked the frequency of the aircraft, then moved to the controllers and spoke to them in English. "Any minute now the approach controller will have to hand over to one of you. I want someone who'll talk that plane down as if nothing's happened here. Who's the volunteer?"

The controllers, eyes clouded with fear, looked at Abdallah. Since occupying the tower, Abdallah had monitored the air traffic in the area and whenever necessary, had transmitted the pertinent signals. That had been routine and easily dealt with. But talking a plane down required a singular skill and the sort of intimacy that pilot and controller developed over time on a regular route.

Idris Ali picked up Abdallah's gun. "Unless I have a volunteer, I shall recruit him by a process of elimination."

The controllers looked at each other in panic. Idris Ali aimed his gun. The controllers, eyes begging, turned to one among them. Idris Ali, moving his gun as if debating whom to shoot, glared at the candidate. The latter mumbled behind his gag and nodded. Abdallah tore his gag off and untied him.

Idris Ali pushed him over to the console and handed him the headset. "What's your name?"

"Eduardo."

"Exemplary talk-down, Eduardo. If that plane gets suspicious and overshoots . . . I don't need to say any more, do I?"

"I'll—I'll do my best." Eduardo arranged his headset and waited in trepidation.

Moments later, AF 205 opened communications in English, the standard language of air traffic control. "Lisbon. This is Air France 205. We are ready to commence our descent. 205."

Eduardo mumbled a prayer, then cleared his throat. "Roger, Air France 205. This is Lisbon. Commence descent. Clear down to flight level five zero at report point Alpha. Prepare to receive Lisbon weather."

Idris Ali tapped him on the shoulder. "Good."

✗

At 12:55 A.M., Platoons S and J, forty men deployed in twenty hired cars at various holding points, prepared themselves for the glorious death apportioned to them by reciting the *Exordium*, the first chapter of the Koran. Then, the gunner in each car checked his RPG-7, a compact grenade launcher, and his Sagger antitank missile, packed in a suitcase.

✗

AF 205, coming in above the Tagus estuary, maintained a perfect descent.

Eduardo, despite his terror, was faultlessly professional. "Five miles from touchdown, Air France 205. You're on the glide path. Clear to land at runway zero-three. On center line. Wind zero-nine-zero at ten knots . . ."

Idris Ali telephoned the fire station. "B and H on to the tarmac!"

✗

At 1:04 A.M., as Platoons B and H sped in their fire engines to their designated locations by the runway, AF 205 landed.

✗

At 1:05 A.M., the suicide Platoons S and J converged on the barracks of the *Regimento de Artilharia* 1. Suleiman, in the lead car, had the honor of firing the first shot at the sentries on duty as his driver burst through the gates. Moments later, the other cars of Platoons S and J spilled into the compound firing a salvo of missiles and incendiary grenades at the tanks, troop carriers and personnel of the Airport Emergency Force.

✗

At 1:07 A.M., AF 205, having covered half the runway, eased the reverse thrusts and proceeded toward the taxiway.

Idris Ali grabbed the headset from Eduardo. "Air France 205. There is a change in landing instructions. You are not to turn into taxiway. Stop at the end of runway."

The captain's voice came through puzzled. "Roger, Lisbon. Anything wrong?"

"Everything's fine, Captain. Do as you're told."

The captain's voice betrayed his suspicion. "What's the problem? Where's the controller who talked us down?"

"He's been relieved. From now on you'll listen to me."

"What do you mean—from now on? Who are you?"

Idris Ali checked the surface radar screen before answering. Platoons B and H, in their fire engines, had flanked the plane and were keeping pace with it. Platoons M and Q had the craft in range from their dugouts. AF 205 was trapped within the WOJ ring. "The Pan-Islamic Army."

"What?"

"If you do as you're told, you'll be safe. . . ."

"Safe? What's going on?"

Idris Ali spoke casually. "Look out of your window! You'll see fire engines on either side of you. Manned by my commandos. They're armed. Ahead of you, you should spot more of my commandos in dugouts. They'll be flashing lights at you. They're armed, too. With missiles. Acknowledge if you see them."

The captain's voice took a few moments to come through. When it did, it was shaken. "I see them."

"Now, stop at the end of the runway. And—no heroics."

✗

Captain Poitevin had no intention of surrendering. The hijackers could not open the doors from the outside, nor force him to open them unless they started shooting indiscriminately. Lisbon Airport, like every international airport, had braced up to the age of the hijack. A special force of armored corps and paratroopers stood by in readiness at the *Regimento de Artilharia 1* barracks for just such an emergency; and, according to instructions issued to all airline captains, required less than ten minutes to go into action. Captain Poitevin intended to give them those ten minutes—if possible, more. He turned to his copilot. "Switch on the hijack transponder. Signal SOS—direct to security headquarters. Use the VHF. Keep the SelCal clear for me."

The copilot applied himself to the radio.

Captain Poitevin glared at the fire engines accompanying the plane. He reckoned he could waste a few minutes stopping the aircraft. At the same time, he could maneuver to face the runway to give himself the chance of an immediate takeoff.

✗

At 1:10 A.M., Platoons S and J had destroyed or incapacitated every armored vehicle within the *Regimento de Artilharia 1* barracks. But the paratroopers in the compound had been quick to regroup and had, in turn, destroyed or incapacitated the WOJ cars. The survivors of Platoons S and J now fought a running battle in the hope of exacting a high price for their lives.

✗

It had taken Captain Poitevin five minutes to turn his plane around and pull to a stop. Idris Ali had watched the intricate maneuver in admiration. And he had been amused by the copilot's frantic appeal to Lisbon Urban Security headquarters, which he had been monitoring on the emergency frequency. The plane's hijack transponder blipping its identity automatically on various European radar screens did not worry him. There was nothing anybody could do.

The officer commanding at Urban Security headquarters, hard-pressed by the havoc raging at the Airport Emergency Force's barracks, had offered to send in the air force from the Montijo base, adjacent to the airport. He had also suggested AF 205 should attempt to take off while ground-attack jets strafed the terrorists. Poitevin, arguing that such a course of action would endanger his passengers and aircraft, had vetoed the suggestion. The OC had been reluctant to drop the idea until he had remembered the thirty national guards and twenty security police assigned to escort the Sacavem cargo. He had duly contacted the national guards and had ordered them to relieve first the plane, then the control tower.

Now, as the national guards moved into action, Idris Ali made his move. "All right. Air France 205. Time to surrender. Switch off engines."

"I shall need assurances first."

"You're in no position to ask for anything."

"Then I refuse to surrender."

"Very well. We'll do it the hard way. I am sure you've SOS'd for help. And you feel confident . . ."

"Let's say, I know you can't hold an airport forever."

"That's debatable, Captain. My men are armed against every eventuality. They are even equipped with SAM-7s. That means they can not only fight off troops, but also down any ground-attack aircraft." He paused for effect. "Are you listening, Captain?"

Poitevin's voice had lost its control. "Yes."

"Of course, what we can do on the tarmac is not your concern. You have to think of your passengers. Incidentally, how many are you carrying?"

"Eighty-nine."

"Including you and the crew, a hundred and one. Right, Captain?"

"Yes."

"Now, here is my final word. Five hundred meters to your left, by the main terminal, there is a TAP Boeing 727. Can you see it?"

"Yes."

"Keep looking."

Idris Ali gestured to Abdallah. Abdallah radioed Hafez. Idris Ali moved to the window. He had barely reached it when the Boeing 727 burst into flames. He stared at it—elated.

✗

As the TAP Boeing 727 turned into a fireball, Captain Poitevin wept. He had seen such a destructive saturnalia once before, in a newsreel, when on September 12, 1970, in Dawson's Field, Jordan, a BOAC VC-10, a TWA Boeing 707 and a Swissair DC-8 had been blown up by the precursors of these terrorists. He remembered that at the time he had blamed the captains for abandoning their aircraft. Now he faced the same dilemma. Worse, he had to save not only his plane, but a hundred people as well.

✗

At 1:22 A.M., Jamal, the last survivor of Platoons S and J, radioed his final signal, reporting an estimated 250 Portuguese dead. Then, joyous at the prospect of impending death, he flung himself at the guns of the four paratroopers who had cornered him.

✗

Abdallah, still monitoring communications, looked up from the console. "Platoons S and J—wiped out."

Idris Ali kept his eyes on the burning Boeing 727. "Be happy for them, Abdallah. They are blessed."

Abdallah, quivering with envy, nodded.

Idris Ali moved to the radio. "Are you looking, Captain?"

Poitevin's voice was tear-soaked. "Yes."

"Incendiary grenades—in case you wondered. Consume steel and people in no time at all."

Poitevin responded querulously. "I get the point."

"So this is what you do. One: switch off your engines. Two: there's a mobile unit moving toward your plane—do you know who they are?"

"National Republican guard."

"Tell whoever sent them that unless they retreat—and fast—you'll be served to worms and maggots."

"They—they may not believe me."

"Tell them how we blew up that Boeing 727. If they still have doubts, tell them they've seen two of my suicide squads in action tonight. That we don't care if we die—which is more than I can say about them or your passengers."

"Very well."

"Three: once the unit retreats, open your forward door. *Only* the forward door. Let my men in—nicely. Four: When my men are in, call your Good Samaritans again. Tell them we, in the control tower, seven commandos and one hostage, demand free passage to the plane; that unless we get it, you'll be blown sky-high. Five: when we're all in, you'll instruct the ground staff to refuel the plane. That's all for now."

✗

Captain Poitevin felt like a child in need of a motherly shoulder. He turned to the stewardesses, but found them as disoriented as when he had summoned them. He wished there were someone beside himself to rise as a tower of strength. He turned to his copilot and passed him the piece of paper on which he had noted Idris Ali's directives. "Ask the OC to follow the instructions."

The copilot applied himself to the VHF transmitter.

Poitevin turned to the stewardesses. "Get back to the passengers. I want you at your best when I address them."

He switched on the passenger address system. How did one tell eighty-nine people they had just flown into disaster?

✗

Lieutenant Fernando Xavier, standing by the troop carrier, watched the national guards and security police under his command—all veteran combatants—halt some two hundred meters from the beleaguered plane and lie low without breaking the pincer formation. He barked into his radio. "We are holding position, sir."

The OC barked back, "I ordered withdrawal, Lieutenant!"

Lieutenant Xavier banged on the dashboard in frustration. "I'm going to use the scrambler, sir. I request you do the same."

He switched on the radio's scrambler.

The OC's voice thundered after a brief pause: "What is it?"

"Sir—we can make mincemeat out of the bastards."

The OC's voice hissed threateningly. "Are you refusing my orders, Lieutenant?"

"No, sir. But I must point out, sir: we can't let that plane be hijacked."

"Overruled!"

"Sir. There's a nuclear cargo aboard. That's why we're here."

"I know what's aboard."

"Can you imagine what might happen if—if terrorists got hold of that cargo?"

"Why should they? This is an ordinary hijack. Only bloodier. How would they know about the cargo? It's top secret."

"All the same, sir . . ."

"Listen to me, Lieutenant. There are one hundred and one people aboard that plane. They're surrounded by fanatics who don't care who they kill—or how many. . . ."

"I'm responsible for that cargo, sir."

"Damn it, man! Don't you understand? They'll fly around a bit, put the fear of God in whomever they can, publicize their cause, then release the plane, the passengers and your cargo. And that will be that."

"With all due respect, sir . . ."

"Lieutenant, if you attack and they blast that plane—what do you think would happen to your cargo?"

"I—I don't know, sir."

"Chances are there'd be a radioactive leak."

Xavier faltered. "I—I didn't think of that, sir. Don't you—shouldn't you, sir, ask the president to ratify your orders?"

"The president has granted me full authority. So get on with it!"

Lieutenant Xavier switched off communications and with a heavy heart, ordered retreat.

✗

On the tarmac, AF 205 opened its forward door. Badran had maneuvered his fire engine beneath it and had raised the ladder. Two stewardesses, nervous hands clasped, stood by to receive the hijackers.

Badran climbed aboard first, pushing the stewardesses inside. His men followed; one remained at the top of the ladder to guard the door. Badran reappeared to signal with his flashlight that the aircraft was under his control.

Platoons M and Q, scampering from their dugouts at twenty-second intervals, boarded next. Platoon H, which had been patrolling the area with the other fire engine, followed suit.

✗

Idris Ali picked up the microphone. "The passengers, Badran?"

Badran's exultant voice came through. "A few hysterical ones. They'll quieten soon."

"Good. We're on our way. Tell the captain to remind the authorities. If we meet any trouble, there'll be a bloodbath."

Idris Ali waved at Abdallah to lead Platoon A out, then grabbed hold of Eduardo. "One last pleasure for you."

Eduardo recoiled with haunted eyes. "No! No—please . . . I did what you asked, please . . ."

"You'll be driving a fire engine. Haven't you always wanted to drive a fire engine?"

Idris Ali pushed Eduardo toward the door, then cast a last look at the control tower.

The huddled controllers watched him, petrified. Idris Ali smiled. He had decided to spare them. His compassion should dissuade the troops on the tarmac from defying orders and putting up a fight.

He waved at the controllers. "Merry Christmas."

✗

Idris Ali savored the slow march to the plane as if it were a ceremonial procession.

Platoon A boarded immediately. Idris Ali whispered a few words to Eduardo. The latter, who until then had behaved like a condemned man, came to life. Full of gratitude, he helped Idris Ali climb the ladder into the plane, then ran around the fire engine, jumped into the driver's seat and drove off at top speed.

Idris Ali paused at the door and stared at the rings of bewildered national guards, security police and ground staff. Smoke from the still burning Boeing 727 swathed the night, a fitting backdrop to his victory. He presented the Churchillian V-sign, then disappeared. The door closed behind him.

Minutes later, the tanker requested by Captain Poitevin arrived to refuel the plane.

✗

At 2:20 A.M., exactly at its scheduled departure time for Caracas, AF 205 took off. On completing its climb, it turned east. During the next eighteen minutes, while still in Portuguese airspace, it gathered as escort a complete wing of F-86F interceptors. These made an attempt to buzz it before it reached the Spanish border; but the pilots were under orders not to endanger the aircraft and the attempt fizzled out, an exercise in futility.

Over Badajoz, in Spain, AF 205 turned south toward the Mediterranean. Simultaneously, it picked up a Spanish squadron of Mirage IIIEE. The squadron escorted it until it cleared the Spanish coast near Almería. This time there was no buzzing; the Spanish authorities merely wanted to ensure that AF 205 did not land in Spain.

DAMASCUS, SYRIA

At 9:35 A.M., AF 205, very low on fuel, was allowed to land, for humanitarian reasons, at Damascus International Airport. Prior to that, it had crisscrossed the Mediterranean, finding all European airports unaccommodating.

At 3:00 P.M., having refueled and provisioned the plane, Idris Ali announced his terms for surrender to President Assad and the French ambassador: the immediate disbandment of the Middle

East peace conference—an unprecedented meeting between Israel, Egypt and Jordan—which had opened in Geneva under the auspices of the U.S.A., the U.S.S.R. and the U.N.; the immediate creation of a Pan-Islamic army; the immediate resumption of war against Israel; immediate and ineluctable pledges from all Islamic countries to protract the jihad until its ordained resolution, the destruction of the State of Israel; and equally immediate and ineluctable pledges from every U.N. member country—especially the U.S.A.—to cut all aid to the Jewish state.

He set a deadline of twenty-five hours for the acceptance of these terms. He considered twenty-four hours a fair limit for his hostages to endure; the additional hour, he declared, should see the Pan-Islamic Army plowing into Israel.

December 25, 1973

DAMASCUS, SYRIA

At 3:30 P.M., the passengers of AF 205 were ordered to celebrate Christmas by singing carols. Exhausted, dirty and ailing from thirty-five hours of incarceration, they tremblingly obliged. A loudspeaker rigged up by Abdallah broadcast their voices.

With that plaintive sound as leitmotif, Idris Ali resumed communications with the authorities and asked whether his terms had been accepted. He received a plethora of disputation. Furious, he announced the immediate departure of the plane.

At 3:48 P.M., AF 205 left Damascus International Airport, still broadcasting the hostages' pitiful cacophony.

ISTANBUL, TURKEY

A *dolmuş*, the shared taxi driven by one of Mossad's men, had picked up Boaz from Küçük Mustafa Paşa Hamamı, the city's most renowned baths. The Memouneh had boarded previously at Balat, with loads of cardboard boxes so that there would be room for only one other passenger. Other Mossad agents, in private cars, provided cover.

From the Golden Horn, they had driven into the congested traffic of Eminönü and were crawling toward the Marmara shore for Yeşilköy Airport. The Memouneh had arrived early that afternoon and would be flying back that evening. Boaz would return to his small hotel near the airport to await departure for Mecca.

During the interlude in Istanbul, Boaz had distracted himself by frequenting various teahouses, listening to natives and foreigners, uprooted peasants and hustling minorities, wanting to feel non-Israeli, non-Jew, non-chosen, non-anything, someone who could have a home in every country, a friend in every street. The Memouneh's news had plunged him back into reality. "You're sure Lisbon is WOJ's work?"

The Memouneh, taut as ever, snarled. "You can't mistake Idris Ali whatever his disguise."

"But Abu Ismail's in Saudi Arabia preparing for the hajj."

"What better place to be? To show clean hands?"

Boaz nodded, conceding the point.

The Memouneh cracked his knuckles. "The question is, why that particular flight? France has bent double to ingratiate herself with the Arabs—why hijack a French plane?"

"Could be retribution against Portugal. For allowing the U.S. arms lift to Israel during the war to refuel at the Azores."

"My guess is they wanted that plane for what it contains."

"Nuclear cargo? Still that theory?"

"Yes."

"In a civil airliner?"

"Not standard practice—but it happens."

Boaz gave him a surprised look. "Any evidence it was carrying nuclear cargo?"

"Not yet."

Boaz stared at the sea, dark as it embraced the night. "Which brings us to Mecca."

"And why I've risked coming to see you."

"You needn't have. I'll kill Abu Ismail—I made that clear."

"I want to make it clearer. You *must*. Whatever happens. That means even if Osman—"

Boaz turned around sharply. "Osman?"

"I've sent him my views on the hijack. So he knows what's at stake. But he's going through hellfire—taking an Infidel into sacred territory. He might falter, crack up, turn mystic. Betray you. If you have to sacrifice him, you must."

Boaz's face turned expressionless. "You needn't have come, Zamora. I accepted that possibility long ago."

MUSCAT, OMAN

At 10:42 P.M., after another seven hours of peregrination, AF 205 was allowed to land and refuel at Seeb Airport, Muscat, in the sultanate of Oman.

At 10:45, through the joint intercession of the International Red Cross, the Red Crescent and the U.N., Sultan Qabus ibn Said permitted the plane a twelve-hour respite so that its exhausted crew could rest. At the same time, various Arab ambassadors to Oman, anxious to mediate on behalf of their governments, urged the hijackers, while sympathizing with them, to reconsider surrender.

Idris Ali merely repeated his terms and, to prove that Israel was a cancer disemboweling the world, released two hostages. One, an elderly Colombian, was in the throes of a coronary; the other, a pregnant Chilean, had suffered a nervous breakdown. They were, for all the world to see, two more victims of the Zionists. But for Israel, they would have been celebrating Christmas in their homes.

December 26, 1973

BENGHAZI, LIBYA

At 7:00 A.M., ARNA, the Official Libyan News Agency, broadcast the following statement:

The Revolutionary Command Council, headed by the custodian of Arabism, Muammar Al-Qaddafi, has decided to offer sanctuary to the brave soldiers of the Pan-Islamic Army now stranded at Muscat. The RCC states that the conditions stipulated by the Pan-Islamic Army are, in Libyan eyes, but legitimate demands. To this effect, the RCC pledges here, ineluctably, to disregard the outcome, if any, of the Geneva peace conference; to mobilize a crack Libyan armored division for the Pan-Islamic Army; to make provisions in the Libyan budget for the equipment of this army; to put all possible pressure on the nations of the world for the dismantlement of the State of Israel; and to head an Islamic rejection front that will confront Israel politically, economically and militarily until the final solution.

The RCC invites the redoubtable soldiers of the Pan-Islamic Army to come to Tripoli, not as fugitives, but as the heroes they are.

The RCC also assures friendship and hospitality to the passengers and crew of the requisitioned plane, guarantees passage to their destinations and undertakes to grant generous rewards for their solidarity.

TRIPOLI, LIBYA

At 7:35 A.M., twenty minutes after the announcement that the hijackers had accepted the Libyan invitation, Noah Manasseh, Mossad's agent in Tripoli, received an instant-action signal from the Memouneh. Noah, a Yemenite Jew with the cover identity of Kamal Amin, an Egyptian official of United Arab Airlines, was ordered to observe the hijackers' arrival and to determine—at all costs—whether they had appropriated any cargo from AF 205 and if so, its specifications.

Rushing to the international airport to join in the fanfared welcome of freedom fighters—a routine occurrence since Qaddafi's reception for the Munich Olympics' terrorists—Noah found it, unexpectedly, under tight security control. The public enclaves had been restricted to all but a hand-picked crowd comprising Libyan troops in plain clothes. The media men, lionized in the past as conveyors of the Libyan gospel, had been limited to those known to be truly xenophobic. But most significantly, the airport had been closed to all civilian traffic; and a large proportion of the ground staff, particularly all non-Libyans, had been given compulsory leave.

This last expedient proved a major obstacle. Despite his cover, Noah, too, had been classified foreign. His protests that in view of the proposed merger between Libya and Egypt—still a political aim despite the rift between Qaddafi and Sadat—he could hardly be considered foreign, did not impress the inscrutable agents of the General Investigation Directorate. They confiscated his airport pass, issuing him a provisional one allowing access only to his office.

Noah soon spotted the focus of the day's activities: a hangar at the farthest end of the airport, guarded by armed civilians—WOJ commandos. According to official statements, the hangar had been reserved for the thorough servicing the hijacked Boeing 707 would need after its odyssey. True enough, from his office window Noah saw a convoy of service vehicles move into the hangar. But he also spotted a heavy-duty transporter—superfluous for any type of aircraft maintenance.

Eventually, while the GID supervised the preparation of VIP lounges for both hijackers and hostages, he slipped out of his office and scampered into the storage shed that provided an excellent view of the guarded hangar.

And he watched the drama unfold.

At 3:15 P.M. Qaddafi arrived with his entourage of bodyguards and jigged about joyously until AF 205's landing at 3:35.

The plane taxied to the terminal building and there discharged into the arms of the Libyan leader first the bedraggled passengers, then the exhausted crew and finally the triumphant hijackers.

For half an hour, crew and passengers were given the limelight and encouraged to praise the chivalrous behavior of their captors. Then they were driven in limousines to the exclusive Libya Palace Hotel, there to rest as the country's guests until the resumption of their journey the next day. Qaddafi spent another half hour in deep conversation with the hijackers' leader, whom Noah had instantly identified as Idris Ali.

Promptly after the departure of Qaddafi, his entourage and the media men, the Boeing 707 was towed to the guarded hangar. Thereafter the airport plunged into a sinister silence.

Night fell.

Noah deemed the dark would give him sufficient cover to steal into AF 205's hangar.

He slipped out of the door. As he paused to plot his course, he felt a gun at his temple.

"Out of bounds, aren't you?"

He was allowed to turn and face his interceptor. "I'm an official of United Arab Airlines—"

Idris Ali ran the barrel of the gun along Noah's cheek. "Which is a network of the Egyptian secret service. We know all about that."

"What—"

Idris Ali prodded him with the gun. "Walk!"

"Where to?"

"We might as well satisfy your curiosity."

Noah tried to look bewildered. "Look—I've had a long day . . . I'd like to get home. . . ."

Idris Ali laughed and pushed him along.

Inside the hangar, Noah was confronted with an unmarked heavy lead casket, dangling on chains at the mouth of the Boeing 707's cargo hold.

Idris Ali spoke effusively. "This is known as a coffin—inside rests our plutonium. Quite a monster. Lives up to twenty thousand years. Or is it forty thousand . . . ?"

Noah, stunned, dropped all pretense of docility. "So—Qaddafi will finally have his bomb."

Idris Ali smiled icily. "The plutonium is ours, Kamal. *We* will make the bomb."

"He'll never let you. He's desperate for a nuclear device. Now that he has the means . . ."

"Well, let's say we've offered to make it for him. And he agreed."

"Does he trust you?"

"He has to. He can't make it openly—not with people like you snooping everywhere."

"Word will get around somehow. . . ."

"If we make it here, but we won't."

"Where then?"

"Ethiopia."

It took awhile for Noah to ingest the fact. "And then what—
you double-cross Qaddafi?"

Idris Ali chuckled. "Oh, more than that, Kamal. Much more
than that."

Noah tensed as the coffin was lowered onto the heavy-duty
transporter and a substitute casket was wheeled to the plane. He
turned to Idris Ali, puzzled. "The other casket?"

Idris Ali smiled, then casually raised his revolver. "A good re-
production. And full of fireworks."

Noah spared his last seconds for his soul. Poor Yemenite Jew
dying far from the Promised Land. Yet lucky Yemenite Jew who
had seen the Promised Land. Who had returned after 2,500 years
to breathe Canaan in every season, to hear music from every
instrument and not just the tin drum permitted his forefathers by
Islam.

Then he raged. This was not the time to die. The seasons were
threatened with extinction.

Oh, Zion . . .

December 27, 1973

TRIPOLI, LIBYA

At 5:00 P.M., the passengers and crew of AF 205, rested and fes-
tooned with bouquets, returned to Tripoli International Airport
that had resumed normal service early that morning. They were
greeted by a large, vociferous crowd and applauded for their submission to the Arab cause.

At 5:15 Captain Poitevin, accompanied by his crew, inspected
the plane. He found the cargo intact, and the electronic warning
mechanism on the lead casket—the only cargo about which he
had specific information—functioning normally; lacking the authority either to handle or open it, he did not inspect it further.

Captain Poitevin and his crew also found the servicing of the
aircraft to have been of the highest standard. Though they
checked that the black box was still clamped in place in the rear
fuselage, they had no way of knowing it was a replacement and
not—as the original had been—indestructible.

At 5:45, they boarded the spotlessly clean plane. Five minutes
later, the passengers embarked.

Captain Poitevin was given immediate clearance and took off
at 6:00 P.M. Instructed by Air France to resume the original schedule, he set a northwesterly course for Lisbon.

At 6:48 P.M., AF 205 vanished.

PART V

Rams Caught in a Thicket by Their Horns

Genesis, 22:13

December 28, 1973

MEDINA, SAUDI ARABIA

The winter rains, brief but heavy, had surged through the wadis. The air, washed, was fragrant. Medina, an oasis at the edge of a vast lava field, and shielded by arid hills, upheld the ether with her minarets. A perfect throne for Allah.

The Faithful who had gathered in Islam's second holiest city before journeying to Mecca seemed beatified by piety and exultation.

The optional pilgrimage to Medina before the hajj was, traditionally, a time when the Faithful reflected on the human condition and sought out spiritual paths to forge the brotherhood of man for the greater glory of The Compassionate. Equally, it was a time of self-adjustment. Within the city which had given sanctuary to the Prophet, the Faithful were expected to live through the beginnings of Islam, seek inspiration in the ordeals of Allah's envoy and attain purity of the soul.

Osman felt engulfed by the demagoguery in the main square of Al-Manakh pilgrim camp.

The orators clung to their proselytes with righteous fervor. Since most lived under some form of tyranny, they were intoxicated by their right to speak—despite the fact that by King Feisal's edict, politics had been restricted to eulogizing the fiction of Islamic unity.

There was one gathering where both the speaker and the topic were of particular interest. At a podium girdled by date palms, Abu Ismail was excoriating the Geneva peace conference. The WOJ

leader, contemptuous of the primary concern of the conference—
the relief of the Egyptian Third Army—had chosen to tackle the
global issue: mankind's deliverance through the final solution of
the Zionist menace.

There Osman stood and listened.

"We have no quarrel with the Jews."

Osman scanned the faces: radical politicians from the Third
World, powerful businessmen from the Middle East, reactionary
theocrats from Muslim states. Opportunists who championed
extremism for personal glory, they were relishing Abu Ismail's hy-
perbole. He was giving them the immutable scapegoat and, by
camouflaging it with a new name, Zionism, offering them a new
charter for anti-Semitism.

"Jews lived with us in harmony throughout the ages. . . ."

Harmony meant having the Jews as *dhimmi*, second-class citi-
zens. Harmony meant suppressing Islam's debt to Judaism. How
could Islam deny that Aaron's tomb lay on the summit of the
adjoining hallowed mountain, Uhud; that the very name of Medina—Yathrib in antiquity—was Jewish, from the Aramaic *me-
dinta*, meaning "the city"? How, except by cleansing the world as
the Prophet had cleansed Medina by massacring its Jews?

"I am, of course, referring to those Jews who adhered to the
true principles of Judaism. With those we can continue to live
harmoniously. But the Zionists are racists and deserve no mercy."

The racist element would find fertile soil in the African mind.
Genocide as a human right. Goebbels could not have done it
better.

But the big lie also threatened Jordan. Served to the poor Muslim who, cowering under economic, political and social injustices,
merely needed an outlet to channel his overwhelming hostility,
the big lie was a time bomb. The Jew was determined to survive.
Sooner or later Muslim hostility would seek another channel and
turn the Faithful back against each other. Arab blood would
swamp Arab blood. And lest it bleed to extinction, there would be
need for another scapegoat. That would be Jordan, Islam's pariah.

"The Koran has listed the characteristics of the Zionist so that
we can recognize him. Apostasy. Warmongering. Self-aggrandize-
ment. Pride. Deception. Lust. Envy. Tyranny. Usury. Theft. Im-
morality. Cowardice. Fratricide. Parricide. Infanticide. Uxoricide.
Homicide. Genocide."

That was the traditional touch. By listing a host of evils and
naming the Koran as the source, Abu Ismail was rendering his
statement incontestable. For everything was written in the Koran,
and only the recipient of revelations, an *arif* like Abu Ismail, could
winnow the secret truths.

"It is our sacred duty to bring the Zionists to judgment before the justice-loving peoples of the world."

Osman stopped listening. The words did not matter. The man did.

Osman's visual knowledge of Abu Ismail had been restricted to occasional observations from the periphery of a security cordon. Thus, he had felt compelled to come to Medina and audit the man's physical essence, his power as well as his frailty. The body, no matter how disciplined, could not erase the reflections of the mind; eyes and skin registered fear, limbs anticipated action.

And, for the past two days, during the traditional orisons, he had kept a close watch.

On Wednesday the devotions had progressed through the sacred mosques: the Mosque of Quba, the first in Islamic history, where the Prophet had been vouchsafed a view of Mecca; the Mosque of the Two Qiblahs, where the Prophet had changed the prayer direction from Jerusalem to Mecca; the Mosque of Al-Dir'a where the Prophet had donned his armor for the battle of Uhud; and the Mosque of Al-Raya where the Prophet had unfurled his standard for Khandaq, the decisive battle against the Meccans. Each mosque, because of its historic association, had been a perfect setting in which to stir religious zeal. Abu Ismail had acted self-effacement with distinction.

The next day, the laudations had concentrated on dramatic shrines: the Tomb of Hamza, the Prophet's uncle who had fallen in the battle of Uhud; the sacred cave where the Prophet, wounded, had taken refuge; the length and breadth of the ditch, Khandaq, which the Prophet had dug around Medina for the glorious battle; and the shrine of Al-Mustarah, where the Prophet had rested on his way to the battle of Uhud. Throughout, the mood of the multitude had been martial. At each venue, Abu Ismail had emanated an aura of humility, as befitted a standard-bearer.

Today, at the Prophet's Mosque, during the Friday service which, as the only congregational prayer stipulated by Islam, was a conduit for political exhortations and had, over the centuries, inspired the Faithful to take the field against the Infidel, Abu Ismail had brilliantly colored his image. Climbing the pulpit in the manner of a caliph, he had brandished a sword and an olive branch. Then, shouting "Allah!" and chopping the olive branch with the sword, he had called for jihad. The simple but spectacular gesture had enflamed the pilgrims.

And yet it had been at the Prophet's Mosque, before Mohammed's Tomb, the focal point for all pilgrims, that Osman had finally seen the true Abu Ismail. While all, Osman included, had shed tears of redemption, Abu Ismail had stood vacuous, glazed eyes fixed on the majestic green dome as if it were a blurred landscape.

It had been a brief moment. But it had revealed that beneath his armor Abu Ismail was soulless, lacking even dust. And the revelation had produced another revelation.

Not once, during his stay in Medina, had Abu Ismail reflected doubt. Yet, for a mystic who lusted after The Merciful—as the tapes of his communion at Mount Nebo had indicated—the specter of man's formidable judge, The Doubter, Al-Munafiq, should have been as real as the very existence of Paradise. But Abu Ismail had lived his days impalpably, like a spider who wove webs without understanding nature.

And in the light of these revelations, Abu Ismail's other affectations had fallen into perspective. The exaggerated arthritic limp was not the sympathetic pain of a savior, but crude pantomime. The reluctance to mingle with other pilgrims was not the mystic's compulsion for solitude, but the reticence of a phantom. Only the absence of his bodyguard, Nazmi, and his chief of staff, Idris Ali, had indicated a positive characteristic: fatalistic courage.

"Israel, by virtue of its structure, is a closed racist society linked to imperialism. Therefore the aim of the Arab revolution is to liquidate this entity in all its aspects, political, military, social, economic and cultural, and to liberate Arabism completely."

The paraphrased principal resolution of the May 6, 1970, Palestinian National Assembly had concluded the speech.

Osman walked away. The temptation to reevaluate Abu Ismail as a lesser foe was dangerous.

LISBON, PORTUGAL

At 5:30 P.M., the Lisbon Emergency Center received a report from the island of San Pedro, Italy, that the previous day a group of fishermen had observed a great explosion in the air some miles south of their fishing grounds. The reported location lay exactly on AF 205's flight path over the Mediterranean.

TRIPOLI, LIBYA

At 8:00 P.M., Colonel Muammar Qaddafi won the distinction of being the first head of state to deplore the tragic fate of AF 205. Extending his condolences to the relatives and friends of the passengers and crew, he disdainfully dismissed allegations that there had been a bomb on board. Islam's freedom fighters, he declared, were not inhuman fascists like the Israelis who, if the world needed reminding, had shot down a defenseless Libyan airliner over Sinai in February 1973. He attributed the rumored explosion to British-American-Zionist-Imperialist propaganda.

December 29, 1973

JIDDA, SAUDI ARABIA

Saudia flight 888 from Istanbul landed at Kandara airport and parked at an apron by the new hajj terminal.

Osman, compulsively munching mastic on the observation deck, watched the pilgrims disembark. Some kissed the tarmac, honoring it as the threshold to Mecca; others proclaimed the *ni'ia*, the formal vow affirming the pilgrim's intention.

One man, long-haired, bearded and pale, wandered about in a daze, impervious to taxiing aircraft, intoning repeatedly the pilgrim's joyous declaration, *"Labbaik, Allah, Labbaik!"*—"Here I am, Allah, here I am!" Only when the Wahabi official assigned to escort the passengers through quarantine, immigration and customs had run after the man did Osman recognize Boaz.

His spirits sank. There was no turning back. Like Spain's conqueror Tariq, who had arrested retreat by burning his armada, he had reduced other options to ashes. Could he, a humble soul, find the strength to walk through fire?

He could vindicate the assassination, irrespective of other considerations, on religious grounds. By proclaiming himself Al-Mahdi, Abu Ismail disseminated apostasy. The concept of a savior rested on the Shi'a claim that the imamate descended by right to the House of the Prophet. The idolatry mythified one Mohammed Al-Mahdi, the twelfth imam designate who had disappeared at the age of five, in a grotto at Surraman-Raa, in the ninth century, and who would remain Hidden, Expected, Living until the end of time, when he would reappear in Immaculacy to purify man and redeem the world. But the ineffable recitations of the Koran did not prophesy such a coming. Islam had no need of a savior since it had already submitted to the Rule of Allah. Consequently, Islam reconstituted by one claiming superiority over the Prophet would no longer be the True Religion.

The sanction to fight the apostate came from Allah. The Koran commanded: *"Kill them wherever you find them." Wherever* meant even in the sacred precincts of Mecca.

Still, Osman feared damnation. Since November 2, when he had come upon Abu Ismail's tapes and had confiscated the one delineating Operation Dragons, he had desperately sought a source which might offer guidance. But finding the Arab world incapable of distilling truth through the dense layers of historical detritus, he had not dared confront any of his people with the anathema Abu Ismail personified.

Worse, even armed with the truth, he had proven himself only marginally better. Instead of acting decisively, as Allah's instrument should, without temporal or eschatological fears, he had prepared for battle in trepidation, mitigating his destiny, like an insurance-minded merchant, by resorting to the old Arab subterfuge of unholy alliances: *He who is the enemy of my enemy is my friend.* Thus, he had recruited Boaz to deal the deathblow while he, Osman, dug a gossamer foothold in the hereafter by performing the hajj, a devotion that absolved all sins past, present and future.

Shakily, he pressed the Koran to his heart. Fear of damnation was underscored by another fear. He could not swear, even at this stage, that he would maintain his resolve, that he would not betray Boaz. And that would be betraying Allah's Will—the ultimate sin.

✗

Boaz stood before the immigration officer and softly recited the *Fatiha*, the opening chapter of the Koran.

" *'In the Name of Allah The Compassionate The Merciful . . .'* "

He wondered whether there was truth in the Islamic tradition that the mere pronouncement of Allah's name rendered a person a Muslim. He did not want to slight the stern and jealous God of the Jews, but there was comfort in the appeal and fortitude in the sound of the gentile Name.

The immigration officer, unimpressed by Boaz's devotion, scrutinized his passport.

Boaz waited patiently, as one respectful of authority, and surveyed the Hall of Pilgrims. Despite its modern splendor, the numerous posters in various languages—PILGRIMS, SAUDI ARABIA WELCOMES YOU—the hall emanated severity. Packs of dour *Motawa*, Saudi Arabia's religious police, hovered over the pilgrims; and fierce national guards, the paramilitary elite once known as the White Army, sealed all entry and exit points.

The immigration officer, indicating that Boaz should wait, picked up his telephone and called for someone from Al-Moukhabarat.

Boaz felt the unfamiliar stir of panic. Had İskender Ağa, who had procured the passport and visa, informed on him? Unlikely. İskender Ağa was not one to tarnish his honor.

There was, of course, another person who could have betrayed him: Osman. But he clung to the conviction that the Saudis would then have pounced the moment he had stepped out of the plane.

It was possible he himself had blundered. But how?

He had prepared himself assiduously. He had read and reread the Koran; memorized whole passages, waded through piles of literature on the hajj, its rituals, its significance; studied copious psychological reports—Western and Islamic—on religious ecstasy in general and the hajj pilgrim's behavior in particular. He had befriended venerable old hajjis to absorb their reminiscences; ingested every scrap of intelligence Mossad had evaluated. Attentive to detail, he had perfected the demeanor of an ailing man, the serenity of a fatalist; for the past ten days, following a chemical diet, he had contracted the pallor of a pietist.

Nonetheless, Al-Moukhabarat had been summoned. Perhaps a random check—a much publicized feature of Saudi Security to deter undesirables. Too fortuitous.

Boaz considered the quarantine clearance. It had preoccupied him throughout the planning stages as one of the toughest hurdles. His wounds from Aaron's booby-trapped corpse were barely healed. There were other scars. Any astute observer would wonder why a middle-aged Turk should be so pockmarked.

To his surprise, the quarantine officials, pathologically vigilant for Western adventurers, had concentrated solely on his circumcision.

Al-Moukhabarat arrived in the person of a major, a resplendent, unsmiling youth. He inspected Boaz's passport at length, conferred in whispers with the immigration officer, then ordered the latter to summon the "turncoat." As they waited, the immigration officer and the major ran the full spectrum of grimaces and glares. Boaz fidgeted and offered humble smiles.

Turncoat was soon revealed as an elderly Levantine with barricaded eyes. Either a Copt from Alexandria or a Greek from Beirut who had tossed about hither and thither until his conversion to Islam—forced or voluntary—had anchored him to Saudi Arabia. A man, as the soubriquet "turncoat" indicated, held in contempt not only by his own but also by those whose religion he had embraced. Boaz classified him as dangerous: one who might fortify inferior status with free-floating hatred.

The major briefed Turncoat, demanding clarification, as Boaz had feared, of his scars.

Turncoat addressed Boaz in moderate Turkish. "You are Turkish?"

Boaz beamed a smile. "Yes. You, too?"

Turncoat shrugged noncommittally. "You are from Istanbul?"

Boaz gave him an innocent look. "No. Çukurca."

"Where's that?"

"Anatolia. Southeast. Near the Iraqi border. A small town."

Turncoat relayed the information to the major. The latter consulted a map of Turkey.

"Your passport—and pilgrim's visa. They were issued in Istanbul. Why?"

"No passport office—and no Saudi Arabian hajj visa office in Çukurca."

"What work do you do?"

Boaz pointed to his passport. "Carpentry."

The major signaled that the map did show Çukurca.

Turncoat blinked in irritation, then pointed at Boaz's ticket. "You came on a scheduled flight. Expensive for a carpenter."

Boaz glared at the implied insult. "I'm here to perform the hajj. You think I care about expense?"

"Cheaper by charter. There are many from Turkey. . . ."

Boaz simulated confusion.

Turncoat smiled, point scored, and put on a chilling voice. "Can you prove you are a Muslim?"

Boaz rasped with suppressed fury. "You dare ask me such a question!"

Turncoat, conditioned to cower before authority, toned down his voice. "We have to be sure."

Boaz drew himself up proudly. "I am Nuri Aslan, son of Murat Aslan. I am from a family that has performed the hajj for generations. Should you know anyone who passed quarantine at Et-Tur, Egypt, in 1950, before performing the hajj, ask him about my father. He will tell you how my father advised the men on how to make their women fruitful with sons."

With Boaz towering over him Turncoat wavered between docility and aggression. The major, impressed by Boaz's tone, asked for a translation. Turncoat complied.

The major looked at Boaz with growing interest. Boaz had submitted a genealogical reference which, for the Muslims of the Middle East, identified the speaker as a man with established roots, therefore a worthy coreligionist. Since the honesty of a man undertaking the hajj should not be doubted, such references were hardly ever challenged; but had the major decided to check, he would have found them substantiated. There had been a Murat Aslan—now deceased—who had held court at Et-Tur in 1950 on how to procreate sons; the information had been filed by Mossad in 1967 when, with the occupation of Sinai, Et-Tur's records had fallen into Israeli hands.

The major appeared satisfied but Turncoat, keen to dispense his authority, continued with the interrogation. "According to our quarantine inspector, you have scars all over your body. How did you receive them?"

Boaz flinched. "Fighting."

"Turkey hasn't had a war for a long time."

Boaz fidgeted uneasily.

Turncoat turned on him like a predator. "Well? How do you explain it?"

Boaz started to shake, then falling to his knees, grabbed Turncoat's sleeve. The gesture petitioned a favor which, by tradition, could not be refused. "I seek your graciousness."

Turncoat, surprised, related the request to the major and, overzealous like most converts, expressed the desire to grant it. The major, curious himself, agreed.

"Ask."

"You are wise to question me. I am more than I seem to be. I am a warrior."

"How—warrior?"

"A righteous one with a righteous cause."

"Be specific."

"I am not an enemy of Saudi Arabia. However, it is possible you may not sympathize with my cause. I beg you: whatever you think of me, permit me to perform the hajj. I have not long to live."

Turncoat translated the exchange. Boaz sensed the change in attitude. Righteousness, even as a boast, had to be taken seriously.

The major spoke briefly.

Turncoat translated. "Your request will be granted if you satisfy us you are not an enemy of this kingdom."

Boaz smiled gratefully, then switched to Arabic. "I shall be an open book. I shall even address you in the language of angels. My passport provides my name, my trade and the country of my birth. But it does not specify the fire which consumes me. I am a Kurd. I have in me the blood of Saladin, the scourge of the Crusaders. I am distantly related to Mullah Mustafa al-Barzani, the leader of the Kurdish nationalist movement. All my life I have struggled for our legitimate rights. I have run the risk of imprisonment in Turkey and the risk of death in Iraq when on countless occasions I smuggled arms and provisions to my people. For the past two years I have fought in the ranks of *Pesh Merga*. On eleven occasions I have suckled the bullets of the Iraqi army. The scars are there for you to see. I have fresh wounds from shrapnel, which I received two months ago. Soon I shall be strong enough to resume the fight. Since the Iraqis are planning a big offensive, and since we intend to fight to the last man, I do not expect to live out the year. I shall welcome death. But I would die with open eyes and troubled spirit if I did not perform the hajj, the fifth pillar of the Faith. I beg you, do not send me to Allah's bosom until I am a hajji."

Boaz stopped, face tear-drenched, body trembling, but defiant. He had savored the grandiloquence. Arabic, that most seductive tongue, affected the speaker as much as the listener.

The major, the immigration officer, even Turncoat, of whom Boaz might have expected a degree of cynicism, looked subdued. None had accepted death for a shadow. Now, confronted with a true warrior, they felt diminished.

In compensation, they indulged their hatred for the Iraqis. To the Saudis, the Iraqi Ba'athists were progenies of the Devil; jinn, hungry for power, pursuing radical socialism laced with terror and genocide, who threatened to deliver the Arabs to soulless Russia. Whoever fought them was blessed.

The major, impulsively, saluted. "Go, pilgrim. And may Allah protect you."

Boaz kissed his hand, then paid the same homage to the immigration officer and Turncoat. "Thank you. Thank you. Thank you."

They gave him a copy of *Manasik al Hajj*, the manual of pilgrim devotion, and waved him on.

Boaz encountered no difficulties at customs. His rucksack containing his prayer mat, his pilgrim's garb, a camper's tent and a few changes of underwear received careful inspection. But the customs officer showed little interest in the few items of toiletries. One of them, a spray deodorant canister, contained in a false chamber 500 units of concentrated insulin.

BEERSHEBA, ISRAEL

Unlike its counterpart at the Tel Aviv Ha-kirya which had become an enclave for politicians and ministers, the Southern Command war room in Beersheba was the domain of the military—the professionals. Here, in an underground bunker resembling an indoor stadium, a world map, known as "the Table," lay pinned down like an apocalyptic Gulliver, its threads of intelligence from electronic spy systems depicting up-to-the-minute pictures of besieged Israel.

Kidan found the Memouneh seated in the gallery, inanimate except for his eyes. The Memouneh, rumors said, had actually wept when the Mossad cell in Libya had reported that Noah's body had been fished out of the harbor.

"Well, Kidan—how goes it?"

"I'm still upright."

"That's what I call strength."

Kidan grimaced. It was strength. None of that cloth-rending paranoia that had afflicted the nation with the Yom Kippur War. "At least we know for sure, Zamora. You were right. Abu Ismail's going nuclear."

The Memouneh stared at the multicolored, multishaped dots blinking from the Table. Each designated the neighboring forces and showed their deployment under various pacts. The squares represented naval craft and were divided into various categories: warships denominated by national flags; merchant shipping marked by the insignia of their maritime company; private boats identified by their port of origin. The circular dots represented aircraft. Those capable of military strike bore the emblem of the particular nation's air force; those engaged in civil aviation carried the logos of their airlines; the private aircraft, where possible, had their registration numbers. A cursory glance showed a proliferation on land, sea and air of Russian tactical strike forces, and in the Middle East, Russian support units hand in glove with Israel's enemies. The few Stars of David that represented, in a variety of designs, the Israeli army, navy and air force as well as ZIM and El-Al, looked as vulnerable as wasps in a beehive.

"Are you humoring me, Kidan? Just about everybody else has reservations. . . ."

Kidan lit a cigarette. Until Noah's death, he had been ambivalent about the nuclear-attack theory; at times, he had disputed it as preposterous, at other times he had seen it as plausible; but mostly he had disregarded it as peripheral to the fight against Abu Ismail. "If I convince you . . ."

"We'll form a double act—the new Moses and Aaron. It's too heavy a burden for one person."

Kidan met the Memouneh's eyes and belatedly saw an artisan of the oldest Jewish profession, the cross-bearer. Powerful, solitary, begging for the sleep of the earth. It was not Kidan's way of exercising power. But it led to the top of the mound where he belonged by right.

"I've gone through every report on Operation Dragons, Zamora. Muddy waters—until Lisbon. Now, it's staring us in the face. They hijacked AF 205 for its cargo. To conceal the evidence, they blew up the plane and killed Noah. We know for certain the cargo was special. We've had El-Al check the Orly computer. The entry specifies ingots—that's French defense ministry code for strategic material. . . ."

"But the French have not confirmed it. I've been to them cap in hand."

"The French consider themselves accountable to no one, Zamora. But we have concrete evidence from our French cell. There was a consignment of plutonium delivered to Orly from the Chinon Nuclear Reprocessing Plant on the twenty-third. Destination: Portugal. We know Portugal's Sacavem plant has contracted Chinon to reprocess its waste biannually. We've also found out that at the time of the hijack, there was a heavy transporter at Lisbon Airport with a national guard escort, waiting to take delivery. Moreover, since the disappearance of AF 205, French naval commandos have been scouring the Mediterranean, mainly the seabed. In other words, searching not for survivors, or bodies, but for something specific. Nothing could have survived the blast intact except a plutonium coffin."

Kidan stubbed out his cigarette and lit another one. The case he had outlined was convincing. "Just to ram the point home, Zamora, we may be asked whether it's conceivable for a nuclear cargo to be transported on a scheduled passenger flight. The answer's yes—and we've got it on computer. Numerous instances. On at least one occasion, a U.S. plane, transporting enough nuclear material to make an A-bomb, was hijacked to Cuba—though in that instance, the hijackers weren't interested in the cargo."

Dejectedly, the Memouneh scrutinized the Red Sea region on the Table. "We knew nuclear terrorism was inevitable. It's the fanatic's obvious progression. . . . and we've played it wrong. We've tried to cover the world—look for WOJ under every stone. Carried on like CIA or KGB—when all we've got is seven dwarfs. We've unearthed nothing—not even in Ethiopia since Kevork Dedeyan's brief glimpse. We've dissipated our energies. That's not our style. Direct approach, Kidan. Kill Abu Ismail first—then ask questions. That's what we have to do. We have two options. The first is already in play at Jidda."

Kidan tried to keep his face expressionless. He was disconcerted, not so much by the surprise, but because he knew instinctively that the move involved Boaz, and that there was a good chance of Operation Dragons being rubbed out before he could put his signature on it. "Boaz?"

"Yes. Abu Ismail is performing the hajj. . . ."

Kidan bridled. "You think Boaz can get farther than Jidda Airport?"

The Memouneh pointed at two circular dots on the Table situated on the Red Sea and bearing El-Al markings. "You see those El-Al 707s. One's flying to Johannesburg; the other's coming back. Both are equipped with long-range electronic eavesdroppers, loaned by the air force. The planes crossed paths at the nineteenth latitude, east of Suakin, at nine-thirty-three Saudi Arabian time. For thirty-five minutes prior to that, the southbound plane, now past Massawa, had been monitoring Saudi Arabian Al-Moukhabarat communications. The northbound plane now approaching the Tropic of Cancer has been doing the same. Boaz arrived at Jidda at eight-forty-five Saudi Arabian time—one hour and ten minutes ago. By now, he's either passed immigration and customs or he's been caught. Since the capture of an Israeli spy would immediately burn Al-Moukhabarat's wires, and since such an activity has been absent, I assume he is now one of the pilgrims."

Kidan, against the grain, was captivated by the boldness of the venture. "For how long?"

"I expect long enough to return as the first Jewish hajji. We may not hear from him for a week. But five days from now, we should be celebrating Abu Ismail's death."

"Fail or succeed Boaz won't come back—you know that."

"Do you care?"

Kidan paused, thought about it, pursed his lips indecisively. "I can't say. . . ."

The Memouneh smiled, wearily. "I'm hoping Osman Nusseibi will act as his guardian angel."

Kidan filed the fact with grudging admiration.

The Memouneh turned to the Table and watched the northbound El-Al plane fly out of electronic range from Jidda. He passed a set of earphones to Kidan, then donned his own. For some minutes they waited in silence. The headphones and the master teleprinter confirmed there was still no extraordinary activity from the Saudi Arabian Al-Moukhabarat. Nonetheless, for the next seven days, systematic monitoring would continue.

The Memouneh resumed the conversation, looking less tense. "Now the second option. What we don't really know is whether WOJ devised Operation Dragons independently or are acting as Qaddafi's surrogate force. Therefore, we must consider that even if Boaz kills Abu Ismail, either Idris Ali or Qaddafi or the two together might still make that bomb. So—we may have to strike in a big way."

"Raid Tripoli? Can you see Golda agreeing to that?"

"It's unlikely the bomb would be assembled in Tripoli—or any other city. Disregarding the dangers of failure and fallout, Libyan cities are teeming with agents. Equally, to maintain secrecy, the bomb cannot be assembled in any of the training camps WOJ shares with Qaddafi's other pet terrorists. They'll pick a desolate spot. Maybe in the Sahara. Maybe in a neighboring country like Chad. Maybe even Ethiopia. We can be in and out before anybody starts screaming."

"What about afterward? When they shout bloody murder?"

"We'll be guilty of conducting a limited action with a limited objective. There'll be the usual invective from the usual quarters. But since nobody wants Qaddafi to have a bomb, we'll make the world secretly happy."

Kidan lit yet another cigarette. "You hope."

The Memouneh picked up Kidan's cigarette, took a puff, then returned it in the familiar gesture of one who, having given up smoking, succumbs to the occasional temptation. "These are your orders, Kidan. You'll anchor yourself to this war room. If Qaddafi or Idris Ali sets up a base for the bomb, you must be the first to know. You can liaise with whomever you see fit, use any special services. If and when you locate a possible base, I want an assault plan for it. Only remember—there's no margin for error. We need blueprints that are infallible as well as flexible."

Kidan cast his eyes over the war room. His lair, at last. He thought he ought to be joyous, but instead he felt panic. The front line offered an ocean of sand and precious few laurels. He wondered how sand tasted.

December 30, 1973

JIDDA, SAUDI ARABIA

At 1:30 A.M., the shops and banks closed and the hubbub abated as if soothed by divine command. The Airport Pilgrim City that had looked like a refugee camp in a vast shopping center, now throbbed with pious repose.

In the male rest room, where he had found a corner, Boaz woke up instantly. He gathered his belongings and took leave of an old Senegalese who, earlier, had insisted on sharing his supper with him. The Senegalese had expressed the desire to die during the hajj, and thus achieve the most sanctified death a Muslim could hope for. Boaz had empathized. In the absurdity of life only faith and death provided constants.

Out in the shopping area, Boaz walked toward the mosque. Halfway there, he spotted Osman in the guise of a wordly Levantine, staring at the strange sight of some Bahrain matriarchs in burkas discussing, as if in a fashion show, the striking blue dresses of two Kikuyu girls.

At the washbasins of the mosque, while performing the requisite ablutions, he caught a glimpse of Turncoat. This was his second sighting of the man since the encounter at the immigration desk. When he had been breaking bread with the old Senegalese, Turncoat had been drifting around the rest rooms.

He placed his sandals by the entrance to the mosque and walked in.

Night prayer was not a stipulated daily prayer, but a voluntary devotion—hence most meritorious. It had been influenced by the Christian practice of vigils in Syria and Iraq. It assuaged the ultraorthodox as fair compensation to Allah. The Deity had at first demanded fifty daily prayers, and Mohammed, advised by Ibrahim, had bargained him down to five.

As he recited the verses and genuflected, Boaz reviewed the situation.

Coming out of customs, he had caught sight of Osman arguing volubly with a taxi driver over the fare to Mecca. This had signaled that nothing extraordinary had happened to warrant a change of plans. Boaz, in turn, had alluded to his precarious passage through immigration by approaching an official guide and asking him the way to Mecca. Boaz and Osman had agreed that in the event of the merest brush with Saudi Security, Boaz should consider himself under surveillance. Boaz had thus indicated that he had put himself on probation and that he would walk the full distance to Mecca to provide proof of piety. Then, they had made their separate ways to the pilgrim city.

There, in the opulent branch of the Riyadh Bank, joining the long line at the foreign exchange window, they had struck up casual conversation. They had discussed the trek to Mecca. Osman had doubted the wisdom of undertaking such a journey beneath a blazing sun. When Boaz had reconfirmed that he would walk, Osman had advised him to start immediately to benefit from the cool of the night. Boaz, grateful for the suggestion and anxious to rest before starting off, had taken leave effusively. They had made sure that much of the conversation took place within earshot of two national guards. For good measure, Boaz had bought some provisions for the journey.

Boaz concluded the salat and feeling peaceful, wondered whether the tranquillity had emanated from prayer. The stereotyped phrases, the diffusing cadence of Arabic had inexplicably fused the Lord with Allah.

Coming out of the mosque, he surveyed the square. Turncoat was still there, chatting to a patrol of religious police. Osman was there, too, near the exit, seated in front of a scribe.

Boaz put on his sandals, heaved his bag onto his shoulder and proceeded toward the exit. He passed Turncoat and salaamed respectfully, receiving a vague response.

He walked past Osman, pretending not to notice him.

Osman called after him: "Brother! Brother!"

Boaz stopped, turned and smiled.

Osman caught up with him. "You're off, are you? May Allah walk with you."

"Thank you."

Osman, like one anxious to consolidate a friendship, prolonged the conversation. "I was sending a letter to my family . . . you should do the same. You won't have time during the hajj."

"I have no family."

"Oh. I am sorry."

The exchange concerning the scribe alerted Boaz that Osman had observed some activity from Saudi Security. Osman had no way of telling if this was directed against Boaz, but he was urging utmost caution. "I hope we meet again."

"I should be honored." Boaz walked through the exit.

There was still a great bustle outside the pilgrim city. The airport was handling charters around the clock. Waves of pilgrims, unsettled by jet-lag and oppressed by the humidity, languished about.

As Boaz weaved through the crowd, a taxi driver swooped upon him. "Jidda! Three riyals!"

Boaz glanced at Turncoat. The man had followed him and now stood by an official car. "Thank you. I am walking."

"It's twenty-three kilometers to Jidda. Seventy-three from Jidda to Mecca. "You'll walk all that way?"

"Yes . . ."

"Good sir. I bow before your piety. But I must tell you: a pilgrim is not required to walk to Mecca from the airport. It is sufficient to walk from Jidda. It is even sufficient to walk from the sacred boundary."

Boaz hesitated. He had accepted the 100-kilometer walk to Mecca stoically, as a phase of the mission. But not averse to reducing the tedium legitimately, he became, for Turncoat's benefit, yet another victim of Jidda's wily taxi drivers. "Are you sure?"

The taxi driver beamed a smile. "I'll drop you at the traffic circle where Mecca Road begins. All for three riyals."

Boaz hesitated a little longer, then nodded agreement.

He scrambled into the taxi and perched on a jump seat. As the taxi roared off, he turned around to salute his fellow passengers— all Indonesians—and watched, through the back window, Turn-coat's car align itself behind the taxi.

Ten minutes later, after the kind of perilous ride Boaz would expect from an Israeli *sherut*, they reached Mecca Road intersection. Boaz paid his fare, commending the driver on his choice of colorful tassels, cushions and curtains that had transformed his taxi into a pious vehicle. He wished good luck to the Indonesians who had booked rooms at Al-Haramain Hotel; they had become morose, having been told by the driver that during the hajj, advance reservations never guaranteed a room, and that even if they did, the price was sure to have tripled.

Boaz stepped out of the taxi and waited briefly for Turncoat's car. As its headlights caught him, he started walking toward Mecca.

He saw the last of Turncoat at kilometer 2. Having parked his car, the man was hurrying toward the Jidda offices of the Ministry of the Interior, no doubt to issue instructions to security forces along Mecca Road.

MECCA ROAD, SAUDI ARABIA

Boaz maintained an average speed of seven kilometers an hour.

The first hour was the hardest. That was unexpected; as part of his perennial training he had often run fifty kilometers a day in the Sinai, where similar climatic conditions prevailed. Now, overnight, age had caught up with him. He saw the humor of it: he was on his last mission, and Fate had synchronized it so that he would deal his most telling blow just before obsolescence.

With the month of *Dhu'l-Hijja* already in its sixth day, and the hajj due to start on the eighth, the pilgrim traffic was heavy. Those who wished to enter the Holy City on foot, as the Prophet had done at the time of his only pilgrimage, had congested the road.

Some, eager to show their zeal beneath the harsh sun, awaited the day in white tents; others, like Boaz, availing themselves of the night, walked; yet others, the weary, the elderly and the invalid, encamped by the roadside and waited patiently for the commencement of public transport at sunrise.

Most of those who walked did so in groups, often competing to

outchant one another with exultant declamations. Whenever
Boaz overtook them, he was asked to join the group. He refused,
offering a mystic's humility and appropriate gratitude. Often he
regretted doing so. The men and women from the four corners of
the world, surging like seraphim summoned by the Lord, canopied
the way with a consecrated aura. At times, the repeated affirma-
tions of the uniqueness of Allah, and His supreme power over
man, made Boaz wish that he, too, were a Muslim. He identified
the wish as the desire to assimilate. He had nurtured it all his life.
That was why he had soldiered. Within the legions of the army it
had been possible to find an identity. That had sufficed as a reason
to live until the realization that what he really sought was sanctity.
Sanctity that lay on these pilgrims like pollen. Had it not been too
early to forget the Holocaust, or too late to divorce the pilgrims
from their holy war against the Jew, or too perfidious to defect
from the New Masada that was Israel, he might well have considered performing the hajj as his very own pillar of faith.

At kilometer 6, alongside the economics school of the King
Abdul Aziz University, a unit from Al-Moukhabarat stopped him.
While they checked his passport, he sang, like a dervish, a song of
union with Allah. When they told him to move on, he lingered
long enough to hear them report to headquarters that his conduct
appeared to be that of a true pilgrim.

At kilometer 7, near the Al-Mahjar Isolation Hospital, he was
stopped again, this time by a Royal Guard patrol. They checked
his vaccination certificates for cholera, smallpox and yellow fever.
Boaz treated them to rousing verses from the Koran. The Royal
Guards, fierce desert warriors lauded by King Feisal as *Ikhwan*,
brothers in faith, showed deep respect for the recitation and sent
him on, full of praise.

At kilometer 10, he met three more patrols: a police squad car
at the agricultural station; officers from Al-Moukhabarat at the Ein
Aziziya reservoir intersection; and a religious police unit by the
roadside restaurant. He passed their scrutiny by singing Turkish
folksongs and appearing unobservant of their presence.

Three hours later, at first light, past Hadda, he spotted another
religious police unit. Again he preempted their attention. He
stopped, pulled at his hair, held it before his eyes and, satisfied
that he could see it, declared it was time for the dawn prayer. He
took out his prayer mat, drew a semicircle on the sand in the
direction of Mecca, and performed *al-fajr* with those pilgrims who
had heard his call.

He was stopped for the last time by armed national guards at
kilometer 29. These, protecting the television and radio transmit-

ters, proved very thorough. They examined his passport, visa and vaccination certificates and searched his person and belongings. Throughout it all, he hummed a medley of Kurdish songs—and all the more fervently when one of the guards, inspecting his spray deodorant, came close to unlocking the secret chamber. Finally, courteously, he was allowed to proceed. He sensed he had passed muster and sang as one possessed.

At 9:40 A.M., he reached kilometer 51 at the sandy valley of Wadi Sharif by the foothills of the main Hejaz range. An uninterrupted line of trucks, buses, coaches, taxis and private cars crawled past, counterpointing their passengers' euphoric declamations with their strident horns. The pilgrims who had spent the night in the open responded with equal fervor.

They were within reach of the boundary post where, before entering the sacred territory of Mecca, they would have to halt, undergo a final check, perform purificatory ablutions, and don the pilgrim's garb. So near to fulfilling the journey which they had covenanted at birth, every man and woman presented a portrait of beatitude. Countless voices recited the *Shahadah*, the Confession of Faith: *There is no other God but Allah! Mohammed is the Prophet of Allah!*

Boaz pitched his tent and breakfasted lightly. The *Shahadah* continued to echo from the firmament. He had heard this, the first pillar of Islam, on countless occasions, mostly as the war cry of Arab armies, frequently from the lips of dying Arab soldiers. In essence it was the same cry as the Hebrew *Shema: Hear O Israel, the Lord our God, the Lord is One!* And like the *Shema*, it elevated man to mystic realms, while tragically setting him apart from his brothers.

Before lying down to a brief rest, he gazed at the last checkpoint less than a kilometer away. There, all being well, he would meet Osman at 3:00 P.M.

JIDDA, SAUDI ARABIA

Osman entered Sheikh Latif Ibn-Omer's diwan as one who, though entitled to hospitality as his birthright, is nonetheless grateful for it.

An ancient Nubian, obviously a freed *mamluk*, slave, led him to his seat, pointedly appraising him. Osman decided to accord the Nubian due respect. Prior to the abolition of slavery in 1962, the *mamlukin*, in obedience to the teachings of the Koran, had been treated as family members. Those who had chosen to stay with their masters after freedom had often become counselors;

their advice, undefiled by personal gain, was considered invaluable.

Sheikh Latif Ibn-Omer, unaffected by the Saudi disregard for punctuality, entered promptly at 10:30.

Osman placed his right hand on his heart in the customary devotional gesture. Sheikh Latif greeted him regally, then sat on his austere chair with the dignity of a Wahabi prince whose ancestors had restored orthodoxy to Islam by freeing it from its cult of innovation.

The Nubian served coffee.

Osman, assuming an air of great confidence, appraised Sheikh Latif.

The pillar of the Boycott of Israel bureau, Sheikh Latif was the legendary righteous man among Saudi royalty. Many international companies, blacklisted for trafficking with Zionists, had found him as immovable as Allah's curse. He was unaffected by wealth since, in addition to his high office, he was also one of the small band of agents who monopolized the kingdom's imports. And such was his piety that, irrespective of the demands of state and commerce, he served the Faith during every hajj as *Mutawwif*, secular guide to pilgrims. But, although his status entitled him to gather under his wing the elite, he scorned the prerogative. Instead, he formed his own group, picking only people renowned for the extremity of their politics toward Israel.

It seemed inconceivable that such a man could be exploited, but that was Osman's task. For Sheikh Latif had selected Abu Ismail for his group and, unless Osman joined that group, the mission's chances of success would diminish considerably.

Sheikh Latif, scrutinizing Osman's visiting card, beamed as if in the presence of a long-lost relative. "Permit me to know your name perfectly."

"Izzat Jadid. From Lebanon."

Sheikh Latif blinked sadly. "Brave is the Lebanese who carries a lamp in his hand."

Osman displayed hurt. It had been necessary to assume a Lebanese identity. But much as fermenting Lebanon was the butt of every Arab's contempt, those Lebanese who could prove their worth were doubly honored. "I know my measure, Sheikh Latif."

Sheik Latif smiled appeasingly. "I meant no affront."

Osman took the offensive. "I should like to present my case."

Sheik Latif looked up warily. "A man who rushes with his plea can only be one of two things: an opportunist or a firebrand."

"Sheikh Latif, I am here to beg a favor. I could have forced you to grant it by abusing tradition—simply by kissing your sleeve. Instead, I wish to convince you with honest words."

"You speak like a firebrand."

"Judge me. I will be brief. We both have to leave for Mecca."

"Present your case then."

Osman paused dramatically, then fixed his eyes upon Sheikh Latif. "I come to you because you are a true Muslim. Because you fight the Zionist menace, and you understand the essence of our Faith: that it is universal. You must, therefore, abhor the fact that a large part of the world remains Infidel."

"Alas."

"Why do we permit it? Islamic law stipulates that to fulfill Mohammed's task, every infidel domain must be considered a territory of war; that there can be no peace with the Jew or the Christian or any other; that at the most only a truce is permissible —and that for a maximum of ten years as an expedient to hone our swords, whet our blood and strengthen our will. Do you agree?"

"Yes."

"I ask further: Can it be Allah's will that Israel should grow by our jugular like cancer? Is it Allah's Will that some Arabs should worship a creature said to be the fruit of a Jewish virgin and Allah's seed? Have we so offended Allah that He should strike us with retribution worse than the fires of hell?"

"It is possible."

"Venerable Sheikh, I beg to differ. Every *Sura* of the sacred Book, except the one entitled 'Repentance,' commences with the words: *In the Name of Allah, The Compassionate, The Merciful.* How can so perfect a Deity inflict such punishment as Zionist-Christian domination of a world destined to echo the muezzin in every corner?"

Sheikh Latif pursed his lips, at a loss himself.

Osman continued with utmost fervor. "No. The Infidel in our gullet is not a punishment. It is an irritation put there to goad us to jihad. Allah is urging us to cough, so that we can spit out the unbeliever and redeem the world."

Sheikh Latif blinked and nodded. Then, unexpectedly, he burst into tears. "Your tongue captivates me."

"Not my tongue, Sheikh Latif. Your own heart—because it recognizes the truth."

"Yes. I have been beating my head against daggers because I don't know how I—or anybody—can make our brothers see the truth. My old slave will tell you, only this morning I wailed in the direction of Al-Quds because there, tomorrow, the Jew will elect a new government."

"We can make sure it is their last. The Jew has his vulnerable spot. Not only can we kill him, but we can, at the same time, reclaim my country, Lebanon, from the Christian!"

Sheikh Latif's eyes blazed. "How?"

"My people, much as they have been polluted by the Christian sucking our entrails, have defended the Faith. Daily, we are growing in strength. Our ranks are filling with Palestinian brothers. Tomorrow we can drive the Christian into the sea and reclaim the cedars for Allah. The next day we can purge the Jewish existence in Palestine."

"Money—is that what you want?"

"No. A general. One to equal Khalid ibn al-Walid, the scourge of the Byzantines."

Sheikh Latif stared at him in surprise. "You're not suggesting . . . I have no experience in military matters."

"No. You are needed where you are."

"Who else? King Feisal?"

"King Feisal, may Allah protect him, is already fighting the feudal lords. We need a chieftain, equally zealous, to fight their serfs. One who can forge Lebanese Muslims and Palestinians into an invincible sword."

"Is there such a man?"

"There is. Abu Ismail."

Sheikh Latif thought for a long time, then blinked and nodded. "Yes. I see that. But how can I help you?"

"Abu Ismail has allowed himself to wear blinkers. Magnificent as is his single-mindedness for the destruction of Israel, he is proceeding through a forest of thorns. I should like to direct him to the clear path. The way to the enemy's underbelly is through Lebanon."

"You want me to talk to him?"

"I doubt whether as Mutawwif you would find the time. But if I could talk to him . . ."

"Can't you?"

"If I joined your group . . ."

Sheikh Latif glanced at the Nubian. The latter, inscrutable, served Osman a dish of peeled figs. Sheikh Latif rose and embraced Osman. "I should be honored . . ."

Osman took Sheikh Latif's hand, kissed it and pressed it to his eyes.

ASH SHUMAYSI, SAUDI ARABIA

Invocations to Allah detonated the very air. Boaz surged on, a particle in a tidal wave of sun-scorched, weary, humble, ecstatic pilgrims. He had witnessed such ecstasy once before: in the faces of hysterical Jews streaming to the Wailing Wall in the aftermath of the battle for Jerusalem in June 1967.

Ahead, on either side of the road, lay two colossal tents, sign-posted respectively for men and women; these housed the basins where the pilgrims had to perform their purificatory ablutions. Beyond stood the last checkpoint and the *alamein*, the twin pillars that marked the boundaries of *Al-Haram*, the Sacred Territory.

The checkpoint had been set up in a semicircle. Large sign-posts in Arabic, Malay, Urdu and English indicated the area was restricted to Muslims only.

The main barrier spanned the road like a border post and processed the long line of vehicles. Simple turnstiles, erected off the road, dealt with pedestrians. They were all manned by officers of the Royal Guard. The whole complex was ringed by crack units of police, religious police, national guard and members of the frontier force. These, in turn, were linked to an outer ring of paratroopers in scout cars guarding the periphery of Al-Haram. Sand clouds on the horizon indicated that an additional force of light tanks patrolled the desert routes. Boaz was reminded of the Saudi boast that it was easier for an infidel to extract the Hundredth Holy Name of Allah from the camel who alone knew it, than to infiltrate the precincts of the Holy City. He went into the tent to cleanse himself.

The basin, a plastic container as large as a family-size swimming pool, had a length of pipe with some fifty taps running around it; water was pumped through from a tanker parked nearby; the drainage system funneled the dirty water into a small pool outside, where under the hot sun, it quickly evaporated. Pilgrims considered it a vast improvement over the past when they had had to purify themselves with stone or sand.

Boaz undressed, washed all over, then again washed his mouth, nostrils, face, arms and feet. He took his time, listening to the pilgrims' gossip. He realized he was filing information which might prove useful for Mossad. Though his flesh had accepted death, his spirit had not.

He put on sandals cut at the heel and the instep, then donned his *ihram*. The white, unsewn garb—two lengths of cotton draped around the body so as to leave the head, hands, right shoulder, right arm, feet and ankles uncovered—transfigured him. The Muslim glorified the ihram both as raiment, which rendered all the Faithful equal, and as the vestment that would serve as his shroud. Wearing it, a man felt favored by God, assured of resurrection. Such sentiments were equally seductive for the Jew, and

Boaz, convinced that he had put on his last vestment, felt as free as the dead.

He transferred his watch, wallet, passport and toiletries into a *mizuda*, the simple cotton bag that the pilgrim, forbidden to display any adornment, used for his personal belongings. He packed his clothes and walked out.

His objective was to reach the checkpoint a few minutes before afternoon prayers. Earlier he had observed that prior to the noon prayers, the forbidding Royal Guards had become neglectful of their duties in their zeal to perform the devotion. By reaching the checkpoint just before prayers, he hoped to ensure an expeditious processing. He did not fear a confrontation but, at the threshold of the Sacred Territory, he was wary of Osman.

Osman had alighted from a taxi soon after 3:00 and, declaring that he would walk the rest of the way, had dismissed his driver. No one had considered his behavior irregular; the sighting of the Sacred Boundary had inspired a large number of pilgrims in cars and buses to do the same. But Boaz had noted a change. The nod signaling success with Sheikh Latif had been curt and anguished.

Throughout the planning stages Boaz, suppressing his doubts about Osman, had shirked the key question: How could Osman, who regarded the Faith as sacrosanct, carry out a mission that would damn him for eternity? That he had seemed to support such a burden lackadaisically had been unnatural, if not suspicious.

Now, seeing Osman visibly in torment, reduced to another misguided Judas, Boaz had to face the inherent dangers.

The common Judas, if he were to believe the psychiatrists, bridled his protesting soul at least until receipt of the blood money; the uncommon one, often in search of redemption, remained inconstant. If Osman fell into the latter category, computer evaluations had indicated that on at least two occasions he would be subject to maximum stress and possible crack-up: on the point of entry into the Sacred Territory; and after the assassination. In the first instance he would feel a desperate urge to recant before treachery became irreversible. In the second, having fulfilled his objective, he would crave expiation.

Boaz, though as distrustful of computers as of the men who programmed them, had not taken the warnings lightly. Thus he had planned to pass through the checkpoint before Osman. After the assassination, retribution was assured—one way or another.

Boaz timed his move perfectly and reached the checkpoint just as the Royal Guards began to pick up their prayer mats. They waved him through impatiently, then closed the barriers. He crossed the *alamein* at a run.

Once on hallowed ground, he spread out his prayer mat. He caught a glimpse of Osman, on the other side of the boundary, also preparing for prayers, looking bereft.

Boaz prayed, unable to distinguish between Allah and the Lord of the Universe. And he witnessed, like Peter, John and James, a transfiguration—not of a deity, but of humanity. The miracle emanated from the mellowed earth; for though penned in by one religion to the exclusion of all others, Baoz felt it belonged to all mankind. Sanctified earth contained the Almighty's breath. That was why shrines had remained sacred throughout man's religious evolution, and why cities like Mecca and Jerusalem would remain holy until the last of days.

SACRED TERRITORY, SAUDI ARABIA

Boaz stopped at the King Abdul Aziz well, near the ruins of an old Turkish fort. He filled his cup, squatted by the roadside and sipped his water as one attuned to the desert. Then, he waited.

Osman duly arrived, lined up at the well, helped himself to a few cups of water, gulped them down like a city dweller, then sat on a stone. As he wiped perspiration off his neck, he looked at Boaz in recognition. "Brother, we met last night."

Boaz stood up. "Indeed. Indeed."

They smiled humbly, in the spirit of the pilgrimage, and started walking, chanting prayers. When clear of the throng, Osman hissed venomously, "You pray with great devotion."

"The only way."

"If it is to Allah."

"God by any name is God."

Despairingly, Osman scanned the wilderness. Before entering the Sacred Territory, the arid land, the winding road infected by traffic, had seemed to carry all the ills of the times. But, once inside, the air had been transformed to an ether filled with the victuals of salvation. And he had wept because Boaz's presence had defiled it. Yet somehow the ether was still there—intact. "Does it help you. Boaz—praying?"

"It hasn't killed me."

"It may, yet."

Boaz squeezed Osman's arm affectionately. "Wait till we're through."

Osman gazed at the land that was as dear to Allah as a cosmic eye.

Boaz wished he could offer some solace, pronounce, like the

Talmudists, a distillation of wisdom. "Was it difficult with Sheikh Latif?"

"No."

"Latest on Abu Ismail?"

"In Mecca. Arrived yesterday. At the hotel I'll be staying."

"Still alone."

"Yes."

"I don't understand it. No Idris Ali. Even more puzzling, no bodyguard, no Nazmi."

"They'll show up. When they've tidied up the Air France caper. We proceed as planned. Strike at the climax of the pilgrimage. On the tenth of *Dhu'l-Hijja*. If we fail, we resort to the contingency plan. Hit at the Great Mosque. On the thirteenth—a week from now."

Boaz faced Osman. He had decided, irrespective of the psychiatrists' predictions, to test him for himself. "We could strike tomorrow. In the Sanctuary. With Nazmi and Idris Ali absent, we'd have a free hand."

Osman's voice shook. "No, Boaz! No! The proscription against shedding blood in Mecca. We said we'd honor that."

"You got around that long ago, Osman. It's not an unqualified prohibition. What's that passage in the Koran against the apostate?"

Osman replied faintly. " '*Kill them wherever you find them.*' "

"Wherever!"

"But it goes on to say: '*Do not fight them within the precincts of the Holy Mosque unless they attack you there*' "

"By calling himself Al-Mahdi, Abu Ismail is attacking Islam right there in the Sanctuary! You said so yourself!"

"Boaz, we agreed to respect Mecca's sanctity!"

"We also agreed to be flexible."

Osman argued defiantly. "If we move tomorrow, how will you get near Abu Ismail?"

"I'll find a way."

"There is no way—except as we planned. Working around the hajj. Circumventing the Saudi organization . . . filtering through the groups."

"It'll be tough, I agree—"

"The groupings are rigid. You know that. Arranged according to country, race, tribe, sect, occupation, class—like stones in a pyramid. Each remains a unit under its particular Mutawwif. Easy to control. Easy to supervise."

"Even so . . ."

"It'd be impossible, Boaz. First thing tomorrow morning you'll be assigned to a group—hopefully a respectable one. But nothing like Sheikh Latif's—Abu Ismail's—near the top of the pyramid. You can't jump from one to the other just like that. You have to maneuver with extreme delicacy. Freewheeling between ceremonies. Acting the ingenuous believer who's been separated from his group. . . ."

"A bold charge, Osman—"

Despair crept into Osman's voice. "Boaz, listen. We decided Abu Ismail should seem to die of natural causes. That blatant assassination would spawn an even greater monster: a martyred saint. Even your experts advised us we should wait for the day of the Great Sacrifice. A day so charged with religious fervor that people suffer coronaries. And some literally will themselves to death because that's the supreme moment of the hajj—the apogee of their lives. The perfect day to die."

"So? Death comes at the wrong moment. It happens all the time."

Osman wailed. "You won't see reason, will you?"

"All I see are scruples on the sanctity of Mecca. Now, I respect that—but you're sanctioned to ignore it! So—"

Osman's voice quivered, barely under control. "You agreed we should hit at Wadi Aranah—in the secular zone! Why go back on it now?"

"I gave you my reasons."

"They're not good enough."

"If I can kill Abu Ismail tomorrow—would you stop me?"

Osman rattled his words confusedly. "Yes—no. He must be killed." He stopped sharply and faced Boaz. "You don't trust me —that's the reason for this turnabout, isn't that so?"

Boaz remained silent.

Osman smiled bitterly. "I don't blame you. I myself have doubts—every second."

"I know. . . ."

Osman rasped. "You know nothing! You can't imagine—nobody can—what I'm going through!" He paused, deep in thought, then mumbled hesitantly. "There's a parable, a true story. I repeat it to myself—over and over again. It disperses my doubts. It might yours. Would you like to hear it?"

Boaz faced him, intrigued. "Yes."

Osman spoke, letting his eyes wander over the wilderness. "It's the tale of a Bedouin rais, an ally of the Hashemites in the days when we controlled the Arabian peninsula. This rais, passing through Kuwait early in his youth, befriended a pearl diver. Enchanted by the diver's youngest daughter, Hussa, he promised to marry her the day she first washed her hair, meaning the day she ended her first menstruation. After five years, having waited in vain for word, he returned to Kuwait. He found that the pearl diver had died, his wife remarried, his children scattered. He inquired after Hussa, and discovered that she was living with a *sha'ak*, a woman who loves both sexes. He banished the *sha'ak* and reclaimed Hussa as his betrothed. This caused quite a sensation. Hussa's distant relatives, slaves to honor, intervened. They demanded as a condition of marriage the prescribed punishment for a lapsed girl: forty days of incarceration on a daily diet of one cup of water and a handful of dates. If Hussa survived, it would mean Allah had forgiven her. The rais reluctantly agreed. But knowing that Allah had more pressing obligations than repairing man's stupidity, he fed Hussa secretly. So, they married. And for some years they lived a blissful life. The rais, a most sensual man, found Hussa a perfect twin-soul. He even felt grateful to the *sha'ak* for making Hussa such a knowledgeable paramour. But the *sha'ak*, not so forgiving, waited to avenge herself. Her chance came when the rais went on an important raid. Confident that the passionate Hussa would be prey to temptation, the *sha'ak* commissioned a wily pimp. For a while Hussa resisted the pimp's solicitations. Eventually frustration consumed her, and she agreed to a tryst with a discreet prince. But, at the house of assignation, instead of the paragon she had been promised, she found a multitude of men —lechers who had heard of her past and were determined to sample the favors that had induced the rais to forgo other women. They abused her. Then, boasting about their exploits, branded her a daughter of sin. Hussa's relatives, incensed by the dishonor she had brought upon the family, charged her with adultery, as the *sha'ak* had anticipated, before the shari'a court. Hussa, facing a death sentence, wrote to her husband, confessing her improbity and appealing to him to be her sole judge. Her relatives, afraid that the rais might forgive her, prevailed upon the court to execute her without delay. She was stoned to death. When the rais returned, he, naturally, put all those who had abused her to the sword, including the *sha'ak* and the pimp. But his grief never abated. And until his death, this is what he preached: honor, duty, even religious laws, are the misguided offsprings of moral insensibility, that these had shackled the Muslims to the twin pursuits of shame and revenge, that nothing can compensate for the loss of what is most precious and that, consequently, happiness, as defined by poets, would never perch on the Arab shoulder."

Osman fell silent.

Boaz reflected on the story. "Am I to equate Mecca with Hussa?"

Osman faced him. "If you had a wife whom you cherished more than life and honor—as I do—you could. Easily. No impurity can defile what is sanctified. Because impurity is transient, sanctity eternal. And, in terms of Mecca, any desecration is preferable to its destruction."

"Destruction?"

Osman avoided Boaz's eyes. "That's what it would amount to if Abu Ismail established his theocracy. Now, can we assume you trust me—and confirm procedure?"

Boaz sighed, as sure of Osman as he could possibly be, yet troubled by all Osman had left unsaid. "All right. We keep to the plan."

Osman let his tension seep away. "Thank you. Let's just walk, like we're on basic training." Without waiting for a response, he surged forward, praying that Allah saw him, chest bared in obedience to His Will.

✗

Though the road had climbed steadily, they had averaged more than ten kilometers an hour. They had held the pace not because they were exceptionally trained soldiers but because the pilgrim masses, eager to catch sight of Mecca, had set a fast tempo. They had refrained from speaking, taking refuge in the stark beauty of the igneous rocks that colored the wilderness.

Shortly before sunset, the pilgrims' exultant declarations of arrival reached a crescendo. Osman and Boaz pushed forward and suddenly, shimmering like a mirage, Mecca confronted them. They stood transfixed.

Osman shouted compulsively, "Here I am Allah, here I am!"

Boaz echoed him.

For a moment, Osman forgot the conflicts and passions that had brought him to the Holy City. It sufficed that he had reached it; it almost did not matter that he was there to save it for the generations of Muslims to come. He wept tears of joy.

Boaz, too, felt enthralled. Sprawled over two wadis, surrounded by seven hills, white Mecca, hennaed by the sunset, did not look incorporeal. Not like Jerusalem. There were no city walls to suggest it had been defended by zealous men throughout history. It spread over the hills, quite arbitrarily with slums and rich suburbs. It emitted the usual smells of Arabia: food, ordure, dust and exhaust fumes. Only the Great Mosque, dominating the city center, reflected a mythical aura. It was, in fact, a city like any other—and its throbbing life, more than anything else, highlighted its holiness.

There, unlike the austere Jerusalem, the supernatural was accessible to men; one could touch God even from the gutter.

December 31, 1973

MECCA, SAUDI ARABIA

The seventh of *Dhu'l-Hijja* was the day the pilgrims inaugurated the hajj by performing the rites at the Great Mosque.

Boaz had to join a group not too distant—literally and in spirit —from that of Abu Ismail.

The assignment of pilgrims to groups had taken many hours. There had been the inevitable chaos of an exultant multitude; the endless negotiations between pilgrims and secular guides as to who should join which group, according to origin and social standing, conducted in subtle nuances in order not to contravene the doctrine that all the Faithful were equal in the eyes of Allah.

Boaz had used the confusion to advantage by shunning the ordination and withdrawing to pray so that when, finally, the groups had been sorted out, he and a few other pietists would be left as outsiders. This unusual strategy, courtesy of Jordanian Intelligence, had been aimed at securing one of the worthier guides who made it a tradition to scour the encampments for the most pious among the lesser pilgrims. The inclusion in such a guide's group established the pilgrim as meritorious and allowed him, at least for the duration of the hajj, to rub shoulders with Islam's elite.

The strategy had been sound. Boaz, having impressed one Zaki Kutbi, a learned imam from Afif, had been invited to join Kutbi's group of the ultrapious. Soon after 10:00 A.M., he set out for the Great Mosque.

✗

Abu Ismail sat in the foyer of the Egyptian Hotel and watched Sheikh Latif gather the cream of Islam—cream being the euphemism for excreta; for these were men who had abandoned the desert for the quagmire of international boardrooms, who had betrayed name, honor and tribe for the Infidel's contempt.

The spectacle was bearable only because they would soon perish. The pomp and ceremony were the death dance of these worshipers of Mammon, arse-lickers of rulers, lip-servers to Allah.

They would be engulfed by the fires of hell like graven images. They would be replaced by men with prodigious genitals; spunk that bore the strain of the warrior. The Faith would no longer be contaminated by midget souls perforated by the profanities of the West, programmed to bully or kowtow, frown or smile, condemn or forgive as self-interest demanded.

Abu Ismail rebuked himself. He was being peremptory. There was one among the mutants worthy of preservation. They had been introduced earlier on. Osman Nusseibi was the name, though Sheikh Latif had called him something else. A good man, fearless, powerful—a son of the desert. He recalled the brief conversation.

"*I am your servant, Abu Ismail.*"

"*I am honored.*"

"*May I seek a favor?*"

"*You may.*"

"*Judge my devotion during the hajj. . . .*"

"*To what purpose?*"

"*To form an alliance.*"

"*I do not seek an alliance.*"

"*You need fearless men.*"

"*Fearless men wait for the call.*"

"*I shall remain by your side. Like the face of the moon I shall shine with love for Allah. Like the dark of the moon I shall nurture hatred for the enemy. And you shall call me. There are not many like me.*"

Abu Ismail believed that, if only because he knew Osman Nusseibi to be a cornerstone of Jordanian Intelligence. There might be much to gain from such an allegiance.

He stiffened, suddenly confused. How did he know Osman Nusseibi was with Jordanian Intelligence? Indeed, how did he know his name was Osman Nusseibi and not the alias he had used? No one had told him.

He directed a troubled glance at Osman Nusseibi, sitting opposite, smiling courteously, but with eyes that burned holes in a man's soul. Why was he staring like that? To impress? To prove he had more fight in him than an army? They would talk again—soon; they would discuss how to defeat the Jew. So why did he glower?

He fidgeted. He had seen those eyes before—then, too, looking dangerous. Where? He could not focus on the memory. Some years back—in Jordan. During the pitch-black September of 1970 when King Hussein had driven the fedayeen from their strongholds. He could remember a desk. A hut—shell-marked and full of rubble. Osman Nusseibi interrogating. He could remember another name: Tawfiq Tal. Who was Tawfiq Tal? What was the interrogation about? What was he, Abu Ismail, doing there? There was another dim memory: he was talking about Nablus, shouting, "My birthplace, my home, before the Zionist took it away from me." What was that about? Why did he, Abu Ismail, claim Nablus as his birthplace when he was born in holy Hebron?

He felt nauseous. It always happened when memory started playing tricks on him. A psychosomatic manifestation, the doctors had called it: the body's adjustment to the levitation of the mind. The fissure of memory was the sign of a prophet. The warriors had accepted it as such. They had expected it of Al-Mahdi. And what little discomfort it caused was easily remedied by medication.

That reminded him. He signaled the hall porter for some water. It arrived immediately. He took out eight assorted pills, his daily ration, and gulped them down.

He felt better. Amnesiac or not, he was Al-Mahdi. Performing the hajj as the next caliph. The world was his. The doctrines to rule it were his. He was the savior. Soon to establish Allah's kingdom on earth. Soon to reign supreme over the final and definitive theocracy. The rest did not matter.

He smiled at the man opposite, tried to think of his name. It had slipped his mind. But he remembered Sheikh Latif's introduction: an enemy of the enemy; therefore, a friend.

"Your Excellence . . ."

Sheikh Latif stood before him, wringing hands, dispensing adoration.

He smiled graciously. "Yes?"

"We shall be leaving soon for the Great Mosque. Perhaps you wish to attend to natural functions. . . . It will be a long day. . . ."

Abu Ismail nodded. Sheikh Latif withdrew. Abu Ismail rose, steadied himself, then walked to the rest room.

Osman stood up, strolled about casually, then stopped by Abu Ismail's table, He took out a handkerchief, pretended to blow his nose, then, swiftly covering Abu Ismail's glass with his handkerchief, picked it up, emptied the remaining water in a cuspidor, and slipped the glass into his cotton bag. Still casually, he walked to the stairs—and hurried to his room.

He returned shortly—without the glass.

The Great Mosque, which had given its appellation, *Al-Haram*, to the Sacred Territory, was still undergoing reconstruction that had started in 1965. Even so, it was awe-inspiring. The massive walls, surrounded by open spaces—leveled to accommodate the fleet of pilgrim buses and official cars—held the bustling city at bay and highlighted the Sanctuary's aura. Coming upon it from a maze of narrow streets shaded by old buildings and intricately carved wooden balconies, the vision of the white marble lodestone of Islam was, for Boaz, as dramatic as seeing Death in a bridal gown. He marveled at the colored geometrical designs that embellished the gateways, and the exquisite calligraphy which decorated the ramparts with quotations from the Koran. He lent exultant voice to the exclamations canopying the air.

As it was incumbent on all pilgrims upon arrival at Mecca, he had tried to visit the Great Mosque the previous night and conduct a reconnaissance. But the strict control which regulated the peregrinations of half a million or more pilgrims had not yet been enforced, and the milling masses had made the Sanctuary impenetrable.

Now, as the guide took them around the exterior walk, he surveyed the scene. Security arrangements were tight. Armed units of police, national guards and paratroopers patrolled the area under the aegis of the religious police. These last, equipped with radio, manned every conceivable point of the compass. They would be on duty day and night.

The Great Mosque had twenty-four gates. Four led, respectively, to the library, archives, the shari'a court and the madrasa. Of the remaining twenty, five, Bab Ali, Babel Abbas, Bab en Nebi, Bab el Cait Bey and Bab es Salam, were located along Al-Mas'a, the covered path also known as Hagar's Way. Since this was a ritual zone, those five gates were used as exits. Of the fifteen gates offering access into the Sanctuary, one, Bab Ibrahim, served royalty, heads of state and other important personages. The other fourteen accommodated the rest of the pilgrims according to the ranking of their groups.

Boaz and his group lined up at Bab er Rahma, the Gate of Blessing. Boaz was well pleased. As the central and most prominent of the seven gates on the southwest wall, it was reserved for highly select groups. Moreover, Bab er Rahma held a strategic position, offering an unrestricted view of the main plaza where the official motorcades stopped; and being only five gates away from Bab Ibrahim, it conducted the pilgrims into the same quarter of the Sanctuary as the elite. With Abu Ismail privileged to go through Bab Ibrahim, Boaz expected to catch sight of him either outside or inside the Great Mosque.

His expectations were fulfilled sooner than he had hoped. Shortly before his group reached the gate, a convoy of Cadillacs, bearing Sheikh Latif's party, arrived at the main plaza. Boaz disengaged briefly from the line so that Osman, who had jumped out first from the lead car, could spot him.

Then he directed his attention to Abu Ismail. The last time he had seen the WOJ leader had been in Beirut Airport when, but for the Memouneh's perverse decision to abduct Abu Ismail together with George Habash, he would have killed him.

He observed Abu Ismail long enough to register his purposeful gait—obviously rejuvenated by the hajj.

*

Boaz had imagined that entering the Sanctuary, which only a handful of non-Muslims had seen before him, would generate a sense of achievement.

Instead, he stood humbly before Islam's holiest place and realized that his elation was transcendental. The Sanctuary had instantly reduced him, in spirit and in flesh, to a mere supplicant. As he listened to the rumbling murmur of the thousands who prayed and circumambulated, he felt at peace. He understood why the Faithful wished to die in Mecca. Whoever set foot in Al-Haram found himself in the presence of God; who, in his right mind, would wish to let go of Him and return to the inhumanity of man's world?

He knelt down behind his guide to offer the customary thanksgiving prayer. "O Allah . . . I have come from a far country with transgressions . . ."

Architecturally, Al-Haram was a vast rectangle surrounded by a belt of cloisters. Marble and granite pillars, supporting pointed arches and domes, separated the enclosure and the cloisters. Within the cloisters two further lines of pillars supported a second tier of galleries, also pillared, where pilgrims could linger either as spectators or to offer additional prayers. This flat-roofed second tier supported in turn four of the seven minarets. The remaining three, added to the main edifice, completed the harmony. The minarets—sturdy towers compared to the pencil-thin design perfected by the Turks—their balconies painted green, the color of Islam since the Fatimids, their total of seven denoting completeness, conveyed both the adoration of the Faithful and the eternity of the Faith.

The enclosure itself was even more imposing. Prayer areas strewn with innumerable carpets converged to the marble-floored vortex, which held at its center the Kaaba. This was the palladium, fixed as the qibla, the direction in which Muslims prayed five times a day. This was the House of Allah, built by Ibrahim and Ismail on Allah's command as a replica of His abode in Heaven. This was the edifice which in pre-Islamic times housed 360 gods, one for each lunar day, and which contained the *hajar al aswad*, the meteoric Black Stone received by Ismail as the cornerstone. This was the shrine to which even the Jews had sent offerings before their banishment from the Arabian peninsula.

The Kaaba, draped by the black silk kiswa heavily embroidered in arabesque calligraphy with the Confession of Faith, was, as its appellation signified, a cube-shaped edifice, eighteen meters high. Yet it emanated the supernatural. Some of the Faithful attributed the phenomenon to the breath of Allah that resided in it and instructed man through the symbolic shape of the cube on the perpetuity and immutability of Truth. Others ascribed it to the presence of the Black Stone which, being of heavenly origin, was the depository of Allah's Will. Yet others believed that a second stone on the western corner, known as *hajar al as'ad*, The Stone of Luck, reviewed their destiny at the very moment of their presence before the Kaaba. For Boaz, the phenomenon evinced itself in more incongruous terms: the Sanctuary teemed with pigeons yet none perched on the Kaaba; none dared defile the kiswa.

As if by itself the House of Allah would be too dazzling to behold, Al-Haram contained other shrines. Opposite the Kaaba's northern wall, a semicircular white marble parapet called *al-hatim* and meaning knowledge of the Koran enshrined the *Makam Ismail*, the Place of Ismail. The space between the parapet and *al mataf*, the pavement on which the circumambulation was performed, glorified the ascent of Ismail and his mother, Hagar, to Heaven. A few paces from the eastern wall, a pagoda with a small dome sanctified the *Makam Ibrahim*, the Place of Ibrahim, and contained a stone on which the patriarch was said to have stood while building the Kaaba. At the other end of the eastern wall almost directly opposite the Black Stone, a majestic flight of stairs led down to the Holy Well of *Bi'r Zem Zem*. Beyond stood the gates that gave access to Hagar's Way, the enclosed route which ran between the ancient hillocks of Safa and Marwa.

The guide rose and beckoned his group forward. They genuflected again in the space left vacant by the preceding group to offer another prayer of thanksgiving.

"O Allah . . . Keep me protected from the fire."

Boaz turned his thoughts to prosaic matters.

Progress to the Kaaba would be slow. There were numerous groups ahead of them and yet more groups coming from the other gates. One of the groups poised to perform the circumambulation was Sheikh Latif's. Boaz surveyed the path that separated him from Abu Ismail.

One practicality became self-evident. Should he be forced to resort to the contingency plan and kill Abu Ismail in Al-Haram at the end of the hajj, he would have to stop freewheeling and rejoin his own group. For, though a pilgrim separated from his group would be allowed access into the Sanctuary, he would be directed to the farthest corner of the enclave where any movement would be subject to the discretion of the organizers. Boaz's group was sufficiently near Sheikh Latif's; the attempt to infiltrate a nearer group, at the risk of conflict with that group's members, would offer little advantage.

The distance from Abu Ismail, as it stood now, was about fifty meters. But it covered an area choked with pilgrims, genuflecting in obeisance: the men weeping in joy; the women forbidden to veil themselves in the Sanctuary and for once able to expose their faces reflecting, according to tradition, inner paradise. Not a soul would shift eyes from the Kaaba lest the eternal moment be profaned.

Consequently, a sudden dash would be feasible. He would be spotted, of course. Immediately. For the Sanctuary was under constant surveillance from the administration building. There, behind vast glass windows, religious police lookouts scanned the area with field glasses. Moreover, there were closed-circuit television cameras everywhere. The system had been installed originally for the reconstruction of the Great Mosque, to enable the non-Muslim architects and engineers, forbidden entry to Mecca, to supervise the work through television screens from outside the city limits. Since then, the Royal Guard had extended it to cover every corner of the Sanctuary. Increasingly alarmed by attempted coups against King Feisal—five involving the Saudi Air Force; fourteen initiated by tribal and religious fanatics—and aware that the king would be at his most vulnerable within the precincts of the Great Mosque, the Royal Guard would be ultravigilant. Nonetheless, Boaz felt confident. Given the time lapse between the issuing of orders and their application, he should have enough margin to reach Abu Ismail. Conceivably, there would be a clash or two with the religious police, but even discounting any help from Osman, he would be able to handle that. On the day, with King Feisal also performing the Al-Haram rites, both the religious police and the Royal Guards would be tightly ringed around the king, and not all that amenable to giving chase to an apparently disoriented pilgrim.

Boaz surrendered to the general exultation. He wished he could love the pilgrims. With the temporal world shut out, they were what men should be: cherubs.

✗

Sheikh Latif directed Osman to the eastern corner of the Kaaba. There, before the Black Stone, accessible to the pilgrim through a slit in the kiswa, he had to commence the *tawaf*, the circumambulation.

Osman paused. He saw himself in the flesh. A true Muslim, upholding the five pillars of Islam. A man who testified to the Oneness of Allah and his sole prophet, Mohammed; who observed the prescribed prayers; who gave voluntary and obligatory alms; who celebrated the Feast of Ramadan; and now, a man who was performing the hajj, having diligently prepared for it by abstaining from sexual relations, hunting, the uprooting of plants and the shedding of blood.

He felt his flesh conflagrate. This time, he saw himself in spirit: ethereal, variable, billowing, a cloud bearing judgment. A man whom Allah forged periodically to purge His world.

He moved forward. His mind, determined to imprint the moment for life and eternity, recorded the features of the Black Stone, the one relic still extant that had been touched by the Prophet.

Momentarily, he felt alienated. The Stone did not look unique, did not reflect the Divine Will that had fashioned it from the dust of Heaven. It was not even black, but the color of dark amber. Built into the masonry in a ring of brown cement, mounted on a silver setting less than a meter in diameter and shaped like an inverted oval bowl, with the heads of silver nails visible on its surface, it looked as vulnerable as any relic; and it bore, like a tablet, the chronicles of floods, fire and man.

It was, he realized, this very vestige of time that illumined the Stone's sanctity. For though it had been broken and ransacked, burned and desecrated—even carried away as spoils of war by the Carmathians, though it had been abused recurrently by internecine warfare and despoiled by seekers of remission, it had remained inviolate, like its Creator. If anything, the scars emphasized the smoothness of its surface, immaculately polished by the lips of generations of men and women who had kissed it since the days of the Prophet.

And so, at last, he could see the Stone as it was: a fount that rendered mankind pure; the Right Hand of Allah stretching out to the Faithful. He could believe that on the Day of Judgment it would grow two eyes and a tongue to give testimony on behalf of those who had adored it.

He kissed it and felt Allah's breath.

He started circumambulating. His bare feet fused with the sacred ground. His senses wished for total nudity, in the manner of the pre-Islamic pagans, so that he could unite with the Merciful in full sensuality. Hands raised, palms pointing outward toward the Kaaba, he circumambulated counterclockwise. He completed the first three circuits at speed, emulating the Prophet's determined run before the hostile Quraish. He completed the remaining four at a solemn pace. Each time he touched the Stone of Luck. At the end of each circuit, he kissed the Black Stone and moved to the place of refuge situated between the Black Stone and the door to the Kaaba. There, aware of the Divine Presence behind the door, he pressed himself against the wall, clung to the kiswa and prayed: 'O Allah, save me from the fires of *Jehennem*; deliver me from evil deed. . . .'

At the last circuit, he declaimed the prescribed prayer in tears of joy: "O Allah, grant me a perfect faith. . . ."

He moved to the Place of Ismail. There, to conceive Allah's wrath, he recalled how Adam had erected the earthly Kaaba with stones from five sacred mountains while ten thousand angels guarded the edifice, and how Allah had sent the flood to destroy even the Kaaba because of man's insubordination. And he thanked Allah for His compassion, for His mercy to man, for commanding Ibrahim and Ismail to reconstruct the Kaaba, and for sending the Angel Jibril to guide Ismail to Jebel Qubais, there to find the Black Stone.

He advanced to the Place of Ibrahim. At the very spot where the patriarch had stood to pray and offer submission, he prayed: "O Allah, you know my thoughts—even those hidden. Enable me to die a Muslim."

And since the ritual at the Place of Ibrahim permitted the worshiper a personal supplication, he pleaded: "Grant me the courage, O Allah, to maintain an alliance with the misguided Jew, so that we can save Islam's eye. And then grant me the strength to expiate my sin."

He progressed to the Holy Well that Jibril had disclosed to Hagar so that young Ismail could survive in the wilderness and reach manhood, thereupon to sire a great nation. Osman drank the sour water, the very elixir of Allah's compassion, with abandon.

He returned to the Black Stone to kiss it again.

For a while he remained transmogrified, a mighty rock washed by the pilgrims' prayers in rainbowed sprays. Finally, he drifted behind Sheikh Latif out of the Kaaba, through its most famous gate, Bab Ali, and on to Hagar's Way.

Indeterminate moments later, he found himself at the starting point for the *sa'i* ceremony. Still barefoot, still light in limb and mind, he ran between Safa and Marwa, the two hillocks where, according to tradition, Hagar and Ismail lay buried. And he commemorated Hagar's distress. The patriarch's mother had run the same course under a merciless sun in the hope of sighting a habitation, a caravan, or even a solitary traveler who would give water to her parched son. He ran thrice rapidly, and four times slowly. He completed the course at Marwa; and there, his heart bursting, he repeated the *Tauhid*, the Testimony to the Unity of Allah. Then he wept. He had completed the rituals prescribed for Al-Haram.

✗

Later, when Sheikh Latif disbanded the pilgrims, Osman returned to the earthly world. He walked to the hotel behind Abu Ismail and, seeing him uplifted by the day's rituals, found it inconceivable that he could be enemy.

He lingered at the hotel until Abu Ismail retired to his room. He noted that Idris Ali and Nazmi had still not arrived. It annoyed him that Abu Ismail should feel so safe in Mecca; deep down, he regretted having stopped Boaz from killing him that morning.

✗

Toward midnight, Boaz and Osman met at the panoramic terrace on the heights of Wadi Misfala. They greeted each other guardedly.

"Did you perform the rites, Boaz?"

"Yes."

Osman felt a sharp pain. "How did it feel?"

"I was deeply moved."

Osman searched Boaz's face for signs of irreverence.

Boaz continued in a tremulous whisper. "I felt near to God— nearer than I have ever felt."

"I think I can understand that."

Boaz nodded. "Abu Ismail?"

"At the hotel."

"Still alone?"

"Yes."

Boaz shook his head, perplexed.

Osman brought out a set of black-and-white prayer beads, a popular souvenir of the hajj. "For you. As a keepsake."

"No. No keepsakes."

Osman shook his head. "Why? Because you've given up on life?"

"It is as if you've given them to me. The gesture counts—as always."

Osman growled. "Don't you ever have doubts—about yourself? Your yearnings?"

"Not about my yearnings."

"We Arabs have a concept: *Al-Munafiq*. The Doubter. The Despoiler. I remember reading once about a North American mythical animal, the Hidebehind, a creature that you can never see because whichever way you turn, it's always behind you. The Doubter is something like that—but infinitely more threatening. He inhabits man's mind, his innermost recesses. You can't destroy him. But you can learn to live with him. To accept his persecution. To judge your achievements against his contempt for you."

"The point, Osman . . . ?"

"You seem to be free of The Doubter."

"I may have defeated him."

"You can't. Not unless you flush out your soul. Turn into a zombie. Like Abu Ismail."

"He's hardly that."

"Wait till you see him at close quarters. An empty shell. But that's irrelevant. The point once more: why should *you* be an empty shell? Renege on life?"

"You're out of your depth, Osman."

"Perhaps because if I come to an ocean, I see it as it is. An ocean—not a pool. And, since obviously I can't swim across it, I take a boat. I forget about depths—unless, of course, Allah sinks me, but then it's Allah's Will, and who am I to complain?" Defiantly, Osman offered the prayer beads again. "Take them. For their symbolism."

"Thank you. No."

Osman shook his head sadly. "See you tomorrow then."

"Without fail."

January 1, 1974

AMMAN, JORDAN

At 8:30 A.M., Zaynab Ghaffar, Osman's trusted secretary, a middle-aged matron of Junoesque proportions, entered the telecommunications center of the Jordanian Secret Service and proceeded to the interception section. A security guard examined the red tag that authorized her to handle classified material, then handed her a file.

The file contained transcripts of the previous night's communications between CIA Middle East headquarters in Beirut and CIA general headquarters in Langley, Virginia. These communications, transmitted by satellite, were religiously monitored by the Jordanians in the belief that on occasion the CIA knew more about what was going on in the Middle East than the local intelligence services.

Before his departure, Osman had rearranged the duty roster so that on this day Zaynab would be assigned the task of delivering the communications to Ciphers for decoding. She duly signed the duty book and left.

She did not go directly to Ciphers as procedure stipulated, but stopped at Osman's office.

There, she unlocked a cabinet with a key entrusted to her by Osman. Behind a pile of documents she found a sealed envelope. She tore it open and took out a single sheet of paper. She noted the sheet was identical to those used by Telecommunications for intercepted material, and that the short typed column of figures appeared to be in a CIA code. She inserted the paper into the file she had collected from Telecommunications, locked the cabinet, fed the empty envelope into the shredder and walked out.

At 8:45 A.M., she reported to Ciphers, and delivered the file to Mansour Assad.

As she returned to her office, Zaynab finally allowed herself to wonder why Osman had ordered her to plant into the CIA transcripts, on the eighth day of Dhu'l-Hijja, a sheet of false information compiled and coded by him, and to hand it specifically to Mansour Assad, known to be a Libyan agent but kept unpurged for the purposes of disinformation.

She had not been instructed as to the nature of this particular deception, but she was sure that as a CIA report it would be accorded due respect by Tripoli, and acted upon. Osman, whom she worshiped like a prodigal son, was a master strategist in cat-and-mouse games.

MECCA, SAUDI ARABIA

Boaz woke up in harmony with the world. There would be more of the spiritual nourishment he had imbibed at the Kaaba. For this was *Yaum al-tarwiya*, the Day of Moistening, the day the pilgrimage moved some eight kilometers from Mecca, to Mina, there to stand and bear witness to Allah.

He spent most of the morning relaxing in a shaded corner, as one reliving the fateful encounter with Allah. He rejoined his group to return to the Great Mosque for the afternoon prayers. Then they set out for Mina.

The exodus from the Holy City became a majestic pageant. Emotionally, it surpassed even the arrival. For on this occasion, pilgrims had neither the choice of locomotion nor the margin of time, but had to walk at the prescribed hours. And so they surged like a mighty river, contracting and expanding as the terrain dictated, leaving behind a city populated merely by children, the infirm, a garrison of soldiers who had performed the hajj in previous years—and, Boaz thought, the footprints of those who would not return.

AMMAN, JORDAN

The intercepted CIA transcripts had been, in the main, evaluations on the results of the Israeli general election of December 31: Golda Meir's Labor coalition had suffered a reduced majority; the Likud, a right-wing grouping critical of the government's handling of the Yom Kippur War, had made significant gains—trends which might make Israel intransigent in future negotiations.

But for Mansour Assad, the single item that broke the routine eclipsed the sum total of the month's intelligence. Using a highly sophisticated code only recently deciphered by the Jordanians, but providing no field reference, it had simply stated:

OSMAN NUSSEIBI, HIGH-RANKING JORDANIAN INTELLIGENCE OFFICER, AT PRESENT PERFORMING THE HAJJ UNDER ALIAS IZZAT JADID, PLANS TO ASSASSINATE THE WOJ LEADER ABU ISMAIL.

Assad imagined that most people would be inclined to dismiss the item as improbable. He did not. Through his activities at Ciphers, he had been privy to Osman's obsession with Abu Ismail. The problem would be to convince Qaddafi and WOJ. On second thought, neither, no matter how incredulous, could afford to reject such vital intelligence.

MINA, SAUDI ARABIA

As darkness fell, the pilgrims reached a narrow defile beyond the picturesque town of Mina. They performed the combined, shortened sunset and evening prayers, as prescribed for travelers at all times. Then they set up tents. Later, anxious to prepare for the momentous day ahead, they strolled about in search of friends, kindred spirits or solitude.

Boaz made his way to the crest of the gorge and sat down to

stare at the vast expanse of hurricane lamps shimmering like stars in a fallen sky. At least half a million people—yet they were merely a fraction of the Faithful who called for Israel's destruction. What was the point of killing one among them?

"The eternity of Islam. Does it frighten you?" Osman towered above him, highlighted by the crescent moon.

"A bit."

"Do you sometimes wish you could kill us all?"

"No."

"Inconceivable, isn't it—genocide?"

Boaz sensed the pity in Osman's voice. He also sensed the strain. Osman was cracking up in large fissures. "Not to those who've experienced it."

"Idris Ali has arrived."

Boaz nodded.

"According to Sheikh Latif, he came directly to Mina. Some pilgrims do that and perform the Kaaba rites after the Great Sacrifice."

"Any other WOJ?"

"A man called Abdallah . . ."

"In place of Nazmi?"

"Abdallah is one of their best platoon leaders."

Boaz shrugged. "We knew Abu Ismail would have protection. We planned accordingly. Nothing's changed."

"No. But don't waver. Don't worry about Idris Ali or Abdallah. I'll take care of them. Whatever happens—kill Abu Ismail. Just remember: genocide—some people worship it."

January 2, 1974

MINA, SAUDI ARABIA

A splash of amber daubed the sky. The last murmurs of the morning prayers abated. Eyes remained transfixed on the eastern horizon, some dilated anxiously as if afraid the day might be stillborn.

Then, as the enclosing hills started to blush in colors of damask rose, the Faithful galvanized and declaimed their presence. Souls swayed, grew into a maelstrom. A space opened up at the vortex, revealing the royal house of Ibn Saud. One of King Feisal's entourage raised a spear. When the rising sun attained its length, the pilgrims cried out and started to move. The hills resounded, the firmament rippled.

Fear gripped Boaz. The throbbing humanity conjured up apocalyptic images; the tumult objectified the Day of the Lord. For all he knew, mankind was rushing to bitter judgment; nations were crumbling in battle cries and cosmic upheavals; souls were being thrown at the deathless worms of Gehenna. And why not? What was there to save in man?

He strode forward in the wake of his group. The fear increased. He prayed for his soul to be saved. His mind mocked him: all who are proud and high, lofty and tall, shall be the first to fall down. He remembered Osman's words about The Doubter. Inhabiting the mind's innermost recesses. Was that The Doubter mocking him?

He paused. He had been running. He had managed, unwittingly, to detach himself from his group. His body had executed a tricky maneuver simply, as if in contempt of the woolly mind that would have accomplished it laboriously. Now, he could freewheel toward Abu Ismail. But the fear remained. All-embracing. You shall die without a whiff of sanctity. So said Providence, and so it would come to pass. If he could accept that, if he could smother his aspirations, if he could fear, instead of the death of the soul, the death of the flesh, the pain of crushed limbs—if he could die like a true sinner, he might perhaps die in hope.

He started to walk again. He looked around. No one took any notice of him. He increased his pace. The march was taking them to Mount Arafat, sixteen kilometers ahead. Before it ended, he had to be within striking distance of Abu Ismail. The WOJ leader, as befitted his status, was following King Feisal's retinue—somewhere ahead.

AL-TARIQ AL-ARAFAT, SAUDI ARABIA

By the time the pilgrims had reached the Bazan boundary pillars beyond Muzdalifa, Boaz had moved into the thick of the main throng.

At the free territory of Wadi Aranah, he surged forward again. He reached Namirah with the vanguard throng. At Namirah, known as the mosque without a minaret—since the Saudi reign a description no longer applicable—the noon service was to take place. Boldly, he moved to the enclosure reserved for overseas imams. He sat down, as one summoned to Allah's presence, and immersed himself in meditation. When the main body of pilgrims came, a few of the imams cast curious looks at him, but none dared disturb him.

He watched the royal entourage arrive. Abu Ismail's group took its place not far from King Feisal's enclosure. He maintained observation during the prayers and traditional sermon. Throughout,

Idris Ali and Abdallah flanked Abu Ismail; Osman hovered in the background in the manner of an admirer. King Feisal's phalanx of bodyguards, overstretched by having to guard the House of Ibn Saud as well as other Muslim heads of state, did not extend their duties as far as Abu Ismail's group.

Immediately after the noon sermon, the pilgrims continued toward Mount Arafat. They had to reach it by 2:00 P.M.

Boaz threaded his way to the forefront.

MOUNT ARAFAT, SAUDI ARABIA

The low, conical hill of Mount Arafat stood diffused in the afternoon sun. The heat, cauterizing even breath, cascaded down the slopes as if to subject the Faithful to a trial by fire.

The pilgrims settled on the plains, wave after wave, to perform the most sacred rite of the pilgrimage—the *waqfa*, the ceremony of standing and bearing witness at the very spot where Ibrahim had taken Ismail for sacrifice, where Allah had shown mercy, and where the Prophet Mohammed, otherwordly with the premonition of death, had delivered his farewell address.

Boaz, among the first to reach the site, had rooted himself at a vantage position—again at an enclosure reserved for overseas imams—within sight of Abu Ismail's group.

From now on he had to remain within close proximity of Abu Ismail. Though he was by now a familiar face to the imams whose patch he shared, they might seek to return him to the humbler ranks. The only way was to preempt them by emerging as a lone mystic who communed with Allah on planes beyond tradition or reason.

He took the pill that the Mossad laboratories had concocted to induce frenzy. He would unfold himself as a sufi, exhibit symptoms of transcendental love, the ecstatic readiness for self-annihilation. Such men were respected, even by the Wahabis. The imams would not dare censure him. He would be left untouched —scorned by some, revered by others.

The pill did its work. For four hours, until sunset, as the multitude recited the prescribed prayers, counterpointed the sublime words with joyous cries, waved their holy garments and wept with joy, his face took on the mien of a deep trance. Occasionally, saliva frothed from his mouth; twice he collapsed, prostrate, as if intoxicated by the Divinity's love. The intense heat added a realistic dimension to the charade; the fervor of the masses acted as camouflage. No one challenged him.

He compensated for his charlatanry with the compassion he

felt for a number of people who died from the heat, and for the few distraught women who left the plains declaring themselves unclean because they had started menstruating. For the latter the pilgrimage would be null and void. *Waqfa* was the one rite above all others that rendered a person a hajji.

MUZDALIFA, SAUDI ARABIA

Osman was a hajji—at least in Allah's eyes. A man housing truth as he would a beloved wife. Flesh finally vested with aura. As the Prophet had urged, he had allowed himself to die before his death out on the plains of Arafat. The soul he had carried through the *nafr*, the rush back to Muzdalifa, was immortal. Now he could treat the world as a tree beneath the shade of which a wayfarer briefly shelters before moving on. Now, he could even hope for forgiveness for violating Mecca's sanctity.

The pilgrims were congregating in the vicinity of Mashhad, Muzdalifa's minaret without a mosque. Before sleep they had a last duty to perform: a brief excursion to the nearby Wadi Muhassab where they had to collect forty-nine stones with which to lapidate the devils during the next three days.

He approached Abu Ismail's tent. The hurricane lamps highlighted the silhouettes of the WOJ leader, Idris Ali and Abdallah. Earlier, during the short interval between sunset and evening prayers, there had been a fourth man. Osman had identified him as Tahir Said, WOJ's peripatetic agent in Saudi Arabia. His sudden and brief appearance had signified that the news of his intention to kill Abu Ismail had filtered through from Amman.

He paused as he confronted Boaz, calmly waiting to go to collect stones.

Boaz clasped him, surprising him. "Congratulations, Hajji."

"Thank you." Elated, Osman looked toward Abu Ismail's tent. "I'll give them ten more minutes. They must have discussed me fully. Now, let them see me make a move."

Boaz offered his hand. "We may not talk again."

"Why not?"

Boaz shrugged. How could he explain a Jew's death wish to a man who believed in the Will of Allah? Muslims had no concept of suicide; self-destruction was permissible in the course of martyrdom, revenge or vendettas of honor—but not to banish despair. "Things may go wrong."

Osman rasped, "Listen to me. You'll get the chance to kill Abu Ismail—that I promise you. But that may not be the end. . . . You think you know what Operation Dragons is! You don't. I do."

"Go on."

"As I said, killing Abu Ismail might not be the end of it. Cataclysm—that's what's facing your people and mine. So you make sure you keep yourself available!"

"Tell me what you know."

"When I have to."

Boaz shook his head resolutely but felt his determination waver. "On second thought, Osman, I don't want to know. Once I complete this mission, I'm my own man. I retire."

Osman shook his head bleakly, then walked off.

"Tawfiq Tal. Who was Tawfiq Tal?"

Idris Ali and Abdallah looked up. "Who?"

"This Osman Nusseibi you have been talking about. He was interrogating a man called Tawfiq Tal."

Idris Ali stared deep into Abu Ismail's eyes. They had been cloudy throughout supper. Now they were clearer. "When?"

"I cannot remember. Long ago—in Jordan."

Idris Ali clasped Abu Ismail's hand. "Why didn't you tell us before?"

Abu Ismail searched their faces. "Who was Tawfiq Tal?"

"We don't know."

Abu Ismail gazed at them unseeing, pensive. "I saw him at our headquarters. In the sick bay. Swathed in bandages."

Idris Ali exchanged glances with Abdallah. "We'll check. Might be one of Nusseibi's agents."

Abu Ismail closed his eyes. "Yes."

Idris Ali released Abu Ismail's hand. "Al-Mahdi. It's been a day like no other. You have communed with Allah. You have subjected your frail limbs to heavy duty. You must rest."

"I do not hurt. I am not even tired."

Idris Ali offered him some pills and a glass of water. "Al-Mahadi. You must conserve your energy—for Islam's sake."

Abu Ismail swallowed the pills. "It is my memory. Worries me at times."

Osman's shadow, looming outside the tent, interrupted them. Idris Ali and Abdallah jumped up and flanked Abu Ismail.

Osman came in, noting the aggression in Idris Ali and Abdallah. He spoke humbly. "Rais! Great Chief . . ."

Abu Ismail turned away as if Osman were invisible.

Idris Ali stepped in between. "Who are you?"

"A friend. Izzat Jadid."

Abdallah moved forward to close ranks with Idris Ali.

Osman ignored them. "Abu Ismail. It is an auspicious night, and we ought to discuss auspicious matters. If we were to collect the devils' stones together. . . ."

Idris Ali spoke in a deadly murmur. "Abu Ismail is in meditation. Perhaps one of us can go with you. . . ."

Osman smiled politely. "I only deal with leaders. There'll be another occasion—no doubt." He left abruptly.

Idris Ali turned to Abdallah. "That was him. Osman Nusseibi. Let's go!"

Abdallah's eyes flashed. "I can take him on my own. You look after Al-Mahdi."

Idris Ali glanced at Abu Ismail, deep in dreams, and nodded reluctantly. "It must look like an accident."

WADI MUHASSAB, SAUDI ARABIA

There were two schools of thought concerning the collection of stones for the devils. The ascetics argued that any would serve; the luminaries urged that a pilgrim had to be selective, and pick only those stones which, by their distortion and ugliness, reflected man's hatred for evil spirits.

Boaz, siding with the ascetics, collected his stones quickly, then moved into the thick of the crowd to watch over Osman. Boaz had been tailing him ever since he had left Abu Ismail's tent with Abdallah in hot pursuit.

Osman had chosen to be fastidiously discriminating. He had discarded most of the stones found on the dry riverbed as either too small or too smooth or too ordinary, and had moved toward the slopes. Abdallah had followed him quite openly.

When Osman continued up the slope, Boaz scrambled higher up the hillside. Camouflaged within a rock cluster, he waited.

Some fifteen minutes later, Osman clambered up, breathing raucously. Abdallah, in pursuit, moved swiftly, barely heard. Boaz remained ultra-alert.

Suddenly, as Abdallah closed in, Osman disappeared. Boaz strained to hear Osman's breathing, but could not. He smiled. Osman had found the cave they had selected for this ploy from Jordanian ordnance maps dating from the Hashemite rule of the region. He did not need help. When he reappeared the next day, he would not be underestimated.

Boaz stalked Abdallah until the latter gave up the search. He could have killed the man easily. But that would have prompted Abu Ismail either to flee or to seek protection from King Feisal.

January 3, 1974

MUZDALIFA, SAUDI ARABIA

Osman returned to Muzdalifa and Sheikh Latif's group moments before the requisite standing at the Mashhad. Boaz had already regained the overseas imams' enclosure. The pilgrims were in a state of hyperexcitement. It was *yaum al-nahr*, the Day of Slaughter.

After the standing and the morning prayers, the multitude set out for Mina for the climax of the pilgrimage.

As soon as they left Muzdalifa, Abu Ismail and Abdallah took up position next to Sheikh Latif, at the front of the group.

Idris Ali dropped back and sidled up to Osman. "Abu Ismail tells me you want an alliance. Why?"

"I told him my reasons."

"Tell them to me. I screen all potential recruits."

Osman gave him a sideways glance. "You won't screen me."

"Your confidence deceives you."

Osman chuckled. "Whether you like it or not, I mean to get him."

"You'll need to kill me first."

"That's a condition I can meet."

"How? By running away . . .? Hiding?"

"You should see my chest. Full of scars. I shall be facing you —rest assured."

"Look at my mizuda."

Osman glanced at Idris Ali's cotton pouch and noted the sharp point of a stiletto knife. "I see it."

"We won't always be on sanctified ground."

"No."

"They must have been scraping the sewers—those who sent you."

Osman shook his head contemptuously. "You're still reading me wrong. I take orders from nobody. I want Abu Ismail. And I'll have him."

Idris Ali twitched and clutched his bag. Osman grabbed his hand, squeezed hard until Idris Ali grimaced. He beamed a smile and turned on his heel, leaving Idris Ali taut with fury.

Not far behind, Boaz drew nearer to Shiekh Latif's group. He had been watching Osman and Idris Ali. Osman had undoubtedly pushed the WOJ trio on the defensive. And panic lurked there.

MINA, SAUDI ARABIA

They reached Mina at midmorning and joined the long line that led to *Djamrat al Aqaba*, "The Great Devil." This structure, a thick, white pillar enclosed by a low circular wall, had been erected on the spot where the Devil, in the form of a benign old man, had intercepted Ismail and had urged the boy to flee and save himself from his father's knife. Ismail had driven the Devil away by casting seven stones, and it was incumbent on the pilgrim to emulate the Patriarch by stoning the pillar.

They had to wait in line for an hour. Throughout that time, Idris Ali and Abdallah, monitoring Osman's movements, flanked Abu Ismail tightly. Conversely, Abu Ismail, suffused by elation, seemed indifferent to the threat of death.

Osman remained alert, but ecstatic. The *rami*, the stoning of the Great Devil, was a duty he was determined to perform zealously. He would miss the rites scheduled for the next two days when two other pillars, the Middle One and the Little One, exemplifying the Devil's second and third attempts to tempt Ismail, were also to be stoned.

Thus when their turn came to stone the Great Devil, only Osman scaled the fervor demanded of the occasion. He rushed forward, pushing people out of the way. He bellowed seven times with unbridled fury; after each proclamation, he cast a stone. "In the Name of Allah, the Compassionate, the Merciful! Allah is Mighty!"

Then, having had the satisfaction of seeing Idris Ali and Abdallah curl like porcupines, he flashed them a beatific smile. The latter performed the stoning meekly, then hastened Abu Ismail away, almost brushing Boaz as they passed.

✗

The completion of the *rami* inaugurated *'Id al-Adha*, the Festival of the Great Sacrifice.

The pilgrims poured forth onto the plains of Mina. Now they could solicit Allah's boundless mercy by commemorating Ibrahim's willingness to sacrifice his son, Ismail; now they could slaughter their own ram in the thicket.

Men and women declaimed their presence, wept unashamedly, ululated, rubbed their holy garments on the sacred soil and held them up for the heavens to see. The rush lacked only the indiscriminate rifle fire with which pilgrims, in pre-Saudi days, used to express their euphoria. The prohibition of this last practice —indeed, the prohibition against any arms—had arisen from the fact that such demonstrations had resulted in fatal accidents, often contrived to seal blood feuds.

And the plains of Mina engulfed them.

Flocks of sheep and goats, herds of camels and horned cattle brought in by livestock merchants since early morning and lying tethered as far as the eye could see, counterpointed the chants of the Faithful with woeful bleating.

Sacrificers converged with their animals toward a smooth rock, the Altar, which still bore the fire of Ibrahim's touch.

There, by the newly dug drainage troughs, *hallal* slayers stood ready to advise the sacrificers on the ritual laws of slaughter or to offer their services to those too fainthearted to perform the rite. There the Faithful ascended in full passion. Joyous shrieks detonated the air; the earth reverberated with the hum of the trucks and refrigerated transports, contracted by the Red Crescent to load up the carcasses. The offerings would be distributed among the poor as *sadaga*, fulfilling Allah's command that proscribed the pilgrim from consuming more than a third of his sacrifice.

As if to provide a boundary for this awesome canvas, gaudy booths of traders, fortune-tellers, prostitutes, scribes, jugglers, fakirs, bards and barbers laced the plains with a riot of color. For these camp followers, business would be brisk. The implementation of the Great Sacrifice would launch *Ayyam al-Tashriq*, the Days of Drying the Flesh, when the pilgrimage would be celebrated with festivities. Those pilgrims who had performed the rites at the Kaaba would revert to the state of secularity, remove their ihram, wash, shave, cut hair, pare nails and resume secular clothes. They would recommence normal life, but to savor their triumph they would linger on hallowed ground to glimpse, through earthly pleasures, all that awaited them in the hereafter. For as hajjis, safeguarded even from future sins, they would be destined for Paradise.

✗

Sheikh Latif proved his all-embracing qualities as mutawwif by guiding his group swiftly through the pandemonium to the stall of a respectable shepherd with whom he had dealt for years. Thus the group purchased their sacrificial animals without the tedium of bargaining, and felt assured that the animals were without defect and of the right age.

Abu Ismail bought a camel as expected of a leader. Though the camel, because of its value, would have served as many as seven supplicants, Idris Ali and Abdallah chose to make propitiation individually and purchased a goat apiece. Osman procured four sheep, three to be sacrificed by proxy on behalf of his wife and daughters. Sheikh Latif, as befitted a prince, also acquired a camel, then led the drive to the Altar.

Boaz, now maintaining a distance of some twenty meters, bought a sheep from the same shepherd and drove it in the wake of Sheikh Latif's group.

✗

The Altar, Osman saw, was the Palm of Allah—or, if conceivable, the Womb. There, suffused with dust, blood, tears and clamor, the Faithful died and simultaneously experienced rebirth. There, in a new universe, the soul drank life-force, the body levitated, the mind atomized to gather Allah's infinite requirements, and the spirit stood immune to The Doubter.

And there, Osman knew, Idris Ali and Abdallah would consider Abu Ismail most vulnerable. The exigencies of the ritual, the emotional impact of assuming the mantle of Ibrahim and of propitiating personally to Allah, was such that for a large number of pilgrims the moment was hazardous. Many who sacrificed their animals personally suffered injury either by mishandling the knife in exultation or by fainting at the sight of spurting blood. Some simply died of intense excitation. Under such circumstances, a bold assassin would have promising options.

Consequently, to keep the WOJ trio under pressure, Osman chose to have his offerings slaughtered by one of the ritual butchers. That put him at the end of the group's line. He hovered there while Abu Ismail, Idris Ali and Abdallah slew their animals.

Abu Ismail performed the rite as if born to it. He shouted the prescribed invocations in a rapture. Then he laid down his camel expertly on the blood-soaked, gelatinous surface, drew its head round to its flank and cut the jugular vein at the point where the neck met the body—seemingly in one languid but precise movement. He received hearty approval from the crowd.

By contrast, Idris Ali, anxious at leaving Abu Ismail protected only by Abdallah, declaimed the invocation at speed, then slew his goat quickly and ferociously, cutting, as prescribed, immediately behind the jawbone, but heavily. He, too, drew approval from the crowd; flamboyance was as acceptable as finesse.

But Abdallah, daunted by Osman's presence, faltered in his invocations, nearly rendering the sacrifice carrion; then, trying to make amends, he slaughtered hesitantly, almost mutilating the goat. The crowd, attributing his clumsiness to the awesomeness of the occasion, sympathized and refrained from berating him.

When his turn came, Osman moved as if he were the reincarnation of the patriarch Ibrahim. He faced the crowd, his feet solidly planted in the pools of blood, his chest encompassing the girth of the Altar.

"I delegate the slaying of my sacrifice to my worthy brother, the lawful slaughterer of animals. For such is my love of Allah that I must forgo this, the greatest privilege bestowed on man, and spare unnecessary suffering to my offerings—Allah's creatures themselves. Few men in my exalted state could be sure of dealing a clean cut."

Then, as the multitude endorsed his sentiments, he took his place next to the butcher to officiate. With a resounding voice he invoked the *Tasmiya:* "In the Name of Allah, The Compassionate, The Merciful . . ." He continued with the Blessing on the Prophet. As the butcher prepared to slay, he turned piously toward Mecca and repeated thrice the *Takbir.* Finally, in abject humility, his hoarse voice barely audible, he requested Allah to accept the sacrifices on behalf of himself and his family, and apportioned two-thirds of the carcasses to the poor.

When the animals were slain, he regained his place. Trembling, he faced the WOJ trio. He had concluded the pilgrimage. And the enemy stood before him. He shouted frenziedly into their faces: "Now strike the hour of doom for Allah's enemies."

His exuberance drew the crowd's applause. Osman imagined he saw Abu Ismail shrink into a clot of blood between the groping figures of Idris Ali and Abdallah, then float down the drainage trough into a sea of hellfire.

Behind them, Boaz offered his sacrifice. He found cutting the throat of a helpless animal incomparably more repulsive than killing a man.

AL-TARIQ AL-ARAFAT, SAUDI ARABIA

The pilgrims took the road back to Mount Arafat to assemble for prayers and sermons at the place of the Prophet's last discourse. It had been announced that a caucus of alims would divulge their wisdom; and that King Feisal would deliver an important speech.

Past Muzdalifa they marched, shouting the immortal dialogue between the Messenger of Allah and the Faithful.

" *'What day is this?'* "
" *'The day of sacrifice!'* "
" *'What place is this?'* "
" *'The holy place!'* "

" 'What month is this?' "
" 'The holy month!' "
" 'O Allah, be my witness.' "

❃

The moment Sheikh Latif's group crossed Muzdalifa's boundary pillars into the free territory, Osman approached the WOJ trio. Briefly he scrutinized Idris Ali and Abdallah, then glaring at Abu Ismail, he snapped finger to mouth, the sign of revenge. A moment later, he pitched into the crowd and disappeared in an ocean of faces.

Abdallah turned to Idris Ali. "What's he up to? Ambush?"

"Maybe. We mustn't lose him, Abdallah. After him!"

Abdallah waded into the crowd.

Behind them, Boaz reduced the distance to ten meters.

Osman found the going easy. The crowd, continuously declaiming, were spellbound by the heavy cadence of the sublime language. They cared little for a hajji who pushed past them.

Osman and Boaz had been confident that Osman's flight would draw at least one of Abu Ismail's bodyguards. The WOJ trio, far from judging the ploy as pathetically obvious. would consider it as a wily move to keep them in place while Osman prepared his attack.

Osman, plotting his course meticulously, weaved in and out of the crowd, now showing himself to Abdallah, now disappearing, now looming behind, now ahead. It was a tricky operation and, executed in a thick forest of entranced pilgrims, it elicited all his skills. He kept the hunt going for some twenty minutes. By the end, he had lured Abdallah to the outer periphery of the pilgrim masses. At a point where the ancient volcanic desolation warped into a maze of huge boulders, he detached himself from the crowd and melted into the wilderness.

Abdallah followed.

Keeping out of sight, Osman scampered from boulder to boulder. Satisfied that Abdallah was well entrenched in the wasteland and moving cautiously for fear of ambush, he circumvented the rocks, regained the road and dived back into the crowd.

He backtracked toward Abu Ismail to deal with Idris Ali.

As he approached them, he saw that Idris Ali, disquieted by Abdallah's prolonged absence, was rigid with tension.

He paused a moment. The next time he saw Abu Ismail the man would be dead.

He shot forward and confronted the WOJ leader and his chief of staff like an apparition.

Idris Ali, bristling, brought Abu Ismail to a halt.

Pilgrims pushed past, some urging them to move on.

Idris Ali scanned the crowd in search of Abdallah. Osman mocked him with a mournful look. Idris Ali reacted with disbelief. Osman chortled, shrugged, then swiftly changed his expression to menace. Idris Ali, incensed, lunged forward.

Abu Ismail held him. "Where are you going?"

Idris Ali hissed, almost disrespectfully. "Stay here—you'll be all right!" He extricated himself from his leader's grip and rushed toward Osman.

Osman took to his heels again.

Boaz waited until Osman and Idris Ali had vanished into the crowd, then moved forward. Carefully handling the hypodermic syringe concealed in his mizuda, he fixed the capped needle and disconnected the tiny clamps that had held the plunger in place.

He drew alongside Abu Ismail. For some moments he stared at the man, gazing at his drugged eyes and wondering how such a pitiful body could aspire to kill indiscriminately. He dismissed the thought. Hitler had been such a creature. He uncapped the needle and grabbed Abu Ismail's hand. "Rais! Rais! Rais!"

Abu Ismail stared at him with glazed eyes.

Boaz abandoned himself to the blinding light that navigated his mind through conflict and stress. His hand, inside the mizuda, jabbed the needle into Abu Ismail's wrist and injected intramuscularly 500 units of concentrated insulin. During those few seconds, his voice, reverberating like an alien sound, begged Abu Ismail to recruit him. Then, as he pulled the needle out, he focused again.

Abu Ismail was still looking at him; in his enraptured state, he had not even felt the needle. "Are you a warrior?"

"Yes, Rais . . ."

"Then go—to combat."

Boaz kept close to him. The drug required twenty minutes to take effect. After that, not even a massive dose of glucose would help. Another ten minutes . . . Death. "I shall walk by your side, Rais!"

"There is no need."

"I must prove my worth. You're in danger, Rais."

Abu Ismail stiffened. "How do you know?"

"Your men—they've deserted you. But I shall not. I worship you. You are vulnerable. Let me walk by your side."

Abu Ismail wavered, looked anxiously toward Sheikh Latif.

Boaz grabbed his hand and kissed it. "He can't help you. I can. Trust me."

Abu Ismail relaxed. "Tell me—who are you?"

"Your slave, Rais."

Abu Ismail nodded, accepting the homage.

They walked in silence for some ten minutes. Abu Ismail started to falter. Boaz gauged the sweat—profuse, induced partly by the heat, partly by the insulin.

"Warrior—I feel unwell."

"The heat, Rais."

"How awful everything is . . . The world. The Jew. The Arab."

"Yes, Rais."

"I had a wife . . . children . . ."

Confusion had set in. The insulin had started to act. Soon there would be disorientation.

"But then violence . . . I had the call . . . violence, warrior— organized, indoctrinated. That's what teaches the masses truth. . . ."

"A cleansing force, Rais. Liberates us from despair. From in- action. Makes us proud—fearless."

"You know . . ."

"Your *War Rule*, Rais. I've read it."

"What *War Rule?*"

Boaz scrutinized him. Disorientation. "Our most sacred tract —after the Koran."

"Oh, yes . . . I forgot. . . ."

"The day of sacrifice, Rais. It's a wonder we can remember our own names. . . ."

"Yes . . . I remember Tawfiq Tal, though. . . . Do you know Tawfiq Tal?"

"Who is he, Rais?"

"A true warrior . . . Dead now . . . He haunts me. . . ."

"Warriors must die, Rais. There is no need to be haunted by them."

"There is much I want to say . . . only I cannot stir my thoughts. . . ." Abu Ismail's limbs began to lose coordination. "I feel . . . I am not myself. . . ."

"Just walk, Rais . . ."

"Yes. . . ."

They walked for another few minutes. Boaz, heart thumping, waited for the next phase: loss of consciousness.

Suddenly, Abu Ismail grabbed his arm. "Tawfiq Tal . . . You must know Tawfiq Tal! Never mourned . . . the poor bastard . . ."

Abu Ismail collapsed, short of breath, his face distorted with pain.

Boaz yelped. "Help here! Help here!"

Abu Ismail convulsed briefly, then passed out.

Sheikh Latif was the first to rush over.

Boaz met him with a tearful face. "He collapsed. . . . Look after him. I'll find a doctor."

Sheikh Latif bent over Abu Ismail, uncertain what to do. More pilgrims converged.

Boaz slipped away.

✗

From a distance, Idris Ali, still in pursuit of Osman, noticed the commotion. He plowed back through the crowd toward his commander.

Osman lingered long enough to watch Idris Ali and Sheikh Latif carry Abu Ismail's body to the roadside. There a distraught Abdallah joined them. Idris Ali sought the Royal Guards and asked for an ambulance. When it came, the doctor in charge declared Abu Ismail dead.

MOUNT ARAFAT, SAUDI ARABIA

It was late afternoon. The plains of Arafat teemed with hajjis. They had imbibed the alims' wise sermons. Now it was the turn of the politicians. King Feisal stood at the rostrum. Numerous loudspeakers conveyed his vision to the Muslim world.

In the forefront of the mass, separated from the king by a large company of Royal Guards, Boaz stood and listened.

"The Zionists are the enemies of Allah! They have no connection with Al-Quds. Therefore they must be driven out!"

The words were familiar, even welcome. Perhaps, in the eyes of those who could differentiate between truth and lie, they would justify what he was about to do.

For a moment, he thought of Osman. A true friendship. Like Theban soldiers of antiquity. A mighty unit of two. He felt proud to have conducted himself honorably.

He surveyed the Royal Guards. Given the element of surprise he should be able to carve his way through to the king. There he would keep the guards at bay by holding the king in a stranglehold. He would need barely a minute—time enough to declare his message. Then a sharp jerk to break the fragile royal neck. And seconds later, his own death at the hands of the Royal Guards.

It would be a personal gesture. He owed no debts—neither to the State of Israel nor to any man.

Two zealots, a monarch and a commoner, would prove in death the equality of man, of race, of faith—on holy ground, before the Single God's eyes. And perhaps another voice, stronger than his own, would tell the world that power is evil, that even the Lord prays He should be spared using it.

As King Feisal paused and the multitude burst into applause, Boaz lunged forward.

At that very instant, Osman struck Boaz down with a swift blow. The hajjis who saw Boaz fall thought he had been overcome by the heat. Osman, radiating a philanthropic air, dragged Boaz away.

Book Two

PART VI

If a Falcon Hunts Mice He Is Worthless.

Arab proverb

January 4, 1974

DJIBOUTI, T.F.A.I.

Madame Expo—the most liquid woman Montblanc had ever known—lay rippling on velvet cushions. She always smiled; and always looked a man in the crotch. Her self-christened name had been inspired by the 1958 Brussels World Fair that she had visited with the French roué who had transformed her from an Issa beauty into a magnificent odalisque.

She wafted kisses at his crotch. "You are a good man, Montblanc. I loves you." She regrouped her mountainous breasts; her cyclopean vagina, clean-shaven, winked lasciviously. "Is true. You make much investigation for my friend Giovanni Varchi."

Montblanc dropped his eyes in commiseration for the Italian adventurer who had died in Aden soon after the South Yemenis had confiscated his boat, the *Succubus*. He had had dealings with the man. There had been mutual respect, and great discretion from Varchi when some of the enterprises had obviously been CIA business. Schoenberg, still troubled by the ramifications of the WOJ–ELF connection, was anxious to find out why the South Yemenis had impounded the *Succubus*, then sold it to Musaddiq Hamdi, ELF's Aden-based officer, and what the ELF, either conjointly with WOJ or as its agent, intended to do with the boat, having taken great pains to dispose of Varchi.

"I misses him, Montblanc. Always he would sit there. And admire maybe an hour my Klondike. He call it Klondike because he quarry for gold very deep. Then he lie down on Madame Expo.

184

And he stay for hours. Doing boom-boom with him like having
mad love in dreams. As God intended." Madame Expo slowly
dabbed the tears on her smiling face, then sprayed herself with
Old Spice, her latest acquisition from a grateful client. "You want
information, Montblanc?"

"Isn't that why you called me?"

"Also to see you. Or I thinks you one man who want only
information from me."

Montblanc smiled, his eyes riveted on the cascading folds of
her pelvis. "Information I can handle."

"Don't be that man Freud I hears all the time. Undress. I
whispers happenings."

"Madame Expo—I need my wits."

"Undress. Madame Expo has reputation. No man stay here
with clothes."

Montblanc undressed.

His erection increased her smiles. "You think wits you will have
carrying that?" She shook flesh-cascading arms. "Come to love
queen, Montblanc."

He went to her. She gurgled, stroked his penis with shower-
light fingers, then immersed it in her mouth. Her tongue streamed
serenades; he cavorted like a dolphin. She stopped pertly. Montblanc watched her legs part. The cleft summoning him was a la-
goon.

"First I baptize you."

His mouth was sucked in. His face inundated. He drank greedily.

She pulled him up, submerged his head within her breasts, and
chortled. "Now, inside Madame Expo. So she can treasure you."
She whirled her velvet legs and engulfed him. "Don't think what
happen down there. It happen in good time. When you no expect
it."

"I like expecting it."

"Surprise is better. Madame Expo surprise the best. I gives
guarantee. Now we talk."

Montblanc felt himself rolling. "Yes, Madame."

"You know since Varchi's death I keep lips to ground. I has
international clientele. Captains. Industrialists. Merchants.
Fighters . . . So. Yesterday. I has old lover. He sell foodstuff. I
asks: Anything not standing like good cock?"

Montblanc, drifting with her undercurrents, barely heard her.

She bit his ear. "Listen. Yes—he say. One man buy enough
rice for an army. But he buy bit here, bit there. Expensive when
there is wholesale."

Montblanc tried to take in the information. Wondrous waves buffeted him.

"And more strange: this rice is for smuggling to Ethiopia. By caravan. Very secret."

Montblanc erupted.

Madame Expo, gyrating with abandoned shrieks, collected his torrent, patting him as if he were a baby suffering from gas. "Naughty boy, Montblanc. You makes us joy quickly. You hear what I says?"

Montblanc, breathless, cast his lips on a rocklike nipple. "Who's the man doing the buying?"

"Yusuf the Afar. You knows him?"

"Yeah. Snake dressed up as man. Just rice—nothing else?"

"No. It puzzle my merchant, too. Ethiopian eat teff. Rice luxury—normal only for Italians and Arabs. I also asks about Varchi. My merchant—he hear that assassin who have Varchi's boat, Hamdi—preparing to sail. I puzzles maybe rice for Hamdi?"

Montblanc pulled himself up. "Could be. That's good information."

Madame Expo stretched languidly. "You no go yet. Kiss belly button. And we starts again. This time we eats each other slowly —true feast. Is included in price."

Montblanc did not have time to respond. Her legs, locking around his waist, pulled him down. He plunged his lips into her belly.

January 5, 1974

BEERSHEBA, ISRAEL

The air in the war room hung heavy with perspiration, cigarette smoke and the collective stale breaths of people working around the clock. The men milled about with wide grins, the women smiled like grandmothers at weddings. The Memouneh, entering, was reminded of other war rooms at other times when Israel had achieved miracles.

Kidan, wearing arrogance like a medal, shouted from the gallery above the Table. "We've done it, Zamora. Abu Ismail's dead. Confirmed—by electronic eavesdropping."

The Menouneh ran up to the gallery. "When?"

"I think as planned—January third. But the signals are yesterday's—picked up by the Johannesburg-bound El-Al. We've sifted them through the computer. Extraordinary intelligence communications from three centers: Mecca, Riyadh, Jidda. Makes good listening."

The Memouneh grabbed a set of earphones and punched the replay button on a console.

There were eighty-three conversations between various Saudi Al-Moukhabarat operators concerning Abu Ismail. Conversations 1–13 referred to the sudden death by heart attack of a prominent Arab leader on the road to Mount Arafat. Conversation 14 reported unofficially that the dead leader was Abu Ismail. Conversations 15–31 continued referring to Abu Ismail by name and urged all parties concerned to establish positive identification; three conversations in that batch, 22, 27 and 29, inquired whether foul play was suspected. Conversations 32–35 were strict directives from the chief of the Saudi Al-Moukhabarat that all material should be classified top secret and that news of the death should be censored until further notice. Conversations 36–78 reported eyewitness accounts of Abu Ismail's sudden collapse. Conversations 79–82 featured the Al-Moukhabarat chief again, issuing further directives that communications should thereafter be conducted in writing as a countermeasure against eavesdropping. The last recording refused permission for an autopsy.

The Memouneh laid aside the earphones pensively. "No mention of Boaz. That's hopeful."

Kidan, eager to wear the laurels, drew up a chair. "Conclusive, if you ask me."

"These were recorded yesterday, you say. Anything since?"

"No. They're still maintaining silence."

"Why should they?"

"Like they said. To stop eavesdropping."

"By whom?"

"Russians. Iranians. The so-called revolutionary Arab states. Us. The Americans, Everybody's a potential enemy to the Saudis."

"So is Abu Ismail. His messianic movement threatens them. Why should they care?"

"The Arab mind. Forever devious."

"Clichés, Kidan."

Kidan fidgeted. "For God's sake, Zamora. They've named the victim. They suspect foul play. What more do you want?"

The Memouneh nodded several times, distractedly. "Keep monitoring. If Abu Ismail is really dead the lines will get hot again. There'll be much buck-passing. Then we'll know for sure. And news of Boaz—the merest whiff—I want it. If he doesn't come back—we'll have no cause for celebration."

Kidan waited for the Memouneh to leave, then hissed. "Fuck Boaz!"

January 6, 1974

GODA MOUNTAINS, T.F.A.I.

The hills were strewn with the fossilized remains of a prehistoric forest. In the surrounding gulleys, a number of marabout shrines, tombs of holy men, offered hints of the supernatural. Somewhere a spring gurgled, reminding Corporal Weber of the thaw in his native Bernese Oberland.

He stretched and felt pain. His hands and feet were still tied to stakes. Semiconsciousness that had provided relief dispersed; panic returned. He twisted his head toward his men. Robic, Druon, Cuccelli lay tethered alongside, unconscious, faces blistering under the blazing sky.

He twisted in the other direction. Three Afars were sitting on their haunches, staring vacantly into the distance. The fourth, Yusuf, with his distinctive frizzled hair dyed ginger with henna, was upright and staring at the sun.

Fear tore through Weber's genitals. Yusuf, though honed by a *lycée* education, was the most ferocious Afar chieftain for generations. When he had taken a third wife, he had presented his bride, as traditional dowry, a dozen severed genitals of Issa warriors when a pair would have sufficed.

Weber searched for saliva that did not taste of death. "Yusuf— if I don't report to HQ soon, there'll be a full alert."

Yusuf turned languidly, his voice friendly. "I'm counting on that, Corporal. I want them to find you."

Weber screeched, "They'll come in helicopters. Kill you—and your men."

Yusuf chuckled. "First, they will have to catch me. Second, they will have no reason: your deaths will look like a tragic misadventure. Third, they would not dare touch me. Fourth, those who have sent you will learn the lesson. I, Yusuf, go where I please, do what I please. They try to stop me—more French blood."

Weber started weeping; his tears, barely liquid, dried as specks of salt. He cursed himself for letting Lieutenant Schoenberg talk him into intercepting Yusuf. The Afar had been leading an unusually big caravan—fifty camels secreted out from the outskirts of Djibouti and deviating from the desert routes right up to the Ethiopian border, near Mount Moussa Ali, where Weber had finally caught up with him.

And the felony? Smuggling ten tons of rice for someone in Assab, Ethiopia. Nothing else. Weber and his men had checked every fifty-kilo sack. Hardly the sort of contraband to alarm Military Intelligence. Nobody had dared touch Yusuf on the countless arms-smuggling runs to the ELF. Now . . . for ten tons of rice . . .

A shadow crossed Weber's eyes. He focused on Yusuf, standing over him. He felt enraged. He could have killed Yusuf: ordered his patrol to fire when Yusuf had resisted arrest. Instead he had hesitated and found himself facing the Afar guns.

Yusuf was pointing at his shadow. "It's past two. The sun will be hitting the bees' nests. They'll be maddened in minutes. . . ." He signaled to his men. They sprang up and cut loose Robic, Druon and Cuccelli.

Hope surged in Weber. "You're letting us go?"

Yusuf smiled and produced a bottle and a sponge. He saturated the sponge with the liquid from the bottle and knelt beside Weber.

Weber smelled a heavy perfume. "What's that?"

Yusuf started rubbing Weber's bare arms and legs with the sponge. "Rosewater. The bees here are spoiled. They feed on rare flowers. They have to be seduced. They'll love rosewater. I do."

Weber saw, at the extremity of his vision, that Yusuf's men had also sponged down Robic, Druon and Cuccelli, and were in the process of putting on protective clothes. Then he understood. The Afar slow death.

He screamed and struggled with his bonds as Yusuf squeezed the sponge over his hair. He heard a distant buzzing. To his surprise he remained lucid. "They'll get you, too, Yusuf! You're also smeared with rosewater!"

The buzzing became a drone. Weber suddenly felt free. Yusuf had cut his bonds. He sprang up. Yusuf, standing at a safe distance, grinned, then pointed at the primitive flag of faded cotton which marked a marabout grave. "I shall be there. The bees respect that tomb. The marabout used to talk to them. They never trespass."

Weber stared witlessly. The buzzing reached a terrifying pitch. Weber caught sight of a dark cloud in the distance. He grasped Yusuf's words and ran to the marabout tomb.

Reality distorted. Bees, larger than he had ever seen, billowed in an ever-expanding tornado. They converged in straight lines from every direction, somehow avoiding collision, and dived at the insentient Robic, Druon and Cuccelli. They burrowed briefly on their bodies, then, upon a mysterious signal, flew off to vacate space for other bees and to realign for another run.

Through it all, Yusuf sauntered, joking with his masked men, his bare face teeming with bees.

Weber, hypnotized, registered Yusuf's approach only when he was upon him. A scream rose in his throat. For a split second he saw Yusuf standing by his side, free of the bees that had infested him. The next moment, the bees looped and swarmed on Weber.

Weber collapsed, screaming. The drone enveloped him. Far away he heard Yusuf's amiable voice. "I forgot to mention, Corporal. Though the bees respect this tomb, they hate intruders. All except me. You see, I am their friend. I buried the marabout."

Weber spent his last seconds trying to tear the hundreds of bees, dead or dying, out of his hair and eyes. Then, as his body, ravaged by toxin, began to distend, he succumbed to shock and died.

January 7, 1974

ADEN, PEOPLE'S DEMOCRATIC REPUBLIC OF YEMEN

The submarine *Khanjar*, "Dagger," scrubbed clean and adorned with Libyan and PDRY flags, lay moored at Military Pier. She had sailed into Aden a few days before to the announcement that she had been seconded to the PDRY navy as Libya's gesture of solidarity with revolutionary brother states. In official celebration of this event, she had her hatches open to the diplomatic corps.

Her commander, elaborating on his new commission, wished to make clear on behalf of Colonel Qaddafi that the *Khanjar*'s presence at the mouth of the Red Sea should serve as a warning to French, American and British imperialists—all Zionist henchmen—that Islam's sword was unsheathed.

Getachew Iyessous, who had wormed himself into the Ethiopian delegation, reviewed the submarine's capabilities. Not exceptional. Speed: 15 knots surfaced, 18 knots dived, respectively, 1½ and 2 knots faster than the specifications of her class. Standard navigational, radar and sonar systems. Twelve torpedo tubes—eight bow, four stern—and a 20mm Oerlikon cannon mounted on the deck. Big deal, as Jameson had summed up after studying reports from the Defense Intelligence Agency, which had evaluated the *Khanjar* during her passage to Aden.

The *Khanjar*'s moderate capabilities did not allay Getachew's apprehensions. In an area heavily monitored by the superpowers, she would become another statistic in the arms buildup and, to all intents and purposes, ignored. Seen from another perspective, she would achieve the anonymity requisite for clandestine operations. Moreover, before his departure for Aden, Sanbat had briefed him on a routine Mossad report filed in November, when the *Khanjar* had left Tripoli, stating that her crew might include WOJ commandos selected for naval warfare training. Consequently, Getachew had paid special attention to the men. Captain and company had not only betrayed rudimentary proficiency indicating a crash course in seafaring but they had also displayed what Getachew's air fraternity called earth-minds: senses that lacked the sweep which pilots and sailors extracted from their elements. He was convinced they were WOJ commandos.

That assessment had dovetailed with a further disturbing factor. Another objective of his visit had been the evaluation of the ELF cell in Aden, and the extent of its reported links with WOJ. He had managed to take an excursion around the peninsula to survey the villa at Cape Ras Marshaq where Musaddiq Hamdi, ELF's Yemen-based officer, was headquartered and where he kept the motor yacht *Succubus* berthed.

The villa had appeared deserted, though rubble of building material had corroborated reports that it had been renovated to accommodate a large number of people.

Nor had he caught sight of the *Succubus*. The boat's absence had correlated with the mystery of Yusuf the Afar's rice caravan that had cost the lives of a French Legionnaire patrol detailed by Schoenberg. Getachew could now assume that the rice was intended for WOJ and that with the *Khanjar*'s arrival, Operation Dragons had moved into the Horn of Africa.

January 8, 1974

TRIPOLI, LIBYA

The gardens of the WOJ villa, stretching over seven acres, had been landscaped in the eighteenth century by the Karamanli dynasty in the exotic spirit of the Ottoman Empire's Tulip era.

Abu Ismail favored the mock oasis situated in the center of the grand design. There, in the pure sand, clear pool and languid date palms, the mystic could understand why the Jew's boastful God and the frail Christian Trinity were mirages, and why the Faithful had taken many more centuries to discover the true Lord of the Universe. Allah was a hidden oasis; one had to journey through the wilderness almost forever before He could be found.

He pivoted on his cushions until comfortable. The pain in his limbs had dispersed. It confirmed, as he had often suspected, that the arthritis was simply a manifestation of his doubts. He opened his eyes.

Al-Munafiq, The Doubter, Phantom of Ash, was crawling in the sand in the shape of an insect. *"You are lanced with profanity, Abu Ismail. You have abjured the hajj and assumed falsely the title hajji."*

"I saved myself for Allah's glory."

"There can be no justification."

"Al-Mahdi, until secure on his throne, must assume he is always under threat. The doctrine of taqiya grants him dispensation from religious duties."

"Doctrines are men's work. Forged for their convenience."

"But always through Allah's guidance. The truth was revealed to me on the summit of Mount Nebo. And again—last night."

The Doubter began to retreat as one who bled from a wound.

Abu Ismail bludgeoned him with his fresh revelation. "I transfigured as a single green lily in a miasmic swamp where men wallowed in their excrement. A glorious bird, part peacock, part eagle, plucked me and carried me to the violet clouds above Islam's pillars. First the angels built me a throne, declaiming that Mecca, the ancient abode of pagan gods, was like the alchemist's gold: painted stone. A terrible truth, Al-Munafiq, but the truth. Mecca's status as Islam's holiest city was forced upon Mohammed until such time as Al-Quds, the place of assembly for the Final Judgment and Resurrection, could be reclaimed."

The Doubter retreated farther.

Abu Ismail thundered so that it could hear him. "That is not all. As I sat on the throne, the archangel Jibril came to stud me with precious stones. He assured me my renunciation of the hajj, my assumption of the title hajji were for the greater good of the Faithful."

The Doubter buried its head in the sand.

"There is more still. After Jibril, the Prophet himself came to sit by my side. And he informed me that though he, Mohammed, had been obliged to perform the hajj, I, Al-Mahdi, being a Savior and an altogether different messenger of Allah, was exempt from the duty."

The Doubter burrowed into the sand and disappeared. Truth was the one force it could not challenge.

✗

Idris Ali, waiting for Abu Ismail to descend to earthly plains, faced his own demons. Not self-doubt. He had always known his full measure—and that had kept constant. But anguish and resignation. Because the very constancy that spared him from doubts had reached its earthly limit and could not leap beyond.

It was the Meccan episode that had brought the demons to the surface.

He could not be blamed for the death of Abu Ismail's double. How, with just Abdallah lending support, could he have thwarted a concerted attack? In any case, the double had been sent to perform the hajj simply to provide Abu Ismail and WOJ with an alibi for the AF 205 hijacking.

But Mecca had been humiliating. Osman Nusseibi had defiled him with defeat. The humiliation could have been prevented if Abu Ismail had not, insensitively, refused a larger escort on the irrelevant scruple that he did not wish to alarm the Saudis with a show of strength.

The hajj had also exposed the shallow roots of his strength. Instead of Allah's breath, which he had sought earnestly, he had found man's pathetic acceptance of the supernatural. This, despite the fact that under Abu Ismail's teaching he had learned to look upon the Faith as the elixir that made men indomitable—and the special few immortal.

Thus the Faith had proved to be vapor. Or, as he now had to accept, the Faith could not envelop him. Simply because he himself had lost his soul during those years when Russian indoctrination had irradiated his marrow.

What mitigated the anguish was his rationality. Marxism, it could be argued, was another faith. One which reduced the world's conflicts and aspirations to a single dimension; cut through Creation's basic duality of matter and spirit; wrenched history from the Deity to give it substance, movement, control and direction. In fact, a simpler ideology than Islam for the harnessing of mass frustration and alienation.

So in reality, nothing was lost. He could still exist as Abu Ismail's heir, still aspire to equal, even surpass, the WOJ leader. Clone immortality by the application of reason.

Yet he felt cheated. He envied Abu Ismail his transcendental plains, his constant struggles against doubt. For Abu Ismail had the courage to wage the greater jihad that was not fought against enemy hordes, but against the self. And that courage could not be grafted because it was the very ichor of the soul. How could a man be complete without it? And what weight did he have without a soul?

Abu Ismail opened his eyes and scrutinized Idris Ali.

"Have you been watching over me like the angel who guards the navel of the earth?"

"How else, Al-Mahdi?"

"Your face reflects a mind that has strayed."

Idris Ali forced a smile. Had Abu Ismail, from his cloud of revelation, glimpsed his soullessness? He colored his eyes with devotion. "Self-recrimination, Al-Mahdi. I am still enraged by Tawfiq Tal's martyrdom."

"A thought for you, my son. Islam's sword is like the surgeon's blade. It heals by cutting out that which must die."

Idris Ali nodded, wondering whether the words carried a hidden threat. "I shall be guided by it."

"That is my expectation."

Idris Ali kissed Abu Ismail's hands. "Your orders for the day, Al-Mahdi?"

Abu Ismail signaled Nazmi, who had stood hawklike behind Idris Ali throughout the afternoon, to serve refreshments. "Contact your Russian. Inform him we have fulfilled our part of the agreement."

"Yes, Al-Mahdi."

"Commence operations at the base."

"Yes, Al-Mahdi."

"Announce to the world that we have returned from the hajj. Deny any culpability in the Air France hijacking. Label the accusations directed at us as Zionist dust thrown at the eyes of justice-loving peoples. Declare that having walked in the footsteps of the Prophet, our hands are as clean as the day our mothers bore us."

January 9, 1974

SHARM AL-SHEIKH, ISRAELI OCCUPIED SINAI

Despite the radio distortion, Gideon, Mossad's man in Amman, spoke with a lively voice. The Memouneh envied that. His own sounded tired. He had to stop dreaming about retirement.

"Absolute silence."

"Have you tried the direct line?"

"Nothing."

"His home?"

"Shuttered. The family's away. No one knows where. I even tried his secretary. She worships him . . . Silent as the tomb."

The Memouneh switched off the tape recorder. He knew the conversation by heart. He was listening for something to do. He moved to the window. It was a beautiful morning; the haze had lifted but the sand, blown from the desert, covered sea and sky with a grainy print.

Down at the docks, men worked and laughed, preparing berths for the long-range missile-boats scheduled to enter service in the Red Sea by the spring.

He looked out at the straits. The six Bartram coastal patrol boats had skirted round Tiran island and were breaking formation; four would deploy north into the Gulf of Aqaba; two would proceed east as far as the Saudi island of Umm Qusur. All six would scour allocated sectors until further notice. But they were merely insurance. In an emergency, Boaz would attempt to divert to the Saudi coast somewhere near Qadhima, eighty kilometers northwest of Mecca, then proceed north along the coast. The Memouneh did not expect him to have reached the Gulf as yet—not unless he had secured a plane. At best, he would be somewhere around Yanbu', the ancient port of Medina. That was where he had sent his main rescue force, five Dabur patrol boats.

He returned to the table. The ashtrays were full from the briefing session. He picked up a butt and lit it. His desk had still to be run. The trial of the Mossad hit team that had killed an Arab waiter in Norway, mistaking him for Black September's Ali Hassan Salamah, had started in Oslo. That, too, was an emergency: transcripts to be analyzed, recommendations made to the defense lawyers, suggestions formulated for the Foreign Ministry on how best to exert pressure on the Norwegians for minimum fuss and minimum sentences. But he could not concentrate.

As an act of faith, he was assuming Boaz was still alive. Amman's silence suggested that the Jordanians were covering up Osman's death. If so, could Boaz have survived? What of his Greek romanticism, his vision of martial perfection? As in the Theban army, structured in units of two; if one fell, the other, bereft, made certain he died too.

There was another possibility. Amman's silence could also indicate Osman had reneged and betrayed Boaz.

The telephone rang. Kidan's voice cackled. "There's been a press release—from Abu Ismail!"

"I heard."

"He can't be alive. . . . If he is . . . Then Boaz is . . ."

The Memouneh was surprised that Kidan could be overcome. "Presumed *missing*."

"That entails full alert. Search parties . . ."

"Already set up. Navy is deployed. Rescue helicopters standing by."

"That's what you've been up to? I wouldn't have bothered. He's dead. Must be—"

The Memouneh slammed the telephone down. Israel had the worst and the best in the world. The worst ran desks; the best died.

January 11, 1974

TAIF, SAUDI ARABIA

There shall flow in it rivers of unpolluted water, and rivers of milk forever fresh: rivers of delectable wine and rivers of clearest honey.

So the Koran described Paradise; and Taif, it was said, came nearest to the description. Osman could not contest it. The city, perched on the Meccan highlands, gleamed as if scrubbed by dew. Gardens echoed the ripples of pools, roses scented a man's breath.

He reverted to the reports. The first had been photocopied from the Saudi Al-Moukhabarat files; the second was a coded telex from his secretary in Amman.

The Saudi report related the events following Abu Ismail's collapse on the road to Mount Arafat. How Idris Ali and Abdallah had taken immediate charge and how, within minutes, they had refuted the attending doctor's pronouncement of his death and had forced the ambulance to proceed to Jidda instead of to a hospital. At Jidda, they had taken Abu Ismail to the house of WOJ's agent, Tahir Said. There, claiming that the WOJ leader was suffering from exhaustion, they had remained ensconced until the official end of the hajj. On that evening, under cover of darkness, they had driven the prostrate Abu Ismail straight to his private jet, bypassing immigration controls on King Feisal's dispensation. Idris Ali, the report concluded, had further prevailed on the king to suppress all inquiries on the premise that Abu Ismail was a symbol of hope for the Arabs and that the least doubt about his health would demoralize the Faithful in the holy war against the Jew.

The telex from Amman informed Osman that the fingerprints on Abu Ismail's tumbler, dispatched by him, had been positively identified as those of Tawfiq Tal, a Palestinian guerrilla, born in Nablus in 1930, taken prisoner during the civil war of September 1970, and exiled from Jordan in February 1971.

Osman pocketed the reports. Part of his mind preached that he should treat defeat in the same way as he would victory—as an illusion. Another part mocked him: only a fool could think he had understood the Divine Will. But surprisingly, his soul stood unscathed. The Prophet had said: die before your death. He had done so. The Prophet had also said: the holy warrior is the one who fights himself. He had done that, too—was still doing it.

He walked over to Zubair who stood humbly amid the rose-
bushes, admiring Allah's art. "It's time, Zubair. Please attend to
the travel arrangements."

Zubair's eyes shaded with gloom. "I'll be sad to see you go.
Everything's ready. It'll take you four days. A roundabout route—
but safe."

Zubair, Osman's man in Saudi Arabia, was peerless. It was he
who had whisked them away from Mount Arafat; he who had
delivered the Al-Moukhabarat report. Osman kissed him on both
cheeks, then moved into the house.

Zubair squatted by the roses and listened to the birds. He believed they alone knew the secret of the flower's beauty.

He felt he ought to run amok.

He could not move. The drugs induced lethargy. But where
was his fury?

"Boaz . . ."

He focused on Osman. Hated face: open, full of brotherly love,
tortured. Always ministering to him.

"Boaz, we have to leave."

Boaz tried to scorch him with his eyes, but he only had a few
embers left.

Osman brought out a hypodermic set, fiddled with it indecisively. "I'd rather you had your wits about you. But I'll drug you
—if I must."

"You can do better than that."

"Fratricide?"

"Don't be melodramatic."

"The Arab vice."

"A favor . . ."

"Perhaps, one day. In the battlefield. Anyway, I promised the
Memouneh I'd bring you back."

Boaz felt nauseous. How typically treacherous. "What did he
offer you in return?"

"Not the West Bank, I assure you. Drugs or not, Boaz?"

"What did he offer you?"

Osman faced Boaz squarely. "What I offered him. Full support. Until we wipe out Abu Ismail and Operation Dragons."

Boaz looked away, focused on the garden, watched Zubair
sprinkle the pool with rose petals. "I thought I had dreamt it,
Osman. Is Abu Ismail really alive?"

"Yes."

"Who did I kill then?"

"A double. Real identity: Tawfiq Tal. Palestinian guerrilla."

Boaz remembered the ramblings of his victim. *"Do you know Tawfiq Tal? A true warrior . . . Dead now . . ."* And the pathetic remark: *"I had a wife . . . and children . . ."*

"Do you have proof?"

Osman waved the telex. "Just in from Amman. Fingerprints match Tawfiq Tal's. I'll check voiceprints when we get back. But that'll be just to confirm. I ought to have remembered him, Boaz. I interrogated him. Now I shall never forget him."

Osman's anger charged Boaz. He managed to haul himself up, wave a useless arm, refusing to believe.

"The fingerprints. How—where did you get them?"

"Abu Ismail—Tal—took some pills before leaving for the Sanctuary. I picked up his glass. Sent it on to Amman."

Boaz tried to drive off the last of his confusion. "You knew it then? All along?"

"No. Just suspicions."

"What suspicions?"

"I stuck pretty close to him. In Medina. He looked younger. Free of doubt."

"His face. His features . . ."

"Perfect match. But then I haven't seen him close-up many times."

"You should have told me about your suspicions!"

Osman gazed at the garden. He wished he could seek shelter there—immerse himself in peace with his wife and family. Alas, he also had a country. "We'd have killed Tal anyway."

Boaz realized that he could walk and that his arms had strength. "Liar! That's been your secret! All along!"

Osman bellowed. "You think I've damned myself just to kill a robot?"

Boaz grabbed Osman by the throat. "Why did you damn yourself then?" He tightened his grip, waited for that nonmoment when another Boaz killed. It did not come.

Osman stood motionless. "Live and see."

Boaz dropped his arms, walked to the window. Zubair was sitting by the pool, watching the petals float, and smiling. Boaz envied his pure madness. "That's why you saved me? So that I can continue killing? That's some morality."

"It's served you well enough."

"I'll kill Abu Ismail. That's all I'll do."

"That'll be enough."

Lacking tears, Boaz punched the wall. There was no end to this fight.

January 13, 1974

ASSAB, ETHIOPIA

Ischii Watanabe knew he was drugged. His limbs moved in slow motion, strangely graceful; his mind lay thick, glutinous, inert. A few words escaped the mire, like jets of hot sulfur.

"There is no morality. No truth. No conscience. Only power. Everything is permissible."

He trembled. The self was still seismic. It had to be made whole. And such was the dynamic of wholeness that only the outcast achieved it. That, he now knew, was the inalienable truth. He had been whole when as a *Rengo Sekigun* he had been feared and respected. Fragmentation of the self had occurred only when he had ceased to be an outsider. When the guilt of killing, like a tumor, had atrophied his brain.

"Conflict is the language of man. Violence is what is best in us."

The trembling persisted. It would take some time to become whole again. But he had rejoined the path. He would arm himself with power. Wrest redemption. Rise in strength.

Abdallah helped him out of the plane. The hot air blotted out everything.

✗

Assab airport had a twice-weekly service to and from Aden with connecting flights to Addis Ababa. Despite this international status, it was a sleepy little airport—a couple of Nissen huts on a desert patch—famed only for its officious functionaries who had successfully arrested the illicit traffic of *chat*, the local narcotic plant. Yet on this Sunday it was ringed by Captain Wolde's paratroopers as if threatened by a full-scale attack.

Kevork Dedeyan hovered, alert, tense.

Wolde and his men had been deploying in the area for the past week, scouring for guerrillas—ostensibly because Assab, Ethiopia's second port, was part of Eritrea and a declared objective for liberation by the ELF. Except that there were no guerrillas in the region. The ELF, bogged down in northern Eritrea, was, as yet, unable to open a second front. The Danakil wilderness, surrounding Assab, was one of the hottest and most inhospitable places on earth; supplying a force through this volcanic hell of craters, canyons and vast deserts was beyond the ELF's present capabilities.

That left Yusuf's activities which had cost the lives of four of Schoenberg's men. Dedeyan, having once observed Wolde receiving arms from Hamdi and Idris Ali at Massawa, could only link

Wolde's presence to Yusuf's caravan. Consequently, when his own incursions into the wilderness for signs of Yusuf had proved barren, Dedeyan had kept track of Wolde as his only lead to whatever was afoot.

Dedeyan knew the undertaking had exposed him. Wolde, instead of scouring the uncharted wilderness, ideal for guerrillas, had deployed on the plains. Dedeyan, unable to conceal his Land-Rover's tracks, had been forced to allow Wolde to intercept him on a couple of occasions. Though his documents as a researcher for the Belgian Meteorological Society had been valid, Wolde's suspicions had not been allayed. On the second occasion Wolde, declaring the area dangerous, had assigned a few men to escort Dedeyan back to Assab, thus preventing him from monitoring the troops' activities for two days, the tenth and the eleventh.

Now he had encountered Wolde again. And Dedeyan had renewed his hopes that Wolde's sojourn in the desert had not been significant; that his subversive business had centered all the time on Assab airport; and that this had something to do with the WOJ unit which Getachew had reported having arrived at Aden by submarine.

Dedeyan took position by the iron railings to survey the DC-6B from Aden.

He should have been running. His infallible sixth sense warned him that this time Wolde would pounce on him. But he had to see what or whom the plane had brought. He could just do it. Passengers had to walk some seventy meters from the plane to the arrivals hut. He should have time to photograph them as well as the unloading of the cargo, then put the film in the envelope, already stamped and addressed to Sanbat, drop it in the mailbox, regain his Land-Rover and disappear.

He took out a cigarette, lit it and, holding the lighter absentmindedly, activated its miniature camera.

✗

The decision to sneak Watanabe through Ethiopia's side door had not been taken impetuously. Watanabe was needed at the Danakil base ahead of the main force to plan the storage layout for the plutonium and the high explosives as well as the safety measures that would have to be applied·to protect them from the infernal heat.

Originally, Abu Ismail had planned to transport Watanabe either with the *Khanjar* or the *Succubus*. But Watanabe, haunted by guilt, had responded negatively to the WOJ indoctrination, plunging, even when drugged, into abysses of acute hysteria. A tense sea voyage, much of it at night to evade the Ethiopian coast guard, followed by a tricky beaching, could have ruptured his frail hold on sanity. An overland passage through Sudan and northern Eritrea, suggested by Idris Ali, had been rejected as beyond Watanabe's physical resources. A parachute drop was also rejected for the same reason. That had left a swift journey by air, via Aden, with risks of detection mitigated by Wolde's presence at Assab.

But Abdallah, chosen to act as Watanabe's nurse, had been racked with misgivings. Even if the world had forgotten the Japanese terrorist, Abdallah was a wanted man. The Lisbon hijacking had not been forgotten. His description would be circulating throughout the world and might have percolated even to this hell-hole.

He rebuked himself for his anxiety. The only possible threat, the Armenian-Belgian meteorologist whom Wolde had reported as a possible enemy agent, would be disposed of without further ado.

Watanabe was beckoned to the immigration desk. Swaying on his feet, he presented his travel documents. His passport, supplied by *Rengo Sekigun*, identified him as Yukio Kato; other documents declared him a doctoral candidate at Tokyo University working on a thesis on Lalibela's rock-hewn churches. The vaccination certificates for typhoid, cholera, smallpox and yellow fever, perfectly forged, included the postscript that Kato was an epileptic and that in case of any malady, treatment should take into account a history of anticonvulsant medication. On perusing the last, the immigration officer dropped his parody of Western thoroughness and waved Watanabe through. In Africa, as elsewhere, the unsophisticated mind still regarded epilepsy as the sacred disease of visionaries.

Abdallah presented his Algerian passport and documents identifying him as a pharmacologist attached to the World Health Organization. The immigration officer stamped the passport after a cursory scrutiny.

Abdallah nudged Watanabe toward the exit. He felt ashamed for having nurtured fears. There had been no justification, not even the fact that his concern had been not for his person but for the safety of Operation Dragons. How could he have doubted Abu Ismail's words? Allah's Will always prevailed like daybreak. Allah's revolutionaries evolved in a crucible where only those most submissive to His command flourished. That was why a victim of imperialism like himself could rise from the dust of Palestinian camps and emerge as a torchbearer.

✗

Blood pounded Dedeyan's temple. He could smell danger, pungent like rotting garbage. Yet he had stolen away from the airport in good time. No one had followed him. For all he knew, the Assab episode was a red herring. The only cargo that had been unloaded from the Aden plane had been animal skins, one mailbag and some battered pieces of luggage. As for the passengers—just a few. Two people of interest: a young Arab and an emaciated Japanese. He had duly photographed them and mailed the film to Sanbat.

He started whistling, gratingly. To bolster his confidence, he laid his gun on the passenger seat.

The Land-Rover raced with its shadow. The road held the coast. Beyond, the Haleb archipelago undulated in the haze. The sea reflected the jade of mangroves. The wind whisked the sand, bent the palm trees. He was approaching the new church, built outside Assab by the sea—a heroic edifice with a golden dome and twin bell towers. Attuned to the wilderness because churches enriched any landscape.

A few kilometers more and he would reach the desert road to Addis Ababa. Then open space where he could spot trouble from far off.

He stopped whistling. A glint of metal in the mimosa shrubs opposite the church. He craned for a better look. He detected a massive frame: Wolde's dour sergeant, Ketema. The glint of metal sharpened. A bazooka.

His blood stopped pounding. He found himself catapulting out of the door, rolling on the ground, scurrying toward the church through the billowing dust. He heard the explosion. He dived behind a dune, looked back. He saw the Land-Rover enfolded in the vortex of a fireball. He crawled backward. He felt dizzy. He had hit his head on a rock. He touched water. He slithered into the sea.

He swam underwater, bobbing occasionally for breath, until he felt he was safe. He surfaced, looked back. The church stood before him like the majestic seat of an abandoned civilization. Nothing moved except a column of smoke in the distance. He scrambled ashore.

Instinct made him undress, bury his clothes in the sand, run into the church, and scamper up one of the bell towers. Like a chameleon changing color, unaware that intellect and memory had deserted him.

Abdallah bundled Watanabe into the World Health Organization Land-Rover, then embraced Idris Ali. The latter had parachuted into Eritrea on the night of January 10–11 but already looked as weathered as a Danakil tribesman.

Captain Wolde approached them. "My sergeant just radioed. The Armenian—blown."

Idris Ali rasped. "I said discreetly. No repercussions—"

Wolde grinned. "There won't be any. We'll blame it on the ELF."

Idris Ali grinned in turn, full of approval.

Wolde tarried. "That's it. Unless you'd like us to escort you through the wilderness . . ."

"Thank you. No."

Wolde kept an inscrutable face, but registered the rejection. WOJ were keeping the location of their Danakil base secret. Even Hamdi who had collected the rice from Yusuf at a deserted cove south of Assab had been forbidden to carry it farther than another deserted cove near Barassoli. "We'll keep in touch then."

Idris Ali nodded, then jumped into the Land-Rover.

✗

Dedeyan listened to the night. Cicadas. The sea washing on the shore. But the enemy were around. He could smell them.

He stared at the half-moon and judged it was near midnight. Wistfully, he gazed at the Haleb archipelago. He had considered swimming to one of the islands, living off the mangroves and wild-life. But there was no fresh water there and the sea was infested with sharks. He could not remember how he knew all that—but he knew. What else he knew, he could not remember. Memory and body, past and present, had separated.

He faced the desert. Before sunset, while the enemy horde had first searched the church, then dug in around it, he had surveyed the plains from the bell tower. He had seen birds of prey, hyenas and the odd dust trail of wild herds. The desert was alive. He could survive if he reached it.

He listened again to the night, this time concentrating on the solitary building that stood to the right of the church. He had identified it as a rest house for priests. Now, it contained the enemy. Soldiers. They and their guns were asleep—the silence confirmed that. But there were others scattered about, guarding the approaches to the road.

He inspected his naked frame: dirt and thick body hair had turned it black.

He moved forward stealthily, smelling the air. Close to the enemy. One jerked up, turned in his direction. He snarled and ran off on all fours, first sideways, then at full stretch, like a hyena. A voice cursed and threw stones.

He ran into the desert—for a while on all fours, then upright. He abandoned himself to his senses, knowing they would lead him to food and water—now his only priorities.

January 15, 1974

JERUSALEM, ISRAEL

The Memouneh's red telephone, used for incoming calls with special code references, bleeped. He picked it up.

"We are back. Your falcon is with me."

"Unharmed?"

"Yes."

"When will I see him?"

"Soon. Salaam."

The line went dead. The Memouneh replaced the receiver. Osman's voice had been lifeless. Natural—after a failed mission. But Boaz was safe and there was cause for rejoicing in that.

Wearily, he reverted to the report on his desk. From Sanbat. Informing him of Dedeyan's disappearance. Enclosed two photographs as Dedeyan's leavetaking. Abdallah of WOJ. Hiroshi Anami, alias Ischii Watanabe, of the Japanese Red Army.

January 17, 1974

DJIBOUTI, T.F.A.I.

The desert sprawled, seeking a sea that had dried up in prehistory. Only guffaws from Yusuf's band, squatting by the barbed-wire barrier that encircled Djibouti, broke the lizard silence.

Schoenberg scrutinized the troops standing in line on both sides of the track. There were few guns in sight; the men, in regulation shorts, open shirts and kepis, looked bored and appeared to be the usual mixture of *troupes de marine*, gendarmes and Legionnaires that turned up every Monday and Thursday to search the Addis Ababa train for illegal immigrants. Yusuf could not have detected that the detail had been reinforced.

The Afars converged on the freight car. Schoenberg's company casually broke rank and encircled them. The Legionnaires Mrozek, Estienne, Landrieu, Ockwirk, Pellerin, Quesada, Richter and Ulrich were tough veterans, loyal above all to their regiment—and to Schoenberg, with whom they had fought in past campaigns. They had unhesitatingly agreed to lend him an unofficial hand, regretting only that they would not be allowed to avenge their comrades killed by Yusuf, for fear of triggering an open war.

The Afars boarded the freight car. They would be unloading the bales of *chat* which Yusuf imported under special license. The dispensation, obtained on the grounds that the narcotic plant was a vital Afar staple, summed up the present French colonial strategy. Anything to keep the Afars peaceful.

Yusuf left his men to complete customs formalities. Schoenberg waited until he entered the first-class car, then darted after him. He caught up with him next to an empty compartment and bundled him in.

Yusuf spun around menacingly. "What's going on?"

Schoenberg slid the door shut and pulled down its blinds.

Yusuf, fury mounting, bellowed. "What is this?"

Schoenberg raised his silencer-fitted gun. He was taking a great risk grappling with Yusuf. But at least the Afar's pugnacity put personal morals into perspective. He pointed at the window. "Take a good look, Yusuf. Your men are surrounded. Raise your voice again and they're dead."

Yusuf observed the white kepis encircling the freight car. Shuttling between anger and incredulity, he forced a grin. "Are you mad? Who are you?"

Schoenberg switched on the lights, pulled down the window blinds, and aimed the gun at Yusuf's forehead. "Name's Schoenberg. Lieutenant. Military Intelligence. Sit down."

Yusuf, managing to find caution in his anger, obeyed. "Lieutenant, I warn you—"

Schoenberg fired a round into the headrest, close to Yusuf's head. "Just so you understand, Yusuf. I'd like you to provoke me."

Yusuf, shaking off shock, snarled. "What do you want?"

"What I really want is to avenge my comrades. The four you killed."

Yusuf eyed him defiantly. "What are you talking about?"

"But I'll make a deal with you. I want information."

Yusuf shrugged contemptuously. "You *are* mad."

"The rice you smuggled into Ethiopia. Who was it for? Where did you deliver it?"

"What . . . rice?"

Schoenberg fired another round, hitting the headrest a few centimeters from Yusuf's cheek. "I'd be happy to do it the hard way, Yusuf."

Yusuf's fury overrode panic. "There'll be war if you harm me!"

"Some of us would love a war, *mon pote*. I grant you not the governor-general—but with so many corpses in his hand, it would be a *fait accompli*."

"And what would happen to you?"

"I'd probably get a medal."

"Don't fool yourself! You're as much fodder for the old hens in Paris as we are. Deprive them of their colonial gains and they'd turn on you. Peck out your guts."

Schoenberg nodded and smiled. "You've read all the right books, Yusuf."

"Go bury yourself, Lieutenant. You can't touch me."

"On the other hand, I'm a good learner, too. I could stage your death. Put you and your men in a smuggler's boat, sink it out at sea, feed you to the sharks—it'd be more credible than killer bees."

Yusuf's anger faltered. "I'll tell you this much—the rice is no threat to France."

"I'll be the judge of that."

"I took it—to Musaddiq Hamdi."

"Where?"

"To his boat, the *Succubus*. In the Bay of Assab."

"Go on."

"That's all."

"Everyday smuggling?"

"Yes."

"So why murder a whole patrol?"

Yusuf's voice tightened. "It had to be—secret."

"Why? What's so special about rice? Who was it for?"

"ELF."

"That still doesn't warrant killing four Legionnaires."

"That was the deal. Secret—at all costs. I honor my deals."

Schoenberg spat at him. "Life's cheap, eh, Yusuf?"

Yusuf met his eyes. "Some lives—yes."

Schoenberg's finger twitched on the trigger. "How do you know the rice was for the ELF? Did you see them?"

"No. The ELF's in the north—around Massawa. . . . Hamdi was going to take it to them."

"Couldn't trust you, eh?"

Yusuf bridled. "Everyone trusts me. Hamdi's business was se-cret. That's all."

"What about Captain Wolde? He was in the area."

"Nowhere near the coast. Up in the desert."

"Nothing to do with Hamdi?"

"I don't know. I didn't ask."

"What about WOJ?"

Yusuf stared at him, surprised. "WOJ?"

"No sign of them?"

"No."

Schoenberg fought to hold the initiative. "Hamdi didn't mention them?"

"No."

"Think again, Yusuf."

Yusuf rose. "I've told you all I know, Lieutenant. Consider that a victory."

Schoenberg felt deflated. Deep down he had known the confrontation would be futile. Nothing Yusuf revealed would bring hope of retribution to the unquiet corpses of the four Legionnaires and Mossad's Dedeyan. WOJ would have taken no one into their confidence.

He debated if he dared kill Yusuf. If he did, the Afars would rebel, France would suffer, more Legionnaires would die. If he did not, Yusuf would seek to avenge his humiliation. He lowered his gun and walked out. "We'll cross paths again, Yusuf."

Yusuf waited until Schoenberg jumped off the train. Then he raged. "We will, Schoenberg! We will!"

January 18, 1974

PAPHOS, CYPRUS

The sun lay on the sea in its winter coat. The beach, snaking dramatically through rocky points, was deserted. Anybody who saw them from the cliffs above would think them hardy tourists.

The last time the Memouneh had met Dr. Charles Quinn, professor of mathematics at the American University, Beirut, and CIA's Middle East station chief, had been on the second day of the Yom Kippur War. On that occasion, the encounter had been tense and punctuated by recriminations against American and Israeli Military Intelligence, both of which had failed to predict war despite the billowing storm that had gathered. Yet even under strain, Quinn had been sparkling, rattling off data like a computer.

The Quinn who walked beside him now was a different man; eyes sunk and lusterless, hair thinned out, muscular girth reduced to flabbiness, hands shaky, cheeks rouged by heavy drinking. Though Mossad agents in Lebanon had reported Quinn's disintegration, linking it to the mysterious suicide of Professor Talat Fawzi, the Memouneh could not have conceived such a metamorphosis. He had assumed that even if Quinn's feelings for the physicist transcended friendship, he would have borne Fawzi's loss with the fortitude expected of a professional. But bereavement had crushed him. Quinn was fading away, not like an old soldier but like a widow seeking burial beside her husband.

Yet, the Memouneh hoped that Paphos, Aphrodite's legendary birthplace and a favorite spot of Quinn's, would inspire the American by way of a poignant valediction. "Shall I kick off, Charlie?"

Quinn drank a hearty mouthful of ouzo from a hip flask. "Sure, friend."

"You've received our last communication on the WOJ buildup in the Horn of Africa. I'd like your views."

"I'm not a strategist."

The Memouneh hated indulging a man he had so respected. "If that were so, Charlie, I wouldn't stand here cap in hand. I need your help."

Quinn grunted, shook his hip flask to gauge its level. "All right. In a nutshell, for what it's worth: Abu Ismail's set his sights on Saudi Arabia. That's why WOJ is in the Horn of Africa."

The Memouneh, surprised at the evaluation, pondered a moment. "Saudi Arabia? That's stretching it a bit, isn't it?"

"If you were a religious fanatic trying to set up a global theocracy, not at all. Saudi Arabia is where Islam's Holiest of Holies is. And where the sand turns to gold."

"What about Israel? He wants Israel off the map. More than that, he wants Jerusalem."

"Sure he does. And if he gets Saudi Arabia, you people won't have a snowball's chance in hell. He'd have the oil—and the world would do his dirty work."

The Memouneh watched the waves rolling toward the beach. Quinn, he believed, might not be off target. The unorthodox perspective merely corroborated the obvious: every strategy hurled against the Jewish state, whatever its objective, augured a precipitous end. "Then all the more reason for my request, Charlie. Let's team up."

Quinn chuckled nervously. "You're kidding."

"We've done it before."

"Times change."

"Time's still with us. You can't let Abu Ismail take Saudi Arabia —not unless you can run the American Dream on Coca-Cola. Our interests coincide. You need us as much as we need you."

Quinn spoke into his flask. "Let me put it this way. Bedfellows change. Even marriages made in heaven flounder. . . ."

The Memouneh curbed his irritation. "I want men, Charlie. Top-notch men who understand the Arab mind. Who have insight into religious fanaticism. You've got such men."

"So have you."

"Most of ours are still at the front. Even if we could pull them out, we can't infiltrate them where we want them. Not overnight. We've lost our anchors inside WOJ, in Libya, and now in Ethiopia."

Quinn looked away. "Kevork Dedeyan—yeah, I heard. That's the way it crumbles sometimes."

The Memouneh rasped. "What's happened, Charlie?"

Quinn hissed. "You know damn well what's happened. The rot's set in. Watergate. Impeachment on the horizon . . ."

"I meant what's happened to you, Charlie? The rot's set in for some time. But you weren't part of it."

Quinn took another mouthful of ouzo. "Well, you can see what's before your eyes."

"What's before my eyes?"

"A wreck."

"Come on, Charlie."

Quinn bellowed. "What d'you want me to do?"

The Memouneh looked hard into Quinn's eyes. "Tell me you'll fight on our side."

"I'll tell you this: you can't get blood out of a stone. That's what we are—the company *and* yours truly."

The Memouneh kicked at a seashell angrily. "One final point. WOJ have plutonium. From that Air France plane—"

"That's only your theory, Zamora."

"Ask the French why they're scouring the Mediterranean seabed. And why Pompidou ordered them to keep searching—indefinitely, if need be."

"We did. They're searching for the plane's black box."

"They're trying to find the plutonium, Charlie. They suffer from your complaint: the ostrich syndrome. They know it's not there, but they don't want to know. So they pretend it is there."

Quinn, dejected, sat on the sand and faced the sea. "You no doubt have a plane to catch, Zamora. I'll stick around for a bit."

The Memouneh flared. "Plutonium, Charlie! They could blow up the world! Don't you care?"

Quinn stared at his flask. "If you must know, Zamora—no. Serves us right."

The Memouneh walked away.

When he looked back from the clifftop, Quinn was lying on the beach, waving his flask at the waves. A casualty of love—probably cursing Aphrodite whom he had worshiped in the past. On such frailties the fate of the world rested.

January 19, 1974

AMMAN, JORDAN

It was time to leave—though Boaz wished he could stay longer.

Osman lived on the outskirts of the diplomatic quarter in a modest villa near the Intercontinental Hotel. In September 1970, during the Civil War, the hillside had been invaded by contingents of the Palestinian Popular Front. Since Osman had been fighting with the Special Security Squads, the task of defending his house had fallen on his wife, Samia; she had not surrendered it.

Samia was a progeny of those Circassians who had migrated from the Caucasus in the nineteenth century and, having re-founded Amman, had settled there. She had thus inherited the spirit of mountains and thunder. Osman, in awe of her qualities and anxious that Boaz should hold her in equal esteem, had introduced her as his pioneer woman, self-consciously using the Hebrew word *chalutz*.

The cognomen was apt. She was, in the Biblical sense of the world, not only a forager but also liberation personified. The man at whose side she stood could never lack strength, nor suffer isolation. For the first time in his life, Boaz had wished to share his life with a woman, had begrudged, even coveted, another man's wife. Then, to assuage the guilt, he had envisaged her as the sister he would have cherished—though the thought had disinterred great pain.

He finished his coffee. Osman and Samia exchanged a longing look. Husband and wife had been reunited that morning, when Samia had returned from Aqaba where Osman had placed her in safekeeping at the king's summer palace. Their daughters, Fatma and Hatijeh, had already discreetly left.

"I ought to go."

Osman jumped up, almost with indecent haste. "I'll get the car."

Left alone with Samia, Boaz became diffident and took to studying the room. It was simply furnished. There was plenty of air and light, and the walls seemed whitewashed with perennial laughter.

He and Osman had spent most of the past four days in Osman's office, compiling the dossier on the Mecca operation for King Hussein, which Osman had placed in an electronically protected safe to be handed over to the monarch in the event of his death. The work had thawed their tension, and they had reaffirmed their peculiar friendship. There remained a residual indignation rooted in the fact that Osman still refused to disclose the secrets of Operation Dragons. Boaz had finally decided that this was not due to Osman's distrust, but to a superstition that demanded that evil should be buried lest mere mention give it substance.

That had led to a surprising realization: that to some extent failure, and to a greater extent the hajj, had transformed him. He was reborn in a way that seemed to have destroyed his individuality, that had reduced him to cosmic dust. Within this insignificance, he could tolerate Islam's fatalism and the Jewish concept that had preceded it. It was incumbent on man to live—if need be by subterfuge, and irrespective of hardship or injustice—in order to serve God: martyrdom would come anyway, either when man refused to transgress prime prohibitions or when God was found absent.

One immediate result of this transformation had been a sense of harmony—a relief he had only experienced during long swims when he had felt part of the sea. Consequently, he could now feel life did concern him. He could see beauty and nobility in a woman. He could look back, pleasurably, on a simple meal, hastily prepared and willingly shared.

"Boaz . . ."

He turned to Samia, happy that she had saved him from silence.

"May I talk to you . . . in earnest . . . ?"

He hesitated, surprised. "Of course."

"You're quite different . . . not like other Israelis. Not arrogant . . ."

Boaz forced a smile, disappointed by the banality of the comment. "Are we arrogant, Samia?"

"Often. Though I've never understood why."

"Perhaps what you call arrogance is our way of deceiving ourselves. We want to believe in our strength."

"Is strength so important?"

"Weakness has never served the Jew."

"And yet, Boaz, all that the Jew has given to this world he has given in weakness."

"Blind acceptance instead of defiance. Is that what you recommend?"

"Isn't that what you want? For yourself?"

Boaz held her eyes, saw how beautiful they were. How mistaken he had been to think her capable of banality. "What I want is unattainable. Conversely, I fear weakness."

"By strength I don't mean the capacity to survive. If that can be achieved by strength, then you and your country need every bit of it."

"What other strength is there?"

"The strength to live. Or, by my definition, the weakness that fears death, that runs away, if it can, to avoid it."

Boaz smiled ruefully. "I hear Osman's voice. His brother's keeper."

"Have you that weakness, Boaz?"

"For the months ahead."

Samia shook her head in despair. "Why not for the rest of your life? Like your people—for centuries?"

Boaz dropped his eyes. He had long ceased identifying with his people. He fought for them, was zealous for their survival, looked, felt, behaved and remembered like them. But his soul had been severed. If he had a people at all, it was in the chords of the bouzouki, in the music of its composers, in a distant time which, like Olympus, was born in Greece but had never existed.

Samia's voice sounded as if she had read his thoughts. "Then let me beg a favor, Boaz. . . . Spare yourself."

"Why should you care?"

"To start with: my husband is working with you. I want to entrust him to you. Secondly, there is hope in your friendship. For Arabs. And for Israel."

He envied Osman again. If there was any hope, it suckled at her faith.

"Will you, Boaz?"

"I can't answer that. There's a part in me—just born—that wants to. But it may not, as you put it, be weak enough."

"I'll pray it becomes so. So will Osman."

Boaz hid the emotions he would have liked to show behind a feeble smile. A moment later, Osman returned. Boaz suspected he had been lingering in the hall outside, listening.

"Ready, Boaz?"

Boaz went to Samia, kissed her hand and placed it on his forehead. "May Allah watch over you all, Samia."

She lowered her eyes graciously.

As Boaz left the room, he felt he had turned into a rock. One he could use as a foundation for his soul.

PART VII

Out of the Paw of the Lion, into the Paw of the Bear

1 Samuel, 17:37

January 24, 1974

QOUARA, ETHIOPIA

Sanbat surveyed the *masgid*, the Falasha synagogue. It was a circular hut like the ordinary *tukul*, but had been built with thicker branches and denser layers of mud. On one wall, a white cloth draped the Ark of the Law; next to it, a wooden cabinet held the *Orit*, the Falasha Bible. The other walls were bare. Above, on the domed ceiling, the Star of David, woven in coarse grass, served both as a celestial shield and as the reflector of the Lord's design.

This was the first time she had set food in a *masgid*. She felt in such a niche the soul might stumble upon Elijah preparing for the Day of the Lord.

She picked up the *Orit*. Lovingly copied by anonymous ancestors, it contained—in addition to the Holy Scriptures—Apocrypha and Pseudepigrapha which, the Falashas claimed, enlightened them above all mankind by chronicling unerringly the Advent of the Messiah.

She put the *Orit* back, afraid that its vision might possess her, and moved to the narrow window in the western wall. She pondered the strange world that might have been hers.

The village and its revered monastery were situated on the summit of an *amba*, a flat-topped hill with almost vertical escarpments. It was here, at the highest peak of the region, legends told, that Gideon, the last Falasha king, had deposited copies of the sacred writings. That had been early in the seventeenth century, when the black Jews had come near to extinction at the hands of the Ethiopian king Susenyos. Then and since, the *amba* had remained inviolate, a symbol, like Masada, of Jewish zeal.

The settlement, named Bagerond, "Treasurer," after King Gideon, encouraged few visitors. It had taken Sanbat four days to reach it. Traveling from Asmara to Gondar by Land-Rover, she had stopped at Falasha villages along the needle-sharp Simen Mountains to seek clearance through a hierarchy of wise men. Then, having proceeded by mule around the northeastern highlands of Lake Tana, she had been obliged to prostrate herself for a day and a night at the foot of the *amba* to impress that her mission warranted the attention of the highest authority.

During the obeisance, she had been asked to immerse herself in prayer and perceive the structure of the Universe as depicted by the panorama: the skies for the Lord; the harsh highlands for the House of Israel; the fertile plains for the Christians; the mystic regions for the Muslims; the polymorphous nether ends for the pagans. Only the person who could embrace this arcane order would survive in perpetuity. Sanbat had found the esoteric philosophy repugnant—a psalm of death rather than hope. Only once, when led up the tortuous snakepath, had she wished to lean on the knotted muscles of roots and feel that eternity was truly the human birthright. But she had shaken off the spell. The Falasha tree was withering, whereas she, a transplant, had the chance to survive.

That she had returned to the land of specters on battle orders was a macabre irony. The directive had come from the Memouneh. The arrival at Aden of the submarine *Khanjar* with a WOJ complement, followed by Yusuf's delivery of a large consignment of rice to WOJ's surrogates, the ELF, had been evidence enough that WOJ had chosen Ethiopia and the Horn of Africa as its next theater of war. Reservations on this evaluation had been dispersed by Captain Wolde's mysterious activities in southern Eritrea culminating in Kevork Dedeyan's murder—allegedly by the ELF. Dedeyan himself, stalwart to the end, had provided positive proof by photographing in Assab the arrival of WOJ's Abdallah with Hiroshi Anami, alias Ischii Watanabe, the *Rengo Sekigun* high-explosives expert.

The evaluation demanded drastic action. But in the wake of the Yom Kippur War the imperative had proved beyond Mossad's resources. Even an immediate measure such as restructuring the Ethiopian cell—reduced after Dedeyan's death to one agent, Sanbat—had been abandoned. Mossad did not have a reserve of black agents; even if it could redeploy those operating in other African countries, it could not wait for them to assimilate to their new surroundings. The same condition, with compounding difficulties, applied to its other agents, including those of Yemenite and Arab origin. For these were certain to be subjected to close scrutiny both by the disaffected elements in Ethiopia and by the Libyan, Algerian and Egyptian spies monitoring Ethiopia's estrangement from Israel from within the OAU.

An interim remedy, collaboration with the ISS through Getachew Iyessous, had proved, at best, circumscribed. Although Getachew did supply some manpower under the counter, these could not be expected to operate or alter course beyond their ISS briefs. Moreover, the ISS was already overstretched: in addition to the ELF, it had other secessionist groups to contend with—notably Somalia's clients in the Ogaden, the Western Somali Liberation Front. Also sniffing carrion in the prevailing unrest were the superpower vultures, Russia and China.

As an instant remedy, the Memouneh had sought collaboration from the CIA—in vain. Thus, more in desperation than as sound strategy, he had had to turn to the Falashas.

Such an obvious consideration did not automatically promise success. The Falashas were an entity apart. Claiming to practice a fundamental Judaism, which had remained unchanged since the time of Solomon and Sheba, they regarded themselves as the true descendants of the Chosen Race, the purest of the Tribes, the guardians of the Faith, and rejected the rest of Jewry as Gentile. Conversely, world Jewry classified the Falashas as non-Jews on the doctrinal point that they lacked knowledge of the Talmud and the Mishnah. Thus, relations between Israel and the Falashas, tentatively established in the early fifties, had been restricted. Israel had sent some instructors to teach the Falashas Hebrew—a language unknown to them—and a few agriculturalists to improve their farming. The Falashas had reciprocated by sending some children to Israel for higher education but had suffered great disappointment when most had chosen to settle there, undergoing conversion as prescribed by the Chief Rabbinate. Israel had barely redressed the balance by mediating with the emperor on occasion to improve the Falashas' living conditions. It had taken the Yom Kippur War to change the perspective for both Israel and the Falashas. Israel, wounded and all the more anxious to prepare against future conflicts, was now inclined to consider the Falashas as part of the Diaspora. And the Falashas, with Israel and Ethiopia forced into opposite camps, had found themselves once again as isolated as when the mists of history had segregated them as immigrants.

It was this sense of isolation that the Memouneh had hoped to exploit. Over the past twenty years the Falashas had acquired a wider grasp of politics. They could compare the expedient, self-interested groupings of nations with their bitter struggles against Christians and Muslims. Imbued with the Old Testament, they could visualize genocide. The educated among them had realized that the war against one Jew concerned all Jews. Already a number, picking up ancient arms, had volunteered to fight for Israel. The rest had to be convinced.

The meeting with the Falasha elders had taken place the previous night. It had been the eve of *Sanbat*, the Falasha Sabbath. There had been twelve *kahen*, priests with similar functions to rabbis, from various communities; twenty *manokse*, monks from the *amba* monastery; and the *Telleq Kahen*, the High Priest of Bagerond, as great an eminence as the High Priest of the Second Temple.

At first the elders had been wary. The *kahen* had pronounced their distrust of Sanbat as a Falasha-born who had assimilated with the Hollow Jew—hollow for abolishing such intermediaries of the Lord as priests and monastic institutions. The *manokse* had rejected her origins outright, arguing that having left her homeland when still a baby, she had not undergone clitoridectomy, an equivalent rite to circumcision, and could not be a Falasha. The *Telleq Kahen*, sniffing her body with distrust—though she had cleansed it, as prescribed, with nothing else but water—had declared her soiled by the wilderness surrounding *Beta Israel*.

But Sanbat had insisted against all dogma that a Falasha remained a Jew—whatever the transgression—until the Day of Judgment. Laying out symbolic offerings of a gun and a plow, she had related the plight of Israel and had offered them two choices: to stone her to death or to consider her petition.

Her defiance had triumphed. None of the elders had been able to dismiss the sheer physical will of an outsider who declared herself one of them—yet was not in either the flesh or the spirit, and yet again seemed to possess the authority of that formidable widow of antiquity, Judith.

Their deliberations had taken a whole night. As often happened in communities debating survival, they had resorted to mysticism. They had sought the hidden meanings of words and actions and had found, as they had expected, that these invariably held menace for the Jew. At daybreak the High Priest, bemisted—by foreboding or the supernatural or body vapor, Sanbat could not tell—had chosen to speak.

Pronouncing that he embodied the collective voices of the angels, he had drawn attention to the peculiar name of the Israeli emissary, Sanbat, the very name of the sacred day, which had existed in the Lord's mind before Creation, and had been transformed into the deity known as Luminous, Glorified, Beautiful, Resuscitating, Beloved, Guardian. Such a coincidence could only be devised by the Divine Will and meant that the mortal Sanbat should be seen as an apparition of her deified namesake. Since no Falasha could refuse *Sanbat*'s commandments, the strayed children of Israel must be helped.

The Elders, no strangers to a voice possessed by angels, had ululated in unanimous agreement.

There the mission had ended. And there Sanbat should have started planning for the strenuous week ahead when she would teach surveillance techniques to those Falashas chosen for the task. Instead, she had allowed herself to venture deeper into the supernatural and there seek out the answers to her future. She had arranged an audience with Abbew Abba Yaqob, a hermit who, after long years in the wilderness, had attained clairvoyance.

She moved away from the window, trembling. She could no longer delude herself that her desire to consult an oracle was merely a device which, like the tossing of a coin, would decide whether to exorcise or to reclaim Boaz. She was in earnest. Yet like most Israelis, she dared not look into the future for fear of losing the present. Conversely, a present haunted by Boaz had become intolerable.

She had tried to keep in touch with Boaz, first directly, then through mutual friends and finally through official channels. She had met with a screen of silence until the Memouneh, prone to dressing crises with verse, had sent her a Chinese poem, underlining the phrase "cloud-hidden, whereabouts unknown." She had assumed that Boaz had found his suicide mission.

At first she had reacted with infantile anger as when her husband had been shot down, unable to accept that the loved man, idolized as superstrong, was in reality weak and mortal. Later, she had turned spiteful, arguing that if the strong deliberately weaken themselves to consummate a death wish, they forfeit adoration. She had upbraided herself for not resuming life in its most primitive sense—demanding nothing more from a man than his seed. After all, in her sexual fantasies she always imagined herself as a passive but bountiful vagina in need of plowing—like good earth. In the end, she had had to admit that for her fantasies to take color, she needed Boaz to do the plowing.

"Child . . . "

Sanbat spun around toward the voice. Abbew Abba Yaqob, the Most Venerable Father, carrying a body that had shrunk down to two enormous white eyes, stood before her. It seemed natural, Sanbat realized with shock, that a man who could see into the dark ages of the future, and farther, into the chaos of the mind, should be blind.

She rose hastily. "Yes, Father . . ."

He enveloped her with the fog of his eyes, than ran his hands over her face to imprint her features to memory.

She drew out a parcel. "I have brought an offering. Clothes, sandals, salt."

The hermit squatted down. Sanbat noticed his left arm, mangled by leprosy. Legend told that the Most Venerable Father had chased every disease to its lair to conquer it in the name of the Lord. It was easy to believe. Covered in a tattered colorless shamma, chin resting on skeletal knees, he looked as indestructible as a termite mound. His good hand gathered sand. "Dust. Can you carry dust, child?"

The voice was clear and resonant—unmistakably the voice of Truth.

"If you show me how . . ."

He poured the dust into her hand. "Does it burn?"

Sanbat felt her hand sear. "Yes."

Abbew Abba Yaqob's mouth dribbled. "During Creation, the Lord required dust. The Earth refused to give it, knowing that man would contaminate it. The Lord sent his archangels, Germael, Aksael and Bernael. The first two returned without the dust because Earth had pleaded with them, invoking the Lord's glorious Name. Bernael ignored the invocation. He secured the dust."

"I can't understand parables, Father."

"The dust has been contaminated."

"Give me hope, Father."

"The Lord our God, the Lord is One."

She knelt beside the hermit, took his hand, ran it over her breasts so that he could touch her despair. "I have a man . . ."

"I see him. He is measuring the limits of Hell."

"What does that mean?"

"There was a great eagle named Tani. The Lord sent it to Hell so that it could see the punishment awaiting man. Tani returned with wings hung down, breath frail and bones showing like plumage. He had only seen a corner of Hell. He had understood: no sin remains hidden."

"Is life a sin?"

"For some men life and death are the same."

"Will he want me? Must I renounce him?"

Abbew Abba Yaqob jumped up, surprising her with his agility. He started whirling, cackling, tearing off his shamma. Sanbat stared at his shrunken body. It was said that Abbew Abba Yaqob had forty layers of skin, each a chronicle of man's evil deeds. There was not a patch that did not bear a deep scar. But the worst was the genital area: hairless and wrinkled like a decayed fruit, flat like a woman's. Abbew Abba Yaqob had been unmanned by the knife, cauterized by fire, interred by clay. He seemed, as he whirled in the flickering light of candles, the last of the Suffering Servants.

He shrieked, pointing his stumped wrist. "What you must know is this: you must return to these highlands. The Lord needs your womb."

Involuntarily Sanbat glanced at his groin. He caught her look with his sightless eyes, stopped whirling and stooped over her. From her squatting position she could see the abomination in detail. She heaved and brought up bile.

"You understand, child. I have known all there is to know. I know what awaits the world. The Falasha will be shredded."

Sanbat sank back on her heels.

"That is not the worst, child. I am the Second Noah. I speak of calamities that shall surpass the Deluge."

"Don't tell me any more."

"You wanted to look into the future. Look! The Twelve Tribes —what is left of them—are mobilizing for the journey to Jerusalem's fortress. For a final stand!"

Sanbat crawled backward toward the door.

The hermit blocked her way. "Look! The hatred for *Beta Israel* floods every corner. Look! The Last of Days! The last battle! Jerusalem falls! This time, the Twelve Tribes die to a man! That is the Lord's Will!" The hermit grabbed her hair, pressed her face onto his loins. "After the destruction of *Beta Israel!* Look, destruction of all Creation! The way to destroy Evil! Look, the Lord needs witnesses. Strong witnesses! Ten good Falashas. Give the Lord your womb!"

Sanbat choked on putrified flesh. "No!"

"Then—perish!" He let her go.

Sanbat remained conscious long enough to wonder if Boaz had ever encountered Abbew Abba Yaqob. That would explain his despair. Then it occurred to her that every Jew had encountered Abbew Abba Yaqob. Every Jew had the vision of the Last of Days.

February 1, 1974

ABU RUDEIS, ISRAELI OCCUPIED SINAI

Across the Gulf, on the west bank of the Suez Canal, the Israeli troops were continuing their withdrawal in accordance with the disengagement agreement signed with Egypt.

The country was sighing with relief. But not the Memouneh. Disengagement agreements meant the end of one round and a brief respite before the next. The camp where he had found Boaz temporarily billeted, an enclave of Spartan dormitories for tourists, had on view symbolic spoils of the Six Day War: a shot-down MiG-21, a T-55 tank, AA guns, APCS—all Egyptian. They would be replaced by symbolic spoils of the Yom Kippur War and, probably, of other wars to come. Then one day the camp would revert to the Egyptians, would house once again oil technicians, and the symbolic spoils would change markings, become Israeli. Masada would fall again; God would reexhibit the Jew's ashes as proof that life was a divine experiment quite meaningless to the guinea pigs.

They sat in the shade of the T-55, drinking cola and eating army rations. The Memouneh's eyes had sunk deeper—signs of a migraine—and he panted in the heat.

This was the first occasion since Boaz's return that the two had met in private. The previous meeting, Boaz's debriefing, had stagnated. The expedition to Mecca had so caught Mossad's imagination that almost everybody from top brass to minor department heads had stormed headquarters to receive the facts direct from Boaz. Thereafter, Dr. Kissinger's "shuttle diplomacy" had kept the Memouneh in the thick of security problems, while the navy had commandeered Boaz to fight the blaze on three of Abu Rudeis's offshore rigs, still raging after a stray hit from an Israeli Skyhawk during the Yom Kippur War.

They had exchanged pleasantries and discussed the ramifications of the disengagement agreement. To Boaz it seemed they were behaving like Odysseus and Telemachus, reunited after a decade, both aching to restake claim on the other, but unsure as to how the other had fared, waiting for a first embrace.

As with Odysseus, it fell to the Memouneh to dispense wisdom. "How was it really, Boaz?"

"The mission? A smooth failure."

"I mean Mecca. Tell me about Mecca."

"What? That it is sanctified? That it dispenses love, brotherhood? That it turns pilgrims into saints? Men into angels? That Islam is a glorious religion? Mecca is so many things. . . ."

"What is it in essence?"

Boaz reached down and sifted the sand through his fingers. "Why do you want to know?"

"Because I hope—against hope. That as you look back on it, it will change you. It might even change me. It's infectious—all that ails you."

Boaz stared into the Memouneh's eyes. They were glazed, dehumanized, which, according to Mossad myth, was a device perfected in Mandate days to hide the inner man. It had fought off Goliath then; it fought off weakness now. Unaccountably the old warrior inclined his head as if in resignation. The gesture, the first sign of vulnerability Boaz had seen in the Memouneh, confused and frightened him. "The Jew's revolt. That's your motto! Have you abandoned it?"

"It needs motivation, Boaz."

"Mecca?"

"Yes."

"No, Zamora. Mecca means hundreds of millions of Muslims. Mecca means Mohammed is the only prophet. That the Infidel—we—have taken the wrong path. Mecca means universal brotherhood—but only under the Crescent. Mecca offers us no hope."

"What is there in Mecca that immerses one in Truth? So far you've described movement. A sea raging. Waves breaking. Plankton tossed here and there. But what is the *force* . . . ?"

Boaz could not think how to answer. But the Word escaped. Like his Nazarene hero before the adulteress, his finger wrote on the sand.

The Memouneh stared at the two letters—both the Hebrew *Yud*. "God?"

Boaz scored the letters repeatedly.

The Memouneh growled. "Then tell me about God!"

Boaz saw the passion in the Memouneh's eyes. He held up his head, wondering how the words would come. They came in an avalanche.

"I saw Him—blasphemous as that sounds. He was there inside the Kaaba. And He was outside. Everywhere. He was inconceivable—as we believe Him to be. But He had substance. A formidable breath that caressed you. Beauty, divided and subdivided, yet infinite—landscaped on every face. He spoke soothingly. Individually, to every man. I asked Him—are you Allah? I heard Him say: 'I am the One God. . . .' "

"And?"

"That's it. Does it help you?"

"Yes. I never believed in Him. Perhaps I can now—if He spares us. Failing that, I might be able to fool myself."

"The truth is: He is not exclusive. He has many children. We're one of them."

"But will He let us live?"

"I don't know."

"Let's hang on and find out."

Boaz smiled. "Don't worry about me! Keep throwing me at Abu Ismail. I'll get him in the end."

"And then?"

"We'll see."

"Coming from you—that's optimism."

Boaz gazed into the distance. "It's a question of bosoms really. Whichever proves more attractive. His or . . ."

"Israel's?"

Boaz pursed his lips and left the question dangling.

The Memouneh stood up. "It's been good, Boaz . . ."

"Is that it? You just came for a chat?"

"And to see you."

"What about Abu Ismail?"

"In Tripoli."   .

"Operation Dragons?"

The Memouneh looked away. He did not want to talk about Dedeyan. That was for his nightmares. Where all his men died, running into a minor desolation to avert a major one. "There are indications it's moving to Ethiopia."

"What about me? I'd rather fight Abu Ismail instead of an oil blaze. Why not Ethiopia . . . ?"

"I'd like to keep you in the background until things heat up. Unless you have personal reasons."

"Personal reasons?"

"Sanbat. She's in Ethiopia. Talking of attractive bosoms . . ."

Boaz shook his head sadly.

The Memouneh nodded, started to walk away, then stopped. "Boaz, we have a clear picture of what Operation Dragons will be. So I want you to take some special courses. I'm working on the clearances. Don't take risks with that oil blaze. Some of God's children need you."

February 4, 1974

HARAR, ETHIOPIA

Ethiopia, a land like ancient Rome where every rumor was true, had been resounding with one that sounded like an augury of Nostradamus: *The king of beasts will roar a few times, then he will be caged and he will die.* The *king of beasts* was Emperor Haile

Selassie, the Conquering Lion of Judah, the Power of the Trinity, the Elect of God. And the prophesied end of his long reign was no longer inconceivable—the plague that had long been incubating in the country's marrow had erupted in boils.

Recriminations continued over the 1973 famine in Wollo province, which the government had tried to cover up in an insane pretense to show Ethiopia trouble-free. Rising prices, particularly that of oil, and the cost of the Eritrean war were wreaking havoc with the frail economy. The armed forces and the teachers' association had already demanded substantial pay increases; members of the Confederation of Labor Unions were about to do the same. And most threateningly, the *Dergue*, the junta of unknown officers whom some people saw as saviors in the mold of Fidel Castro's Eighty, had begun its offensive for its declared creeping coup. There had been a revolt during Christmas in the Negele camp near the Kenyan border which, though quelled with promises of better conditions and salaries, had given proof that the Imperial Army's loyalty to the throne had been eroded.

Boding additional ills was the WOJ–ELF grouping with which Captain Tewodoros Wolde—in Getachew's estimation a charismatic Dergue member—had formed an alliance, no doubt to further his own ambitions.

Getachew, clinging to his belief that only the throne could keep Ethiopia united and independent, had applied himself to reversing the tide. Isolated in the ISS, already riddled by Dergue sympathizers, he had petitioned the emperor for a special force to flush out the conspirators. The eighty-two-year-old monarch, claiming he held absolute power by divine right, had rejected Getachew's warnings as outlandish but, in recognition of Getachew's concern, had assigned an aging Imperial Bodyguard, Sergeant Imru, to assist him in naming "the dogs that dared bark."

In desperation, Getachew had approached Al Jameson for a CIA unit. Jameson, hampered by both America's post-Vietnam mood of nonintervention and the present troubles of Watergate, had complied with one combatant, himself—and that unofficially.

The imperative for action had presented itself immediately. Captain Wolde had been invited by the Harar military academy to give lectures on guerrilla warfare. Since the invitation, extended over and above recognized experts, had smacked of string-pulling by powers unknown, Getachew had speculated that Wolde had come to attend the extraordinary meeting that, according to the grapevine, the Dergue had planned for some time.

The surveillance on Wolde had started at noon when the latter had made his way to Harar's old quarter, an area still enclosed literally and culturally by a wall and as prohibitive as when, less than a hundred years earlier, it had stood as Islam's third forbidden city.

Getachew and Jameson, familiar figures in Imperial Army circles, had decided to preserve anonymity by operating in the background. They had separated at the marketplace; Jameson kept as his bearing the three-gabled wooden house where the poet Rimbaud had lived his damnation, and which had become an attraction for tourists. Getachew progressed along the larger houses of silversmiths and basket-weavers. Sergeant Imru held the center. The objective was to tail Wolde to the Dergue's lair, then pepper the area with miniature cameras. They hoped to have identified all the Dergue members by that evening.

Despite their expertise, Getachew and Jameson found the going difficult. The lanes of the old quarter climbed or descended haphazardly; alleyways intersected sharply and suddenly. The houses, whitewashed and squat, overlapped more often than not, obstructing the view. Their feet trailed in effluvia. The locals, hostile toward strangers, either blocked their way or jostled them.

Only Sergeant Imru progressed satisfactorily. Dressed in the stifling heat in thick trousers, shoes and a heavy shamma, thus covering feet, legs, arms and hands, he looked like a leper trying to hide his affliction. People allowed him passage for dread of contagion. The danger was that he generated revulsion. The Hararis had restricted the lepers to the periphery of the six gates and Sergeant Imru feared that the barrage of invective might arouse Wolde's suspicions.

But Wolde marched on. People made way for him. He was in uniform, and his hand rested on his holster. The Hararis knew a killer when they saw one.

✗

Wolde had spotted Sergeant Imru as far back as the marketplace. The latter's gait had the unmistakable grit of the Imperial Bodyguard. Wolde had been informed of Getachew's audience with the emperor by a Dergue member in the higher echelons of the ISS.

The Dergue had not been unduly worried by Getachew's offensive. Ethiopia was a country where even time could be hidden. The Dergue was adept at that or it would not have survived. Getachew could be disarmed with some ingenuity. That was the dynamics of subversion: one could strike like the flea.

Wolde deprecated that philosophy. He belonged to the school of wholesale solutions. But such solutions required heavy armor. And while he forged his by collaborating with Russia, WOJ and

the ELF—all of them future targets—he needed to harness himself to the Dergue's line. He had agreed to defuse Getachew and
Jameson circumspectly. But at least Sergeant Imru could be eliminated with panache.

He turned into an alleyway. Six hefty Gallas, recruited by a
Harari police inspector seeking to join the Dergue, were waiting
for him. "The one in leper's guise."

The Gallas slunk away, seemingly intoxicated by *chat*.

Wolde stopped by a bar bearing the legend "Charle D. Gaul."
The bar's owner beckoned him. "Best cabaret. The Smokers. Very
exciting."

Wolde glanced back at the Gallas. They had encircled Sergeant
Imru and, claiming to be vigilantes on the lookout for lepers, were
shouting abuse. He walked into the Charle D. Gaul.

The commotion continued. The Gallas turned violent. Ser-
geant Imru hit back. He was strong and brave—a hero of the
Italian war—but he was one against six, fists against heavy clubs.
He collapsed after a series of blows on the head.

Both Getachew and Jameson, having kept their line, saw the
incident. By the time they could push through the crowd, the
Gallas and Imru had disappeared.

Police whistles blew shrilly from various directions.

Getachew pointed at the Charle D. Gaul. "In there, Al. Stay
with Wolde, I'll see to Imru." He ran into the nearest alleyway.

Jameson hurried into the bar. The owner looked pleased at the
way business had picked up.

✗

The Charle D. Gaul, despite its name, had little to distinguish it
from other Ethiopian bars. It had a few tables, a regular clientele,
some haggard-looking barmaids and a tiny area that served as a
stage. Wolde was sitting at a front table, salaciously watching the
Smokers. The latter, three Somali women, had just started.
Naked, and gyrating to an indistinguishable piece of music, they
had inserted cigarettes into their vaginas and were in the process
of lighting them.

Jameson was not a prude; during his tour of duty in Africa he
had seen the act often enough. It still sickened him. The women
were invariably withered hags, their vaginas like sore wounds, with
pierced lobes that had kept the orifice strapped for chastity when
they had been young and marriageable.

He sat at a table farthest from the stage.

✗

Getachew found Sergeant Imru on a rubbish heap in an alleyway —garroted with piano wire. He did not have to call the police. They were lying in wait. A revolver barrel tore open his eyebrows. He passed out.

✗

Wolde had summoned the bar's owner and was whispering to her. The latter grinned, took some money, shuffled over to the principal Smoker and muttered something to her. The Smoker grinned in turn and spoke to the other two. They continued gyrating but at a faster tempo, pointing at cigarettes now half smoked.

Jameson realized the gestures were for his benefit. He forced a smile. The Smokers rushed over, put their arms around him and, taking the cigarettes out of their vaginas, tried to push them into his mouth.

He saw Wolde rise. He struggled to get up. The Smokers fell upon him, covering his face with terrible vaginas.

"Let go! For chrissakes let go!"

Giggling, they scratched his arms and stubbed their cigarettes on his body. He started punching.

✗

When Wolde came out, the police were waiting. He nodded. The police saluted smartly and stormed into the bar.

Briskly Wolde walked on. Behind him, Getachew was being bundled off. In a few moments Jameson would be in custody. Both would be jailed, charged respectively with murder and unruly behavior and released only after much haranguing. Not quite the fate they deserved. But they were important people, and their deaths would have caused repercussions. There would be another time.

He quickened his pace. The Dergue had arranged to meet in an abandoned house near the city wall where hermits fed hyenas. It was not an auspicious place. But it was safe. Few Hararis would venture there during the day for fear of offending the Hyena-Men. Conversely, at night, when the hyenas were fed, there would be a crowd, but by then the Dergue would have concluded its meeting and taken its momentous decisions—some of which would earn for him Abu Ismail's gratitude.

He felt elated. He had taken another step toward the reclamation of his beloved Ethiopia.

February 6, 1974

HANISH KEBIR, ETHIOPIA

They had left Aden two nights ago at midnight, with the submarine escort. The voyage had been pleasant, even though they had been cramped for space. The men, all technicians, had been jovial, and the virgins, as ever, accommodating.

Now the *Succubus* lay at anchor in a cove in the Great Hanish, hidden from view of passing ships. Some of the complement swam; others lounged on deck; a few dozed on the beach in the shade of gigantic black rocks that looked like old wrecks washed ashore.

Professor Talat Fawzi stood on the foredeck relishing the breeze, tracing the reefs that grooved islandward and watching the *Khanjar*'s periscope, a mile out at sea.

The submarine acted as watchdog. WOJ were taking no chances on their human cargo. Since leaving Aden, the *Succubus* had not crossed paths with any vessel—an exceptional feat of navigation in so busy a sea.

Next to Fawzi stood the ubiquitous shadow, in this instance Hamdi. Again WOJ were taking no chances. The Red Sea abounded with tales of people who, finding themselves on a doomed ship, burst into death songs and threw themselves overboard. Since Fawzi knew the *Succubus* ferried doom, even swimming was forbidden to him.

An unnecessary precaution. He had not contemplated suicide, though he knew his life's orbit had been broken. In fact, the gravitation toward death had induced serenity. When his double had shot himself in full view of the setting sun, Fawzi had seen that not all death's faces were ugly; that whatever Freud's theories on the death instinct, the return of organic matter to inorganic state had sublimity; that death was the only way to transform the flailing man into a pulsating quasar.

There were moments when the past haunted him. He bemoaned his separation from Charlie Quinn who, as friend, colleague and confidant, had shared so much of his intellectual isolation.

Sometimes he brooded over Charlie's tenderness, remembered those moments of horseplay when the American's manly touch had had a feminine quality. Fawzi had realized, very early on in the relationship, that Charlie dared not admit his homosexuality. Unrequited love, as always, had created barriers. Now, from the death side of life, Fawzi saw how easy it would have been to smash them. He was, after all, a sensual man. And flesh was flesh. He could have knelt before Charlie, partly in charity, partly out of carnal curiosity, and partly for the possibility that the intimacy might have created something startlingly new.

Sometimes, also, he thought about Charlie's CIA connection. The fact had ceased to be a secret long ago. At the time, Fawzi's soft spot for the Americans had been conditioned by the belief that only the U.S. could promote a stable era out of the present mess. He had also nurtured the intellectual's pride that valued freedom of the mind above other considerations and consequently defined the Russian oligarchy as the time bomb that would destroy humanity. Once Charlie had tested his sincerity; he had confessed his CIA post, offering a spate of lame theories as justification. They had often discussed the unholy pragmatism that oiled the CIA and had agreed it was a necessary evil. On one occasion Fawzi had even joked that whereas the U.S. could dismantle the CIA if need be, not even the monolithic Supreme Soviet could liquidate the KGB except with a peculiarly selective nuclear device.

That witticism had now taken substance. A nuclear device that would destroy not only the CIA and the KGB but also the future, was being prepared. And he was in charge of it. His old self, meek with humane considerations, would have sought Charlie's help, would have devised a ruse to contact him. His new self, by contrast, gloried at having been chosen for the task. And not because of the WOJ indoctrination. That had merely disclosed Abu Ismail's vision of the Last of Days which Fawzi had believed to be inevitable.

He had reached the decision without much deliberation. Privy to the nature of Operation Dragons, he had convinced himself that nobody else, certainly no other physicist, could or would nurse the project to its proposed end as decisively as he. It was, if he could for once be unscientific, Allah's Will. Irrevocable.

The decision had also revealed what had remained a mystery to him—the purpose of his life and genius. He would die soon, and for a good reason. Someone would remember his name, pronounce it in awe. Allah, proven to have eyes, would pluck him off the contaminated earth and plant him in Paradise.

"You might get sunstroke."

Abdallah had appeared at his side, reservedly servile.

Fawzi gave him a friendly smile. "I'm enjoying the breeze."

Abdallah pointed at the virgins on the deck. "You'd get more enjoyment out of them."

Fawzi eyed the women and chuckled. They too had substantiated his salvation. He had savored them all, first one by one, then in any number his fantasies dictated. He loved them all. His desire never abated. It was rampant now, though he had not ceased fornicating since their departure from Aden.

"Go on, Talat. Make the most of it. Soon you'll be too busy."

"How soon is soon?"

"We sail again at sunset. We land sometime tonight."

Fawzi rubbed his hands excitedly, then summoned the first three maidens.

February 8, 1974

ZARQA, JORDAN

Osman held his head at an angle to stabilize the pain. A momentary relief; then the pounding started again. He moaned in fury. "I can take it. It's only pain."

Samia squeezed his hands. "Yes, *ayyuni.*"

He forced his eyes open. Hesitantly, he focused on his wife. "Where am I?" He noted his speech was slurred. He also saw his right leg was in traction.

"Infirmary. At Zarqa barracks."

"Since when?"

"Yesterday. You've been under sedation."

Osman managed to look out of the window. The tanks were on the parade ground, but without their crews. A unit of the king's Guards was on patrol. "Am I—is it serious?"

Samia tried to sound casual—as he would expect of her. "Bad —but not serious. Fractured femur with septic gash. And you've been shot in the mouth. The bullet went through your cheeks. . . ."

Osman tried to disperse the clouds that hung low in his head. The effort aggravated the pain. "The king . . . ?"

"He's still talking to the mutineers. . . . He's offered them a raise. They've more or less accepted."

Osman closed his eyes. The clouds lifted slightly. He remembered, in patches, the last few days. The thick air of conspiracy that had brought him to Zarqa. The long silences every time he probed the officers' mess for a clue to the ringleaders. Then, finally, on Thursday: the tanks, screeching, churning dust, armed . . . flying female clothing on their aerials. . . . A declaration that the men, withheld from the common enemy in the Yom Kippur War, had been reduced to women. "We squashed it then. . . . The mutiny?"

"Oh, yes. You stopped the tanks with your body."

"Did I?"

Samia looked away so that he would not see how weak she was, how she feared for his life, how she fought off premonitions that the interminable squabbles over an ancient land would one day claim her man. "So they say."

More of the clouds cleared. The tanks beginning to move. Nothing between them and the Hashemite throne. So he had jumped onto a jeep, driven to the gate and blocked the way. Nose to nose with the lead Centurion's gun barrel, breathing diesel fumes and weapons grease. That was when he had been shot. He remembered hanging on to the steering wheel. Arguing, mouth full of blood. Then, in fury, driving the jeep straight at the Centurion. The agony of his shattered leg. The rest remained vague. The Centurion had not moved to crush the jeep. At some point the engines had been switched off; crews had alighted. Sheepish. Defused. "Who . . . ?" His mouth had dried up. He tried to salivate. He coughed, tasted blood and medicine. . . .

"Who shot you? A Palestinian sympathizer. He's surrendered. . . ."

"Who was behind it? Do they know?"

"WOJ is what I heard. . . ."

"WOJ don't have to resort to this. They have a final solution in mind."

"Final solution?"

Osman managed to seize the threads of the conversation. He had lived with his secret for so long that suppression had become an involuntary reflex. "What final solution?"

"That's what you said—about WOJ. . . ."

"Did I? Figure of speech . . ."

Samia looked into his eyes. A deep secret, quite separate from those official ones. He had wanted to talk about this one. Now, at his weakest, he had held back again. There would never be another opportunity. "I understand. . . ."

He raised her hands to his lips, then stopped. His mouth was like pulp.

She persisted with the gesture, placed her hands gently on his mouth. "I love your lips, Osman."

He smiled. "You're my blessing, Samia."

She lowered her eyes. "And you are mine."

He dropped her hands, closed his eyes. The hammering in his head rose another pitch. He felt faint, fought against it. "When will they let me out?"

"Soon."

"Tell them tomorrow. Or I'll discharge myself—"

"You'll discharge yourself when they've mended you."

"There's much to do."

"It will have to wait."

Osman felt weakness envelop him. Thoughts stampeded through his head. WOJ had not been behind the mutiny. Other Palestinian agitators—from Beirut, from Damascus, from Baghdad. Weeds that the king would root out. But WOJ was still the ultimate threat. And they were regrouping. In Ethiopia, the Memouneh believed. Osman knew for certain. Ethiopia was the right place—perfectly located for the target. The countdown had probably begun. Concerted action should be taken. . . .

He fell asleep.

Samia adjusted the pillows and sat back. She urged herself to rejoice. Osman had had a miraculous escape. The gash and the cheek wounds would heal in a couple of weeks. The leg would take another two to three weeks. Yet she felt severed from life, like a widow.

February 12, 1974

REHOVOT, ISRAEL

On January 31 four members of the PFLP and *Rengo Sekigun* had attempted to blow up the Shell oil installations in Singapore and, having failed, had hijacked the ferry *Laju*, holding its passengers hostage. Declared motive: to denounce the Israeli elections as a crime against Palestinian rights. On Feburary 3, three Pakistani terrorists had hijacked the Greek ship *Vori* in Karachi. Declared motive: retaliation against death sentences on two Arab terrorists who had killed five and injured fifty-five at Athens airport in August 1973. On Feburary 7 other members of the PFLP and *Rengo Sekigun* had seized the Japanese embassy in Kuwait. Declared motive: to secure the release of the Singapore terrorists.

Intelligence reports, still filtering in, suggested that the operations had been masterminded by WOJ. Mossad evaluations, however, refuted the connection on the grounds that none of the groups involved owed WOJ favors. Both theories had to be cross-checked.

That would have been enough to keep Kidan tied to his desk. But there was more. In the Oslo verdicts on the Lillehammer affair, Norway's leniency toward the Israeli hit team—prison sentences ranging from five and a half years to one, and one acquittal —had incensed the Arab world. WOJ and other Palestinian groups had threatened retaliatory action, and measures had to be taken accordingly.

There was still more work. Sanbat had filed reports on the intelligence amassed by the Falashas. Though these offered no clues to WOJ activity in Ethiopia, they still had to be processed through the computer in the hope that one snippet dovetailed with another.

Yet, Kidan had had to drop everything and deliver Boaz to the Weizmann Institute of Science.

"Different from Mecca—eh, Boaz?"

Boaz surveyed the luscious gardens, the concrete-and-glass monoliths of faculties and laboratories, and the constant rush of the country's brainpower. Another world with another pulse.

"Let the Arabs catch us if they can. Look at it—twenty-first century already."

"It's man-made, Kidan."

"What's that mean?"

"Mecca will always be there."

"Is that meant to be profound?"

Boaz ignored him, quickened his pace. That made Kidan all the more resentful. Operation Dragons was slipping out of his hands. He hated himself for shirking a showdown with the Memouneh when the latter, clinging to the archaic belief that the conflict would be decided in single combat between Boaz and Abu Ismail, had brought Boaz into the war room. Now, carrying unorthodoxy to ridiculous lengths, the Memouneh had pressed Boaz to a crash course in nuclear weaponry.

"This is all a waste of time—you realize, Boaz? In the end we'll have to go in. Raid Libya—or wherever. You've seen the plans. That's what I've been doing while you were sightseeing in Mecca."

"Pat yourself on the shoulder."

Kidan hissed. "Where do you think you're stepping? Into my shoes?"

Boaz stopped, but instead of the brittleness that Kidan had wished to provoke, he displayed amusement. "Turds can share the same sewer quite happily. Why can't we, Kidan?"

"Another profound statement?"

Boaz shook his head in exasperation. "What do you want me to say? God save Israel from your plans?"

The sudden emergence of a group of men from the central library prevented Kidan from responding. "Fuck, there's our lot! Don't think you've had the last word! The blackie's your man. God knows how he came out of Oriental stock. But then we all know history has turned its back on the best of us."

Boaz ignored him and noted Matityahu, a young, frail Cochin Indian, standing apart from the worldly deans and bodyguards.

Those who knew swore that Matityahu was the genius who would, one day, devise Israel's ultimate deterrent. The Memouneh, always obsessed with choosing the best, had moved heaven and earth to get him. Matityahu would teach Boaz the intricacies of nuclear weapons—from the standard ones to the crude dirties that could be homemade with the right amount of fissionable material.

Boaz empathized with Matityahu's visible isolation. Resentment against a fate that had cast him as the new Moses. What sins had Matityahu committed to deserve such disfavor?

The groups met. Boaz left Kidan to talk to the deans and proffered a hand to Matityahu. The other's grip, though weak, had warmth. "We'll start immediately, Colonel Ben Ya'ir. We have a lot of ground to cover. "I—I read your file. I'm overawed by your accomplishments. I feel privileged—"

Boaz winced, shocked that such a mind could be seduced by the cult of the warrior. "Please, Professor . . ."

Matityahu nodded shyly and led the way to the Institute of Nuclear Science. Kidan, the deans and the bodyguards stayed back to discuss security arrangements.

Boaz felt disturbed by the fact that he could carry the horror of his mission impassively—unlike Osman, who had carried it alone, and with saintly consideration for others. But then Osman was born to be tested against evil. He never shirked the ordeal—his bravery during the Zarqa mutiny was proof of that. Every generation produced such men and one trembled for them, as Boaz had, until reassured that Osman's injuries were, miraculously, not too serious. And every generation produced expendable soldier-ants like himself. Ironically, in the final analysis, the soldier-ants had the better bargain. They lived and died with greater ease.

February 19, 1974

ADDIS ABABA, ETHIOPIA

Getachew was into his third bottle of *kati kala*, the local brew guaranteed to perforate any stomach. Jameson, deciding that in so much *vino* Getachew's depression was genuine, wondered what had made him suspect Getachew, why he had woven theories that the Harar episode had been a Machiavellian ruse to discredit him and get him out of Ethiopia. He, too, was in his cups, and hardly in a state to trace the roots of his misplaced suspicions. Something about the Dergue and its complement of patriots . . . Getachew was a patriot, therefore a candidate for the Dergue; Jameson was

CIA, one of the pillars that supported the Imperial Throne; so what more natural than that he should be compromised?

"What will happen to you, Al?"

"It won't be the firing squad."

That was what his boss, Gentleman Jim, had said. Instead, it would be an obscure think tank analyzing data or playing war games. With countless others just like him. Gentleman Jim, so called because he had been army heavyweight champion, represented the new Uncle Sam. The gelded giant. Withdrawing soldiers from the field, abandoning God to those who denied Him. Prophets of freedom called the malady, crisis of confidence; woolly intellectuals defended it as liberalism and nonintervention. Jameson summed it up differently. Nobody wanted to be his brother's keeper anymore. "I'm surprised we got out of jail."

Getachew shuddered as he remembered Harar prison. It had taken them two weeks to get out. This, despite pressure from the emperor and waffled pleas from the U.S. Embassy. Getachew had had to admit that the Dergue's influence had increased even beyond his most pessimistic assessment. "I'll miss you, Al."

"Get to know Montblanc in Djibouti. Good man. Also in case of emergency try Lieutenant O'Brien. Defense Intelligence Agency. At Kagnew. Real whiz kid."

"It won't be the same."

The jukebox recommenced with "Tekeza," the hit of 1972 now a classic. It meant "nostalgia." Jameson staggered to the porch. The sun was up, balancing like a heavy crown on Mount Entoto. The air was fragrant with the breath of eucalyptus trees. Tiny jets of firewood—or was it frankincense?—stoked the day. And the day would take him to Asmara, thence to Washington. Disgraced.

"Addis Ababa—New Flower. I used to dream about this city, Getachew. When the world was a colorful high school atlas. . . . I came here by choice. Volunteered. I had such expectations."

Getachew joined him on the porch. "They have fallen short?"

"Civilization, you see. The way I figure, life has less value now than it did ten thousand years ago. I expected to find an old wisdom here—primeval. Some source which would evolve us—not toward perdition but eternal survival. But it's not out there, is it?"

"No."

"What is out there, Getachew?"

Getachew craned his neck. The Debre Zeyt road stretched toward the high-rise blocks of the modern metropolis like a lazy anaconda. The nightclubs were still active. Yet uptown the streets were littered with stones, broken glass and burned cars; hospitals full of wounded students—some barely in their teens. The riots that had started the day before were gathering momentum. Ostensibly, students were supporting the teachers' strike called for the eighteenth—but the undertones were ominous. "You really want to know, Al?"

"I really want to know."

Getachew directed his eyes at a small group of people, homeless and hungry, scavenging at the side of the road. They often found scraps which a young poet had said were alms from weeping ancestors buried beneath. "Graves. Waiting to be filled."

Jameson remembered Sergeant Imru's belated funeral. An ornate parchment scroll of divine invocation had been tied to his feet to guide him through his journey to Heaven. One grave had already been filled. "Yeah, that's what I see, too."

Getachew drank from his bottle. "Do you—really? But you come from a world where there are no graves—only Elysian Fields."

"What about Vietnam?"

"Lost opportunity. You never thought of the Vietnamese."

Jameson felt nauseous. The criticism, though harsh, was justified. He felt ashamed for having doubted Getachew. "I'll come back. . . ." He met Getachew's hopeful look. "If need be as a civilian. I promise you."

"It won't be much fun sharing the same grave."

"I don't know, buddy. If you're hooked on poker, a grave's as good a place as any to while away the time."

Getachew guffawed. "I'll keep you to your promise, Al."

Jameson laughed heartily. He had not done so for a long time. It took the sting out of the eunuch's summons home.

ASMARA, ETHIOPIA

The Lockheed C-5A Galaxy, Jameson's transport home, was being loaded with equipment and files in the U.S. Air Force hangar. At the other end of the airport, in the international terminal, Russian observers were, as usual, manning binoculars. Next to Jameson stood Sanbat, solicitous.

Jameson, hung over, was reminded of the leavetaking so common to overseas personnel. The GI going home, leaving behind a much-loved household; greedy eyes waiting to scavenge, and a sympathizer standing by disconsolate.

"Nice of you to see me off, Sanbat. How did you pass security?"

"Just walked through."

Jameson winced. That, too, fitted the picture. When the menage breaks up, who cares who walks into the house?

"I'm here officially, Al. My request comes straight from my chief."

Sanbat sounded as if she were extracting her words from her nerve roots. Jameson had a good idea of her heavy loads. Interminable hours manning the Asmara office; surveillance at airports; desperate pursuit of clues on WOJ and Dedeyan's murder.

"We have different interests, Al. But there are times when they coincide. It's such a time now. Against WOJ. The Sons of Light against the Forces of Darkness. Irrespective of anything."

Jameson grimaced at the Biblical language. "Irrespective of Ethiopia too? The riots? The Dergue?"

"Whatever happens, Ethiopia will still be here—mauled, perhaps, but alive. If WOJ have their way, it will be the Dark Ages for everybody."

"Okay, Sanbat—cut the commercials. . . ."

"When you get back, dig into your archives. Nothing happens in this world without a record of it somewhere in your files. Sooner or later you'll find it."

Jameson looked away thoughtfully. The Galaxy, loaded now, was undergoing final checks. "Find what?"

"Where the WOJ lair is. What they're up to. Target, date, deployment. We're convinced, when you find it, you'll join forces with us. Have a good trip. *Shalom.*"

She kissed him on both cheeks. Incomprehensibly, Jameson felt a deserter.

February 24, 1974

THE DANAKIL ALPS, ETHIOPIA

Idris Ali surveyed WOJ's new outpost—designated by Abu Ismail as "the penultimate tent before Allah's abode." The technicians, more prosaically, had named it "Little Petra" after the hidden Nabatean city in Jordan.

On the clearing where he stood, affectionately dubbed *maidan*, converged sixteen ravines; their high and jagged cliffs of maroon and red sandstone stood as the petrified remains of a prehistoric waterfall. The maidan and most of the ravine beds had eroded extensively. Not so the clifftops which revealed narrow strips of sky, now barely visible above the camouflage netting. The sun, even at midday, penetrated only in wisps of light.

Four of the ravines offered little width. The remaining twelve, each possessing caves of various sizes, were in use. Four, with rock pools solving the problem of cooling water for the machinery, would accommodate the factory. Another four quartered the technicians and the virgins. The virgins' quarters also served as field kitchen and refectory. Drinking water brought from Aden was rationed to give the supply shuttle maximum space for the large quantity of oil required for the generators. The ninth ravine,' an oasis of rock pools and desert vegetation, sheltered the livestock and the beasts of burden. The tenth provided private quarters for Professor Talat Fawzi and Ischii Watanabe. The eleventh, the most arid, had been selected as infirmary and burial ground. The twelfth, farthest from the factory, served as command HQ.

Idris Ali studiously observed the task force. The virgins and the technicians had worked indefatigably to clear the area. Now, relaxing on the maidan, they looked like nomads squatting over good pasture. Fully conditioned by drugs, they had fathomed the substance of the mission and were as resolute as a tribe on the march.

Idris Ali's attention lingered on Fawzi and Watanabe, engrossed in a game of chess. Since one would make the bomb and the other devise the high-explosive chambers, the fuses, booby-traps and trigger mechanisms, they were, for the present, the two most important people. Fawzi, provided with a miniature library to complement the attentions of the virgins, displayed exemplary goodwill. Not so Watanabe. Only drugs, which now included heroin, moderated his hysteria.

Idris Ali cast another look at the maidan. He had relished the last six weeks. Setting up the defenses, installing the generators that provided electricity and air conditioning, erecting the system of mirrors that magnified the available light, and soundproofing the outpost against aerial listening devices, had crowned his ingenuity.

He turned to Badran, promoted to second-in-command. "Final briefing on the defenses."

Badran led the way up a rope ladder to the top of the highest ravine.

Badran and the other Lisbon veterans, still maintaining platoon formations A, B, H, M and Q, formed the nucleus of the defense forces. Platoon A, whose commander, Abdallah, had been commissioned to run the supply shuttle from Aden to Barassoli, had a new leader. Each platoon now had six warriors apiece. Five new platoons, D, F, G, N and W, also of six men each, constituted reinforcements. All had parachuted into Eritrea on the night of January 10–11 from a DC-6B secured from Qaddafi and operating as a cargo carrier between Tripoli and Aden. They had made their way separately to the outpost—in the process acquiring from Wolde and Hamdi such essentials as vehicles, livestock and provisions—well in time to receive the technicians and the virgins.

They reached the top of the ravine and scanned the Danakil Alps encircling them.

Badran indicated a strategic peak. "That's where Platoon D is deploying. They have unrestricted views over every channel that might be passable. Machine-gun nests at vantage points. Enough dynamite in the rocks to detonate the whole mountain."

During his reconnaissance in November Idris Ali had already assessed that the southern perimeter offered little threat. The terrain, strewn with dead craters and fissures, was practically impassable. He had even considered leaving it undefended, but with so much at stake, caution had prevailed. "I can't see any of the men. Excellent."

Badran pointed to the west. "Platoons F and G over there. You won't see them either. Well spread out. Machine-gun nests. Mortars. Dynamite to cover all the gullies."

Idris Ali surveyed the western ridges, dominated by Ramlo, an active volcano and the Danakil Alps's highest peak, some twenty kilometers away. Granite sheets, basaltic lava clustered like columns of weird, misshapen timber, and volcanic plugs standing sentry over sandstone canyons in shades of dark patina sketched the perimeter. Jubal Wallace, the Australian explorer whose papers and maps had led WOJ to this region, had described the landscape as the most chaotic on earth. Beyond, the ridges descended sharply onto gravel plains, thus offering a perfect view over an approaching force.

Idris Ali turned to the north. The terrain was similar. There Mount Dubbi dominated the volcanic activity. Around it, sheets of fire blazed in the craters as if perpetually ignited by the sun. Beyond, the terrain plunged toward the Dallol Depression as a dazzling desert of salt, remnants of a severed ocean that had evaporated under intense heat.

Badran pointed at the ridges. "Platoons N and Q. They're spread out to cover the desert approaches. Also armed to the teeth. The western and northern platoons maintain visual contact as well as radio, and can lend assistance to each other if need be."

Idris Ali nodded. The northern perimeter, too, opening up to flatlands, precluded a surprise attack. Two platoons could hold an army at bay indefinitely. "Excellent. The gorge now."

Badran led the way.

The gorge at the eastern perimeter was the most vulnerable stretch. It opened onto a wadi which cut through a range of basalt peaks to meet the sea at the secluded cove near Barassoli, some fifty kilometers away. Thus it constituted the outpost's lifeline. The terrain to the cove where the *Succubus* and the *Khanjar* would put in was either rock or shifting sands. WOJ convoys could travel through it without leaving a trace. By the same token, an enemy force could push inland for a surprise attack undetected. Consequently, the wadi and the gorge had to be defended in depth, and for this purpose they had been allocated four platoons.

They reached the high ground overlooking the gorge. Badran pointed at the wadi beyond. "Platoon A is farthest out. They're dug in at the escarpments overlooking the coastal plain. Electronic devices placed all around—and monitoring. Platoon A will act as our trip wire. Should an enemy approach, it'll let them through, then backtrack to attack them in the rear. Platoon H is spread out in the wadi. Platoon W is deployed on the peaks. And Platoon M at the entrance to the gorge. All equipped with machine guns, mortars, dynamite. Plus SAM-7s—in case of an aerial raid."

"Good."

"That leaves my platoon B. We form the last line of defense. At Little Petra. Fully equipped—plus radioactive material."

Idris Ali scanned the area again, concentrating this time on the clusters of rock columns on both sides of the wadi which offered convenient niches to conceal the Land-Rovers and fuel storage tanks.

"Right, Badran. Maneuvers for the next few days. Simulated attacks on the base. Get the platoons fluid, able to reinforce any given position. Let's consolidate."

Badran could not hide his excitement. "We're ready, then?"

Idris Ali smiled. He remembered how in pre-WOJ days in Russia, when he was still a neophyte in terror, he had often fantasized a secret hideout like a SMERSH complex in a James Bond film, where he could perpetrate ingenious operations to repoliticize the world as he saw fit. Now he had forged fantasy into reality. What the WOJ base lacked in Bondian gimmickry it compensated for with deadly functionalism: invisible from sky or land, impenetrable except by hyenas and lizards, impregnable to any force save an earthquake or a volcanic explosion. "Yes. We're ready. Signal Abdallah to pick me up. Then alert Tripoli I'm coming to get the plutonium."

February 27, 1974

LEIPZIG, GERMAN DEMOCRATIC REPUBLIC

The *Liedermacher* sang about a pregnant scientist's dilemma over whether she should selfishly bear the child she wanted or have an abortion and continue serving the state. The students from Leipzig's Karl Marx University listened devotedly as if, Ivan Mikhailovich Volkov mused, the song had been composed by Bach and the lyrics taken from Luther's disputation. Banal art and the affectation it generated depicted for him the future envisioned by Russia's ruling gerontocracy: a commonwealth of obsolete robot workers.

He returned his attention to Idris Ali. They had not met since November; the communications he had received had invariably echoed Abu Ismail's otherwordly tones, making him wonder whether Idris Ali had disintegrated. He need not have feared. Idris Ali looked as complete as when he had put his signature on him. Undoubtedly his masterpiece. He could not have had better material: a formidable spirit drifting through the maze of Arab aspirations, amoral, fearless and exceptionally receptive to parapsychological manipulation.

Yet, Idris Ali was under stress. That had manifested itself in his criticism of the venue for the meeting, despite Volkov's assurances that their casual encounter in Leipzig would seem coincidental since both were on legitimate business—Idris Ali to purchase medical supplies, Volkov at a conference with East German colleagues —and that not even their worst enemies would expect them to plan the reconstruction of the world in a crowded beer hall.

The stress, Volkov realized, was rooted in Idris Ali's ambition. And that was heartening.

The Liedermacher finished to boisterous applause. Volkov drew his chair closer to Idris Ali, filled the glasses with vodka, then offered a toast with a skeletal hand. "They'll sing a different song when the fire consumes them."

Idris Ali raised his glass. Volkov, sitting like Death reviewing the day's harvest, reminded him of Abu Ismail—inebriated by tomorrow's nectar. It never occurred to them that tomorrow was always spawned by today. All the better. The seekers of tomorrow would clear the field. He, Idris Ali, the man equipped to seize today, would be the one to plow it.

"To business, Ivan Mikhailovich. We have to seal our alliance."

Volkov's puny eyebrows danced. "Sealed. You will have my full backing—unless you fail to manufacture the bomb."

"The umbrella?"

"Three of our best soldiers. Admiral Yuri Tiblyashin, flag officer of the Soviet Indian Ocean fleet. Air Force General Alexei Larinchev, commanding officer of our only air base outside the Warsaw Pact—the Tu-22 Soviet bomber squadron, Baghdad. And Marshal of the Red Army Sergei Yeliseev, commander of land forces. A formidable combination. You'll have their files."

"You've taught me to distrust files."

Volkov chuckled and gulped down his drink. "Let me sum them up for you. Admiral Yuri Tiblyashin. A throwback to old Russia. A passionate man of aristocratic bearing, monk's asceticism and hussar's obsession for glory. He dreams that Russia, like the Christ he secretly prays to, will blanket the world. He realizes our alliance will create chaos. Chaos will undermine the West. That would crown his aspirations."

Idris Ali nodded.

Volkov refilled his glass. "Next. Air Force General Alexei Larinchev. A great tactician. He's familiar with Islamic fanaticism. He knows that Muslim wrath harnessed—total jihad—would carry anybody to victory. Not as bold as Yuri Tiblyashin, but very ambitious. He'll snuggle behind any slipstream."

"If he's not bold, he may pull out."

"He won't. I've promised him the Defense Ministry. He sees that as the perfect perch from which to shoot down his rivals—including me."

Idris Ali sipped his drink. "Truly misguided."

Volkov smiled, drank heartily. "Finally, Marshal Sergei Yeliseev. Russia's most decorated soldier. What makes him even more special is that he's apolitical. Consequently, he's never been involved in power struggles. Conversely, he sees such struggles as the crucible in which the men of the times are forged. He has served every leader loyally. And he will serve me from the moment I wrest the leadership. He understands that is inevitable. He has gauged the support I have within the hierarchy. He knows that I shall be riding, as you once put it, an invincible dragon."

Idris Ali nodded. "Sounds good."

Volkov reclined in his chair, not at all perturbed by Idris Ali's restraint. The best time to analyze a man was when doubt haunted him. Idris Ali, face shining with sweat, high on adrenaline, was still functioning like a well-oiled automaton. That was what counted. Reservations and doubts would crumble when he unveiled the throne he had built for Idris Ali since completing him.

"The finer details, Ivan Mikhailovich. We must create diversionary tactics for the next two months—while we make the bomb. The enemy will be ferreting. We must confuse them as to where and how Operation Dragons will strike. Even more important, we must smokescreen Ethiopia. That won't be easy. The situation there will deteriorate. There'll be disturbances—some of them violent, engineered by Wolde at our request."

"What have you planned so far?"

"With the exception of the Ethiopian disturbances—which

must appear as national unrest—we'll take credit for every operation going, terrorist or otherwise. For instance, we've already claimed we were behind the Zarqa mutiny in Jordan."

"Pity it failed. Osman Nusseibi—getting to be a thorn in your side."

"His time will come."

"Of course."

"You must substantiate our claim. State them as facts through the Russian news media."

"Rest assured."

"Now, early in March, Israel should complete her withdrawal from the west bank of Suez. We'll threaten to celebrate that in our inimitable way in Cairo, Tel Aviv and Amman. We also have intelligence on several hijacks from Beirut. We'll hitch on to those as well."

Volkov nodded approval.

Idris Ali continued. "On to April. April needs careful handling. By then, we'll be at the final countdown. Keeping very low in Ethiopia. Qaddafi has been planning Sadat's assassination—we've asked him to postpone it until April. He's agreed."

"Excellent. That should preoccupy everybody—Arabs, Israelis, Americans . . ."

"Quite. But we'll appear to be concentrating on Israel. Nearly all the Palestinian groups are preparing operations for the Jew's Passover and Israel's Independence Day. Some promise to be bloodbaths. We'll put our names to every single one."

"Admirable."

Idris Ali drained his glass but remained primed. "Finally—the big lie. We'll launch it as soon as we find the perfect platform. Abu Ismail will personally warn the world that Israel has nuclear capability—and that she's planning a strike against the Arabs to force them into a peace treaty."

Volkov pursed his lips. "I'm still uneasy about that. It could prove premature—give the game away."

"We'll be fighting Mossad and everyone else whatever they think the game is. The issue is world opinion. The big lie will generate sympathy for us *and* brainwash the world for what's to happen."

Volkov conceded the point. "You'll need proof of Israel's nuclear capability."

"It's an open secret."

"Solid facts would sound better. How about the Lillehammer affair? While questioning the Israeli hit team, the Norwegian secret service uncovered some interesting facts. For example, in

1968 Israel secured two hundred tons of yellowcake—uranium oxide—capable of yielding weapons-grade material. . . ."

"Documented?"

"Absolutely. We make sure we get our facts right."

"That's perfect."

Volkov straightened up. "Nothing else to iron out? Reservations?"

"None on the planning."

"The planning's impeccable—your work, isn't it?"

"Yes."

Volkov paused dramatically. "Come, dear comrade. We can see into each other's mind. You didn't come here just to seal our alliance. You came to reassess me. To make sure I am what I was. And, by the same token, to show me you are still what you were. To put it more bluntly: your reservations have nothing to do with your plans or my contribution to Operation Dragons. They center on Abu Ismail. You want to take over."

Idris Ali met Volkov's gaze, but remained impassive.

Volkov dropped his voice to a tantalizing whisper. "Now, if you're waiting for me to ask you to take over . . ."

Idris Ali felt an intensity he had experienced only once before —at his first killing. Today—and its dependent tomorrow—was within his grasp. "Go on. . . ."

Volkov patted Idris Ali's shoulder with the nearest emotion to affection he had felt for anybody. "I'm asking you. Take over. We've had enough of senile men bending to the wind from their graveside. The world wants us—stalwart young men."

Idris Ali smiled. "So be it."

Volkov raised his glass. Idris Ali followed suit. They drank ceremoniously.

"It can't happen immediately, Ivan Mikhailovich. . . ."

"It *mustn't*. Abu Ismail is well entrenched. Besides, for the moment, he's a useful figurehead."

"Yes. I thought when we leave Ethiopia with the bomb . . ."

"I agree. The best time. He'll be isolated. And vulnerable."

Idris Ali laughed and projected himself into the future. It was imageless—but bright as the center of a prism. Ingathering color. It contrasted sharply with the past. The dour days of apprenticeship with the KGB. The somber mysticism of Abu Ismail. Two mighty currents, seemingly repelling each other. He had not known how they would coexist, if at all. Which way he would have to jump. Now, suddenly, the currents had fused. Irresistibly.

Volkov watched him indulgently. Pretender's daydreams. Arabian-night fantasies.

March 1, 1974

TRIPOLI, LIBYA

" 'Allah has knowledge of all your actions.' "

The words, echoing, gave a final resonance to Abu Ismail's prayers. Idris Ali repeated the invocation. He had managed to summon tears; he imagined his face to be formidable.

The men started shunting the forklifts. Idris Ali moved to the DC-6B's cargo hold. As the machinery was loaded, he checked the heavy-duty parachutes harnessed to each crate.

Abu Ismail, seated on a high chair and flanked by Nazmi, conferred with his sixth sense. He had hoped this moment would be as fragrant as a leave-taking in a rose garden. But Idris Ali had spoiled it, reducing occasion and place to sordid human dimensions: illicit work in a derelict hangar at a disused end of Tripoli International Airport. Idris Ali, whom he had elevated to heirship, had returned from the Russian a different man, an impetuous Aladdin brandishing the Kremlin's contaminated lamp. The Eater of the Dead, scurrying to bury Allah's green world, to devour sun, water, pasture and desert, had bitten into Idris Ali's soul. All of which was evident in the tears that held no substance, in the expressions of loyalty grossly tainted with unnatural pride.

Abu Ismail sought comfort from the excruciating pains in his arthritic limbs. They, at least, had substance. Like growing pains, they were forging bones, multiplying cells so that he could stand on the Day of Glory as the giant he was, in flesh as well as in spirit, purged of doubt, immune to betrayal.

"Al-Mahdi. We are ready to load the plutonium."

He turned to Idris Ali standing before him, drenched in honest warrior's sweat. He nodded.

Idris Ali prostrated himself. "Al-Mahdi, I shall justify your trust in me. Only death can cause me to fail."

Abu Ismail pulled Idris Ali up and gazed deeply into his eyes. They appeared clear, like springwater, and momentarily he was dazzled by the artifice. "Remember—an arrow that has left the bow cannot be summoned back."

Idris Ali kissed Abu Ismail's hands. The gesture exposed yet again the Eater of the Dead, lying in the depths of Idris Ali's retina, yelping with its wide, evil mouth.

Abu Ismail thundered: " 'Permission to take up arms is hereby given to those who are attacked, because they have been wronged. Allah has power to grant them victory.' "

Idris Ali moved ceremoniously to the plutonium coffin. He

checked the parachutes; satisfied, he signaled the warriors to load it onto the DC-6B.

Abu Ismail closed his eyes for a further assessment of the Eater of the Dead. The question remained—could it be exorcised? He knew the answer. But, like a father hoping his delinquent son would reform before the ultimate betrayal, he had decided to hold back the hour of disownment. The blow, merciless and final, could be delivered anytime.

March 2, 1974

THE DANAKIL DESERT, ETHIOPIA

The air rippled with sulfur fumes. Within the hour the sun would deaden everything; nothing would move but creatures with the sturdiest lungs.

The DC-6B, emerging from the west, caught the sunrise and sparkled like a celestial eye. Badran signaled the men to light the fires, then checked his watch: 5:53 A.M.

✗

Idris Ali, strapped into his seat behind Abbas and Isa, WOJ's senior and support pilots, counted the seconds. Abbas had to descend to below radar range, circle the area for some four minutes to complete the drop, then climb again and proceed to Aden according to his flight plan. The brief disappearance from the radar screens —Ethiopian as well as American at Kagnew base—had to be justified. On January 10–11, the previous occasion when the DC-6B had descended below radar range to drop the WOJ task force, admission of a navigational error and subsequent apology had sufficed. But as the same excuse, in view of the secessionist war in Eritrea, might arouse suspicion, Idris Ali had instructed Abbas to provide a plausible reason which would satisfy any curiosity.

He tapped Abbas's shoulder. The senior pilot, who had learned his flying at Hamble, in England, switched the radio to the South Eritrea air traffic control center's frequency and summoned his best English accent.

"Five-Alpha-Delta-Yankee-Delta-November-Foxtrot-Three-Three-One-Three calling South Eritrea . . ."

"South Eritrea . . . Go ahead, Five-Alpha-Delta-Yankee . . ."

"South Eritrea . . . We are having trouble with the pressurization system. . . . Request clearance to descend to flight level seventy . . . Five-Alpha-Delta-Yankee . . ."

"Five-Alpha-Delta-Yankee . . . Request granted. . . . Clear to descend flight level seventy. . . . South Eritrea standing by . . ."

Abbas glanced back at Idris Ali and winked. He commenced the descent.

Idris Ali looked out of the window. The drop area, even from eighteen thousand feet, looked like a scrap heap for Allah's discarded designs.

✗

There had been twenty-eight crates parachuted; the last, the plutonium coffin, was still in the air. The men were already driving the Land-Rovers to pick them up. The DC-6B turned out of its last circuit, waggled its wings in salute and climbed away at full throttle.

Badran listened on his radio to the conversation between Abbas and South Eritrea air traffic control. The latter had voiced its concern over the plane's problems and now sounded relieved by Abbas's assurances that the malfunction had been rectified. Abbas requested a new flight level and confirmed the next reporting point.

✗

Idris Ali positioned himself by the open hatch, drew breath and launched himself.

For a while he free-fell, imbibing the dawn's henna hues over the earth that awaited to receive him as its master. Nearer the ground, he pulled his cord and dealt with the opening shock expertly.

He landed strongly, as a conqueror should.

PART VIII

Truth Sits upon the Lips of Dead Men.

MATTHEW ARNOLD, *Sohrab and Rustum*

March 8, 1974

KIBBUTZ TEL KATZIR, ISRAEL

It was Purim, the Feast of Esther, when it was incumbent upon the Jew to drink until unable to differentiate between "Blessed be Mordechai" and "Cursed be Haman": to laugh at customs, institutions and self through children's satires. Yet this Purim the merrymaking was strained.

Following the Gromyko-Assad saber rattling, the country was on Red Alert. Above, on the Golan Heights, Syrian and Israeli artillery were spewing fire. The kibbutzniks prayed for the boys entrenched in the snow; some still mourned loved ones who had fallen in the Yom Kippur War.

The Memouneh, standing by the window of his chalet, sought a burst of mental energy that would sharpen his brutalized mind to omniscience.

The kibbutz, at the southeastern tip of Kinneret, the sea of Galilee, was his birthplace and where he had directed incursions into Syrian territory in the bitterness before the Six Day War. Occasionally, he had plowed the fields under fire from enemy pillboxes to savor the defiance bequeathed to the Jew by the Scriptures. Now the pillboxes lay derelict; but so, alas, did the strength of the pioneering years. Time seemed to be defeating both Jew and Arab. He dared not admit it, but staring across the lake at Tiberias, clouded by the storm that had risen as suddenly as the one described by the Evangelists, he was gauging the air, searching in its heaviness the density that would herald the Messiah. Had he been

247

a Christian, he would have implored Jesus to choose this moment to walk over the waters for his Second Coming. There was need for divine intervention.

He turned to Osman. "How's the leg?"

Osman limped to the tray of drinks and poured himself a large arak. "No problem."

The Memouneh picked at a bunch of grapes and waited.

Osman was far from fit. He had had a steel rod implanted into the femur and had come out of traction only ten days earlier. He needed more physiotherapy. Yet he had discharged himself from the hospital and had instructed his secretary to tell King Hussein that he was taking indefinite leave and to hand the monarch, in case of his death, his personal file on Operation Dragons. Then, putting through a priority call to the Memouneh, he had presented himself at the Sheikh Hussein Bridge. Even more ominous had been the fact that he had not dared contact his beloved wife in case she should dissuade him from coming. The Memouneh had whisked him to his kibbutz, wondering what further horrors were in store.

Osman hobbled over to the Memouneh. His stiff knee protested, empathizing with his mouth, still rigid with traumatized nerves from the bullet wound. "There's something I know that you don't, Zamora."

The Memouneh spoke gently. "I gathered as much."

Osman gazed at the storm raging over the lake. "I can't raise the heart to tell you."

"The heart is seldom wise, Osman. For years most Arab intellectuals—you included—have said, even publicly, that the Arab's greatest enemy is not Israel but the superpowers—Russia in particular. That it is they who want to devour you, either by subversion or by their alien cultures. Yet reason has been rejected by the Arab heart. Israel has remained the enemy. The Arab heart still cherishes the Koranic dictum of everlasting war. We still keep each other at arms' length. Join hands only secretly—like this—hoping that it's not too late. Think, Osman, if we'd ignored the heart, if we'd been rational, self-interested even, think what might have happened."

"Speech time, Zamora?"

The Memouneh regretted his outburst. What was the use of recriminations? Events took their course and became history. The past did not relate nor teach a.lesson; it merely provided a mold for a state of mind. And the mold broke arbitrarily, according to the whim of time. "Sorry. I didn't mean to. I'm haunted by the fact that Jew and Arab could have turned this part of the world into a Garden of Eden. . . ."

"That may yet happen. But if Operation Dragons succeeds, there won't be a Garden of Eden anywhere. . . ."

"A nuclear attack on Israel? Who'd shed tears over it?"

"*If* the target is Israel."

The Memouneh looked up sharply. "If? Where else?"

Osman gulped down his arak. "Give me Boaz, Zamora. We've got the nose. We'll call you in for the kill."

The Memouneh fixed his eyes on Osman. "What do you know?"

Osman compulsively poured another drink. "Look, Zamora. I've been tearing my hair since Mecca. Searching for a lead. I've had men running in circles. Dead-ends everywhere! All right—we're not Mossad standard. So I turn to you. But you're not doing any better! You're at your wits' end—not to mention casualties. Meanwhile, time is ticking by! In fact, there's not much of it left. So let's not sit anymore. Give me your battering ram! Now—before it's too late!"

"Tell me what you know."

Osman took a deep breath and engaged the Memouneh's eyes. "The target. I've known it—since November . . . when Abu Ismail was meditating on Mount Nebo. You remember the tapes? You didn't have the whole batch. I kept one. It contains Operation Dragons's objective. No one has heard that tape. Not even the king . . ."

The Memouneh held his breath. Beads of sweat had erupted on Osman's forehead. The bullet scars on both cheeks had turned into purple dimples.

"It's been . . . I—I've often wanted to share its secret. I nearly did—with Boaz."

"Tell me. . . ."

Osman sat down wearily. "I ought to, I agree. If something happens to me . . . you ought to know. But . . . one condition."

"No conditions!"

"One condition, Zamora. You'll keep it to yourself."

"Why?"

"For the same reasons that I've kept it secret. To start with, no one would believe you. Second, if it becomes common knowledge, it will trickle back to Abu Ismail. He'll take appropriate measures. We'd never see daylight again."

"I'll promise this much. I'll keep it to myself until I judge secrecy would be counterproductive."

Osman pondered a moment, glanced at the ubiquitous tape recorder, then picked up a newspaper. "I won't have it on record." He scribbled a word along the newspaper's margin, tore the piece off and showed it to the Memouneh.

The latter's face lost the last of its color. "I don't believe it."

Osman burned the piece of paper with his lighter. "That's why WOJ have dug in in Ethiopia."

"I don't believe it, Osman!"

"Think about it. It will make sense. It's the only target that will establish Abu Ismail as Al-Mahdi."

The Memouneh sat frozen. Horror at such a pitch had afflicted him once before—on that fateful day when, as a lieutenant in the British Forces Jewish Brigade, he had walked into Belsen.

"Let me have Boaz, Zamora. Now!"

March 9, 1974

THE DANAKIL DESERT, ETHIOPIA

Sanbat and Bayyu, her Falasha escort, faced the Kabele spring, but at enough distance to disclaim drinking rights. They had a good view of the chunks of meat they had placed by the water.

It was late afternoon; the desert still smoldered. The Dankali band who had brought them stood wanly by the sacks of teff given as payment; the married women, distinguished by their black head scarves, disregarded the supper chores; the young girls, breasts bare, neglected the camels. They watched in silence.

Sanbat was near exhaustion. She had been traveling for the past twenty hours, in a hired, furnace-hot Volkswagen, from As-mara to Sardo by way of Dessie, and from Sardo on the desert trail that led to Lake Afrera. She had barely kept dehydration at bay; to make matters worse, she was menstruating heavily and painfully. Consequently, when she first caught sight of the man peering from above an escarpment, she thought she was hallucinating. "Did you see him, Bayyu?"

"I saw something. . . ." Bayyu craned forward. An itinerant trader, he had proved one of Sanbat's best Falasha recruits. Charged to investigate Kevork Dedeyan's death, he had amassed enough evidence to link the murder with Captain Wolde's unit. Then, having established through police contacts that no trace of Dedeyan's body had been found in the charred Land-Rover, he had considered the possibility that Dedeyan might have escaped. The rumor of the mysterious white man of the desert had sent him scurrying to Sanbat. "Wait . . . He come down."

Expectation overrode Sanbat's exhaustion. She took a salt tablet, sat on her haunches and surveyed the spring with binoculars. She caught sight of three spotted hyenas sauntering down the lava terraces. She waited, revolted yet fascinated by the ugly creatures.

The rumor about the Hyena-Man—as the Dankalis called him
—had originated from a band of salt quarriers who had claimed to
have seen a sun-scorched male, indisputably the reincarnation of
a heroic ancestor, watering at the spring with a pack of hyenas as
if he were one of them. When Sanbat had decided to check, Bayyu
had negotiated with the Dankalis, spinning the tale that Sanbat
was a hyena worshiper who, having once held the precious stone
in the eye of the creature, was compelled to feed them wherever
they approached man. The claim, Mossad's free adaptation of an
ancient Egyptian cult, had impressed the tribesmen: the region
abounded with stories of strange ascetics consorting with hyenas.
The teff had clinched the deal.

"Look, Sanbat—over there."

Sanbat directed the binoculars to where Bayyu pointed. She
saw the shadow, moving forward stealthily, stopping, head gyrating as it smelled the air, moving forward again. Her heart
pounded. It was a man, naked and spotted by sun blisters but
definitely Caucasian. She directed her attention to his penis: un-
circumcised—therefore not a Muslim. And finally she noted the
body hair: thick and extensive—unlike any of the desert tribesmen. "It's him, Bayyu. . . . I think . . ."

Bayyu looked at the Hyena-Man dubiously. "What you do
now?"

"Let him get near."

They waited as the man cautiously approached the spring.
There he paused, sniffed about, then casually stood up and looked
at them. He watched for a long time, immobile. From that distance his eyes seemed to reflect the orange luminosity of an
animal. The hyenas next to him watched too, teeth bared. Eventually, the man, with a perfect imitation of the hyena's cry, rushed
to the spring. The hyenas followed. They drank for a while. The
man, on all fours, lapped at the water instead of scooping it up
with his hands. Finally, he moved back and inspected the chunks
of meat. He picked them up and threw each hyena a piece, then
sat down and munched the one he had kept for himself. Occasionally he grunted and received resonant responses from the hyenas.

Bayyu whispered. "This man is born to hyenas. It cannot be
your man."

Sanbat protested doggedly. "Must be. He's a white man. Must
be."

"How he has stayed alive?"

Sanbat had been considering the same question. True, Dedeyan had had training in survival, but who could have envisaged
survival in such conditions? Moreover, the Kabele spring was some

200 kilometers from Assab over one of the most inhospitable terrains in the world. How could he have trekked across volcanic mountain ranges and arid plains? How could he have acclimatized to temperatures above 50 degrees centigrade? How could he have tamed the hyenas to hunt with them? How could he have triumphed over the pack to become their leader? How—in the space of a few weeks? "I'm going to talk to him. . . ."

"No, Sanbat. The hyenas . . ."

"They're supposed to be cowards—aren't they?"

"These spotted ones. They are fearless. They have iron jaws. They are stronger than lions. They attack. They kill."

Sanbat hesitated. But bravery, or exhaustion—she could not tell which—urged her on. She rose.

The man and the hyenas formed a pack. Her courage drained. She stood transfixed, unable to go forward or squat down again.

Man and beasts bared their teeth. Sanbat heard herself shout in English. "Kevork! It's Sanbat! Sanbat Abraham!"

The man growled. Then, flailing his hands protectively, he turned to the hyenas. The latter listened attentively to his growling and obediently sauntered off with their meat. The man remained, teeth still bared.

Sanbat edged forward. "I'm coming over. It's all right, Kevork! You're safe!"

The man screeched. *"Anchi lij, hid!"*

Sanbat stood still. The response in Amharic meant "Little girl, go." She thought she had detected an accent. She tried to sound comforting, like a mother, a loved woman. "Kevork! It's me . . . Sanbat . . ."

"Hid!"

Sanbat ventured a step. "You know me . . . Sanbat Abraham!"

The man bellowed. *"Yellem!"*

Sanbat stopped. The "no" had been menacing. "All right. You come over here."

The man howled. *"Hid!"*

Sanbat switched to Amharic. "Kevork, listen to me. . . ."

The man reverted to screeching, then ran off.

"Kevork! No!"

The man disappeared in the lava flows. Sanbat stared at Bayyu, distraught. Bayyu dropped his eyes. Sanbat turned to the Dankalis. The men moved forward. The eldest placed a rectangular salt bar at Sanbat's feet and muttered something in Tigrean.

Bayyu translated gravely. "Sanbat, they are amazed Hyena-Man talk to you. They think you are blessed because Hyena-Man no harm you. The salt bar—for them is money—is their gift of respect."

"Then ask them to help. We've got to go after him."

Bayyu transmitted Sanbat's request. The Dankalis grinned. The eldest spoke briefly.

"He says nobody finds Hyena-Man. Only if Hyena-Man shows himself."

"Nonsense!"

"Is true, Sanbat. In this desert whole tribes can burrow and never be found."

"But we had him—almost. . . ."

"I think he not your man."

"He was! I heard him! His accent . . ."

"His accent of this region."

"How can you tell? He hardly spoke. . . ." She let her voice trail, realizing that Bayyu could ask the same question.

He took her arm and drew her away. "If it is your man, he no want to come back. He prefer new life."

Sanbat protested weakly. "How could he?"

"It is said by wise people, wild animal has better life than man."

Sanbat turned to the lava flows. The setting sun had plunged the ranges into shadow. There was no trace of the man. Only distant hyena laughter. The stillness suggested he had never appeared, or if he had, only as a mirage. She walked away. Her menstrual pains gave substance to agonies she could feel but not understand.

March 10, 1974

YAVNE, ISRAEL

Like everywhere else in Israel, Yavne had an evocative history. It was at the Roman camp there that Rabbi Johanan ben Zakkai had relinquished Jerusalem and had asked Titus for Yavne and its scholars. It was also there that the definitive canon of the Holy Scriptures had been formulated. Now Yavne housed the Sorreo Nuclear Research Center. For some of the founding fathers, like the Memouneh, such a leap was profanity; for others, like Kidan, it denoted fulfillment: Rome, which had scattered the tents of the Jew, had perished; but its victims had returned—stronger, wiser and armed with the doomsday sling. For those who belonged to the Middle East in spirit, like Boaz and Osman, the center was the sign of contagion of the human sickness.

They had been allocated an office overlooking the sea. Boaz stood at the window, grateful for the sound of the waves; Osman sat in the armchair, massaging his stiff leg; the Memouneh sat at the table and cracked his knuckles.

Boaz had been considering Osman's proposition. "If you were fit, Osman, I'd say yes—let's run amok. We've got the nose. . . ."

The Memouneh smiled. Boaz had used Osman's very phrase. So different from each other. Yet so similar—like two epic poems.

Osman straightened up. "That's settled then."

Boaz turned to face him. "But I'm not risking you—"

"Don't play my brother's keeper with me, my brother!"

"You do. You *did*."

"And don't be an eye-for-an-eye Jew."

Boaz ignored him. "I can go solo, Zamora."

The Memouneh picked up Osman's cigarette and puffed it greedily. "This is too difficult to go solo, Boaz. You'll need all the muscle you can get."

"There's Sanbat and her Falashas."

"The Falashas are scouts—good ones. But they're not trained to strike. You can't throw them in the fray."

"All right, give me the best hit team you've got. Osman's not fit!"

The Memouneh handed the cigarette back to Osman. "Osman knows all the ins and outs, Boaz—like you. Anybody else coming in cold wouldn't have the confidence to improvise. You two would make a perfect team."

"And Osman, my dear friend, is gaining strength by the hour."

Boaz turned to Osman viciously. "Cheap is it, your life?"

"Like yours."

"Is that what your wife and daughters say?"

Osman raised his cane and waved it threateningly. "That's enough!"

The Memouneh compared the fiery little dispute with the re-union earlier on. Boaz, summoned from the laboratory, had been visibly shocked by Osman's ravaged face and heavy gait. Then, submitting to Osman's brotherly embrace, he had looked blessed. "I want Osman to have a crash briefing on nuclear weaponry. You can fill him in on the finer points as you go along."

Boaz shrugged in disgust, turned away to gaze at the Mediterranean.

The Memouneh continued. "Now, I won't leave you without backup. I'll have a special squad standing by ready to move. Also, we have two *Reshevs* going into service in Sharm al-Sheikh. They'll be sailing around the Cape. They should be in the Red Sea within the month. I'll get clearance to keep them in reserve."

Osman rose eagerly to his feet. "That sounds fine. When do we leave?"

"When we can get around the general strike."

"What general strike?"

"In Ethiopia. The country's paralyzed. Airports closed."

"Can't we jump?"

Boaz growled. "With that leg?"

The Memouneh hastily defused another flare-up. "No, Osman. Even if you could, I wouldn't have the sanction to arrange it."

Osman sat down, looking aggrieved. Then, as affection conquered his anger, he turned to Boaz and burst out laughing. Unable to resist, Boaz responded with a smile. The Memouneh watched them, envious of their friendship.

March 13, 1974

THE DANAKIL ALPS, ETHIOPIA

"The tests have been comprehensive. I have my calculations. We can achieve chain reaction."

The news was sublime, but Idris Ali maintained a formal attitude. "Are you well?"

Talat Fawzi smoothed his hair, and concealed the tufts that had stuck to his hand. "I'm fine."

"The vomiting? Diarrhea?"

"Better."

"Are you taking your cysteine pills?"

"For what they're worth."

Idris Ali answered vehemently. "They're worth a lot. Cysteine is an amino acid that provides substantial protection against irradiation. It produces anoxia—competes for oxygen with normal cell constituents. Reduced oxygen renders living systems more radiation-resistant. Decreases the rate of ionizing."

"Well memorized. But I'm not worried."

Idris Ali gave him a suspicious look. "Why not?"

"For the same reason you're not. The mission is vital to me."

"I identify with the mission, Professor. You were pressed into it."

Fawzi met Idris Ali's look sternly. "True. But I have seen the light. It is time for Islam to unleash cataclysm. I thank Allah for having chosen me to engineer it."

Idris Ali grunted. Fawzi was repeating his indoctrination. The rest—the arrogance and pomposity—were merely vestiges of Fawzi's former self. He turned to Mustafa, the metallurgist. "What about the technicians?"

Mustafa, shaky even as he sat, answered resolutely. "We're well."

Fawzi interjected matter-of-factly. "Only four in the infirmary."

"Serious?"

"Difficult to say at this stage. I wouldn't worry."

Idris Ali's mouth twitched. "I do. I care for you all."

Fawzi nodded as if the remark were self-evident, then gestured toward Watanabe, sitting to his left. "He's the one you should be concerned with. For one thing, he doesn't believe in Allah."

Idris Ali directed his attention to Watanabe. "He will. Won't you, brother?"

Watanabe's glazed eyes glinted as if focused on a distant vision. "Of course . . . If He gives me what I need . . ."

Idris Ali scrutinized him for signs of rebellion. He saw none. The last time Watanabe had burst into disorderliness had been a week ago, when his favorite virgin had inadvertently wandered into the factory during a test and had contracted the sickness. Idris Ali had dealt with the situation promptly by refusing him heroin. Thereafter, Watanabe had behaved like a lamb. "You'll have whatever you need, Watanabe. How about your progress?"

"I've finished the blueprints. I'm ready."

Idris Ali turned to Fawzi. "When can we start assembling, Professor?"

Fawzi reflected a moment. "When we get a new bomb casing."

"We have a bomb casing."

"It's defective."

Idris Ali faced him sharply. "Defective?"

Fawzi turned to Mustafa. "You'd better explain."

Mustafa fidgeted uneasily. "I don't know how to. It's corroded. Brittle. Perhaps the conditions here. Maybe the effects of the tests."

Idris Ali stared at them, incredulous. "We've made that casing to specifications!"

Fawzi rasped. "Your specifications were for a conventionally produced nuclear weapon—perfect if we were assembling it at a plant. We're not. Our bomb is somewhat exotic, the conditions quite eccentric. We have to compensate for a number of factors."

"Professor, are you telling me we can't have a bomb because of the casing?"

Fawzi shook his head. "No. If worse comes to worst, we could improvise something with the alloys we have here. But a new casing would simplify our task. Get one as soon as you can."

Idris Ali responded to the order with imperceptible hesitancy.

The project had been worked out to the minutest detail. He did not relish a setback. A moment later, he composed himself. His trepidation could only be due to the brain-frying heat. He could take setbacks in his stride. "All right. You can go. Mustafa, you stay behind."

Fawzi and Watanabe left the cave. Idris Ali watched them cross the maidan toward the virgins' quarters. They had lost weight and strength; their gait had deteriorated. They now sought out the virgins for companionship—which proved they were flotsam. He despised them. Scientists were modern slaves. Ready to jump to orders. That being so, he wondered why he distrusted them.

He turned to Mustafa. "The casing—could it have been sabotaged?"

Mustafa blinked a few times, horrified. "Sabotaged? How?"

Idris Ali paced about. "Impossible, I know. Still . . . Tell me— what happens if we can't get a new casing in time? If we have to improvise one?"

"I—I don't know. . . . There'd be risk to the tampings. Might dissipate the fissionable material—stop it going critical. Also, there'd be little to protect the various mechanisms, fuses, detonators. The casing is a shield, really—essential for something precision-built."

Idris Ali pondered awhile. "But a shield—no more?"

"Basically—yes."

Idris Ali waved dismissively. "Thank you, Mustafa."

Mustafa rose and with heavy steps left the cave.

Idris Ali returned to his desk. Composing his signal to Abu Ismail, he notified definite feasibility and requested delivery of a new bomb casing.

March 14, 1974

ASMARA, ETHIOPIA

"It's good to have you here, Boaz. Really good."

Boaz shifted uneasily, offered a smile, then concentrated on his tea. Sanbat was sitting next to him, closer than she needed to, showing too much leg and, when leaning forward to catch his eye, too deep a cleavage. She had voiced her pleasure at his being there incessantly. Boaz, having initially attributed her sentimentality to relief at receiving support in Ethiopia, could no longer dispute the fact that beneath her controlled hysteria she still loved him. "Good to see you, too."

She beamed as if prepared to believe anything he said.

To preempt further banalities, Boaz turned to Osman and Getachew, both busy at the radio console. He caught Osman's eye.
Osman had instantly guessed Sanbat's passion. He had even re-
proached Boaz for his cool cordiality. The look was still reproach-
ful. It angered Boaz. He gulped down his tea, pushed his cup to
Sanbat. "Can I have some more?"

Sanbat jumped up. "Of course." She took his cup, collected
Osman's and Getachew's and went into the kitchen.

Boaz tried to unwind. It had been a tedious few days. The
Ethiopian general strike had been called off the night of the tenth
after the labor unions' demands had been met and after the emperor, in a press conference, had declared his willingness to support reforms and to tolerate political parties. Boaz and Osman, in
their respective cover identities of Greek merchant and Iranian
geologist, had scrambled to Rome to catch a connecting flight,
only to find that the Ethiopian civil aviation authority employees
were continuing their strike, keeping both Asmara and Addis
Ababa airports shut. Early that morning, after three days at
Fiumicino with little to relieve the boredom except meticulous
attention to their elaborate disguises, they had boarded Ethiopian
Airlines flight 703 to Asmara which had been permitted to break
the strike for lack of hangaring facilities in Rome.

They had not been met at the airport and had proceeded separately to the safe house where Sanbat and Getachew Iyessous
had been waiting for them.

Getachew closed channels and came to sit opposite Boaz. "I've
got a plane—a Siai-Marchetti."

"Clean?"

"Perfectly. From the mapping mission. One of the advantages
of being ex–air force. You can cash in on old favors. I've also
made arrangements to refuel at Makale—that's in Tigre, the adjoining province to Eritrea. My homeland. Wolde hasn't much
jurisdiction there."

"Excellent."

Sanbat returned with the tea. Getachew gallantly helped her
serve it. Boaz noted the friendship. It had been welded, Sanbat
had said, after Dedeyan's misadventure. Getachew, fearing that
Wolde might have linked Dedeyan with her, had kept closer contact. Boaz wondered whether the friendship might turn into love.
It would be a good match—and it would take Sanbat off his back.

Getachew himself had presented Boaz and Osman with a priority decision. During their preparations, considering the possibility
that they might at some point have to clash with Getachew, they
had familiarized themselves with his psychotechnic profile. They

had been impressed—all the more when they had met him. What they had had to find out had been whether Getachew's patriotism coincided with their mission. Should they have nursed the slightest suspicion that he was using Sanbat to keep his eye on Mossad, either to thwart its efforts or in the misguided belief that the WOJ operations in Ethiopia might benefit his country, they would have had to dispose of him.

"You know about Alexander and the Gordian knot, Boaz?"

Sanbat answered for Boaz, making him wince. "Anything Greek Boaz knows, Getachew."

Getachew slammed the edge of his hand on his knee. "That's what's needed. One stroke with a sharp sword."

Boaz looked up. "Where?"

"Captain Wolde's neck."

Boaz pondered. Wolde, apparently, had begun reaping rewards from his collaboration with WOJ, and probably from a chain of masters extending to Russia. He seemed to have unlimited funds. His paratroopers received enviable bonuses. His unit, a law to itself, was superbly equipped. Above all, a great deal of propaganda was being disseminated about him. Apocryphal stories comparing him to his namesake, the charismatic nineteenth-century emperor Tewodoros, had already caught the imagination of the younger elements in the army. Soon he would be in a position to gain control of the Dergue, and move against the emperor. Hence Getachew's impatience to tackle him.

"Wolde's neck will have to wait, Getachew. We can't match his force. Even if we could, we might precipitate civil war."

Getachew waved his hands desperately. "Have you ever thought . . . I mean, if, as you say, WOJ are preparing a nuclear device . . . Have you ever thought Wolde might want it for himself?"

Boaz nodded. "But how would he get it?"

"Grab it as soon as it's assembled."

"That's underestimating WOJ. They'll have taken countermeasures. Fail-safe devices and so on. Besides, they're keeping the location of the base secret."

"You're going by Schoenberg's interrogation of Yusuf. Wolde's not Yusuf."

"To Abu Ismail, everybody's a lackey. Even Qaddafi. Believe me, Getachew—we have to undo this particular knot bit by bit. WOJ first—because if they make their bomb they'll be a greater threat to Ethiopia than Wolde."

Getachew lowered his head dejectedly. "Time—that's what worries me. You don't know the state the country's in. . . ."

Osman hobbled over from the radio-console, sat down and compulsively started to massage his leg. "Zubair has secured a sambouk. Shipshape to the last nail. He's just left Jizan. He'll reach the Ethiopian coast early tomorrow morning."

Boaz nodded, pleased. His esteem for Zubair, who had helped them out so astutely in Mecca and Taif, had risen as high as Osman's. He unfurled the map of Eritrea. "All right. We'll start tomorrow. Sanbat and I by boat along the coast. Getachew and Osman by plane over the Danakil. Every nook and cranny that might harbor the WOJ base, we investigate. . . ."

March 17, 1974

MADRID, SPAIN

"It is my pious belief that he who worships Allah must renounce the politics of man. For years, honoring this belief, I have abstained from the power struggles of the godless. Today I renege on my belief. I do so humbly, in this country which has remained, despite imperialist Zionist pressures, a close friend to the Arabs."

Abu Ismail paused. Film cameras whirred, photo cameras flashed. Otherwise the silence was absolute. He could see the reporters were dazzled by his immaculate white *zibun*, awed by the damson in his turban, which identified him as a hajji.

"I renege on my belief, may Allah forgive me, to warn not only my brothers-in-Islam but also those who, as worshipers of the single God, I consider my stepbrothers."

He listened to his words echo in the Luz Palacio Hotel's conference room. It was fitting that such a capitalist temple should provide the setting for his last appearance in the West. After the advent of the theocracy, it would be enshrined. On a grander scale, Madrid—once Moorish Majrit and Islam's outpost in Europe—would assume symbolic importance for its role in repairing history to Allah's Design.

"To all of you I cry out: The Zionist threat is no longer the Arab concern. It is your concern as well."

He had timed his speech well. A fortnight ago the Israelis had completed their pullout from the Suez Canal. Once again the world had started to envisage a Middle East settlement. Now, following Idris Ali's signal from the Danakil, it was time to prepare the world for the Last Days.

"The Zionists are preparing a nuclear holocaust."

He noted that none of the reporters—except the two accredited to the English newspaper, the *Jewish Chronicle*, but in reality stringers for Israel's *Maariv* and the *Jerusalem Post*—showed surprise or concern. He smiled. The press, as usual, would grab the story, then ask questions.

"I have proof. In 1968, through a series of subterfuges, Israel purchased two hundred tons of uranium oxide from Belgium, loaded it onto a ship called *Scheersberg A*, transferred it to an Israeli boat in the Mediterranean and delivered it to their nuclear weapons plant in Dimona, in the Negev desert."

"Are you giving us facts, sir? Or polemics?"

He looked up. The heckler was one of the Jewish reporters. He smiled again. He had hoped for just such a question to electrify the atmosphere. "I consented to give this press conference with the proviso that I would refrain from answering questions. However, I shall make an exception and answer yours. I am giving you facts. Facts that can be checked with Euratom—they are still investigating the theft. Facts which can also be checked with the Norwegian secret service—they were the first to discover the perfidy."

The conference room was in uproar. The Jewish reporters, now joined by Scandinavians and Americans, were standing up, shouting at the platform. Other reporters were struggling with the security guards to leave the room and file their copy. The gathering was ready for the master stroke.

He thundered. "I have more to say. Please, your indulgence."

Silence descended.

"Israel, created by a world in chaos, believes by her demonic logic that if she is to survive, the world must remain in chaos. But we all know that the world, by the grace of justice-loving peoples, has embraced order. Israel is determined to destroy that order. To this end, she has her nuclear weapons poised over all Islam!"

Shouts of disbelief and mockery filled the room.

Abu Ismail bellowed into the microphones. "Take heed! Israel will celebrate her next Independence Day by wiping out the Sacred City of Mecca. . . ."

He glared for a final moment, then turning his back on the pandemonium, walked away from the rostrum.

March 18, 1974

BEYLUL, ETHIOPIA

They had anchored in a secluded creek. The surrounding desert had offered ideal conditions to camouflage the plane under netting amid the sand dunes. They were halfway between Assab in the south and Barassoli in the north, at a deserted stretch of the coast-line.

Osman sat at the prow, mauling a Transworld radio set, striving to find a trustworthy station for authoritative analyses on Abu Ismail's press conference. He had caught the news the previous night on the BBC World Service and had been monosyllabic ever since. Almost every station had elaborated on Israel's nuclear potential but had treated Abu Ismail's warnings of an impending attack on Mecca as hysterical. Moscow and Tripoli had expounded on Israel's history of crimes against humanity as an indication that such an atrocity would be characteristic of the imperialist Zionists. Not one station had bothered to analyze Abu Ismail's possible motives in making the statement. No one had postulated that he might be perpetrating a gross deception to create a pretext for Terror.

Sanbat felt sorry for Osman. She had warmed to him. A brave man, ready to undertake any task, despite his still-ailing leg. Also a compassionate man. He had talked about Boaz perceptively; had begged her to save him before he destroyed himself. She had promised to do her best. He had gratified her by assuring her that her best would certainly triumph. His words had fed her hopes.

She moved down the deck.

Getachew was at the wheelhouse communicating over the radio with Schoenberg in Djibouti. He had little to report.

Having secured the mapping mission's monoplane three days before, they had rendezvoused with Zubair near Gulbub, north of Massawa. Boaz had taken command of the boat, and Zubair had returned to Saudi Arabia in the sambouk that had escorted him.

Thereafter, Osman and Getachew, Boaz and Sanbat had conducted a thorough search of the Danakil and the Eritrean coast, respectively by plane and sambouk. They had kept a close watch on Wolde and his paratroopers, still operating in the vicinity of Assab; and they had monitored the radio frequencies for a stray signal from WOJ—in vain.

The search for the WOJ base had proved equally fruitless. From the air, the Danakil had disclosed none of its secrets. Desert wasteland interrupted either by volcanic ranges or impenetrable mazes of petrified detritus.

One discovery, made by Boaz and Sanbat, had temporarily raised their hopes. A cove near Barassoli, judging from some patches of diesel oil on the water, had sheltered a boat. Odd tire marks on the beach of the cove had further indicated that a number of vehicles and men had deployed there. But as the tracks had vanished into the desert, they had been unable to search inland.

Their disappointment had been compounded by the fact that the cove was some 120 kilometers north of Assab Bay where Yusuf had delivered the consignment of rice to Hamdi; that, moreover, nearby Barassoli was a fishing village with a growing sea-salt industry, and that the tracks could be attributed to engineers surveying for new installations.

For Boaz and Osman, who had come to Ethiopia to shoot arrows in the air in the hope of hitting something, the venture had been demoralizing. The Danakil, they feared, would defeat them, for it was a theater of war where neither the battlefield nor the enemy was visible.

Now, in desperation, they had decided to attack—just the two of them—the next available target: Cape Ras Marshag, in Aden, where the *Succubus* lay at anchor by a seaside villa designated by Getachew as WOJ's likely headquarters. The strike could be made stealthily by sea, thus avoiding any international repercussions. They were still in the dhow season; countless craft running to the northern monsoon, shuttling between the Red Sea and the Arabian Peninsula, would provide excellent cover for the operation by preserving the sambouk's anonymity. The objective was to reach Ras Marshag, some 230 nautical miles away, during the night—weather conditions permitting. There they would storm the *Succubus* and capture Hamdi and any WOJ commando on board. One among them would know the location of the base. Schoenberg would help by maintaining aerial surveillance of the *Succubus*—a favor he had been rendering, unbeknown to his superiors, by inducing friendly pilots in the French air force at Djibouti to violate the PDRY air space accidentally.

Sanbat approached Boaz.

He was tuning up the sambouk's engines, working meticulously and, Sanbat thought, sensually. He had been delighted with the boat, named *Aziz*, "dear one." The sambouk, according to Zubair, could outrun most Coast Guard patrol boats and had won her combat sails on countless smuggling expeditions. Boaz, eulogizing her classic shape inspired by Turkish galleons, had briefed them on her capabilities. The main engine provided a spectacular turn of speed of 23 knots. The auxiliary wing engine was capable of 10 knots. There was a full complement of navigational instrumentation on board, including radar and sonar, and ample reserve fuel. And being a smuggler's boat, she also had an anti-radar device sophisticated enough, Boaz judged, to cloud most screens in the area.

Sanbat watched him work. He had been pensive but placid, sympathetic to Osman's anxiety in the wake of Abu Ismail's press

conference. When she and Getachew had made the obvious comment, that Abu Ismail had lost his senses to rely on propaganda
for such absurdities, Boaz had, uncharacteristically, intervened
sharply. If he, who had so briefly tasted the sanctity of Mecca,
found the idea horrendous, Osman, a devout Muslim, must be
tormented. The mere mention of such an obscenity, even for the
purposes of sensationalism, reflecting the sickness of the fanatic
must make Osman despair. Out of respect for Osman's sensibili-
ties, he asked that no further mention be made of Abu Ismail's
rantings. To Sanbat, the responsiveness of his outburst had been
heartening.

Since then, though not paying particular attention to her, he
had not avoided her. That had encouraged her to attempt a proper
farewell before she and Getachew flew off to Asmara, there to
monitor the spate of signals that would pour out of Jerusalem,
Djibouti and the *Aziz*. If she showed him she was near him, would
always be close at hand, he might reach for her.

"What is it, Sanbat?"

She did not think his affability was forced. "Getachew's about
to finish. We'll be off."

He wiped the oil from his hands. "You be careful now. Stick
by him. He's a good man."

She smiled, pleased. He was concerned—though from a distance. It would do, for now. "You, too. Be careful."

"Sure."

She fastened on the mellowness in his eyes. "I'll have you inside me, Boaz. Whatever happens. Before I die. Before you die."

She paused, fearful of her words that had caught even her
unawares. Boaz's warmth waned—not ominously but sadly. As if
in acceptance.

March 19, 1974

THE DANAKIL ALPS, ETHIOPIA

Idris Ali studied the blow-ups of the photographs taken by Platoon
A at the farthest post overlooking the coastal plain. They showed
an anchored sambouk and a man and a woman surveying the
cove's beach.

Badran pointed at a detail. "The boat's from Jizan. You can
read its port of registration. The woman's black—Ethiopian. The
man—definitely not Saudi. Could be a Westerner on a holiday
cruise."

"Then why was he scouring the cove?"

"They can't be agents! How could they have picked up our trail?"

Idris Ali paced angrily. "Maybe that Armenian Wolde killed. Maybe a leak somewhere. The fact is: they have picked up our trail. And they're not alone. That Siai-Marchetti that kept flying over—Wolde spotted it, too. On one occasion tipping its wings to a craft at sea—the sambouk, no doubt. I've had Wolde check the plane. Registered with the mapping mission in Asmara. Taken over a few days ago by an ISS major."

"What do we do?"

"They haven't located us yet, and they can't—that's one good thing."

"They'll keep on looking. We've got to neutralize them."

"We can't risk a sortie. What worries me is if they've tracked us to the Danakil, what else do they know? Where might they ferret next? What's the news from Abdallah?"

"He's just received the bomb casing."

"Good. Signal him to sail immediately. I don't want him stationary. Tell him to stand by for further orders. He's not to put into the cove until my clearance. Then signal Wolde—tell him to keep an eye on the sambouk."

March 20, 1074

BARASSOLI, ETHIOPIA

The Ethiopian Airlines DC-6 disappeared beyond the northeastern ridges of the Danakil Alps. A few minutes earlier, it had flown low over Barassoli to observe the *Aziz* lying at anchor in a tiny inlet. The plane had obviously come from Assab—there were no other airports in the area—but it should not have been flying over Barassoli. Ethiopian Airlines did not have a service between Massawa and Assab; its only northern Red Sea route was to Taizz, North Yemen, once a week on Thursdays. There was the possibility that it had been chartered, but Boaz thought it unlikely. Ethiopia was in turmoil; there had been a change of cabinet; the armed forces were demanding trials for ex-ministers; airports were being watched closely in case any members of the Establishment tried to flee abroad; charters were all but suspended.

Osman came out of the wheelhouse, drenched in sweat. "That was Schoenberg. He managed a reconnaissance flight this morning. The *Succubus* is sheltering at Perim Island."

Boaz pondered. The *Succubus* had sailed from Aden at sundown yesterday, about the time Osman and Boaz were clearing the Bab el Mandeb Strait, thus thwarting their plan of attacking her at Aden. Schoenberg, who had worked miracles maintaining surveillance on the motor yacht, had been unable to coerce his pilot friends to mount night operations and chart her progress. Montblanc, trying to remedy matters, had asked Langley for reconnaissance planes from the U.S. Gulf Fleet, but had been defeated by CIA red tape. Facing the fact that they could not have identified the *Succubus* at night from all the crafts sailing in the area, Boaz and Osman had been forced to change plans. They had turned tail to the vicinity of Barassoli, there to lie in wait for the *Succubus* in the belief that she would lead them to the WOJ base. That plan still held. "Perim's halfway here. She'll probably sail again at sundown. So we can expect her before sunrise tomorrow."

"Schoenberg says the sub *Khanjar* has also put to sea. He fears she might be on escort duty. His pilots looked out for her at Perim. No signs. She could have been submerged, though."

"I haven't forgotten the sub."

Osman followed Boaz's glance at the equipment on the deck. "So that's why we're lugging all this."

"It's the Greek in me. I distrust gifts—particularly from Libya to South Yemen."

Osman nodded. "Any other auguries?"

Boaz hesitated a moment, then mumbled. "The WOJ target. I understand now why you've never told me."

Osman leaned against the mast, despondently. "You saw through it—Abu Ismail's press conference. . . . How can you believe it? I still can't."

"It has its logic. Destroy Mecca with a nuclear device. Blame the atrocity on Israel—the only enemy capable of nuclear strike. At one stroke you'd have the whole Muslim world up in arms. Not a lip-service jihad, but the ultimate. Within weeks Israel would be overrun. Jerusalem, as the seat of the Last Judgment, would become the new Mecca, and Abu Ismail, as Al-Mahdi, would establish his theocracy."

"But Mecca, Boaz—how can he destroy Mecca?"

"He doesn't care about Mecca. He wouldn't even perform the hajj. Mecca, for him, is an ancient pagan site. Jerusalem is his sanctified city."

Osman nodded miserably. "But—everything would rest on his say-so. How does he expect to convince the Faithful that Israel is the perpetrator of the atrocity?"

"Come on, Osman! Put yourself in the shoes of a simple, devout Muslim. Indoctrinated to hate Israel all his life. Do you think he'd give her the benefit of the doubt? Could he think the unthinkable—that not the Jew but a misguided Muslim destroyed the cornerstone of Islam?"

"Don't underestimate the simple, devout Faithful. . . ."

"Osman, you yourself still can't believe it. You kept it secret from everybody. Why? Because you didn't think anybody would believe you . . ."

"Also to spare them—the profanity . . ."

Boaz nodded sadly. "And you expect the Faithful to think twice? In the midst of hysteria that defies imagination?"

"No . . . You're right. . . . What I don't understand, though, is why he made it public. Why didn't he keep it a secret?"

"It's good strategy. If he fails to destroy Mecca, his words will be forgotten as fanatical ramblings. If he succeeds, he'll have prepared the world."

"You read him better than I do."

Boaz shrugged.

"It's a relief, Boaz. Not to be the only man carrying the secret. . . . I've been wondering—what changed you . . . ?"

"Changed me?"

Osman faced him. "You've mellowed. Overnight. Toward me. Sanbat. Even toward yourself. . . ."

Boaz smiled sadly. "Perceptive of you."

"The question is: How did it change you?"

Boaz gazed at the sea. "I don't know. We're confronting Evil. Against that, even as killers, we're sanctified. We're Satan's adversaries, if you like. No doubt, Abu Ismail thinks the same—that we are evil. Maybe that's how it should be. So that we can fight it out. Before God. And let Him choose the winner. Meanwhile, it's given me strength, reason, purpose. Even a sense of belonging—not to a country, an ideal or an objective—but to man. I almost feel human. . . ."

Osman patted his shoulder affectionately. "I'm glad, my brother."

Boaz responded to the gesture by ruffling Osman's hair. Simultaneously he caught a sparkle in the sky. The plane had changed course for Assab. "It had a good look at us."

Osman watched the plane receding in the southern horizon. "Who do you think it was?"

"Wolde, I expect. We'd better weigh anchor."

"Where to?"

"Out to sea."

Osman's face tautened. Boaz grimaced, feeling contrite. The trip to and from Bab el Mandeb had taken over twenty-four hours. They had labored hard, slept little. Osman had not complained once—but the strain on his leg must have been unabating. "I'm sorry, Osman. If it is Wolde, he'll come gunning."

"Or chase us by plane."

"He can't do that. There are no military airfields here. And not even he can requisition the DC-6 as a bomber."

"What about the *Succubus?* Where do we lie in wait?"

"We'll play it by ear."

Osman shrugged, then beamed. "I couldn't have rested, anyway. I'll start up."

Boaz watched him hobble toward the wheelhouse, then moved to winch the anchor. He had become indifferent to Osman's pain. Not out of callousness. Loving a frail brother meant that his frailty had to be ignored. Otherwise the relationship was devalued.

PERIM ISLAND, PEOPLE'S DEMOCRATIC REPUBLIC OF YEMEN

The pile in the arsehole of the world was how British servicemen had described Perim Island. It was an apt summation for a wind-lashed lava block that divided the Strait of Bab el Mandeb into two treacherous channels.

Abdallah and Hamdi had anchored the *Succubus* in the harbor.

Sitting on deck, staring at the African continent some ten miles away, Abdallah felt pleasurably tense.

Wolde, instructed to check the whereabouts of the sambouk *Aziz*, had spotted her once again in the vicinity of Barassoli. Against that, Abdallah had observed the odd French reconnaissance plane, flying over Perim. Put together, these facts indicated that the enemy had linked Barassoli with the WOJ base and were now lying in wait for the *Succubus.*

It was imperative to delude the enemy that the WOJ base was outside mainland Ethiopia. Once that was achieved, Abdallah could deliver the bomb casing. Then, even if more enemy hounds were sent, WOJ would be invulnerable—for they would have the bomb.

He reviewed the plan he had worked out with Idris Ali.

He would sail before sundown. The French would spot him. They would note his speed—twelve knots, comparable to his journey from Ras Marshag—and relay the information to the *Aziz.* The latter would expect the *Succubus* at Barassoli, some 110 nautical miles away, in the early hours of the morning. Instead, he would be at the Hanish Islands, after a leisurely voyage that would enable the *Khanjar*—now lying submerged off Turbah, at the tip of the Arabian Peninsula—to surface and recharge her batteries. The enemy, having drawn a blank at Barassoli, would start search-

ing again. Conceivably, French reconnaissance units would lend
a hand. If so, Abdallah would more than satisfy their curiosity by
simulating clandestine activity, using some of the crew of the
Khanjar—by then submerged again. If not, he would be careless
with his radio and allow the enemy to discover his position. Either
way, the *Aziz* would assume that the WOJ base was at the Hanish
Islands and, impatient after a frustrating game of cat-and-mouse,
would proceed there—to become fodder for the sharks.

March 21, 1974

RAS RAHMAT, ETHIOPIA

Osman thundered. "They could stay there forever—and we could
stay here forever!"

Boaz controlled his anxiety. "But there's nothing at Hanish!
Nothing on any of the islands!"

Osman slammed his hand on the navigational charts. "There
are caves! Grottos! Hundreds they could be holed in!"

"It's a trap, Osman. They're trying to lure us there. . . ."

Osman lit a cigarette and hobbled over to the side. He gazed
unseeing at the tiny atolls spread like a tiara around Ras Rahmat,
the tip of the peninsula, which sheltered the coves of Barassoli. At
another time, in another world, he would have imbibed the view
romantically—as a tropical paradise. "On the other hand, Boaz,
maybe that's just what they want. For us to fear a trap. We stay
put, twiddle our thumbs. They carry on happily. Safe in their base.
That's of course assuming the WOJ base is not at Hanish Kabir—
which we daren't assume. Certainly not with the evidence before
us."

Boaz pored over the charts again. All the previous day, and all
night, they had kept watch on Barassoli. Wolde—or someone—
had spotted them by plane but had not deployed there. Nor had
the *Succubus* or the *Khanjar*. He and Osman had to consider,
therefore, that Barassoli had no links with the WOJ base; otherwise
there would have been some action against the intruders.

Boaz remembered their panic that morning as they had tried
to figure out where the vessels had gone; the long deliberations
until they had picked the Hanish Islands, fifty nautical miles directly east, as the likeliest destination. The time spent painstak-
ingly confirming it, first by intercepting a signal from the islands,
then prevailing on Schoenberg to conduct yet another reconnaissance. Schoenberg's fliers had not only spotted the *Succubus* lying

at anchor off Hanish Kabir, but had also reported significant activity from boat to shore.

"The way I see it, Boaz, we have two alternatives. Either you get the Memouneh to send his commando force on to Hanish—"

"He'd never get clearance. Not without irrefutable proof it's the WOJ base."

"Or we walk into the trap."

"What about the sub?"

"She's there, too. Even if Schoenberg's boys couldn't spot her."

"I know she's there. The point is, there are reefs around the islands. She could be submerged behind any one of them. Which would make our sonar practically useless. We'd be sitting targets."

"I thought we were battering rams. . . ."

"Osman, I'm trying to open your eyes to—"

"The dangers? All right, I'm scared stiff. So, enough talk! Let's go battering. . . ."

Boaz hesitated a moment, then nodded stoically.

HANISH KABIR, ETHIOPIA

The *Succubus*, according to Schoenberg's information, lay in Hanish Kabir's southwestern bay. It was the perfect location for any unloading—if she was unloading; and it offered unrestricted surveillance on any vessel approaching from the Ethiopian coast to the west.

Consequently, Boaz and Osman had decided on a long detour to the north along a busy sambouk route, turning southwest off the North Yemen coast to come upon the island on the blind side, from the east.

Approaching midnight, they were hugging the island's southern coast toward the western bay. They had switched off the lights, shut off the engine and hoisted the sail. Boaz had taken the helm, leaving Osman to monitor the radar and sonar. Both had donned wet suits.

Coming up to the bay's southern isthmus, Boaz lowered the sail and let the sambouk drift.

Moments later Osman whispered. "Boat on radar. Dead ahead."

Boaz grabbed the infrared binoculars and scanned the swell. He had expected to see the submarine, but instead found the *Succubus*. She had moved out of the bay and was heaving to a mile or so out at sea. Boaz scanned again for the submarine, this time in the bay as they rounded the isthmus. He saw nothing. "Anything on sonar?"

"Not yet."

Boaz redirected the infrared binoculars onto the *Succubus*. She had all her lights on, blatantly offering herself as bait. He adjusted the focus, picked up two figures leaning over the railings, staring into the horizon as if discussing the phenomenon that was the sea. No others on deck.

Osman rasped. "What are they doing out there?"

"They've given themselves room to maneuver. Wouldn't be wise to be cornered inside the bay."

"Waiting for us?"

"Yes."

Boaz checked the radio compass, then the wind. Their original plan was still operational, with minor improvisations—if Osman had the stamina. "Can you swim as far as the *Succubus*?"

Osman did not allow himself a whiff of doubt. "Sure."

Boaz made up his mind. No scruples. Soldiers had to face death squarely. "Off you go."

Osman pulled on his aqualung. He moved swiftly to the stern, keeping well below the bulwarks so as not to be seen by anybody scanning the sambouk. He pulled on his flippers and goggles and signaled readiness.

Boaz scrambled over and helped him overboard. Osman, not trained as a frogman, eased himself down clumsily, knocking his injured leg and growling in pain.

Boaz tried not to show concern. "Deep as you can. Watch out for the sub, torpedoes, debris and sharks."

"Sharks?"

"If you see any, stay put. They should swim by. At least, that's the theory."

Osman forced a smile. "Now you tell me."

Boaz lowered a waterproof bag containing Osman's gun and belongings. Osman tied the bag to his belt, gave the thumbs-up sign and dived.

Boaz rushed back to the wheelhouse. He checked the sonar. Negative. He allowed Osman enough time to clear the sambouk, then fired the engine. Still warm from the long trip, it responded immediately. He gave it full throttle, set course directly toward the *Succubus* and locked the helm.

He donned his scuba gear and a belt of charges. He waited by the stern, eyes zeroed in on the sonar. He permitted himself to enjoy the spray that washed over him. He listened to the creaking timber, admiring the ancient skill with which the sambouk cut through the swell. Alas, she would die.

The submarine pinged on sonar. She had been lying in wait,

beyond the northern isthmus. The captain had picked up the sambouk and, as Boaz had expected, decided that she was on an attack course against the *Succubus*. Within a minute or so, sambouk and submarine would clear their respective isthmuses; the submarine would be in position to fire a torpedo.

He packed the infrared binoculars in a waterproof bag containing his gun and belongings, zipped it up, pulled down his goggles, grabbed his flippers and dived off the port side, keeping clear of the periscope by staying in line with the poop.

He surfaced immediately in the wake of the sambouk. He watched her making headway toward her doom, then wet his goggles and bit on his mouthpiece.

He dived, carefully negotiating rock shelves, feeling his way through the dark depths to the seabed. He waited—not for long. A muffled explosion, followed by heavy waves of sound, shook him; distorted patches of brightness wavered on the waterline above. He sensed movement behind him, pulled his knife, veered around. A piece of metal, still spinning, plummeted down. He recognized it as a blade of the sambouk's propeller. He waited for the rest of the debris to sink, then moved to the surface.

He bobbed up amid floating rubble. He scanned the waterline. Except for a section of the poop miraculously afloat, there was little left of the sambouk. Then, at the mouth of the bay, the submarine's conning tower rose. As he had anticipated, the *Khanjar* was surfacing to check for survivors. He noted her course, waited until the hatch flew open. When the gun crew scrambled toward the cannon, he dived again.

He swam some five hundred meters, guided by the sound of the *Khanjar*'s engines, and met her almost head on. Keeping clear of the propeller, he listened to the muffled shouts above. Satisfied that the crew were conducting a thorough search, he unhooked the limpet charges from his belt, set the timing mechanisms and placed them along the hull—six of them. He checked that they had stuck securely, then started swimming toward the *Succubus*.

✗

He surfaced fore of the *Succubus*'s starboard bow. He trod water, adjusted his vision, scanned the swell and listened. He could not see Osman. The *Succubus* was still brightly lit, and the two men whom he now recognized as Abdallah and Hamdi were still on deck—on the port side—discussing the submarine's exploits. The submarine, having searched the vicinity of the sambouk's wreckage, was now altering course toward the *Succubus*. Boaz checked his watch: 11:26 P.M. Four more minutes.

He sensed movement beneath him. He dived, barely controlling a primordial fear of sharks. His leg touched a smooth object. As it pitched, he drew his knife. His hand felt the cold touch of a cylinder. He spun the thrashing mass around and stared into Osman's eyes, racked with pain, beneath the goggles. He held him tight, as much in relief as to stop him from pitching about. Osman pointed at his leg. Boaz ran his hand over it, felt it stiff with cramp. He signaled Osman to relax. Pulling him toward the *Succubus*, he massaged the leg. The stiffness eased.

He dragged Osman to the bows, signaled he should hold tightly, then pointed at the *Khanjar*.

A moment later, the submarine shot out of the water. The sound of the explosions reverberated. Within seconds the sea around her burned in patches of oil. Boaz and Osman watched mesmerized as waves of screams, then sounds of further explosions buffeted across.

Boaz whispered. "Stay here."

Osman's voice croaked. "You'll need help."

"With that going on?"

The submarine's tail had risen above the sea; the propeller still whirred furiously as if anxious to send her down to the depths. Men on fire ran up the bridge, screaming. Some jumped into the sea and flailed the waters, as if already in the jaws of sharks.

Boaz took off his goggles, flippers and scuba gear and let them sink. He untied the waterproof bag and passed it to Osman. He put his knife between his teeth and lurched to grab hold of the anchor, secured halfway up the bow. For a second he stood suspended, then pulled himself up. He climbed swiftly onto the railings, peered over carefully, then jumped onto the starboard deck.

He crouched low and listened. Abdallah and Hamdi, still on the port side, were hurling strange, guttural sounds. He clambered forward carefully over the boards, slippery under his wet feet. He took his knife out of his mouth, held it steady. He rounded the bridge. He saw Abdallah and Hamdi rooted in place, fists in the air. Ahead of them, the sea opened up and swallowed the *Khanjar*'s fin.

He moved forward, ready to pounce. Something clanked behind him. He veered around. Osman was crawling by the railings, trying to clamber up on one good leg while seeking to retrieve the knife he had dropped. Boaz veered again toward Abdallah and Hamdi. They had heard the noise and turned around.

Boaz thundered ferociously, like a Greek hero on the Trojan field. "*Abdallah al-Fedayeen al-Jihad!*"

The shout made Hamdi scamper around the other side.

Osman shouted. "Leave Hamdi to me!"

Boaz edged forward.

Abdallah, who had been staring at him as if he were a demon, fulminated. His hand pointed to the sea. You did that?"

Boaz grinned. "Yes."

Abdallah screamed. "The sharks are eating them!"

Boaz heard sounds of grappling behind him. He whirled swiftly without losing sight of Abdallah. He saw, peripherally, Osman felling Hamdi and keeping him pinned down with his knife. He smiled. "I could feed you to the sharks, too, Abdallah, but I won't."

Abdallah bellowed. "Who are you?"

"Boaz Ben-Ya'ir. Colonel. *Zahal.*"

Abdallah sprang forward. Boaz caught the glint of metal. He spun sideways, noting the weapon—a curved Danakil knife. He steadied himself.

Abdallah lunged. Boaz jumped back and crashed against the cabin door.

Abdallah sniggered. "I'll cut you up, Jew!"

Boaz threw away his knife. "I'll take you alive!"

Abdallah lunged again.

Boaz jumped aside and kicked. He caught Abdallah in the pit of the stomach. It barely winded him, but it gave Boaz a split second to divert his knife arm. They grappled. Boaz kneed him in the groin. Abdallah staggered back, dragging Boaz with him. Boaz's hand remained locked on Abdallah's. Abdallah butted him. Boaz ignored the pain. At Abdallah's second attempt, he ducked and struck Abdallah's throat. Abdallah's hand slackened. Boaz put a lock on the knife hand, jerked the arm, and dislocated it. Abdallah howled and dropped the knife. Boaz drove his knee yet again into the stomach. Abdallah tried to kick. Boaz grabbed the leg, twisted it and pulled it out of its socket. As he fell on the deck, Abdallah kicked with the other leg. Boaz took the kick on his stomach and locked his hands on the foot. He swung right and left, then jerked, pulling that, too, out of its socket. He stood back, breathing easily.

Abdallah writhed on the deck, three out of four limbs hanging limp from their joints; then, desperately, he lunged with his good hand at the knife on the deck and threw it at Boaz. Boaz catapulted sideways. Abdallah thrust his body at him, trying to strangle him with his good arm. Boaz heaved and stood up. Abdallah clung to him. Boaz cantered backward and slammed Abdallah against the railings. Abdallah wheezed, trying to breathe, lost his grip on Boaz. Boaz let go, turned, locked his hands and hit Abdallah across the face with all his strength. Several of Abdallah's teeth spun in the air; others embedded themselves in his hands.

Abdallah stared at him with glazed eyes; then he tried to smile. "I tell you, Jew. Nobody takes me alive."

He leaned back and let his weight plummet him over the railings into the sea.

Boaz rushed forward.

Osman's voice thundered behind him. "Boaz!"

He spun around. Osman, limping heavily, dragging Hamdi by the hair, pointed at the sea.

Boaz looked. The sea between the *Succubus* and where the submarine had sunk was writhing. Torn corpses of sailors bobbed alongside circling sharks.

"It's mob feeding time down there, Boaz."

"We need Abdallah! He'll provide all the answers!"

Osman pointed again. Abdallah had surfaced and, using his one good arm, was swimming sideways toward the sharks. "Not a chance!"

Boaz clambered over the railings.

Osman let go of Hamdi, grabbed Boaz and pulled him down. "We've got Hamdi!"

Boaz heaved and threw off Osman. He moved to the railings again, then stopped as he heard Abdallah's screams. A moment later, Abdallah disappeared amid a mass of fins.

Son of Man, Can These Bones Live Again?

Ezekiel, 37:3

March 23, 1974

TRIPOLI, LIBYA

" 'You bring forth the living from the dead and the dead from the living.' "

Abu Ismail had pared Allah's Book to its very essence. The recitations sparkled with the light of other worlds, resounded like tombs breaking open. The command room felt dank as if already infested by worms.

Nazmi, Abu Ismail's bodyguard, felt reanimated. Within the perspective of the World on High, the Blazing Fire and the Garden, defeat had no substance.

WOJ command had had intimations of disaster when communications with the *Khanjar* had been abruptly severed at 11:30 P.M. on March 21. The *Succubus*, requested to report forthwith, had taken half an hour to acknowledge signals. When she had done so, she had failed to provide the null codes for positive identification, thus indicating that she had fallen into enemy hands.

The next day, confirmation of the catastrophe had trickled in through various sources. In the morning Idris Ali, stunned by loss of contact with the submarine and the *Succubus*, had reported that neither had reached Barassoli as expected, following the destruction of the enemy sambouk. At 1:00 P.M., *Galei Zahal*, the Israeli Defense Forces' radio network, had broadcast unconfirmed reports of an Arab warship lost with all hands aboard off the Ethiopian coast. Almost in the wake of this information, a signal from Volkov, quoting a Russian military intelligence report, had imparted the information that Soviet sonar buoys in the Red Sea had recorded a massive explosion in the Hanish Kabir area, the *Khanjar*'s last known position. Finally, toward evening, Idris Ali had had unimpeachable reports from ELF sources that the *Succubus* had been sighted arriving in Djibouti, that of the three men aboard one had been identified as Hamdi, another had fitted the description of Osman Nusseibi, and that the third appeared to be a Middle Eastern man of European bearing; that they had been met and whisked away by Lieutenant Schoenberg of French Military Intelligence. Abdallah's absence had been proof that he had fallen in action.

Throughout those dreadful hours, while Abu Ismail had withdrawn to mystic paths, Nazmi had carried the mantle of the shepherd. He had organized the prescribed prayers, served mourners with solemn banquets and chased away the locusts that had come to prey on WOJ morale.

" *'Peace be on you. Come in to Paradise, the reward of your labors.' "*

Abu Ismail was gliding down from apocalyptic realms to contest, once again, the affairs of men. Nazmi intoned the last declamation and moved next to the holy man.

Abu Ismail acknowledged Nazmi's devotion with a transfiguration. Pain-plundered eyes changed to blazing suns. "The martyr's father is a blessed man, Nazmi. He understands the eternity of the soul—better than the mother who gives it flesh. My seat by Allah is adorned with the flowers of their blood."

"Your children, Al-Mahdi, have one function: to serve the Faith."

"That is why the Infidel always dies as carrion. And why, no matter how many of us fall in battle, we remain triumphant." Painfully, he stretched his arm for Nazmi to help him to his feet. "Come, there is much to do."

Physical weakness, too, was a kind of martyrdom. Though in this instance the feebleness emanated from the two minor operations he had undergone on his return from Madrid. He had had implanted a piezoelectric crystal and an open-contact probe programmed to his heart, respectively, in his upper first molar and beneath his armpit. Both items, microfuses of utmost sensitivity made to his specifications through the auspices of Ivan Volkov, were deterrents against any action the enemy—or a traitor—could conceivably devise on the Day of Glory.

March 25, 1974

DJIBOUTI, T.F.A.I.

The officers' mess, known as *La Popote*, served the best food in Africa. The special lunch prepared for Commandant Alain Tixier had raised gluttony to an art. Brandy had imposed an interlude.

Sanbat, summoned to man communications with Jerusalem, had taken charge of the coffee, attending to Boaz last, calculatingly, in the manner of a wife. Schoenberg, the host, and Montblanc, who had arranged Sanbat's transportation through Kagnew base, Asmara, paced the balcony, stopping occasionally to gaze at the palm-cradled whitewashed arabesque of Djibouti below.

Both Boaz and Osman, reassured by the integrity and commitment of Schoenberg and Montblanc, had warmed to them.

Boaz and Osman had reached Djibouti some ten hours after the engagement with the *Khanjar*. With Captain Wolde likely to be scouring the Ethiopian coast, Djibouti had been the obvious place to retreat to. Schoenberg, stirred by their exploit, had promised all the facilities he could muster.

Their first task had been Musaddiq Hamdi's interrogation. Hamdi, whose ambitions centered on taking over the ELF leadership for his Marxist faction, had agreed to buy his freedom by collaborating. He had told all he knew—from his recruitment by WOJ and his acquisition of the *Succubus*, to his shuttles between Aden and Barassoli, transporting arms to Wolde; water, oil, Yusuf's rice, technicians, women, and Professor Fawzi to the task force; and, on the trip that had led to his capture, one vital piece of equipment, a replacement bomb casing. But Hamdi did not know the location of the WOJ base. He had been neither permitted access to it nor informed of its whereabouts. His deliveries had always been picked up by members of the task force from the secret cove.

However, a man with considerable talent for clandestine work, he had amassed a wealth of pertinent facts.

He had confirmed that the hijack and subsequent destruction of AF 205 had been perpetrated by WOJ and that the operation's objective had been the plane's cargo.

He had disclosed that the *Khanjar* had been commissioned solely to serve as escort to the *Succubus*, and not to deliver the WOJ strike, and that the strike, referred to as the Day of Glory, had been fixed for the end of April.

He had deduced from the dates of the *Succubus*'s support trips that WOJ had executed two aerial drops into the Danakil. One in the second week of January, involving the task force; the other in early March, involving machinery and material.

And he had revealed, on the evidence of a signal sent by Idris Ali to Moscow from the *Succubus*, that WOJ had a Russian connection.

This last fact, a new dimension to Operation Dragons, much as it had alarmed the Memouneh, had not surprised him. Idris Ali's early training with the KGB had always kept that possibility open.

Limited as all this information had been, it had, nonetheless, provided some direction.

The drop dates could be investigated by Getachew, holding steadfast in Asmara, with anomalies, if any, recorded by the Ethiopian Civil Aviation Authority and Air Force Command.

They could determine, on the evidence that the WOJ task force could deploy to and from their cove with relative ease, that the base was located at a manageable distance from Barassoli—at a rough estimate, within a radius of eighty kilometers.

They could assume that deprived of the *Succubus* and the *Khanjar*, WOJ had to establish a new supply line. Though this might be feasible with help from South Yemen or Russia, Abu Ismail would know that any vessel operating between Aden and the Ethiopian coast would come under enemy scrutiny. This factor would restrict him to overland routes and compel him to delegate the task either to Captain Wolde or Yusuf the Afar. Since Wolde could not operate outside Ethiopia, Yusuf was the likely choice. Yusuf could be engaged.

Finally, and crucial to all considerations, there was the bomb casing that Boaz and Osman had found aboard the *Succubus*.

Osman, anxious to start the proceedings, gulped down his coffee and turned to Tixier. "The floor is yours, Commandant."

Tixier nodded solemnly. Tall and taciturn, he was an eminent nuclear expert in France's *Force de Frappe*. He had been vociferously critical of the French government's complacency over the loss of AF 205's plutonium cargo. Dismissing the navy's ongoing search of the Mediterranean seabed as a self-fulfilling delusion, he had tried to convince his superiors that the material had been stolen by the hijackers. Schoenberg's alert had brought him from Toulon in the hope of galvanizing his government with irrefutable proof.

Tixier moved to the shaded balcony and paused before the bomb casing, now dismantled. The others grouped around him.

He spoke softly. "Let me start with a brief introduction. A nuclear device requires Uranium-235 or Plutonium-239. There is not much natural Uranium-235, so this is extracted from Uranium-238, which is quite plentiful. Plutonium-239 is a by-product of uranium fission—that is to say, man-made. The production of weapons-grade material in both instances requires highly complex processes—in terms of finance, technology and manpower—beyond the range of most governments, let alone a terrorist organization. That is the reason WOJ stole the plutonium. They could not have made a nuclear bomb without ready-made material."

He knelt beside the bomb casing. "Bearing that in mind, I have no doubt that this casing has been designed to house an atomic bomb. I won't burden you with all the technical details. The basic facts are these. A nuclear device must accommodate two seemingly incompatible aims. One: it must detonate when wanted. Two: it must *not* detonate when *not* wanted. This means, in essence, that the payload, the power source, the arming, fusing, firing and back-up systems must be so assembled as to function in perfect sequence; simultaneously, they must be protected against unintentional detonation likely to be caused by such mishaps as fragmentation, premature explosion of primary charges, accidental impacts, electrical and chemical interference and so on."

He paused, lit a cigarette, then continued. "To meet such vital specifications, standard weapons contain a plethora of electromechanical permissive-action links and fail-safe systems. The casing itself must be capable, above all else, of housing these ultrasensitive mechanisms. Consequently, the standard ones are manufactured with the sort of precision technology we normally associate with the aircraft industry. The casing we have here is *not* standard."

He faced the people surrounding him. "But unorthodox as this casing is, it is by no means unsophisticated. Quite an ingenious innovation, in fact. The engineers made their own rules in devising a high-strength steel case."

Osman voiced a wisp of hope. "If they've made their own rules, any chance the casing might prove nonfunctional?"

Tixier shook his head. "No. I've examined the compartmentalization carefully. They've made provisions for everything. I should say we're dealing with a bomb much along the lines of 'Fat Man,' the one dropped on Nagasaki. The plutonium warhead will have a belt of TNT charges—imperative for implosion and chain reaction. There are, as you can see, chambers for caps to detonate the explosives simultaneously. There's room for an adequate power source and a backup system for it—two batteries, I think, independently linked to a capacitor. There's provision to house the tamper mechanism—essential for absorbing the implosion, and distributing it equally onto the plutonium masses and maintaining the neutron flux. There's accommodation for other essential systems: arming, firing, fail-safe and, again, independent backup systems for them all. There are compartments for a variety of fuses: proximity, time, barometric and probably a number of unconventional ones serving as booby-traps against neutralization by an enemy. You will also note the casing has stabilizing fins, aerofoils and hooks for parachute lanyards—in other words, it has been designed for an aerial drop." He stood up and stubbed out his cigarette. "Anything you need clarified?"

Schoenberg kicked the casing angrily. "I don't know much about atomic bombs, but I do know that achieving the correct critical mass is not easy. A plutonium bomb has to implode in a particular way. Would that apply to this one?"

Tixier sauntered to the bar and poured himself a hefty measure of brandy. "Let me put it this way. If you have the tools and a good team, but lack such sophisticated equipment as computers, you need, basically, two experts to make a nuclear bomb. One: a physicist who will calculate the amount of subcritical plutonium required—the way it has to be divided for purposes of implosion as well as the exact volume needed to render these portions critical. Two: a high-explosives expert capable of devising a firing system that will use just the right amount of primary charges and will detonate these precisely at the same time. It's true neither of these experts has a margin for error since the slightest miscalculation can alter the nature of the happening and render it a nuclear event —something like a radiation leak—instead of a nuclear blast. But there has been mention of the Lebanese professor of physics, Talat Fawzi, and the Japanese terrorist, Hiroshi Anami, alias Ischii Watanabe. I've studied both their files. I have no reservations on their capabilities. Furthermore, Watanabe is also an electronics expert, capable of devising the most sophisticated fuse systems."

Schoenberg shook his head stubbornly. "They may have Watanabe, but we only have Hamdi's word about Fawzi. Our records say Fawzi committed suicide."

Osman patted Schoenberg's shoulder sympathetically. "The suicide was a substitute. WOJ have been making doubles. We've met one—Abu Ismail's. The Fawzi who died in Beirut is another."

"This Fawzi—is he a WOJ man?"

Boaz turned to Montblanc who had asked the question. "Not as far as we know."

"So they're coercing him."

"If he hasn't been proselytized. Or brainwashed."

"Can't we get at him? Say by radio?"

Boaz and Osman exchanged a glance. The idea had occurred to the Memouneh, too. Theoretically, it was feasible. Stuck in a mountain fastness, the WOJ task force would be dependent on transoceanic radio for distraction. A coded message, one that would be recognizable to Fawzi, could be devised and broadcast continuously. How to determine which stations WOJ would be listening to, and how many of these stations would agree to cooperate, was another matter. "We're checking feasibility on that."

Montblanc nodded and swigged some rum.

Boaz turned to Tixier. "There's something I'd like to clarify, Commandant. This bomb casing is a replacement. That means, the original has developed a fault. So, as things stand, WOJ are without a bomb casing. What would you do in such a situation?"

"I'd ask for another one—immediately."

"You mean a drop? That would be too risky! From the moment we seized the *Succubus*, Israel has been monitoring the area—we have cargo boats and aircraft maintaining electronic surveillance. By the end of this meeting, recommendations from you and Montblanc will have French and U.S. AWACS supporting us. Any drop they try would pinpoint their position."

"Then they'd try by sea—or overland. This Yusuf . . ."

"We're bearing Yusuf in mind. But then again, WOJ would also expect us to be scouring land and sea. They'll know that Israel, at least, will be on intensive alert. For instance, we have a couple of Reshev missile-boats on their way to Sharm al-Sheikh. They'll pass Bab el Mandeb in a few days. WOJ will hear about them from Aden. They'd expect Israel to deploy them. And we would—I have the authority to take over command. Yusuf will have to be very resourceful to get through. . . ."

"I think I can anticipate your next question, Boaz. Can the task force manufacture their own casing?"

"Precisely. Can they?"

"Difficult to say."

"They have the technicians. They have Fawzi. They have Watanabe. They also have tools, vehicles, weapons, ammunition—all of which they can cannibalize—and the plutonium coffin. Can they improvise a bomb casing?"

Tixier took a long time and another glass of brandy to answer. "We must assume they can."

March 26, 1974

DAADATU, ETHIOPIA

The Afars squatted in a group. All wore ivory armlets to indicate they had killed scores of men.

Idris Ali sat in the shade of his Land-Rover and scrutinized them. They seemed an integral part of the wilderness, like acacia stumps. "Is that all? Twenty men?"

Yusuf glanced at the pouch of gold which Idris Ali had brought as payment, but which he had not yet handed over. "It's enough."

"You underestimate the enemy, Yusuf. They've just sunk a submarine. . . ."

"It's easy to sink submarines. Not so easy to move like a lizard."

Idris Ali squinted into the sun. His men had clustered by the livestock. They appeared abnormally affected by the heat and were negotiating with the Afar women for gourds of milk. The bare-breasted young girls, carefree in the shade of a favored oasis, were flirtatious, but the men showed no interest. The older women stood back, wary of the strangers' pallor.

Yusuf interpreted Idris Ali's hesitation as a sign of bad faith. Angrily, he bit his own arm and drew blood in the traditional gesture of death pledged. "Yusuf will kill with his teeth. You have his word."

Idris Ali glared at him, revolted that WOJ had to rely on gold-hungry savages. It should never have happened. Abu Ismail's orders to eliminate the enemy spearhead before it could wreak further damage were, as matters stood now, a panic measure that disregarded several vital facts. That in view of the Israel Defense Forces' broadcast on the *Khanjar*'s fate immediately after the event, there could be no doubt that Israel was leading the chase against WOJ, and that, therefore, the unidentified Middle Eastern man accompanying Osman Nusseibi was an Israeli agent—there had been many such clandestine collaborations between Israel and Jordan in the past. That the nearer Osman Nusseibi and his Israeli shadow sneaked to the WOJ base, the stronger was the possibility of a major action by the Israelis—unilaterally or in conjunction with American, French and Ethiopian forces. That though the base could repulse any assault, sickness among the task force was escalating critically. That even if the base remained secret and inviolate throughout the next four weeks, there was always the danger that a major force could put it under siege by sealing off all entry and exit points. And that would be the end of Operation Dragons.

Idris Ali seethed. With *Khanjar* and her crew lost, WOJ lacked the manpower and logistics to storm Djibouti and capture the enemy spearhead. Deprived of the bomb casing and unable to arrange a drop for a new one because of the risks of detection, the task force had to forge its own. Long ago, during the planning stages, arrangements should have been made to meet such adverse contingencies; a reserve force should have been standing by for immediate deployment.

The failure to do so proved Abu Ismail a lesser man. Now he, Idris Ali, had to redress the situation. And he would do it his way.

He had already solved the problem of the bomb casing by having Ivan Volkov provide him, over the radio, with a blueprint designed by one of his KGB experts.

And he would deal with the enemy. If Yusuf could capture its spearhead, he would interrogate them and, according to the information extracted, plan to divert its forces from the area. Failing that, at the very least, he would have bought precious time.

And once he had redressed the situation, he would take over. With a clear conscience. As the better man. Not as a false Al-Mahdi. "You won't kill them, Yusuf. You'll bring them to me alive. . . ."

Yusuf hesitated, as was obligatory for every conclusion to a transaction. "Including Hamdi?"

"What's special about Hamdi?"

"He's been released. Some of my kin saw him eating money in Djibouti. That means he told them everything."

Idris Ali's eyes narrowed. He had suspected as much when the skies and the Red Sea had festered with French, American and Israeli patrols. But for that, he and his men would not have had to trek for two nights, like fugitives, to this hellhole; but for that, they could have rendezvoused with Yusuf on the coast, got all the supplies they needed instead of rationing themselves to the basic minimum. "He told them what he knew. That's not much, Yusuf."

"Hamdi's not a fool. He always knows more than you think."

Idris Ali spat venomously. That might be true. That could be why they had released him. On the other hand, it could be the old trick. Set him loose in the hope that he would run back to WOJ. Failing that, unnerve WOJ by making them think he had supplied vital information and force them to find out exactly what he had revealed. Either way, to flush WOJ out. "Why do *you* want Hamdi, Yusuf?"

"There are people in the ELF prepared to buy his death."

Idris Ali smiled sardonically and handed Yusuf the pouch. "He's yours."

ASMARA, ETHIOPIA

That morning a group of NCOs had seized the airport, arrested the commander of the Second Division and the commissioner of police and demanded, over Radio Asmara, that they stand trial on charges of corruption.

The revolt had almost caught Getachew flat-footed.

He had been checking records of incidents that might correspond to the dates supplied by Hamdi in relation to the WOJ drops. Air Force Command, buffeted by growing unrest, had proved barren territory. Files that had not been hastily stored or mislaid had lacked appropriate cross-references. Getachew had had to try his luck with the Civil Aviation Authority. Though coercion tempered with bribes had given him access to the records at Yohannes IV Airport, the personnel had been hostile and uncooperative. Nonetheless, after twenty hours of dogged search, Getachew had found two incidents logged by South Eritrean Area Control. He had been searching for further data when the mutineers stormed the airport.

The indications were that the revolt would be short-lived, merely a stage in the creeping coup. But Getachew, uneasily aware that the rebels, to curry favor with Wolde, might arrest him too, had woven his way across to the U.S. Air Force hangar.

Lieutenant Donald O'Brien, looking more like an athletic collegian in the Peace Corps than a powerhouse of the Defense Intelligence Agency, had proven himself as astute as Jameson's assurances. Spreading an effective smokescreen to conceal Getachew's presence, he had cleared the way for a hookup to CIA headquarters. Jameson, with whom Getachew had wished to communicate, had been unavailable. O'Brien, undeterred, had charged Ciphers for a priority signal to his own headquarters, assuring Getachew that the DIA would exhume Jameson, if need be, from the densest scrapheap. "We're ready, sir. Just dictate your message, we'll encode it."

Getachew, though he had memorized the details, consulted his notebook and spoke into the dictaphone. "We've found out that WOJ have dropped personnel and material during two flights over Ethiopia. I believe I can specify these as follows. Dates: January 11 and March 2. Times: oh-oh fifty-one to oh-oh fifty-four for the first; oh-five fifty-seven to oh-six oh-one for the second. Flight call sign: 5A-DY-DNF3313. Squawk code: 3313. Logged flight plan: Tripoli–Aden transit. Airway level: 18,000 feet. Aircraft: DC-6B. Airline: Memleket-Cargo Incorporated. On the first incident, January 11, aircraft dropped below radar level over the Dallol Depression, then, admitting navigational error, offered apologies. On the second incident, March 2, over eastern Danakil, aircraft reported malfunctioning of pressurization system and was allowed to descend. Malfunction was reported rectified on regaining altitude. I have coordinates for the incidents. Latitude 41 degrees 34 minutes north, longitude 40 degrees 25 minutes east for the first; latitude 13 degrees 38 minutes north, longitude 41 degrees 31 minutes east for the second. Recommendation: if Jameson can confirm these data with electronic and satellite intelligence sources, he should prevail on the mapping authorities to survey the Danakil for a location likely to be the WOJ base. Signed: Getachew Iyessous."

March 27, 1974

ISTANBUL, TURKEY

They met on the first-class deck as the ferryboat left Bebek—for the Memouneh the most picturesque village on the Bosphorus. With Cyprus once again churned by unrest, Istanbul had been the next best choice for an urgent meeting.

The day had the quality of summer. The sun danced on Rumeli Hisarı, the fortress on the European bank built by Mehmet II for the conquest of Constantinople; only the mass of jellyfish floating in the water suggested that winter might still take a final curtain call.

"Talat's really alive?" Charles Quinn looked disemboweled, worse than when the Memouneh had last seen him in Paphos. But he was sober.

"Yes. According to Hamdi . . ."

Quinn's sagging cheeks trembled. "I—I knew it . . . deep down . . . Never believed his suicide. I said so in my report. . . ."

"What report?"

"One I filed immediately after . . ."

"I don't understand. You reported that a physicist capable of making a nuclear device was suspected of a fake suicide? Charlie, there would have been alarm bells loud and clear for us all! There weren't!"

Quinn fumbled for a cigarette. "They didn't process it through the computer. They—thought I'd flipped. They were very . . . commiserating. . . ."

"Did they know your feelings for Fawzi?"

Quinn lit his cigarette before answering. "Maybe. I guess, sometimes, I made it too obvious. . . ."

The Memouneh nodded bitterly. A speck—that was all it took to tilt the scales. One man's emotions, wrongly weighed, held the world to ransom.

The ferryboat was moving toward Kandilli on the Asian bank. The hills on both sides of the Bosphorus changed hues kaleidoscopically. In an effort to calm himself, Quinn pointed at a cluster of buildings by the ramparts of Rumeli Hisarı. "That's the American College—Robert College, as it was known when I started my academic career. I could have taught there. I might have been a doyen by now. . . . And loved it . . . There're not many places more beautiful than Istanbul. Instead—I chose Beirut. . . ."

"Why?"

"I thought I'd be more at home in Lebanon. A country half Christian, if you follow. I thought it'd be more stable. Ironic, isn't it? *Kismet*, as Talat used to say . . ."

The Memouneh nodded sympathetically. Quinn threw away his cigarette. "Beirut's been hell, Zamora, I don't mind telling you —particularly after the Company signed me on. But because of Talat, it's also been heaven. That's why I can't bring myself to cut out. . . ."

"I understand."

Quinn turned around sharply, sensing indulgence. "Sure you do. Or you wouldn't have brought me here with Talat as the carrot."

The Memouneh parried aggressively. "Would you have come otherwise? After the brush-off you gave me last time?"

"What about Talat?"

"You want him alive? Rescued?"

Quinn's eyes glinted. "What is this? Blackmail?"

"Sentiment might compel you to move heaven and earth. . . . Nothing else did. . . ."

Angrily, Quinn lit another cigarette. "What about Talat?"

"I've been checking on him. He's never shown himself to be an extremist. . . . Nor a WOJ sympathizer. Could he have been converted?"

"Intellectually? No. But torture a man . . . brainwash him . . . Who can tell?"

"Knowing him as you do, do you think he'd make the bomb?"

"He's their prisoner, for Jesus' sake!"

"I've known prisoners—so have you—who've died rather than collaborate. Would he make the bomb?"

Quinn had suppressed the question ever since receiving the Memouneh's message. Timorously, he reexamined his friendship with Fawzi: the carefree moments, the exchanges of political views, aspirations, insecurities . . . "Yes."

The Memouneh's eyes glazed. He had hoped for a different answer.

Quinn grimaced. How could the Memouneh, a soldier, understand the unstable mind of a genius? The exultation and the hopelessness that competed for dominion. And ultimately, the horror of living in a world abandoned by God. "If he feels desolate . . . beyond redemption . . . If his despair of mankind gets control . . ."

The Memouneh pondered a moment. "If you talked to him . . ."

"Talked to him . . . ?"

"Say if you had a code. Something that would catch his attention. Bearing, unmistakably, your signature. We have computers that can do anything. . . ."

"And?"

"Transmit that. Through various bands. Between programs."

"Telling him what?"

"That help is at hand. To hold out. To sabotage the bomb."

Quinn, captivated by the idea, pondered over the possibilities. "There's a hole right through that."

"Several."

"No guarantees he'd receive the signals."

"None. But we can try the radio stations WOJ are likely to tune to."

"If they do at all. If they allow Talat to listen . . ."

"It's worth a try, don't you think?"

"I'll say it is. Can you come up with such a code . . . ?"

"We have. A combination of an Anglo-Saxon rune, Bragg's Law and Anderssen's famous chess game, 'The Immortal Partie,' set to a twelve-tone musical piece by Dallapiccola. It's way beyond me, but I understand you and Fawzi spent a lot of time playing such games. . . ."

"Yes, we did . . ."

"That's our first favor from you, Charlie. . . ."

The Memouneh left the statement hanging. The ferryboat had stopped at Kandilli and had taken on more passengers. As he waited for Mossad agents on cover duty to screen the newcomers, he checked his watch. He had arranged to get off at Beşiktaş, beyond the Bosphorus Bridge, and drive on to Yeşilköy Airport. The meeting had to be resolved by then.

One of the Mossad agents signaled clearance.

The Memouneh resumed, brusque and businesslike. "You'll have the code on the way to the airport, Charlie. But there's more . . ."

Quinn shot him a look. "What do you mean, the airport—"

"No beating about the bush this time."

"Just hold on a minute. You giving me orders?"

"You want to see Fawzi again? Well, the chance lies with us.

And there's no conflict of loyalties! You tell your boss that—the president too, if you have to!"

Quinn, antagonized by the tone of command, protested. "Now, listen—"

"We'll get you to Yeşilköy for the Pan-Am flight. You'll be in New York tonight, in time for a connection to Washington. Get some sleep on the plane. Might be days before you sleep again. . . ."

"You crazy son of a—"

The Memouneh crushed the invective with a staccato burst. "You'll start transmitting to Fawzi immediately. Along with the code, we'll be providing you with recommendations as to which stations to go through—and how. If your boys can improve on those—all the better. But, even more imperative—the moment you land, you start hustling! I don't care how you do it, which door you knock on. But by tomorrow I want your satellites over Ethiopia. I want photographs. Black-and-white, color, infrared, low-speed, high-speed. I want thermographs, line scans, holograms, three-dimensional maps. I want every conceivable electronic intelligence the U.S. can provide. And without delay!"

"You don't want much, do you?"

"Charlie. We've got to locate the WOJ base. We've tried conventional surveying—we've sent our planes. So have the French. And, thanks to your colleague Montblanc, even some of your boys in Asmara. Waste of time. Like looking for a grain of wheat in a sand dune. You're our last hope. If that doesn't move you—you're Fawzi's last hope. . . . I'm sorry to be so rough, but I haven't got the strength for delicacy. . . ."

Quinn saw, despite his anger, that the Memouneh was not exaggerating. The man's strength had ebbed; he had shrunk, was shrinking. Simultaneously, he felt himself broaden. In a flash of memory, he saw himself as the relay runner he had been in his youth: last to go, bursting with strength, picking up the baton from an exhausted teammate. That, he decided, was how he should be. "Hell, Zamora—why not? Time I got myself into a scrap . . ."

March 30, 1974

CANBERRA, AUSTRALIA

There were about a dozen exercise books, and they had been preserved as codices of great importance. But to Jameson, surrounded by the tomes and maps of the Teachers' Library, they seemed incongruous. Exercise books were tools for schoolchildren, not explorers.

". . . The Wallaces settled here as missionaries, you see. Jubal's after the Biblical hero who invented music. But we all called him by his nickname: Dunes."

"Why Dunes?"

"For sand dunes. He was the greatest explorer of deserts—our Great Sandy, the Gobi, the Kara Kum, the Empty Quarter, the Sahara, and the Danakil . . ."

Dr. Madge Lawler's fingers, resting on the exercise books, trembled. Jameson guessed she had had a bad night. Madge Lawler, he had been warned, had been Wallace's woman and since the latter's murder, inconsolable.

"Tea?"

"I'd hate to trouble you, ma'am."

She moved toward the door. "I want some myself. Browse, if you wish. Leave anything you take out on the table. I'll put them back later."

"I make a point of admiring from a distance, ma'am. I'm often clumsy in the presence of splendor."

She stopped, softened by his humility. "I'm sorry. I was being officious. It's just that—they've decided to name this library after him . . . I've taken it upon myself to keep it in trim."

"I understand."

She left him with a grateful jerk of the shoulder.

Jameson walked to the bay windows. The grounds of the School of Advanced Studies of the Australian National University harmonized with Sullivans Creek, West Lake and Capital Hill beyond. There was a hint of autumn in the air, and the garden city of Canberra seemed to welcome it with colors newly invented. He could well have forgotten, but for the stench of death and desperation he carried with him, that outside this idyllic setting there were continents on fire.

Since his return from Ethiopia, he had not ceased ferreting through the convolutions of Operation Dragons. Checking on the fate of AF 205, he had discovered, he was sure, how WOJ had secured classified information on nuclear cargo movements—the bizarre death of a clerk in the International Atomic Energy Agency in Vienna.

The principle that a nuclear device required the guidance of a capable physicist had led him to Dr. Charles Quinn's jeremiad on the doubtful suicide of Professor Talat Fawzi.

Various dossiers, willingly provided by Mossad, had completed the picture with reports on the recruitment of Watanabe, the women and the technicians; the deaths of Aaron Levi and Noah Manasseh, Mossad's agents within WOJ and Libya; and the assassination of Abu Ismail's double in Mecca.

Thereafter, convinced that priority lay in the discovery of the WOJ base, he had had himself transplanted through the arm-bending tactics of Gentleman Jim, his boss, to the National Security Agency at Fort George G. Meade, Maryland, to check the mass of electronic intelligence.

The task of sifting through those records with no specific data except the maximum boundaries of the Danakil had consumed much precious time, even with an expert team at his disposal. The search, in fact, would have foundered but for Getachew's signal of the twenty-sixth, providing references to the flights of a Libyan DC-6B on January 11 and March 2. Satellite photographs relating to the coordinates had revealed that in both instances the aircraft had circled a narrow sector of approximately twenty-six kilometers radius, executing in the process sizable parachute drops.

Much as the last had generated hope of a breakthrough, he had remained despondent, convinced by his knowledge of the Danakil that surveying even a small high-probability area might prove impossible. His fears had been confirmed after the sudden appearance in Washington of Dr. Charles Quinn.

Quinn, regenerated by the news that his friend Fawzi was alive, had mobilized every intelligence department and, in the past sixty hours, had subjected the Danakil to intensive surveys by spy satellites and planes.

But the Danakil, brandishing its volcanic face, had defied infrared, low-speed and high-speed photography, line scans and three-dimensional maps. Holograms of the light waves emanating from the earth's crust, and thermographs capable of recording heat emissions of a human colony had been useless. The active craters had blurred all readings.

The surveys were still continuing, by the grace of Quinn's tenacity and by the fact that some radioactivity had been recorded in the atmosphere over the search area. Modifications were being improvised to sensitize equipment to the singular conditions, and experts were still hopeful. He was not.

Instead, he had taken an unlikely diversion to pursue a hunch.

Since he had begun his investigation of incidents hitherto unexplained, but which might bear the WOJ stamp, one had been howling for close scrutiny: Jubal Wallace's murder.

He had been the first to admit the hunch was a desperate one. Wallace's murder had never been linked, officially or unofficially, with any subversive group, let alone WOJ. There had been no witnesses to the crime, and the case had remained unsolved. But the brutality of the deed, linked to the fact that the murderer had destroyed Wallace's photographs, films and manuscript on the Danakil, the region he had recently explored, had struck him as a carefully executed killing. This perspective, evaluated in the light of Idris Ali's incursion into Ethiopia at the time of his meeting with Captain Wolde, had offered a highly plausible motive for the murder. Simply that WOJ, needing a base in the Danakil, had sought it in Wallace's manuscript.

"I've been instructed by the Department of Defense to offer every assistance . . ."

He veered around. Lost in thought, he had not heard Madge Lawler come in. He hurried to the table where she had sat down with the tea. "As long as it doesn't get too painful for you. . . ."

"The pain's constant. Go ahead. . . ."

He used his gentlest tone. "It concerns, as I've mentioned, Professor Wallace's book on the Danakil. . . . I believe you've taken over . . ."

"I felt it my duty—as his amanuensis. He regarded it as his greatest work. It will be some time before I finish it. . . ."

"Does that mean not all of his papers were destroyed?"

She pointed at the notebooks. "I have only these. His notes in the field . . . He had left them here. . . . They're quite adequate. Day-to-day accounts. Summaries of the geographical areas. . . ."

"Do the areas include the Danakil Alps?"

"Most of the book is about the Danakil Alps. The rest of the wilderness, the Awash valley, had already been explored—by Thesiger and others. The Alps were virgin territory."

He felt his throat dry up. "Dr. Lawler, I think you're about to answer many people's prayers. We need a reference—"

"What sort of reference?"

"A vast cave. Or a chain of caves. A hidden valley. A subterranean complex. I don't know. An area so secluded that it cannot be spotted from land or air, but suitable enough to accommodate a hundred people or more, and relatively accessible from the coast. . . ."

Madge Lawler smiled. "Oh, that. Shangri-la."

He moved to the edge of his seat. "What?"

"Dunes used to daydream about it. Danakil's mystery realm. The seat of a lost civilization. There's a reference to it in a twelfth-century Ethiopic poem. He was most disappointed when he found it. It turned out to be a rock maze. Quite remarkable, but a rock maze . . ."

"Where is it? Exactly?"

"I couldn't tell you . . . Well, not offhand."

"I—I'm sorry, I don't follow . . ."

Madge Lawler pointed at the notebooks. "I haven't deciphered all the data yet. I'm progressing step by step."

"What's there to decipher?"

"Dunes's peculiar shorthand."

He hesitated before asking. "How long would it take you to crack the section on the rock maze?"

"Two days . . . Maybe three."

He grabbed her hands like a mendicant. "Start now. Please. We need its exact location. How to get there. Landmarks. Danger areas. Everything."

Madge Lawler looked down at his hands. Jameson's grip had been as earnest as Dunes's used to be. She felt a primeval cry rise in her throat. "Dunes was . . . a remarkable man. Ageless. Like a Polynesian god. You'd spot him straightaway on Bondi Beach on Christmas Day. The way he was killed, Mr. Jameson . . . like a temple torn down—brick by brick . . . Will this reference avenge him?"

"I believe so."

Madge Lawler extricated her hands. "Soon as I can, Mr. Jameson."

March 31, 1974

DJIBOUTI, T.F.A.I.

The European quarter savored the leisure of a Sunday afternoon. Servicemen and their families, refreshed by siestas, converged on *Les Tritons*, the fashionable beach, to catch the last of the sun. Nearby, at the governor-general's villa, preparations were under way for a *poisson d'Avril* garden party. April Fool's Day was a good excuse to reanimate a city stricken with inertia.

Yet there was menace in the air. Schoenberg felt it hovering. He rounded the railway crossing, turned into boulevard de la République and reestablished visual contact with Sanbat, some twenty meters ahead. The menace kept pace.

Schoenberg tried to rationalize. Sanbat was of no importance to the enemy. She had volunteered to return to her room on her own. All he had to do was ensure that she reached it safely.

Boaz and Osman had released Hamdi six days ago. To fatten the bait, they had assigned Sanbat to act as his high-class whore and spend a substantial amount of money. The theory had been that WOJ, no matter how confident that Hamdi did not know the location of the base, would feel threatened by whatever had secured his freedom and blood money. The exhaustive aerial surveillance over the Danakil, the heavy patrolling of the Red Sea, and the fact that a number of counterintelligence agents from SDECE, flown in from France, had been deployed to ferret out Yusuf, would alarm them all the more. They would feel compelled to remedy matters, first by capturing and interrogating Hamdi, then by destroying the enemy spearhead before it could launch an offensive.

Boaz and Osman had not discounted the flaw in their theory: that WOJ might see through the ruse and leave Hamdi to his own devices. But they calculated that Hamdi would not stay put. Wishing to reinstate himself within the WOJ–ELF alliance, he would seek to contact either Aden or Tripoli. In fact, since his release, Hamdi had dropped word at every place likely to harbor an ear. As a result, a growing number of Afars, all Yusuf's kinsmen, had appeared in Djibouti to monitor his movements.

It had been a long and frustrating waiting game—particularly tense for Sanbat who had had to fend off Hamdi's advances.

This morning, just as Boaz and Osman had begun to despair of a development, Hamdi had been contacted by an Afar and instructed to make his way alone to the old city.

The task of tailing him had been undertaken by Boaz, Osman, Montblanc and the French agents—though the last, disoriented city boys, lacked, in Schoenberg's estimation, the mettle of the crack Israeli force which the Memouneh had on standby and which the French government, despite Tixier's recommendations, had refused to have on T.F.A.I. soil. Schoenberg, who was the ideal man to lead the operation in the old city, had had to step down. He was known to too many Afars.

Schoenberg interrupted his thoughts. A black Citroën bearing the *Chambre des Députés* insignia had cruised past the cathedral and turned into the forecourt of the main post office, on Sanbat's side of the boulevard. As a well-dressed African got out to mail letters, Schoenberg instinctively quickened his pace.

The chauffeur drove a short distance, then stopped alongside Sanbat, shouting compliments. Sanbat flirted openly as would have been expected of a sophisticated whore. Then the car door opened, and arms dragged her into the back.

Schoenberg drew his gun on the run and reached the car as the chauffeur revved up. He saw Sanbat, her back to him, embracing a man in the back seat—Yusuf. He steadied his gun. "Sanbat! Duck!"

He saw Sanbat move. He waited for a clear shot. When Sanbat

rolled toward him, he noted she was unconscious. At the same moment, he felt a presence behind him. He turned as the man who had gone to mail letters struck him savagely on the head.

✗

Boaz and Osman were in simple but effective disguise; in abas of peninsular Arabs of whom there was a large community in the old quarter. They moved fast on two flanks, hugging the walls, carrying beneath their garb Chinese submachine guns fitted with silencers, procured by Schoenberg. Boaz, in addition, carried a canvas bag.

The whitewashed houses, leaning against each other across a labyrinth of lanes, offered perfect cover for snipers.

Boaz breathed death in the air. Sunday, for the Muslim Afars, was a working day. Yet the quarter was deserted; even the women had moved children, animals and kitchens indoors.

Osman, too, heard the sound of bones rattling in his ears. He forced his mind to ignore the pain racking his leg.

They paused on opposite sides of an intersection and scrutinized the layout. One lane led to avenue Treize, the old quarter's main thoroughfare; the one they were in ended abruptly, across the intersection, at a courtyard. They spotted Montblanc hidden in a doorway, some ten meters away from it. He signaled them to wait. They melted against their respective walls and surveyed the shuttered windows. Montblanc edged forward, crouched behind a battered oil drum, listened for sounds, then signaled. Boaz and Osman scurried over.

Montblanc whispered. "He's in there."

The house projected a heavy shadow. A few tattered clothes hung on a line in the courtyard. The door was closed, but a faint light slithered through a chink in the shuttered window.

From the canvas bag Boaz pulled out a set of earphones, a miniature directional microphone and a small parabolic dish. He pointed the microphone at the window showing the light, then set up the parabolic dish. He passed the earphones to Montblanc. "See how many voices you can pick up."

Montblanc donned the earphones and concentrated.

He had been the obvious choice for the spearhead. He knew the Afar quarter well, and though a familiar face, he was not associated with French colonial authority. Those who had had dealings with him believed him to be an unscrupulous jack-of-all trades trafficking in anything that would yield a franc. He was also black. Like a stray dog, he could roam without hindrance, wherever mysterious spirits beckoned him.

Montblanc had slunk behind Hamdi at place Rimbaud, and had shadowed him since. The maneuver had enabled Boaz and Osman to maintain maximum distance, as well as the option to counterattack should either Montblanc or Hamdi walk into an ambush. The French agents had been deployed in place Rimbaud and avenue Treize, the two extremities of the old quarter, to block any escape attempt by Hamdi.

Montblanc took off the earphones brusquely. "All I can hear is water. . . ."

Boaz grimaced. "They're not taking any chances, are they?"

Montblanc looked dubious. "It doesn't sound like antibug precautions. . . . Something's overflowing. . . . But . . . running water—they don't have it—not here in the old city. . . ."

Osman fidgeted uneasily. "Maybe it's a special house. What diff—"

Montblanc snapped his fingers. "Jesus, you're right. It *is* a special house. It's the old *hamam*. The baths, built over the Ambuli, an underground stream. It has a pump which taps the water. It's been closed for repairs. . . ." He turned around sharply. "We've been set up. There's another entrance to it—near avenue Treize. They've probably escaped. . . ."

Boaz steadied his gun. "Osman, hold tight! If you hear fireworks, storm!"

Hamdi felt his mind drain. . . . No memories. No truth. No reality even. Except water. Everything confused. Yet he was dying. He knew by his terror. But . . . water. Water more precious than a hundred sons for a man forever with sand in his mouth.

"What did they do?"

Boaz pointed to the hose running from the pump. "Strapped him up. Shoved the hose into his mouth and switched on the pump . . ."

Montblanc felt sick. The thick-stoned floor of the baths looked like that of a slaughterhouse. Chunks of flesh and entrails blocked the troughs and floated on the water that was still spurting from the hose. "Jesus, man, Jesus! I've seen killings, but . . ."

Osman, on lookout at the rear window, spat in disgust. "Used to be an execution reserved for traitors in Palestinian refugee camps." He moved away from the window and smashed the pump with his gun. "There's nobody out there. They've gone. If we had been faster, we'd have had them. . . ."

Boaz squatted on his haunches, rubbed his eyes. His head felt a wasteland. He talked slowly, in desperate need of repose. "We planned wrongly. We didn't think of a second exit. Assumed they'd question Hamdi about us . . . Give us time to pounce . . ."

Osman bellowed. "Excuses!"

"All right, you guys." Montblanc was rummaging through Boaz's canvas bag. He pulled out a walkie-talkie. "Sorry to butt in, but we won't get far on recriminations. The French guys—they might have picked up Hamdi's killers."

Osman snatched at the hope. "That's right!"

Montblanc walked out. "I'll have better reception outside."

Osman followed. "I'll keep you covered."

Boaz remained on his haunches and stared at Hamdi's eyeballs hanging from the torn and bloated face. He could hear Death laugh. As if it had visited Hamdi by mistake. Or if by design, then as a diversion. Because it had not gone away.

On a perverse impulse, he sat on the floor. The slime was, after all, death's fluid. It could turn into a torrent and carry him away. Conversely, it could spend itself like afterbirth, indicate that the Separator of Friends had concluded his labors, that for today at least, no more dead would be born.

Osman returned and knelt beside him. Boaz saw him tremble. "They've got Schoenberg. . . ."

"What?"

"The French boys just heard it . . . Yusuf and his men."

"Sanbat?"

Osman remained silent.

Boaz howled and catapulted himself off the floor. He slipped and sprawled in the slime. He imagined Sanbat, born to Death. Somewhere her body floating through a viscous mass. He thrashed about. Hamdi's slime could carry him to hell. . . . His body for Sanbat's. His soul for hers. Like Judas hanging. Only not like Judas. Not too late.

April 1, 1974

GHOUBET EL KHARAB, T.F.A.I.

Sanbat had come to in the suffocating heat of a shuttered garage. She had been shocked to find Schoenberg sprawled beside her and full of self-recriminations for falling into Yusuf's ambush and dragging Schoenberg with her. Since then, she had kept careful track of their movements.

The garage, on the outskirts of Djibouti, had served as a hideout while Yusuf monitored the police patrol cars. When Schoenberg had regained consciousness, they had driven away, passing through the Douda checkpoint at 6:29 P.M. Warned that lack of cooperation would result in a grenade attack on the sentries, Schoenberg had secured clearance by telling the gendarmes he was taking friends to an April Fool's party at Arta. The gendarmes, Sanbat thought, had been suspicious, but her hopes of pursuit and intervention had floundered when, soon after, Yusuf had abandoned the Citroën, bundled them into a Toyota Land Cruiser and driven off the main road into the desert.

They had reached the periphery of Ghoubet el Kharab, a small village above the southern shore of the Gulf of Tadjoura, at 11:40 P.M., having negotiated some fifty kilometers of very rough terrain at a snail's pace, with headlights hooded to a maximum.

It was 12:23 A.M. now. The Toyota was sheltered in one goat pen, they in another. Yusuf had taken pains not to reveal their presence to the villagers. But he had summoned one Salah who delivered goat's milk to Djibouti. Salah, in Yusuf's debt, had been commandeered to act as messenger.

SOUTHWEST DANAKIL, T.F.A.I.

Updrafts above Lake Abbé, T.F.A.I.'s westernmost border with Ethiopia, had put them on a faultless gliding angle.

Montblanc had spotted several nomad groups on the trails leading to Dikhil, a trading center some 100 kilometers southwest of Djibouti, but had identified them as peaceful Issas steering livestock to the market. Farther along, at the approaches to Yoboki, the desert's main water source, he had investigated other nomadic groups. Again, he had failed to spy Yusuf.

Now, as Olaf Verner banked the sailplane, they seemed to be suspended in a tight turn. Montblanc glanced at the instrument panel. The variometer, a rate-of-climb indicator sensitive to the slightest reduction of air pressure, was rising fast. Earlier, Olaf had singled it out as the instrument that had given gliding the horizon it deserved, comparing it to a bird's inner ear.

Olaf's singsong voice rang joyfully. "We're soaring on a beautiful updraft. A sheer line between air masses. Lake Assal in the distance."

"I want to take a good look around there. So let's not hit the stratosphere."

Olaf's neck seemed to smile. "Stop worrying. We are birds. You'll never feel anything like this again."

Montblanc took the comment in good humor. He liked Olaf.

Heir to a shipping line, he had found mysticism in gliding, and had settled in the T.F.A.I. where the windward slopes of hills, mountain lee waves, clear-air thermals and the peculiar convergences of air masses provided near-perfect conditions for gliding. And he had cause to be grateful. Olaf had agreed without demur to lend assistance when Montblanc, a mere acquaintance, had waylaid him early that morning at the flying club. He had neither objected to his scrambling into the second seat with a load of cameras nor questioned the preposterous explanation that he had been commissioned to conduct an urgent survey on the seasonal wanderings of nomads.

Olaf banked the sailplane. "Best gliding angle toward Lake Assal coming up . . ."

Montblanc watched the turn-and-bank indicator until it leveled, then waited for the altimeter to register a slow rate of descent. He checked the airspeed indicator: 40 knots. "That looks fine."

He craned forward with his binoculars. From the northern shore of Lake Assal a trail led to Mount Moussa Ali, and from there to Eritrea. If Yusuf was moving his captives to the WOJ base, that was the trail he would have to take. And that was where Montblanc, stubbornly refusing to give up hope on Schoenberg, expected to find him.

There had been one lead in the abduction: Schoenberg's declaration at the Douda checkpoint that he and his companions were on their way to a party at Arta. On that, Boaz and Osman, Montblanc and the French agents had turned Arta inside out, while Tixier, assuming command at Schoenberg's desk and deploying every available man, had scoured Djibouti and its environs. Late into the night they had conceded that Yusuf had disappeared into the wilderness, and that unless they could pinpoint his position by aerial reconnaissance, there was no hope of rescuing Sanbat and Schoenberg.

Though the air force was conducting the reconnaissance, Boaz and Osman did not rate its chances highly. Yusuf would be on the lookout for aircraft and would trek accordingly. Montblanc, agreeing with them, had suggested approaching Olaf Verner, who trained daily over the wilderness and whose sailplane was a familiar sight to the Afars.

He adjusted the zooms on the cameras and concentrated on several columns of dust along Lake Assal's western shore. All except one were dust devils—desert whirlwinds. He directed his binoculars at the odd one which rose from a dell like a torn patch of tulle.

His radio cackled. "Montblanc—any luck?"

"Not yet."

"We have a message. And photographs."

"Are they alive?"

"Yes."

Montblanc noted the hesitation in Boaz's voice. "What's the sting?"

"The photographs show them naked."

"Rubbing it in. Means nothing." Montblanc grimaced. Who was he trying to fool? In this part of the world, when captives were stripped naked one had to expect the worst, and more. "What's the message say?"

"Don't worry about it now. Find them, Montblanc!"

While busy at the radio, Montblanc had verified that a number of people were encamped at the dell. Now he could see armed men positioned as lookouts on the eastern ridges facing the trail to Djibouti.

"Can you see an encampment, Olaf? At the dell—eleven o'clock?"

"Yes."

"I'd like a few passes. But I don't want to scare them off."

Olaf banked the sailplane. "How about some loops? They'll think I'm practicing stunts. They may even watch. I would. I'm good at loops."

"Great. As low as you can. And give them a good show."

Olaf's voice tingled with excitement. "Hold tight."

ASSAL RIFT, T.F.A.I.

Yusuf's lookouts, facing the track that circumvented the western shore of Lake Assal, had spotted the glider as it came out of the sun. Now, waiting for Yusuf's orders, they gaped at it as it looped like an albatross possessed by a swallow's spirit.

Yusuf knew Olaf Verner. They had crossed paths once when Verner, on one of his flights, had spied a skirmish between two Afar kinships and had alerted the French. The latter had put an immediate end to the fighting, thus saving the weaker kinship—Yusuf's—from decimation. As a result, there had been a debt owed to Verner. Yusuf had sent word to the Dane to negotiate repayment, but Verner had declared himself satisfied with the kinship's gratitude. Yusuf, contemptuous, had tabulated the debt as still outstanding.

As he watched the glider, it occurred to him he could pay the debt now. His men were well armed. They even had SAM-7 missiles should the French air force try to flush them out. A concerted burst of machine-gun fire would be enough to damage Verner's glider and force him to parachute. Yusuf's men could then pick him up, grant him his life and escort him to Djibouti.

It was a good idea. But Yusuf chose to defer it. Undertaking a diversion at this stage would be unwise. He took one last look at the rolling glider, then walked away. His naked captives in the cave offered a better spectacle.

DJIBOUTI, T.F.A.I.

Within moments of Montblanc's return, Tixier had rushed the negatives for development. Montblanc had gone immediately to file his reports.

When he had finally reached *La Popote*, he had found himself an outsider. Boaz had barricaded himself behind maps of the southwest Danakil; Osman had entrenched himself in the mass of Montblanc's films and photographs. The taciturn Tixier kept Montblanc company for a glass or two, then found distraction in evaluating material from French reconnaissance planes that had been sent over the desert, but off-tangent to Lake Assal—a strategy devised by Boaz to make Yusuf think his hideout was secure.

Boaz, in fact, had taken over. He was making all the decisions. And that rankled with Montblanc. He had good advice to give and had done enough to warrant front-line duty.

He sipped more rum and read yet again Yusuf's message to Osman, delivered personally by a goatherd.

To Osman Nusseibi and the Jew:
You went after Hamdi. A worthless man.
We hold Schoenberg and the woman.
If you want to negotiate for their lives, tomorrow at first light go to Ghoubet el Kharab with the goatherd Salah.
He will hand you a vehicle. Drive it on the Lake Assal trail until it runs out of gas.
Then wait.
Two warnings: do not carry radio and do not involve the French.

Montblanc pushed the note aside. "Negotiations, my drumsticks! Can't you see, you guys! You're on a one-way ticket!"

Osman held up one of the photographs and studied the bullet-hole he had drawn on Yusuf's forehead. "What else can we do?"

"Tell them no deals—and hit them! You don't even know if Sanbat and Schoenberg are still alive. There was no sign of them."

Boaz pushed the maps aside, jotted down a last coordinate and turned to Montblanc. "If I were Yusuf, I'd keep them alive—at least until we get there. . . ."

Montblanc growled. "I'll say it again. You don't stand a chance! Not just the two of you!"

"Who said just the two of us?"

Montblanc stared at him, then grinned. "You bastards! Why didn't you say so in the first place?"

April 2, 1974

ASSAL RIFT, T.F.A.I.

Sanbat lay in the center of a circle of flickering oil lamps. Some of the Afars kept her pinned down; others pummeled her breasts; yet others watched those raping her and waited their turn. Yusuf, standing apart, sharpened his long curved knife.

Schoenberg gazed mesmerized at the grotesque shadows on the wall, insensitive to the ropes that staked his arms and legs. The silence, or rather the mutedness of Sanbat's groans, the faintness of the men's grunts, suggested that the tableau was a nightmare. Except that the basilisk sitting on his chest had death's substance; and the insects crawling over his naked body provided a foretaste of the grave.

He closed his eyes, tried to summon a prayer. He failed, distracted by a sudden, total silence. He opened his eyes. Yusuf towered above him, his gleaming Danakil knife, sharp enough to sever a continent, held like a banner.

"We won't cross paths again, Lieutenant."

Schoenberg tried to shout abuse but could not for lack of saliva.

Yusuf bent over him. Schoenberg turned toward Sanbat. He could not see her beyond the ring of men. He noted, however, that the men had interrupted their activities and were watching Yusuf. They dared not, it seemed to him, breathe. Like him.

A piercing ululation jolted him back toward Yusuf. Quite dispassionately, he observed Yusuf's tongue, admired the speed with which it fluttered inside his mouth to create such a pure sound. Simultaneously he felt his groin convulse. As if his penis had a sixth sense and knew it was about to perish. He remembered something an old Legionnaire had once said to him: "Seeds die to germinate."

"You will surrender life—not a man!"

Schoenberg wished to protest. Manhood did not reside in the

genitals, but in the way a man faced death. Yusuf's knife swung downward. Blood spurted.

Schoenberg heard himself scream. At the same time, he felt himself leave his castrated body and rise. His screams faded. He hung suspended in space, light as a summer cloud. He saw his body on the floor of the cave, still spurting blood. The Afars were clapping; Yusuf threading the penis onto a string. Then, as Yusuf tied the trophy around his waist, Schoenberg realized that his body was still alive down there, and that his consciousness had separated from it.

He spotted a light in the distance. He heard a chant: *Shanti Nilaya. Shanti Nilaya.* He recognized it as the paean of the Buddhists. In Indo-China. All those years ago. When he had fought there. It meant *Home of Peace.*

He proceeded toward the light.

DJIBOUTI, T.F.A.I.

The Legionnaires sat on the tarmac. Some smoked, others sipped beer from cans. They need not have been in battle dress—the sortie did not have official blessing—but they had insisted on a formal turnout.

Boaz studied their faces. Schoenberg's faithful comrades. An NCO, three sergeants and four corporals. Three French, two Germans, one Austrian, one Spaniard, one Pole. Old-timers, still untainted by cynicism, still liege to regimental loyalty and brotherhood. They had shown little interest in the cloak-and-dagger methods by which Tixier had bypassed the governor-general to requisition the plane on the tarmac. They had helped Schoenberg before—most recently when he had interrogated Yusuf. Now, summoned by Montblanc, they chafed to save their friend. They were prepared for the worst. Death, if they failed; possible disciplinary action from the governor-general if they succeeded.

Boaz walked across the tarmac to where Montblanc and Osman were conferring with the pilot, Hugo. Beyond, Tixier was harrying the ground crew to speed up fueling. Boaz checked his watch: 1:22 A.M. Organizing the sortie behind the governor-general's back had consumed valuable time. They were now running against the clock. Montblanc and the Legionnaires had to drop quite a distance behind Yusuf's encampment, and they had to secure an assault position by first light. Failing that, they risked being spotted—which would be calamitous not only for Sanbat and Schoenberg, but also for Montblanc and the Legionnaires, and conceivably for Boaz and Osman, too. Whereas a night operation tilted the advantage in favor of trained men, even a crack unit would find the Afars more than a match in daylight.

He joined Osman, Montblanc and Hugo. Montblanc pointed at a map. "Hugo suggests we drop at this range of high peaks. They'd shield us from Yusuf's lookouts."

"Isn't that too far?"

"Not if we go over the mountains instead of around them. It's almost full moon. Good visibility."

"For them, too. They'd spot the plane."

Hugo interjected. "Unlikely. I'll be coming in on a wide swing from the north. If they spot me, it'll be after the drop. I'll be flying at my ceiling by then—like a routine supply run."

Boaz pondered a moment. Hugo, too, was an old-timer. But unlike the Legionnaires, he had brushed shoulders with Israel in the early sixties, when he had trained her airmen on Mirages. Now flying short-range feeder liners, he was descending from the skies rung by rung. Boaz yielded to his wisdom. "Right. Good luck."

ASSAL RIFT, T.F.A.I.

They had finished with her. For the time being. She was still naked. And cold in the desert night. They had burned her clothes. The terror remained. Multiform. They had not hurt her. Some of the men had been rough—but in passion, not brutality. She ached because their weight had pressed her against the stones on the cave floor. Ironically, the gentlest had been Yusuf. He had been the last. And he had taken his time.

She had been incredulous at the ease with which she had accommodated them all. As if it were natural for a woman to receive so many men.

She felt blighted.

Her body crawled into itself. The watch turned sharply and scrutinized her. They had been alert each time she had moved. Did they think she might try to escape? Did they not see she lacked strength? Will? Could they not understand they had broken her?

She found herself staring at Schoenberg. Still alive. She could see his arm twitching. And a faint rise and fall of the chest. She refused to look at his groin. She could not carry his agony, too. He would die soon. Loss of blood. Gangrene. Or eaten away by insects.

Life mocked her. Surrounded by phalluses. Those she did not want raped her. Those she should not have seen, Schoenberg's, Abbew Abba Yaqob's, lashed her with gaping wounds. And the only one she had wanted remained hidden. Castrated by the mind.

She whimpered. Yusuf had mentioned an ambush. For Boaz. And Osman. She and Schoenberg had been abducted as bait; Hamdi had been a diversion. Did Schoenberg's fate await Boaz and Osman? Hope had run out of seasons.

LAKE ASSAL, T.F.A.I.

The goatherd Salah had judged them lesser killers than Yusuf. He had resisted bribes and threats, contending that if he deviated from Yusuf's instructions, his life would not be his own. Though Boaz and Osman had dragged him to Ghoubet el Kharab by 3:00 A.M.— in a taxi of Salah's choosing as proof that the French were being kept out of the proceedings—he had waited until sunrise before taking them to Yusuf's Toyota Land Cruiser. That had confirmed Boaz and Osman's supposition that Yusuf would be monitoring their progress.

They had left Ghoubet el Kharab at 6:10 A.M. after checking that the vehicle was in running order, had the necessary spares and tools, and had not been wired with a bomb.

In turn, Salah, before leaving them, had inspected their gear for radio or electronic gadgets. He had allowed them to keep their 9mm Browning HP pistols. Yusuf had not forbidden them arms; the unwritten law of the Danakil permitted every man his gun. Or so Montblanc had explained. Osman had thought otherwise. Yusuf was no fool and would not have expected them to venture into his lair like lambs to slaughter. In any case, against a heavily armed outfit, pistols merely preserved appearances.

But they managed to smuggle one important item: a liter of gasoline. Salah, taking it for granted that no man would venture into the desert without water, had not bothered to check their flasks.

Osman had undertaken the driving. Boaz, sharper-eyed, had installed himself in the back as lookout.

For the first forty kilometers, on the asphalt road to Yoboki, the drive had been smooth. On a deserted stretch Boaz had funneled the liter of gas into the tank.

All through the discussions, Boaz had attached special importance to the extra liter. He had reckoned that the stipulation to drive until they ran out of gas gave Yusuf a singular advantage: a dominant location where he would be waiting, prepared. Boaz had been determined to wrest this advantage by stealing a few extra kilometers and thus forcing Yusuf to go after them.

The drive along the Assal trail had been slow and arduous. The terrain, shrub-strewn rockland skirting the Gulf of Tadjoura, had been steep and often at the mercy of huge volcanic boulders precariously perched on the hillsides. They had observed odd nomads at distant vantage points and had presumed them to be Yusuf's bush telegraph.

Past the base of the Gulf, the trail, veering west and descending to below sea level, had deteriorated further. Near-impassable stretches under landslides had offered ideal conditions for ambush. The lack of one confirmed their belief that Yusuf wanted them alive—at least, to start with.

They had reached the Lake Assal plain just before 10:00. Shortly after, winding toward the southern shore, they had negotiated a depression, some two kilometers long and dominated by a range running parallel. They had estimated the depression as Yusuf's preselected rendezvous point, and had had the satisfaction of confirming the fact with the sudden emergence on a ridge of a number of Afars confusedly watching them drive on.

They had finally come to a stop some seven kilometers farther, at the vast salt beach by the western shore of the lake. The spot was adequate, if not ideal: flat on three sides, water on the fourth. Three kilometers ahead lay Yusuf's hideout in the Assal Rift— Montblanc's target. Behind stood Yusuf's vanguard, perhaps even Yusuf himself. The latter would have to regroup and traverse open space to get to them.

There, Boaz and Osman waited, imbibing scenery reminiscent of the Dead Sea: salt beaches enfolding waters which ran the spectrum from jade green to azure blue. A stifling heat, even in the cool season, suggested clay fired by a mighty potter.

Yet it was not a wasteland for mystics. The mountains, compared with Israel's Judean Wilderness and Jordan's Moab Range, offered little spiritual elevation. The lake itself, though highly saline, lacked the stigmata of a final judgment such as God had pronounced on Sodom. Here they could only fester, like blisters.

ASSAL RIFT, T.F.A.I.

Schoenberg returned to view his body. The decision to live or die rested with him. Since his consciousness had separated from his body, he had been blissfully happy. He had followed the light that had appeared and had traveled far. The chant of *Shanti Nilaya*, like a sonorous wing, had enveloped his transcendence and led him to his father and mother. They had greeted him with great love, taken him to a glade reminiscent of the Alsatian countryside of his childhood. They had not talked about suffering. But of serenity. Of the state of grace that exists in life after life. Surprisingly, they had not advised him to stay. His father in particular had been at pains to explain that if he had unfinished business and thus chose to remain corporeal, he would forfeit nothing. He would return later and remain with them forever.

The decision should have been unreserved. He felt no desire to reinhabit his body. But there was unfinished business, and he had returned to the autoscopic state to assess whether he could finish it.

He had timed his return perfectly. From his detached height he could see his friends relieving him of his burden. Montblanc— good fellow. The Legionnaires: old combatants who could teach the god of war a trick or two. Moving to where the Afars whiled away time, snoozing, sculpting wood, and some still raping poor Sanbat. Moving with silencer-fitted guns. Then pouncing.

Schoenberg felt sadness for the first time since his transcendence. The living had to be pitied. Life meant death or killing. Death meant life. He turned toward the light. This time, he ran to it. To rejoin his family before the mayhem below stopped and other spirits rose to distract him.

LAKE ASSAL, T.F.A.I.

"What do you think, Osman?"

Osman, still in the driver's seat of the Land Cruiser, squinted for a better look. The Afars, on camels, galloped toward them from the rear. "It's not a charge. Or they'd have spread out."

Boaz craned forward. The riders were slowing down, still keeping formation. He noted their guns, held upright, stocks on saddles. "They want us alive, all right. Ten of them. Armed with Kalashnikovs. I can see Yusuf, leading from behind."

Osman scanned the mountains ahead. The shimmer had dispersed. The ridges stood in relief in the crimson strokes of the setting sun. He fixed his attention on the area of the Afar camp. Montblanc should have freed Sanbat and Schoenberg; should be poised to send up a flare.

Boaz edged to the door, muscles taut, fear suppressed by the assassin's conditioning. The riders were a hundred meters away now, still trotting, still grouped. Another fifty meters, and they would enter the effective range of the Browning. Boaz and Osman had thirteen rounds each. Providing the pistols did not jam, they had two shots per target. If the enemy remained grouped, that would facilitate matters. They would have a confined space to shoot at, and for some seconds at least, while Yusuf's men tried to disperse, there would be an ineffective response.

There was one unpredictable factor: the camels. If they were unconditioned to gunfire, they would bolt. Then it would be a matter of luck.

Osman checked his Browning, tightened his grip on the door handle. His eyes, locked on the ridges ahead, burned; his parched mouth tasted foul. Somewhere, deep inside, he trembled.

Boaz rasped, "He's cutting it fine . . ."

Osman uttered a hoarse sound in acknowledgment. Montblanc was indeed cutting it fine. He should be up on that mountain range. Watching. Measuring the Afars' approach against the Brownings' firepower. The signal had to go up now, when they had strike advantage. Seconds later, they would be cornered.

"Come on! Come on!"

Boaz's anguished plea echoed within Osman. If there was no flare, that would mean Montblanc had failed. They would have to surrender in the hope of a later advantage.

Boaz hissed. "Thirty meters . . ."

Osman bellowed, spotting the phosphorus flash at the very moment of its ascent. "Now!"

They catapulted out of the Land Cruiser. Osman to the right, Boaz to the left. They rolled, steadied, then fired a burst. They rolled again, steadied again, and fired another burst. When they straightened up, crouched on one knee, seven of the Afars had fallen.

They paused for half a breath, adjusting their aim through camels running loose.

Boaz spotted one of the riders maneuvering to a cover position in the melee, his Kalashnikov ready to spray. He identified the rider as Yusuf and fired at the camel. The animal buckled, throwing Yusuf forward. A burst of gunfire churned the salt, creating a swirling dust that looked like snow.

Boaz sprinted forward. Yusuf was to be taken alive. "Cover me!"

The call had been unnecessary. Osman had fired simultaneously, killing both the remaining Afars.

Yusuf had fallen clear of his dead camel. He was stunned, but still in possession of the Kalashnikov. As he tried to pull himself up, he fired another erratic burst. Boaz dived, rolled, sprang up and zigzagged forward.

Yusuf spotted him, wobbled onto his knees and aimed. Boaz flung himself at him with the sickening thought that he had not been fast enough. A shot rang out. Boaz fell.

He felt no pain. His momentum carried him forward. He scrambled toward Yusuf, surprised that his agility had not been impaired. He made contact and hammered the edge of his hand onto the bridge of Yusuf's nose. He felt the blood.

He took a deep breath and started to search for the wound. He saw it—not on his body, but on Yusuf's smashed shoulder. He breathed more easily.

"Didn't kill him, did I?" Osman was running up stiffly, concerned.

Boaz straightened up. His smile, distorted, looked like a snarl. "No."

They stood side by side, viewing the carnage, fighting off the heaviness of limbs traumatized by adrenaline. Eventually Osman switched his attention to the camels. Those unscathed had trotted off into the distance and were sniffing the air anxiously. Three had been killed; another three lay badly injured and snorting. Osman went over and shot them.

When he returned, Boaz, mesmerized, was holding Yusuf's belt. "Look . . ."

Osman stared at the dried, leathery objects hanging from the belt. Finally he registered the one Boaz had pointed at: putrefying, but still fresh and coated with dried blood. "Can't be!"

Boaz vomited over Yusuf's unconscious face.

✗

Sanbat huddled against a rock. Begged for amnesia. Or madness.

Night had fallen. She shivered. Despite the blankets the Legionnaires had given her.

The lake reflected the moon. The mountains stood darkly behind, blind witnesses. Beneath an overhang, the camels lay grouped in nocturnal shadows, encircling Yusuf like an evil coven. Yusuf, handcuffed, had remained quiet since one of the Legionnaires had bound his shattered shoulder.

Montblanc had signaled Djibouti. A helicopter was on its way to pick them up. The Legionnaires had spread out, keeping watch in case Yusuf had a support group deployed in the area. Merely a precaution. No one doubted they had wiped out Yusuf's band.

Osman, Boaz and Montblanc sat in a group near the water. Next to them lay Schoenberg's mutilated corpse, covered by Legionnaires' shirts.

She forced herself to think of Boaz's tenderness. Even suppressed tears—or had she been mistaken? The way he had held her—like absolution. And Osman? Somber. Shaking his head. In fury. In disbelief. As Montblanc had recounted her ordeal.

Variation on a theme. Superimposed over Schoenberg's castration. Being raped. Unfeeling. Uncaring. Stunned.

Could she ever forget?

There was a palliative. A way to deaden the pain. Revenge.

She let the blankets fall from her, lumbered to her feet and picked up the submachine gun she had been given. She ran toward Yusuf. She heard herself scream in one unending breath. She caught a glimpse of Boaz, Osman, Montblanc. They were bounding toward her. But they would never catch her.

Still screaming, she faced Yusuf. Bolt upright, staring at her. She was glad his eyes reflected the terror of death. She would remember his eyes. All her life. She needed to. She fired. Into his crotch. The full magazine: thirty-two rounds.

April 3, 1974

DJIBOUTI, T.F.A.I.

Boaz squatted on the balcony, listening to the Djibouti night. The bars had closed at the news of President Pompidou's sudden death, and people had flooded the streets to discuss the future of France and the T.F.A.I. The president's death had been the first piece of news they had received on their return.

Boaz lit one of Sanbat's cigarettes. His first smoke in years. He had thought it best to stay with her.

She had broken down—after killing Yusuf. Later, in the helicopter, she had spoken briefly. Murdering Yusuf had been the worst. Or rather, the way she had killed him—literally cutting his body in half by emptying the magazine. Boaz and Osman had tried to console her, even condone the killing. She had not seemed to hear them.

Yusuf's death made little difference to their plans. He had not known the location of the base. He could have led them to Daadatu where he had arranged to deliver them to Idris Ali, but the latter, cautious as ever, had not fixed a definite rendezvous. Yusuf had assumed Idris Ali would have heard of his arrival through Wolde who had men stationed at Daadatu. That would have meant entanglement with a sizable force. And no guarantees that it would have flushed out WOJ.

The second item of news they had received had invalidated that dire option. The message, from Al Jameson to Montblanc with a copy to Getachew, had specified that Jameson had discovered salient information on the WOJ base. Jameson was on his way to Asmara and had requested an urgent meeting on his arrival.

"Boaz . . ."

He sprang up and collided with Sanbat. She had left her bed

and stood clinging to the balcony door. She was drenched in sweat, and she had thrown off her nightdress. The swellings from her bruises had become more pronounced. Earlier, before putting her to bed, Boaz had bathed her. She still smelled of the expensive perfume that he had bought in the hotel shop in the hope that she might feel cleansed by its fragrance. "Yes . . ."

She smiled, relieved, but still clung to the doorframe. "I—I just wanted to know . . . if you were still here. . . ."

"Sanbat . . . Go to bed . . . Sleep . . ."

She shook her head violently. "I can't . . ."

He unclenched her hand from the door and led her back to bed. "It'll do you good. . . ."

She sniggered. "Good?"

He lowered her onto the bed.

She sat up. "Stay with me. Hold my hand."

Boaz sat next to her, held her hand.

They remained silent for a while. Boaz felt the pressure of her hand increase. As if determined never to let go.

"Can you cuddle me?"

He nodded. Awkwardly, he drew her to him and held her.

Her body burned.

She placed her head on his shoulder. "Isn't it peaceful? As it should be?"

"You must rest. . . ."

She began to cry. "You know what will do me good? You. Inside me."

He froze. Aghast.

She moved between his arms, rubbing her breasts against his chest. "That. Only that will heal me."

"Sanbat . . ."

"You don't understand, do you? You think I ought to be full of hate. . . . Hate life. Everything! But I don't want to hate! I want to know—with my flesh—that there are good things! That the best is lying with me. Is inside me. Spreading balm over my wounds. Taking the pain away. Healing me. Don't you understand?"

He nodded. He did understand.

She touched his groin. "And it will heal you, too." She began undressing him. What had she to fear, until she was redeemed again?

"Your sister . . . They have done to me almost everything they did to her. I still breathe—but I'm just as dead. Only you can give me life. Think of your sister. If somebody could have saved her. And wouldn't . . . Think . . ."

Boaz could not think. He could feel he was erect. After an

eternity. Naturally. Lovingly. He held her. She pushed him gently onto the bed. He remembered the Scriptures: *"Son of man, can these bones live?"*

She drew him closer, pulled down his trousers and gently sat astride him. He felt afraid. Fate might be mocking him. If he stretched out now for deliverance, it might be taken away forever.

She kissed him and guided him inside her. She was still hurting. She bore the pain. Transfigured. She rocked gently. He felt deeply imbedded. He cried, silently, aware he had moved into a state of grace. She shuddered. He clutched her. Her nails dug into his back. She bit his shoulder. He received her. And clung to her. And gave himself.

PART X

Fire Storm and Black Rain

and Shadows in Concrete

Descriptions by Hiroshima survivors

April 4, 1974

THE DANAKIL ALPS, ETHIOPIA

Idris Ali studied the chart pinned to the blackboard. He knew its contents by heart yet he kept reading it, as if a fresh perusal might invalidate it.

LETHAL EXPOSURE TO RADIATION (600 REMS PLUS):
Nausea and vomiting after two hours.
Diarrhea, severe vomiting and inflammation of the throat within a few days.
Fever, rapid emaciation and death in two weeks.

MEDIUM EXPOSURE TO RADIATION (200–600 REMS):
No definite symptoms for two weeks.
Loss of hair, loss of appetite, general malaise, fever, pallor and rapid emaciation in the third week.
Death at a ratio of one in two within a month.

MODERATE EXPOSURE TO RADIATION (10–200 REMS):
No definite symptoms for two or three weeks.
Thereafter loss of hair, loss of appetite, sore throat, pallor and diarrhea.
Possible recovery if treatment is available.

CAUTION:
There is no acknowledged safe level of ionizing radiation.
Lethal dose varies considerably according to age and physical condition of the irradiated. Damage to lymph nodes, spleen, blood cells and bone marrow has been recorded even under 10 rems.

Idris Ali moved away from the blackboard. Inspection of the defenses had sapped his strength. His lungs felt scorched. The command cavern seemed like a tomb.

He breathed circumspectly. Oxygen intake had to be moderated. Ionizing radiation tore off electrons from cell atoms. Reduced oxygen made living systems more radiation-resistant. If he could control his breathing, he could fight the sickness.

He paused at his desk, stretched compulsively for the cysteine pills. He swallowed one. He debated whether he should take another. Overdosage could induce oxygen deficiency, impair vital systems, precipitate defective aeration of the blood and sudden death. He was already on maximum dosage—as was the task force. Reluctantly he replaced the bottle.

He had a few minutes before the day's briefing. He should compose himself, wipe clean his doubts, impose a mirage of invincibility.

The platoon leaders were demoralized. They had begun to talk in terms of redemption through conflict. They would have it. Until then, they had to be kept primed.

Equally, he should be coaxing Fawzi and Watanabe through the completion stages. Both experts, stricken with the sickness and walking the hairline between sanity and insanity, had become unpredictable. Recently they had been disrupting schedules by chasing a piece of music from one radio station to another. The tune had been introduced as a program link by Radio Tunis. Its peculiar rhythm had caught on and had started to appear on various African stations and in some BBC overseas broadcasts. Fawzi and Watanabe's obsession symptomatized psychological regression. They now treated their seclusion as an exhilarating fantasy—behavior that unnerved the warriors. But he dared not short-circuit their overloaded brains by hard discipline.

He started pacing about. Anger engulfed him. Safeguards against irradiation should have been incorporated in the planning. The oversight was further proof of faulty leadership.

Or something more sinister. The thought had been haunting him for days. Had Abu Ismail anticipated the sickness? Perhaps even planned around it? After all, the task force was expendable. According to Abu Ismail's *War Rule*, the warriors were already martyred.

The cysteine pills. The supply had been abundant—far beyond crisis requirements. Had Abu Ismail provided it as a blanket palliative for the duration of the bomb's assembly?

The cause of the radiation sickness lay in a peculiar chain reaction—so Fawzi had explained. It had probably started on March 3, when Fawzi and Watanabe had divided the plutonium;

stockpiling three kilos and setting aside two masses of six kilos each as requisite, subject to final load calculations, for a twenty-kiloton-yield warhead. Though the pultonium, still in its stable dioxide state, had been relatively safe to handle, there had been some leakage. It was possible that the glove boxes, where the plutonium had been weighed out, had been faulty.

What was certain was that during the next stages, involving the separation of the pure plutonium, machining it into weapons-grade metal and storing it under refrigeration, there had been careless handling. A string of mishaps—according to Fawzi unavoidable, given the peculiar geography of the base—had scattered plutonium dust and highly radiotoxic plutonium oxide.

Even then the disaster should have been contained. But panic measures had caused further accidents. In one instance, subcritical material had been inadvertently doused with water. In another, negligence of the special racking had disturbed the safe geometry of the stockpile. These had accelerated the decay processes, unleashing further lethal radioisotopes.

As a result, the camp, the livestock, the provisions and the virgins had been contaminated by all four radiation processes: alpha, beta, gamma and neutron. The last had been the most damaging, and the least responsive to decontamination measures.

Thereafter the sickness had galloped. The task force, debilitated by heat, hard work and stress, had fallen easy prey. To date thirty-nine people, a quarter of the full complement, had died. Though the majority of these casualties had been virgins, the toll of technicians and warriors had reached critical proportions and had included the single doctor on the team. At least an equal number were approaching death.

Nervously, he lit a cigarette. Had he underestimated Abu Ismail? Had Abu Ismail schemed it all to dispose of him? If so, how had he triggered the sickness? How was he controlling it? Who was his instrument? Fawzi? Watanabe? One of the technicians? One of the warriors?

It was not just stress feeding his suspicions. Abu Ismail had distrusted Ivan Volkov from the start. Had warned repeatedly that the KGB general was after his soul. Had Abu Ismail, then, foreseen the alliance with Volkov before he, Idris Ali, had contemplated it? Had he consequently commissioned an assassin to eliminate him when the bomb was completed and he had served his purpose?

He refused to believe it. Abu Ismail was not omniscient.

He rose from the desk as the men filed in for the meeting. He scrutinized Fawzi and Watanabe who, despite their racial differences, had begun to look alike, like a man and his dog. Fawzi returned his scrutiny with the burning eyes of a man close to redemption.

As they sat, he noticed that both their flies were undone. He wondered if there was any truth in the gossip that they had become lovers. Both men had manifested high sex drives and could well have preferred homosexuality to the services of the wasting, balding virgins.

He directed his attention to the platoon leaders. Adnan, Abdallah's replacement, exuded an ominous pallor. Of the surviving Lisbon veterans, both Mahmud and Badran looked in good condition. Mahmud, however, carried the silence of deep melancholia. Badran still moved like a tiger. Idris Ali envied him. Badran seemed indestructible. He had taken command over two more platoons, H and Q, following the deaths of Hafez and Qasim, and thrived on the added responsibility. Could he be aspiring even higher?

All the new platoon leaders, Dawood, Farouk, Naif and Walid, were sick: balding, feverish and emaciated. Gamal was absent. "Gamal?"

Walid, Gamal's closest friend, looked up with tearful eyes. "Died—an hour ago."

Idris Ali showed no emotion. "Who wants Gamal's platoon?"

Badran raised his hand. Idris Ali nodded. Badran appeared to expand in girth. Idris Ali ruffled Badran's hair. It was still intact. That annoyed him. But only briefly. Badran would end up burning like a falling star.

Idris Ali distributed the evening's dose of cysteine. "Before we start—any news?"

Badran handed him a signal. "From Wolde. Yusuf has failed."

Idris Ali gave the sheet a cursory glance. Wolde reported rumors of an Afar skirmish in the T.F.A.I. with heavy casualties. It lacked the precision of the GRU report which Volkov had radioed through that morning. Yusuf had died with his men. The Legionnaires who had engaged them had been led by Osman Nusseibi and an Israeli, name unknown.

Idris Ali sat down and faced his men with the vocational bonhomie of a natural leader. "Let's not worry about Yusuf. He hasn't altogether failed. He has bought us time. . . ." He paused and glared at Fawzi and Watanabe who, huddled together, were arguing in whispers over weird figures on a piece of paper. They had left their pills lying on the sand. "Talat. Watanabe."

They looked up distractedly. Fawzi, as ever, acted the spokesman. "Yes?"

"I suggest you do your work in the workshop."

"This is not work. A puzzle."

"Surely not as important as the briefing at hand."

Watanabe giggled, turning his attention to the paper with a mad jerk and cloudy eyes that suggested he had just injected himself with heroin.

Fawzi lowered his eyes as if ashamed of himself. "I'm sorry."

"Put it away, please."

Watanabe fell into resentful silence. Fawzi, his eyes fluid and obedient, put the paper into his pocket.

Idris Ali murmured gently. "And take your pills. Now."

Fawzi did so obediently. Watanabe swallowed them with choking sounds, protesting that he could not wash them down. The little water that had been salvaged uncontaminated was strictly rationed.

The platoon leaders fidgeted uneasily, disturbed by Watanabe's mindless behavior.

Idris Ali motioned patience. "On second thought, Talat, you need not stay for the full briefing. We can discuss your problem first."

Fawzi craned his head in an attentive posture. "We have no problems."

"Let me ask you this: Can you finish the engineering work in two days? Put the casing together?"

Fawzi's demeanor assumed the cool distance of a controlled mind. "Are we decamping?"

Idris Ali hesitated. Whenever Fawzi reverted to his former self, he felt threatened—and his suspicions that the physicist might be serving Abu Ismail reawakened. "We may have to, Professor."

Fawzi pondered. "In two days? I expect we can. Our bomb casing has facilitated the task."

Idris Ali nodded. The makeshift bomb casing, made to Ivan Volkov's specifications, had exceeded expectations. Shaped like a large metal trunk, it looked nondescript, above suspicion, hence safe to transport anywhere. The loss of the original spare, though it had cost Abdallah's life, had proven fortuitous. "Fine, Talat. Have it ready."

"I should point out—the finishing touches are quite delicate. You can't place TNT charges, wire the fuses, set the arming mechanisms in a dark alley. We'll need space, some facilities . . ."

"We have the assault base."

Fawzi looked at him quizzically.

Idris Ali searched beyond the look. In hope of tricking Fawzi, he had referred to the assault base where Abu Ismail would take charge of the bomb. If Fawzi knew of it, it would mean he was Abu Ismail's man.

"I thought this was the assault base."

"This, as Al-Mahdi calls it, is the penultimate tent before Allah's abode. The assault base is the last."

"Well, as long as it proves adequate."

Idris Ali nodded. His suspicions had been unfounded. He would continue nurturing them because that was his nature, but in a minor key. Fawzi was what he was: WOJ's robot—not Abu Ismail's.

". . . I'd hate another mistake. Like the sickness . . ."

"Produce the bomb, Talat. The rest is irrelevant."

Fawzi nodded curtly. "The bomb will work—come what may."

Idris Ali's voice broke through Watanabe's renewed laughter. "That'll be all."

Fawzi stood up and, beckoning Watanabe, sauntered out without a word to anyone. Watanabe followed him sheepishly.

No one spoke. Badran continued chewing his cheroot like the hero in a cowboy film, and the men busied themselves with their appearances.

Idris Ali caught Adnan and Farouk staring in dull horror at hands which had turned translucent. He felt detached sympathy. Though he had kept away from the factory to ward off contamination and had eaten and drunk his own reserves of food and water, it was possible to become equally afflicted. That his hair remained full of vigor, that he was symptom-free offered little comfort. The sickness could be gnawing at his innards. When he raised his flag over that of Abu Ismail's, he might do so half sunk into his grave. He raised his voice—more for his own benefit. "Let's turn our minds to war. . . . I have revised the plans. We will reorganize our depleted forces. . . ."

The men smiled, foreseeing the coveted redemption through conflict.

"If the enemy finds us, you are going to put up such a stand here that the Jew's Masada will be erased from history forever. . . ."

April 5, 1974

MAKALE, ETHIOPIA

Sanbat aligned the truck behind the one driven by Boaz. She turned to Osman and smiled gratefully. He had felt her need to reintegrate and had asked her to drive the first leg.

The afternoon had a legendary quality. The dust-churned plains of Makale struck her as a Biblical domain, an austere boundary dividing the worshipers of two warring idols. Only the aroma of frankincense wafting from boswellia trees offered an illusion of tranquillity. Frankincense, her foster parents had taught her, had protective qualities; in ancient times it had shielded the high priests at the mercy seat of the Ark from the formidable sight of God. So when supervising the loading of the equipment, she had sprinkled the men's packs liberally with it.

Osman lit two cigarettes, passed her one, then turned to the rear window and examined the men at the back.

The latter, tough Tigreans, sat huddled, dreamy-eyed. The leader, once a famous bandit, played dolefully on his *masinko*.

There were fifteen of them. And another fifteen in Boaz's truck. They were loyal followers of Ras Mengesha Seyoum, governor of Tigre, who had distinguished himself as a progressive and compassionate ruler. Getachew, himself a Tigrean, had remained close friends with Ras Mengesha ever since, years ago, they had worked side by side building the road that linked Makale with the Addis Ababa–Asmara arterial route.

With Haile Selassie now fighting desperately for his throne and therefore unresponsive to the WOJ menace, Getachew had found himself abandoned—worse, bereft of the security machinery necessary to smash Operation Dragons. In Ras Mengesha he had sought an alternative, albeit unsophisticated, power base. The governor had responded boldly.

This new development was yet another case of attempting to make, as Jameson had put it, a Tiffany purse out of a sow's ear.

Jameson had arrived in Asmara on the previous afternoon. Boaz, Osman and Sanbat had preceded him in a U.S. Air Force transport provided by Lieutenant O'Brien. Getachew had coordinated the arrivals and had bundled them unceremoniously out of the city. There had been renewed hostilities in Eritrea in the wake of the March 26 revolt, and Asmara was fomenting with unrest. Foreigners, in particular Americans, had become undesirables.

They had proceeded to Makale, into the safety of a reserved wing of the Abraha Castle, a grandiose fortification converted into a hotel.

Makale, Tigre's capital, was the center of the Danakil salt trade and, as such, an even better launching pad for an expedition into the wilderness. Though Tigre had its own secessionist front, the conflict was as yet a minor one. The Tigreans, clinging to a traditionalist heritage, had been more circumspect in embracing political doctrines; moreover, their respect for Ras Mengesha had kept them, in the main, loyal to the throne.

The irony was that for the first time since Abu Ismail had threatened to confiscate the future, his hunters were in a position

to thwart him. For Jameson had returned, after an inspired investigation, with the breakthrough they had almost despaired of
achieving—precise bearings on the WOJ base.

But Ethiopia had no forces to spare. France, more timorous
than ever following the death of President Pompidou, sat three-
monkeys-in-one, in case the revolution in Ethiopia or the impending war with Somalia disrupted her sweet life. Washington
floundered in static as the nation watched Nixon on television—
and Nixon watched the ratings. Even Israel, forever keeping impossible ledgers, hedged, calculating the price of the present
against that of the future.

Yet despite it all, a purse of sorts had been sewn from the sow's
ear. With threads of faith from good men, Getachew and Montblanc. With lining of mauled idealism from Jameson and Tixier.
Trimmed with the rough skin of sacrificial goats—Osman, Boaz
and the Memouneh. And with a frail clasp: Sanbat. All of it tempered with the blood of those who had died.

The purse contained the thirty resourceful Tigreans who,
knowing the Danakil well, would act as scouts. It contained the
crew of the two Reshev missile boats dispatched by Israel in March
from Haifa and around the Cape for deployment in the Red Sea,
and kept loitering, since their passage through the Bab el Mandeb
strait, off Ethiopian waters, by a defiant Memouneh. It contained
Schoenberg's faithful Legionnaires, for whom Tixier had secured
leave and who waited with Montblanc at Moulhoulé, on the
T.F.A.I. coast, for the Reshev boats to pick them up. As the only
frill, it also contained a Hercules C-130E of the U.S. Air Force
tactical airlift squadron, Asmara, that had been commandeered by
Lieutenant O'Brien.

"Do you want to talk, Sanbat?"

"Is that why you arranged to ride with me, Osman? To watch
over me—as you do with Boaz?"

"Not very subtle, am I?"

Sanbat lit another cigarette. "How's your leg?"

"Living."

"Does it hurt?"

"Anything that lives hurts."

"If that were true . . ."

"Isn't it? You—for instance. You are really alive now. Quite a
change."

Sanbat drew on her cigarette. She had been broken and stuck
together again. But, for the first time in her life, she felt whole. As
if fragmentation had been the very process she had needed to
complete herself. The rape would ache forever. But she would

cope. She was, as Boaz had told her tenderly, like a vase from Knossos, found in pieces, then restored. "Can you really see the change, Osman?"

"I can detect hardiness. Before you seemed stunted, wasting with lovesickness. Now you're one of us."

"I won't have much to do. Manning communications, checking supplies, doing odd chores—that's not difficult. . . ."

"It is. When you're under fire."

Osman was right. She felt she had reclaimed the qualities that had caught the attention of first the army, then Mossad. The realization bolstered her faltering self-esteem. Until now, she had seen herself incapable of achieving more than the minimum. Now, she could contribute her share. The carnal obsession with Boaz, which had atrophied vision and faculties, had regenerated itself as a natural sexuality. "But I'm still in love."

"That's different."

"How?"

"Don't you know?"

She nodded. Yet another change. Or rather the accession to another dimension. She had attained a self that she had secretly harbored but had incarcerated behind countless defenses. This new self could feel hurt—live, to quote Osman—and rejoice in the fact. "Yes. I have the strength to fight for him."

"You must, Sanbat."

Sanbat glanced at him, surprised by his vehemence.

Osman turned away, stared out of the window. They were climbing toward Quiha where they would pick up the trail down to the Danakil. The highlands, covered by thorny bush, squat acacia trees and cacti shaped like candelabra, stood in evening shadow. It was a landscape for grazing indefinitely on melancholy. "I have fears, Sanbat . . . that you and I will be the only ones to come out of this alive. . . ."

Sanbat purposely misunderstood him. "Why do you say that? Jameson and Getachew are both experienced. As for Boaz—he's indestructible!"

"He once told me he'd carry on until he has destroyed Abu Ismail. No farther."

Sanbat protested shrilly. "He's changed! He, too!"

"Are you sure?"

Sanbat nodded fervently.

Then she reconsidered. Boaz had not needed to change. Unlike her, he had never been incomplete. He had neither squandered the blessings of unique origins nor rejected another unique set of values. He had come as a Greek, intuitively enlightened, and he had endeavored to be a true Israeli: a plow working a land where the lamb could lie down with the lion. He had fought for the survival of this land and its people. Both on the battlefield and, against tyrants like Kidan, in the corridors of power. He had bled for his people's needs and, as his relationship with Osman proved, he would have bled, had the Arab world given Israel the chance, for the sufferings of the wronged Palestinians. He was intact—in the mold of the classical hero—except for the heel awaiting the fatal arrow. His death wish conjugated rationality with mysticism. The first, in despair of mankind, asserted death as the most logical solution to existence; the second revealed that if sanctity could not be found in life, it had to be found in its aftermath. "If he could be made to see . . . that maybe . . . there's hope in me . . . for him. If he could be persuaded to try a bit more . . ."

"That's why it's up to you, Sanbat."

"Yes . . ."

"It's ironic, isn't it? Compared to maggots and worms, to the gray perpetual thunder of death's domain, life has so much to offer." Osman, carried by a sudden compulsion to confess his innermost secret, turned to her and whispered ashamedly. "I so love life, Sanbat. And so fear death . . . There must be a way to make him understand. . . ." Then, overcoming his momentary weakness, he pointed at the horizon. "Night's falling. I'll take over after Quiha."

April 6, 1974

ASSAB, ETHIOPIA

Captain Wolde conducted a thorough inspection of the patrol craft he had requisitioned.

He knew about boats. Born in a small village on the Eritrean coast, he had spent his youth trawling with his father. When, as an orphan, he had trekked to Massawa, and had gained admission to the state school, he had woven his dreams around the navy. But his teachers, impressed by his brilliance, had decided he would better serve his country as an army officer. Bound by their ruling, and later seduced by his success at the Harar military academy, he had become what he was. Yet he had not forsaken his old dream; one of his priorities, when he deposed the emperor, would be to transform the fleet from a collection of backwater tubs into a formidable force.

The patrol craft, an ex-U.S. PG type, had been far from ship-shape. She had rusted extensively since left idle after the Imperial

Navy's brief mutiny on February 27; the two diesels and the turbine had required servicing.

Wolde checked that the overhaul he had ordered had patched her up sufficiently for a brief outing. It was imperative that for a few days she should look seaworthy and appear to be on legitimate patrol to the Israeli missile boats which, Idris Ali had reported, were lurking off Barassoli.

For the time being, cover for WOJ remained the main consideration. Operation Dragons would enable Abu Ismail to wrest control of Arab wealth and politics. Being a holy man, he would reward his services generously, back Wolde's bid for power with mountains of petrodollars and guarantee Ethiopia's survival as a Christian island in the Muslim sea. Then, one good day, when Ethiopia was strong and fat again, he, Wolde, an excellent student of history, would bite the hand that had fed him and reestablish Ethiopia as an African empire.

The time to collect was approaching. He had few more services to perform. He had already organized the most important one, that of creating four days of confusion in Addis Ababa, from April 22 to 25, by promulgating through the Dergue various grievances against the emperor.

He concluded the inspection. The patrol craft would serve. She could sail that afternoon with the skeleton crew he had chosen from his paratroopers.

DALLOL, ETHIOPIA

The full moon of the spring equinox canopied the sky. It was the first night of *Pesach*, Passover, when Jews were commanded to observe an order of ceremonies, the *Seder*, and recount, at a festive table, the story of their deliverance, the *Haggadah*. It was the night different from all other nights of the year. It celebrated the exodus from Egypt and commemorated the forty years of wandering during which all those who had been slaves to the Pharaoh had died in the wilderness so that their children could worship the Single God as free men in the Promised Land. It imposed the eating of *matzo*, the bread of the poor which, undefiled by leaven, possessed the holiness of Nature and symbolized the harsh demands of liberation that could only be attained through God.

Boaz and Sanbat ate apart from the others. Neither had wanted to do so, but Osman, sensitive to the festival's significance for them, had conducted Getachew, Jameson and the Tigreans to another bivouac.

They had no matzo, so they abstained from bread. They did not conduct the Seder, nor did they recite the Haggadah. But they ate bitter herbs and sanctified their frugal meal with a little wine.

They were surrounded by gullies, salt chimneys and vertical cliffs; the air throbbed with the sound of fumaroles spewing hot brine. They could imagine themselves companions of Moses; conceive that God was with them—deciding whether they, too, should die in the wilderness or live because they had never been slaves.

They did not speak, but they touched hands.

Sanbat interpreted the constant physical contact as another sign of deliverance. She would find the resources to wrestle Death for Boaz's soul and body. God was on her side. He forgave the despair of strong men.

They concluded the meal and regrouped for the second leg of the journey.

Compared with the first, which had taken them down to the Danakil Depression, around the volcano Erte-ale and northeast to Dallol, the second leg was easier: a straight run through the Karum salt plains to the southwestern slopes of the Danakil Alps. But again, to avoid detection by WOJ lookouts, they would be traveling by night. Driving without headlights, even with a full moon, would test their competence.

They set out at 8:00 P.M. This time Sanbat drove with Boaz.

Barring accidents or mishaps, they would set up camp at dawn some eight kilometers from Ramlo, the Danakil's highest peak. There, concealed, they would sweat out the day. The next night, they would move to within striking distance of the WOJ base.

April 7, 1974

MOULHOULÉ, T.F.A.I.

The Reshev's captain, Commander Ilan, a short, burly man with a hairy chest bursting through a half-buttoned shirt, stretched out his hand. "Welcome aboard, Montblanc. Boaz has been singing your praises."

Montblanc smiled. Ilan's accent echoed the Royal Navy; his grip exuded confidence. "What news of Boaz, Commander?"

"Reported last at 5:40 P.M. They'd abandoned their trucks and were about to start on the third leg. They expect to reach a bivouac eight kilometers from the WOJ base by dawn."

Montblanc squinted into the night. "It'll be tough. They'll be climbing all the way to Ramlo. Then around the crater. A rough descent after that. Then climb again. All that at night."

"Is that why you decided against a parachute drop?"

"Mainly. If we'd landed off course we'd have been no better off. Worse, we might have alerted the WOJ base. Then again, Getachew's Tigreans are not trained for a drop. The strike's scheduled for tomorrow night. Is that affirmative with you?"

"Just give us the word, Montblanc. We're one hundred twenty nautical miles from Barassoli. That's about four hours. At a pinch we could do it in less. We estimated going from Haifa around the Cape to Eilat in thirty days. We could have done it with two to spare."

"The men? They won't mind operating on land?"

Ilan glanced at the deck. Some of the crew were dismantling the outboard motors from the rubber dinghies that had picked up Montblanc and the Legionnaires at the beach at Moulhoulé. Others had already made friends with the Legionnaires. "They've all volunteered for the assault force. The same applies to the men in our sister ship."

"I guess they know the enemy."

"They have no choice. But you and your Legionnaire friends could have stayed out. We are privileged to have you."

Montblanc scratched his neck in embarrassment. The compliment was flattery indeed coming from a man who, according to CIA intelligence, had whisked away five Israeli gunboats from French custody in Cherbourg on Christmas Day, 1969. "You don't happen to have some rum aboard, do you, Commander?"

Ilan led the way to the bridge house. "We have a liqueur called Hard Nut—named after Ben-Gurion."

Montblanc rolled his eyes. "That I must taste."

Ilan handed him a bottle, then directed him to the radarscope. "There've been some developments. That bleep is our sister ship. But the other one—near Barassoli—is an Ethiopian patrol boat. According to Quinn, she's been lying inactive at Assab for months. But yesterday she sailed away. We've heard from Sanbat's Falashas that she was manned not by navy personnel but by Wolde and some of his paratroopers. She sailed as far as the T.F.A.I. limits, turned, loitered awhile off Barassoli, then sailed back to Assab. Same routine today . . ."

"You think she might engage you?"

Ilan smiled grimly. "This is a very advanced warship, Montblanc. We're armed with Gabriels. She wouldn't stand a chance."

Montblanc scrutinized the fiberglass containers mounted aft, housing the missiles. The Gabriel, a subsonic sea-skimmer employing semiactive radar homing, had proven infallible in the Yom Kippur War. "She's obviously connected with WOJ. Maybe she's reinforcing the base. . . ."

"There's been nothing on radar. But then, you can't always pick up rubber dinghies."

Montblanc gritted his teeth. He had been conscious of the heavy swell since embarkation. Now, with the sweet almond liqueur invading his stomach, he regretted his foolhardiness. The flight in Olaf's sailplane should have warned him that he had been born a landsman.

April 8, 1974

OFIRA, ISRAELI OCCUPIED SINAI

The Memouneh paced on the tarmac.

Both the Boeing 707 and the Arava 201 had been refueled.

The first, revamped by the air force as a command aircraft with ELINT systems, had served as his tent during the repeated journeys to the Eritrean coast in the past forty-eight hours. The second, a light military transporter, had been commissioned to whisk him to Tel Aviv. He had to decide which to board.

Zeal dictated he should continue watch from the Boeing. Boaz and his group were closing in on the WOJ base. The assault would commence at midnight. But there was an imponderable: the Ethiopian patrol boat under Wolde's command. Quinn was reevaluating the National Security Agency's electronic intelligence to determine whether Wolde was there to extend assistance. If so, he would have to be neutralized. In this, no help could be expected from the Ethiopian government. The situation in that country had deteriorated critically. Discontent was rife despite promises of radical reforms. Troops were in no mood to obey any directive. If Wolde was to be engaged, he should take the responsibility rather than Boaz. Or, if the venture failed, return with firsthand information to urge Golda's cabinet to send a task force.

Intuition, however, curbed his zeal. Instinct told him that Operation Dragons would not end in the wilds of the Danakil. Abu Ismail would have planned his apocalypse so that he, and he alone, would consummate it. At present Abu Ismail was in Tripoli —a fact confirmed by CIA and other sources.

He considered again the emergency in Tel Aviv.

Intelligence flooding in from Lebanon warned that the PLO planned a series of attacks on civilian "soft" targets for the end of Passover, and that these had been instigated by WOJ as a diversion for the run up to Operation Dragons.

Specters, burnished by the death glow of generations of innocents, were crying out: Save one soul of Israel in order to save many souls! That plea, the only skin left on his teeth, took the decision. He started walking toward the Arava.

Kidan, who had been hovering petulantly in the background, rushed over. "Tel Aviv? Why?"

"They're threatening civilians. Children. A series of attacks . . ."

"You think you can intercept them all?"

"No. An odd one always gets through. But we can reduce the number of victims."

"And then what?"

"Then we bury the dead. After that, we bomb their camps. And they bury their dead."

Kidan snorted. "So what's new?"

"Nothing. But I'd like to think we care for our civilians more than they do about theirs. And I'd like to prove it."

"Zamora, you're beginning to believe your own propaganda."

The Memouneh stopped and glowered. "It may be propaganda to you, Kidan; given rope, you'd be Abu Ismail. But the rest of us want peace. For us. And for the Arabs."

Kidan, enraged, growled. "If Operation Dragons succeeds, that will be the end of you, of me, of them, of everybody."

"I'm well aware of that. However, hovering over Boaz without effective ground support would be indulgence. We won't be able to influence matters down there. Merely confirm success or failure."

"But this is our show!"

"Is that what you want, Kidan? Glory?"

"Zamora, I started this. I should be in on the finish. There'll be decisions to be taken."

"Boaz will take them."

Kidan spewed fury. "Hang the world on that Oriental Jew? Yesterday's peasant? How can you—"

The Memouneh dismissed him contemptuously. "As Sanbat would say—because of his soul!"

April 9, 1974

THE DANAKIL ALPS, ETHIOPIA

The ranges looked like giant waves frozen at their final unfurling; the wind, sibilating in strange scales, chased its tail in the gullies. Fumaroles snorted earnestly; the earth chortled like a child at play and shot fireworks through craters and fissures. Moonlight reduced color and fumes to silvery shadows.

Jameson had depicted the landscape as that of another planet. The men gave credence to the description as they trudged in nuclear-biological-chemical protective suits and respirator masks, carrying in their webbed harnesses radios, arms, ammunition, Geiger counters and canisters of decontaminating agents.

To Boaz, however, the wilderness had a greater surrealism. He had visualized it before, in a tale recounted by his mother about a tribe of good men hidden away by the Lord in formidable mountains so that they could survive for the Day of the Messiah protected by fire-spewing giants. The vision had served as a quest until his mother's deportation, then it had been buried. Its exhumation now suggested that the layers of pain armoring him had been lanced. Perhaps Sanbat's conviction that he could fly on her wings toward a state of sanctity had substance.

He surveyed the terrain. Ahead, six Tigreans had blended into the forest of volcanic plugs. He had not liked pushing them forward when fire was about to pour down, but it was essential to maintain the rate of progress. In a wilderness where magnetic intensity rendered compasses erratic, where rocks, plugs, peaks and crevasses piled haphazardly upon one another, disorientation was a major hazard. The Tigreans, born to the mountains, had proven themselves infallible navigators, particularly at night when they could use stars as bearings. Boaz had wanted to traverse the worst stretches by sunrise. The Tigreans would chart a trail.

He scanned the ground below. The remaining Tigreans had taken cover. Osman, Getachew and Jameson were clambering up to the ridge to join him. Sanbat was already in position in a nearby gully monitoring the radio, keeping channels open to O'Brien, Montblanc and Ilan.

He directed his attention to the objective. The cluster of cliffs, which Wallace had named the "Eye of Silence," stood clearly silhouetted against the eastern horizon, some eight kilometers away. It betrayed no sign of life, but the base's existence was now confirmed. During the early part of the night, coming up from their last camp, the scouts had uncovered packs of dynamite placed to blow up the approaches. Disarming them, Boaz and Osman had had evidence of Watanabe's ingenuity.

"All set, Boaz. Everybody's fitted out." Osman's voice, distorted by his throat microphone and Boaz's earphone, summed up the discomfort of the NBC suits.

Contamination was a probability. Although the chance of the WOJ nuclear device detonating during O'Brien's raid was infinitesimal, there was every possibility that the bombardment would disrupt the warhead and scatter the plutonium. Depending on wind conditions, contamination could spread to about ten kilometers. The respirators, filtering air through pads molded into the face-piece and offering protection against chemical, bacteriological and radiological agents, had thus become essential equipment. Furthermore, since Boaz and his men would proceed to the base to mop up, NBC suits, providing body protection, had been deemed equally essential. Jameson, indomitable since rejoining the fray, had brought the equipment with him from the United States.

Getachew, who had been maintaining communications with the Tigreans, drew up to Boaz. "The scouts found a couple of stockades. Possible strongholds for mortars and machine guns. There are signs of a hasty retreat."

Osman chuckled. "They've fallen for it!"

Boaz nodded. That WOJ had withdrawn from the outposts was a relief. He had schemed to achieve that by pushing up Mont-blanc's force of Legionnaires and Israeli sailors from Barassoli during the previous afternoon so that they could be spotted. The coastal plain being the base's most vulnerable flank, he had hoped WOJ would evaluate the advance not as a diversion but as an orthodox thrust, and reinforce those approaches with every available man. O'Brien's raid, due in a few minutes, would seem supportive of the advance and would negate the possibility of a main attack from the rear. Thus—provided O'Brien did not miss his target—Boaz's forces would be able to penetrate the base with only the last leg of the wilderness and possible mines as obstacles; Montblanc would dig in and make a show of preparing an assault to preoccupy the WOJ task force.

That was the plan. But there remained a joker in the pack: Wolde's patrol craft.

The vessel was still within striking distance of Barassoli. The previous day, when the Israeli missile boats had lurked outside Ethiopian waters, and again today when they had penetrated to Barassoli, Wolde had declined to challenge them. On both occasions he had kept a distance of some thirty nautical miles, just outside the range of the Gabriel missiles. His passivity still troubled Boaz. Wolde's reluctance to engage the Israeli missile boats was understandable, but it did not preclude some sort of move, if only to save face with Abu Ismail. A halfhearted engagement drawing a warning shot, followed by an honorable retreat, would have sufficed. It was probable, therefore, that Wolde had something up his sleeve.

"One other thing, Boaz . . . They've found some ground contamination."

Boaz redirected his attention to Getachew. "How bad?"

"They can't read the Geiger counter. But they say it's register-ing."

Boaz turned to Osman and Jameson. "Ground contamination —outside the base? Any ideas why or how?"

Jameson shrugged. "Probably carried . . . wind . . . any-thing . . ."

"Then we must assume some of the WOJ are irradiated. That means they'll be all the more desperate. If the bomb survives the raid, they'll use it to take us with them. So whoever gets there first must neutralize it. Second, keep your distance. Avoid close fight-ing. If your respirator gets damaged, that's bad enough. If you get scratched or wounded, God help you."

They plunged into a brief silence, each nursing his own version of the nightmare.

Boaz checked his watch: 12:09 A.M. Simultaneously, he caught the sound he had been waiting for, the drone of the Hercules C-130E. O'Brien, posing as a supernumerary crew member and carrying palletized loads of forty-gallon drums of gasoline on what had been logged as a fuel airlift to a U.S. naval vessel at Diego Garcia, had reported exactly at midnight. The Hercules would interrupt her flight plan at 12:10 and immediately lose height for a trial dropping run.

Sanbat whispered urgently. "O'Brien's opened communica-tions with Asmara and South Eritrea ATCC. . . . He's signaling Mayday—reporting a control defect. South Eritrea and Asmara are standing by. . . ."

Boaz spotted the Hercules, a shadow outlined against the moon's corona, as she flew over the target and turned. She would perform the same maneuver several times to line up for a perfect run. "Signal Montblanc: stand by with flares."

Sanbat relayed the message. Earlier, Montblanc had reported that spreading his men in a wide arc, he had pushed up to vantage points halfway to the base. He was perfectly poised to provide blanket illumination over the target.

Sanbat reported back: "Montblanc standing by with flares."

"O'Brien?"

"Still playing emergencies with Asmara and South Eritrea. Gave warning of possible crash landing. Requested permission to jettison inflammable cargo over the volcanoes. Permission granted."

Jameson cut in. "Any visual on the target?"

"No. He's going by Wallace's coordinates."

Jameson snorted and reverted to watching the Hercules as she completed another circuit. He observed matter-of-factly that

Boaz, Osman and Getachew had closed ranks to alleviate tension through shoulder-to-shoulder contact, and that he himself, automatically, had pushed against them.

The Hercules started a new run a few thousand feet above the cluster of cliffs.

Sanbat's voice blared harshly. "O'Brien requests flares! This is it!"

"Signal: flares!"

Sanbat started signaling Montblanc.

Boaz barked. "Don't look at the target! If there's a nuclear blast —it'll blind you! Check your respirators!"

The flares lit up the sky. Bright silver, as if the moon had intensified its light.

Boaz cracked his knuckles nervously and edged near Sanbat.

She moved to touch him, then held back. To her surprise, he took her hand and held it gently.

They heard the plane roaring as it passed overhead; O'Brien had jettisoned the palletized loads of gasoline.

They turned their backs to the target. Boaz tightened his grip on Sanbat's hand. He counted the seconds until certain that the free-falling loads had hit ground.

There was no nuclear blast.

He spun around toward the target.

Billowing clouds of fire erupted from the cluster of cliffs. Faintly, he heard the explosions reverberating. The forty-gallon gas drums, fused with incendiaries, had ignited on impact like giant Molotov cocktails.

He saw, captured in a frozen moment, Osman, Getachew and Jameson lean forward in the direction of the cluster of cliffs. The escarpment refracted within a heat shield. Vast tongues of smoke, of ocher and crimson flames rose from the vortex.

Sanbat nudged him. "O'Brien reports sighting movement in the target area."

Boaz scanned the wilderness. It stood primordial, its eternal tremors undisturbed by the bombardment. He allowed himself a deep breath. The gas drums had fallen dead on target. "Confirm bull's-eye, O'Brien. Check Montblanc. Report progress to Ilan."

Time paused for a measure.

When it moved again, Sanbat stood before them somberly. "Montblanc reports two dead. Mrozek and Estienne. Hit by mortar. WOJ opened up to stop the flares."

Boaz and Osman exchanged glances. They had barely known the two Legionnaires. But they had been Schoenberg's friends, and they had fought together. New brothers to mourn.

"O'Brien's signed off. He's reporting to Asmara and South Eritrea that the control defect has stabilized, but that he's abandoning his flight to Diego Garcia and returning to Kagnew to check the aircraft. Wishes us good luck." She walked away. With tears for the two men she had briefly met and who had fought to save her.

Angrily, Boaz stared at the WOJ base. It was still burning. He thought he heard voices screaming. It was his imagination. A glimpse into the immediate future. He spoke gruffly, with his back to his friends. "Five minutes. We've got a lot of ground to cover."

YALTA, U.S.S.R.

From the balcony of the party officials' rest home, Ivan Mikhailovich Volkov had a splendid view of Tsar Nicholas II's Livadia palace where, in February 1945, Churchill, Roosevelt and Stalin had divided the world into spheres of influence. The imperial relic always conjured up a youthful dream: he, installed at Livadia, informing the pathetic leaders of the world how he intended to amend the previous division simply by taking the lion's share.

That day would dawn soon. Yet, since the sinking of WOJ's submarine, he had been forced to reconsider that even he might be defeated by one of history's caprices.

Of primary consideration was Abu Ismail's invitation for an extraordinary meeting in Tripoli.

He could accept the invitation. Officially he was on holiday until May 6. He had planned his leave carefully. No business pending. Every contingency carefully worked out so that from April 25, WOJ's day of attack, to May 6, he would have ten days—incomparably more formidable than those that shook the world in 1917—to collect the dividends on Operation Dragons.

But the invitation intrigued him. He and Abu Ismail had never met. They had never felt the need. What had changed now?

He sighed. He had to accept the invitation. Evaluate what the mad mullah had in mind. If need be, pacify him. The stakes were too high, the end game too near.

But he would give himself a few days. Time to assess Idris Ali's situation. An urgent communiqué early that morning from his man at Russian Military Intelligence Operations Division had reported that a small Israeli force had landed at Barassoli, and that a U.S. Air Force plane, claiming an emergency, had dumped gasoline bombs over the Danakil Alps. The enemy was closing in on the WOJ base. If Idris Ali fell, Abu Ismail would have to be embraced.

THE DANAKIL ALPS, ETHIOPIA

Osman moved up to the rock formation which looked like the seven-headed Hydra where Boaz, crouched, kept vigil before WOJ's aerie.

Boaz's greeting, muffled through the respirator's earphones, sounded like abuse: "Why don't you rest?"

"I can't. How about you? I'll keep watch."

Boaz shook his head. Osman settled down next to him.

The wilderness smoldered, changed face constantly yet remained the same, merely altering the formations of its pockmarks. Some of these had been caused by O'Brien's raid, but it was impossible to tell which.

The cluster of cliffs that sheltered the WOJ base lay directly ahead, a mere kilometer away. Nothing stirred. They had reached the present position, as planned, by sunrise. They had lain under cover since but had maintained alert for WOJ personnel on the run. They had hoped for at least one prisoner to ascertain the situation at the base. But none had come—neither along this flank nor at the eastern end, through Montblanc's ranks. Either O'Brien's raid had razed the base or the WOJ task force, decimated, had chosen to make a stand within its inner sanctum. Daunting as the latter possibility seemed, moving in immediately after the bombardment, in view of the terrain, the distance and the restrictions of the NBC suits, would have been impossible in the nighttime available. Moreover, there was evidence of considerable ground contamination in the area, which suggested that the WOJ bomb had sustained damage. If so, except for the mopping up, the mission had been accomplished.

Osman scanned the cliffs. They offered two routes. The first, traversing several minor crevasses, led to an elevation, parts of which had eroded over the millennia and had collapsed as a natural stairway into one of the base's larger ravines. The second required a direct ascent of the highest cliff to the summit of the cluster, and then an equally hazardous descent into one of the narrower ravines. The first, being relatively easy, had been chosen as the obvious assault route. But Boaz, considering the possibility of WOJ snipers at the heights, had undertaken to create a second line by scaling the alternative route, the rock face, alone.

"Boaz, I'm going up with you. You'll need someone on the rope."

"Not with your leg—"

"My leg hasn't given us trouble so far. And it's almost back to full strength. Anyway, you know I wouldn't let you go alone."

"Why take the risk?"

"What risk are you talking about? For all we know, they're waiting to blow us all up! Even if they're not, we could walk out of here sizzling with contamination!"

"I want you in command. . . ."

"Jameson and Getachew are quite capable . . ."

"Osman, it's night climbing . . ."

"There's moonlight. Come on, Boaz, no argument . . ."

Boaz hissed. "I'll give you a good argument! You've got Samia! Life!"

Osman chuckled. "Ah, the old trick. Well, you've got Sanbat. I suggest we start early. Get there ahead of the others. This is our mess, Boaz. We should do the bulk of the cleaning up."

April 10, 1974

THE DANAKIL ALPS, ETHIOPIA

Boaz led the way. Osman followed on the scree above to provide cover. They held ready their Chinese silenced submachine guns.

Dawn had penetrated the ravine. They had fallen behind schedule.

Initially, their progress had been satisfactory. The climb to the summit of the cliff had proved easier than anticipated. The rock face, chiseled by erosion, had offered excellent hand and foot holds. These had compensated for the limited use of pitons that could not have been driven in securely, particularly nearer to the top, for fear of the noise. Visibility in the moonlight had been adequate. The combined weights of radio, water and rations, decontaminating agents, arms, ammunition, Geiger counter and climbing gear, and the encumbrance of the NBC suit and respirator, had caused surprisingly little hardship. The painstaking minutiae of the ascent had absorbed them completely.

The summit also had proven trouble-free. They had not confronted any WOJ. Scanning with infrared binoculars, they had established that the other peaks, too, had been free of enemy positions. They had found ample evidence of the effectiveness of O'Brien's attack from the mass of debris strewn about. The thick camouflage netting, which had canopied the base against aerial detection, had been reduced to ash. Even more heartening, they had failed to pick up any sound from below. But their Geiger counter, operated for fractions of seconds to minimize sound, had registered ominous levels of ground contamination.

The descent, by contrast, had been rough. The bombing had

all but blocked the ravine they should have taken. They had tried to work their way down by belaying to a projection and rappelling down commando fashion, but the disturbed boulders precariously balancing on crumbling earth had forced them to abandon that route and detour to the other face of the cliff, where the cleft was wider. Though at first glance this other face had seemed ideal for a descent, the cliff dropped down into one of the base's larger ravines where they were likely to encounter WOJ personnel. But having synchronized the attack with Jameson and Getachew for 6:00, they had had no option.

They had resolved to reduce the risks of exposure by taking advantage of the width of the cliff for a fast abseil, aiming to come down at the deepest end of the ravine where they had a chance of surprising the sentries. But there, too, the devastation had proved a bane. Both had come to within a hairsbreadth of being impaled on spikes of basalt blasted out of the rock face like giant maces.

Reaching ground at the deepest end of the ravine, they had found it deserted. They had established brief contact with Jameson, Getachew and Sanbat, only to find that they, too, had been hindered and delayed by the detritus. Having lost the cover of darkness for a dawn attack, Boaz had ruled that he and Osman would go in first, engage the enemy and clear the way for Jameson, Getachew and the Tigreans to strike from the rear. Sanbat had been delegated to report the situation to Montblanc who had remained dug in at the eastern perimeter to block the escape route. Montblanc was to plan his own assault should Boaz's strategy fail.

They were now halfway into the ravine.

They paused near a massive mound of rubble. They could see, about a hundred meters ahead, the clearing, the nucleus of the complex, which Wallace had named the "Temple of Creation."

The explorer had meticulously mapped out the sixteen ravines, giving each a number, starting with the one nearest to noon on a sundial and the rest following clockwise. They could now verify, from the jagged opening of a vast cave immediately ahead, that they were in ravine 11, the complex's fourth largest and the one which, being arid, Osman had theorized, might accommodate the stores. Surveying it now, Osman seemed to have been right. The ravine overflowed with rubbish and sheets in rags.

They cleared the mound. Boaz took the right flank where the cave was situated. Osman took the left and dropped back a pace to provide better cover.

A few steps farther, Boaz stopped. The first thing that had struck him had been the stench of putrefaction. The second, the realization that for the stench to penetrate his respirator, he must

have damaged his facepiece and that he was now exposed to contamination. He whispered into his throat microphone. "Can you
smell something, Osman?"

"What is it?"

"I don't know. We must have sprung leaks. We're being irradiated."

Osman's voice betrayed horror. "So?"

Boaz tried a futile argument. "Why don't you go back? We're
still within safe limits."

Osman's voice shrieked in his ear. "Move, move!"

Boaz hesitated, then edged forward.

His steps sent some chameleons scattering. He noticed that the
ground, blanketed with caustic white ash, was soft and moist wherever it had escaped the fires. The ash, Wallace had noted, was the
residue of volcanic eruptions carried by the winds. When Wallace
had explored the place, the ash had been dry. Boaz wondered why
it should now be moist. Condensation was an unlikely possibility
in an arid canyon where a blistering fire had raged. He prodded a
moist patch. The ash was no longer white but dark purple. An
object crumbled beneath his feet. He identified it, with revulsion,
as a dried piece of intestine. He cast another look at the rubbish.
He could now see it was mainly offal—some inexplicably wrapped
around rags. It seemed the ravine had not been used for stores,
but was a waste pit. That also explained why they had not, so far,
encountered any WOJ commandos.

Approaching the cave, he paused and listened for sounds. He
heard only his heartbeat. Finally, conquering fear, he ran, dived,
rolled over and sprang up at the cave opening, flat against a rock.
He listened. His heart beat even louder.

He glanced back at Osman. Osman did not acknowledge his
look but continued scanning the ravine.

Boaz caught a movement from inside the cave. He fell on one
knee, ready to fire. Behind him he felt Osman do the same.

The shape—a hyena—sauntered out of the cave, moving un-
steadily. It stopped and peered at him with fly-infested eyes. Then
it growled and the sound seemed to come from a larynx cut with
broken glass. Slowly it raised a paw, snarled angrily, then collapsed. It stayed down, twitching and panting in agony.

Boaz stared at the hyena. It had lost most of its coat of short
hair. It kept vomiting a mess of bile, pus and blood. The mouth
was full of sores. "It's sick."

Osman's voice rasped. "It's dying."

The stench of the vomit hit Boaz. He could explain the
miasma. Decomposition. And he could diagnose the animal's sick-

ness. He moved forward again, hoping that action would keep panic under control. "I'm going in."

He launched himself into the cave. Behind him. Osman zigzagged across and took up position by the entrance.

Boaz scrambled out of the light and threw himself down. He stayed put, waiting for a sharp volley. It did not come. The stench was now overpowering. When his eyes adjusted to the dimness, he recoiled.

The cave was a necropolis. Countless bodies, some female, buried in shallow earth, lay partially exhumed and mutilated. Innumerable eyes from scores of hyenas feasting on this horrendous banquet squinted at him. He forced himself to examine the nearest corpse. It bore sickly sores that even the decomposition could not camouflage. And the eyeless head was bald.

The hyenas stopped their feast and turned to him. Instinctively, he backed against the cave wall.

The hyenas grouped and started to advance. Boaz steadied his gun and watched—fascinated despite his terror—as they paused a few meters away—howling, snarling, trying to elect a pack leader. Some were vomiting. Others licked their sores and bald patches.

Slowly, menacingly, one of the hyenas moved forward, then pounced. Boaz shot it dead. The rest broke rank and ran at him. Boaz fired at will. He kept them at bay only because they were too sick to attack speedily. One of the hyenas maneuvered to his flank. Boaz smashed its skull with the barrel of the submachine gun. Other hyenas edged forward. Boaz emptied his magazine, then hurried to reload. The hyenas snarled as if rejoicing in his helplessness.

Boaz saw himself dying. Life mocked him even in death.

A hyena pounced. Again he hit it with his gun, but in so doing, dropped his spare magazine.

Another hyena stood suspended in midair, then catapulted back to fall dead at his feet. Only then did he hear the muffled shot. More muffled shots followed. He turned around and through the distortion of his tears, saw Osman. Illogically, he wondered when he had started crying.

The shooting stopped. Osman's voice blared over the throat microphone. "I've jammed it!"

Horror-struck, Boaz darted his eyes from Osman to the hyenas.

There were five left; they had paused and were glaring at him. One licked the blood off a dead companion. Then, as if Boaz were a delicacy to be preserved, the hyenas turned to Osman.

Terror clouded Osman's eyes as he grappled with his gun. The hyenas inched their way toward him. Osman backed away.

Boaz fumbled for another magazine. The hyenas instantly turned toward him. Boaz kicked at whatever lay at his feet. A severed head hurtled toward the hyenas, the gesture fleetingly reminding him of Samson and the jawbone. Finally, he drove the new magazine into his gun. The hyenas had held back to fight for the skull, teeth imbedded in each others' throats. He emptied the magazine, though he had killed them all with the first rounds.

He edged toward Osman. The latter leaned against the wall, barely suppressing hysteria. "I know what it is, Boaz . . . Radiation."

"Yes. Looks like the whole camp died of it."

"But the hyenas . . . How?"

"Irradiated by eating the corpses . . ."

Osman whined. "Allah . . . Allah . . . Allah . . ." Then he froze, his face distorting with primeval terrors.

Boaz, alarmed, followed Osman's look. And he, too, stood transfixed.

From the depth of the cave, a corpse had risen. It was shaking its head sadly, picking bits of flesh from its skin, handling the bones that clung to it like sacred relics in an ossuary, snarling quietly.

They watched incredulous as the apparition advanced. They realized it was a man. Stark naked, skin sunburned, but Caucasian. Hair and beard balding. Suppurating with numerous sores. Eyes like two beacons, seeing far beyond them. He spoke in precise English, like a colonel addressing natives. "You have killed my children. Are you satisfied?"

Boaz and Osman followed his gestures. He was talking about the hyenas, not the WOJ dead. Boaz regained his composure, nudged Osman. "Keep watch!"

Osman took up position by the cave entrance.

Boaz turned to the man. "Who are you?"

The man inclined his head as if intrigued by the distortion in Boaz's voice through the facepiece. Then he smiled, and for a moment his eyes lost luminosity. He gesticulated at the corpses. "I'm not one of them."

Osman interjected gruffly, in Arabic. "Name—what's your name?"

The man's eyes fulminated again. He continued in English. "I am Anubis. . . . The Pathfinder. . . . The Opener of the Way. . . . I guide souls from this world to the next. I may even be one of God's angels. . . ."

Boaz stepped forward, prompted by the man's clipped accent, and the incongruous precision of speech.

"What about the others?"

"Others?"

Boaz pointed to the corpses. "Hasn't anybody else survived?"

The man shrieked, half-scream, half-laughter, very much like a hyena.

Boaz remembered Sanbat's tale of her encounter with the Hyena-Man.

The man flailed his arms. "Gone. All gone."

Osman bellowed. "What do you mean—gone?"

The man continued to shriek. "Gone . . . I'm here to clean up. . . ."

Boaz forced himself to touch the man's shoulder. Physical contact, as Sanbat had taught him, could fathom a man's soul. "Kevork . . . ? Kevork Dedeyan?"

The man stopped shrieking. He contemplated them for a long time as rivulets of tears flowed from his burning eyes. Then, like a child who had lost and found his father, he clung to Boaz's hand and wailed. "Yes . . . Yes . . . Yes . . ."

FORT GEORGE G. MEADE, MARYLAND, U.S.A.

Quinn broke the seal on his second bottle of bourbon, sank into the armchair and let his eyes wander yet again over the photographs. The blown-up aerial pictures covered the activities of the Ethiopian patrol boat off the Danakil coast on the nights of April 6 and 7. They had been requested by the Memouneh, and Quinn, through the National Security Agency, had duly transmitted them. But more in bitterness than duty. For the Memouneh had been devious in raising his hopes that Talat Fawzi, being a key man, would be kept safe by WOJ—come what may. Yet the Memouneh must have known, as Quinn did deep down, that WOJ would never forfeit Talat. And the photographs proved just that.

THE DANAKIL ALPS, ETHIOPIA

Boaz and Osman, led by the rambling Dedeyan, had penetrated the base without hindrance. They had found the central clearing empty, or rather filled with more corpses, and piled in some order.

Soon after, they had been joined by Jameson, Getachew, Sanbat and the Tigreans, all of whom had arrived unhindered. They had consolidated positions. Boaz and Osman had repaired their NBC suits and respirators, trying hard to convince each other that their exposure to radiation had been below the maximum permissible concentration.

They had spent the rest of the day combing the complex. O'Brien's raid, though it had decimated the base's personnel and

razed much of the superficial structure, had missed the main installations, invariably inside the caves and well protected by sand-
bags. Consequently, they had been able to evaluate the desperate
conditions that had prevailed, particularly in those ravines that
had served as living quarters. They had found the factory, and a
range of sophisticated machinery. In a cave that had apparently
been Talat Fawzi's, they had found notebooks containing calculations and syllogisms; initially they had thought these to be blueprints of the nuclear device, but closer scrutiny had revealed them
as Fawzi's efforts at deciphering Mossad's twelve-tone code, which
Quinn had been transmitting through various friendly radio stations.

Beyond the epicenter of O'Brien's raid, in the gorge leading to
Barassoli, they had discovered heavy-duty generators, barrels of
oil, stockpiles of TNT, three kilos of plutonium dioxide in canisters
and Land-Rovers ready for immediate use. They had also established visual contact with Montblanc. Since Montblanc's force
was perilously close to contaminated ground, Boaz had ordered
him to withdraw down to the coastal plain, there to scour for
possible WOJ stragglers and Wolde's paratroopers.

But they had not found the bomb. Nor had they gleaned any
clues from the mass of papers in Idris Ali's command cave as to
what it looked like and how it had been designed to operate.

Concurrently with the search, they had dug out all the graves,
including the pit that had contained the remains of contaminated
livestock.

The dead had totaled 119. Fifty of these had been the full
complement of women, all victims of radiation sickness. Of the
sixty-nine male dead, forty-three had shown the same symptoms.
The rest had been killed by O'Brien's bombs. At least ten of the
latter appeared to have been in relatively good health.

That had left, according to Idris Ali's personal roster of 133,
fourteen unaccounted for, among them Idris Ali himself and the
two key experts, Talat Fawzi and Ischii Watanabe. According to
Dedeyan, these had left in two groups on separate days.

Where the groups had gone was the issue facing them as they
prepared for the night.

Sanbat sat at Idris Ali's desk. Jameson stood before the blackboard and examined the chart that categorized the levels of
ionizing radiation. At a makeshift table Osman and Getachew mi-
crofilmed the roster, inventories and memoranda. Boaz prowled.
Dedeyan squatted in a corner, covered in ticks and scabs, denuded
of hair, weighed down by the clothes he had been given, and
occasionally vomiting.

Boaz addressed him again. "Kevork, this is important. You said two groups left—on separate days. . . . Can you be specific? When? Yesterday? The day before? Which day?"

Dedeyan watched the facepiece of Boaz's respirator, afraid of its convolutions.

"Kevork, listen to me. . . . There are fourteen WOJ somewhere out there—with a plutonium bomb. You're the only one who can tell us where!"

Dedeyan shrank back and growled.

Sanbat rose and pulled Boaz aside. "Let me question him. He may remember me from the desert. Not feel so threatened. . . ."

Boaz pondered a moment, then nodded.

Sanbat sat down opposite Dedeyan and whinnied like a submissive animal. Dedeyan yelped happily, and retreated into his insanity.

Sanbat held out her hand. Waited.

Eventually Dedeyan gripped it. "I am the Devil. I feed on the damned."

"I know."

"I hold in my eye the *hyaenia* stone. With it I can prophesy."

"I know."

"I am the Egyptian jackal-god Anubis. I guide souls from this world to the next."

"I know."

"I am the Hyena-Man. I cannot be hunted down or shot dead. I cannot be engulfed by fire. I can see by day and by night."

"I know."

Dedeyan released Sanbat's hand and sank back.

Still Sanbat waited. Behind her Boaz, Osman, Jameson and Getachew stood immobile for fear of distracting Dedeyan. They had observed, in the course of the day, that Dedeyan's mythomania invariably produced a catharsis. Moments of lucidity occasionally followed in its wake.

It had been during such moments that Dedeyan had recounted his life in the wilderness. How he had escaped from Wolde's ambush; his days in the desert; how he had found water, like the Bedouins, by tracing salt pools to their freshwater sources; his determination to find a peaceful realm for his hyenas; the wanderings in the wilderness, the discovery of the rock cluster; and the long wait for the offending humans to depart.

How he had established rule over the hyenas had been the only episode that had defied reason. He had told them he had emulated the *dev* of Armenian epics, those giants who could hurl mountains and kill dragons. But even that mythicizing, in the light of his expertise in martial arts, his training to live off any land, his will to survive, had seemed credible enough. Any doubts of his resourcefulness had been dispersed by the fact that, judging from the terminal stage of his sickness, Dedeyan had lived in the base area for a considerable time. He had not only avoided the WOJ lookouts but even more astutely, to safeguard his hyenas, he had dismantled countless explosive charges which WOJ had laid around the perimeter. But for that the assault force would have found the going much harder.

Dedeyan shivered, looked up, peered at Boaz, Osman, Jameson and Getachew, then rested his eyes on Sanbat. "Sanbat, isn't it? You told me your name. . . ."

"Yes."

"I shall impose a favor—when my time comes. . . ."

Sanbat held his hand. "There's still some to go."

Dedeyan smiled, dreamily. "Jews and Armenians—eternal optimists."

Sanbat addressed him solemnly. "Kevork. There are things I must ask you. . . ."

"Yes?"

"This morning—when we reached the clearing—we found twenty-six bodies. Piled up. Do you remember? Recently dead, badly burned. But not yet mutilated."

Dedeyan made raucous sounds as he remembered.

"They were killed two nights ago. During the bombing. Remember the bombing, Kevork? Gasoline drums?"

Dedeyan's eyes darted about in search of the memory.

"Who piled them up, Kevork? Was it you?"

Dedeyan shook his head.

"The survivors then?"

Dedeyan nodded.

"Where are they?"

"They left—after the fires. . . ."

"Where did they go?"

Dedeyan's face started to distort. His hands tried to smooth his features as if to ward off approaching madness. Shakily, he pointed toward the eastern perimeter.

"The gorge, Kevork?"

"Yes. The gorge was not hit. . . ."

"We searched the gorge."

"High. Search high."

"How many of them? Do you know?"

"Eight."

"Did they have the bomb?"

"Bomb?"

"Were they carrying anything heavy?"

Dedeyan's face started twitching. "Only themselves. Heavy . . . Sick . . ."

"The others? What happened to the rest?"

Dedeyan looked up, suddenly lucid. "Idris Ali's group?"

Boaz pushed forward and squatted by Dedeyan. "Yes. Idris Ali's group! Do you know when they left? Where they went?"

Dedeyan cackled. "Days . . ."

"How many days?"

Dedeyan growled. "Remember—when the time comes—your promise!"

"How many days, Kevork? And where? Where?"

Dedeyan shrieked, burst into his hyena laughter.

Boaz grabbed hold of him. "Kevork . . . Answer me. . . ."

Dedeyan snarled, bared his teeth, then pounced on Boaz. Boaz evaded the attack by rolling sideways. Dedeyan rushed at him again. This time Boaz had to thrust him down.

Dedeyan panted on the floor, drooling sickly saliva, and intoned. "I am the Devil. I feed on the damned. I hold in my eye the *hyaenia* stone. With it I can prophesy. I am the Egyptian jackal-god Anubis. I guide souls from this world to the next. . . ." Out of breath, he passed out.

Boaz turned to his friends. They avoided his eyes.

Jameson forced himself to speak. "The heights. We'll have to comb the heights. . . ."

Boaz nodded.

Osman grunted. "We'll do it—Boaz and I!"

Jameson interjected. "You think that would be wise? You guys must be frazzled! When did you last sleep?"

Osman grimaced. "Who'd want to sleep here?"

"You will, and you'll sleep like babes—seeing I'm going to have my say. I'll take a squad of Tigreans. Leave the heights to me."

Boaz objected. "Just a moment."

"Come on, Boaz. You heard Dedeyan. Those men are sick. They might even be dead. Besides, you should stick around here. Montblanc might stumble on Idris Ali—might even need your help. . . ."

Boaz had been considering that very possibility. He could not bring himself to believe that when Dedeyan had said Idris Ali had left days ago, he had meant precisely that. If that was true, Idris Ali would be clear of the Danakil area. On the loose with the bomb. If, on the other hand, he had left a couple of days ago—which would make sense since about that time he would have spotted Montblanc's forces landing—then he would still be out there in the wilderness. Somewhere between the base and Barassoli. If so, he would be cornered, eventually. And conceivably, facing death, he would detonate his bomb to carry his enemies with him. Should that happen, Boaz meant to be there.

"That's a point, Al. All right, go ahead. Take your time. They can't go anywhere. And be careful."

April 11, 1974

THE DANAKIL ALPS, ETHIOPIA

Badran let his tears flow. Idris Ali had assigned him the task of destroying the enemy. He had exulted, confident that he would accomplish the mission. Now he fought off the premonition that his rise to Heaven would be without distinction, without commemoration by poems and songs.

The gorge spread out below him like the thighs of a giantess, visibly in the false dawn only as a dark-tufted shadow. Throughout the night, the enemy had crawled in its folds, like crabs in a whore's cunt.

To the west, the base stood silent. There, too, the enemy was awake. He could see their hurricane lamps flickering. There, too, rummaging for the bomb.

To the east, where the gorge opened onto the coastal plain, there was another enemy encampment. Beyond, off Barassoli, lay their boats. It had been the boats that had fooled him. Had made him think that those moving up to the base were the only force. Had prompted him to move to the heights, and wait for them to advance to the gorge where he sat in ambush. It would have been so simple. A few grenades to detonate the stockpile of explosives. But they had not come. They had stood, at a safe distance.

Thus he had neglected the western perimeter. Allowed another enemy force to enter through the very walls of the cliffs like death visiting a healthy house unannounced. Worse still, he had resisted admitting his misjudgment. Had stuck to the notion that the enemy units would join up, search the base and leave together. Through the gorge. To be slaughtered by him.

He had been vainglorious. The enemy at the east, avoiding the base, had retreated to the coastal plain. Those to the west had dug in. And now a squad was moving toward his position. Foolish, foolish Badran.

He turned to look at his men. They were sleeping. He resented them. Sick men, hiding in shelters, they had survived the bombing. While the healthy ones had sacrificed themselves, trying to save lives. He would have to beat them to wakefulness. Sick or not, they would die on their feet.

He scanned the gorge again. The enemy squad was getting closer. He checked his weapons. A dozen or so grenades, revolvers, some sticks of dynamite. Enough. There was an outside chance. If he dropped the grenades on the gorge as the enemy squad approached, then blew up the ridge he and his men occupied, he might conceivably trigger off a landslide. Bury the base. And all within it.

He started to pray. If The Compassionate had kept him strong and healthy, did that not mean He had chosen him for full glory?

TEL AVIV, ISRAEL

It was 7:00 A.M. on the fifth day of Passover. Tel Aviv's rush hour was further aggravated by early-morning worshipers. Somehow the Memouneh's driver blared a way through.

Next to him, Kidan slammed down the radiophone. "Helicopter ready."

The Memouneh started to tremble. His body, that old, tired sibyl, had already foreseen the end of the day.

The terrorist attack, rumored for some days, was upon them. All his efforts to stop it had failed. Though he had preempted a dozen or so attempts, one had got through. At 6:40 A.M. border patrols had found the trail of three fedayeen heading toward Kiryat Shmona. He hoped he would get there before the atrocity. But deep down, he knew it was already too late.

"What about Operation Dragons?—while you try to sort out this business of Kiryat Shmona?"

The Memouneh glared at Kidan. *"Business?* What sort of man are you?"

Kidan twitched, trying to curb his anger. "For God's sake, let's not start again. There are priorities on Operation Dragons, too!"

The Memouneh nodded. He had not lost sight of Operation Dragons. But at Kiryat Shmona, civilians were threatened. Children, women, mothers, fathers. Whereas Operation Dragons was far away, in the wilderness of Ethiopia—almost unreal. And almost inconceivable. Because though it, too, threatened civilians, it threatened them in masses. In thousands and millions. Inconceivable. Like another Holocaust. Which, on reflection, *was* conceivable. "All right, Kidan. Order Boaz and company to withdraw from the Danakil—soon as they can."

"Boaz will want an explanation."

"Give it to him. Quinn's blowups."

The Memouneh noticed he was shaking even more. A reaction to the long night spent analyzing the radiophotographs dispatched by Quinn. Infrared aerial prints of the Eritrean coast. Blown up. Showing Wolde's patrol boat in the bay of Barassoli. And six men loading what looked like a trunk. Quinn had sworn that one had been Talat Fawzi. Mossad experts had identified the rest: Idris Ali, Ischii Watanabe and three WOJ commandos. The trunk, the Memouneh presumed, was the bomb. The event: a moonlit passage on the night of the sixth. "Also, order the Reshevs home. They won't be needed. Issue a press release. Brief and vague. Announcing their arrival at Sharm al-Sheikh. Mention the voyage around the Cape. Nothing about their deployment off Ethiopia."

The driver had brought them to Sde Dov Airport.

The Memouneh jumped out of the car and ran to the helicopter. His steps already numbed by the number of innocents who would die at Kiryat Shmona.

THE DANAKIL ALPS, ETHIOPIA

Jameson checked his men. They had spread out along the contours of the incline, invisible, but indicating positions with stones strewn casually. He scrutinized the ridge ahead where the WOJ stragglers had taken cover.

The distance was about forty meters. He still possessed the mighty throw of a quarterback; he could raze the ridge with grenades, save himself the marine's charge which, he had believed, he had left behind in the mountains of Korea. But he wanted prisoners.

He felt high on action. Glowing with a feeling of indestructibility. Confident in the speed and power of his body, still in peak condition.

He wanted at least four prisoners. So that he, Boaz, Osman and Getachew could interrogate them separately, play one against the other and extract the single piece of information they needed: the whereabouts of the bomb.

He checked his Ingram M-10. It was not just the adrenaline flowing. He could see himself, at last, in the perspective he had sought throughout his career. The stalwart Yank in shining white armor, saving the world despite itself. It was that clear-cut, if somewhat corny. And here in the wilderness, away from the concrete and steel edifices of seats of power, winnowed from the husks of geopolitics, liberated from abstruse theories, standing man against Evil, it was also the absolute reality.

He hooted a signal to the Tigreans, took a deep breath, held it, and sprang from his shelter. He ran crouched down, spraying bullets to keep the WOJ stragglers pinned down, feeling all the more spurred by the war cries of the Tigreans charging alongside.

He saw several men before him. He noted their deathliness. He saw them drop grenades into the gorge. He saw their leader rise. A massive man. Draped with clusters of tubes. He recognized the tubes as sticks of dynamite. He saw one solitary stick in the man's hand. With a minimal fuse. As the man lit it, he fired a burst. The man's head split open. The body catapulted backward.

He ran as fast as he could. Against the expiring fuse of that one stick of dynamite.

The ridge erupted in front of him. The earth shuddered and collapsed. He felt himself sucked into a void. In the last fraction of his life he wondered whether, down below, Boaz had cleared the explosives from the gorge as he had said he would.

April 12, 1974

THE DANAKIL ALPS, ETHIOPIA

"I am the *sharapet* of the Hayk! Do you know what that means?"

"Commander in chief of the Armenians."

Dedeyan looked up, surprised. "How did you know?"

"You told me before."

"I am also waterborn. Not earthborn. Did I tell you that, too?"

"Yes."

"Am I rambling?"

"Not anymore."

"Total clarity—before death. Is that it?"

Boaz pulled him up closer so that Dedeyan's head would rest on his lap. "Yes."

Dedeyan watched the cave walls undulate, like ripples on water. "They're still moving—the walls."

"Must be nice to see."

Dedeyan closed his eyes for a moment. "Did I tell you also . . . I know the *Devils of Sassoun* by heart? That's our epic. . . ."

"Yes."

"Strange, isn't it? For someone in our line of business . . . But then . . . it's such a different world . . . the epic. . . ."

"I know what you mean. When I was a boy, I used to know one, too . . . *The Iliad*. I still remember chunks of it. . . ."

"Recite me some . . ."

"In Greek?"

"I don't mind. . . ."

Boaz hesitated a moment, then obligingly started with the invocation. " 'Sing goddess, the wrath of Achilles Peleus' son—' "

"Sorry to interrupt. Just one question. I had asked you a favor —will you do it?"

"I have already."

Dedeyan turned to him, puzzled, then pointed to Boaz's revolver. "How?"

"There are other ways. More peaceful . . ."

"Like what?"

"Overdose. Heroin. Barbiturates. And a drop of LSD."

"Where would you have found those?"

"In one of the caves. Quite a supply. It must have been one way of keeping them sane. . . ."

"I see. . . . Is that why the walls are rippling?"

"I imagine so."

"I'm grateful. I feel marvelous."

"In *The Iliad* Homer says opium induces forgetfulness of the sense of evil. . . ."

"Really? I suppose it does. Thank you." Dedeyan held his hand. "How long—do you think?"

"Not very long."

"You're a good man, Boaz. Good name also. *In strength*— that's what it means, doesn't it? One of the pillars in Solomon's Temple . . ."

"Yes."

"Beautiful colors all around. Beautiful shapes . . . You look like you have a halo. . . . Will you stay with me?"

"Yes."

"Can you go on reciting?"

"If you want me to."

Dedeyan shut his eyes and snuggled close to Boaz. "I'd have preferred Armenian. But Greek will do just as well. . . ."

Boaz started reciting again. He felt at peace. His fatigue, so heavy after so much chasing, so many killings, had dispersed. This was the respite he had sought all his life.

Homer's words added to his sense of peace. He had discarded his respirator and NBC suit—even his undergarments. Like Dedeyan, he had wished to blend into the wilderness naked, a man free of artifice. Complete. A man before the fall of Adam.

The end had come. Not as Nietzsche had advised, at the right time. And not quite as he had wanted. But good enough. A leviathan abandoning the age of the rodent. With fortitude. Beyond the limits Nietzsche could have visualized.

He had killed his last. Not out of hate. But for mercy. He was cradling the dying body of a friend. Not quite his twin, like Osman. But since he could not have borne Osman dying before him, Dedeyan was a good choice. A brother, if not a twin.

Even more important, the regrets had been conquered. The unfinished business of living, the unfinished business of Operation Dragons had been discarded, at one stroke. The end of the pain of life. The end of questions about himself, his country, the world, and his aimless function in the Great Scheme. Let others find the answers through suffering. Redeem themselves. Find sanctity. He had the courage to renounce even that.

Dedeyan trembled in his arms and slipped into coma.

He hugged him tighter and raised his voice. " *'Let the Danaans pay by thine arrows for my tears.'* " A good send-off.

He continued reciting. He would keep his promise to Dedeyan —wait for him to die. In any case, this was a happy moment. He did not mind prolonging it. It had been a good idea to end Dedeyan's life here, in the wilderness, rather than take him back to the Reshev and thence to Israel. He would have died before reaching Sharm al-Sheikh. Even that short reprieve would have been cruel.

He heard his voice rise. It sounded heroic. A good rendition of Homer. For himself, too, a good send-off. Not like poor Jameson —crushed by a mountain, dug out piecemeal, wrapped up in a canvas bag, carried by his twin, Getachew, down the gorge to be dispatched to the States. Not like Jameson's company of Tigreans. Certainly not like Schoenberg.

Dedeyan ceased breathing. Boaz stopped reciting. He put Dedeyan's hands in repose and smoothed the skin around the eyes. He stared at the ravaged face until it seemed to him that the harsh lines, the suppurating sores, had disappeared.

He was ready.

Not quite. The last temptation attacked him. His mind filled with visions of Sanbat, of his hopes of sanctity through her. It might have been possible. But he lacked the resources. Let others ferret Idris Ali from whichever hole he had run into. He could not run anymore. He could not, yet again, start picking up leads. Wolde had dropped Idris Ali at Assab on the night of the sixth. Idris Ali could be anywhere by now. With the bomb. And if he detonated the bomb . . . A world destroyed would be a good world. Conversely, a world ruled by Abu Ismail would be what mankind deserved.

Now he was ready. He hoped Osman and Sanbat would forgive him. Getachew, too. And Montblanc. And the Memouneh.

No, the Memouneh would not forgive him. But if the world

did survive, every year on the seventh of Adar, the traditional date of the death of Moses according to the Hebrew calendar, he would commemorate Boaz's death together with the dead of Zahal whose last resting place, like that of Moses, was unknown. So be it.

He started reciting again. Thunderously. He picked up his revolver. Raised it toward his temple.

The barrel of a submachine gun sent the revolver flying. He dropped Dedeyan and jumped to his feet.

Osman stood before him. "You bastard! That's why you sent us ahead! Did you think you could fool me?"

"Get out, Osman! Go! Go!"

Osman thundered. "If death is such a panacea—why condemn us to life? Why not all of us? Together! Grand finale!"

Boaz growled desperately. "Your lives are sacred. Mine—not—"

"Delusions of grandeur—"

"You can't stop me!"

Osman called out. "Sanbat!"

Boaz spun on his heels as she walked into the cave. He roared, more incensed by her tears than her presence. "Get out! Get out! Get out!"

Osman lowered himself to the ground. "We're going to share the spoils, Boaz. Life or death!"

Book Three

I Am a Bow in Your Hands, Lord, Draw Me Lest I Rot; Do Not Overdraw Me, Lest I Break; Overdraw Me, and Who Cares If I Break.

NIKOS KAZANTZAKIS, *Report to Greco*

April 15, 1974

THE GAMBELA RESERVE, ETHIOPIA

Idris Ali set up his radio under a camouflage awning.

Rain blanketed earth, sky and the viridian of the thick tropical vegetation. The Baro River undulated westward in a wide sweep.

The location, at the southwestern extremity of Ethiopia, was another hellhole. But here at least he could purge the claustrophobia of the Danakil, breathe, immerse himself in water and see the skies run with heavy clouds. He could even distract himself by studying the crocodiles on the riverbanks; sleeping long hours, striking swiftly when necessary, they divested creation of its mysticism.

The rain stopped. The grass steamed. It would be a brief respite: the infernal insects had not bothered to come out.

He caught sight of Fawzi and Watanabe at the doorway of the principal *tukul*. Ghostly. The advanced state of their sickness had produced hydrophobia. Though this kept them indoors and made surveillance easier, it perturbed Mahmud, Qabus and Wahbi. The three warriors, fully fit and chosen as escort for that very reason, believed Fawzi and Watanabe had contracted rabies from the scavenging hyenas at the base and had urged that with the bomb completed, they should be disposed of.

They were right. The final procedure, the arming of the bomb, could be carried out by anybody. But Abu Ismail wanted Fawzi and Watanabe alive throughout the countdown in case modifications were necessary. Much as Idris Ali resented it, he still had to obey orders. The final phase required Abu Ismail's presence. The WOJ leader's charisma and the weight of his leadership were essential to get Operation Dragons airborne.

Watanabe made faces. Fawzi pulled him away. Idris Ali spat in disgust. Watanabe's puerile antics and the blatant homosexual conduct of the two men sickened him. He would have relished feeding them to the crocodiles.

He checked his watch: 12:55 P.M.

Volkov would be transmitting in five minutes to seal the agreement.

He scanned the ground to make sure he would be undisturbed. Mahmud, the only surviving platoon leader, was at his post, perched on the highest tree. He had a good view over the dirt track and the river. The track, north of the river and running parallel to it, linked Gambela, fifty-eight kilometers to the east, with Jekaw, Sudan, sixty-three kilometers to the west. Now, in the rainy season, it was passable only by cross-country vehicles. Equally, the river, bending sharply northward in a tight arc, ran at its fastest by the encampment. Intruders, whether they came by land or water, would be severely tested by the conditions. A lookout would sight them early enough and enable him to set up an ambush.

He did not expect any intruders.

Though the region had become a nature reserve, the tourist season had ended with the rains. The Imperial Reserves and wildlife conservation officials would be restricted to the immediate vicinity of Gambela. The local inhabitants, in the main Nilotic Nuer and Anuak tribes, were either engaged in sorting the harvested wild coffee, tending the herds or fishing for the Nile perch now spawning. These activities kept them farther east and north where both land and river were more hospitable; not a single native had yet ventured this far down.

The only uncertainty centered on the tiny border garrison and the few customs officials who supervised the river traffic. But once again, as he had foreseen, the rainy season limited the problem. Since the border ran along the eastern reaches of the Sudd, the vast marshland of southern Sudan, and since the rains made the Sudd all the more impenetrable, effectively sealing the border, the garrison had been withdrawn to Gore, the province's capital. By contrast, the customs officers had their hands full in Gambela. The Baro, rising, would soon be navigable to heavy barges, and preparations for the exportation of coffee to Khartoum via the three-river network of the Baro, Sobat and White Nile were already under way.

The possibility that a zealous customs official might be interested in the group's activities was negligible. Though it had been impossible to bypass Gambela, Wolde, assuming the identity of a bored lieutenant, had described his charges as a group of botanists involved in important research. In the prevailing unrest, army escorts for government teams had become commonplace, and the explanation had satisfied official curiosity. By now, their existence would have been forgotten.

The encampment, albeit barely a kilometer off the Gambela–Jekaw track, was virtually inviolate. Concealed by thick tropical vegetation, it was invisible to the eye and indistinguishable from the air. There was only one compass point, the bend in the river, from which a glimpse of it could be caught. This minute chink had been purposely left to provide identification for Abu Ismail and his men, due to come upriver from Sudan. Any other passing eye registering the outlines of the odd thatched *tukul* would presume it to be part of an abandoned Anuak settlement. No one could know that the *tukul*, and four others farther into the bush, had been erected only a few days earlier from rotting cornstalks, and that beyond them lay a reed complex containing guns, ammunition, Land-Rovers and gasoline-powered generators. The supplies had remained undetected since November when he and Wolde had stored them.

Wolde, Idris Ali had to admit, had proved himself an impeccable ally. He had not only evacuated them commendably from under the noses of the Israeli boats, he had also transported them across the country, a distance of some 1,700 kilometers—mostly on rough roads—in less than thirty hours. Then, disdaining rest, he had returned to Assab by the morning of the ninth to resume command of the patrol boat which he had consigned to his trusted sergeant, Ketema. He had remained at sea monitoring and worrying the Reshevs until the twelfth, when the enemy had withdrawn from the Danakil. Thereafter, he had regained Assab and, on the off-chance that Getachew Iyessous might prevail upon the emperor to take action against him, had sent the bulk of his men into the Eritrean wilderness, ostensibly for exercises. He himself, escorted by a crack platoon, had reached Addis Ababa on the night of the twelfth and, taking prearranged leave, had gone to ground. Providing the countdown proceeded smoothly, Wolde would not be required until the Day of Glory when, as WOJ resurfaced, the enemy would be expected to try one last attempt to thwart Operation Dragons.

The radio started receiving at 1:00 P.M. precisely.

Idris Ali decoded the message.

PREPARATIONS SUMMARY:

PARTICIPATION OF ADMIRAL YURI TIBLYASHIN, AIR FORCE GENERAL AL-EXEI LARINCHEV, MARSHAL SERGEI YELISEEV AND THEIR RESPECTIVE FORCES AFFIRMATIVE.

COMPLETION OF GROUNDWORK FOR IVAN VOLKOV TO SEIZE PRESIDIUM AFFIRMATIVE: ALL INFLUENTIAL MEMBERS DIVERTED FROM MOSCOW.

IVAN VOLKOV AT PRESENT DELIVERING FINAL BRIEFINGS TO SUPPORTERS; WILL REGAIN MOSCOW FOR COUNTDOWN ON THE 24TH.

FINAL TIMETABLE:

ZERO HOUR: WOJ AIRCRAFT DEPARTS ADDIS ABABA, ETHIOPIA.

20 MINUTES: SIX SOVIET MIG-25 SQUADRONS, INDIAN OCEAN FLEET, SCRAMBLE MUKALLA, P.D.R.Y., UNDER GUISE ROUTINE MANEUVERS, TO PROVIDE UMBRELLA COVER.

60 MINUTES; WOJ AIRCRAFT ENTERS SOVIET MIG-25 UMBRELLA COVER.

90 MINUTES: WOJ AIRCRAFT JETTISONS DEVICE OVER MECCA.

120 MINUTES: SOVIET NAVAL INFANTRY COMPANY, INDIAN OCEAN FLEET, DEPLOYS IN AN-22 TRANSPORTS, FROM MUKALLA, DESTINATION QATAR.

125 MINUTES: SOVIET MIG-25 SQUADRONS LAND ADEN, P.D.R.Y., REPORT CONFLAGRATION OVER MECCA.

160 MINUTES: IDRIS ALI ELIMINATES ABU ISMAIL. ASSUMES COMMAND OF WOJ.

180 MINUTES: IDRIS ALI LANDS AT HOLDING POINT, NEUTRAL TERRITORY, IRAQ/SAUDI ARABIA.

185 MINUTES: SOVIET TU-22 BOMBER SQUADRON TAKES OFF BAGHDAD, DESTINATION QATAR.

190 MINUTES: SOVIET MIG-25 SQUADRONS DEPLOY FROM ADEN TO PROVIDE UMBRELLA COVER TO TU-22 BOMBER SQUADRON.

200 MINUTES: IVAN VOLKOV TAKES COMMAND OF PRESIDIUM.

220 MINUTES: SOVIET TU-22 SQUADRON ATTACKS DOHA AND UMM SA'ID, QATAR.

240 MINUTES: DOHA AIRPORT OCCUPIED BY SOVIET TU-22 SQUADRON.

270 MINUTES: AIRBORNE SOVIET NAVAL INFANTRY LAND AT DOHA AND UMM SA'ID.

300 MINUTES: SOVIET FORCES OCCUPY QATAR. SOVIET MIG-25 SQUADRONS LAND DOHA AIRPORT NOW AVAILABLE AS TURNAROUND BASE.

310 MINUTES: IDRIS ALI DEPARTS FROM HOLDING POINT.

365 MINUTES: IDRIS ALI LANDS DOHA.

390 MINUTES: IDRIS ALI AS AL-MAHDI, PROCLAIMS JIHAD AGAINST ZIONIST IMPERIALIST ENEMY.

400 MINUTES: U.S.S.R. PREMIER IVAN VOLKOV OFFERS FULL SUPPORT FOR JIHAD.

IF APPROVED CONFIRM CONCORDAT.

Idris Ali read the decoded message several times, then burned it. He had until 2:00 P.M. to signal confirmation. He spent the remaining time considering the imponderables.

During finalization of the plans, Volkov had elaborated on the various scenarios processed by the KGB computer. He had admitted the plan carried a weakness. But, he had argued, weaknesses were inherent to all plans and had to be borne as calculated risks.

The weakness in this plan, according to the computer, lay in the first ninety minutes when the enemy could be expected to intercept the WOJ strike. And, in this context, the principal enemy had been designated as the U.S.A.

The computer had proposed that, irrespective of WOJ efforts, Mossad would amass enough intelligence to assess Operation Dragons as a nuclear attack. Thereafter, it would endeavor to determine the date and target of the attack. Following Abu Ismail's sensational prophecy at the Madrid press conference, of Jewish aims to destroy Mecca on Israel's Independence Day, Mossad would wallow in confusion if not incredulity. Lacking the resources for an effective interception, it would be forced to approach the U.S.A. and delegate preventive measures to her.

The U.S.A. would respond. The National Security Agency would recommend policing action as valid insurance but would contend that the Mossad evaluation was bordering on the absurd. And here the computer had been emphatic: the evaluation's absurdity would compel U.S. military authorities to react reservedly. Even so, they would encounter difficulties. Since the fighters available to the U.S.A. would be Phantoms, F-111As and F-106s stationed in Iran, Bahrain and Diego Garcia, a base would be needed in Saudi Arabia in order to deploy in the operational area. Saudi resistance to such a request would be considerable.

On the possibility that the U.S.A. might activate her vast resources closest to the threatened region, namely the Sixth Fleet in the Mediterranean the Seventh Fleet operating in the Western Pacific/Indian Ocean and the Persian Gulf Fleet guarding the oil routes, the computer had been equally emphatic: logistics complexities would rule out the deployment of these forces.

Thus, the threat of interception would rest at most with a makeshift U.S. Air Force squadron operating on the periphery of Ethiopian airspace. To neutralize such a force, the computer had recommended a massive deterrent—an umbrella of six Soviet MiG-25 fighter squadrons.

These squadrons would be put into operation from Mukalla, P.D.R.Y, by Admiral Yuri Tiblyashin, flag officer of the Soviet Indian Ocean Fleet and one of Volkov's triumvirate.

Evaluating this particular scenario, the computer had estimated an 88 percent chance that the U.S.A. would desist from escalating police action into actual engagement with Soviet navy fighters. On the 12 percent possibility of engagement, the computer had accorded the MiG-25 parity, if not superiority, to the fighters available to the U.S. Air Force, and by virtue of the fact that the Soviet forces would outnumber the U.S. forces six to one, had forecast a very high probability of success.

Since high probability fell short of certainty, Idris Ali's reservations had not been assuaged.

There were other imponderables.

Once the target had been bombed, the computer had predicted, the aftermath would be positively in favor of WOJ and Volkov. The nuclear nature of the attack, combined with the shock that Mecca, Islam's holiest city, had been destroyed, would paralyze the world. Here again, the only power capable of controlling the situation would be the U.S.A. But a concerted action of any kind requiring the president's executive command would, because of the scope of the crisis, impose lengthy deliberations with civil and military advisers. In the course of these deliberations, Volkov would have wrested the political advantage by seizing control of the Presidium. Military advantage, too, would have been seized by the invasion of Qatar by Volkov's coconspirators Admiral Tiblyashin and Air Force General Larinchev.

With regard to the invasion of Qatar and the possibility of an interim U.S. executive order, there would be some risk of engagement with the U.S. naval base at Jufair, Bahrain—a mere forty kilometers off Qatar's eastern coast and a hundred twenty kilometers from Doha. But here, too, superiority of the Soviet forces would ensure swift victory.

By the four-hundredth minute—six hours and forty minutes from the commencement of Operation Dragons—the objectives would have been secured.

On this point, too, Idris Ali had not been totally convinced.

It was inconceivable that the U.S.A. would accept defeat apathetically. But Volkov's computer had been emphatic, evaluating in depth two vital factors: the U.S.A.'s present moral weakness and the chaos that would rule the world immediately after Operation Dragons.

With regard to the first, the computer had listed a plethora of scenarios—with the Vietnam exhaustion and the Watergate crisis as the key constants—illustrating the tortuous paths by which the U.S.A. in general, and Washington in particular, would back away from a global war even if this meant the loss of Middle East oil and economic disaster in the West. Both the U.S.A. and the West, softened by years of bounty, would consider it wiser to retreat into their protective shells, adopt isolationist policies, contrive at any price to secure oil from non-Middle East sources and endeavor, while adjusting to severely reduced energy supplies, to develop alternative sources with which to retrieve power.

The second factor, the computer had predicted, would support the first. The hysteria in the wake of the desolation of Mecca, fanned further by Idris Ali's call for jihad, would convulse the Muslim world. Islamic riots such as had never been seen would engulf the Middle East, Africa and Asia. Any American or Western installation, civil or military, in Muslim countries would be torn apart. Though waves of this hysteria would affect Russia also, the consequences would not be as severe. Russia would not flinch from using her iron fist.

Convincing stuff—if Idris Ali could believe that the U.S.A. and the West were paper tigers.

There were still other imponderables.

The computer had considered it conceivable that the shah of Iran, who never ceased declaring the Persian Gulf *mare nostrum* and who regarded an Islamic revival as anathema, might take unilateral action against Idris Ali to halt the tide of the jihad. The variables of this scenario rested on the as yet unascertainable strength of the religious opposition against the shah, emanating principally from one Ayatollah Khomeini, in exile in Najaf, Iraq. It was probable, the computer had promulgated, that in the wake of Operation Dragons, the inevitable Islamic uprising in Iran might gather instant momentum and topple the shah before the latter could dispatch forces against Idris Ali. However, on the possibility that the shah might prevail, the computer had advised the deployment of a Russian shield. Thus the Soviet naval infantry at Qatar, strategically placed in the Arabian Peninsula, would blunt the shah's attack, simultaneously creating a *casus belli* for Marshal Yeliseev, commander of Soviet land forces and Volkov's third co-conspirator, to invade Iran in a meat-grinder operation.

Still the imponderables remained. And each one hatched countless others—all beyond the reach of the computer.

In the final analysis, the computer itself was an imponderable. Man-fed, as Abu Ismail would judge it. How trustworthy could its visions be? Could it see across trends, scenarios, war games? Could it fathom national aspirations? What of China, for instance? The computer, evaluating China as unprepared for a global struggle, had excluded her from primary action. But what did it know of the quality of Chinese dreams? Or of Chinese fears of Russian hegemony? Then again, could the Americans and the West really agree to live in isolated bunkers while Islamic theocracy, Volkovist communism and free-floating anarchy, together or separately, assaulted them from every quarter?

More to the point. Could the computer probe all the behavioral aspects of man? Would every American soldier, or British, or French, obey his government's orders? Submit to weakness? Accept impotence? What if a nuclear submarine mutinied and fired her Polaris missiles? What if other patriots followed suit and launched ICBMs? What if the Christian, with the Jew wiped out, decided to extirpate Islam with a new crusade?

Or even more basic. What did the computer know of the strengths and weaknesses of Volkov? Could Volkov really take over the Presidium? In one fell swoop, as he had assured Idris Ali? Could he bring Washington to its knees?

Idris Ali checked his watch: 1:56.

There was one forecast that outweighed all imponderables.

On the most crucial analysis, that of Israel, Abu Ismail's *raison d'être* for Operation Dragons and the one country that would put up a fight, the computer had been brief and peremptory.

Since Israel would be accused of perpetrating Operation Dragons, Israel would perish. The accusation pronounced by Idris Ali as Al-Mahdi, and about which Abu Ismail had given ample warning in the Madrid press conference, would be accepted by the world's Muslim population as truth. No force on earth would convince a single soul among the Faithful that the desecration of Mecca could have been perpetrated by anybody else but Israel.

True, the Jewish state would fight her last war as she had often implied—Samson fashion, with her nuclear arsenal. Much of Syria, Iraq, Jordan and Egypt would be devastated. Yet the Islamic hordes would keep marching from the four corners of the world. The jihad, the computer had predicted, would last twenty-one days and claim the lives of an estimated one hundred and fifty million, at a ratio of fifty Muslims for each Israeli. And that would be the end of history for Jew, Arab and God/Allah. The new world would be cybernetic. Rational. Nonspiritual. Perfect.

Weighed against that prediction, imponderables shrank to irrelevance. The outcome could well be left to historic determinism or Allah's Will, whichever proved stronger.

At 2:00 P.M. precisely, Idris Ali signaled his confirmation to Volkov. When he signed off, he combed his hair. Not a single strand stuck to his comb. He started to laugh. Radiation sickness had not touched him. He had been preserved for the future. For who in his right mind, let alone Allah, would entrust tomorrow to an aging, arthritic mystic?

ADDIS ABABA, ETHIOPIA

Boaz, holding a towel against his groin, kept the door ajar. "News?"

"No . . ."

He started to close the door.

Sanbat stopped it with her foot. "May I come in?"

"I'm taking a shower. . . ."

She pushed the door and walked in. "Don't mind me . . . I'll pretend it's friendly. . . ."

"Pardon?"

"Whatever you're hiding behind your towel."

He stared at her with hostility.

She kept up her smile. She must not be intimidated. That was what Osman had advised. Let his fury subside. Then thaw him out. Be brazen. Funny. Seductive. Anything. Get him to respond. "Offer me a drink—or something."

"I'll get dressed."

"Why?"

She saw his anger, braved herself to weather it. She had tried to be brazen before. At Yad Mordechai he had picked her up and dumped her back in her room.

His voice remained controlled. "I don't like parading in the nude. . . ."

She forced a laugh. *Anything*, Osman had said. He copes with life by running away from emotions. Corner him. "You have a point there. I'll join the parade." She shed her clothes. A cotton dress. A pair of white bikini panties. Bra.

He watched her, unable to decide on his next move.

She stood still. She had good breasts, large and firm. Big pointed nipples. Thick, shapely arms. Muscular ebony legs. Not a sex symbol, but a strong woman in whom a strong man could find pleasure and solace. She had blemishes, too: protruding buttocks, stretch marks around her waist and sparse pubic hair that exaggerated, unattractively she thought, the folds of her vagina. But if Boaz could see these as the wear and tear of a good woman, a haven for the weary warrior, a source for the soul to drink at . . .

"Sanbat . . ."

His voice had faltered. She sat down on a chair. Encouraged. Less brazen. Cautious. "Now *you* are dressed. . . . Your towel . . ."

He sat on the bed, deliberately stared at a framed photograph on the bedside table. Getachew's Uncle Zewde, in the tattered uniform of an Abyssinian Irregular at the time of the Second World War. The uncle, dying peacefully in an old-age home, had willingly loaned his apartment as a temporary safe house.

He pressed the towel closer to his groin and directed his anger at himself. "I'm . . . aroused!"

"I am blessed. . . ."

He looked at her, and for a moment his eyes responded. She rose so that he could pull her to him. He shook his head in warning. She quickly sat down again.

He hunched his shoulders, clasped his arms around his body and rocked gently. She managed to stay still. His posture had become familiar. And unbearable. He had retreated to it at the slightest opportunity since the Danakil. Often in visible despair. Occasionally in suppressed rage. Getachew and Montblanc had begun to think he was ill—perhaps contaminated. At times he had been unsteady on his feet. Sanbat refused to believe it. The dizzy spells could be due to exhaustion.

Alternatively, and more likely, he had regressed to his neurosis. If so, it was up to her to save him. The odds were not totally against her. He had tasted her and had not been revolted. Also, he was not entirely broken. The soldier in him was functioning well. He had maintained command. Admirably. Even attending to finer details: supervising decontamination processes, instructing Commander Ilan on the arrangements for the Legionnaires' return to the T.F.A.I., overseeing the storage of WOJ's surplus plutonium canisters in the confines of the missile boats.

And there had been more action to exacerbate the exhaustion. Since the night of April 12, when the Reshevs had landed them on a deserted beach near Assab, they had been ferreting for Wolde, now their only lead to Idris Ali. Sanbat, through the Falashas, had secured intelligence on the layout of the priests' rest house next to Assab's new church, where Wolde had ambushed Dedeyan and where his paratroopers had been billeted. Boaz, Osman, Geta-

chew and Montblanc, leading the Tigreans in a four-pronged attack, had duly stormed it. Wolde and his men, they had
discovered, had decamped. Thereafter, still hoping to catch up
with them, they had hired every available car and scoured the
desert. They had abandoned the search only when Bayyu, coor-
dinating signals from other Falasha lookouts, had informed them
that Wolde was reported to be on leave in Addis Ababa. So, bidding a sad farewell to the Tigreans, who would have been ineffective in the city, they had rushed to the capital.

Sanbat forced herself to provoke conversation. "Montblanc's
out seeking informers in the underworld. Getachew's trying to see
the emperor."

Boaz grunted. Getachew had been trying to see the emperor
since their arrival in Addis Ababa. But the unrest, the strikes, the
string of demonstrations—activated or merely threatened—had
kept the emperor too distracted or too busy.

"Waste of time. The emperor won't listen to him. He's fighting
for his throne. Even if he did, he can't help. He has little power.
Getachew can't see it, but this country's about to collapse. In the
short time we've been in the Danakil, the situation has deteriorated. The Dergue has taken over—bar the shouting. Wolde's safe
wherever he's hiding. The Dergue will block anybody looking for
him."

Sanbat pursed her lips doubtfully. The emperor had just pronounced his grandson Asfa Wossen his heir. The news had convinced the Ethiopian in her that the Imperial Throne was
inviolate. "Osman's out, too. Checking on the safe house."

Boaz stopped rocking. Since the Danakil, he had disavowed
Osman. Pointedly, he changed the subject. "Any news from the
Falashas?"

"They're combing the borders—every available man."

"My hopes lie with them. If they can locate Wolde or Idris Ali
before Abu Ismail gets here, we stand a chance."

Sanbat kept up the discussion. Though he was now oblivious
to her nudity, she was encouraged that he was prepared to talk.
"You still think Abu Ismail will take charge?"

"Yes."

"How will he get here? We're patrolling the sea. The borders
with Sudan and Somalia are closed. He can't just land somewhere
in full daylight."

"Sealed borders won't stop him. North and northwest, the ELF
are in control. They've had help from the Sudan before. There's
no reason why they won't now, particularly when Abu Ismail calls

the tune with cash. South, it's the Ogaden. There the Somalis have the upper hand. There, it's not even just Muslim prepared to help Muslim: Somalis and Ethiopians are historic enemies. West, it's the Sudan again. And mostly, the border is just a line on the map. Endless stretches of wasteland or mountains, unguarded except for the odd frontier post in the middle of nowhere. Southwest, still the Sudan. And this time it's the Sudd. Another wilderness. He's got a million points of entry."

"But he's a sick man, Boaz. He'd never chance a strenuous journey."

"Wouldn't he? If Allah sustained him?"

Sanbat sat still, seeking another topic of conversation. "The safe house can quarter an army apparently. . . ."

The safe house, as opposed to Getachew's uncle's flat, had become necessary to accommodate the special squads Boaz had requested from the Memouneh.

He rasped in sudden venom. "Did he send you? Osman?"

Sanbat pretended not to understand. "I told you, Osman's out—"

"He shouldn't be out. He has no need to check the safe house. Getachew wouldn't come up with a dud."

"Maybe he's fed up. Waiting . . ."

"He's got bullet wounds on his face! A bad leg! And he's white! Conspicuous! I told him! Here in Addis, he and I stay in the background. Let Getachew and Montblanc do the running. . . ."

Sanbat made a helpless gesture.

Boaz shouted. "Is that why he left? For you to put on this show?"

Sanbat forced a pained laugh. "No."

Boaz started rocking again.

Sanbat rose, suddenly angry. "Is that·what you think of me? That I'd act the whore at anyone's bidding?"

"Is that what you've been doing?"

"Yes!"

"Why?"

"To arouse you!"

Boaz flung off the towel and catapulted over to her. "Well, you've aroused me. So what?"

Sanbat clutched him, pressed her face against his stomach, shuddered as she felt his penis throb against her breast. "Can't you understand? I want you to live. . . . You won't forgive me for loving you. I thought you might accept me if I were . . . anonymous. . . . Don't you see, I'd do anything to keep you alive. . . ."

Boaz tried to extricate himself. "Except leave me alone."

She clung to him. "I'd do that, too. If—if I believed you wanted to live."

He stood still. "All right, Sanbat, I understand. But why won't you understand me? Why should I want to live?"

She clung to him desperately. His erection, her only hope. "Look at you."

"Means nothing."

"Means everything. You want me. I'm the first person you've wanted. Take me."

"And then what?"

"Then take me again, and again. And again. Until all you can think of is the honey between my legs! Not death! Not death!"

"I've earned my death!"

She outshouted him: "Kiss my nipples! Bury yourself inside me!"

He tried to push her away. She fell on her knees, clutched at his penis. He pulled her up sharply, lifted her and lowered her onto the bed. "I want to make love to you. . . ."

She dared not look at him. "Am I stopping you? Come. Come into me." She spun her legs about him, locked him inside her. "Be happy, my Boaz, be happy. . . ."

April 16, 1974

HATZERIM, ISRAEL

"We'll bury him in Arlington. With portholes in his coffin! He wasn't pissed up against a wall, you know! He was born the best!"

"They all were."

"You haven't been to Washington lately, old friend. Place is full of guys who killed baboons and stole their faces!"

Jameson's boss, Gentlemen Jim, was legendary for his barracks language. Few apart from the Memouneh knew that it was the professional veneer of a man who could scream only when alone.

Jameson's coffin disappeared into the cargo hold of the U.S. Air Force Boeing 707. The Israeli guard of honor marched off silently.

The Memouneh fumbled for his cigarettes. He had started smoking again. What a travesty to have stopped. Fear of cancer! After the funerals of Kiryat Shmona. After Dedeyan's burial at Mount Herzl, Jerusalem, alongside Israel's heroes.

He registered Kidan's drone behind him, rambling on to Charlie Quinn about the Hatzerim air base and its special importance.

Available to the U.S. as a staging base for troops such as the 82nd Airborne should Uncle Sam decide to police any part of the Middle East.

Quinn was not listening. Jameson's death had hit him hard. A pointer to Fawzi's meager chances. There were no limits to Kidan's asininity.

"Old friend, I gotta get back. Or nobody would know whether he wants a shit or a haircut."

The Memouneh faced Gentleman Jim, offered his hand. "Thanks for rushing over at such short notice."

Gentleman Jim shook hands fervently. "It's final—your decision to go to Ethiopia?"

"It is."

"Great. Anyone else wouldn't know how to organize a fuck in a brothel."

"I hope it's not too late."

"April twenty-fifth—your Independence Day. That's when Abu Ismail will attack—which gives us nine days."

The Memouneh nodded, but not with great assurance. That was the date announced by Abu Ismail during the Madrid press conference.

"Like I said, old friend. I'll crack Washington bang between the legs. I'll have every available plane in the air. I'll seal the target area so that not even a locust can get through."

Again the Memouneh nodded. Now the old fear haunted him. He had never actually heard Aaron's tape—Osman had kept it hidden. What if Abu Ismail had known Aaron had peppered Mount Nebo with microphones? And had fooled him with the tallest story he could think of? A diversion—to paralyze Israelis and Jordanians alike? What if the target was an Israeli city? Jerusalem—as the Memouneh had first believed?

"I've already got the Seventh Fleet steaming. Set sail from the Philippines on the eleventh. It'll take them ten days to get to the Red Sea. In good time. Which brings me to the joker in the pack. The Russkies . . ."

The Memouneh pursed his lips. The possibility of a WOJ-Russian connection had been preoccupying Mossad and the CIA ever since Hamdi had divulged Idris Ali's mysterious communication with Moscow. "I've already stuck my neck out, Jim. I believe there is a Russian connection. I'm also convinced it's not linked to the Russian Establishment. Moscow hasn't been stalking WOJ the way we have. More important, the KGB hasn't been monitoring WOJ —unprecedented for a Russian alliance. That's why we haven't picked up any echoes."

"That means someone's been putting spots on the dominoes."

"My guess is one of Idris Ali's old mentors. Someone high up in the KGB—with a big tail."

"Which makes me fear a fate worse than death, old friend. That's why you need the armies I can put at your disposal. The bigger the balls, the better the man."

The Memouneh's voice regained its resolve. "We've gone over all that, Jim. Armies are no good. If the Russian connection is not sanctioned by the Kremlin, there won't be an overt Russian action. If we start an invasion, we risk a Russian reaction. Alternatively, we might push WOJ into detonating the bomb anywhere. Just give me the men I asked for."

"One dozen *black* CIA agents from Special Operations? To do the soft-shoe shuffle? I've tried sucking that proposition every which way. Doesn't give me a hard-on. You need extra muscle."

"We have extra muscle."

"Twenty Sayeret Matkal boys?"

"That's what Boaz asked for. And only as standby."

"Boaz might have fried his brains, old friend. He can't know for sure what he wants."

"Everybody out there agrees with him—including your man Montblanc."

Gentleman Jim stared for a long time at the desert. He breathed deeply several times, as if seeking the essence of the Negev. "All right! You'll get the CIA-SO boys. But I'm leaving Charlie Quinn here. He's gonna stick to you like a bluebottle sticks to shit. You start having second thoughts, he'll holler, and I'll come riding in with the cavalry!"

ADDIS ABABA, ETHIOPIA

To Getachew, the news on the radio, by its very omissions, was disheartening. The capital was combustive, waiting impatiently for a spark.

Ethiopia's Muslim community, seeking improvements to minority rights, had called a massive demonstration for Saturday, April 20. All over the country dignitaries and their supporters were setting out for Addis Ababa.

The Dergue, too, had announced its own demonstration—not to stifle the Muslim voice, but to prove with a show of strength that the people wished to entrust the affairs of the country to the Armed Forces Committee. This demonstration, blatantly called *Four Days of Confusion*, would commence on Monday, the twenty-second.

Getachew turned off the radio, took another mouthful of *kati kala* and moved to the window.

According to the capital's most persistent rumor, the architect of both the Muslim demonstration and the Four Days of Confusion had been one man, Captain Wolde, the Dergue's pinup soldier. If so, the demonstration was set to prime a process that would not only accelerate the emperor's downfall, but also provide freedom of movement to Abu Ismail on WOJ's D-Day.

Getachew drew open the curtains and stared into the night, out of habit, with a professional eye.

The safe house, squeezed between the Ecuadorian and Ivory Coast embassies and surrounded by eucalyptus trees, represented the only positive gain of the last two days. It was perfectly secluded and defensible. The grounds offered command over the approaches, and the guard hut by the gate provided an excellent lookout post on Airport Road, one of the capital's principal arteries. The house had been empty since its owner, a minor Ethiopian noblewoman, had married one of her neighbors, an Ecuadorian embassy official, and moved to Quito. Getachew had secured it from the agent managing the property with no questions asked. The prevailing unrest had prompted most of the upper class to depart for indefinite holidays abroad, and the market had been flooded with property for rent.

It was a huge, rambling house—of the type he had coveted in the past. To provincial eyes such a habitation signified status—a home which could accommodate wife, children, parents, in-laws, brothers, sisters, their respective families, onward and outward. A field alive with the seeds of its future.

There were no longer traces of his youthful envy. He had renounced status. It invariably fed on injustice. He had also renounced family in favor of country. He had never regretted the condition. But now, this creed, too, had withered. Now, he could not even return to his modest house for fear someone was lying in ambush. He was an outcast in his own homeland.

The emperor had finally seen him. And had dismissed him. The emperor had no time to worry about an Arab terrorist unit. The emperor could not believe Ethiopia and the world stood threatened by nuclear terrorism. The emperor would certainly not trust foreign agents who made such preposterous claims. The emperor was only just awakening to the threats of the Dergue's creeping coup. The emperor had told him that he would be better advised to return to his desk at ISS headquarters and unearth the traitors undermining his absolute, God-inspired rule. The emperor would consider that proof of Getachew's loyalty which, according to army rumors, now stood in question.

He had almost done as he had been bidden—knowing that rumors about his loyalty must have emanated from Wolde, and that if he stepped into his office he would be dragged out on Wolde's orders by some vigilante group, and purged. It had been a great temptation to throw away a life that, overnight, had ceased to have a purpose. He understood now the forces that had brutalized Boaz with cravings for self-destruction. To fall on one's own sword was an honorable way to defy the squalor of an arbitrary morality.

But he had disobeyed the emperor. Possibly he still valued his life. Probably he wanted to sell it dear. Most certainly, he believed he could preserve both his beloved land and the thread that kept it united—the Imperial Throne—by fighting his allies' war.

"Getting drunk, pal?"

Getachew spun around.

Montblanc walked in hesitantly. "Mind if I join you?"

Getachew shrugged, then smiled. "You're most welcome." He offered the bottle. "It's *kati kala*."

"Strong stuff, eh? That'll do nicely." Montblanc took a large swig, then passed the bottle back.

Getachew started to shake. Standing bottle in hand with an American for company, his mind refocused on his grief. He remembered the occasion, after Harar and jail and just before Jameson's departure for home, getting drunk in a bar. Jameson had talked about his aspirations, his subsequent disenchantment. And he had promised to return. To share Getachew's grave, as he had put it. "You're a good man, Montblanc. That's what he said. *In vino veritas*."

"Who?"

"Al Jameson. Who did you think?"

"I thought maybe the emperor. Then I thought if the emperor knows about me, we're in trouble. . . ."

Getachew forced a laugh. "What's happening in there?"

"Osman's taking the night watch. Sanbat's manning the radio. Falasha lookouts have picked up some rumors—various groups at remote corners of the country. Nothing specific yet. Boaz—in his room. Still cool toward Osman." Montblanc paced the room. "It might be a good thing, Getachew . . . a revolution. . . ."

"Sure. If it were carried out by good men . . ."

"Some of the Dergue must be good men. . . ."

"If they are they won't survive. Win or lose."

"Surely if they win . . ."

"They'll be weeded out."

"By Wolde you mean?"

Getachew stared out of the window, suddenly sober. "It's not just Wolde. It's the philosophy that creates the Woldes. Civilization, Jameson called it. The world is a slaughterhouse. Our age has abolished the commandments, detached itself from morality. We're now offered the universe in return for a bit of blood. Well, certainly the promise of blood will be fulfilled. But the universe . . . ? That will go, as it has always done, to a few men in uniforms."

"Come on, Getachew."

"I'll tell you something else. I, for one, would accept that. If I could believe there'd be an extra bowl of soup for the hungry. But if anybody receives an extra bowl of soup he'll receive it not because it's his right, but so that he can carry the men in uniforms. Or—and this is even more frightening—because the uniforms have killed most of those around him. Dead men's swill."

"If I believed that, I'd blow my brains out. . . ."

"Boaz believes it."

"Neither you nor Boaz have the copyright on truth."

"What do you believe in, Montblanc?"

"Corny as it may sound . . . the principles of the American Declaration of Independence."

"You surprise me."

"I surprise many people."

"I wasn't doubting your word. I'm amazed by your innocence. You might as well search for the alchemist's gold."

Montblanc shook his head resolutely. "I disagree. Where do we go from here?"

"Nowhere. We can't even get drunk. At least, I can't."

"We can try. It's one way of whiling away the time."

Getachew grinned ruefully. "What's left of it . . ."

April 17, 1974

TRIPOLI, LIBYA

"Who walks by your side, Mr. Volkov? Ivan the Terrible? Catherine the Great? The Jew Marx? Lenin? Stalin?"

"Do you mean, who has influenced me most?"

"I do not mean that at all. Who walks by your side?"

"I fly my own banner."

"In other words, you walk alone."

Volkov sighed to contain his exasperation. Dialogue with Arabs was a Sisyphean task; whenever you approached the summit, the arguments rolled back. Frustration was further compounded by the fact that they had to converse in English—of which Abu Ismail had better command. "We all walk alone."

"Not I."

Volkov looked up. "Who walks beside you—apart from Qaddafi?"

"Allah."

Volkov lost interest. "Oh, Him."

"Do you not feel His presence by my side? Covering me. Sustaining me like the very air."

Volkov smiled uneasily. "You must forgive me, Abu Ismail. I am an atheist. I can see God only as a drug."

"Ah, the great revolutionary doctrine. The opium of the masses. It surprises me that you, too, should have been brainwashed. Even assuming Allah or religion were an opiate, what of it? Words. Dictates. Denouncements. What do they change? Opium grows. You cannot burn all the fields. And if you could, there would be a new crop next season. When you understand that, you understand everything. You still have a little time left."

Volkov glanced at Nazmi, Abu Ismail's bodyguard, standing by the door, nodding as if privy to a dark secret. "Do I detect a warning, Abu Ismail?"

Abu Ismail smiled for the first time since receiving Volkov. "Allah warns us. Every moment—if you listen. Which is another proof of his immanence."

Volkov spread his arms expansively. "What can I say? I respect your faith."

Abu Ismail blinked, drank some orange juice. Volkov picked up the small cup of Turkish coffee which Abu Ismail had personally poured for him. He took a sip and pursed his lips.

Abu Ismail watched him inscrutably. "Bitter?"

Volkov offered a polite smile. "A little."

"We make it bitter to remind us of our usurped history. And, of course, of the battles ahead. But those who share the bitterness seal many bonds."

Volkov gallantly took another sip. "I can share it."

Abu Ismail blinked again.

Volkov consumed his coffee distastefully and watched Abu Ismail plunge yet again into meditation. The tenth time since the banquet had started. First, the anorexic man took a morsel of the new course in the manner of a good host vouchsafing the quality of his table. Then a pseudopolitical exchange. Then the rush to rest his face on Allah's bosom. The charade would, no doubt, have impressed woolly heads, like those of the gerontocracy in the Kremlin. Volkov had ceased to be amused. Devotion and ritual, whether indulged by lesser people like Arabs or by Politburo sentimentalists, were heirlooms of history. Anathema to the new Russian, armored against passion.

He finished his coffee and reverted, in boredom, to viewing the salon. Furnished like a harem from the Arabian Nights. Fantasy for Rimski-Korsakov. Incongruous with all that extravaganza was the Louis XVI chair—the one Abu Ismail made a point of offering to heads of state. He, too, had sat on that chair. Which had confirmed his initial estimation: that Abu Ismail stood cap in hand, waiting for the right moment to beg. The invitation had merely been an Arab exercise in face-saving.

He still did not know, though, just what Abu Ismail would beg of him. The meticulous care with which he had been whisked away from the airport, the priceless gifts and the royal welcome all suggested a major deal. He kept an open mind. That was the secret to securing better allies.

It did not matter that his deal with Idris Ali had already been sealed. Idris Ali was expendable. Providing, of course, Abu Ismail submitted unconditionally. The returns would be greater. For one thing, Abu Ismail could not live and court history for as long as Idris Ali. He was a sick man. Already halfway to Allah's dung heap.

Volkov felt hot. He loosened his tie, then caught Abu Ismail's eye. Allah's catarrh had come down to earth and was watching him intently. He tried to breathe deeply but found it difficult.

"Time to talk, Volkov."

Volkov stiffened at the abrupt manner of address, but could not protest. He felt he was suffocating. He had eaten too much of the barbarian's food. "Yes . . . Now—"

Abu Ismail cut him short. "I will talk. You will listen."

Volkov nodded. He needed a moment to compose himself. He was nauseous. He could feel his body clenching. He unbuttoned his shirt to ease his breathing.

Abu Ismail rose painfully. "And listen well, Volkov. What I am going to say will remain in this room. Forever."

Volkov twitched, tried to catch his breath, fought gripping fears of a heart attack. He clung to Abu Ismail's words as if their reality offered the remedy to his sudden indisposition. "I'll be . . . very discreet."

Abu Ismail continued as though Volkov had not spoken. "I need not say it, but I want you to know what a fool you have been. . . ."

Volkov felt his mouth run dry. "Fool . . . ?"

"For subverting Idris Ali."

Volkov steadied himself. For a brief moment, as he glared at

Abu Ismail's eyes, he conquered his panic and regulated his breathing. Then, as if kicked from behind, he started convulsing.

"You amaze me, you Russians. You want to devour the world, but look at you, choking as if you had just swallowed a porcupine. Fools, Volkov, fools! Worse than animals. At least animals know what is prey and what is not. Nobody betrays Islam, Volkov, and survives. Least of all Communists . . ."

Volkov gasped for breath. "What . . . ? I don't understand. . . ."

"You do not *understand!* That is your failing, Russian. You do not understand people. Not the Jew. Nor the Christian. Nor the Muslim. Not your so-called satellites. Not even yourselves."

Volkov panted. "I'm not well . . . A doctor . . . please. . . ."

"Will not help. You have been poisoned!"

Volkov, barely registering the remark, collapsed with another bout of convulsions.

Abu Ismail watched him impassively, then continued. "I will tell you, Volkov—to increase the pain—why you so miscalculated. Why everybody is miscalculating. Allah's immanence—you mock it! But the joke is on you. Allah is here watching you die. Embracing me because I am doing His Will. Similarly, outside, the world is mocking me. But there again, the joke is on the world. It will soon crawl . . . as you are crawling now. . . ."

Abruptly, Volkov's convulsions stopped. He pulled himself up, even smiled, realizing he could breathe again. "It's passed."

"A brief respite. The cycles get shorter as the poison spreads."

Volkov darted a look at Nazmi. The bodyguard had not moved nor shown signs of menace. He attempted to laugh. "You didn't invite me all the way here just to kill me. . . ."

Abu Ismail turned to him contemptuously. "There you are. No idea how our minds work. *My* mind works. How Allah ordains His Will. Why should I not have invited you here to kill you? Where else would you be so defenseless?"

Volkov tried to rise, determined, if he had the strength, to strike Abu Ismail down. His legs gave way beneath him. He moaned. "Why should you want to kill me?"

"You have served your purpose."

"Hardly. We're on the threshold . . ."

"Also—for revenge. For subverting Idris Ali. Until you sucked out his blood with your fangs, he was one of Allah's servants."

Volkov shook his head in an effort to clear it. He could not think when he had been poisoned—*if* he had been poisoned. He could not understand why he did not rant and rave. His mind was too busy fighting the pain. "He betrayed me—did he? Reported my last signal?"

Abu Ismail moved menacingly. "What last signal?"

"To Gambela. He must have. How else would you have known?"

"I have known it for months. Did you think I would be blind to what was happening under my own wing? When a demon possesses a servant of Allah, the firmament shakes!"

Volkov sneered. "Servant of Allah? Idris Ali is a little Arab yearning to be a cossack. When I picked him up from the sewers, he ate out of my hands. He hasn't changed, I promise you."

Abu Ismail shook his head sadly. "What a pity for him."

"And for you. If all of Allah's servants are like him . . ."

"They are not."

Volkov, encouraged that his breathing had steadied again, made another attempt to rise. This time he managed to stand up. "Do you really think you—Allah-drunk—can conquer the world . . . ? When *we* are here?"

Abu Ismail moved swiftly and slapped him. Volkov, hardly expecting such agility from an arthritic, collapsed in surprise. "You can move. . . ."

"When I have to. Allah is with me."

Volkov started to convulse again. "Stop talking to me about Allah! We'll trample upon you all. You don't know the Russian might!"

Abu Ismail thundered over Volkov's shrieks. "I know the Russian might. But, more important, I know the Russian mind. Godless men, scheming to become gods! We have nothing to fear from you."

Volkov groaned as his breathing faltered. He tried to cry out, but his jaws locked. He managed to talk through his teeth: "You can't win."

Abu Ismail, moving freely, paced the room. "I will tell you how we shall win. On wings of death! Our noblest inspiration! It is this factor—the call of jihad—the sanction of an Islamic leader, of Al-Mahdi, to sacrifice multitudes for Allah's Will—that raises us above the Infidel. While the Jew and Christian worry how many sons and daughters might die, we laugh and exult. While the damned, like you, try to burgle our house, we burn the house and you with it! That is why even if few of us survive, we shall conquer!"

Volkov had ceased listening to him and was flailing on the floor. He could barely mumble through his clenched jaws. "What . . . sort of . . . poison?"

Abu Ismail turned to him as though distracted by his presence. "Strychnine."

"How . . . how . . . ?"

374 • THE LAST OF DAYS

"In the coffee. You have less than two hours. . . ."

Volkov panted, managed to scream. "Why? We could have . . . together we could have . . . An antidote . . . There must be an antidote. . . ."

"There is none. You will die of asphyxia or exhaustion."

Volkov convulsed again. A part of his mind wondered how he, with years of experience in techniques of assassination, could have fallen prey so easily. The seduction of power . . . "You couldn't . . . You couldn't stand . . . and watch me die. . . ."

Abu Ismail smiled grimly. "I will tell you something nobody knows, Russian. When I was eighteen, in Palestine, I took a wife, Ruqayya. Named after one of the Prophet's daughters. She did her duty immediately and conceived within the month. But at the time of her delivery, she failed. Both she and my firstborn, whom I had named after the Prophet, died within hours. I watched them die. I realized I was watching Allah's Will at work. He had given them to me, and He had taken them away. With good reason. I was to be Al-Mahdi. Allowed to taste worldly pleasures briefly, but never to indulge. Since then I have seen other sons die. Those born of my flesh and ordained to spread the Divine seed, I planted on Infidel soil. Those who by serving me had become my sons, I sacrificed—in continuous battle. Do you think it would disturb me to watch you die? You who have done the Devil's work?"

Volkov tossed about in agony. "Mercy? Have you no mercy?"

"We have one last transaction, Russian. You shall divulge the details of your conspiracy with Idris Ali. You will also provide the data that will activate your support units on the Day of Glory."

Volkov gradually stopped convulsing. He grabbed the Louis XVI chair and managed to pull himself up. He took deep breaths, trying to make the most of another brief respite. He thumped his chest in an effort to disperse the pressure on his heart. Then, as the convulsions started again, he collapsed, frothing at the mouth. "I will. . . . Yes. . . . Only . . . stop the pain. . . ."

Abu Ismail stooped over him. "The codes: Standby. Readiness. Launch. Abort. All of them!"

"No . . . They will abort . . . automatically . . . if you fail to reach . . . their umbrella."

"Radio frequencies. Identification and fail-safe proce-dures . . ."

"Complicated. I—I can't write . . ."

"Just talk. The room is full of microphones. Everything is being recorded."

"Please . . . please . . . Stop the pain. . . ."

"In Russian, if it's easier. We have translators."

Volkov bit his lips and chewed on them until the pain overrode that of the poison. He clutched the chair, spitting blood, panting, scarcely able to breathe. He managed a hoarse whisper. "I won't. . . ."

Abu Ismail signaled to Nazmi. The bodyguard brought a hypodermic needle, pinned Volkov down with his bulk and injected him.

Abu Ismail's eyes blazed. "*Sodium pentathol.* The truth drug. You will talk. I could have given you a pain-killer, too, but I want you to die a terrible death, Volkov! Idris Ali was a son to me! You killed him! This is the punishment!"

He walked out, leaving Volkov thrashing in agony.

Volkov lived for another two hours. And talked. Abu Ismail watched from the command room. At the moment of Volkov's death, he whirled on strong legs and ascended his mystical plains. Allah's martyrs received him with accolades, as their avenger, too.

Al-Munafiq, The Doubter, whose shadow he had seen skulking about in the past few days, dared not appear. Nor did the pains in his limbs.

RAMLA, ISRAEL

The Memouneh studied the faces surrounding him. The twenty men of various ranks were all black, or near enough: Yemenites, Cochin Indians, Falashas. Eighteen were soldiers and had been pulled out from special units on the Golan where sporadic fighting had persisted since the October cease-fire. The remaining two were surgeons with exemplary war records in field hospitals. Every one of them had served with distinction in at least two Sayeret Matkal operations. They were attentive, showing no signs of fatigue, even though, in the past few days, they had hardly slept. Whenever they had taken a breather from exercises, they had had to brief themselves on Ethiopia and on the layout of important cities and installations.

"The country is on the brink of disaster. We could find ourselves operating with relative ease. Conversely, we could be hampered every inch of the way." He stubbed out his cigarette, lit a new one. "Never drop your guard. You will be there as tourists. You will have false passports. While these will pass muster, they're likely to stir things up should you provoke the authorities to check your identities with relevant embassies. We have a safe house, but should we have to move suddenly, regroup and lie low as soon as you can. Always speak Arabic or English. Be extracareful when you count—that's when slipups occur."

He paused, scanned the faces again. Amnon, Avishai, Uri, Dov, Misha, Shimshon, Nehemiah, Dan, Chaim, Emmanuel, Yitzhaq, Aharon, Yigal, Ehud, Zeev, Issahar, Menahem, Shabtai. Some of them were boys. But he saw them as old and heavy-hearted. They were veterans of three wars as well as countless engagements with Al-Fatah cells. Now they were waiting to be sent to Africa, separately via widely divergent routes from European capitals to Addis Ababa. They would change planes, sometimes four times, on tickets purchased in various countries by Mossad from a host of airlines.

The Memouneh continued, pointing at the surgeons. "We have medics, Yonatan and Arik. They are miracle workers. But we do not have full backup. Even if we knew where the action will be, we could not provide it. We shall, however, have equipment and supplies in the safe house. You will all carry first-aid kits. I know if anybody falls, he can depend on his comrades. At the risk of boring you with my usual cliché, I beg you, don't fraternize with enemy bullets." He waited for the brief laughter to subside. "Any questions?"

Major Amnon, senior officer until either Boaz or the Memouneh assumed command, raised his hand. "Just to clarify. Guns, ammunition and equipment are provided by the Americans . . ."

The Memouneh nodded at Quinn to take the question.

Quinn rose from his seat. "Yes. As with the medical equipment. We've assembled quite an arsenal. For security reasons, we preferred to go cloak-and-dagger rather than with a transfer of material from Kagnew. They'll be dispatched direct from Camp Peary, Virginia, in a diplomatic bag. They'll also have an escort—twelve CIA Special Operations agents. Furthermore, as of yesterday, we have at our disposal a Sikorsky S-58T helicopter and a De Havilland Twin Otter 300 utility feeder liner—both registered to USAID. These will be on standby at Addis airport for major operations, if any."

Amnon nodded, impressed.

The Memouneh stubbed out his cigarette. "Anything else?"

The men remained silent.

"Very well. You'll continue with your special exercises until the last moment. You're scheduled to commence departure on the nineteenth—unless I call abort. Each one of you has a round-about route, for obvious security reasons. You will get to Addis just before the Four Days of Confusion. You'll make your way to the safe house on foot—in case the confusion is not all that confused. Kidan has your passports and tickets."

The men rose.

The Memouneh raised his hand. "One other thing. I pray I shall be in a position to call abort. Then again, when you get there, you may just sit and do nothing. I'll pray for that, too. If, however, we do go into action, we may never come back. None of us. If so, we shall die for a good cause—for what it's worth. But certainly in good company."

The men nodded soberly, then moved to Kidan, seated at a desk by the door. They collected their travel folders and left the room in a stream of Shaloms.

The Memouneh caught Kidan's eye. Kidan would not be among those traveling. He had been assigned to investigate a series of bomb outrages in Jerusalem.

The Memouneh joined Quinn. They were departing early the next morning. Their route was relatively short: Tel Aviv to Addis Ababa via Paris and Djibouti.

At the door, Kidan handed him his false passport and ticket. The Memouneh took comfort from Kidan's murderous resentment. At least, as far as the Jews were concerned, the bad men were being left behind.

ADDIS ABABA, ETHIOPIA

They had hired new cars.

Montblanc, at the back of the Fiat 124, kept watch by the rear window. Osman, also in the back, covered the left flank. Boaz, in the front passenger seat, the right. Getachew drove, avoiding main roads.

A tip-off from one of Montblanc's underworld contacts locating Wolde in a bar in the Mercato had sent them scurrying. The suspect had turned out to be a merchant from Massawa, throwing his money at barmaids. They had not spoken since regaining the car.

They approached Maskal Square. They had to cross it before diverting to a labyrinth of narrow streets, and thence to the discreet side entrance of the safe house. Earlier the square had been filling with Muslim crowds, fresh arrivals for Saturday's demonstrations. Police and troops, disoriented by divided loyalties to the throne and the Dergue, had been generally obstructive, particularly against Europeans, cast by Marxist elements as Ethiopia's vultures.

Getachew slowed down as he caught sight of the crowds. "Road blocks ahead!"

Boaz rasped. "Open the windows! And sing—robustly!"

They wound down their windows. Addis Ababa's high-altitude night air, cold even in summer, jolted them.

They started singing an army song which Getachew had taught them. The Muslim crowd would jeer at them. But they hoped the police and troops would look upon them as influential officers on a night out and wave them on. Unless Wolde had come out of hiding and ordered every unit to check every car, in which case they would have to fight their way through. Boaz and Osman, despite their black makeup, would draw attention by their inability to converse in Amharic; Getachew would be wanted by Wolde.

Getachew entered the traffic circle, barely restraining the impulse to accelerate. Boaz, Osman and Montblanc continued singing, hands on the safety catch of their guns. The crowd jeered. Some threw stones.

Getachew, taking the third exit into Africa Avenue, drove toward the road block. Two policemen waved him down. Troops emerged from the dark, guns at the ready. Getachew thrust his head out of the window. "Watch that fucking crowd!"

The police and troops reacted to the command instinctively.

Getachew, accelerating, continued shouting. "I've got important brothers here! Get out of the way!"

The police and troops scampered. Getachew sped into the darkness. Montblanc kept his eyes on the rear window. The police and troops stared after them uncertainly, then, as the crowd moved into Africa Avenue, turned around and closed ranks.

Montblanc tapped Getachew's shoulder. "We're clear."

Getachew exhaled in relief and turned into a side street. The rest of the journey would be quiet.

Osman gave vent to his frustration. "We're chasing dead ends. We'll never find Wolde. He'll lie low until Abu Ismail gets here!"

Montblanc grunted agreement. This was their first sortie since arriving in Addis Ababa. A single, miserable lead. A false one at that. Forcing them all out, despite every rule on cautious procedure, to minimize the risks of failure.

Getachew picked up the argument. "*If* Abu Ismail gets here."

Osman murmured. "He's coming. He has to."

"Why?"

"He needs a plane. To bomb his target."

Montblanc interjected. "He's bringing his own."

"He won't use his own. Too easy to identify. He needs an international airport. Or an air base. Addis it must be."

Getachew remained dubious. "Why not Asmara? Asmara has both an international airport and an air base."

"There are Americans in Asmara. Also, the Four Days of Confusion are scheduled mainly for Addis." He leaned toward Boaz. "You think so, too—don't you?"

Boaz, pointedly snubbing Osman, inspected his gun.

Osman snorted contemptuously. "Achilles is still sulking in his tent!"

Montblanc, disturbed by the continuing hostility between Boaz and Osman, tried to defuse the tension. "What do you think, Boaz?"

Boaz shrugged. They now knew Abu Ismail was coming. A team of Mossad agents, diverted from other Arab countries to Libya to keep watch on WOJ headquarters, had radioed the previous day that Abu Ismail, with sizable commando strength, had left for the WOJ training camp at Al Tawqarah, in the Libyan desert, and that he had boarded a Beechcraft B99, a turboprop light commercial feeder liner, instead of the Grumman Gulfstream II executive jet he normally flew. Since the Beechcraft was more suitable for unsophisticated airstrips and since, the agents had established, Abu Ismail had not reached his purported destination, the indications were that he had departed for the assault point. "Yes! He's coming!"

Osman shouted mockingly. "We got him talking!"

Boaz spoke through clenched teeth. "Where does that get us?"

Osman bellowed. "We can waylay him! We'll have the men! The CIA boys, your boys . . ."

"Where? All I know is he won't come by a conventional route. He's got to stay out of the limelight in case we or the Americans intercept him or in case governments friendly to WOJ delay him with protocol. Equally, he won't come through the front door. It occurred to me he might try to intimidate the emperor by threatening to wreak havoc with the bomb. But his D-Day is the twenty-fifth—eight days from now. Even if the bluff worked, he wouldn't want to give the emperor time to plan countermeasures."

Osman's tone became friendlier. "If we accept what you say—and I do—we're wasting time looking for Wolde. We need to look for Idris Ali! If we find him, we'll know where Abu Ismail will be coming from. Because he will want to take charge of the bomb the moment he arrives. Idris Ali will be waiting near the entry point."

Boaz pushed himself upright. "Which brings me to my initial question: Where?"

"All right. Let's winnow again through our meager harvest. We have a number of possibilities from Sanbat's Falashas. A group of WHO doctors at Alghena—northern Eritrea, near the Sudanese border. Another WHO group at Tesene, northwest, and a FAO team at Metema, west—both also near the Sudanese border. Still near the Sudanese border, somewhere around Gambela, south-west, a group of botanists. Then south, near the Kenyan border, at Moyale—another FAO team. Southeast, at Kelafo, near the Somali border, a group of geologists prospecting for oil. East at Domo and Jijiga, both in the Ogaden, and near the Somali border, two more teams of oil prospectors. Take your pick."

Boaz snorted. "How do we check them all? We haven't the time or the facilities to hop from wilderness to wilderness!"

"Let's check the likeliest one."

"Which is?"

"The most isolated—and the easiest to get through. Moyale on the Kenyan border."

"Waste of time."

Boaz's conviction surprised Osman. "Why?"

"As a terrorist leader, Abu Ismail is *persona non grata* in Kenya. He wouldn't risk it. Second . . ." Boaz paused, allowing his sixth sense to take charge. The presentiment had been lurking in his mind for some time but he had not considered it simply because he had not dared trust his intuition as anything more than the raw nerve ends of a good soldier who anticipates the enemy and moves accordingly. Now it struck him again. And this time he knew it was valid. He knew his enemy. "Second—he won't choose an easy way."

"He's not in a position to choose. He's a sick man."

Boaz twisted around to face Osman, hostility forgotten. "Don't you see, Osman? He sees himself as a savior. And a savior must have a trial by fire. Prove himself to himself. Like Moses before the Red Sea. Like Jesus on the Cross. Like Mohammed at the battle of Uhud. Abu Ismail will choose the most difficult route."

Osman computed the possibilities. "There are two choices. Via the Sudd. Or the Ogaden. Gambela or Domo. Which one?"

Montblanc interjected. "The Ogaden's more difficult. Harsh terrain. Restricted area. Running the gauntlet of local tribes, Somali troops and the Ethiopian army."

Getachew contradicted him. "The Sudd's just as bad. It would be almost impassable now, in the rainy season. . . ."

Osman arbitrated. "Let's check them both. Let's have the Falashas concentrate around Gambela and Domo. . . ."

Boaz nodded. "Aerial reconnaissance, too. O'Brien should manage that. I expect both regions offer perfect hideouts, but we might get lucky."

Getachew interrupted the discussion by braking suddenly. Osman, Boaz and Montblanc swung their guns as a figure, suspended in the air, loomed ahead.

They gaped at it. A bearded Ethiopian in a mock uniform of the emperor hung from the branch of a tree, bearing a banner in Amharic.

Boaz whispered. "What's it say?"

Getachew translated. " 'Four Days of Confusion.' Hold tight—in case it's an ambush."

He accelerated, then stopped at a safe distance and looked back. "I knew the man . . . officer of the Imperial Bodyguard. The rest of the placard said he had been executed for being loyal to the emperor. Now we know what's in store."

April 18, 1974

THE SUDD, THE SUDAN

The papyrus rising in delicate wisps of tulle multiplied obsessively and glazed the horizon green. Occasionally purple eruptions of water hyacinths blotched the verdant expanse, revealing a new contender for the marshland.

Silence. Or rather, the ear ceased heeding the heavy rain, the gurglings of the swamp, the busy chatter of the water birds, the snorts of hippopotamuses coming up for air, the sudden stirrings of crocodiles seeking the sun whenever it stilled the rains and pierced through. The groans of the *sudds*, the decomposing vegetation that gave the wilderness its name, clustering, breaking and clustering again at the whim of the currents, provided a sinister pulse.

For those traversing this protean labyrinth, the silence betokened a primordial struggle: life's stoic acceptance that Creation exacted for its miracle the urge for decomposition.

Nine of the men endured it as such. The tenth, Abu Ismail, did not even hear the silence.

He wore a canvas cap emblazoned with the initials of the United Nations Food and Agriculture Organization. Except for his life jacket and a scarf tied around his loins, he was naked. His skin, coated with thick insect-repellent cream, shimmered. He cradled a Beretta BM59 rifle as if it were a child.

To Abbas, his pilot, he looked like Death, undraped and resting. Legs folded and tucked under; eyes drawing fire from the sun, darkness from the rain. The sack of millet which served as a cushion, and which bore the name of a Sudanese wholesaler, incongruously accentuated the supernaturality of the image. It provided proof that Al-Mahdi could inhabit the earth and the heavens at the same time.

Abu Ismail was inhabiting both realms—but not for the reasons Abbas presumed.

On earth, he was struggling against pain, failure and death. This was his first mission in the field since the late 1940s. All his accomplishments had been achieved either by the proxy of other powers or from the security of his headquarters, on the shoulders of giant warriors. He had forgotten that at the front line a man was often dispossessed of his love for Allah and faith in His Will, that with death and physical pain tugging at his elbow, he required superior brands of courage and spirit to discount his life.

And inconceivable as it seemed, he who loved Allah most, he who was Allah's Chosen, was in danger of disintegrating before the most contemptible human frailty, fear. He believed the Sudd sought to destroy him. If not by decomposing him in the fetid heat or by choking him with clouds of insects, then simply by engulfing him with its greasy rain.

Navigation was barely possible.

Whenever they cleared a channel, the *sudds* rushed menacingly to reclaim the ooze, or scurried ahead to lie in wait below the waterline like treacherous reefs, or spread out, frothing with white spume, before closing in like a sand drift. Even on the odd occasions when they came upon a clear stretch, the slime, as if to repel encroachment, resumed its Nilotic nature and flung the canoe at sudden whirlpools or at mud flats dissolving in the rain as quicksand.

Xenophon, the guide recruited from the South Sudanese Liberation Movement, was steering. Nazmi and the six-man squad, chosen for the Day of Glory, experienced an altogether different baptism of fire by constantly prizing the canoe from the clusters of rotting papyrus and water hyacinth.

To escape this reality and so control his fear, Abu Ismail ascended the heavens. But instead of respite, he found himself cornered by The Doubter, Al-Munafiq.

Here in the Sudd, The Doubter argued, Allah's ways did not seem mysterious, but haphazard. Here, Allah showed Himself not ineluctable, timeless, orderly and wise, but fickle, transient, chaotic and unsure. To support his argument, The Doubter pointed out the profligacy with which Allah wasted water on useless, faithless life.

Abu Ismail patiently explained. The Sudd was neither a challenge Allah had failed to meet nor a corner of the earth He had forgotten to put into final shape. What The Doubter failed to understand was that Allah created everything for a purpose. The Sudd was, in fact, the cornerstone in Allah's Design. The Sudd was a hazard created for the sole purpose of testing the true Al-Mahdi, as Eden had been created to test Adam. The Sudd had stood untouched by time—and judging by its green expanse, as a vast banner of Islam—simply to transport Allah's Deliverer to the Last of Days. The Sudd was where Al-Mahdi would become Allah's Image . . . or perish as a false savior.

"Hold tight! Hold tight! Hold tight!"

Abu Ismail gathered his divided self.

The current had accelerated. The walls of papyrus stalks had receded. The channel was clear, winding through a maze of islets that had suddenly appeared.

Xenophon, who had shouted the warning, was pointing ahead at an expanse of rocks spread across the water like mines.

Abu Ismail turned to Abbas. "Where are we?"

Abbas consulted his map. "Approaching Machar, I think."

Abu Ismail nodded. Machar was a riverine settlement on high ground, some twenty-five kilometers from the Sudan-Ethiopian border and perched where the main stream of the Sudd flowed into the Baro. Xenophon had briefed them that this stream, unnamed and barely distinguishable from myriad tributaries, lost itself in an islet-strewn delta a few kilometers before Machar. "We're making good progress, Abbas."

"Yes, Al-Mahdi." The confirmation did not carry conviction. Abbas was staring apprehensively at the rocks ahead.

When his eyes adjusted to the curtain of rain, Abu Ismail also saw the frothing waters and the spray rising to meet the downpour. He realized that his fears had been projections, like radar beams bouncing back, of this singular hazard. And that his conviction, so assuredly put to The Doubter, now stood before the eye of the needle.

Here, Xenophon had warned, the stream imitated that stretch of the White Nile south of Mongalla, which broke into cataracts. Except that here the cataracts compensated for their stunted falls —eight meters at most—by hurling water and debris savagely through a narrow chute, thus making the rapids one of the most treacherous in the world. This phenomenon had been pantheistically described by the locals as the tyranny of a midget seeking the majesty of a giant. For, oral tradition explained, the stream envied the White Nile as a humble man envies his king, and resented bartering water with the Great Vein of Africa through the Baro, the Sobat and the even more formidable western reaches of the Sudd.

Still on the villainy of this petty tyrant, Xenophon had recounted tales of South Sudanese guerrillas broken on these rapids.

The guerrillas, known as *Anya-Nya* after the deadly scorpion of the region, had been the unsung heroes of the little-known but relentless war of 1963–72 that had been waged by the Christian South Sudanese against the government of the Muslim North. Through the desperate conditions of that long war, these men had attempted to smuggle arms and provisions from Ethiopia, a country sympathetic to their resistance to Islam, using this particular route. Nearly all who had attempted the journey had perished at the rapids ahead. Those few who had not, among them Xenophon himself, had survived for one reason only: they had had the protection of the pagan deities which ruled the rivers and which they had been permitted to worship alongside Jesus by wise missionaries —like the Irishman who had christened Xenophon after the Greek historian. The same pagan deities, Xenophon had assured Abu Ismail, would watch over them on this crossing too—but not without giving them a taste of the power they wielded.

"Hold tight! Hold tight! Hold tight!"

Xenophon's shouts faded as the roar of rushing water enveloped them.

Abu Ismail dropped his rifle and clung to the sides of the canoe. Endowed at the very moment of his trial with a million eyes, he registered the various images simultaneously.

He saw his warriors check their life jackets, grip their paddles and brace themselves for the ordeal ahead. He respected their fear and the steadfastness with which they controlled it.

He saw Nazmi, growing daily in stature, slither over to his side, life and limb ready to protect him.

He saw Xenophon mold into the contours of the canoe's nose and bark instructions at the six warriors ranged behind him. He felt some compassion for Xenophon. A legend among the *Anya-Nya*. A resourceful man, he had performed his tasks efficiently— particularly the delicate operation of homing the WOJ Beechcraft in the middle of the night to a disused landing strip near Garwang, fifty kilometers to the north. Abbas had been full of praise. After a five-hour flight, and having covered some 1,600 kilometers from Libya's southernmost border with the Sudan, the Beechcraft had reached the limits of her range; she would have eaten up precious reserve fuel in a risky search over the Sudd for the rendezvous point, but for Xenophon's excellent flare path and talk-down.

He saw Abbas—a daredevil who could fly any plane, who had held his own against Israeli fighters and who would provide the wings for the Day of Glory—whimper as he faced water, a lesser element than air.

But above all, he saw himself. Suddenly calm. His emaciated

legs, fastened against the hollow of the canoe, bulging with prodigious powers. His arms rippling with the breath of Allah. His spirit levitating. Fear of pain, failure and death evaporating. Unshackled of doubt. Truly The Chosen One.

A moment later, the horizon turned upside down.

Images engaged each other.

Water for sky. Rocks as missiles. Slime attacking eyes, nose. Burning throat.

Hands gripping. Water. Air. Wood. Flesh.

Legs flung to extremity. Bruising. Holding strong.

Body floating, sinking, floating again.

Men spilling out. Disappearing into murky depths. Rising up. Traces of blood.

The boat. Frothing. Tossing. Catapulting. Somersaulting. Creaking. Screeching. Splintering.

Xenophon shouting, pushing water, rock, slime. Holding men steady. Shouting orders.

Nazmi clutching his hair. Floating with him. Dividing the water.

Sounds of hell. Men's agonized cries.

Silence.

DEBRE ZEYT, ETHIOPIA

The U.S. Air Force Lockheed C-5A Galaxy long-range military transporter landed at Debre Zeyt airfield at 6:15 P.M. It contained some arms and spare parts ordered by the Imperial Air Force and eight crates of various sizes marked as diplomatic bag. Its personnel, a crew of five, a relief crew of another five and one courier, Brian Coover, disembarked at once. A complement of twelve men, all black, who had traveled in a partitioned compartment on the rear upper deck, remained hidden.

The arrival of the arms a month ahead of the delivery date delighted the officers on the base. The formalities for the transfer of cargo and the clearance of the diplomatic bag took a few minutes. The captain, however, made sure that the ensuing interlude for refreshments and the filing of flight plans for the Galaxy's next port of call, Abadan, in Iran, took a full half hour.

During that time, the twelve CIA-SO agents slipped out of the Galaxy and disappeared, under cover of night, into the fields beyond the airfield perimeter. The base's single security barrier, a barbed-wire fence, did not present them with any problems.

Between 7:15 and 7:25 P.M. the ground staff, supervised by Brian Coover, and John Queensberry, the consular affairs attaché who had come to take delivery of the diplomatic bag, transferred the eight crates into an embassy van.

They left the base at 7:30, traveling south for two kilometers to reach the junction with the main highway to Addis Ababa. Sam Greig, the accredited embassy transport officer, took extra care before performing the right turn for the capital. While he waited, Coover and Queensberry counted four Fiat 124s among the Addis Ababa-bound traffic. A fifth Fiat 124, courteously flashing lights, let them through. Moments later, as it overtook the van, Queensberry recognized the driver, Montblanc, by his massive frame. The flashing lights had signaled that the twelve CIA-SO agents had been successfully picked up by the preceding Fiats.

At 7:40 P.M. the van turned into a concealed turnoff on a deserted stretch of the road. The five Fiats were waiting. The twelve CIA-SO agents, plus Montblanc, Getachew, Boaz and Osman, took less than a minute to transfer the eight crates containing guns and medical supplies into the Fiats.

Another minute was devoted to inflicting gashes and bruises on Coover, Queensberry and Greig. The trio would display these in the days to come, acknowledging with some relief that the brigands who had robbed them could have been more brutal or, worse, could have held them hostage, an act growing in popularity the world over. The U.S. Embassy would offer rewards for the capture of the brigands and for the return of five hundred blank passports which it would claim to be the only items of importance stolen.

April 19, 1974

JEKAW, THE SUDAN

It continued to rain. This time, it was a blessing. It kept away the mosquitoes, soothed the pains, blackened the night and hid them from the sight of all but Allah.

They had camped on a mudbank downstream of Jekaw at a point which would have been no-man's-land had there been sense in erecting frontiers in such an inhospitable wilderness. But they were on the Baro. Immediately west lay Ethiopia. Sixty kilometers beyond, as the river twisted, stood the last tent before Allah.

Abu Ismail performed the night prayers. For once the communion, cherished because it was supererogatory, did not consume him. He was so replete that an additional rapture, no matter how pure, was like another bud in a flower-strewn garden.

He lived and relived his trial at the rapids. He searched the heavens time and again for The Doubter so that he could declare:

See, I am The Chosen One! Or declaim one of Allah's names: *En Al-Haq!* I am God!

It had been a severe trial. Four of the six-man squad had received minor injuries: strained limbs, bruised ribs. Not serious enough to prevent them fighting on the Day of Glory. The other two, who had been thrown off the canoe, had suffered concussion but were recovering well. Abbas had broken his nose but that, too, was a minor injury. He would be able to fly on the Day of Glory.

Nazmi, like Abu Ismail, had survived the ordeal unscathed. This, despite the fact that he had thrown himself into the water in Abu Ismail's wake and had been buffeted alongside his leader throughout the worst stretches of the rapids. Nazmi the lion-hearted had thought Abu Ismail had been washed away. He was, of course, still callow. He had not perceived that Abu Ismail had engaged the rapids willfully because as Al-Mahdi it was incumbent on him to conquer the storm at its vortex. Allah, however, had exulted in Nazmi's devotion and had cocooned him within the Prophet's blessing.

Only Xenophon had suffered serious injury: a multiple fracture of the right arm and three broken ribs. This was further proof that Allah had kept His Eyes on His Faithful. It was immaterial that Xenophon had brought the canoe out of the rapids, still watertight and requiring minimum repairs to cracks and splinterings; or that he had sustained his injuries while attempting to help the two platoon members who had fallen overboard. Xenophon was a Christian: Allah's enemy.

Abu Ismail concluded his prayers. The elation remained. Enhanced by the fact that his prostrations had not hurt. His once-arthritic limbs had been transformed in the course of this one day into pillars of strength. He was cured of his affliction. Cured of his fears. He now stood as the supreme warrior. The taste of action still sweet in his mouth. Impatient for more.

Nazmi came up to him and kissed his hands. Affectionately, Abu Ismail patted his head. He had sent Nazmi to reconnoiter the border and during that short absence had realized how much he had grown to love him. Truly, Allah's gift as replacement for Idris Ali.

"The border's clear, Al-Mahdi. No lookouts or encampments on either side. Jekaw is asleep. We can slip by without being seen."

"Excellent. Prepare to set off."

"Xenophon?"

Abu Ismail turned to look at Xenophon, stretched out near the boat, disdaining Muslim company and nursing his injuries with a bottle of *zibib*. "Attend to him."

"Fodder for crocodiles. No remains."

"That will do."

Nazmi retreated to the shadows.

Abu Ismail closed his eyes, ascended the heavens once more in search of The Doubter. See I have arrived! *En Al-Haq!*

The Doubter did not emerge. He had died. He lay buried in the Sudd.

ADDIS ABABA, ETHIOPIA

The Memouneh sniffed the air. "So this is the smell of Africa."

Boaz cast a cursory glance at the swirling dust. "Eucalyptus. Frankincense. Burnt wood. That's the smell of Africa. You're smelling dust. Crowds. Half of Ethiopia is in Addis. . . ."

"So I see. Tomorrow's Muslim demonstration. The Four Days of Confusion . . . Everything nicely on the boil . . ."

Boaz scanned the street. It was off the main road but not deserted. Children, brought by demonstrators and sent out of harm's way, played in dark corners. Boaz tightened his hand on his pistol. Children also fronted for muggers, particularly at night.

The Memouneh and Quinn had arrived from Djibouti on time, despite the congested air traffic. Their false identities, respectively West German industrialist and Canadian coffee wholesaler, had pushed them through immigration and customs with salutary speed. Even in such troubled times, Ethiopia had need of foreign businessmen. Boaz and Montblanc, each using three CIA-SO agents to form a protective cordon, had established visual contact as soon as the Memouneh and Quinn had come out of the arrivals building.

In keeping with their identities, the Memouneh and Quinn had tried to make hotel reservations from the airport, knowing from their last communication with Boaz that all the hotels were full with Muslim dignitaries. They had duly decided to try the Italian pensions near the airport and had set out gruffly, on foot.

Boaz and Montblanc, still covered by the CIA-SO agents, had caught up with their respective charges to escort them personally to the safe house.

"You look well, Boaz. One of Sanbat's signals intimated you were unwell."

Boaz shook his head. The weakness and giddiness that had afflicted him on the return from the Danakil had disappeared, suggesting that the condition had been exhaustion rather than contamination. Now he felt fitter than ever. Sanbat's flesh had seen to that. "What else did she intimate? A moment's aberration? The old wound playing up?"

The Memouneh shook his head. "No. Did it?"

Boaz left the question unanswered.

The Memouneh changed the subject. "Any developments?"

"A second tip-off on Wolde's whereabouts. Negative like the first. Aerial reconnaissance for Idris Ali and Abu Ismail negative. O'Brien flew over both the Ogaden and Gambela regions several times. Desert ranges and jungle. You could hide the whole of Israel in either. The Falashas are still ferreting, but it takes days to scour a few kilometers. . . ."

They reemerged on Airport Road about a hundred meters from the front entrance of the safe house.

Boaz slowed down and surveyed the crowds and traffic. Peaceful. He saw, ahead, Quinn and Montblanc go into the safe house. The CIA-SO agents in the crowd were breaking formation. "All clear."

The Memouneh cast a final look about him. "Still no Russians. Not at the airport. Not in the city. Nowhere."

Boaz nodded. He had kept a special eye open for Russians who might be preparing to assist Idris Ali and Abu Ismail. The CIA-SO agents, too, upon arrival, had deployed to sniff them out—a game at which they were experts. "They're not about. Waiting for the aftermath, no doubt."

The Memouneh sighed. "What a rational world—for those who can see it rationally."

THE GAMBELA RESERVE, ETHIOPIA

"It was too dangerous a journey, Al-Mahdi."

Abu Ismail, revolted by the Eater of the Dead, leering from Idris Ali's shoulder, kept his eyes closed. He managed, however, to hold Idris Ali's hand paternally on his lap. The Christian's prophet had suffered his betrayer. He, Al-Mahdi, a better prophet, would divert the betrayer's sting onto the betrayer.

"There were other places you could have come through, Al-Mahdi. Safer places. Why take such a risk?"

"It was not a risk. Nothing, nobody can touch me."

Idris Ali looked away, pretending to be distracted by Nazmi, who was preparing the night potions. He had been wary of Abu Ismail's estimation of Nazmi, had even considered the possibility of Nazmi superseding him on the Day of Glory. But Nazmi was ponderous in his movements, even clumsy. Hardly the caliber of a chief of staff. A devoted slave, no more.

Nazmi served them hot milk.

Idris Ali deferentially waited for Abu Ismail to start drinking.

At last, the honey-and-almond-sweet reunion was coming to an end. Everyone except the night watch had gone to sleep. Abu Ismail's six-man squad, in particular, had collapsed with exhaustion. They had had to paddle sixty kilometers against the current, nursing injuries and under incessant rain. It had taken them fourteen hours. By contrast, Abu Ismail looked neither tired nor under strain. That annoyed Idris Ali. This was not the time for the old cripple to have a remission.

"I cannot tell you, my son, how glad I am to find you in such good health. That plague at the Danakil base—I was deeply apprehensive. Allah has answered my prayers."

Idris Ali looked up. Abu Ismail was staring at him with luminous eyes. He could not see beyond, so he assumed they reflected joy. He dropped his head in reverence. "Allah always answers your prayers, Al-Mahdi."

Abu Ismail, assuming a casual air, examined the *tukul*'s primitive interior. "Anything I should know?"

"I don't think so."

"No problems? No alarm signals from Volkov?"

Idris Ali hesitated. "From Volkov? No—nothing."

Abu Ismail, controlling his impulse to strike out, patted Idris Ali's hand. The slate was clean at last. He had given Idris Ali one last chance. It was not to be. Idris Ali had fused with the Eater of the Dead. It was time for the exorcism.

"Good."

Idris Ali tried to cover up his moment of hesitation. "In any case, in the event of an emergency, Volkov would have signaled you—not me."

Abu Ismail finished his drink and rose. "I shall retire. I suggest you do the same."

Idris Ali gulped down his drink and rose, too. "As soon as I've checked with the watch."

Abu Ismail smiled to indicate approval of his diligence. Idris Ali responded by kissing Abu Ismail's hands. Abu Ismail blinked. Like Christians degrading themselves with Judas kisses. But it was the last ignominy he would have to suffer.

ADDIS ABABA, ETHIOPIA

Ayyuni,

Zaynab—your secretary, my guardian angel—told me I could send another letter. So here I am, breathless as a fifteen-year-old.

I will have to ramble on, my Osman. I have so much to say. I'll probably say only a fraction. But you will feel my breath in each word.

I am writing this sitting on the bed. Our sanctuary. The only place where you and I can shut out the world. Where we unite. Where we make love. Where we just sit and hold hands. Where we talk. Where we laugh. Where we sleep and dream of each other while our bodies touch. Yet often I hate this bed. Filled more with the soldier's memories, than with his presence. I have cried so many times in this bed. I have felt anchorless so often. I so love you, my Osman. I so resent that you and I were born to fight for Allah, throne and country. It may be blasphemous—but nothing, nothing should justify the absence of a man from his wife's side. Have you ever thought? We have been married more than eighteen years. To be precise: 6,658 days. Have you spent 1,001 nights with me?

Change of mood. Allah stands watch over me like a father. I am sure He is watching over you, too. I, your woman, can only survive with you by my side.

A happier note. The other day an old Gypsy came around, selling flowers. I bought some and offered her food. She kept saying I was a lucky woman, that I would have uninterrupted happiness for the rest of my life. I suppose she was being grateful. But I believed her. When I made coffee, she offered to read my fortune. I let her. I was afraid, I must admit. She said I had great anguish because you were away. Well, that's true. Then she said you'd come back. Very soon. And you'd never go again. That you'd get a bigger desk and sit at it forever. I am convinced she is right. About time, Ayyuni.

A funny episode. Hatijeh saw some Scandinavians wind-surfing at Aqaba where she had gone for a weekend with her class. Well, our daughter's in love. With all the Scandinavians! She has decided to marry a viking. I quote her: "Imagine going to bed every night with the sun by your side." Imagine that. What do Scandinavians know about the sun, locked in their dark land? I told her if she had any sense, she should find herself a man like her father. Then she would have the universe in her bed.

Bed. I am possessed by our bed. I want you in it. I want you, night after night. Hold you as if I had just given birth to you. Suckle you. I so love you, my Osman. I want you in my flesh. Forever.

A disturbing note. I didn't want to mention it, but I feel compelled. I keep dreaming about you and that tortured man, Boaz. Battling. Side by side. He dies every time. Horribly. You try to save him. But you fail. You explain: no one can save a man who wants to die. Is this prophetic? Is there no way you can save him? I say this, would you believe it, with jealousy. Because I feel you and Boaz have a special closeness. So he has claims on you and takes something away from me. Yet I also rejoice in that. Such friendship, such brotherly care between enemies is the only hope for the future. If you and he can sow those seeds, perhaps one day all the wives in the world might have their husbands in their beds.

Zaynab has arrived to take this. So I'll close. I know I shall see you soon. I shall count the seconds. When I clasp you, I shall never let you go. I love you, Ayyuni, my Osman, my man, my boy. Keep safe.

Samia

Osman caressed the letter. Samia reflected his secret yearnings, his soldier's weariness. Yet she had made him what he was. His strength emanated from hers. A mere paper containing her breath uplifted him. Since the Memouneh had delivered the letter, he had regained his spirits. He no longer felt crushed by the long wait. These frustrating days in Addis Ababa would prove uncritical. They would pick up Abu Ismail's trail. They would engage him. And they would triumph. And then—maybe—he would retire from the field.

"Not bad news?" Boaz stood by the door, keeping his distance but concerned.

"No. From Samia."

"You suddenly disappeared. I thought . . . Is she all right?"

Osman felt tempted to show him the letter. He desisted, fearing Samia's reference to Boaz might unleash demons temporarily under control. Mending fences was a laborious and delicate process. "She's fine. Thank you for your concern."

Boaz turned to leave.

Osman tried to keep him talking. "What's happening?"

"The watch is watching. The others are in their rooms—biting their nails."

"No change in the orders for tomorrow?"

"No."

Osman made a wry face. Tomorrow promised to be another day of frustration. Covering the Muslim demonstration, city centers, main roads, arrival points, airport—all in the hope of spotting Abu Ismail's arrival, but not expecting it. "What do you think of the SO boys?"

"They're good. Why the small talk, Osman?"

Osman faced him, gravely. "I'm trying to resurrect what we had. . . ." Impulsively, he pushed Samia's letter into Boaz's hands. "Here, read this. It might knock some sense into you!"

Boaz hesitated, then leaned against the wall and read the letter. "What do you want me to say?"

"Tell me her vision is true—untarnished. That she sees what you and I are. A unit of two. Like the formations of ancient Greeks you so admire. And that she sees beyond that. She sees what our friendship means—not only in terms of Arab and Jew. But in universal terms. Husbands in their wives' beds—forever and ever. The only hope . . ."

"I don't deny it. But she also proves my point."

"What point?"

"The need for innocence. Purity. Sanctity."

"Yours for the asking, Boaz . . ."

"By killing?"

"By fighting the killers. By soldiering."

"Wives and soldiers don't go together. A clean sweep of all killers, soldiers included. Break the sword—every sword. Then you might attain Samia's Utopia."

"There is no Utopia. But there is life—yearning for dignity. And to uphold life you have to live. Nothing can be changed from the grave."

"To each his own deliverance."

"What puts you above other men, Boaz? Above your own people?"

"My people have nothing to do with it."

"It's not for me to say. . . . But as your army never ceases reminding you, deprive the Jew of a sword and he faces extinction. Forge him into a Maccabee, and he will survive. . . ."

"A soldier forever?"

"A heavy burden. But that is the heritage of your Chosenness. The Will of your Lord."

The words, echoing the early Zionist creed, found their mark. The Jew was the world's conscience. That was why he had survived for millennia. And why he had continuously faced persecution. Now, however, the world worshiped extermination. It could no longer tolerate conscience. Did not see the need for it. Some, like Osman, knowing nothing could live without conscience, fought to protect the future. How could he help them?

Catharsis caught up with him. He felt as vulnerable as when he had stood in the Yad Mordechai museum in front of the Nazi deportation list that had borne his mother's name. He mumbled, resolute that he should not cry. "I'm sick of it all. Battle fatigue. Shock. Despair. Enough! Enough! Enough! Don't you understand?"

"Of course I understand. I am your brother. And your enemy. How can I fail to understand?"

Boaz protested. "My brother. Never my enemy."

Osman moved to him, placed his arm around his shoulders. "I am your enemy. I will remain your enemy until our people make peace. And though I do not want to kill your people, I will do so if Allah willy it. So you see—even against me, you may need a sword."

Boaz faced him. "And you say death is not preferable to that?"

"It is. But who has the right to indulge in preferences?"

April 20, 1974

THE GAMBELA RESERVE, ETHIOPIA

Abu Ismail examined the bomb. A trunk divided into compartments: 1.65 meters high. 0.65 meters wide. 1.70 meters long. Made to measure for the passenger door of a Super VC-10.

He redirected his ear to Watanabe's persistent giggle and atrociously accented English. Watanabe had been droning on about the functions of the various compartments, the improvised but ingenious accommodations for the warhead, primary charges, detonators, power sources, arming, firing and permissive-action mechanisms, fuses, booby-traps and backup systems. Abu Ismail had hardly paid attention. He had checked the bomb thoroughly during the night. He was satisfied every specification had been incorporated. It had not been the technicalities that had forced him to recruit Fawzi and Watanabe, but the precision mathematics necessary for chain reaction. Allah's Chosen could master technicalities, but he could not be expected to balance weights and figures like a street vendor.

"*Pièce de résistance . . .*" Watanabe had picked up a small metal box containing two switches which would render the bomb superior to any device produced. "This fuse box—most vital component. The bomb is not armed yet. So we are safe to test if you want."

Abu Ismail addressed him paternally. "I do, Ischii."

Watanabe's giggles escalated a decibel. "This makes sure enemy won't try silly heroics. . . ."

"Get on with it." The terse command came from Idris Ali.

Abu Ismail rebuked him. "Let him enjoy his moment of glory."

Watanabe chortled. "Yes . . . Yes . . ."

Idris Ali grimaced, wavered on his feet, then leaned against a chair.

"Are you not well, my son?"

Idris Ali rubbed his eyes to clear his vision. He had had a bad night. Full of nightmares. One, the most disturbing, still haunted him. Nazmi, wearing a gas mask, had crept into his hut and had sprayed him from an aerosol canister. BZ psychochemical gas. Absurd . . .

BZ was an incapacitating agent. WOJ had left their stock in Tripoli. They could not use it in any operation for fear of incapacitating their own men. BZ produced temporary paralysis, blindness, deafness, maniacal behavior.

"The heat—I think . . ."

Abu Ismail looked concerned. "I am afraid you will have to bear it, my son."

Idris Ali tried to focus. Angry with himself. It was guilt gnawing at him. Nightmares were false air, false light. Harmless. Abu Ismail's admonishments, the hysterically pronounced sentences of death, the macabre tortures beneath bizarre landscapes—none of these could touch him. Besides, there was no cause for guilt. He, Idris Ali, was the better man. He rasped, trying to hold himself steady. "I'll be all right."

Abu Ismail, still looking concerned, searched the faces surrounding him for an explanation of Idris Ali's condition. Nazmi raised innocent eyebrows. Mahmud, Qabus and Wahbi stared back, puzzled. Abbas and those of the six-man squad not on guard duty looked disapproving. They were still nursing the injuries they had received in the Sudd's cataracts. They expected Idris Ali to bear ailments as they did, without a murmur. Only Fawzi, at the far end of the *tukul* sitting with his legs tucked under, looked shaken. But Fawzi, thoroughly indoctrinated by WOJ philosophy, revered Idris Ali as a *mujaddit*, an innovator, a man second only to Al-Mahdi.

Abu Ismail turned to Watanabe. "Your *pièce de résistance*, Ischii . . ."

Watanabe waved the fuse box. "Outside on mudbank are two charges. Very small. Ready for detonation. This fuse box: two switches—like push buttons. One. Two. I switch on. Both fuses armed."

Abu Ismail nodded.

Watanabe rummaged in his pocket and brought out a small box. He opened it, took out a tiny pair of pliers and a hexagonal piece of ceramic no bigger than the head of a thumbtack. He pointed at the ceramic. "Here a piezoelectric ceramic. *Piezo* is Greek word meaning 'press.' So piezoelectric means production of electricity by application of pressure. How? Pressure distorts dipoles which are positive-negative pairs of atoms, and distortion creates electrical field. This ceramic has identical qualities as piezoelectric crystal fitted in your tooth, Abu Ismail. It contains a transducer—a device which interchanges types of energy. So, pressure on crystal produces electricity for transducer. Transducer produces ultrasonic wave. Ultrasonic wave emitted to detector—here, in fuse box. Detector activates trigger mechanism. And boom—explosion. Understand?"

Abu Ismail nodded pleasantly. "I understand."

"Practice even more simple. For you to make boom—all you do is bite on your tooth. I show you." Watanabe picked up the ceramic with the pair of pliers. "Charge is on mudbank. Fuse already armed. I have ceramic. I press with pliers. Hard—like bite on ceramic in tooth."

Abu Ismail turned to the *tukul*'s window just as a wisp of smoke rose from the mudbank. The rain muffled the sound of the blast.

Watanabe giggled hysterically. "Good, eh . . . Good, eh . . ."

Abu Ismail smiled. "Very good."

Watanabe moderated his mirth and pointed at the second switch. "Now this other—it is for the heart probe you have implanted in your body." Again Watanabe rummaged in his pockets and produced a gadget no larger than a coin. "Here, a replica of the probe. Battery-operated like pacemaker. But with miniature transmitter. Principle similar to electrocardiogram. Probe picks up heartbeat, turns it into steady electrical charge. This charge part of bridge circuit holding transmitter in nontransmitting condition. The cessation of heartbeat—in your case, the stoppage of blood circulation—causes bridge circuit to activate transmitter. In this device, transmission timed at forty seconds. Circulation of blood every four seconds—so it gives circulation ten chances to recommence. If no circulation in forty seconds, transmitter signals fuse box. Activates trigger. And boom! I demonstrate?"

Abu Ismail nodded.

Watanabe moved to a cage containing a rabbit. "Our guinea pig." He took out the rabbit and clipped the probe onto its back. "I attach probe instead of implant. No difference." He held the rabbit up and giggled. "Somebody kill it, please."

Abu Ismail turned to Idris Ali. Idris Ali, swaying precariously, declined, shaking his head. Abu Ismail turned to Nazmi.

The giant bodyguard picked up the rabbit and with a twist of his hand broke its neck.

Watanabe giggled at a higher pitch. "I don't know rate of rabbit blood circulation—but difference unimportant."

Abu Ismail turned to the window and stared at the mudbank. "What's the range of the transmitter?"

Watanabe's reply was lost first in the blast on the mudbank— like the first one, a mere wisp of smoke—then in Idris Ali's heart-wrenching groan.

"Abu—"

Abu Ismail veered around with feigned alarm as Idris Ali collapsed. "What happened?"

Nazmi seemed baffled. "He passed out, Al-Mahdi."

Fawzi, looking horrified, moved across, wanting to help. Idris Ali lay unconscious, his body twisted and rigid.

Abu Ismail stooped over Idris Ali and stroked his forehead. "Idris Ali . . . My son . . ."

Nazmi took Idris Ali's pulse and appeared to be even more puzzled. "Pulse is all right. . . ."

Abu Ismail rose, looking grim. "Take him to his quarters. See to him."

Nazmi signaled to Abbas. They picked up Idris Ali and carried him out.

The warriors tried to conceal their shock. Watanabe had stopped giggling at last and retreated into a corner, shaking as if Idris Ali's collapse augured his own. Fawzi remained immobile, crouching on the spot where Idris Ali had fallen, traumatized eyes staring into demons' pits.

Abu Ismail sighed, then turned to Watanabe. "You were about to tell me the range of the transmitter."

Watanabe giggled feebly. "Oh, yes. Normally four hundred meters. Your probe is three times more. It can be extended, if you want, with repeater transmitters."

"One point two kilometers is ample. Thank you. Leave me now —all of you."

The men, with Watanabe helping Fawzi, filed out.

Alone, Abu Ismail dropped on his knees and wrapped his arms around the bomb. His bomb. He delighted in the smell of the components. Indefinable. But fragrant. Like the perfumed breath of Allah.

ADDIS ABABA, ETHIOPIA

The Memouneh paced the room with a pot of coffee and replenished the cups of Boaz, Osman, Getachew and Ellis, the commanding officer of the CIA-SO contingent.

The day had been frustrating. The Muslim demonstration had been peaceful; the participants, determined to prevent a premature eruption of the Four Days of Confusion, had voiced grievances with dignity and left.

They had not sighted Abu Ismail or any WOJ commandos among the crowds; nor Wolde and his paratroopers among the troops on duty.

For those covering entry points and the airport on the possibility that Abu Ismail might dart in during the demonstration, events had been even more tedious. All scheduled flights had been delayed until after the demonstration because of the number of staff attending it.

By contrast, late afternoon and evening, hit by the mass exodus of demonstrators, had been hectic. The roads and bus terminals had been congested, making the task of differentiating between incoming and outgoing traffic guesswork. At the airport, the delayed arrivals of scheduled and chartered flights had created similar chaos.

Now, approaching midnight, the situation had eased. Quinn, Montblanc, Sanbat and the CIA-SO agents were still deployed; Boaz, Osman, Getachew and Ellis had been summoned for an emergency meeting.

On the agenda were four signals received in the course of the day that suggested a breakthrough.

The first, from Gentleman Jim, was a tránscript of a National Security Agency ELINT report detailing the movements of Abu Ismail's Beechcraft on April 17–18: from Tripoli south to El Uweinat, an oasis on the Libya–Sudan border, then, after a brief stopover, to a disused airstrip near Garwang, one of the few high-ground villages in the eastern Sudd; and a return to Tripoli via the same route following an even briefer stopover at the oasis. Total time of operation: sixteen hours eleven minutes.

The second, from Bayyu, coordinated Falasha reports of rumors from migrant South Sudanese of a covert excursion into the Sudd undertaken by one Xenophon, a renowned guerrilla, and a group of men alleged to be FAO officials.

The third, via Israel from Mossad agents in Tripoli, confirmed the return of Abu Ismail's Beechcraft on the eighteenth, empty save for one Isa, Abu Ismail's most trusted pilot after Abbas. The agents further reported that within two hours of landing, Isa had departed with a complement of eight men for Entebbe, Uganda, this time in Abu Ismail's executive jet, the Grumman Gulfstream II.

The fourth signal, also via Israel but from Mossad's agent in Kampala, had confirmed the arrival of the Grumman Gulfstream II at Entebbe in the early hours of the nineteenth, and reported that the nine men had checked in at the Lake Victoria Hotel, ostensibly for a week's holiday.

These signals, dovetailed to the presence of a botanical team, as yet untraced in the Gambela Reserve, had allowed them to formulate a conclusive evaluation. The WOJ commandos at Entebbe were either a reserve or a support assault force, enjoying Idi Amin's hospitality until required to move. The FAO team reported in the Sudd was Abu Ismail's contingent. The botanists were Idris Ali and his men. Somewhere in the Gambela Reserve, the two contingents—or all three—were about to meet.

The Memouneh sat down. "At least we know where they are—roughly. . . ."

Getachew gesticulated defeatedly. "Roughly is no good. Much of the area is tropical jungle."

"We could try smoking them out."

"They'll come out anyway. And if Osman's theory still holds, they'll come to Addis. For those in Entebbe, it's only an hour's flight. All we can do is lie in wait. . . ."

Boaz shook his head. "Even if we lie in wait we're still faced with the problem *where*. For all we know, Wolde has supplied them with helicopters. They could land on the roof of the Organization of African Unity building without our being any the wiser."

Getachew grimaced, yielding the point.

Osman thumped the table. "I agree with Zamora. We should try and smoke them out. We'll have to go out there!"

The Memouneh interjected. "Except that we can't abandon our position here. Addis is our last line of defense."

"I meant some of us. Leave you standing by with the main force here. If we can engage Abu Ismail in the bush, we could seize the advantage. If he gets to Addis, the advantage is his."

"What you propose, Osman, demands jungle experience. We're thin on that—"

A deep, solemn voice joined the argument. "That's not so, General." Ellis, the stocky CIA officer, drawled on in his New Orleans lilt. "You don't become an SO without jungle-warfare training. Me and my men had a bellyful in the Panama Canal Zone—in hellholes that'd make Gambela Reserve look like Central Park. If that doesn't qualify us, here's more: we're all 'Nam veterans."

The Memouneh considered the point. "Thank you, Ellis. I should have thought of that. Your requirements?"

"Six men. Bradley, Harrison, Joyce, Laszlo, Pietrangeli, Williams. One helicopter."

The Memouneh looked at Boaz, Osman and Getachew. They posed no objections. He turned back to Ellis. "First light tomorrow?"

Ellis nodded. "Right."

April 21, 1974

THE GAMBELA RESERVE, ETHIOPIA

Fawzi stroked Watanabe's forehead and hummed what had become a precious tune, the Dallapiccola theme. He could now enjoy it for its melody. He had deciphered it. A coded message from Charlie Quinn. Asking him to sabotage the bomb. Charlie should have known better.

He heard a groan. It startled him. Watanabe was asleep. He turned sharply and stared at Idris Ali, lying rigid on a straw mat. Idris Ali's presence in the small *tukul* that had been his and Watanabe's confused him.

Then he remembered. He and Watanabe were not in their *tukul*, but in Idris Ali's. Idris Ali and Watanabe being sick, it was best, Nazmi had said, to keep them together.

Fawzi sighed. He had come to say good-bye.

The relationship with Watanabe had been sterile, but functional. Something to do during leisure hours. Leave-taking caused little pain.

He cast a last look at Idris Ali. Probably radiation sickness. Though there had been no signs. No balding, vomiting, fever, emaciation. None of those afflictions that had become chronic with everyone else. But then, who knew the vagaries of radiation sickness?

Painfully, he left the *tukul*. They were letting him go. He could not believe it. And, despite his elation, he felt disturbed. Was he distrusted? Or had the WOJ leader decided that with the completion of the bomb, his usefulness had come to an end? Or was it a reward? Had Abu Ismail detected his secret desire? That he was dying and wished to die at home? In surroundings precious to him. With his books. Records. The sea air mingling with the cedars. Little escaped Abu Ismail's eyes.

Nazmi guided him into the command *tukul*.

Abu Ismail greeted him effusively. "You have my blessing, Professor."

Fawzi stoked his hope. "Are you really letting me go?"

Abu Ismail held out a travel folder. "Your passport. Money— enough to see you home. Details of your reservations. You will have to get the tickets yourself."

Fawzi took the folder. As speedily as he could, he checked the contents. Passport. His own. Two thousand U.S. dollars in cash. Details of reservations neatly typed out on a piece of paper: Gambela–Addis Ababa–Rome–Beirut. They were really letting him go. "Thank you . . . Thank you . . ."

"It is we who should thank you: Allah and Al-Mahdi."

Fawzi gesticulated, trying to convey all his emotions at once. His body shook, his legs weakened. Nazmi held him steady.

"One last thing, Professor."

Fawzi looked up, afraid that Abu Ismail might change his mind. His eyes focused on Abu Ismail's hands, holding a small silver dish containing a single piece of Turkish delight.

Abu Ismail smiled. "To sweeten your departure."

Fawzi waved weak hands. "I—I can't eat . . . I'm sick."

"This contains medicine. A miracle drug."

"What?"

"Eat it! It will make you better in no time."

Fawzi took the sweet. The miracle drug, he suspected, was a narcotic that had sustained Watanabe. LSD? STP? One such. He munched compulsively. If it would keep him going until he reached home.

Abu Ismail patted him on the shoulder. "Allah be with you."

As Nazmi led him out, he stuffed a piece of paper into his travel folder. "This is our address here. Keep it safe. Send us a card saying you got home."

Fawzi nodded, barely registering the absurdity of the statement.

ADDIS ABABA, ETHIOPIA

Boaz cleaned his gun and listened to the BBC world news.

There had been an assassination attempt on Egypt's President Sadat, leaving twenty-four dead at the Cairo military academy. The attempt had been financed by Qaddafi and masterminded by a group calling itself the Islamic Liberation Organization. The name had betrayed Abu Ismail's hand and endorsed the Memouneh's theory: that the attempt was a diversion for the last phase of Operation Dragons.

Sanbat came in, flushed, sweaty, drained by heat and fatigue. She had been on surveillance duty at the airport. She would resume another shift in four hours. She smiled, trying to suppress her anxiety. "Osman said Ellis spotted them."

"He spotted a Land-Rover on the Gambela–Jekaw road. We don't know yet if it's WOJ. He's tracking it. He'll report again when it reaches its destination."

"If you have to move out, when will you go?"

"Depends on WOJ defenses. If they're heavily fortified, we might have to wait for the Sayeret Matkal. They'll start trickling in this afternoon."

Sanbat started undressing. "I'm going to take a shower. Would you like to wash my back?"

Boaz stared at her breasts. "Very much."

"I've asked Osman to let us have as much time as possible."

Boaz kissed her nipples.

She pulled him with her. "Shower first. I want to taste good."

THE GAMBELA RESERVE, ETHIOPIA

The rain had stopped. It did not help Nazmi. The dirt track was still a channel of thick mud, and the raised cloud ceiling allowed the helicopter to stalk from high altitude.

He did not want to lose the helicopter. Not on this trip. But he resented the fact that during the morning, when he was taking Fawzi to Gambela and needed to avoid detection, the conditions had also favored the helicopter. Then squatting clouds and lashing rain had forced him to drive for cover into the bush every time the helicopter appeared over the jungle.

It had been a great achievement to deposit Fawzi on the 12:25 flight to Addis Ababa unobserved and with minutes to spare. Had Fawzi missed the flight, Abu Ismail would have forfeited one of his vital moves against the enemy.

They had first spotted the helicopter, a Sikorsky 58T with USAID markings, early that morning, sweeping low from the northwest and flying toward the Gilo River, a tributary of the Sobat–White Nile, south of the Baro. One such run, unorthodox though it was, might not have aroused Abu Ismail's suspicions: there were some Peace Corps volunteers in the area who might have required a drop. But the overflights had not ceased, either over the length and breadth of the Baro or, as Nazmi himself would vouch, over the Gambela–Jekaw road.

Given the Sikorsky's basic performance—maximum range: 770 kilometers, cruising speed: 148 kilometers per hour—and allowing for some 500 kilometers and a three-and-a-half-hour flight from Addis Ababa, where USAID hangared their helicopters, it had left the capital at first light. The timing, indicating a military mind, and the fact that since reaching the area the helicopter had flown for six and a half hours over a terrain approximately 50 kilometers wide and 100 kilometers long, refueling twice at Gambela, respectively at about 10:00 A.M. and 3:00 P.M., had convinced Abu Ismail that it was on a scouting mission. Nazmi, on hand in Gambela, had been instructed to investigate further and had spied on the helicopter during its second refueling stop. His observations had confirmed Abu Ismail's suspicions. The helicopter's seven-man crew were not USAID employees. Their gait and casual alertness, and the fact that they were all black instead of the racial mixture favored by American organizations for overseas service, identified them as a special unit.

That meant the enemy had traced the WOJ assault force on its own initiative—a day before Abu Ismail's planned move to that effect.

But when Nazmi had radioed to confirm the setback, Abu Ismail had remained unperturbed, stating that for victory to have a unique substance, Al-Mahdi's adversaries had to be formidable.

Then, in an equally sonorous tone, he had ordered Nazmi to leave Gambela when the helicopter took off, to proceed openly on the Gambela–Jekaw road to draw attention, and to act as quarry until he reached a particularly dense stretch of jungle halfway to the WOJ encampment.

Nazmi leaned forward. Beyond the curve of the road he could see the scrub thickening. He had a good idea what awaited the helicopter.

Past the curve of the road, he spotted the WOJ Land-Rovers: three parked off the dirt track. Mohammad, Shamsedin and Tahir, members of the Day of Glory platoon, were walking around aimlessly, their slovenly behavior matching the sloppy camouflage of the vehicles. A fourth man, Riyad, was squatting on the ground as if defecating. Nazmi scanned the foliage, trying to spot the last two, Ferid and Said. He could not. All praise to them.

He checked his mirror and saw the helicopter dropping height. He flashed his lights, blasted his horn. The men scampered into the bush. Nazmi, joining in the charade, screeched to a stop and catapulted out.

He took cover. The helicopter flew past, very low. A moment later, two silvery darts streaked out of the bush.

The pilot maneuvered desperately against the missiles. He evaded the first, but not the second. The helicopter hung momentarily suspended in the air, then fell in a ball of orange flame.

ADDIS ABABA, ETHIOPIA

Quinn sat hunched in the back of the car and kept his eyes on the arrivals exit. But for Montblanc keeping the engine running, his hold on reality would have been tenuous. Fawzi had come back from the dead.

He had arrived during the afternoon. The airport had been even more chaotic, trying on the one hand to cope with the disruption of schedules still prevailing after Saturday's demonstration and, on the other, to accommodate the flux of people wanting to leave before the onset of the Four Days of Confusion.

With Ellis and six others dispatched to Gambela, Quinn and the Memouneh had had fewer men to deploy for a work load that had quadrupled by the regular, albeit delayed, arrivals of the Sayeret Matkal.

They could not have missed Fawzi. But they had been lucky to stumble on him before he had drawn attention to himself.

One of the Sayeret Matkal surgeons, Yonatan, having arrived from Douala, had chosen to go to the men's room before the long walk to the safe house. There he had come upon a man, sick, delirious and prostrate. Despite orders to maintain a low profile, he had tried to get him to the airport infirmary. The man had resisted. His rantings in Arabic and the repeated references to Beirut had intrigued Yonatan. He had checked the man's documents. The name on the passport, Talat Fawzi, and the occupation, professor of physics, had forced him to break cover and approach Sanbat, who was back on another shift.

Sanbat had assigned two CIA-SO agents to cover Fawzi, then had alerted Quinn and the Memouneh. Quinn, summoning Montblanc from his observation post at the bus terminal, had rushed to the airport.

Now the CIA-SO agents were coaxing Fawzi out of the arrivals lounge. Yonatan had joined Quinn and Montblanc in order to attend to Fawzi.

Montblanc slammed the car into gear. "Here they come!"

Quinn watched like a hawk. The CIA-SO agents, arms around Fawzi, acted like Samaritans helping an elderly invalid.

Montblanc stopped the car by the arrivals exit just as the CIA-SO agents brought Fawzi out. Quinn opened the door. The agents pushed Fawzi in. Yonatan pulled him down onto the seat. Montblanc eased away, keeping an eye on the mirror. No one had shown interest in the incident. The CIA-SO agents dispersed casually to resume surveillance.

Quinn stooped over Fawzi. "Talat . . . It's me . . . Charlie . . ."

Fawzi stared back with wild eyes but did not register Quinn. Then he heaved and vomited.

Yonatan pushed Quinn away. "Move to the front."

Quinn, dazed, climbed over awkwardly to the front seat. He stared into a void shadowed by horrors. Fawzi was a wreck. A skeleton. Balding. Covered in scabs. The muscular hands wasted. The eyes sickly, protruding like buboes. He would not have recognized him but for the tiny scar on the chin running across the dimple, and the large brown birthmark on the temple.

He became aware of the wetness, smelled the vomit. All over his clothes. He groaned. "Oh, my God . . . my God . . ."

Montblanc rasped. "Keep cool, Charlie."

Quinn turned to him viciously. "Look at him!"

Montblanc tried to sound reassuring. "He'll be all right."

Quinn twisted around. "How bad is he?"

Yonatan held Fawzi tightly and rocked him like a baby, hoping that the child in the man would find comfort in the embrace. "I don't know yet."

Quinn rested his head against the window. "Oh, my God . . . Oh, my God . . ."

Montblanc drove the car off the road into a dark lane. He kept the engine running while he made sure the area was deserted, then turned the key and pulled the hand brake. "All right, let's strip him. Clothes, shoes, everything. Yonatan, check every orifice. Also check for implant scars. . . ."

Quinn gaped at him. "What the hell—"

"In case he's bugged, Charlie . . ."

Quinn nodded, ashamed. He had forgotten about elementary precautions.

THE GAMBELA RESERVE, ETHIOPIA

"It's not radiation sickness, is it?"

Abu Ismail handed Idris Ali a mirror. "Impossible. Look at yourself."

Idris Ali held the mirror to his face. His hands shook as if burdened by a heavy weight. He welcomed the discomfort. It was proof he had shaken off the paralysis. He focused on his face. Gaunt. Black rings under the eyes. Signs of debility or the ravages of panic. He dropped the mirror, turned to Abu Ismail. "What's the matter with me, then?"

"Tropical fever. Or a chill . . . The rains . . ."

Idris Ali pulled himself to his elbows. Panting with the effort, he took a moment's rest. He darted his eyes from Abu Ismail to Nazmi to Abbas, then trembled in sudden alarm. "What's the date?"

"Twenty-first."

He felt relief. "I'll be all right by the twenty-fifth."

Abu Ismail rose from the floor. "I am sure."

Impulsively, Idris Ali grabbed Abu Ismail's hand. "You won't leave me!"

"Of course not."

The excessive sweetness in Abu Ismail's voice failed to convince. "But you're going now!"

"To start preparations . . ."

"So soon—"

"The first bulbul always catches Allah's ear. We will be back to pick you up. . . . Mahmud, Qabus and Wahbi will stay. They will attend to your needs. See that they also rest—I want them strong and fresh for the Day of Glory."

Idris Ali cast glances at the three men. They were standing humbly at attention. If Abu Ismail intended to abandon him, he would not leave three valiant warriors behind. His doubts abated. "And me. I'll be strong and fresh, too."

Abu Ismail replied with his back to Idris Ali. "You before everybody else."

A vestige of suspicion prodded Idris Ali. "What about Fawzi? Watanabe?"

Abu Ismail turned and pointed at the bundle of blankets in the far corner. "We have put Watanabe here so that you can monitor him. Keep him drugged, or he is likely to get out of hand. Fawzi's death hit him very hard."

Idris Ali reacted with shock. "Fawzi died?"

"Unfortunately. As we were releasing him."

Idris Ali tried to clear his mind. He had almost forgotten about Fawzi's release. One of Abu Ismail's improvisations. A subtle one, too. Fawzi, expendable now that he had made the bomb, was to be used as bait. Let loose and conspicuous by his condition, he would have been picked up by enemy agents searching for WOJ. This would have allowed Wolde to spot the agents and neutralize them before the Day of Glory. "How did he die?"

Abu Ismail shook his head sadly. "He went mad, poor man. Probably wanted to be included in the Day of Glory. While Nazmi was driving him to Gambela, he tried to return to camp. Threw himself out of the car. Broke his neck."

"What about the enemy? How will we flush them out?"

"I will think of something else."

"Why not release Watanabe? He'd be as good as Fawzi. . . ."

"He is too unstable. Likely to turn violent and get killed. Besides, I want him to set the fuses on the Day of Glory."

"We can all set the fuses."

"Yes. But he is the expert."

Idris Ali sank back, unable to think of other points.

"Do not worry, my son. Just get better. That is our main concern."

"I shall. You have my word."

Abu Ismail smiled graciously and walked out.

Idris Ali watched his gait: sprightly, almost youthful, betraying no signs of arthritis. An inexplicable rejuvenation which, Idris Ali felt, threatened him.

✗

Later, after Abu Ismail, Nazmi, Abbas and the six-man squad had taken the road to Dembidollo, Idris Ali started thinking again. Two things disturbed him: Fawzi's death; and the nightmare he had had about Nazmi spraying him with BZ gas.

On the first, he interrogated Qabus, Wahbi and Mahmud extensively. Except for one detail, that the incident had been witnessed by the six-man squad out on exercise, they could not elaborate. Idris Ali was left wondering why the squad had been sent out on exercise when they were supposed to be lying low at the encampment.

On the second, his thoughts remained unresolved. He kept remembering the dream as if it had actually happened.

April 22, 1974

ADDIS ABABA, ETHIOPIA

Montblanc, Quinn and Yonatan had found no transmitters in Fawzi's clothes or shoes, nor on his person. This suggested that WOJ had not released him in the expectation of pinpointing the enemy headquarters. Conversely, they had found among Fawzi's travel documents a crude map of the Baro River showing precise markings of an encampment.

Yonatan and Arik, the other surgeon, had attended Fawzi throughout the evening and night. Their prognosis had been grave.

On the question of his possible recovery from radiation sickness, they had given him a marginal chance, and that only because, unable to estimate the rem dosage, they could not judge the range of complications.

They had diagnosed the uncontrolled psychic energy and the perceptual distortions that terrorized Fawzi as effects of a megahallucinogen, probably STP, a synthetic chemical related to amphetamines.

There they had admitted defeat. Megahallucinogens in general, and STP in particular, were long-acting drugs. Their hold on a healthy adult could last a week; on someone as seriously ill as Fawzi, much longer, assuming that fatality due to respiratory failure could be prevented. There was no antidote to STP. Psychedelic inhibitors merely intensified the delirium; known remedies for mild hallucinogens actually compounded the toxic effects. All they could do was stand by with a catheter and stimulate the heart should it falter.

The prognosis had scuttled the hopes of a thorough interroga-

tion. The team required precise details. If Fawzi could answer
questions, the replies, like his perceptions, were bound to be distorted. Even if Fawzi could tell them whether he had solved the
Dallapiccola code and subsequently sabotaged the bomb, no one,
least of all the Memouneh, would be prepared to accept his word.
With a nuclear bomb in the balance, they could not risk being
misled or misinformed. If Fawzi had been brainwashed, he might
say precisely what Abu Ismail had programmed him to say.

Nonetheless, the Memouneh was adamant about implement-
ing some form of interrogation. Fawzi might provide a snippet that
could offer a tactical direction. Thus, they had settled on the next-
best thing: subjecting Fawzi to a group discussion during which
some pertinent argument might penetrate his trauma.

They had had to wait until the morning for a relatively calm
phase in the STP cycle.

The delay had been agonizing. The downing of Ellis and his
men had plunged them into despair. The agony had been compounded by the fact that they had lacked both the means to satu-
rate the Gambela Reserve with airborne forces and the authority
to commission the U.S. units at Kagnew base, Asmara, to do so
unilaterally. The single option, that of using the USAID Twin
Otter to drop the Sayeret Matkal in the vicinity of Ellis's crashed
helicopter, had had to be discounted. WOJ, anticipating such a
move, might either have been waiting for them with more missiles
or have moved camp.

Morning, counterpointing their impotence, had unveiled the
first of the Four Days of Confusion.

Addis Ababa had come to a standstill to watch the duel between
the emperor and the Dergue. The airport, following the arrivals of
the scheduled international flights—on which the last of the Sayeret Matkal had squeezed—had closed to all traffic except military
aircraft and planes operated by foreign-aid organizations. The bus
terminal had restricted service to short-distance routes. Much of
the population had spilled into the streets in response to rumors
that rebel tank units would storm the capital. These developments
had further complicated the surveillance of the airport, main road
junctions and the bus terminal, now shared by the remaining CIA-
SO agents and the Sayeret Matkal.

They sat in a wide circle. The group comprised the Memouneh, Sanbat, Getachew, Major Amnon, Montblanc, MacDonald
—the CIA-SO deputy commander—Osman, Boaz and Quinn.
Fawzi, strapped to his bed, occupied the center of the room, with
the doctors, Yonatan and Arik, in attendance. The latter had advised that the deliberations be conducted by units of two so that
Fawzi would not be confused by a babel of voices.

The Memouneh began by addressing the group. "O'Brien managed to send a plane over the Gambela Reserve. They spotted a wreckage some thirty kilometers west of Gambela. I'm afraid Ellis and his men must be presumed dead. Ellis's last message was that he was tailing a Land-Rover on the Gambela–Jekaw Road. Then we heard Harrison, the pilot, shout: 'Missiles!' " He paused to light a cigarette and gauged Fawzi's reaction.

The latter remained submerged.

The Memouneh continued. "We must assume Ellis came very close to spotting the WOJ hideout, and that the hideout itself is well defended. I should think the missiles were SAM-7s—they offer exceptional mobility. The fact that WOJ possess SAM-7s makes me wonder what else they might have. Bigger missiles? Rockets? Something that can accommodate a nuclear warhead?"

Fawzi twitched.

Quinn, interpreting the reaction as a response, picked up the cue. "I doubt it. Anything capable of accommodating a nuclear warhead would be too cumbersome to carry around."

"Well, we know they needed a bomb casing. We intercepted their spare. It's possible that rather than improvise one, they found somebody to supply them with a missile. The Russians, perhaps. We know Idris Ali has Russian support."

"If Russians were involved we'd have spotted them. Then again, not even Russians would back nuclear terrorism. Otherwise they'd have given WOJ a rocket complete with warhead and spared them the agonies of making a bomb."

"I take your point. We should discount missiles."

They paused and looked at Fawzi. He seemed to be listening, trying to focus.

Boaz picked up the discussion. "Missile or bomb, what's the difference? They've planned a nuclear attack. They intend to carry it out."

Osman joined in. "There *is* a difference. The bomb might not work. Fawzi might have failed."

"That's not our evaluation. All those people killed by radiation sickness . . ."

"Could have been sabotage. Maybe Fawzi—"

Fawzi started groaning.

Quinn picked up the discussion. "Sabotage is a possibility. We asked Talat to do just that—transmitted a musical code from a piece by Dallapiccola."

Montblanc interjected. "Hey, man, that's bullshit. A musical code?"

"We know he received it. Boaz found papers in the Danakil showing he tried to decode it. Listen . . ."

Quinn whistled the Dallapiccola melody.

Fawzi, suddenly animated, tried humming the refrain.

Quinn turned to Fawzi, excitedly. "That's it, Talat. Did you decode it . . . ?"

Fawzi stopped humming and stared intensely, trying to gather his thoughts. Then he screamed and started flailing his limbs.

Yonatan and Arik restrained him. Yonatan whispered. "Don't address him directly. Let him join in when he wants to. He won't if he feels threatened."

The gathering waited for Fawzi to calm down.

Getachew started the next round. "I think you're raising false hopes. Even assuming Fawzi decoded your message, you think they'd have let him sabotage the bomb?"

"They'd have had to be physicists to monitor him."

"Look, explain this: Abu Ismail isn't a fool. Why do you think he released Fawzi? Because Fawzi has served his purpose. Because Abu Ismail was satisfied that the bomb was functional."

Fawzi started laughing.

The talking stopped. They stared at him. Yonatan signaled they should go on.

Montblanc picked up the argument. "I think none of you guys can see what's staring you in the face. They've released Fawzi to set a trap."

MacDonald teamed up with Montblanc. "That's stretching it, I'd say. They gave him his passport. They gave him money. They even gave him a flight schedule that'd take him home. That doesn't smack of a trap. . . . More like compassion."

Fawzi mumbled. "Home . . . Beirut . . . Home . . . Please . . . let me go home. . . ."

They stopped expectantly. Yonatan signaled them to continue.

Amnon took up the conversation. "I agree with Montblanc. WOJ have never shown compassion. Why should they now? And particularly a few days before their operation? They wouldn't risk it. One indiscretion from Fawzi—and they're done for."

Sanbat engaged him. "Not if Fawzi's one of them. They wouldn't expect him to be indiscreet."

"Why should he be one of them? We know he's not a fanatic. Quite the contrary . . . A humanitarian . . ."

Fawzi started screaming, his arms jerking. "Horrors . . . horrors . . . Riders of the dragon . . . Fire enfolding itself . . . Please . . . let me go . . . Beirut. . . . Let me die . . . at home. . . . See . . . the Last of . . . Days . . . home . . ." Exhausted, he collapsed back on his pillow, breathing with difficulty.

The Memouneh whispered to Yonatan. "What did that sound like? Hallucinations or fact?"

Yonatan shrugged, uncertain.

The Memouneh pondered a moment, then resumed the discussion. "I'm inclined to agree with Sanbat. They've released Fawzi because he's one of them."

Osman opposed him. "You know WOJ better than that. There's no room for compassion. Men are expendable. The cause is not. They would not have risked his falling into enemy hands—which is just what happened!"

"We're not Fawzi's enemies. . . ."

"How do we prove that to him?"

"By letting him go home."

Fawzi agitated again. "Home . . . Beirut . . . Please . . . Please . . ." His eyes rotating, he tried to pull himself free from his strappings. "A sick man's water—our acts and words . . . Poison —our faith . . . The dreams of the hopeless—our hopes . . . The sun of death—our sun . . . Sorrow . . . our holy ground . . . Every day a day of judgment . . . because . . . evil is what is best in us. . . . This is the age of the assassins. . . . The paths of glory lead to the grave. . . . I say enough. . . . Enough . . ."

Quinn, disturbed, whispered to the Memouneh. "He's quoting —paraphrasing some of his favorite sayings."

Fawzi thundered. "Charlie—"

Quinn turned to him, glowing with hope. "Yes, Talat . . ."

"Home . . . I want to go home. . . ."

"You will, Talat. . . ."

Fawzi screamed. "Liar!"

Quinn glanced at Yonatan. Yonatan nodded uneasily that he should continue.

Quinn toned his voice to its gentlest. "I'll take you home myself —I swear it."

Fawzi focused on him. "The bomb—that's what you're interested in. . . ."

"Only because you made it, Talat . . ."

Fawzi shrieked with laughter. "I made it . . . Height: 1.65 meters. Width: 0.65 meters. Length: 1.70 meters . . . For a Super VC-10."

"Is it functional, Talat?"

Fawzi started crying. "I'm dying, Charlie. . . ."

Quinn forced himself to ignore the plea. "The bomb, Talat— will it work?"

Fawzi started laughing hysterically. "Will it work . . . ? It'll work, Charlie. . . . It'll surprise everybody. . . . A masterpiece."

Quinn held his hand. "Where is the bomb, Talat?"

"Safe—with Abu Ismail . . ."

Boaz pushed his way through. "Excuse me, Charlie. . . . While he's lucid . . ."

Quinn moved away.

Boaz waved Fawzi's map in front of his face. "Talat, see this? It's a map! Of the Baro. Exceptionally detailed. It shows an encampment. . . . It was among your papers—in your passport. Did you draw it?"

Fawzi started coughing and spluttering. "I . . . can't remember. . . ."

"Talat—tell me! Is this the map of the WOJ hideout?"

Fawzi wheezed and tried to catch his breath. "I don't know. . . ."

Boaz shook him roughly. "Look at it, Talat! Is this the map of the WOJ base?"

Fawzi stared at it in horror, then started to flail. "They gave it to me."

"Who?"

"So that I can send them postcards. . . ."

"What?"

"Postcards . . . Postcards . . ."

Boaz slapped him. "Talk sense!"

Fawzi's eyes clouded; a moment later he started convulsing. He pushed Boaz away, screaming.

Yonatan hissed. "You shouldn't have done that!"

Quinn squared up to Boaz. "You inhuman son of a bitch—"

Boaz muttered. "We had to know!"

Fawzi, still screaming and in convulsions, started banging his head against the bedpost. "Home . . . I want to die . . . home. . . ."

Yonatan and Arik tried to hold him down but Fawzi, struggling with superhuman strength, managed to extricate himself from the doctors' grip and, smashing his head viciously against the bedpost, knocked himself unconscious.

Quinn sank onto his chair and held his head in his hands.

The rest, in despair, stared at Fawzi.

Finally, the Memouneh addressed the doctors. "Take him to his room. Let me know when we can try again."

Yonatan and Arik wheeled Fawzi's bed out.

The Memouneh turned to the gathering. "Well, what do you think? Are we wiser?"

Getachew slumped further in his seat. "He made the bomb. It'll work. He said so."

Quinn muttered, trying to compose himself. "He said it would surprise everybody. . . ."

Montblanc paced the room. "Most important—he said it was made to fit a VC-10. That gives us something to work on."

Boaz interjected. "Let's not get bogged down with postmortems! We know where Abu Ismail is! We can go and get him. . . ."

The Memouneh, pensive, lit another cigarette. "That's just what Abu Ismail wants. He's released Fawzi knowing we'd find him. He's drugged him out of his mind, so that we couldn't make head or tail of what he says. But he's planted a map, showing every bend in the river, beckoning us to go after him. He's waiting to deal with us as he's dealt with Ellis and his men."

Boaz stared down at the Memouneh. "He's there. With his assault force. We've got to hit them before they move on again."

"If they cut us down—that's it! We've got nobody to stop them."

"I know that. But we can't afford to sit it out! I'll go—with a few men. You and the main force stay here for a last stand!"

Osman stood up. "Boaz is right. We must go!"

The Memouneh snapped. "Don't rush me!"

"As of now, I revert to being my own man, Zamora. I'm going out there—whatever you say or do!"

The Memouneh gazed at his cigarette. "I admit we can't sit it out. And it'd be better to fight them out there than here in Addis. Who would you want, Boaz?"

"Getachew, for a start. He can guide us."

Getachew stood up. "Ready."

MacDonald interrupted. "I think for the rest the honor falls on us Yanks, sir. We'd like to settle scores. . . ."

"You have duties here. . . ."

"Surveillance! Any of your guys can take over. And it's not only the action we want, sir. I figure your boys have more experience with last-ditch stands than we have. You'll need them if we don't come back. No sense dividing them up now . . ."

The Memouneh nodded.

Montblanc interjected. "Count me in, too."

The Memouneh shook his head. "No. I need one old head here."

Boaz looked at Osman. "Why not two? If Osman changed his mind—"

Osman waved a warning finger. "Not a chance."

Montblanc tried a last gambit. "How about drawing lots?"

Osman repeated his gesture to Montblanc. "Sorry, Montblanc. Decided."

Montblanc resignedly nodded agreement.

The Memouneh stared at his palms. "All right. Some don'ts. You don't fly anywhere near the encampment. I suggest you come up from the south. They know you'll be coming from Addis so they're likely to expect you from the east. Land somewhere between the Baro and the Gilo. Then trek." He paused, stubbed out his cigarette. "I'm sure you'll know what to do if you have no alternative to detonating the bomb. . . ."

Osman spoke uneasily. "We will. Question of numbers. Fewer people there than here . . ."

THE GAMBELA RESERVE, ETHIOPIA

Watanabe sat opposite, a crumpled, emaciated Buddha, eyes closed and inscrutable. Idris Ali aimed his pistol and let the hammer fall on an empty chamber. The mock execution failed to distract; like the previous ones, it had drawn no response from Watanabe, heavily drugged.

Idris Ali pulled himself up. His legs were weak, but no longer shaking. His arms and hands, as his aim proved, were back to their former strength. His sight and hearing had returned, and his temperature had dropped to normal. He had ridden the fever—if fever it had been.

He paced the *tukul*. The dream in which Nazmi sprayed him with BZ gas continued to haunt him. He had checked the stores and burrowed through every inch of the encampment. He had not found a single canister of BZ—or a likely container that might have stored it. Nor had Mahmud, Wahbi and Qabus seen any. But the suspicion remained. Even the most pertinent argument, that his brief illness had burned out, as tropical fevers did, failed to bolster reason. The effects of BZ gas were also of short duration.

And with the suspicion grew the irrational thought. At some point, either during his illness or just before, he had lost a vital battle and now stood to lose everything.

Yet was the thought irrational? The penultimate phase required the transportation of the bomb to Addis Ababa so that WOJ could dictate terms to the emperor. But Abu Ismail had departed with it—earlier than had been planned—ostensibly to give himself a greater margin for the move. The counterargument that the bomb was useless until armed, and that the man Abu Ismail had chosen for the task, Watanabe, had been left behind like Idris Ali to await Abu Ismail's return, failed to satisfy.

One further fact disturbed him. He had tried to raise Ivan Volkov for advice and reevaluation and had failed. Obviously,

Volkov was still briefing his supporters. He would return to Moscow on the twenty-fourth. If Abu Ismail intended to betray them, they would have little time to plan countermeasures.

Reluctantly, he returned to his place and picked up his pistol again. At the least, he would perfect his aim for that one shot he held for Abu Ismail.

DEMBIDOLLO, ETHIOPIA

Abu Ismail felt himself vested with the awesome power of the large crate at the back of the Land-Rover. His bomb. No other Commander of the Faith had been in such harmony with his weapon.

He caught sight of Nazmi and Abbas coming up the hill draped in shammas, like natives. They were not being followed. The six-man squad, spread out at various cover points, had not signaled danger.

He had not expected any. They had left the encampment at night. They had traveled slowly, without lights, conscious of their vulnerability on the Gambela–Jekaw road. Beyond Gambela, on the road north to Dembidollo, there had been little to fear. If the enemy had intercepted Fawzi, they would be coming from Addis Ababa to the east and proceeding southward in the opposite direction.

The sun, filtering through the closed windows, heightened his euphoria. He gazed at the forested mountains shimmering in the brilliant light. He marveled again at Allah's infinite imagination. They were merely sixty-five kilometers north of Gambela, but they could have been in another realm. They were on high land—above the Nile basin. Rain and tropical vegetation had been replaced by sun and clear alpine sky.

Nazmi and Abbas entered the Land-Rover. They kissed his hands and humbly received his affectionate caresses.

Nazmi spoke with an assertiveness acquired since his trial in the Sudd. "The plane's on schedule. It left Addis at eight-fifteen and at the moment it's doing its usual hops to Jimma and Gore. It's due to land here at eleven and then continue on to Beica and Asosa, farther north, at eleven-fifteen. That's exactly as the timetable. It should keep to the timetable on the return journey. Leave Asosa at twelve thirty-five, stop at Beica, and land here again at thirteen thirty-nine for departure at thirteen fifty-four—all that's confirmed. But the airport personnel are not sure whether it will be allowed to continue to Addis. Addis Airport is closed. In fact, our plane left just before the shutdown. If it remains closed, air service may be terminated here. The Four Days of Confusion—"

"Are for our benefit, Nazmi. There'll be no trouble. We'll land at Addis whether it's open or closed."

Nazmi nodded, accepting the assurance without reservation. "Pertinent details: Monday is a busy day. There'll be passengers from Asosa and Beica, and some from here. Usual lot: landlords, merchants, provincial officials . . ."

"Soldiers?"

"None in Dembidollo. Those at Asosa and Beica we know are deployed near the northern border with Sudan. But the plane would have two security men."

"Communications?"

"As per Idris Ali's reconnaissance. One radio for air traffic control in the manager's office. A small telephone exchange in Dembidollo. Both easy to deal with."

"Personnel?"

"Ten. Including four police in charge of screening passengers."

Abu Ismail turned to Abbas. "Any problems for you, Abbas?"

Abbas smiled and prodded the bruises around his broken nose to show that he was untroubled. "None."

"The airport?"

"It's hardly that. A vast field, barely cleared."

"You will be able to take off?"

"The plane's a DC-3. I can lift one of those off the tip of a pencil."

Abu Ismail nodded, then pointed at his watch. "We shall move after the noon prayers."

THE GAMBELA RESERVE, ETHIOPIA

In accordance with the Memouneh's advice, Boaz, Osman, Getachew, MacDonald and his men dropped into the bush south of the Baro some twenty kilometers from the point where the river turned northwest toward Sudan and where, Fawzi's map had indicated, the WOJ encampment lay.

They stopped briefly to watch the Twin Otter disappear into rain clouds safely above missile range. The pilot, Sam Greig, transport officer at the U.S. Embassy, would land at Gambela and visit the American Presbyterian Mission on the pretext of making arrangements for evacuation in the event of political upheaval. He would delay his departure until Boaz's task force returned from the attack on the WOJ encampment.

There had been some delay. Bearing in mind the possibility that WOJ might have lookouts at Addis Ababa airport, or might have activated Wolde, they had decided that the sudden excursion in a USAID plane of eight men heavily laden with packed cases would be too dangerous an undertaking. Consequently, they had left Addis Ababa by car, directing Greig to fly out alone and to rendezvous with them at a Peace Corps model farm airstrip at Ginchi, a townlet eighty kilometers west of the capital. The diversion had cost them two hours. Head winds had caused the flight to take half an hour longer than the estimated two.

Boaz set a hard pace. They had four hours before sundown, and he was determined to reach the Baro by then. The night would be moonless. It was imperative to cross the crocodile-infested river with some residual light still available. They could assume Abu Ismail would discount such a perilous move, slacken guard at the riverbank and redeploy his warriors on a radius covering the Gambela–Jekaw road.

Getachew led the way. Daubed with ash and cattle dung—the Anuak deterrent against insects—and heavily armed, they looked both in harmony with the bush and threatened by it.

DEMBIDOLLO, ETHIOPIA

Abu Ismail sat on a boulder outside the hut that served as a terminal. Abbas leaned against the wall a few paces behind.

Tahir, Riyad, Ferid and Said, dressed in jeans and heavy parkas, had accompanied Abu Ismail as far as the security gate and now waited behind the rope barrier with relatives or servants of the other passengers to watch the plane land and take off.

Abu Ismail was not ignored. He was an important technician —or so people thought, hearing him explain at the check-in desk that his crate, weighing seventy-three kilos, contained precision instruments that he had used for surveys for the Blue Nile Irrigation Scheme, a development project sponsored by FAO.

The ground hostess announced the arrival of Ethiopian Airlines' domestic flight 251 and its subsequent destinations.

Looking up, he spotted the DC-3 approaching from the northwest and checked his watch: 1:33 P.M. The plane was on schedule. He glanced at Abbas, saw him study the approach intently. He reverted his attention to the airstrip. At the farthest end of the field his other warriors, Nazmi, Mohammed and Shamseddin, were measuring the elevation of the ground like seasoned engineers. They had had no difficulty in securing access to the perimeter. The airport manager, impressed by the fact that the Blue Nile Irrigation Scheme included the construction of a concrete runway at Dembidollo, had hardly bothered to check their forged survey permits.

The plane touched down.

The baggage loader sauntered out, pulling a trailer. Two ground crew shunted the steps toward the disembarkation point.

Abu Ismail watched the progress of the baggage loader. The bomb in its crate looked as innocent as the luggage accompanying it.

He stood up.

In the hut's lounge, Tahir edged toward the airport manager's office, which also served as the air traffic control office, and contained the only radio in the area. He waited for communication between the airport manager and the DC-3 pilot to terminate. Neutralizing the radio would take seconds. It would be as easy as when he had cut the telephone wire from a pole outside the townlet, thus isolating Dembidollo from the rest of the country. No one had yet fathomed why the telephone had gone dead.

At the far end of the field, Nazmi, Mohammed and Shamseddin regained their Land-Rover.

In the lounge, Riyad, as if anxious to wave at an arriving passenger, climbed onto a bench. He had a clear view of the four policemen who had conducted the security check. Casually, he unzipped his parka and clutched his PM-63 Polish machine pistol with a 40-round magazine.

Ferid and Said, disengaging themselves from the crowd, took vantage positions in the lounge, their machine pistols also at the ready. They would deal with any bystander who offered resistance.

The plane stopped some fifty meters from the terminal hut.

Abu Ismail stood at the center of the hut's terrace to command operations.

Abbas sauntered onto the airstrip and, like an enthusiastic plane watcher, moved toward the DC-3.

At the far end of the field, Nazmi started the Land-Rover and drove toward the plane. Mohammed and Shamseddin, poised at the passenger side and the back, steadied their guns, also PM-63 machine pistols.

The door of the DC-3 opened. The ground crew pushed the steps to the door. An air hostess secured it. A few passengers gathered at the doorway.

Abu Ismail glanced back.

Tahir slipped into the airport manager's office.

Riyad, Ferid and Said signaled readiness. Abu Ismail held his hand steady, commanding them to wait.

The passengers alighted. The two security men and the crew followed.

As the last of them touched the ground, Nazmi drove to the

blind side of the DC-3 and brought the Land-Rover to a screeching stop. The security men spun around, caught by surprise.

Abu Ismail dropped his hand.

Mohammed and Shamseddin shot the security men before they could pull out their guns. By the time they had also shot the pilot and copilot, who had tried to rush at them, Nazmi had climbed the stairs to cover those passengers who, traveling farther, had stayed in the plane.

In the terminal hut, Riyad shot all four policemen. A warning burst from Ferid and Said froze the rest of the people. In the manager's office, Tahir, who had taken his cue from Riyad to kill the airport manager, proceeded to smash up the radio.

Abbas reached the plane at a run and climbed up the steps. Nazmi waited for him to enter the cockpit, then ushered the passengers out.

Abu Ismail smiled contentedly. The engagement had taken less than a minute. It had borne the mark of Al-Mahdi.

He walked toward the plane. The screams of those left alive rang in his ears. He cherished them as the first strains of victory.

Nazmi led his captives toward the terminal hut where Riyad and Ferid were herding their prisoners into the manager's office. Tahir, joined by Mohammed and Shamseddin, who had run ahead with explosives, started wiring the windows and door to prevent the hysterical crowd from trying to escape.

They took five minutes to load the bomb and take off.

THE GAMBELA RESERVE, ETHIOPIA

They waded in torrential rain a kilometer upstream of the WOJ encampment, where the Baro was about forty meters wide and the current, approaching the major bend, picked up speed.

They had observed earlier that the mudbanks by the WOJ encampment were virtually undefended. Only two lookouts: one on top of the tallest tree, another in a foxhole some twenty meters above the bank. Slack as these precautions had seemed, they had made sense. Crossing the river at the bend, swimmers, no matter how strong, would have had to compensate for the strong current and their efforts would have attracted the attention of both the WOJ guards and the crocodiles. The alternative, a slow, cautious swim across, would have carried the swimmers downstream and presented them with a trek back through terrain offering the defenders countless opportunities for ambush.

By contrast, the particular stretch upriver offered two advantages: thick vegetation and a favorable current. The first proved excellent camouflage; the second, Boaz had calculated, would carry them, at a steady stroke, very close to the WOJ encampment. This would allow them to maintain surprise. The two WOJ guards, together with any others that might be detected, would be picked up simultaneously with the attack by Tripps and Underwood, MacDonald's sharpshooters, planted on the bank opposite the encampment with sniper rifles fitted with telescopic night sights.

They swam in an arrowhead formation. Boaz led, Osman and Getachew followed; MacDonald, Oates and Vernon formed the third line. They used a stroke improvised by Boaz that simulated the swim of the hippopotamus. The heavy waterproof bags containing their weapons were harnessed to their backs; looking like powerful humps, they completed the image of a monstrous triangular animal.

They swam grimly clutching knives in both hands, barely able to suppress panic, particularly when driftwood or rotten vegetation brushed past or entwined them. Their main hope lay in the timing of their crossing. More likely than not, in early evening the crocodiles would still be on the mudbanks or beneath foliage, extracting the last of the day's heat before moving into warmer depths.

It took them four minutes to reach the opposite bank. But for a desperate urge to get out of the water when near the shallows— where they could actually see a few crocodiles—they would have landed dead on target.

Boaz, drained by fear like his companions, resisted the temptation to rest; gesticulating at the men to unpack, he edged forward to survey their objective.

He could barely see the tiny *tukul* which, according to Fawzi's map, was nearest to the river, and had been left disused to give the impression of an abandoned settlement. He judged they had landed some hundred meters short of the encampment.

He scanned the waterfront with infrared binoculars. The guard at the foxhole had shifted position and seemed more concerned with the relentless rain than a possible attack.

An old fear lapped at Boaz's consciousness. Too quiet. Too still.

He surveyed the thick vegetation. According to Fawzi's map, the main compound, four other *tukuls* and a reed complex for stores, lay some thirty meters beyond the disused *tukul*. They were perfectly concealed and he could only estimate their positions. The larger *tukuls* would serve as quarters for Abu Ismail and Idris Ali—and those were the primary targets.

Boaz returned to the men. They had unpacked and were ready. Getachew, Vernon and Oates had donned twin-cylinder napalm-fueled flame throwers capable of twenty seconds of continuous fire. A fourth flame thrower lay prepared for Boaz. He strapped it on. Fired in short bursts at the *tukuls*, the flame throwers would flush out the WOJ commandos and allow Osman and MacDonald, both armed with submachine guns, to deal with them. Tripps and Underwood, on the opposite bank, would pick up those running for cover.

Boaz, using signs, gave his estimation of the likely clear paths to the *tukuls*, and assigned assault positions. They would move by the shortest route, but well spread out: Osman, Getachew and Vernon through the thick foliage; Boaz, MacDonald and Oates down the exposed riverbank. The pelting rain would stifle sound —though for those deployed on the bank, maintaining footing on the squelching mud would be severely testing.

Boaz signaled attack.

Osman, Getachew and Vernon made for the bush.

Boaz, MacDonald and Oates allowed Osman's column time to clamber through the foliage, then moved.

They progressed slowly, zigzagging from one cover position to another; lying still; listening. As they approached the encampment, MacDonald and Oates grew in confidence. There had been no movement behind them, no hoarse whispers. Boaz's soldier's instinct nagged: WOJ, if it had set up an ambush, had since changed its mind. He dared not think of the corollary: that WOJ had lured them to a dead end.

They paused within fifteen meters of the tiny *tukul*. Boaz could see the WOJ commando in the foxhole—bludgeoned by the rain, trying hard to keep alert.

They could now see the four *tukuls* in the main compound. There was light only in the central and largest one. Bright, fluorescent—battery operated. Boaz checked his watch: 5:07. Even assuming that the WOJ task force, marking time and bored with inactivity, might have retired early, it was unlikely that they would have fallen asleep.

Discounting the alarming possibility that the unlit *tukuls* were empty, the only explanation was that WOJ commandos lay in wait within to catch intruders in cross-fire as they moved to the lighted *tukul*. If so, other WOJ would be ready to close in from the bush extending to the Gambela–Jekaw road, the encampment's main line of defense.

The *kraaank* of a heron pierced the air. It was Osman's signal denoting attack readiness. Boaz swiftly delegated objectives to MacDonald and Oates, then signaled Tripps and Underwood on the opposite bank with another heron cry.

The next moment, two shots cracked the night air.

Boaz, running toward the lighted *tukul,* saw the sentry in the foxhole slump. The sound of a body falling through branches assured him that the other visible sentry, on top of the tree, had also been killed.

Monitoring the movements of MacDonald and Oates, as well as those of Osman, Getachew and Vernon storming out of the bush, he aimed the nozzle of the flame thrower at the lighted *tukul.* He dived for cover as the burning jet streaked onto the target.

Oates, Getachew and Vernon had fired almost at the same time, picking the other three *tukuls.* They, too, dived for cover.

The *tukuls,* though sodden with rain, caught fire as the napalm, thicker than gasoline, burned with intense heat.

Boaz, Oates, Getachew and Vernon scrambled to vantage points, leaving Osman and MacDonald room to spray anybody stumbling out of the blazing *tukuls.*

For a few seconds a macabre stillness reigned. Then a scream wavered in the air.

A moment later a man rushed out of the lighted *tukul,* partly aflame, firing his submachine gun blindly from the hip. His voice reverberated with a torrent of Arabic. "Betrayed! Betrayed! Betrayed!"

Another voice—Osman's—thundered above him. "Idris Ali!"

The WOJ chief of staff spun around, waving his gun and screaming. "Yes! Idris Ali! The better man! Al-Mahdi! The better—"

His body shattered as Osman fired a burst.

They stood still, listening to the crackle of the intense fire. Boaz and Osman glanced at each other. Both tried to pretend that Idris Ali's words had been the rantings of a dying man.

A high-pitched sound, part laughter, part scream, rose from the central *tukul.*

Boaz and Osman whirled around. Watanabe, immolating, stared at them through the window. Serene in horrendous death.

Boaz bellowed. "Mac, Getachew—take the road! Vernon, Oates—downriver! Osman—come with me! We still have to find the bomb!"

They scampered toward their objectives.

As Boaz and Osman approached the reed complex, a shrill voice rang out. "Allah! Allah! Allah!"

Boaz and Osman dived for cover.

Two grenades sailed through the air.

Boaz fired in the direction of the voice.

The bush burst into flames.

A figure—Wahbi—ran out, on fire but still shouting. "Allah! Allah! Allah!"

Osman fired a burst.

Wahbi slumped.

The grenades he had thrown exploded harmlessly.

Boaz and Osman sprinted forward.

Wahbi, dying, found the strength to prime another grenade.

As he moved to the reed complex, Osman's weak leg twisted under him.

Wahbi's last grenade detonated.

A burning pain streaked through Osman's spine. He stared in disbelief at the shadowy night, registering the smells that in the heat of the fighting he had ignored: cordite, charred flesh, napalm, burning vegetation. Then a different aroma enveloped him: Samia's perfume. Mingled with sweat. Hers. And his. The fragrance of their lovemaking. And he tasted terror. Bitter. That of death. He cried out. "Not now!"

His legs buckled. He fell.

PART XII

He Who Kills a Man Is an Assassin;
He Who Kills a Million Is a Conqueror;
He Who Kills All Is God.

JEAN ROSTAND, *Pensées d'un biologiste*

April 23, 1974

ADDIS ABABA, ETHIOPIA

Captain Tewodoros Wolde stood near the green-tinted windows of
the air traffic control tower. His shadow would reinforce his paratroopers' sense of occasion.

He had briefed them boldly, proclaiming that there were great
dangers within and without the gates of the empire, that anarchy,
spawned in the palace's stagnant waters, was flooding their country
and that once order was restored, the Dergue would reclaim their
future.

They would lay down their lives for him as their forebears had
done for Emperor Tewodoros. But this Tewodoros would
triumph. The charisma which charged the paratroopers today
would carry the Dergue tomorrow, and all Ethiopia thereafter.

He surveyed the Haile Selassie I International Airport. Ideally
compact.

On this flank, the west, facing Airport Road and the capital,
three buildings stood next to each other: the international terminal, the airport authority offices and the domestic terminal. The
control tower, where he had set up headquarters, rose immediately in front of the central building, at the edge of the apron.
From the apron, taxiways branched north and south, undulating
toward the runway that bisected the perimeter diagonally from
northeast to southwest. Service centers for catering, ground staff
and cleaners were in various bungalows at the southwest. Fuel

424

farm at the northwest; maintenance hangars, air cargo and mortuary at the southeast.

Outside the perimeter there were thick woods directly north, fields to the east and almond groves to the south.

The runways and taxiways were fully lighted. Four M-41 tanks and four AML-245 armored cars cordoned the perimeter. An air defense battery, dug in at the eastern zone, commanded the descent paths around Mount Entoto. Twenty paratroopers dug in at strategic points formed a second line of defense.

Outside the compound another M-41 tank blocked Airport Road; four other armored cars covered the filters that served the terminals. His crack platoon, ten men under Sergeant Ketema's command, were deployed on motorcycles as mobile support force for both the airport and its approaches.

He checked his watch: 2:45 A.M. They had moved in at 11:00 during the night. Waiting made him curiously breathless.

He glanced at Fisseha, senior approach controller and one of the skeleton staff he had retained to keep the airport operative.

Fisseha shook his head to indicate the absence of traffic on his radarscope.

Wolde frowned. Abu Ismail was scheduled to land at 3:00 A.M. There were no adverse weather conditions. The plane should be approaching. It was uncharacteristic of Abu Ismail to fall behind schedule.

He and Abu Ismail had maintained radio silence since noon the previous day as a precaution against interception. He had kept abreast of events by monitoring Ethiopian Airlines' radio signals. He had ascertained the successful hijack of Flight 251 first by the severance of communications at Dembidollo, then through anxious signals from Gore, the plane's next scheduled stop. The 9:00 A.M. radio news, reporting the investigation of Ethiopian Airlines officials despatched from Gambela, had provided confirmation and details.

During that time, keeping to his own schedule, Wolde had emerged from his hideout at Zuquala, an ancient monastery by the crater lake of a dead volcano sixty kilometers south of Addis Ababa—a spot chosen as much for its seclusion as for the fact that a similar monastery had forged his namesake and hero, Emperor Tewodoros. By 7:00 he had assembled his men, transported during the afternoon from Eritrea to Debre Zeyt air base by the Dergue cadre within the Imperial Air Force. Within an hour he had requisitioned tanks, armored cars and the air defense battery from the NCOs of the Addis Ababa-based Fourth Division, the Dergue's staunchest supporters.

He checked his watch again: 2:50 A.M.

Abu Ismail, having decided to arrive in Addis Ababa at the capital's dead hour, had planned to lie low with the hijacked DC-3 in a secluded valley by the foothills of Mount Tuca, some four hundred kilometers west of Addis Ababa. It was possible the DC-3 had failed to execute the tricky maneuvers of landing or takeoff. If so, he, Wolde, faced a debacle. The Dergue members to whom he had promised the emperor's dethronement by the twenty-fifth would sacrifice him peremptorily to preserve the momentum of the creeping coup.

Fisseha shouted. "I have a blip!"

Wolde rushed to the radarscope. "Hijacked plane?"

Fisseha worked the identification switch on the radar. Next to the blip the plane's Squawk ident number, emitted by its transponder, appeared. "Yes. There it is: 251. What do I do?"

"Wait for them to open communications."

Wolde returned to the windows and permitted himself a smile. Nothing had gone wrong. And once Abu Ismail landed, nothing could go wrong. He scanned the perimeter again. He could sense his men's vigilance; they had relished occupying the airport. Compared with the heat, sand and monotony of the Danakil, the deployment had provided excitement.

The pretext for occupying the airport had been easy to formulate. The Dergue's request for the arrest of former cabinet members, which he had initiated as the opening gambit to the Four Days of Confusion, had been rejected by the emperor—as he had expected. The Dergue, incensed, had mobilized and sealed off the capital to prevent the ex-ministers from escaping. Wolde, acting as front-runner, had insisted on securing the airport personally and had directed his fellow conspirators to occupy such key installations as radio and telecommunications, police stations, Imperial Bodyguard barracks and territorial army bases. The operations, perfectly dovetailing, had restricted the emperor to the confines of the Jubilee Palace.

Since then, as he and Abu Ismail had foreseen, the hijacking had provided a suitable emergency to entrench his forces. The news that a number of people had been ruthlessly killed at Dembidollo had prompted Ethiopian Airlines to request high security alert at every airport. His forces, already on the spot at Addis Ababa airport, had complied by sealing it. As further justification for the move, Abu Ismail had prompted him to spread rumors that the USAID Twin Otter that had hastily departed from Addis Ababa the previous morning might have provided support for the Dembidollo hijackers, and that its complement should be held for questioning upon the plane's return.

In fact, the Twin Otter had become an important issue. Abu Ismail had disclosed that the plane had transported a number of Israeli and American agents—as well as Wolde's old enemy Getachew Iyessous—for a raid on the WOJ base at Gambela. He had flushed out these agents by using one of his own men, Fawzi, as bait and expected them to be ambushed by Idris Ali who had stayed behind in Gambela for that purpose. If, however, Idris Ali failed, the American and Israeli agents would most certainly rush back to Addis Ababa. In which case they had to be captured and interrogated on the enemy's plans against both WOJ and Wolde's Day of Glory. Then they could be executed. It was imperative, therefore, to keep Addis Ababa airport under control while fellow officers in the Dergue maintained close watch on all the airstrips near the capital.

The radio crackled. "Addis Control . . . This is Ethiopian 251 . . . Are you receiving me?"

Fisseha turned sharply to Wolde. Wolde indicated he should respond.

Fisseha operated the radio. "Ethiopian 251 . . . This is Addis Control. . . . Receiving you . . ."

Abu Ismail's somber voice resonated authoritatively despite the distortions of radio. "Addis Control. This is Hajji Abu Ismail, leader of WOJ. Listen carefully. This aircraft is under my command. I can destroy Addis Ababa. I urge you neither to intercept us nor obstruct our landing."

Wolde, feigning fury, pushed Fisseha out of his seat and took charge of communications. "Listen, Hajji, whatever—"

Abu Ismail's voice thundered: "Do not interrupt. You are not in a position to threaten or negotiate. This is my directive. Contact the emperor. I have conditions to stipulate. When I land, I want him ready to receive my commands. Is that clear?"

"Now hear this! Addis Ababa airport is under military control. This is Captain Tewodoros Wolde, commanding officer. I urge you to surrender. . . ."

Abu Ismail's voice sounded patient. "You do not seem to understand, Captain Wolde. I repeat: I can destroy Addis Ababa!"

"That's preposterous!"

"True, nonetheless! I can provide proof—and I shall. But only to the emperor!"

"I am not prepared to disturb the emperor—"

Abu Ismail's voice became stern. "Make sure you do, Captain Wolde—by the time I land. I will dictate terms only to the head of state."

Silence ensued.

Wolde raged. "He's bluffing! I should shoot him down. . . ."

Fisseha looked stunned. "And if he's not?"

"What can the emperor do? He has no power! We have!"

"The hijackers don't know that."

Wolde pretended to reconsider. "On the other hand, I'd rather blast them on the ground than in the air. So, why not? Let them speak to the emperor. It might prove the perfect diversion." Brusquely, Wolde resumed communication. "Ethiopian 251. Do you read me?"

Abu Ismail's voice responded gently. "Perfectly, Captain Wolde."

"I grant your request."

"Very commendable, Captain. I shall hand you over to my pilot. You will provide him with landing instructions."

Wolde beckoned Fisseha back to the console. "Take over."

He paced the room in elation. The charade of hostility toward Abu Ismail—witnessed by Fisseha and recorded on tape—would absolve him, should it ever become necessary, of any charges of collaboration with WOJ. Abu Ismail's strategy of insisting on negotiating only with the emperor would also serve to relieve him of the responsibility for the next forty-eight hours. The emperor, Wolde reminded himself, was not totally ineffective. For one thing, affairs of state were still in the hands of his government. For another, the Jubilee Palace possessed means of communicating with the outside world. The emperor, even if he failed to rally support from loyal forces, had the option of approaching heads of friendly states. Abu Ismail, knowing this, had deemed it imperative to neutralize the emperor's power base by forcing the monarch to accept, as head of government, WOJ's immutable conditions. Haile Selassie, whatever else might be said of him, was a patriot. He would never forfeit Addis Ababa. No Ethiopian would, irrespective of his politics. Wolde himself had had to consider the issue carefully when WOJ had sought his collaboration. Had he ever believed Addis Ababa would be seriously threatened, he would have fought WOJ with all his might. He still would if ever Abu Ismail attempted to carry out his threat.

Outwardly, the emperor's capitulation would bestow on Abu Ismail, albeit briefly, absolute power over Ethiopia. He would control the two major forces in the land: the Dergue, through Wolde; the emperor and anti-Dergue elements through his threat to the capital. But such a situation would strengthen the Dergue's hand. Haile Selassie, more exposed than the Dergue, would emerge from the crisis compromised. In the confusion of the aftermath of Operation Dragons, the Dergue would depose and liquidate the emperor. For those Ethiopians still worshiping him, the liquidation would be blamed on Abu Ismail. For those undecided on the Dergue's merits, the emperor's negotiations with Abu Ismail would serve as proof of weakness. For the clergy, always prepared to meddle in politics, the emperor's collaboration with a Muslim fanatic would be anathema.

In the background, Fisseha commenced the talk-down.

Wolde picked up the telephone and dialed the emergency line to the Jubilee Palace.

✗

The U.S. Embassy's cipher room had not been designed for a crowd. They sat on the floor. The Memouneh smoked; Quinn rattled his loose change; Sanbat scribbled compulsively on a pad; the ambassador rested his head between his hands; and Burns, the cipher officer, chewed gum furiously.

They seemed all the more demoralized by the consoles and decks of the sophisticated communications and scrambler network. They had open channels to Gentleman Jim at Fort Meade, Maryland; to O'Brien at Kagnew base, Asmara; and to various U.S. air force and naval commands in the hemisphere. Through the National Security Agency headquarters they could hook up with every major head of state, including Brezhnev, should the Memouneh request it. But all that, they felt, was irrelevant.

The conversation between Abu Ismail and the emperor, on continuous playback, recommenced. Abu Ismail, wanting to ensure his demands would not be misunderstood, had insisted that all communications be recorded.

Haile Selassie:
You have been informed by Captain Wolde of my claim: I can destroy Addis Ababa.

I have in my possession a nuclear device of twenty kilotons yield.

This bomb is the Arab deterrent against the Jew.

No doubt you have heard my warnings that the Jew intends to destroy Mecca in two days' time on his so-called Independence Day, to redeem his defeat in the Ramadan war and establish, by the measure of his sick mind, superiority over Allah's children.

Only one strategy can prevent the Jew from perpetrating this atrocity: the threat of retaliation.

This is my objective.

If the Jew destroys Mecca, I shall destroy Tel Aviv.

This cannot be done from Ethiopia.

But it can be done from Iraq whose sons are the most valiant in all Islam.

I demand the freedom and facility to transport my device to Iraq.

This is a reasonable demand.

However, judging by your past associations with the Jew, you are bound to be unreasonable. You are, like the rest of the world, in the Jew's pocket.

I must, therefore, give you no choice.

If you attempt to stop me, I shall destroy Addis Ababa.

Your people will die a horrendous death—as my brothers shall in Mecca. If you cooperate, you will save Mecca; you will even save the Jew—but, above all, you will save your flower of a capital.

I hope the equation is clear to you.

A long pause ensued. The emperor had apparently been too bewildered to reply. Eventually, Abu Ismail had continued in the same imperious tone.

To practical matters.

Your first impulse will be to doubt the existence of my bomb.

I advise you to consult the French, the Jew and the American.

From the French I took plutonium. The Jew and his lackey, the American, endeavored to stop me at every turn. They should provide proof beyond doubt.

Should you still disbelieve them, find one Talat Fawzi, eminent physicist. He made the bomb. I released him two days ago so that he could supply you with such pertinent data as yield capacity, radius of destruction and fallout characteristics.

He is, I expect, under custody—either yours or the Jew's or the American's.

You cannot dispossess me of my bomb.

I urge you to be absolutely clear about this.

My bomb has a number of booby traps. Any attempt to wrest it from me would cause it to explode.

It also has two special fuses.

The first is a piezoelectric crystal implanted in my tooth. This means that even if you take possession of the bomb or capture and incapacitate me, I can detonate it merely by biting on the piezoelectric crystal.

The second fuse is even more elemental. It is a heart probe which monitors my blood circulation.

This has been transplanted into my body. Should you kill me, the bomb will detonate within forty seconds of my death.

I foresee you might consider these last two claims beyond credibility.

I urge you to consult experts.

They will confirm feasibility.

You have two hours to do so.

At oh six hundred hours precisely, I shall specify my conditions for a harmonious collaboration.

The tape, on loop, returned to playback.

Quinn snapped. "Do we have to listen to it again?"

Burns looked at the ambassador. The latter nodded agreement with Quinn. Burns switched off the tape.

Quinn groaned in despair. "We know the fuses are functional. Jerusalem confirmed feasibility. So did Gentleman Jim. We might as well tell the emperor and get on with some thinking."

The ambassador turned to the Memouneh. "You call the shots, sir—at least, until Gentleman Jim rescinds the order."

The Memouneh checked his watch: 5:41 A.M. "We'll wait. Until five fifty-five."

Quinn spun toward him. "What's the sense in that?"

"I want the emperor to sweat, Charlie. He's an old man. He needs time to digest facts. When we get back to him, I want him crushed."

"You think that'll help?"

"Yes. I don't know what Abu Ismail's conditions will be, but they're bound to be awesome. I want the emperor to turn to us as his only hope."

"He's begging—already!"

"Not yet. He's *consulting* us. He's also trying to think how to go it alone. That would be his instinct. We don't want to be blocked. Or crowded out. Or waste time in endless conferences rushing here and there. Or be pushed aside when things get critical. We have to play Abu Ismail our way. The emperor must give us a free hand. He will—but only if he realizes we're his only hope."

"And if he doesn't?"

"We tell him he loses Addis Ababa. We tell him there's an agent at the airport ready to kill Abu Ismail. We tell him the agent is an Israeli who doesn't give a damn about Addis if it means saving Israel."

"Would he believe it?"

"Wouldn't you?"

Quinn frowned uncertainly.

The Memouneh pressed his point. "You're half inclined to believe it now, Charlie. Even though you know that if we fail, your fighters will shoot Abu Ismail down. But you suspect we'd rather not risk his slipping through your hands. That to preserve the

Jewish state we'd blow up Addis and Abu Ismail first, then face the music."

Quinn hesitated. "Would you?"

"You won't believe me if I say no. At the moment, I don't have the directive. But even if I did, I doubt I'd be able to carry it out."

"You *doubt?*"

"All right. Let's say there's a possibility I might. Which proves my point. No one can take that chance."

Quinn nodded.

Sanbat rose to fetch more coffee.

The Memouneh watched her leave, not without admiration. She had borne the news from Gambela with great fortitude.

The last twelve hours had been as bad as any the Memouneh had experienced during his harrowing tenure of office. The details of the WOJ hijack had reached them through Sam Greig well before the radio news. Greig, waiting at Gambela to airlift Boaz's company, had been on the spot when the investigating Ethiopian Airlines officials had returned from Dembidollo. Getachew's chilling signal reporting Osman's death had followed in its wake. Then Captain Wolde had materialized.

Abu Ismail had chosen his quisling well. Wolde's occupation of the airport had been efficient. It said much for Montblanc and the six Sayeret Matkal on surveillance in and around the compound that they had managed to slip out of his dragnet without mishap.

The Memouneh could take comfort only from the fact that a seventh Sayeret Matkal, Emmanuel, one of the two Falashas in the company and fluent in Amharic, had managed to slip into the international terminal as a member of the skeleton staff. If Emmanuel could keep evading Wolde's patrols or, better still, find a hole to hide in, he would operate as lookout.

Then there had been two more signals from Getachew. The first, following a thorough search of WOJ's Gambela base, had confirmed that Abu Ismail had decamped with his bomb. The second reported that Greig had duly flown the USAID Twin Otter to the base, but instead of landing it on the Gambela–Jekaw road as previously arranged, had crashed it into the Baro on Boaz's order. A cryptic coda from Boaz had urged that the plane's fate should be conveyed—somehow—to Abu Ismail.

As soon as Montblanc and the six Sayeret Matkal had regained the safe house, the Memouneh, Sanbat and Quinn had transferred to the U.S. Embassy. The move had been instigated by Quinn who had argued that the Memouneh now required an inviolate command post from which to conduct operations, and that the embassy, with its diplomatic immunity, was the only option. The embassy's communications system, unlike the equipment in the safe house, had the range and authority to engage and monitor every conceivable source.

The fact that the Memouneh was privy to the dialogue between the embassy and the Jubilee Palace—and that through O'Brien's surveillance aircraft operating around the clock from Kagnew base, he could monitor Abu Ismail's signals both from the DC-3 and on the field—had proved the wisdom of the move. Also of vital importance, the embassy's receivers permitted him to monitor Soviet Embassy communications. WOJ's Russian connection, the Memouneh still suspected, would come into play before or during Operation Dragons.

The switch to the embassy, however, had heightened his sense of doom. He was prepared to believe he had finally reached the Masada which had haunted him all his life. This one merely happened to be far from home and different from what he had imagined. Osman's death underscored the belief and eroded the remnants of hope. Moreover, he had left Montblanc and the Sayeret Matkal at the safe house to preserve their freedom of movement. And he felt he had deserted them. Quinn, heartbroken at having to abandon Fawzi, who had been too ill to be moved, had understood. The Memouneh dreaded that if he managed to return to Israel, he would do so with only one survivor—Sanbat, if, that is, she managed to remain sane, listing the dead as they fell.

Sanbat returned with the coffee, passed the mugs around, then sat beside him.

He noted her attempt to smile, then checked his watch: 5:55. He turned to the ambassador. "Your Excellency . . ."

The ambassador nodded and picked up the telephone.

The Memouneh's voice urged confidence. "As I said, we need a free hand. Make the most of the Twin Otter. Say it's been shot down like the USAID helicopter. Say that proves how ruthless WOJ are. Urge the emperor to tell Abu Ismail you're furious, particularly as there have been no survivors!"

The ambassador tried to shake off his confusion. "Don't worry."

Quinn interjected. "Zamora, aren't we likely to muddle the issue with that plane? We don't even know why Boaz destroyed it!"

"No doubt he thinks Wolde and Abu Ismail are waiting for it to return."

"So they'll stop waiting. What will that change? And why destroy the plane just to make them think that? If you ask me, he's flipped! Osman's death was the last straw! We know—"

The Memouneh cut him off abruptly. "Perhaps. We'll see." He nodded to the ambassador.

The ambassador breathed deeply and started dialing.

The Memouneh turned to Sanbat. She looked away. Her despair reminded him of a wounded soldier he had once assisted in another war. When he had cut the clothes off, the youth's insides had fallen out. The boy had averted his eyes as Sanbat did now. Her wound was Osman's death. She remained whole, only because her training held her together. She did not know what Boaz would do. Nobody did.

AGARO, ETHIOPIA

Boaz had reached the eye of the storm.

And the storm was unfurling as that cloud in the scriptures that Elijah had pointed out to Ahab, and which had billowed to cover the firmament.

He would become fixed in the eye. Ground into a cyclopean lens, he would collect fire and immolate Abu Ismail.

He turned to Osman, pressed the rigid hands. He had held them all night. They were cold now. He gazed at Osman's eyes. He had been unable to close them. But who could say the dead did not need eyes? There was much Osman had to see before they put earth over him. He mumbled. "I know Abu Ismail now, Osman. Formidable. But he makes mistakes. He has a flaw."

"What?"

The voice disoriented him. He searched Osman's face. A distraught death mask. Then realized that the speaker was Getachew, in the front seat. He looked up, saw Getachew's concern, and inclined his head apologetically. "Sorry. Talking to myself."

"What mistakes?"

Boaz shrugged, reluctant to talk. "We're still alive."

Getachew nodded grimly.

Boaz cast a look at the roadside. He caught sight of Tripps, squatting by a tree, defecating. Farther up, MacDonald and Underwood were jacking up the other Land-Rover. Vernon, Greig and Oates were pumping spare tires. He turned to Getachew, no longer distracted. "Anything serious?"

Getachew shook his head. "Only tires. One's punctured. The other's torn."

Boaz frowned. "That's five spares gone!"

Getachew stared at the woods stretching from both sides of the road. "We're just outside Agaro. The road will get better. We shouldn't have any more problems."

Boaz looked at the Michelin road map on his lap. WOJ, whose Land-Rovers they were using, had supplied each vehicle with one. He glanced at his watch: 6:25 A.M. "We're due to check with the Memouneh in five minutes. Might as well do it here."

Getachew nodded. "I'll set up the radio."

As Getachew got out, Boaz watched MacDonald and Underwood. They were now left with seven spares. He could have taken more. The WOJ stores, comprehensive, had had dozens. But he had preferred not to overload the Land-Rovers, particularly as he had given priority to fuel—enough to get them to Addis Ababa: twelve jerricans for each vehicle. He reverted to the map. They had traveled halfway. The worst stretches were behind them. Barring exceptional bad luck, the spares should be adequate.

They had made good time: six hundred-odd kilometers in just over nine hours. Mostly at night. The Land-Rovers had been in perfect condition. He had wondered at first why Abu Ismail had left them intact at the base. Then he had remembered Idris Ali's howled epithet: "Betrayed!" Whatever his reasons for exposing Idris Ali, Abu Ismail must have promised to return and Idris Ali must have believed him, thinking a betrayer would not have left some means of escape or pursuit.

But in his attempt to deceive Idris Ali, Abu Ismail had made a mistake. Having set up Fawzi, he had rightly expected the enemy to come by air. But he had been wrong to assume the enemy would leave the same way.

Abu Ismail must have expected them to depart immediately after the engagement with Idris Ali in order to get to Addis Ababa ahead of him. His delayed arrival at Addis Ababa early that morning supported that theory: he had not wanted the enemy warned by lookouts of the trap he had laid. Presumably, he had expected them to land at about midnight, straight into Wolde's hands. With the enemy thus captive or destroyed, he would have had a clear path for the last lap.

In that context, Abu Ismail had made another mistake. He had assumed the enemy would send all its combatants to Gambela, leaving behind only such peripheral operators as lookouts, and minor agents attached to the U.S. Embassy or USAID. He had not considered the enemy would have gathered a sizable force. He had been satisfied by the lack of precedent. Israel, whatever the provocation, had never before dared send a task force overseas. She had always resorted to a few select hit men. Though the same could not have been said about the U.S.A., it was reasonable to expect that she, too, would keep a low profile in the wake of international denunciations on the CIA's role in the overthrow of Chile's President Allende. The misconception was proof that the

Divinely Guided One did not walk flawlessly through his maze of clouds.

Thus, he had allowed Boaz a thread of initiative. Instead of returning to Addis Ababa with the Twin Otter, Boaz had ordered Sam Greig to ditch it into the Baro. Then, spared the trouble of finding alternative transport, he had resorted to the unexpected: the overland return in WOJ's vehicles.

There had been two routes available: one through Nekempt, north to east, another through Jimma, south to northeast. The distances had been 919 and 998 kilometers respectively. The first, served with relatively better roads, required fifteen hours; the second, between eighteen and twenty. He had chosen the second partly because it was good strategy to be perverse, but mainly because the longer route, mostly forested, provided concealment from the air.

The salient point was that Abu Ismail would be confused for some precious hours. The Twin Otter having failed to return to Addis Ababa, he would demand a search. Wolde or the Dergue would forage outlying airstrips. Foiled, they would extend the hunt to Gambela and discover the Twin Otter's wreckage. Conceivably, Abu Ismail might dismiss the matter there, accepting that the plane had crashed trying to take off from the only place it could have landed, the Gambela–Jekaw road—a plausible thesis, considering the hazards of flying out at night from a strip of jungle road barely suitable for vehicles. Conceivably, too, he might presume the plane's complement had either died on impact or drowned. If so, Boaz and his men should enter Addis Ababa unchallenged some time in the afternoon.

If not—and it would be characteristic of Abu Ismail to distrust the plane's fortuitous end—there would be roadblocks on both routes from Gambela. By that time, barring breakdowns, Boaz and his men would be near Addis Ababa. And they would have the option of abandoning vehicles and trekking over the hills. They would still be on time to engage Abu Ismail.

Getachew, looking grim, returned and handed him a sheet of paper.

"From the Memouneh. Abu Ismail's demands of the emperor."

Boaz read the decoded text.

ONE: ADDIS ABABA AIRPORT WILL REMAIN CLOSED TO ALL TRAFFIC UNTIL TOMORROW, APRIL 24. THE EXPLANATION FOR THIS WILL BE FOR VITAL REPAIRS TO THE RUNWAY. ALL INTERNATIONAL FLIGHTS WILL BE DIVERTED TO ASMARA. ASSURANCES WILL BE GIVEN THAT THE AIRPORT WILL RESUME NORMAL SERVICES APRIL 24.

TWO: ABU ISMAIL'S PRIVATE JET, AT PRESENT AT ENTEBBE, UGANDA, WILL BE THE ONLY EXCEPTION TO THE ABOVE. IT WILL BE GIVEN CLEARANCE TO LAND WHEN IT ARRIVES AT ADDIS ABABA.

THREE: THE SENIOR DELEGATE TO THE ORGANIZATION OF AFRICAN UNITY FROM EACH OF THE 41 MEMBER STATES WILL BE HANDED OVER TO WOJ AS HOSTAGES. IN THE CASE OF ANY DELEGATE'S LEGITIMATE ABSENCE EITHER A MEMBER OF HIS FAMILY OR TWO OF HIS SUBORDINATES WILL BE TAKEN IN HIS PLACE. UTMOST DISCRETION WILL BE USED IN THE ROUNDUP. THE ORDER FOR THE ARRESTS WILL BE ISSUED BY THE EMPEROR PERSON-ALLY AND CARRIED OUT BY THE IMPERIAL BODYGUARD. THE OAU DELEGATES OR THEIR REPLACEMENTS WILL BE DELIVERED TO ADDIS ABABA AIRPORT BY A COMPANY OF THE EMPEROR'S MOST LOYAL BODYGUARDS. THE BODYGUARD ESCORT WILL THEREUPON SURRENDER UNCONDITIONALLY.

"Interesting."

Getachew stiffened. *"Interesting?* If we arrest the OAU dele-gates we'll be declaring war on virtually every African state."

"If Abu Ismail succeeds, every African state will have other things to worry about."

Getachew grunted. "You know what this means? We'll have our hands tied. We can't touch Abu Ismail's plane—not with the OAU as hostages."

Boaz pondered for a moment, then glanced at Osman and nodded as though he had been given good advice. "Among the OAU delegates—is there anyone friendly toward Ethiopia? Really friendly?"

"I should think so. None of the Arabs, but certainly some of the Africans."

"Ask the Memouneh to find the friendliest—and compromise him. . . ."

"Compromise him?"

"I want at least one of our boys among the hostages—two if at all possible. Tell the Memouneh I'm thinking of the Trojan Horse. It's one of our assault blueprints."

"I can guess what it is. Can it work?"

"I don't know what will work. But let's sow where we can. Another thing: I'm sure the Memouneh has thought of it, but tell him if Abu Ismail intends to open the airport tomorrow he must have his eye on one of the flights. We know from Fawzi the bomb's made to fit a Super VC-10. That gives us a few moves—like finding out which carrier and then coercing one of the ground staff to help out."

"You're giving me hope, Boaz. . . ."

"We won't fail."

Getachew moved to send the signal, then stopped. "Wouldn't you like to get out a bit? Stretch your legs?"

"No."

"If it's . . . I can sit with Osman. . . ."

"Thanks, Getachew. But no." He frowned with a sudden thought. "Is he starting to smell?"

"Not yet."

Boaz turned toward the sun, already steaming the earth. "It'll be a hot day . . . You won't mind . . . ?"

Getachew shook his head, then walked away.

Boaz cradled Osman in his arms.

He had chosen to believe his friend was present. Listening, evaluating, advising, guiding. He did not know whether the belief was anchored in his own mysticism or was a trick of the mind, to enable him to live with Osman's death. It did not matter which. It stoked him now as it had stoked him after his sister's death. The truth was that if the dead did oversee the living, then Osman was with him. Osman was not one to abandon friends, even in the sanctity of his death. Osman, as ever, would seek to break through his loneliness.

There was another reason for Osman's immanence: the order of *kapparot*. The ancient Jewish belief that demanded, as part of the ritual of atonement, the transference of a man's sins to a substitute. The order, at its symbolic level, imposed the sacrifice of a pure life so that a man's scarlet soul could become as white as snow. It was the only phenomenon that could possibly explain Osman's death.

The equation was simple. Osman, the innocent, had been sacrificed for Boaz, the sinner. The One God—Adonai or Allah—had decreed that the better killer should execute His Will. Man, for reasons that only the Deity could justify, would survive—for the time being.

ADDIS ABABA, ETHIOPIA

By 7:55 A.M., the company of Imperial Bodyguards commissioned to arrest Julius Habyarwanda, Rwanda's economic chargé d'affaires at the OAU, had sealed off the dilapidated block where Habyarwanda lived in a two-room apartment.

They waited until 8:15, the time specified by WOJ for the simultaneous arrests of the OAU hostages before the delegates had left home for their offices.

Montblanc, who had arrived at Habyarwanda's apartment minutes before the Imperial Bodyguard, watched them take position from the window.

His reluctant host, still sleepy-eyed, examined his press card. "Journalist—you say?"

Montblanc moved away from the window and set up his tape recorder. He had twenty minutes to befriend Habyarwanda. His French, a Joseph's coat of exotic accents from Martinique, Puerto Rico, the U.S.A., the Foreign Legion and Djibouti, compared with Habyarwanda's Belgian French, had already mesmerized the chargé d'affaires. A worldly, professional attitude would impress further. "From Haiti. Radio Port-au-Prince. Investigating the possibilities of a coffee cartel for small states such as ours against the world economic crisis. I spent much of yesterday in Africa Hall, looking for your ambassador."

"He's away at Kigali, our capital. I'm the only member of our mission here."

"So I found out . . ."

"Anyway, the ambassador wouldn't have been able to help. I'm the economic expert. In fact, I've just submitted a report to the U.N. Economic Commission for Africa, on your very subject." Habyarwanda moved to his desk, rummaged through his papers and handed Montblanc a photocopied document. "The tip of the iceberg."

"Pardon?"

"Our troubles, Monsieur . . ."

"Philippe Mercier . . . Would you mind if I recorded our interview? I don't want to misquote."

Habyarwanda's manner warmed. "Do, please . . ."

Montblanc switched on the tape recorder. "You were saying?"

Habyarwanda assumed a studious frown. "Our troubles, Monsieur Mercier, are misleading. After all, Rwanda is one of the poorest countries in the world. Also one of the most densely populated. If our bowl of sorghum is reduced to half, it means nothing to the rest of the world. After all, who has heard of Rwanda? Who cares? But the world is blind, Monsieur Mercier. They cannot see that our bowl reduced by half portends a terrible depression. Eventually, pro rata, everybody's bowl will be reduced by half. After all, we're only the tip of the iceberg."

Montblanc nodded. "I see. . . . Most enlightening . . ."

Habyarwanda smiled. "That's just a general outline. There are imponderables, variations, geopolitical factors—which I could expound. . . ."

"I should be very glad if you did. . . ."

"If you are not in a hurry . . ."

"No hurry at all. My plane leaves this evening—if the airport opens, that is . . ."

Habyarwanda shook his head disconsolately. "There you are.

This country's troubles? After all, what are they? Economic. Why? Because its economy has no shield, nothing to counterbalance it against the oil crisis." He checked his watch. "I must get ready. Will you join me for breakfast?"

"If it's no inconvenience."

"None at all. It will be very simple. After all, we are a poor country. You see how I live. . . ."

"Very honorable. I shouldn't say this, but you should see some of our diplomats."

Habyarwanda smiled again, pleased with the compliment. "Integrity, Monsieur Mercier. It's the only luxury for the enlightened poor. I'll put the coffee on." He disappeared into the kitchen.

Montblanc returned to the window. Some of the Imperial Bodyguards were converging on the building. He examined as a final check the thick strip of plaster covering the deep cut on his finger. The cut had been self-inflicted. The strip of plaster was vital ordnance against WOJ.

He sat down, rewound the tape recorder, pressed the playback button and started listening to the recorded conversation. Habyarwanda, on his way from the kitchen to the bathroom, looked impressed. Montblanc felt convinced he had won him over. At the very least, the Rwandan would vouch for him should any OAU delegates question his identity. Whether that would pass muster with Abu Ismail was another matter.

At 6:05 A.M. the emperor, advised by the Memouneh through the American ambassador, had accepted Abu Ismail's demand for the arrest and delivery of the OAU hostages. Long before that the Memouneh had been working on the possibility of infiltrating some of the Sayeret Matkal among the delegates. By 6:30, having considered every possible variable, he had had to abandon the option. Being black, none of the Sayeret Matkal could pass as an Arab diplomat; and none bore the slightest resemblance to any of the African delegates,

Then the Memouneh had investigated the possibility suggested by Boaz, of compromising a delegate friendly to Ethiopia. He had soon rejected the idea. Such a move would have necessitated disclosing something of the prevailing situation, and there were no guarantees that the delegate would not panic and consequently provoke Abu Ismail to countermeasures.

Thereafter, with time running short, there had been a brief open forum between the personnel at the U.S. Embassy and those at the safe house.

It had fallen to Montblanc to come up with the present ploy. Included in the equipment brought by the CIA-SO team had been a series of documentation tailor-made for every member of the task force. Because of Montblanc's Caribbean background and command of French, the CIA had produced for him a set of Haitian papers identifying him as a journalist from Port-au-Prince. Haiti, enjoying a boom in coffee exports, had begun establishing contacts with other coffee producers, not only in Latin America, but also in Africa, particularly with Ethiopia, Uganda, Rwanda and Burundi, for all of which coffee was a vital cash crop. Haiti was determined to escalate the prices as oil producers had escalated theirs. As a result, Haitians had become less of a rarity in Addis Ababa, headquarters of the OAU.

The ploy had required one last condition for success: a gullible delegate whom Montblanc could legitimately approach. Julius Habyarwanda, on his own in Addis Ababa, had been singled out by the embassy computer as the likeliest.

He was young, fiery and, as a devout Catholic, not pro-Arab. He was also an idealist and a man of moral courage. He was one of the few Hutus who had not bloodied his hands in Rwanda's bitter conflict between his tribe and the Tutsis. He was politically immature and insecure in the turbulent waters of global economics. He was inclined to compensate for this weakness by championing popular grievances. Finally, he had only just started his term in the OAU and had not yet adopted the caprices of high office toward obscure journalists.

Montblanc had received the go-ahead at 7:20 A.M. He had left the safe house immediately.

Habyarwanda emerged, dressed and carrying two cups of coffee. As he laid them on the table, Montblanc respectfully switched off the tape recorder.

The doorbell rang.

Habyarwanda turned to Montblanc. "Did you bring a colleague?"

Montblanc shook his head. "No."

Puzzled, Habyarwanda opened the door.

Four Imperial Bodyguards entered. Their sergeant, waving a warrant, declared his business in officious English. "Mr. Julius Habyarwanda—you are under arrest."

Habyarwanda responded in poor English. "You say—what charge?"

"You will be advised not to resist."

Habyarwanda protested. "I member of OAU. I diplomatic immunity have."

The sergeant ignored him and turned to Montblanc. "Who are you, please?"

Montblanc presented his press card.

The sergeant examined the card, then, troubled, looked around the room, spotted the telephone and walked over to it. As he dialed, his men grabbed hold of Habyarwanda.

Habyarwanda raged. "You not know what you doing! I warn you!"

Montblanc tried to intervene. "I can vouch for him. He's a diplomat."

The Imperial Bodyguards ignored him.

The sergeant spoke hesitantly into the telephone. Montblanc caught the gist of the Amharic and was reassured that the sergeant was speaking to the emperor's office. The emperor had been briefed to communicate with Abu Ismail during this call and report that a journalist was present at one of the delegates' houses. It had been assumed with a degree of certainty that Abu Ismail would order the journalist's arrest in order to suppress the news of the OAU delegates' roundup. At this stage of Operation Dragons, Abu Ismail would not want Ethiopia exposed to African fury and world scrutiny.

The sergeant received his orders impassively. He replaced the receiver and beckoned Montblanc. "You are under arrest, too."

Montblanc stared at him in horror, then grabbing his tape recorder, tried to run out. The sergeant barked an order. One of his men struck Montblanc across the back with his baton. Montblanc collapsed, almost enjoying the pain and started to whine.

✗

Emmanuel, the Memouneh's sole lookout at the airport, had found the perfect niche: the duty-free sales manager's office off the international departures lounge on the first floor. The office, like all the others, had been locked. He had master keys should he need to make a quick exit. The air-conditioner outlet provided a convenient hole for his radio aerial. The window, overlooking the apron, offered an excellent view of the compound; venetian blinds minimized the chances of his being seen from the outside.

The possibilities of being intercepted seemed remote. Though every hour or so a company of what sounded like three men patrolled the empty lounge and checked the offices, so far, they had not bothered to open the doors and look inside. Should they do so, Emmanuel would have time and surprise on his side to knock them out, drug them, drench them with whiskey, break open the cashboxes and move with his gun and radio to another niche. When found, the guards would appear to have been looting. Incoherent, seemingly drunk, they would be unable to offer a plausible story.

Emmanuel watched the eight WOJ commandos on the apron. They had arrived from Entebbe at 11:37 in Abu Ismail's executive jet, the Grumman Gulfstream II flown by WOJ's second-string pilot, Isa. Within minutes, they had started unloading toolboxes, planks of wood and metal tracks. Emmanuel, preparing to report to the Memouneh, surmised they would act as ground crew to prevent possible sabotage of the WOJ plane.

✗

The emperor's lions prowled in their cages. The Lion of Judah himself prowled in the throne room. The gardens of the Jubilee Palace droned with the fury of captivity. The sound reminded Yitzhaq, the second Falasha in the Sayeret Matkal, of the wail of hopelessness he had heard among his people before he had emigrated to Israel.

The drone was the collective voice of the OAU hostages, herded into the summerhouse. They had been allowed to register their protests to two protocol secretaries—inside the building, so that their hysteria would not draw the attention of the reporters who had been gathering outside the palace gates like vultures since the start of the Dergue's progressive bid for power.

Yitzhaq checked his watch: 12:15 P.M. There were still hours to go. Abu Ismail had demanded delivery of the hostages at 5:00 P.M. Why the WOJ leader had insisted on a delay when all the hostages had been rounded up by 8:30 A.M. was a mystery.

The long wait worried Yitzhaq. Abu Ismail's demand for an Imperial Bodyguard escort for the OAU hostages had given the Memouneh an excellent gambit. Through the Americans he had prevailed upon the emperor to include Yitzhaq as a member of this company. Yitzhaq had duly reported to the captain of the bodyguards, Major Afewerk, at 8:30; by the time the hostages had been rounded up, he had gained the trust of the ten men selected. By now he should have been inside the airport, locked up by WOJ and forgotten, so that he and Afewerk could plan how to break loose at zero hour.

✗

The photographs showed the Twin Otter's severed tail sticking up from the Baro's shallows; the current frothed against the USAID markings. The main fuselage was not in evidence, though the dark shadow in midstream suggested it had sunk there. There were no bodies discernible in the mangled wreckage. Other photographs taken upstream and downstream had failed to record corpses.

Abu Ismail turned to his pilots, Abbas and Isa. "Is it possible?"

Isa, who had taken the photographs, replied without hesitation. "To crash on takeoff? Very easy."

Abbas scowled, annoyed at Isa's assurance, so characteristic of his youth and inexperience. "Possible—yes."

"But you have reservations?"

Abbas nodded. "If it could land on that narrow road, it should have been able to take off. If it had crashed on landing, I'd have no reservations. . . ."

Isa protested vehemently. He had been detoured to Gambela while flying in from Entebbe to find out why the USAID plane had failed to return to Addis Ababa. He had accomplished his mission. Most competently. "I flew over the river several times. Thick vegetation, tropical rains. A bog in the jungle. Anything could have gone wrong. A gust of wind could have toppled it over."

Abu Ismail snapped back. "There should have been corpses."

Isa pointed at the photographs. "With respect, Al-Mahdi, between the current and the crocodiles, there'd be nothing left."

Abu Ismail pondered another moment, then dismissed the pilots with a wave.

He moved to the plate-glass windows of the control tower. Nazmi took position by his side to scrutinize the airport compound. He did not expect trouble, particularly with Wolde keeping his paratroopers on their toes, but having climbed the ranks as a sniper, he could never be at ease when his leader stood before a window.

"What do you think, Nazmi?"

"I think they crashed. I can't see any other explanation."

Abu Ismail watched the eight commandos who had arrived with Isa unload equipment from the Grumman. He admired their efficiency. They would service and equip the Super VC-10 expertly. "I distrust gifts—even from Fate." An inner voice, hiding within the retina of his soul, had been worrying him, warning him there was another explanation, that the enemy had purposely destroyed the plane to dupe him. It was, of course, the voice of caution urging him to check the roads from Gambela, reminding him that as Al-Mahdi, it was incumbent upon him to consider even the unlikeliest possibility. "We have to know for certain, Nazmi. Order Wolde to arrange surveillance on the roads from Gambela. There may be an odd survivor trying to get back."

"Yes, Al-Mahdi."

Abu Ismail checked his watch: 12:28. He felt uneasy and wondered whether this was because the OAU hostages were not due to be handed over before 5:00. There could be no danger in shunting them to the Jubilee Palace for the day. Wolde had requested the move so that the hostages could confront the emperor. The emperor's refusal to release them would show him to be insane and justify, in African eyes, the Dergue's coup. This placebo for Wolde was good policy—and not without psychological advantages for Operation Dragons. After their futile remonstrations, the hostages would be agitated. When delivered to the airport, they would be exhausted and all the more vulnerable to the greater shock awaiting them. They would cower instantly, like sheep disciplined by a shepherd's dog.

Still, he remained uneasy. There had been the odd moment when the voice of caution had sounded like Al-Munafiq. Which was absurd. He had destroyed The Doubter in the Sudd.

GHION, ETHIOPIA

Ghion, famous for its hot springs and a mere 120 kilometers from Addis Ababa on an unusually good road, was a popular resort with the Establishment. Getachew had predicted that some of these, if they had not already left the country, would be weathering the Four Days of Confusion at the spa, while keeping close contact with their underlings. They would thus have news of the latest situation in the capital and be able to assess what concerned Boaz most, the security measures at the main entry points. Consequently, MacDonald and Oates, acting as producers planning a sequel to *Shaft in Africa*, a film much loved by Ethiopians for having been shot in their country, and accompanied by Getachew as their official escort, had gone to the Ras Hotel to be lionized over a leisurely lunch by the hotel pool.

Boaz had directed the Land-Rovers to a disused picnic site near one of the lesser springs. Greig, Vernon, Tripps and Underwood had spread out to keep watch.

From Agaro on, they had made excellent progress. A steady fifty kilometers an hour. No flat tires. No mechanical troubles. No patrols. No roadblocks. They had reached Ghion at 12:20. It would take two hours or so to drive to Addis Ababa. He would set departure in accordance with Getachew's report. If the roads were clear, they would attempt to reach the capital before sundown to snatch a brief rest prior to planning the final moves. If the roads were guarded, they would wait for darkness.

At 1:00 he had reported progress to the Memouneh and had, in turn, received encouraging news on the infiltration of Montblanc, Emmanuel and Yitzhaq. At present, the Memouneh was working on recruiting a fourth man, an outsider and in many respects the most important element: a member of British Airways' staff.

Boaz felt confident that these men, backed by the Sayeret Matkal and the CIA-SO, would level the odds. After that, victory or defeat would rest with an altogether different creature. A specter. Al-Munafiq. The Despoiler. The Doubter.

He had been formulating a rough plan. Osman, by whose side he had remained, had continued to inspire him.

It had been Osman who had instructed him about The Doubter. In Mecca. Enveloped by Holy Breath. This ghoul of Muslim mysticism penetrated the soul's innermost recesses, mutilated the spirit. That was the key to Abu Ismail. And Osman had known it. The Chosen One's fatal flaw. No matter how much he believed in his Chosenness, he still had to face Reason. And Reason was a scourge—always. The Doubter's ultimate weapon.

Boaz fanned the flies away from Osman's open eyes. There were signs of decomposition in the swelling face. And the heat threatened worse. But the sun, smoothing Osman's features, wrestled with the ravages of death. Boaz clung to the illusion that Osman was smiling.

Abu Ismail might think he had defeated The Doubter—perhaps in the Sudd, during his trial by ordeal. But The Doubter always returned. This time, he would return incarnated in Boaz.

ADDIS ABABA, ETHIOPIA

The Memouneh peered at Hugh Llewellyn who was sipping his fourth bottle of beer or, as he had put it, his second pint. There had been a natural integrity in Llewellyn's firm handshake, which the Memouneh had thought encouraging.

A short, stocky man, Llewellyn was a British Airways ground engineer at Addis Ababa airport. Though not chief inspector, he had, as the expert on turbines and compressors, the authority to ground a plane. A gruff personality, obsessed with safety, he was popular with both colleagues and air crews.

He had been approached with meticulous care.

Basing deliberations on Abu Ismail's intention to open the airport the next day, the Memouneh and Quinn had agreed that one of the day's scheduled flights, incoming or outgoing, had been chosen for seizure. They had already confirmed, by investigating Fawzi's measurements of the WOJ bomb, that of all the jetliners in service on African routes, the Super VC-10 had the most convenient egress for a bomb. Cross-checking this fact with the aircraft scheduled for service on the twenty-fourth, they had reduced

the options to a single flight: a British Airways incoming from the
Seychelles Islands and outbound for Nicosia, Cyprus, and London. This evaluation had been further supported by the fact that
the BA VC-10, in accordance with her schedule, would file a flight
plan for the main air route over the Red Sea, an ideal course for
the WOJ target, Mecca. She would thus be identified on Saudi
Arabian, U.S. Air Force and Navy radars as a nonbelligerent civil
transporter.

To some extent, Abu Ismail's choice had suited the Memouneh and Quinn. The British government had been approachable.

Through the auspices of the U.S. ambassador, they had invited
his British counterpart and the Secret Intelligence Service officer
at the British Embassy to an extraordinary meeting and had
briefed them on Operation Dragons. The British had declared
their readiness to help.

There had been initial problems to solve.

London's first consideration had been the safety and welfare of
the VC-10's passengers. They had argued that the problem had a
simpler solution, that the flight from the Seychelles could be diverted elsewhere on some pretext, thus not only protecting the
passengers from risking their lives as hostages, but also thwarting
Abu Ismail.

The Memouneh and Quinn, supported by Gentleman Jim
from Fort Meade, had prevailed with a detailed argument. The
VC-10 passengers did not risk being taken as hostages, since this
unenviable fate had already befallen the OAU delegates in Addis
Ababa. In all likelihood, the passengers would be herded into the
terminal building upon disembarkation, there to await the outcome of Operation Dragons. If Abu Ismail succeeded, the lives of
those passengers, whether diverted elsewhere or safe in London or
the Seychelles, might be forfeited anyway in the ensuing world
conflict. But if the Mossad-CIA task force succeeded in defeating
Abu Ismail, the passengers would only suffer the inconvenience
of some anxiety and a minor delay. If the British Airways VC-10
were not made available to Abu Ismail, there was no telling what
he might do, as he still reserved the option to destroy Addis Ababa
or direct his attention to another airliner carrying equally innocent
passengers. Great consideration should be given to the fate of the
OAU hostages both for humanitarian and political reasons, since
if the Mossad-CIA efforts failed, the WOJ plane would be shot out
of the skies by the U.S. Air Force. There was always an outside
chance that Abu Ismail might evade the U.S. Air Force; and that
thereafter the task force had perhaps the only opportunity to stop
him from committing his atrocity.

When London had finally delegated all decisions to Addis Ababa, Miles Whittemore, the SIS officer, had been commissioned to find a British Airways employee able and likely to help. In a short time, Whittemore had compiled information on all British Airways personnel at Addis Ababa, recommending that Llewellyn should be approached first.

Llewellyn swirled his beer and faced the Memouneh. "You're sure those are the bomb's measurements—1.65 meters high, 0.65 meters wide, 1.70 meters long?"

The Memouneh nodded. "As sure as we can be."

Llewellyn helped himself from the Memouneh's pack of cigarettes. "Yes—that'll fit in snugly by the VC-10's passenger door. But that doesn't mean they'll be going for ours."

The Memouneh pointed at a collection of timetables. "There are five international flights scheduled for tomorrow morning. East African Airways 972 from Nairobi; Ethiopian Airlines 704 to Paris via Asmara and Rome, 772 to Bombay, 724 to Athens via Khartoum and Cairo; and British Airways 054 from Seychelles to London via Addis and Nicosia. The British Airways plane arrives at ten fifty-five. Only one flight precedes it—the Ethiopian 704 to Paris departing at seven-thirty. Are you with me?"

"Yes."

"We assume that the flight to Paris will be canceled. WOJ would not want the airport cluttered with passengers and staff. We also assume when the next plane, BA 054, lands, the airport will close again. For the same reason. All other incoming planes will be diverted."

"But what makes you so sure it's BA 054 they're after?"

"That's obvious. It's the only Super VC-10. The others are Boeings."

"It's not so obvious. East Africa, to my knowledge, has four Super VC-10s. Who's to say they won't use one of them tomorrow?"

"Why should they? If the timetable—"

"Means nothing. The scheduled plane might be grounded for one reason or another. Or your friend Abu Ismail might have twisted someone's arm in Nairobi to schedule a VC-10 instead. What then?"

The Memouneh stared into his palms. Llewellyn's point was a good one and had occurred to them, too. They had investigated the possibilities and had taken appropriate measures. Of the four Super VC-10s operated by East African Airways, one was being overhauled in London; the other three were on their way to Frankfurt, West Germany, Port Louis, Mauritius, and Karachi, Pakistan. CIA and SIS, conjointly, would ensure through their counterparts in those cities that the planes would be grounded on a technicality for as long as necessary. But the Memouneh chose to keep these arrangements to himself. Llewellyn, if he had judged him right, was ruled by his heart. The Memouneh had to be seen with his back to the wall, but defiant. "Then God help us, Mr. Llewellyn. We'd have our hands tied."

Llewellyn grunted and swigged his beer.

The Memouneh sat in silence. Llewellyn was still suspicious, still aggressive. The Memouneh had advised Whittemore to approach him carefully just in case Abu Ismail, taking into account that Mossad or CIA might resort to sabotaging planes, had initiated surveillance on the airport staff.

Whittemore had been devious. Llewellyn, he had established, had a passion for singing. Fabricating a story that the British Embassy were forming a choir, and using a mutual acquaintance to pass the word, he had lured him to St. Matthew's Anglican Church for an audition. Having made sure that Llewellyn had not been followed, Whittemore had introduced himself as the cultural attaché; then, stating that the auditions would be held elsewhere, he had whisked him to the U.S. Embassy. Thus, Llewellyn had found himself in a large conference room—thrown, like a Christian to the lions, at the U.S. and U.K. ambassadors, Quinn, Sanbat and the Memouneh. He had begun to thaw only after the Memouneh had dismissed the others, had briefed him on the situation and run the tape with Abu Ismail's demands.

"Unless . . ."

The Memouneh looked up hopefully. "Unless what, Mr. Llewellyn?"

Llewellyn stubbed out his cigarette and opened another bottle of beer. "Well, I could pull rank with the East African gang. When it comes to VC-10s, they think we're the cat's whiskers—which we are. . . ."

"That might work if it was an option, Mr. Llewellyn. But we're convinced the only ground staff that will be allowed into the airport will be your team. The personnel of other carriers will be superfluous, and a possible threat."

"What makes you so sure they'll let us in?"

"If a British Airways plane is coming in and the ground staff is barred from the airport, there would be repercussions. You are all conscientious people. You'd realize there was something wrong. You'd raise hell with every authority concerned. You'd try to confer with London. If you didn't get through—which is likely under the present chaos—you'd contact the embassy. Am I right?"

"Yes."

"WOJ definitely would not want that. Alarms and strange rumors would put them at risk. They'd want to ensure an appearance of normality. They can do so only if they admit you into the airport. And, of course, in the process, keep you under control."

"I see what you mean. The sods . . . Well, maybe they've got a thing or two coming. . . ."

"Does that mean . . . ?"

Llewellyn shook his glass at him. "Don't push me. Tell me what you want me to do. . . ."

The Memouneh's voice became businesslike. "The Super VC-10, like all jet aircraft, has warning lights for every one of its doors. Am I right?"

"Yes. Standard. Located on the flight engineer's console."

"They light up whenever the particular door opens or is not properly shut?"

"That's right."

"The tail section has two doors: the rear passenger and the rear servicing and emergency exit."

"Yes."

"The rear passenger door is of no use to us. It will be blocked by the bomb. But as we only need a tiny space to get in, the rear servicing and emergency exit door will serve perfectly."

"Get in, did you say?"

"Yes. Providing you can sabotage its warning light."

"You mean—go up onto the flight deck—?"

"You won't be allowed anywhere near the flight deck. When WOJ take command of the aircraft, they'll keep everybody away. They've brought their own engineers. Besides, even if you could manage to get at the flight deck, it wouldn't serve our purpose. The doors are checked during the captain's preflight check. We want the light to go out of action when the plane is taxiing—not before."

Llewellyn, engrossed by the problem, stared into his beer. "You don't want much, do you? Let's see . . . You have three options: you'd need to either tamper with the contact switch at the door, or bugger up the particular electrical circuit or fiddle with the fuse. Now, the contact switch of the rear servicing and emergency exit door is beneath the door structure. You'd never have time to tamper with it between preflight check and taxiing. That's assuming you could get to the door. Same goes for the electrical circuit—even if you could find your way through the maze of wiring. The fuse is your likeliest bet. It's located at the gangway end of the flight engineer's console—you might be able to get at that."

"Wouldn't even attempt it. The cockpit will be well guarded."

Llewellyn pursed his lips. "Short of asking the captain to smash the warning light bulb—which you can't, and which would give the game away—there's no way."

The Memouneh smiled. "We've thought of one. Convoluted —but just about feasible."

Llewellyn stared at him, gripped by doubt and fascination. "I can't see how in Addis . . ."

"We'll start the ball rolling in the Seychelles."

Llewellyn gave him a puzzled look. "If you're going to the Seychelles, why not do the job properly? Put in a few commandos?"

"No sense in that! We can't engage Abu Ismail—not with those triggers implanted in his body."

Llewellyn helped himself to another cigarette. "How will you start the ball rolling in the Seychelles?"

The Memouneh brought out a small box, opened it and pointed to a tiny bulb wrapped in cotton wool. "This is identical to the rear servicing and emergency exit door's warning-signal bulb. We've made a series of these in Israel—for almost every type of aircraft. Part of our measures against hijackers. So we came well prepared. What's special about this bulb is that it has a miniaturized electromagnetic self-destruct device—no bigger than a pinhead—imbedded in its bayonet. The bulb functions normally— once. For the duration of the first application of power. On the second application, the self-destruct mechanism instantly causes the power to overcharge the filament and break it."

"Let me get this straight. This bulb burns bright when the door's opened for the first time . . . ?"

"Yes, and for as long as the door remains open when the aircraft's on the ground."

"So the crew see it functioning perfectly. The door closes during the preparations for takeoff . . ."

"Unlikely to be opened again before the plane reaches its next destination."

"Right. When the door closes, the light goes out, as it should. Next time the door opens, the bulb's blown. No warning light."

"Simple microelectronics."

Llewellyn shook his head in admiration. "That's fantastic. Go on."

"First, we put one of these bulbs in in the Seychelles."

"And it burns out here—as soon as the plane lands and the rear servicing and emergency exit door opens. . . ."

"That's right. That's essential."

"To stop the captain from rectifying the fault in the Seychelles . . . ?"

"And to present WOJ with a genuine defect when they take possession of the plane."

Llewellyn pondered a moment. "Has it occurred to you—you might be going to all this trouble for nothing? They might not even notice it. It's such a minor fault."

The Memouneh shook his head decisively. "Oh, they'll notice it all right. They're not amateurs. And they'll be extravigilant on any fault at any entry point. They'll want to make sure they can't be touched. That's precisely what we want—to make them feel impregnable. In order to do that, we must contrive to make sure the fault seems genuine, but minor."

"Easier said than done."

"We'll have to be clever. Some bluff and counterbluff. And a bit of sleight of hand."

"Come again?"

"Correct me if I'm wrong. In the plane's logbook there's a special section. Snag sheet, defect log, squawk book—whatever you call it. Where the flight engineer notes malfunctioning systems, if any. At the end of every stage, he or the captain presents the engineers—you—with this log. Right?"

"Right."

"Now, if you can contact the captain or the flight engineer as soon as the plane lands and ask him to insert in the log that the rear servicing and emergency exit door's warning light appears to be suspect . . ."

"He'll wonder why. Ask questions."

"He'll know why. He'll see WOJ. He'll realize there's nothing he can do to save the plane. But his instinct will be to fight. He'll grab the chance. No questions asked."

Llewellyn was beginning to smile. "You've thought of everything, haven't you?"

The Memouneh tried not to betray his uncertainty. "I pray we have."

"Go on."

"It's imperative the log entry specifies: one, that the warning light was found defective in the Seychelles; two, that the flight engineer replaced the bulb with the spare the plane normally carries; three, that he will check it again when he lands at Addis."

"Yes."

"When WOJ take possession of the aircraft, they'll see the entry and make a point of checking it. When they open the rear servicing and emergency exit door, they'll find that the warning light is not functioning—because it will have been blown."

"I'm with you."

"They'll want to rectify the fault. What would be the procedure?"

"They'll check the bulb."

"They'll note its filament is broken."

Llewellyn became excited. "That will puzzle them. Because it's the spare—or so the log says. They'll wonder if there's something wrong with the circuit."

"They'd check the circuit?"

"Oh, yes."

"If it's okay?"

"They'll check the contact switch by the door."

"If that's okay, too?"

"They'll assume the spare was defective."

"Not too farfetched?"

"No. Spares get knocked about. You get duds often enough."

"Fine. What would they do then?"

"They'll check if there's another spare in the plane."

"There won't be. We'll make sure in the Seychelles."

"They might consider carrying the defect."

"Not WOJ. And certainly not on what would be for them a historic flight. They'll go looking for another spare bulb."

Llewellyn spoke breathlessly. "Only one place would have it. British Airways. Us."

The Memouneh pointed at the bulb on the table. "So, you'll give them this."

Llewellyn chuckled. "I like it. *They'll* replace the bulb. Poetic justice—right?"

The Memouneh smiled.

Llewellyn frowned with a sudden thought. "What if they have a spare themselves? You said they have their own engineers. . . ."

"Then we're sunk. But I doubt whether they'll bring spares for warning lights—particularly one for the rear servicing and emergency exit door. They'll bring vital spares, if any. Anyway, that's what I'm banking on. . . ."

Llewellyn stubbed out his cigarette excitedly. "Have you tied up the Seychelles end?"

"We shall have by tomorrow. With Addis airport in WOJ hands and with roadblocks at every exit point, we can't do much from here. But the Americans have a man in Asmara. Since we can't supply him with one of these bulbs, we've arranged for the U.S. Air Force to deliver it from Israel—via Cyprus, so that no one will get suspicious. BA 054 is scheduled to leave the Seychelles tomorrow morning at eight forty-five. Our man will make it—just."

Llewellyn downed his glass in one go, by way of exclamation. Then he sat back and grinned. "Might work . . . Might just work . . ."

"Providing you get to the crew first and the defect is logged."

"Shouldn't be impossible . . ."

The Memouneh relaxed slightly. "One other point. It might seem strange to have just the warning light malfunctioning. If we can add a couple of other minor faults . . ."

Llewellyn's excitement had dispersed all his doubts. "Oh, there'll be a few anyway. I've yet to see a plane land without some silly thing having gone wrong. And if this proves the exception, you leave it to me. . . ."

The Memouneh smiled, proffered his hand. "I'd be delighted to."

Llewellyn shook the hand, then started on another pint.

The tape containing Montblanc's interview with Habyarwanda, interrupted by the Imperial Bodyguards, came to an end. Abu Ismail switched off the tape recorder and looked up pensively. "So you're the journalist? . . . The emperor panicked when he heard about you. . . ."

Montblanc swayed on weak knees, stared helplessly at Abu Ismail's platoon guarding him, then mumbled hoarsely. "Oh . . ."

Abu Ismail turned to Nazmi. "Have we anything on him?"

Nazmi looked up from a pile of documents. "No."

Abu Ismail studied Montblanc's Haitian passport, press card and other identification. "You arrived . . . when?"

Montblanc swayed even more precariously and whined, "Three . . . four days before . . . Is stamped on passport . . ."

They were speaking in English, and Montblanc's French accent seemed to irritate Abu Ismail. "Yes. But Ethiopian immigration has no record of it."

Montblanc did not rise to the bait. Abu Ismail, though in possession of quite comprehensive documentation on each of the OAU hostages, did not have Ethiopian immigration records. With Addis Ababa in chaos, no one knew or cared whether the records had been filed with the police or awaited dispatch. "No?" He stared uncomprehendingly, on the verge of collapse.

Julius Habyarwanda rose to hold him steady, then turned to Abu Ismail. "Why you question him?"

Abu Ismail snapped sharply. "Sit down!"

Habyarwanda stood his ground. "Stop persecuting him! Look him! He very worried man. What you expect?"

Abu Ismail blinked, then smiled. "I did not expect such a coward. A big man like that."

Habyarwanda tried to reason. "Fear . . . After all, understandable."

Abu Ismail, pursing his lips, turned again to Montblanc's papers.

Montblanc stared sheepishly around him.

The OAU hostages, seated on the floor of the customs hall, were all watching—some almost enjoying his discomfort; others with sympathy. Including Habyarwanda, there were fifty-four of them: twenty-eight delegates and twenty-six substitutes, two for each of the thirteen who were away from Addis Ababa at the time of the arrests. Nineteen of the substitutes were women: nine wives, ten secretaries.

By contrast, the Imperial Bodyguards—Yitzhaq among them —who had been pushed to the farthest end of the hall and made to squat with hands over their heads—glared at him with contempt. Wolde and his sergeant, Ketema, were standing watch over them with Russian Degtyarev RPD light machine guns. The bodyguards, having recognized Wolde and Ketema and incensed by their collaboration, seemed to be looking for an excuse to charge at them—despite the emperor's orders to refrain from any conflict. Montblanc averted his eyes. He did not want to provoke them with his whining. Wolde and Ketema would welcome the opportunity of mowing them down.

"Tell me . . . Philippe Mercier . . . How's Papa Doc these days?"

Montblanc turned to Abu Ismail in trepidation, gesticulated weakly and managed a croaking voice. "He—dead. With Baron Cimeterre . . . our Lord of . . . cemetery . . ."

"Oh, yes . . ."

Abu Ismail dropped Montblanc's papers into the pile of photographs and files of the OAU hostages. The latter, Montblanc assumed, had been collected by Wolde and the Dergue intelligence unit and demonstrated once again Abu Ismail's meticulous approach to detail. The hostages' roll call had been far more exhaustive than either Montblanc or the Memouneh had anticipated, and Montblanc realized his fate hung on frail threads. The fear he had acted with such bravura had become real.

Abu Ismail glared at him. "I am in two minds about you. . . ." He pointed at the OAU hostages. "You are a bad example to these people. A coward. A man unworthy of life."

Montblanc held a handkerchief to his mouth as if he were about to vomit. "Please . . ."

Habyarwanda interjected. "You will no harm him. After all, he is in my protection."

Abu Ismail rasped. "Be quiet!"

Habyarwanda defied him. "He taken from my house. That makes him guest of Rwanda. Harm him—and you give account to my government!"

Abu Ismail stared at him menacingly, then started to laugh.

Montblanc whimpered. His admiration for Habyarwanda, such an insecure politician, had grown as the day had progressed. Swiftly, almost naturally, the leadership of the hostage group had settled around his simple and unequivocal stand. Toward Montblanc in particular, he had manifested exemplary devotion even though, to his disappointment, Montblanc had disintegrated in noticeable stages from a stolid journalist to a sapless reed. He had repeatedly declared that he held himself responsible for Montblanc's fate and that he would defend him with his life. Montblanc could see himself diving in desperation at the machine guns if only to save the foolhardy Rwandan.

Abu Ismail stopped laughing. "You are a brave man, Julius Habyarwanda. An ant against a lion. It is not common among the unbelievers."

Habyarwanda angrily shook his head. "What you know of belief?"

"I know Allah."

"And I—Jesus."

Abu Ismail smiled. "You challenge me in a domain where I am invincible. It is foolish. Also commendable. I shall take up your challenge. We shall put Allah and Jesus to the test. I shall reprieve you and your journalist until the dawn of the Last of Days. You will see Jesus forsake you as Allah forsook him." He waved a dismissive hand. "Take them away."

Nazmi pointed his gun at the hostages. "Line up. Four abreast."

The hostages rose.

Nazmi turned to the six-man platoon. "To the hangar."

Shamseddin, in charge of the commandos, shouted. "Start walking!"

Montblanc, still keeping close to Habyarwanda, cast a quick glance of relief toward Yitzhaq. He turned just as Abu Ismail nodded a signal to Wolde. A moment later, Wolde and Ketema opened up their Degtyarevs on the Imperial Bodyguards.

The hostages screamed.

Montblanc coiled up, his fury urging him to action.

Next to him Habyarwanda bellowed. "Why . . . ? Why . . . ?"

No answer. Not even fanatical mutterings from Abu Ismail. Montblanc was instantly recommitted to reality. This was the way of the world. Reason had long departed.

MOUNT WECHECHA, ETHIOPIA

Getachew's excursion to the Ras Hotel at Ghion had been fruitful. He had returned with two vital pieces of information: almost every faction contesting Ethiopia's future had organized wide-scale riots for the next day, and the Dergue forces, using riots as an excuse, had put up checkpoints on every major road leading to Addis Ababa. Consequently, Boaz had delayed departure from Ghion until late afternoon.

They had reached Sabata, a village some twenty kilometers from Addis Ababa, at nightfall, and had branched off onto a track which skirted the eastern reaches of Mount Wechecha. They had thus avoided the checkpoint at the intersection of the Ghion and Hosana roads, six kilometers ahead. A shopkeeper in Sabata from whom Getachew bought old clothes and shammas had revealed that the troops seemed specifically on the lookout for foreigners. The disclosure had proved Boaz's contention that Abu Ismail would not have been entirely satisfied by the fortuitous fate of the Twin Otter. He should, however, assume them dead or at least of no threat to Operation Dragons by the following morning when the checkpoints reported no sightings.

They had progressed on the track, which the local peasants used for the market in preference to the roads where their beasts risked being run over.

In the caverns of a disused quarry, they had hidden the Land-Rovers, changed into peasant clothes and shammas and built a litter from eucalyptus branches for Osman.

Boaz scrutinized the men, sitting silent and pensive. There was a long way to go yet: five kilometers to Addis Ababa and at least another five through its suburbs in a roundabout route to avoid patrols. The men felt consumed by fatigue, but their dour expressions showed they were also determined. He checked his watch: 7:08 P.M. "We should reach the safe house by twenty-two hundred."

The men nodded.

Boaz took charge of Osman's litter and turned to Getachew. "You lead."

ADDIS ABABA, ETHIOPIA

Abu Ismail surveyed the airport from the control tower. It was brilliantly lit except for the hangar which accommodated the OAU hostages. That stood closed, dark, and now that night had fallen, chilly. Microphones planted in it to eavesdrop on possible resistance were silent. The hostages, stupefied by the tranquilizers in their rations, had fallen asleep—including the hysterical Haitian journalist who had ended up vomiting his food. The hostages, in effect, had been broken. Tomorrow, bludgeoned by despair, cold, sedatives and debility, they would be meek as lambs at the slaughter.

On the apron stood the DC-3, still housing the bomb, and his private jet. These were being guarded respectively by his special squad and the warrior-technicians who had arrived from Entebbe. Equipment brought by the latter stood in neat piles, so that the minor work required to transfer the bomb and accommodate it in the Super VC-10 would take little time.

The technicians had confirmed the data for the bomb. It would be dropped at 2,000 feet. Its rate of descent, parachute-retarded, would be 25 feet per second; it would hit target in 80 seconds. Separation distance from the 20-kiloton bomb had been determined at 6.6 miles, though with the aircraft moving away from the blast at 300 knots, they would have another 2.2 miles to evade the shock waves. Overpressure for the Super VC-10 had been estimated with generous allowance as 0.5 pounds per square inch. That meant the plane would be safe from the blast at 3.65 miles from ground zero. They would be twice that distance on detonation.

Behind him, Nazmi took a radio message. "From our observer in Johannesburg. The KLM flight left Amsterdam on schedule. It's due in Johannesburg tomorrow morning at seven hundred hours local time. It should leave for Cairo via Nairobi and Jiddah at eight-thirty. Barring delays, that is . . ."

"We have considered delays. Once it leaves Johannesburg, Admiral Tiblyashin will monitor it on radar. We will time our move accordingly."

"We fix zero hour as it departs Nairobi?"

"No. Later. We have to range with it soon after our departure. We shall need to compute its progress against weather conditions. We will fix zero hour when it enters Ethiopian airspace."

"It will have my prayers for a smooth passage, Al-Mahdi."

"Rest assured. It will keep to schedule. If it does not, we shall pick an alternative. There are several: Air France, TWA, South African Airways, Air India. You must understand, my son, the principle of dovetailing with another commercial airliner is merely insurance—in case we encounter trouble. Say an American plane manages to escape the Russian net. He will be reluctant to fire at two civil airliners flying side by side. He will not have the confidence that his missile will hit the right plane. And should he be reckless enough to try, we will be able to take evasive action, using the other airliner as a shield. In the process, we shall have wrested the time to direct a MiG onto its tail. Therefore, it does not matter which plane we hide behind. Were it not for the fact that the Jew's planes are always in contact with their defense forces, I would have bestowed the honor on an El-Al from Johannesburg to Tel Aviv."

Nazmi lowered his eyes as if reprimanded. "I understand, but . . ."

Abu Ismail smiled like a loving father who had talked too harshly to his son. "But you fear something will go amiss. Trust your faith. Tell me—the Russians . . . Nothing yet?"

Nazmi, cherishing his leader's smile, reverted to full efficiency. "They're due to report at ten o'clock. A few minutes still . . ."

Abu Ismail helped himself to some coffee. He realized he was tense. Berating Nazmi on the function of the KLM plane was proof of it. The boy knew every detail. He wondered whether the tension was a shadow cast by The Doubter. He rejected the thought. He had triumphed over Al-Munafiq. If further proof was needed, his limbs were devoid of pain—youthful.

He was tense for a good reason: he disliked waiting on other people's decisions. He knew Volkov's conspirators would not panic just because he had brought the date of Operation Dragons forward one day. Why should they? They were under Volkov's orders. And the complex series of codes Nazmi had sent them had borne Volkov's signature.

Volkov's conspirators should, in fact, be delighted. By bringing the date forward, Abu Ismail was sparing them a possible engagement with the U.S. Air Force or any other foolhardy air force that might dare challenge WOJ. Volkov himself, had he been alive, would have approved.

The strategy was simple and effective. He had predicted in Madrid that Mecca would be destroyed on the Jew's Independence Day, April 25. The Jew had tried his utmost to stop him. Having failed, the Jew was likely to draw in the Americans. According to latest intelligence reports, the Americans had already spread a net over the Red Sea. Though this measure could be neutralized by Russian MiGs, the danger of an American fighter streaking suicidally at the WOJ plane had remained. Abu Ismail had reduced that danger simply by bringing the date forward. The Americans would be caught off guard.

In the final analysis, the change of date was an overindulgence: like the KLM Boeing 747 with which the WOJ VC-10 would dovetail; like Abu Ismail's third insurance policy, the Grumman Gulfstream II, piloted by Isa, to be sent on a decoy flight seemingly on a mission to an Israeli target. At the end of the day, none of these insurance policies would prove to have been needed. With the enemy ensnared, he would have a clear run to Mecca. He would even fulfill his prophecy. His bomb would be dropped sometime after sunset, at the commencement of the Jewish day and on the twenty-sixth anniversary of the birth of the accursed State of Israel.

Volkov's conspirators would rejoice in their luck, mock Abu Ismail as either too insecure or, geopolitically, too naive. Only later, and too late, would they understand that the collaboration had been on Abu Ismail's terms from the very beginning. That he had chosen to use the Russians as janitors to his theocracy. That once he, Al-Mahdi, accused Israel of destroying Mecca, the Russians would become debris, too. Because all Islam, taking up arms for the jihad, would destroy like a mighty earthquake not only the Jew, but every despicable hand that had touched the Jew. High up on that list would be the godless Russians who, irrespective of how they persecuted the Jew now, had supported the creation of the Jewish State.

Nazmi shouted excitedly. "The Russian signals, Al-Mahdi!"

Cautiously, Abu Ismail wrapped his glorious aura around himself.

Nazmi's voice echoed from a great distance. "Admiral Tiblyashin: affirmative! Air Force General Larinchev: affirmative! Marshal of the Red Army Yeliseev: also affirmative!"

Abu Ismail glowed triumphantly.

Nazmi moved across in awe and kissed his hands. "They will wait for you to pronounce zero hour."

Abu Ismail caressed Nazmi's hand tenderly. "Leave me."

Nazmi obediently withdrew.

Abu Ismail turned toward the plate-glass windows and resumed his survey of the airport. This time he saw it—unmistakably—as his last tent before Allah.

Incongruously, the perimeter, surrounded by Wolde's troops

like pilgrims encamped for the hajj, conjured up the specter of Mecca. He remembered the festive spirit among the paratroopers after Wolde and Ketema had recounted their gratuitous massacre of the Imperial Bodyguards and assured them that the path to the throne now lay open. Savages. Slaves. It was their brothers and distant cousins, embracing Islam under false pretenses, who had brought Mecca, the contaminated old whore, to the abyss.

He, Abu Ismail, had never been to Mecca. That was another great distinction—proof of the Savior's strength. It had not been easy to nurture that strength. As a lover of Allah, he had been expected, time and time again, to perform the hajj. The little people had failed to understand, as he had understood, that the so-called fifth pillar of Islam was not only irrelevant but tainted. He had been criticized, calumnized, ostracized. But he had held to his faith.

He knew Mecca in his heart. Had known it always. The holy city of the Faithful was in reality still that desert hole of old, still the house for pagan idols. Three hundred and sixty of them entrenched in the Kaaba. The True Holy City was Al-Quds, the Jew's Jerusalem. The Prophet himself had preached that prayers should be directed there. But he had failed to convince his followers. Consequently, Allah had deferred the conquest of the True Holy City until the advent of Al-Mahdi.

For only Al-Mahdi could perceive that the Faithful, naive or blind, still worshiped the pagan deities. Only now he called them by different names—like tribe, nation, race, honor. Islamic divisions and murderous feuds were proof of that. All would come to an end in twenty-four hours. By an upheaval promised repeatedly by Allah in His Holy Book. By the hand of Al-Mahdi, the Savior. The house of the pagan deities would fall so that the Faithful could be shepherded at last to the True Holy City.

He held up his vision, daring The Doubter to challenge it. It hung without shadow. The Doubter remained dead.

✗

The last lap had been uneventful. They had reached the safe house soon after 10:00 P.M.

They had attended to Osman's remains. The doctors, Yonatan and Arik, had washed the body and placed it in Formalin.

They had showered.

They had discussed developments with Amnon and his company of Sayeret Matkal.

They had heard of another death: Yitzhaq. The Memouneh's lookout at the airport, Emmanuel, had observed Wolde's paratroopers piling the corpses of the Imperial Bodyguards into a commissary truck.

They had been briefed on the progress of the Four Days of Confusion. Confusion had turned to anarchy. The government had issued a strict warning on radio and television forbidding strikes, marches and demonstrations, and threatening severe measures against civil disobedience and unrest. There had been no mention of WOJ, nor of the fact that Abu Ismail held Addis Ababa to ransom. The last had been in accordance with the Memouneh's directives to the emperor through the American ambassador. In order to avoid pushing Abu Ismail into a dangerous corner and, furthermore, to safeguard the task force's options, blanket secrecy was imperative.

They had received confirmation that the Memouneh had recruited a British Airways engineer to handle the warning-signal bulb and that Lieutenant O'Brien, having received a similar bulb from Israel by the grace of the U.S. Air Force, had left Asmara for the Seychelles in a Hercules.

Thereafter, MacDonald and his men had retired for a brief rest.

Boaz and Getachew had proceeded to the American Embassy to finalize plans with the Memouneh and Quinn.

✗

For Boaz there had been a letter. From Osman. Sealed and left with Sanbat.

> *My Brother and Friend,*
> *I don't know why I'm writing this. If you come to read it, I shall be dead or dying. Which is inconceivable to me.*
> *I suspect the culprit is Samia. Rereading her last letter now, as we prepare to leave for Gambela, I see how much one can put into the written word and between the lines.*
> *If this is a farewell, several things must be said.*
> *One: I love you. As my friend. As my brother.*
> *Two: One of us must live, Boaz.*
> *Three: After Abu Ismail there will be other madmen. You must keep fighting. For me. For my honor. For the innocence, purity, sanctity and faith for which we have both searched.*
> *Four: Will I be forgiven for taking you to Mecca? Perhaps. Mecca should be open to the world. Nowhere else can men be so inspired. You saw Islam's loving side there. Young, vibrant, living, giving. The side that Abu Ismail seeks to destroy. You came very close to God there. I know.*

Five: It will be a very lonely world for you without me. It would have been for me if you had died—even though I have Samia, my children and Allah. I don't know what to advise to alleviate this loneliness. Ascetism, withdrawal from life will not help. Much as you love your God, you are angry with Him for having made you what you are. But then, as I said once before: What makes you so special? Everybody is angry with God. But anger is bitter food. Conceivably, you might find salvation in Sanbat. You won't find it in death. Death, unless it comes peacefully in the winter years, is horrible. That's my heresy.

Six: Not least. I don't know what to suggest for Samia. If she can have a brother in you, she might find some meaning in this waste. I am tempted to seek an epigram that will reflect my love for her. Sentimental Arab that I am. That's ridiculous. What I have to say of Samia she already knows.

That's all. If you're reading this, mourn me. I might have been a better man if I had lived another day.

May Allah preserve you, my Brother and Friend.

Osman

April 24, 1974

ADDIS ABABA, ETHIOPIA

They served breakfast at 7:30 A.M.: cheese and tomato sandwiches, coffee and tea.

The OAU hostages, heavy-headed and chilled after a night on the hangar's concrete floor, ate mechanically.

Montblanc watched the WOJ commandos on duty. Two, from the complement of Abu Ismail's executive jet, did not worry him. They had been assigned the menial tasks: heating and serving the food they had brought in refrigerated boxes, emptying the slop buckets, arranging the order for washing at the single tap allowed to the hostages. They had come to ignore Montblanc's endless trips to drink and to urinate. Montblanc had had to explain that he suffered from a pernicious bladder disorder and had to flush his system regularly. Some of the hostages, having observed this peculiar behavior since assembling at the Jubilee Palace, had confirmed his distress as genuine.

Montblanc, however, needed to establish the fact with Abu Ismail's special squad, who were always armed and who took turns guarding the hostages. These six, Montblanc guessed, would remain on duty in the VC-10.

He had succeeded, he thought, with Tahir and Mohammed, who had stood guard during the night. At first they had been contemptuous of his whimpering cowardice. Later, when he feigned incontinence, they had pitied him.

The relief guards, Ferid and Said, appeared tougher. It was to be expected. They had not faced a cold night and they had had some sleep. Also, they seemed to have been briefed about Montblanc and concentrated on him more than the others. He had barely managed to exchange his sandwiches and coffee for Habyarwanda's empty tray. Starvation was a necessity if he was to remain sharp and unsedated.

Montblanc rose and instantly faced the barrel of Ferid's machine gun. He mumbled. "I—I need to go . . ."

Ferid mocked him. "Little big boy wants wee-wee, eh?"

Montblanc tried dignity. "May I—please . . ."

Ferid turned to Said, still mocking. "What do you think?"

Said, ignoring Ferid's game, motioned to Montblanc. "Go. . . ."

Ferid hissed his annoyance. "Just this once!"

Said rebuked him. "Let him be—the poor bastard . . ."

Ferid did not respond, but Montblanc registered the callousness.

As he urinated, he pondered. He had had to make himself conspicuously despicable. The plan was a good one. But it contained an inherent weakness. Such behavior provoked antipathy, as was evident in Ferid's response to it. Success or failure could rest on the vagaries of a bully.

✗

Plans had been finalized, and the offensive had received its official name, "Operation Osman." The deliberations had lasted until the early hours. After that, Boaz and Getachew had gone to sleep— their first rest in over seventy hours.

At 8:00 A.M., Sanbat woke Boaz with coffee, fruit juice, toast, a six-egg omelet, glucose tablets, stimulant pills and a timid kiss. Boaz responded with a touch on her hand.

She watched him fight off exhaustion. She searched for signs of his pain, for a clue to what he would do after the operation was over. He had shown her Osman's letter. Yet she felt he would abandon himself to some macabre ritual, as he had after Dedeyan's death, and that she was looking at him for the last time.

He took the pills without comment and washed them down with the fruit juice. He started eating—to her delight, with appetite. "What's the latest, Sanbat?"

"O'Brien has switched the bulb, and removed the existing spares. Smooth as anything. No WOJ lookouts. The VC-10 was hangared for the night, and the British Intelligence Service at Seychelles provided full assistance."

"Good. What about here?"

"It's going to be a day of riots."

"Despite the government's warnings?"

"More like in defiance of them. People are gathering everywhere. Rumors of some shooting even."

"Our end?"

"Organized. I've alerted all the Falashas in or near Addis—except Bayyu—to join in the rioting and to deploy as near the airport as possible."

"And Bayyu?"

"He's at the safe house. We've secured a dilapidated truck—and cornmeal. Two of MacDonald's boys will escort him to the veterinary station beyond the airport's eastern perimeter."

"Does Bayyu think it's feasible?"

"He says the cornmeal is likely to attract every sparrow in Addis."

"Good. What else?"

"The Ethiopian Airlines seven-thirty flight to Paris has been canceled. As we'd predicted. That's confirmed both by Emmanuel and by our monitoring of air traffic control. But the airport's officially open—though of course there's nothing scheduled before the British Airways."

Boaz poured himself some coffee. "You want some?"

"I didn't bring a cup."

Boaz offered his cup, then poured his own into the juice glass. He faced her with a gentle smile. "How do you feel, Sanbat?"

"Tense."

"We won't fail."

"And very worried."

"About me?"

"Natural, isn't it?"

"I'll come through."

"And after that?"

Boaz looked away. "Is Getachew up?"

"Yes. Quinn's attending to him."

"We have a little time. Can you stay with me for a while?"

Sanbat touched his hand. "Of course. The Memouneh's in charge of the radio. . . ." She pointed to the table where she had laid the various containers of cosmetics. "We thought I should help you make up. Cover every little fold . . ."

Boaz smiled. "I just want to look at something that's alive . . . and beautiful . . . and offers hope. . . ."

Sanbat placed his hand on her face, then brushed it with her lips. He had made an immense effort in reaching out to her. She felt more hopeful. "Please do . . . please . . ."

✗

Fisseha, the senior approach controller, who had spent the night in custody with the rest of the skeleton staff in the administration offices, had been brought to the control tower at 6:00 A.M. He had been ordered first by Wolde, then by the emperor, to cooperate fully with WOJ.

At 6:10 he had declared the airport open and instructed the Ethiopian Airlines operations center and the Addis Ababa air traffic control center—neither situated at the airport, but near Debre Zeyt, and therefore unaware of the WOJ occupation—to be prepared for normal air traffic. Then he had personally relayed the information to British Airways at the Seychelles.

At 7:00 he had announced the cancellation for technical reasons of ET 704 to Operations Center and to the Addis Ababa air traffic control center. He had requested that the information be conveyed to the various air traffic control centers en route to Paris.

At 7:30 he had instructed the airport manager, also in custody, to order British Airways ground hostesses and maintenance engineers to report for duty as scheduled at 10:00 A.M.

Thereafter, he had sat in his chair in terror, wondering whether Nazmi would really kill him, as he had threatened, if for any reason BA 054 failed to stop over at Addis Ababa.

Fisseha's reprieve came at 8:55 when the telex reported that BA 054 had taken off from the Seychelles following a ten-minute delay; but weather conditions being favorable, it would make up the lost time en route and that the estimated time of arrival should stand as scheduled as 10:55 A.M.

He handed the message to Nazmi, then sat down to await his next nightmare: talking down BA 054 calmly. The slightest mistake that might make BA 054's captain suspicious would, he knew, cancel the reprieve instantly.

✗

At 9:00 A.M., Addis Ababa, in the words of the "Voice of the Gospel" radio newscaster, looked like a rose stricken by mildew. Large pockets of demonstrators, ranging from dissatisfied students and workers to various ethnic and political pressure groups, had erupted in the streets in search of a riot.

Stones had been thrown at schools and government buildings, taxis and buses. These, the demonstrators had declared, served only as a prelude.

Those demonstrators unfortunate enough to confront Imperial troops or Dergue forces at key points were injured as nervous soldiers opened fire. Realizing that the day would have a momentum of its own, that neither the demonstrators nor the troops would have a chance of identifying friend or foe, a number of rioters had scattered toward safer points away from the city center. Some had spilled onto Airport Road.

One group in particular, ten Falashas, moved as near the airport as Wolde's troops ringing it would permit. There they appeared to disband and disperse north and south, into the countryside.

✗

At 9:05 A.M., Bayyu, Tripps and Underwood left the safe house through the side entrance in the dilapidated truck procured by the American ambassador from USAID. Their load contained such agricultural items as wire mesh, an old plow, spades, fertilizer, and two twenty-five-kilo sacks of cornmeal. Underwood took the wheel. Tripps lay concealed with his gun in the truck's load.

Ten minutes after their departure, the Sayeret Matkal company with MacDonald, Oates and Vernon drifted out at three-minute intervals. Dressed in loose-fitting shammas, perfect garments for concealing their Imperial Army uniforms and webbed harnesses accommodating their equipment, weapons and ammunition, they deployed on the periphery of the crowds and advanced toward the airport.

Tension was acute. They were moving too early. But the growing chaos in the capital threatened to push more and more demonstrators into the Airport Road. The Memouneh, afraid that this might draw further troops to the area and so curtail the task force's freedom of movement, had wanted them to be clear of the safe house in good time.

They would be in their appointed positions in the woods and groves north and south of the airport, where the Falashas had dispersed, between 10:30 and 11:15.

The medics Yonatan and Arik, scheduled to leave last, each in a well-equipped Fiat 124, would set up station at an abandoned scrapyard, half a kilometer southwest of the airport.

Fawzi, loosely but securely trussed to his bed, would sleep through the next twelve hours. Now in the fourth day of his megatrip, exhaustion had gained the upper hand.

The only other occupant of the house, Osman, dead and safe, would await his burial.

✗

Boaz's makeup, one of the items in the special equipment brought by the CIA, had consisted of a special blend of brown theatrical body rub and a black vegetable dye used by Navajo carpet weavers. The liquid, meticulously applied to the whole of the body, had created a perfect imitation of the Amhara's burnished coloring. Talcum powder mixed with aluminum dust had heightened sheen and would also serve to prevent smearing. A wig of crinkled hair had completed the disguise; a spray of local spices had added a natural African smell. The effort, with Sanbat's help, had taken over an hour.

At 9:25 A.M., Boaz and Getachew completed their preparations.

They wore tank crew's battle dress and webbed harnesses. They had equipped themselves with commando knives, binoculars, stun grenades, earplugs, Smith and Wesson .38 revolvers—with a spare for Montblanc—that had been adapted for use inside aircraft, special silencers for the .38s, belts of pancake bullets, disk-shaped suction clamps each hooked onto a nylon rope thirteen meters long, and a field radio. In addition, Boaz had included carefully folded lengths of black drapes, and Getachew an orange wind sock of the sort used at airports for gauging wind direction.

The Memouneh, Quinn and Sanbat had supervised in silence, restricting themselves to confirming the communications codes.

At 9:30, covering their uniforms with shammas, Boaz and Getachew slipped out of the American Embassy. Both Sanbat and the Memouneh chose to interpret the casual departure as a good omen.

Five minutes later, their Fiat 124, with Getachew at the wheel, entered the maze of Addis Ababa's northern suburbs and edged toward the airport.

✗

At 9:55 A.M., Hugh Llewellyn arrived at the airport staff entrance and found it manned by paratroopers. He recognized Wolde, standing in the background, from photographs shown to him by the Memouneh. Sergeant Ketema, in charge of the checkpoint, waved him to the security hut, outside which three other British Airways ground engineers, Illingworth, O'Leary and Matthews, paced sullenly.

Llewellyn exuded good cheer. "Don't tell me they've closed the bloody place again!"

Illingworth, a wispy man with an ever-troubled face, shrugged disconsolate shoulders. "God knows. I had to abandon my car, didn't I? Foot it half the fucking way! You seen the crowds?"

Llewellyn slapped him on the shoulder. "Never mind, boyo.

Go to Africa and find adventure. That's what the bloke at the careers office said!"

O'Leary, nursing a hangover, grunted. "It's ten o'clock in the morning, Taffy. Do you have to act like you've just been to chapel?"

"What's up then?"

Matthews, senior engineer, spat in disgust. "Your guess, mate. . . ."

Llewellyn turned to Sergeant Ketema. "Hey—you gonna let us in or not, Sarge?"

Sergeant Ketema responded by steadying his submachine gun. Wolde checked his watch, then moved over to them. "Your passes, please."

They handed over their passes.

Wolde scrutinized each one carefully. "There is a security alert. You will be allowed to enter, but you will be confined to your section. You will carry out your duties when necessary."

Matthews raised his eyes to heaven. "Fucking hell!"

Wolde pointed at the hut. "Please go in there. You will be searched for arms."

Llewellyn tried to maintain his good spirits. The doctored warning-light bulb given him by the Memouneh had been fixed to a tiny flashlight serving as a key ring. The Memouneh had assured him the trinket would pass any inspection, but that did not subdue his fears.

✗

At 10:05 A.M. Boaz and Getachew reached a deserted stretch east of the northern suburbs. They parked the car off the road, punctured two of the tires, then abandoned it. Anybody spotting the car would assume its passengers had gone to seek help; considering the riots, no one would be surprised if they had failed to find any.

They continued eastward on foot for about a hundred meters. Satisfied there had been no one to observe them, they moved into the woods situated beyond the airport's northern perimeter.

✗

At 10:10 A.M., from the duty-free manager's office in the departures lounge, Emmanuel observed the British Airways ground engineers proceeding under escort to their duty room. He paid particular attention to Llewellyn. The latter paused momentarily and scraped one of his shoes, as if he had stepped in some tar. Emmanuel immediately signaled the Memouneh that Llewellyn was safely through with the doctored warning-light bulb.

✗

At 10:15 A.M., BA 054, en route from Seychelles, entered the southeast Ethiopia flight information region and tuned its radio to the first very high frequency omnidirectional range transmitting beacon to set course for Addis Ababa.

Senior approach controller Fisseha, trembling, reported its progress to Nazmi.

The latter, ebullient, switched on the intercom to the controllers' rest room where Abu Ismail had retired. "It is arriving, Al-Mahdi. . . ."

✗

At 10:20 A.M. Bayyu, Tripps and Underwood, having traveled a convoluted route through the suburbs, reached the veterinary station, situated half a kilometer from the airport's eastern perimeter.

Bayyu settled down in front of the station's closed door, holding a piece of paper which identified him as a farmhand sent by his landlord to fetch rinderpest vaccine for cattle. The note, suggesting that Bayyu was an illiterate peasant, was protection against the remote possibility of his encountering an official. The embassy had reassured the Memouneh that the British veterinary surgeons, running the station on behalf of FAO, would be on field duty in the Awash valley throughout the day.

Tripps and Underwood, armed with sniper rifles, dug in at vantage positions. They had been commissioned to neutralize the possible threat of Wolde's men intercepting Bayyu before or during the assault. Should such an emergency arise, it was hoped that the incident, having taken place well outside the airport perimeter, would be construed as another disorder of this third day of confusion.

✗

At 10:30 A.M. Boaz and Getachew set up watch in the branches of a densely foliated tree at the edge of the woods bordering the airport's northern perimeter.

Five Falashas and two Sayeret Matkal had taken positions in the trees behind them; six more Sayeret Matkal, the rest of the complement allocated to Boaz's flank, had signaled that they were approaching the woods without hindrance. The Sayeret Matkal would spread out to cover points right and left, leaving the Falashas at the center. Boaz and Getachew would remain at the extreme left to give themselves room to maneuver.

Boaz raised his binoculars and surveyed the airport.

About a hundred meters ahead, facing the center of the woods with its 75mm gun, stood an M-41 medium tank. Its crew of five, sitting around the turret, looked far from alert; whenever they scrutinized the woods, as obviously they had been assigned to do, they did so casually. They were, it was easy to see, troops who had not faced action and did not expect to.

Two more M-41s, with crews looking similarly relaxed, were in position at the eastern and southern extremities. A fourth stood on the apron in front of the terminals; a fifth, barely visible outside the compound, covered Airport Road.

Between each tank, at points north-east south-east, south-west and north-west, AML-245 armored cars, each manned by a driver and eight troops, maintained positions of support.

An air-defense battery dug in at the eastern perimeter completed the hardware.

Boaz disregarded the air-defense battery. It guarded the air approaches, and would not be involved with ground action. He also discounted the M-41 on Airport Road and its support of four armored cars. These were covering the approaches from the city. If his assault went according to plan, they would know nothing about it. If it did not, they would be superfluous. The armor within the airport would have enough power to wipe out the task force.

He concentrated on the armor.

The emplacement of the tanks at precise compass points suggested that Wolde's knowledge of defensive rings was theoretical. The M-41 on the apron was virtually redundant; its counterpart on the other side of the terminals, guarding the city approaches, had absolute advantage of terrain and could repulse any attack, except that of superior armor. Similarly, the M-41 at the east faced open terrain which any attacking force would reject for its lack of cover. That particular sector could have been satisfactorily secured by a single lookout, releasing the M-41 to provide support either at the north or the south where the tanks faced dense vegetation. In fact, at the southern position, the strict adherence to the compass point had put the tank there at a disadvantage by placing it twenty degrees right of the groves where Amnon and his contingent would be deploying.

Obviously the theory had been that the four tanks, given the 75mm gun's 800 meters effective range against slow-moving targets, would each cover ninety degrees of the circle; the task of intercepting fast-moving targets would fall to the four armored cars positioned at forty-five degrees between the tanks. Here again, theory had shortchanged practice. For one thing, the airport compound was not a perfect circle but a rough rectangle approximately five kilometers from north to south, and six kilometers from west to east. Consequently, the rigid deployment, despite armored-car support, left exploitable chinks. Moreover, it restricted the tank gunners; if they were to avoid damaging the airport or hitting their own forces, they would have to fire with exceptional precision.

In the final analysis, however, these weaknesses reduced the odds merely fractionally. The ring remained a formidable obstacle —certainly one that could not be engaged openly nor eliminated with antitank missiles. Any such move would alert Abu Ismail. The ring had to be broken imperceptibly. The tanks at the northern and southern ends had to be captured; the rest of the armor had to be kept lulled.

Boaz directed his attention to the airport's second line of defense: the twenty paratroopers dug in at strategic points along the perimeter and runway. He studied the four strung out parallel to the woods. Unlike the tank crews and armored-car troops, these were Wolde's own men—veterans of the Danakil. They were, Boaz could see, exceptionally alert despite their long vigil. Eliminating them simultaneously was essential.

Finally, as a third line of defense, there were three special squads: Abu Ismail's own platoon standing watch by the DC-3, the support platoon that had arrived from Entebbe, and Wolde's crack ten-man platoon led by Sergeant Ketema.

He discounted the first two as of no immediate danger. He would confront Abu Ismail's platoon inside the plane—not before; they were assigned to the bomb, and they would stay with it until takeoff. The support platoon, at present congregated around the Grumman Gulfstream II, would have their hands full, if Emmanuel's information was correct, preparing the Super VC-10 for its mission. That left Sergeant Ketema's platoon, acting—also according to Emmanuel's information—in a supernumerary capacity both inside and outside the airport compound. At present, they were around the terminals, guarding the British Airways personnel and the airport's skeleton staff. It was imperative they remain at the terminal area at the time of the assault.

He switched his attention to the layout of the airport.

The terminals, standing next to each other, facing west toward the city, had a modern elegance: plate-glass windows interspaced by slender columns upholding wide, shallow bowls that formed the roof.

But the modernity stopped there. The outlying hangars were antiquated and in disrepair. The apron, runway and taxiways were in need of maintenance. Boaz and Getachew had been briefed that the runway, in particular, had an unsatisfactory surface which, added to the sluggish aerodynamics of heat and high altitude, made takeoff a nightmare.

The airport also lacked sophisticated aids. It had no surface radar scanners; it could not afford them. Which was fortuitous. Nor did it have the instrument landing system radio transmitters which, placed at the end of the runway, facilitated landing by providing heading and approach-slope indications.

These deficiencies, singly or together, frequently plunged the airport into frantic activity either to preempt a hazard or to prepare for an emergency. An analysis of the incident log of the previous six months—supplied by the U.S. Kagnew Base—had indicated that at almost any given time, ground crew had been found bustling around the compound.

Such conditions, Boaz had felt certain, were exploitable. If a sudden and unexpected emergency occurred, Abu Ismail would certainly be fastidious rather than cavalier. He was bound to know that one of the airport's worst disasters had occurred through negligence when a jet on takeoff had crashed into a hydraulic jack left on the runway and had disintegrated, killing forty-two.

Boaz surveyed the runway.

It was long—over three kilometers, according to his briefing, to compensate for the low air density of high altitude and hot climate. It bisected the airport diagonally, extending from northeast to southwest to provide approach and departure paths clear of the surrounding hills. It contained regulation threshold and touchdown markings at each end, as well as pairs of runway visual range points signaling prevailing visibility along the grass verge. None of the RVR points, however, was bulky enough to provide cover.

Boaz concentrated on the threshold markings designating takeoff positions. He scrutinized the clusters of concrete grid slabs that had been laid down around the holding points to prevent soil erosion from jet blast. These monoslabs offered some cover and, more important, would fall behind the cockpit's line of vision once the plane passed the holding position. Providing Boaz and Getachew synchronized their move with that of the plane, they would have at least thirty seconds to scramble to the tail and another thirty before the plane reached takeoff position. And if, as the long-range weather forecast indicated, the wind direction favored the northeastern end for takeoff, they could take advantage of a little luck: the monoslabs at the northeastern end were slightly higher.

He directed his attention to the taxiways. Two for jets and several minor ones for propeller aircraft. The jet taxiways extending from the apron had been recently widened, but were still, according to Kagnew experts, below par. A pilot would need to reduce taxiing speed to about twenty kph to avoid careering into the grass and a bog-down; a plane moving for takeoff, weighed down by fuel and passengers, might have to reduce speed even further, possibly down to ten kph.

He felt more confident. The airport model used during the planning had lacked the correct elevations. The terrain, especially on the northern flank, sloped considerably between the woods and the taxiway. The incline would offer adequate cover for an advance not only to take account of the armor in the field, but also against possible lookouts in the control tower.

✗

Llewellyn pointed to the clock. "It's ten-forty. Are you going to let us out or not?"

The guard remained inscrutable and kept his gun trained on him. Llewellyn bit his knuckles anxiously. His nerve was waning. The guard's attitude indicated that Wolde had tagged him as a troublemaker. They could choose to make an example of him. He would crack then, he knew. Much as he hated Fate for having thrust such a responsibility on his shoulders, he felt proud. It was a good feeling. It would be even better if he succeeded.

He glanced at Illingworth, O'Leary and Matthews. They were playing cards.

He worried about them, too. They had been puzzled when, acting the zealous employee, he had insisted on inspecting the workshop to make sure nothing belonging to British Airways had been damaged.

He had been too quick for them to see anything. In the rest room he had taken the doctored warning-light bulb out of the key ring, marked it and hidden it in his mouth. Then, as he checked the spares tray, he had coughed, covered his mouth, taken the bulb out and dropped it in. The guard escort had paid little attention; they had searched him at the gate and declared him clean. They had watched him merely to make sure he would not try to escape or attempt sabotage.

But the boys knew he was up to something. They probably resented him for not taking them into his confidence. He had been sorely tempted. It was not that he distrusted them, but it would have taken too long to explain. It had taken the Memouneh long enough to convince him. Then again, resentment or not, the boys would back him up, automatically.

Wolde, the other guard who had gone to fetch him, and a third man entered. He recognized the last from the Memouneh's photographs: the WOJ pilot, Abbas.

Wolde faced him angrily. "My man says you wish to see me. . . ."

Llewellyn hoped fear would give substance to his pretended anger. "BA 054 is due to land at ten fifty-five. That's in less than fifteen minutes! We've got to get ready to turn her around. Your men refuse to let us out."

"That's their orders."

"Well now, you can change their orders! We've got to set up equipment. She's only stopping over for fifty minutes."

"You won't be servicing her today. Another crew will take charge."

Llewellyn looked stunned, then turned to Illingworth, O'Leary and Matthews. To his relief they looked angry. He felt less alone. "Another crew? With due respect, boyo, this is a Super VC-10. A delicate lady. There's no one in Addis except us who knows how to keep her in trim."

Abbas laughed. "Ground crews. Same everywhere. Like you were married to them."

Llewellyn turned to him contemptuously. "Who're you when you're at home?"

"WOJ."

"What?"

"We control the airport."

Llewellyn turned to his friends as though shocked. They had crowded behind him supportively.

Matthews barked. "Are you telling us you're hijacking our plane?"

"Requistioning it."

Llewellyn turned to Wolde. "And you're cooperating with them?"

Wolde nodded curtly. "The emperor's orders."

Llewellyn snorted. "We're to cooperate as well, is that it?"

"Of course."

Llewellyn took a deep breath. The time for the first bluff had come. He turned to Matthews. "Matt, you know what this means? . . ."

Matthews looked at him quizzically.

Llewellyn continued before he could respond. "You think . . . We ought to tell them, don't you think?"

Abbas, catching Llewellyn's anxiety, moved forward. "Tell us what?"

Llewellyn fidgeted, put more urgency into his voice. "Matt, we've got to . . ."

Matthews played along, uncertainly. "You think so . . . ?"

"Or they're likely to be trigger-happy. They're WOJ, Matt. They don't fuck about. . . ."

Abbas spun Llewellyn around. "Tell us what? What are you talking about?"

Llewellyn looked desperately at Matthews. The latter exchanged looks with Illingworth and O'Leary, then, to Llewellyn's relief, nodded. "We'll leave it to you, Taffy."

Abbas held Llewellyn by his overalls. "Is there something wrong with BA 054?"

Llewellyn mumbled, as if reluctantly. "No—but . . . You'll—you'll have a hard time hijacking it. . . ."

Abbas forced a laugh, stung by doubt even though the statement sounded preposterous. "Really? Why?"

Llewellyn spoke with great difficulty. "If—when she lands—we're not there to meet her . . . the captain will know . . ."

"Will know what?"

"Something's up."

"How?"

"New regulations . . . Security measure . . . Since that Lisbon hijack . . . we—the ground crew—we're there to give the thumbs-up if you see what I mean. . . ."

"What'll happen if you don't?"

"Straight off, the captain hits the emergency hijack transponder. That blips the flight's squawk sign at air traffic control centers, alerts the world . . ."

"I know what it does. What else?"

"Providing there's no ground fire or aerial interception, he tries to taxi back to the runway. And if he can, takes off instantly."

Abbas pondered a moment, then turned to Wolde. "I want these men out on the tarmac to receive the BA 054. Check them again for weapons."

Wolde, annoyed that a snag had arisen, resisted Abbas's request. "I doubt whether any captain would risk—"

Abbas snapped. "The emergency hijack transponder—I don't want that activated. I want passengers and crew out of that plane as if it's a routine stopover."

Wolde made a face, then shouted orders in Amharic to the guards. The guards pushed the engineers against the wall and started searching them.

Abbas towered over Llewellyn. "You'll behave normally. If you provoke the passengers or crew to any heroics, or if I find the emergency hijack transponder switched on, we'll shoot everybody. Is that understood?"

Llewellyn nodded, trying to control the trembling in his legs. Then, as Abbas and Wolde marched out, he sighed with relief.

While the guards searched them, O'Leary mumbled. "What're you playing at, Taffy?"

Llewellyn winked. "Not with my cock, boyo—I promise you."

Illingworth looked troubled. "Shouldn't push our luck—"

Matthews hissed. "Belt up, lad. Do as the man says."

At 10:55 A.M. BA 054 landed.

As it taxied, Abu Ismail scrutinized the men on the apron. His support commandos, Amir, Hilmi, Rahman, Ayub, Fahd, Ziya, Niyazi and Bahadur, dressed in dungarees and commissioned to service the aircraft, were in position, manning mobile steps, maintenance van, catering truck, baggage car, sanitary servicing vehicle, chocks, ground power unit and refueler. His pilots, Abbas and Isa, stood by a supervisor's jeep as representatives of customs and immigration. His Day of Glory platoon, except for Mohammed and Shamseddin who were guarding the OAU hostages, were armed and ready to intervene in case of resistance. Wolde's Sergeant Ketema and six of his paratroopers deployed as security officers. Wolde himself, with two other men, stood guard over the British Airways ground engineers whom Abbas had brought out of their quarters.

The role of the engineers as signalmen to British Airways captains was obviously a recent innovation. Otherwise WOJ intelligence would have known about it. That such a detail could have scuttled Operation Dragons either by alerting the world or by forcing WOJ to storm the aircraft had been a great shock. He had even wondered momentarily whether the artifice had been the work of The Doubter. Ridiculous, of course, but it rankled that so near to total victory he should still be preoccupied by doubt.

He watched anxiously as the Super VC-10 arrived on the apron and cut her engines. Commandos rushed to place the chocks against the wheels; others pushed the mobile steps against the doors. But the doors did not open. His head spun.

Abbas materialized by Llewellyn's side. "Why aren't they opening the doors?"

Llewellyn looked blankly at him. There was nothing untoward

in the delay. The crew were taking their time and the hijackers were ultraimpatient. He felt it was a good hand to play.

He directed his attention to the cockpit. He could see Captain Malcolm Boyd in the left-hand seat, already busy with his logbook. The fact that the captain had turned out to be Boyd delighted him. Ex-RAF, a bold pilot turned into a fussy old woman as British Airways training stipulated. Llewellyn could depend on him.

He pretended alarm. "I don't know. . . . Maybe he smells something . . . wondering why we're standing here doing nothing."

"What should you be doing?"

"Plugging in the auxiliary power unit, for a start . . ."

Abbas pointed at the WOJ crew positioning the ground power unit beneath the aircraft. "We're already doing that. . . ."

"That's what I mean—you're doing it all. We're standing here like spare pricks at a wedding."

"What's your procedure—after plugging in the power?"

"Well, one of us should be talking to him—getting an overall report on the flight. . . ."

"From the ground?"

"Yes. . . ."

"Go on. . . . But remember, I'll be right behind you. . . ."

Llewellyn nodded, then pointedly composing himself, hurried toward the plane's nose.

Abbas followed him.

Llewellyn's legs shook. The exchange with Abbas had been brief, but it had felt endless. Throughout, he had expected the doors suddenly to open, had agonized over the prospect of having to devise another ruse to contact Boyd. He was still running against the clock. The doors were bound to open any second.

He felt thankful that Boyd's side window was open. He shouted. "Hullo, Captain . . ."

Boyd waved from his lofty height. "How're tricks, Taffy?"

"Great. Good flight?"

"Fine."

"Snags?"

"Usual odd niggles. Nothing serious."

Out of the corner of his eye Llewellyn saw the doors open. His heart sank. He turned toward Abbas. To his relief, he saw the WOJ pilot point him out to Wolde, then run up the steps to take charge of the plane.

He seized his chance. "Captain, imperative! Enter into snag log: rear servicing and emergency exit door warning light was suspect at the Seychelles. Spare bulb fitted—but dodgy. System to be checked at Addis. Make sure they see it!"

Boyd looked at him sharply. "What?"

Llewellyn saw Abbas push past the passengers gathering at the door. "Be seeing you, Captain."

A moment later he saw Abbas burst into the flight deck. He turned around just as Wolde reached him. He tried to look defeated. He felt exultant. He had accomplished his task. The next phase depended on Boyd. After Abbas's charge into the cockpit, Boyd was likely to be formidable.

☒

As Abbas took possession of the plane, Nazmi moved to Abu Ismail and kissed his hands. "Your wings of victory, Al-Mahdi!"

Abu Ismail savored the words. His head stopped spinning. He felt his arms expand, as if they had truly grown wings. "Instruct the controller, Nazmi. He is to declare the airport temporarily closed. All flights are to be diverted to Asmara until further notice. Reason for closure: unserviceability of runway due to minor incident. Instruct him also to inform British Airways at Nicosia and London that 054 has had a tire burst on landing, that it incurred some damage to the nosewheel oleo strut, that repairs are under way and that departure will be delayed by a few hours."

"Yes, Al-Mahdi."

"Instruct my warriors to start work on the VC-10. We shall pause at noon for our last prayer before Glory."

Nazmi sat at the radio console.

Abu Ismail smiled serenely, mocking The Doubter, although it was a dead enemy.

☒

It took four minutes for the seventy-three passengers of BA 054 to disembark.

At 11:10 A.M. Sergeant Ketema and his platoon led them into the transit lounge, there to join the British Airways ground hostesses, the airport's skeleton staff and those other passengers joining the flight at Addis Ababa. All the latter had been taken into custody immediately upon their arrival at the airport.

Sergeant Ketema beckoned Angela Peters, the senior ground hostess.

She rose nervously. She had been briefed earlier by Captain Wolde to announce that flight 054 would be delayed by some twelve hours and that due to prevailing security arrangements, all passengers had to remain in the transit lounge—and that those violating the order would risk being shot.

☒

Captain Boyd resigned himself to the hijacking and turned to Abbas. "Will you be keeping my logbook?"

"For the time being. This aircraft is our concern now."

"I should like to complete it."

"Haven't you already?"

"A final point."

Abbas handed him the logbook.

Captain Boyd opened the snag sheet. He read over the entries he had completed with his flight engineer. Four items: malfunctioning windshield wipers, difficulty in tuning the radio, suspected malfunctioning of the rear servicing and emergency exit door warning light, one nosewheel indicator light unserviceable. Against the first and second he had marked "AD," meaning "allowable deficiency," with brief notes indicating that until arrival in London, the windshield wipers were to be compensated for by rain repellent and the radio by the alternative and auxiliary sets. Against the nosewheel indicator light entry he had recorded use of the bulb changeover switch on the approach to Addis Ababa, and that he would replace the defective bulb, in Addis Ababa, with the spare the plane carried. Against the third item, he had placed a cross and a note explaining that the rear servicing and emergency exit door's warning light had been flickering while the aircraft was on the ground at the Seychelles, that the spare had been fitted, but that it, too, had appeared to be on the blink, and that the system should be checked at Addis Ababa.

For a moment he wondered whether that particular entry was too elaborate and in danger of arousing WOJ suspicions. He decided it was not. He had no idea how Llewellyn and the security forces by whom he had obviously been briefed intended to exploit the warning light, but he reassured himself that if he were the WOJ pilot, he would most certainly do something about it. Moreover, he had put the fault between three genuine snags; a cursory check on those would prove positive and confer authenticity on the warning light's failure.

Briskly he wrote a fifth entry: "T/Ds hijack flight," then handed back the logbook.

Abbas gave him a puzzled look. "What's T/Ds mean?"

Boyd got up from his seat. "Turds."

Abbas stared, wondering whether to laugh or to strike him.

Boyd did not give him a chance to do either. "I surrender my aircraft. I expect humanitarian treatment for my crew and passengers. And I hope you rot in hell!"

*

At 11:25 A.M. from the groves bordering the southern perimeter, Amnon signaled both Boaz and the Memouneh that his contingent of Sayeret Matkal, Falashas and MacDonald, Oates and Vernon were in assault position.

⚔

At 11:30 A.M. Emmanuel signaled the Memouneh that the passengers, captain and crew of BA 054 had been locked in the transit lounge adjacent to the international departures lounge, and that the WOJ support crew had started work on the VC-10. Judging from the tracks and pulley system being laid at the rear passenger door, he surmised that the work entailed the installation of a bomb chute.

As a postscript to his signal, he reported that his lookout spot close to the transit lounge had become vulnerable and that the chatter of passengers would reduce his chances of an early warning of approaching sentries. In the event of discovery, he expected to have time to dispose of his radio and create enough confusion to suggest that his activities were those of a lone, misguided dissident.

⚔

At 11:40 A.M. the Memouneh signaled Gentleman Jim at Fort Meade that the Mossad-CIA assault force was in position at Haile Selassie I International Airport and that the countdown for the first move stood, as planned, for 12:02, when WOJ would be expected to perform noon prayers.

Gentleman Jim's reply acknowledged affirmative and informed the Memouneh that he had put into operation the following positive control measures to intercept the WOJ plane, should the assault force abort mission or fail.

1. Three U.S. Air Force F-111A bomber/interceptor squadrons of twenty aircraft each, equipped with large weapon/avionics payload, operating from Hatzerim Air Base, Israel, and in deployment since 6:00 A.M. over the Red Sea sector between Ethiopia and Saudi Arabia in a special turn-around rota that guaranteed interception of the WOJ plane by no less than thirty aircraft at any given time of day or night.

2. Two U.S. Air Force F-100 interceptor squadrons of twenty aircraft each, operating due to restrictions of range from Djibouti, T.F.A.I., and Jizan, Saudi Arabia, under pretext of arms sales promotions and in deployment since 9:00 A.M. in a special turn-around rota that guaranteed interception of the WOJ plane by no less than fifteen aircraft at any given time of day or night.

3. Two U.S. Navy aircraft carriers of the Seventh Fleet summoned from the Philippines as of April 11, each with a complement of two F-14F fighter squadrons of twenty aircraft each, on full alert in the Red Sea as of 1:00 A.M., time of sail-through the Strait of Bab el Mandeb.

4. Four U.S. Navy nuclear submarines of the Seventh Fleet on escort duty to aircraft carriers, on full alert in the Red Sea as of 12:30 A.M., time of sail-through the Strait of Bab el Mandeb.

5. All-encompassing surveillance systems to alert and direct both the U.S. Air Force and U.S. Navy forces comprising:

   a. Major NSA surveillance and warning satellite systems locked on North-East Africa as of 6:00 A.M.

   b. Major back-up interceptor control systems locked on Northeast Africa as of 6:00 A.M.

   c. Three U.S. Air Force AWACS aircraft, operating on permanent rota from Hatzerim Air Base, Israel, over Red Sea sector.

   d. Two SR-71A strategic reconnaissance aircraft, operating on permanent rota over Red Sea sector from bases Diego Garcia, British Colony, Indian Ocean, and Naples, Italy.

✗

At 11:45 A.M. Nazmi came out onto the apron. He directed every WOJ commando to the drinking-water supply truck parked near the Super VC-10 and joined them in the ablution of the mouth, nostrils, face, arms and feet.

At 11:55, he issued the commandos with the white ihrams and new prayer mats that had been stored in Abu Ismail's executive jet. He then placed a prayer mat of emerald green, also new, at the fore for Abu Ismail.

Neither Wolde nor the paratroopers brought in from the periphery of the apron to provide a security cordon nor Sergeant Ketema's platoon delegated to guard the control tower, the passengers and crew of BA 054, the airport skeleton staff, the British Airways maintenance engineers and the OAU hostages, observed that the worshipers faced not Mecca, as prescribed, but a point northwest of Mecca.

To Wolde and his men, however, the spectacle of a band of Muslims preparing to pray on soil which was part of a Christian capital, and which they had occupied, albeit technically and temporarily, proved painful. The fact that the troops had been forced not only to tolerate the offense, but also to provide protection to the desecraters, compounded the injury with insult. The remorse

Wolde felt was salved by the certainty that the unholy alliance would tomorrow reclaim Ethiopia's future.

At 11:58, Abu Ismail, dressed in a dazzling white ihram, emerged onto the apron.

At 12:00 precisely, he commenced the noon prayers.

✗

At 12:01 P.M. Boaz received two signals.

The first, from the Memouneh, who had been monitoring the field radios of both WOJ and Wolde, informed him that communications between Wolde, the tanks and the paratroopers in the second line of defense had remained at a minimum, involving nothing more than quarter-hourly reports of "all quiet."

Boaz welcomed the news. The more secure the enemy felt, the better.

The second signal, from Amnon at the southern perimeter, informed him that Amnon's targets, the tank crew at the southern flank and the four Ethiopian paratroopers dug in beyond, were suitably lulled by inactivity.

Boaz checked his contingent. The eight Sayeret Matkal, perched on various trees for a clear line to target, were glued to the sniperscopes of their silencer-fitted rifles waiting for Boaz's order to fire. The five Falashas stood tense, but poised to hurtle across the hundred meters that separated them from the M-41.

Getachew, who had been racing his binoculars between the armored cars at the northwest and those at the northeast, reported urgently. "The troops are all watching the prayers, Boaz."

Boaz took a final look at the targets. The tank crew were still sitting on the turret. The heavy heat haze of the midday sun made it difficult to ascertain what precisely they were doing to while away the boredom. To some extent the haze would camouflage their death throes. He felt sorry for them. They looked like children in uniform playing war games.

He directed his attention to the paratroopers in the second line of defense. All were lying prone. By contrast to the tank crew, they would not significantly alter position when hit.

Boaz raised his rifle, aimed at the paratrooper at the extreme left and placed his finger on the trigger. "Getachew—it's go! Signal Amnon!"

Getachew rasped the order into his field radio.

Boaz barked at his men. "Now!"

They fired.

Simultaneously, the five Falashas broke into a crouched run.

Getachew flashed his binoculars from the armored cars to the control tower.

Boaz dropped his rifle, raised his binoculars. Behind him, four Sayeret Matkal, Avishai, Uri, Dov and Misha, already down from the trees, darted forward.

The remaining four kept their guns trained in case any of the tank crew or paratroopers had escaped the first salvo.

Boaz scanned the field. All the targets had been shot through the head. Except for the commander who swayed precariously by the edge of the turret, the tank crew had slumped into a pile, their fall from the tank prevented by the paraphernalia spread around the turret. The paratroopers in the second line of defense lay still.

"Control tower, Getachew?"

"Fine—so far."

Boaz continued scanning the field. The Falashas had covered a quarter of the distance. Their objective was the M-41 tank. They would be virtually clear at the halfway stage where the upward-sloping terrain would conceal them.

The four Sayeret Matkal, highly trained men in peak condition, had overtaken the Falashas and were running up the slope. The difficulty for them lay beyond the tank. They had to traverse another hundred meters to reach the paratroopers' dugouts. The terrain was quite open. They would have to crawl, pacing themselves with no guidance except their sixth sense, plus a meek prayer that their mottled fatigues would provide adequate camouflage.

Boaz ordered the remaining Sayeret Matkal. "Shimshon, Nehemiah, Dan, Chaim—take over!"

The four scrambled down the trees and spread out at the edge of the woods.

Boaz sprinted forward. "Let's go, Getachew!"

Getachew darted from behind him.

They ran as fast as they could in a crouched position toward the M-41. Boaz's sense of timing, precise after years of warfare, estimated that twenty seconds had passed. Another ten seconds, and he and Getachew would be on the slope and near safety. Their objective, like the Falashas', was the tank. The Falashas would act as the original crew. He and Getachew would hold position there and take care of Wolde's signals. Later, they would lure Wolde.

They reached the slope, clambered up. Boaz counted twenty-eight seconds. Faster than he had estimated. The Falashas had attained the tank. Avishai, Uri, Dov and Misha were crawling forward to the paratroopers' positions.

Another eight seconds and Boaz and Getachew scaled the tank with the dead crew serving as cover.

Getachew dived down the turret hatch.

Boaz rasped into his field radio. "Shimshon?"

Shimson's voice crackled. "All's well . . . Carry on. . . ."

Boaz turned to the Falashas flattened around the tank. "Stand by."

He grabbed the corpse of a crew member and pushed it down the hatch into Getachew's arms. Simultaneously, one of the Falashas climbed onto the turret. Boaz grabbed a second corpse. The Falasha helped him drop it down the hatch. Another Falasha climbed onto the turret. They repeated the maneuver for the other three corpses. Each time one disappeared, a Falasha scrambled aboard.

When all the Falashas had climbed onto the tank, Boaz sent them down the hatch. "Put the crew's uniforms on—quick as you can. Then come up."

He took position by the turret-top machine gun and checked his watch: fifty-seven seconds. He scanned the terrain ahead. Avishai, Uri, Dov and Misha had another fifty meters to crawl.

✗

At the southern perimeter, MacDonald reached the paratrooper whose position he was to occupy. He covered the corpse with the length of camouflage netting he had wound around his waist and assumed guard.

Along his line Ehud, Zeev and Issahar had also reached their positions.

He looked back. Oates and Vernon, sprawled on the turret like bored troops, had lit cigarettes; Amnon lounged behind the machine gun. Two of the Falashas, now in uniform, were also on the turret, playing cards. The other three had ensconced themselves inside the tank with the dead crew and two of Amnon's men, Menahem and Shabtai. The remaining two Sayeret Matkal, Aharon and Yigal, were in the grove, keeping them covered.

He craned forward and gazed at the northern perimeter to observe how Boaz and his company were faring with the same maneuver. But the heat haze, which had helped the action considerably, diffused the terrain.

He checked his watch: 12:05.

✗

At 12:07 P.M. Boaz reported to the Memouneh that the northern perimeter had been secured without mishap.

The Memouneh reported in turn that Amnon had achieved the same objective at the southern flank.

Boaz and Getachew settled down to wait for the next move.

✗

At 12:35 P.M. at the end of the noon prayers, Abu Ismail summoned his warriors to hear his last sermon before the advent of theocracy. He stood upright, aware that his flesh was stronger than a caliph's sword and that his spirit stretched like a granite mountain beyond the firmament. He had sensed the hostility the prayers had generated in Wolde's men, and he had let it ignite his blood so that his words danced on the flame's edge.

"My warriors. You stand before Allah on His Day of Glory. You stand as bearers of the Day of Judgment. Today we have prayed not toward that house of harlot gods Mecca, but toward Al-Quds, that holy mount upon which Allah set up his first tent. By our particular devotion, we have declared to Al-Quds that we have begun the march for the last jihad, that before the advent of the next moon, we shall have delivered the sacred stones from the diseased hands of the Infidel. Today, my children, you escape the milkless teats of an old world. Tomorrow, my holy warriors, you will reconstruct the world in the vision of the Prophet, ensure its eternal youth with the wisdom of creation. Tomorrow, my beloved brethren, you will no longer merely submit to Allah, but you will unite with Him day and night, insatiably, in the most sublime act of love. Tomorrow, my holy sons, you will possess a religion that has been saved from the profane ways of the Jew, of its godless lackeys, the Christian, of its mother of corruption, the West. Tomorrow, my saved children, you will imbibe religious fulfillment and self-respect in your faith. Prepare for heaven on earth, my sons. . . ."

The warriors thundered. "We are prepared!"

Abu Ismail spread his arms. "This is our war cry. We have no god but Allah! We have no leader but the Prophet! We have no constitution but the Koran! We have no way but Jihad! Our supreme desire is death for the glory of Allah! The Savior of the Faith is Al-Mahdi!"

The warriors declaimed seven times: "Al-Mahdi! Al-Mahdi! Al-Mahdi! Al-Mahdi! Al-Mahdi! Al-Mahdi! Al-Mahdi!"

Abu Ismail levitated. He penetrated the clouds. Only briefly did he wonder whether The Doubter lay in wait for him. He continued to ascend. He reached the sun. He stood before the Godhead. He touched It. It smiled.

✗

At 1:00 P.M. Emmanuel reported to the Memouneh, Boaz and Amnon that the WOJ support team had completed work on the rear passenger door and had commenced servicing the VC-10.

✗

Twenty minutes later, Nairobi air traffic control center informed its South Ethiopian counterpart that KLM 320 from Johannesburg had completed its first stage, and should be expected to enter South Ethiopian flight information region at the estimated time of 3:03 P.M.

South Ethiopian air traffic control center relayed the information automatically to Haile Selassie I International Airport.

The report pleased Abu Ismail. KLM 320's punctuality ensured that there would be no delay, and eliminated the option of having to find another flight as his shield.

✗

At 1:34 P.M. Abbas, accompanied by his chief maintenance engineer, Hilmi, burst into the British Airways duty room. The ground engineers, impervious of their guards, had taken to dozing.

Abbas clapped his hands impatiently. "One of you!"

Llewellyn, who had been feigning sleep, rose dazedly. "What's up?"

Abbas pointed to BA 054's snag sheet. "I'd like your views on this."

Llewellyn, trying his utmost to remain calm, studied Captain Boyd's entries on the snag sheet. "Looks straightforward to me."

"We've opened the rear servicing and emergency exit door. The warning light's not functioning."

"It should. It says they put in a spare in the Seychelles."

"It also says the spare appeared to be dodgy. It's dead now."

"Have you checked the door for pressure leaks?"

"Yes. It's okay. We've also checked the contact switch. Perfectly functional."

"Checked the electrical circuit?"

"Yes. Nothing wrong with it."

"Then what are you worried about?"

"There's something wrong with that system. And I want it corrected."

"If the door, the contact switch and the circuits are all okay, that leaves one other possibility."

"What?"

"The bulb. You've got a defective bulb."

"Yes. But why? According to the snag sheet, it was replaced this morning. Why should it go so soon?"

"Well, the captain's report more or less says so. Dodgy."

Abbas glanced at Hilmi. "Can't be anything else—you're sure?"

"Spares get knocked about. Aircrews treat them like they're unbreakable. Use another spare."

Abbas looked annoyed. "We haven't got one. They must have used the last."

Llewellyn shook his head. "It's always the little things, isn't it? Every time I go for a dirty weekend, I stuff my bag with rubbers . . . but I always run out—"

Abbas was not listening. "Have you got one?"

"I expect so."

"Get it."

"Spares are in the back room."

Abbas gesticulated to Hilmi to follow Llewellyn.

Llewellyn moved on hollow legs. He glanced quickly at Illingworth, O'Leary and Matthews. Illingworth, who was responsible for electrical parts, had begun to get to his feet.

Matthews, determined to give Llewellyn the rope he obviously wanted, moved across to Illingworth. "Illy, you got a smoke on you?"

Llewellyn stopped by the door to the back room. "While I'm at it, anything else you want?"

Abbas shook his head. "No."

"I saw other snags mentioned. Another light?"

"We've taken care of them. The other light was the nosewheel indicator. We found a spare for that in the plane."

"Shows you—we get things right most of the time." He went into the back room.

Hilmi followed.

Llewellyn took his time, rummaging in the spares tray. Finally, he picked up the self-destruct bulb given to him by the Memouneh and handed it to Hilmi.

$$\mathcal{X}$$

At 1:46 P.M. Emmanuel reported to the Memouneh, Boaz and Amnon that Llewellyn had stood by the window of the duty room with his face against the glass to signal the successful handover of the self-destruct bulb to WOJ engineers.

$$\mathcal{X}$$

At 2:00 P.M. Montblanc, who had drunk vast quantities of water throughout the morning, used the slop bucket for the last time. A few minutes earlier, Shamseddin and Riyad had announced that the OAU hostages would have no lunch as the airport caterers had failed to turn up.

The announcement had not surprised Montblanc. The hostages were well sedated by the previous meals and no longer preoccupied WOJ. That, in turn, meant that departure time was approaching.

Montblanc staggered back to the tap and drank to replace the liquid he had discharged. He then moved next to Habyarwanda and curled up on the floor. He could retain his urine easier in that position.

✗

At 2:05 P.M. Hilmi reported to Abbas that the VC-10 had been serviced and refueled and stood ready.

Abbas glanced at the new warning-light bulb of the rear servicing and emergency exit door. It was working satisfactorily. Nevertheless, he memorized its position on the flight engineer's console. He would keep an eye on it in case it registered a live circuit during the flight.

✗

At 2:16 P.M. Nairobi informed South Ethiopian air traffic control center that KLM 320 was on its second stage from Johannesburg to Amsterdam and that it would enter the South Ethiopian region at the estimated time of 3:03.

South Ethiopian air traffic control center relayed the information to Haile Selassie I International Airport.

✗

At 2:20 P.M. Abu Ismail ran a final check on the weather reports that had been relayed from regional and international stations. Both the terminal area forecast and the meteorological aerodrome report specified ceiling and visibility unlimited and clement weather for a 450-kilometer radius of Addis Ababa. Two significant meteorological conditions had been issued for Africa: haboobs, quick-rising sandstorms over the Sudan and thunderstorms over the Congo—neither affecting KLM 320's route.

Abu Ismail turned to Nazmi. "We can expect KLM 320 over Addis Ababa at about fifteen thirty-five. Our zero hour will be fifteen thirty."

Nazmi savored the moment. "Yes, Al-Mahdi."

"Signal Admiral Tiblyashin, General Larinchev and Marshal Yeliseev to that effect. At fifteen hundred hours inform British Airways London and Nicosia that BA 054 will resume flight at fifteen thirty. File a plan that will correspond to that of KLM 320, but make sure it is within safety regulations. I do not want British Airways to fear collision. Instruct Isa to prepare the Gulfstream for departure at fifteen hundred hours. He is to file a flight plan for Cairo and Baghdad immediately. I want maximum advance warning for the Israelis. I want them alarmed by the fact that my plane will be close to their airspace. Even if they think it is a decoy, they will scramble. That will be sufficient. A full-scale deployment of the Israeli Air Force would be adequate evidence to incriminate the Jew as Mecca's desecraters. Tell Isa to avoid the haboobs over the Sudan. I do not want him to fail with this flight."

"Yes, Al-Mahdi."

"Alert our warriors at Tripoli. We shall return to base immediately after the raid. At zero plus five hours."

"Will you still delay revealing yourself as Al-Mahdi until tomorrow?"

"Yes. I want the Faithful's fury to gather momentum. I also want the Russians in an untenable position with their forces exposed and paralyzed. I want chaos in the Kremlin—the Presidium at each other's throats."

"What will Qaddafi do when you reveal yourself as Al-Mahdi?"

"Qaddafi will have been engulfed by the Faithful. Go, Nazmi. Announce zero hour. Order Wolde to be doubly alert."

Nazmi bent down and kissed Abu Ismail's feet. "Yes. Al-Mahdi."

Abu Ismail kissed Nazmi's forehead. "You have been my chief of staff but briefly, my son. Yet you have ascended to Heaven's gateway. I could not have wished for a better companion."

"I shall never fail you, Al-Mahdi. You are my father, my guide, my Savior."

✼

At 2:35 P.M. Gentleman Jim alerted the Memouneh that WOJ's Russian connection had finally come into play.

Signals had been picked up from Abu Ismail to Soviet bases in Mukalla and Baghdad and to Marshal Sergei Yeliseev's headquarters in Moscow. The National Security Agency had succeeded in decoding the signals. All had borne the authorization of KGB General Ivan Volkov, a past mentor of Idris Ali. The first had ordered the Soviet MiG-25 squadrons of the Indian Ocean Fleet to provide umbrella cover for the WOJ VC-10; the second and third had activated countdown for the Soviet Tu-22 bomber squadron, Baghdad, and Marshal Yeliseev's land forces on the Iranian border for the subsequent phases of Operation Dragons. Zero hour had been declared as 3:30 P.M.

Gentleman Jim reassured the Memouneh that following these signals, U.S. Air Force and Navy contingents in the Red Sea had received a presidential directive to engage the Soviet MiG-25 umbrella. The U.S. forces' first priority would still be to destroy the WOJ VC-10 over the Danakil at zero hour plus fifty minutes. This move would be executed on the assumption that Boaz, Getachew and Montblanc, expected to infiltrate the WOJ aircraft at zero hour, had failed to redress the situation. The move would also safeguard against the remote possibility of failure against the Soviet forces.

There had been one final undertaking. The CIA computer, depicting KGB General Ivan Volkov as the leader of an ultrahawk faction in the Soviet Union, had suggested the possibility that the Soviet forces commissioned to assist WOJ might be rebel troops recruited by Volkov to provoke a coup d'état. On this evaluation, the U.S. president had been advised to instigate direct talks with the Soviet premier. If the Soviet forces assigned to assist WOJ lacked official sanction, the Soviet premier could be expected to intercept effectively. If not, the U.S. president would assert his government's resolve to foil the Soviet-WOJ alliance come what may. Such an ultimatum, it was expected, would be heeded if only because, deprived of the element of surprise, the Soviet forces would face a debacle.

✗

At 2:40 P.M. Captain Wolde boarded his jeep to inspect the airport's outer defenses. His spirits had begun to lift. His unholy alliance would be terminating within the hour. He did not even resent the imperious manner with which Nazmi had commanded him to heighten vigilance.

He drove toward the northern perimeter. A zealous signal from the commander of the M-41 stationed there had requested him to inspect that position first and rouse the crew who had become restless by the inactivity.

He had seen how Abu Ismail's sermon had electrified the WOJ commandos. He wanted a similar reaction from his men now that the time to depose the emperor was approaching.

✗

At 2:45 P.M. Emmanuel reported to the Memouneh, Boaz and Amnon that WOJ personnel had commenced loading the bomb onto the VC-10. It was being placed at the rear passenger door and except for the parachutes harnessed to it, it looked like an ordinary trunk with a number of antennae sticking out of its sides. Judging by the care with which it was handled, it seemed, as Abu Ismail had warned, extensively booby-trapped.

*

The man who claimed to be an Israeli officer pointed at his watch. "It is fourteen fifty, Wolde. Zero hour minus forty minutes. You'll have to decide."

Wolde scanned the northern perimeter, still stunned that the zealous tank commander who had summoned him was his old enemy, Getachew Iyessous, and that somehow the traitor, with his Israeli and American henchmen, had secured both the northern and southern perimeters, killing in the process two tank crews and eight of his paratroopers. His eyes scurried between the two armored cars positioned at the northeast and northwest.

The Israeli officer called Boaz shook his head. "They can't help you, Wolde. Before they could load one shell or advance one centimeter, my gunner would hit the VC-10. And that would be the end of Addis. The end of us all."

Wolde faced him defiantly. "You're bluffing!"

"The stakes are too high, Wolde. If the choice is between the destruction of Israel and that of Addis, you'll appreciate Addis stands no chance. . . ."

Wolde protested. "They're not going to Israel. They are going to Iraq."

Boaz remained impassive. "Actually, they intend to destroy Mecca. But my threat stands. If I have to save Mecca or Addis, I'll save Mecca."

Wolde, barely controlling his fury, turned to Getachew. "You'd let him do that, Getachew? You'd let him destroy Addis?"

Getachew, who had been squatting by the tracks of the tank, rose and faced him. "No, Tewodoros. If Addis is destroyed, it will be you who will have destroyed it."

Wolde's body rocked with fury. "Me?"

"You can prevent it. I can't. Even if I could kill this man and his platoon, there's another tank at the southern perimeter. Even if I could stop the other tank, who'll stop the rest?"

"The rest—who?"

"American, Israeli, French, British—you name them, Tewodoros. What you would call Zionist-imperialist forces. They're circling Addis. They know nothing about Abu Ismail's boobytraps and sophisticated fuses. Or if they do, they don't care! They're under orders to destroy the VC-10 the moment it takes off."

Boaz hardened his tone with menace. "You're caught between

two fanatics, Wolde: Arab and Jew. If you want to save Addis, you have no alternative."

Wolde pondered. He did not believe the Israeli would carry out his threat and destroy Addis Ababa. Nor did he believe the man was a fanatic in Abu Ismail's mold. Fanaticism of that stature had a physical presence—like a cloud of locusts. Even so, Wolde was a realist. And a realistic evaluation of the situation told him he would have little to gain by rejecting the Israeli's offer. Abu Ismail was not aware of the developments and would stay ignorant. The Israeli held the initiative; he would have first strike and knock out the remaining tanks and armored cars. Even if Wolde could escape mayhem and summon assistance from other Dergue forces, the final victory would be empty. He would have lost his credibility and his power base. "If I help you—what then?"

Getachew replied sharply. "You'll at least prove yourself a patriot."

"Prove—"

Getachew spat in Wolde's face. "You know what I think of you, Tewodoros. I will make only one promise. One day we will fight to the death. But I would rather we did so before the eyes of our beloved Ethiopia—not as makeweights to foreigners. If you cooperate now, I'll let you fight another day."

Wolde held his ground, then with equal venom spat back, "So be it."

Boaz moved between Getachew and Wolde. "You'll cooperate then, Captain?"

"What do I have to do?"

"Very little. You will not, needless to say, divulge our presence to WOJ. You will instruct your paratroopers at the runway and apron that two of your men—that is, Getachew and I—will be taking new cover positions during the VC-10's takeoff and that they need not pay any attention to us. You will instruct the armored cars likewise. You will further instruct your platoon at the passenger terminal to move away from the control tower. After the takeoff some of my men will deploy there; I don't want them to meet resistance. Finally, when the birds appear—"

"Birds? What birds?"

"Sparrows, mainly . . ."

"I don't understand . . ."

"A bird can explode an engine. A flock of birds can cripple a plane. Birds have been responsible for crashes."

"Yes, but—"

"When Abu Ismail sees his takeoff path crowded with birds, he'll want them dispersed. He should ask for the bird-scaring jeep to clear the runway. If he doesn't, being a staunch ally, you'll advise him to do so. You'll personally take charge of the jeep. You'll drive here for extra hands. That's all. Getachew and I will do the rest."

"I don't know if this airport has a bird-scaring jeep."

"It has. In the maintenance hangar. Complete with bullhorns, tape recorder, sound-effects cassettes and shotguns."

Wolde shook his head in disbelief. "What makes you think there will be any birds?"

"We'll just call them. They'll come."

✗

At 2:57 P.M. Abu Ismail's executive jet, piloted by Isa and carrying Amir, Rahman, Ayub, Fahd and Bahadur of the WOJ support platoon, taxied to the runway.

Emmanuel reported to the Memouneh that there had been no ceremonial leavetaking even though with the Israeli Air Force on full alert, the plane could not expect to reach its destination.

At 3:00 the Grumman Gulfstream II took off. As it turned north, it received its last signal from Abu Ismail: "Tomorrow in Al-Quds!"

✗

At 3:05 P.M. Nazmi addressed the OAU hostages. "I shall be forthright. We, the Warriors of Jihad, are on a portentous mission. The world wants to stop us. We cannot be stopped. We need not have burdened ourselves with you as hostages. We have done so against the possibility that the emperor or his Zionist imperialist masters might attempt to intercept our aircraft. You august members of the OAU are our guarantee they will not dare do so. That is all. I specify these facts because I want to make sure you will obey orders. For those still defiant, I need only say we are not bound by the conventions of international diplomacy. If you cooperate you will be freed as soon as we land at our destination. If not, you will be killed. We believe you will cooperate. Those of you who are Muslims will realize that the glory we shall achieve for Allah will be the glory you have wished for your countries. Those who are not Muslims will exult equally because our mission will deliver you from the Zionist-imperialist yoke. Is that clear?"

Nazmi paused. Though his question was rhetorical, the OAU hostages, fuzzy and lethargic from the sedatives they had consumed, searched each other's faces in the hope that one could provide an answer.

Montblanc, huddled next to Habyarwanda, and in discomfort from his full bladder, mumbled weakly. "Yes."

Nazmi smiled appreciatively at him. "Good. You will start boarding soon. However, just to make sure no one smuggles objects that could be used as weapons, I must ask you to undress down to your undergarments. . . ."

A few of the women muttered, stupefied. "Undergarments . . . ?"

Nazmi inclined his head politely. Undressing the hostages was not really necessary. But Abu Ismail had specified that the measure had psychological value and ensured control. A man in his underpants seldom generated the will to resist; a half-naked woman, more often than not, withdrew into a corner to safeguard her modesty.

At 3:06 P.M. Sanbat relayed Boaz's signal to Bayyu, ordering him to start scattering the cornmeal.

At 3:07 P.M. at the veterinary station beyond the eastern perimeter, Bayyu set to work. Tripps and Underwood kept him covered from their vantage points.

Bayyu carried the twenty-five-kilo sacks some distance so that neither the truck nor he and his companions would intimidate the birds. Then he spread the cornmeal in an extending arc toward the airport. At the edges of the arc, he made two mounds large enough to attract flying birds. He completed his task in three minutes.

At 3:11 P.M. the Day of Glory platoon led the OAU hostages toward the VC-10. Befuddled by drugs, disquieted by their state of undress, the hostages stuck close to their captors like confused children seeking the protection of adults.

At 3:14 P.M. Boaz spotted some sparrows east of the runway. "They're coming in."

Getachew smiled. "The Marines, as Al Jameson would have said. . . ."

At 3:17 P.M. Montblanc and Habyarwanda entered the VC-10 through the forward passenger door.

As Montblanc, who had maneuvered to embark last, had hoped, they found the first-class section, five rows with two seats at each side of the aisle, filled. They progressed past the bulkhead into the economy section.

Montblanc surveyed the economy-class cabin. During the planning, he had memorized the interior of the Super VC-10, as he had the interiors of every other jet carrier likely to touch down at Addis Ababa. The economy class had nineteen rows each with three seats at either side of the aisle; three more seats on the right-hand side behind the nineteenth completed the accommodation: 117, excluding the first-class cabin.

It was imperative that he should sit three-quarters of the way toward the tail to give himself an adequate margin for action.

He noted with relief that the WOJ commandos supervising the boarding were allowing the hostages to sit as they pleased, providing they did not go beyond the seventeenth row where a green curtain sealed off the bomb egress and the remaining seats, the latter presumably reserved for some of the commandos. Thus, the fifty-four hostages pushed into economy class had taken either the aisle or the window seats of each three-seat unit, leaving the middle one empty. Some elderly hostages and a few of the women had even been allowed sole occupancy of three-seat units.

Montblanc hurried to the fifteenth row, sat by the window and summoned Habyarwanda to the aisle seat. Then, resuming his meek attitude, he coiled up and closed his eyes. He wondered whether he would be able to hold out for the next ten minutes or so. The walk from the hangar had pushed him to the verge of incontinence.

At 3:18 P.M. Abbas and Hilmi, the latter acting as flight engineer, completed checking the sixty items of the prestart checklist. The checklists had been printed on parchment and were destined to be housed in Al-Quds's silver-domed Al-Masjid Al-Aqsa, specified by the Koran as the Most Supreme Mosque, as documents of Islam's historic flight. Consequently, Abbas logged every item with a flourish.

At 3:19 P.M. Abu Ismail, who had been watching preparations from the control tower, rose from his seat. "It is time."

Nazmi turned to Fisseha. "You know what is at stake. You

have your orders. From Al-Mahdi. From the emperor. And from Captain Wolde. Obey them!"

Fisseha nodded meekly.

Nazmi moved quickly to Abu Ismail's side to offer his arm as support. Abu Ismail shook his head and walked lightly on legs liberated from arthritis.

At 3:20 P.M. Boaz and Getachew synchronized watches with Emmanuel in the passenger terminal and Amnon's unit at the southern perimeter. They then jumped off the tank to wait for Wolde and the bird-scaring jeep.

They had kept their eyes fixed on the eastern horizon. Flocks of birds circled above the veterinary station; others, attracted by the movement, followed. Some of the smaller flocks flew low across the runway at a point where the plane would have passed Velocity One, the decision speed, and would have committed itself to Velocity-rotate, the precalculated takeoff speed. Faced with such a situation, no pilot would commence takeoff until the runway had been cleared of birds. Some would even delay departure until the flocks dispersed completely, to ensure safety during the climb out at Velocity Two.

Ironically, a long delay would work against Boaz and Getachew. WOJ would have time on its hands. They would walk about, chat, check or bully the hostages. That would make Montblanc's task impossible.

That was the worst possibility. But it would not happen. Boaz's confidence rested on his conviction that his life had been extended for this particular hour.

Another assurance, provided by Mossad's computer, on the time it would take an average surge of sparrows to devour fifty kilos of cornmeal, he had found incredible. The computer, predicting first bite within a minute of the spraying of the cornmeal, had calculated that the feast would last eighteen minutes and that the birds would disperse four minutes later. Counting the first bite at 3:11, that meant the cornmeal would be consumed by 3:29 and the birds would clear the area by 3:33.

At 3:21 P.M. Abbas completed the twenty-two items of the crew-at-their-stations checklist, leaving the forward passenger door warning signal to be checked during after-start.

Hilmi left the flight deck to supervise the starting of the engines. He would collect Ziya and Niyazi, the two maintenance engineers who had stayed behind for preflight tasks. He would then return, shut the forward passenger door and declare the aircraft ready for its historic flight.

✗

At 3:22 P.M. Abu Ismail, flanked by Nazmi, emerged onto the apron.

Captain Wolde stood at attention in front of the VC-10 with Sergeant Ketema's platoon lined up as a guard of honor.

"Parting of our ways, Captain Wolde . . ."

"It is, Your Excellency."

"I shall demand one further service. Keep the airport sealed and remain in radio contact for another hour."

"Rest assured."

"I leave Ethiopia in your good hands. Your revolution is blessed by Allah. We shall meet again."

"I hope so."

Abu Ismail caught the edge in Wolde's voice. "Doubts, Captain?"

Wolde smiled ruefully. He wanted to warn Abu Ismail of the Israeli presence at the airport. But in the past minutes he had observed that the tanks at the northern and southern perimeters had trained their guns on the VC-10. "Doubt is the measure of man, sir. . . ."

Abu Ismail glared with formidable eyes. "It is not my measure, Captain Wolde."

Wolde looked blankly at Abu Ismail, then extended his hand. "Good luck."

Abu Ismail bristled as if Wolde had blasphemed. Disregarding the proffered hand, he turned away and started ascending the steps to the forward passenger door.

Wolde seethed but remained at attention. He could not guess how Getachew and the Israelis planned to hit Abu Ismail, but he almost wished they would succeed. And destroy each other.

He turned his thoughts to his predicament. He had been reconsidering the situation. Though it was true the infiltrators held the advantage, the condition was not irreversible. The Israelis were on foreign ground and would move out in the wake of the WOJ plane's departure. In all likelihood, they would be evacuated by the Americans with a transport from Kagnew Base. But until the transport's arrival, they would be vulnerable, no matter how well dug in. Particularly to an attack by the Ethiopian Air Force.

He could strike after the WOJ plane's departure. He had to strike. He could not storm the Jubilee Palace, depose the emperor and assume leadership of the Dergue without having cleaned up the airport first. His future, if not his life, depended on a successful strike.

He turned to his sergeant. "Ketema. When the plane prepares to take off, move to the control tower. Contact Debre Zeyt base. Tell them to scramble. Tell them to tune in on our channel. I shall want them for a limited action."

Ketema looked startled. "Against WOJ?"

"No. I'll explain later. Just contact Debre Zeyt—and wait for me!"

✗

At 3:24 P.M. Abu Ismail and Nazmi entered the cockpit.

Abu Ismail sat behind Abbas in the navigator's seat. Nazmi sat in the first officer's seat to the right of Abbas.

Abu Ismail took out his prayer beads. His murmured invocations soothed the tension.

✗

At 3:26 P.M. Addis Ababa air traffic control center reported that KLM 320 would be overflying Addis Ababa, en route to Jidda, at 3:35, on schedule.

✗

At 3:27 P.M. Abbas and Nazmi completed the after-start check.

Abbas turned to Hilmi, seated at the flight engineer's console behind Nazmi. "All okay?"

Hilmi confirmed. "All okay."

Abbas clipped his takeoff data sheet onto the console in front. He had marked the all-up-weight, temperature, cross-wind, head-wind and runway allowance in bold letters. The takeoff data sheet, too, would be preserved as a historic document.

The aircraft, its engines whining, was ready for departure.

Abbas contacted the control tower, exaggerating the English accent he had acquired in London during his studies. He used standard code in order not to betray the plane's new masters to any eavesdropper monitoring the Addis Ababa air traffic control center frequency. "Addis . . . Speedbird 054 ready to taxi."

Fisseha's voice, shaking with strain, replied instantly: "Speedbird 054, you are clear to taxi. Turn right into northern taxiway. Clear to runway."

Abbas scanned the airfield. A moment later, he spotted the birds swarming across the runway. He sat up sharply. "Addis, have you seen all these birds? Can you clear them from the runway?"

"054. We see the birds. We'll try and clear them. We have a bird-scaring jeep. I've contacted the officer in charge. . . ."

"Addis, do hurry up. I don't want delays."

"054. Will do our best."

Abbas shook his head in disgust. *Birds*—moments before zero hour.

Abu Ismail leaned forward. "Why are you troubled by the birds, Abbas?"

Abbas turned around apologetically, as if personally responsible for the mishap. "Too many of them, Al-Mahdi. If they get sucked into the engines, we could crash. . . ."

"Are we to be delayed?"

"Minimally, Al-Mahdi. They should scare easily."

"They are Allah's creatures, Abbas. They will go. Proceed to the runway."

Fisseha's voice prevented Abbas from replying. "Speedbird 054. Bird-scaring jeep will commence operation now. Captain Wolde has taken personal charge."

Abbas, spared from contradicting Abu Ismail, smiled. "Thank you, Addis. Proceeding to runway. 054."

✗

Boaz and Getachew tautened as the aircraft started taxiing. A moment later they spotted Wolde in the bird-scaring jeep, speeding past the apron toward the northern perimeter.

"This is for dead friends, Getachew. . . ."

Getachew nodded grimly and took out the orange wind sock from his pack.

Boaz blared into the radio. "Emmanuel—to control tower! Quick as you can! Watch out for Wolde's men!"

Emmanuel acknowledged instantly. "Right."

Getachew started blowing up a small balloon glued to the inside of the wind sock.

Boaz switched channels. "Amnon—move to terminal! Secure area! Liberate British Airways passengers and crew when you can! Mop up five minutes after takeoff!"

Amnon's voice rasped. "Right!"

Boaz pocketed the radio and concentrated on the approaching bird-scaring jeep.

Getachew tied up the balloon, waited for the VC-10 to enter the taxiway, then released the wind sock. It trailed on the ground for a moment, then lifted gently and floated into the air. WOJ would spot it, but they would dismiss it, the Memouneh had assured him, as a wind sock that had worked itself loose from its pole. Such mishaps occurred even in the most efficiently run airports.

Getachew turned to Boaz. "I want another man in the jeep!"

Boaz turned to him questioningly.

Getachew met his eyes impassively. "I have my reasons!"

✗

Emmanuel inched open the duty-free manager's office door.

The corridor was clear. It did not surprise him. Since noon, soon after his signal to the Memouneh expressing his fear of discovery, the guards had not bothered to check his section. They had had their hands full with the British Airways passengers.

He steadied his Swiss Hammerli .22. Despite its cumbersome length, its long and thick silencer, it had stopping power, good penetration and excellent balance.

He squeezed out of the door. His legs felt heavy, his body stiff. He had been cooped up for some forty hours. He had not slept and had not ceased his observation.

Halfway down the corridor, as he reached the plate glass of the international departures lounge, he slowed down. On the other side a corresponding length of plate glass sectioned off the transit lounge. Any of the guards looking in his direction would see him. Streaking past that stretch would attract attention and arouse suspicion. He had to walk, casually and brazenly, and hope that if the guards saw him, they would assume he was associated with WOJ.

He held his gun conspicuously, but pointed its silencer-fitted barrel down. He walked at a steady pace.

He cast surreptitious glances at the transit lounge. Most of the passengers had congregated at the windows and were watching the departure of the VC-10. Some looked angry, others disoriented. A few men, those of the airport skeleton staff not on duty, were obviously agitated. He counted the guards: two, members of Sergeant Ketema's platoon. They looked bored. One of them caught sight of him. Emmanuel, noting the man's puzzled look, hurried his steps. The guard craned his head for a better look. Emmanuel pretended not to have noticed him. He reached the hallway and ran down the stairs three at a time.

He paused at the ground floor and scanned the check-in stations. Deserted. He observed four paratroopers outside the terminal deployed around the M-41 blocking Airport Road. They presented no threat. They were watching the approaches from the city.

He ran to the arrivals lounge. Also deserted. He scurried through the exit onto the tarmac.

He took bearings. The terminal complex, three buildings adjacent to each other, minimized distance. The international terminal outside which he now stood formed the right wing, and the domestic terminal, smaller in size, the left. The middle building, as large as the international terminal, housed the airport offices. The tower stood some ten meters in front of the middle building. A small garden enclosed it. Beyond the tower stood the DC-3 hijacked at Dembidollo. Farther beyond, on the verges of the apron, four of Wolde's paratroopers lay stretched out.

Emmanuel concentrated on the paratroopers. They were watching the taxiing VC-10. Were they to look toward the terminals, their vision would be partially blocked by the DC-3. They would only see his legs and assume he was one of the airport's skeleton staff on duty.

He darted toward the control tower. As he crossed the space between the international terminal and the office building, Sergeant Ketema, with two members of his platoon, came around the domestic terminal. Emmanuel flattened himself against the nearest wall.

Sergeant Ketema and his men marched into the control tower.

✗

Captain Wolde stopped the bird-scaring jeep by the M-41. He had already switched the tape recorder on, and an earsplitting cacophony blared out.

Boaz signaled Avishai, the extra man Getachew had requested. Avishai scrambled from his dugout forward of the tank.

Getachew jumped onto the jeep.

Wolde shouted above the din. "I thought you said there'd be two of you!"

"We miscalculated."

Avishai arrived. Boaz pushed him into the jeep, then jumped in himself.

He shouted to Wolde. "Runway holding point! Fast as you can!"

Wolde accelerated.

Boaz and Getachew each grabbed a bullhorn and howled through it. Avishai picked up a tin can and started beating on it. Boaz checked his watch: 3:29 P.M. The time, as predicted by the computer, when the cornmeal would be consumed and the sparrows would start dispersing.

He looked at the runway. The sparrows were still flying across it. So much for the computer.

✗

Abbas completed the fifteen items of the taxi checklist, then surveyed the runway. He could see Wolde streaking ahead in the bird-scaring jeep. Three men from the northern unit were with him. Like exuberant children, they were beating on a tin can and yelling through the loudspeakers. They were doing a good job—certainly better than whoever had attended to the wind sock now floating in the air. The birds, petrified by the sounds, were flying off in panic.

✗

Montblanc had spotted the orange wind sock, Getachew's signal that the operation was on. Everything now depended on him.

He heaved as if stricken with nausea and grabbed the paper bag in front of his seat. He admired the zeal of the WOJ support crew; not only had they serviced and refueled the plane, but they had spruced up the interior better than most cabin maintenance teams.

He forced up some bile and groaned as if debilitated by the effort.

Habyarwanda extended a comforting hand. "I wish I could help you, my friend."

Montblanc cast a quick look around the cabin.

The WOJ platoon had taken final positions.

Mohammed and Shamseddin, guarding both the entrance to the cockpit and those hostages seated in first class, were sitting on the floor between the galley and the forward passenger door.

Tahir, Riyad, and Ziya and Niyazi, the two commandos from the support platoon who had joined the flight, occupied aisle seats on the fourth, eighth, twelfth and seventeenth rows of the economy-class section.

Ferid, the bully, and Said were at the tail, behind the curtain which screened the bomb.

All the WOJ commandos had changed guns and were now armed with Smith and Wesson .38 revolvers, with rounds of pancake bullets developed for use inside aircraft. The bullets, pliable on impact, spread over the target's body, minimizing the damage to the cabin. Boaz and Getachew would be using identical weapons.

Montblanc breathed deeply. To reach the toilet at the tail section, he had to get past the four WOJ in the economy class and then Ferid and Said. His bladder felt near to bursting.

He sensed the aircraft slow down to take the last bend in the taxiway. It was time.

He lumbered up. He tried to get past Habyarwanda and into the aisle. Simultaneously, he found himself facing Niyazi's gun.

✗

Emmanuel allowed Sergeant Ketema and his two men time to climb halfway up the control tower, then scurried over.

He took cover by the door, listening for sounds. The footsteps were still ascending. He dived in.

Sticking close to the wall, he crept lightly up the stairs.

He paused on the fourth floor and listened. Two men had stopped at the sixth floor; the third was moving up to the last, which housed the airport control center.

He continued climbing, faster now. He reached the fifth floor, edged around to the next flight until the paratroopers came into his line of vision. They were blocking the stairs to the control center. They were not expecting intruders. They had lit cigarettes.

Emmanuel streaked up the stairs. One of the paratroopers looked up in surprise. Emmanuel shot him through the head. The second paratrooper did not have time to react. Emmanuel shot him through the head, too.

As they fell across the landing, he moved past them and sprinted up to the control center.

He kicked the door open and burst through. He took a moment to gauge the activities of the two men inside.

The air traffic controller, with headphones and microphone, was standing by the window watching the VC-10's progress.

Sergeant Ketema was about to operate the radio. As he turned around, Emmanuel shot him through the chest.

He pointed the .22 at the petrified controller. "Stay calm! Carry on with takeoff procedures."

Fisseha uttered in terror. "Yes . . . Yes . . . "

Emmanuel took up a position facing both Fisseha and the door. He took out his radio and reported to Boaz, Amnon and the Memouneh.

With the control tower secure, the Memouneh could instruct the U.S. Air Force AWACS to jam the frequencies between Addis Ababa airport and the VC-10, once the hijacked plane had departed. Abu Ismail would have little cause to maintain communications with the airport, but it was best to make sure he could not. The jamming would not arouse suspicion. Interference on the region's radio frequencies had exasperated many pilots.

✗

Boaz nudged Wolde as the bird-scaring jeep approached the runway threshold markings. "We'll get off by those monoslabs."

Wolde slowed down, turning to Boaz. "I must continue along the runway! That's the procedure."

Getachew interjected. "Avishai will do that. We need you."

"What for?"

"The pilot knows you. We want him to think everything's normal."

Wolde stopped the jeep by the monoslabs. Boaz jumped out. Getachew handed Wolde the tin can and prodded him.

Wolde hesitated. Without the jeep he would be stranded in the middle of the airfield and hard-pressed to reach the control tower ahead of the Israelis. But he had no choice. He jumped out of the jeep.

Getachew followed with the loudspeakers.

Avishai took the wheel and sped down the runway.

Boaz and Getachew, keeping Wolde ahead, scampered to the monoslabs. They recommenced shrieking through the loudspeakers. Wolde, reluctantly, beat the tin can.

Boaz watched the VC-10. It was approaching the holding point. It would be at takeoff position within one minute. He glanced at the runway. There were fewer birds flying across it. Either the computer was right, or the infernal din was proving effective.

✗

Montblanc faced Niyazi, Ziya and Riyad. Some of the hostages, cowed by Tahir's gun, glared at Montblanc with hatred, afraid he might provoke the commandos to fire.

Montblanc continued pleading. "I am sick man . . . please . . . I must go toilet. . . . "

Riyad prodded him with his gun. "Later."

Montblanc doubled up and relaxed his bladder. He was standing just above Habyarwanda in a position that would direct his urine over the Rwandan. It was a pity to do such a thing to someone who had shown such fortitude, but it would be effective. He cast one last mournful look at the commandos. "Please . . ."

Riyad prodded him again. "No! Now sit down!"

Montblanc made as if to move back to his seat, then stared aghast at his underpants. "Oh, my God! Oh, my God!"

Habyarwanda, reacting in shock as the urine splashed on him, shrieked in horror.

Niyazi, Ziya and Riyad stared in disgust.

Tahir edged toward them.

Montblanc wailed.

Habyarwanda, regaining his composure, directed his anger at the WOJ commandos. "What sort of people are you? He's sick man—after all! Don't you have pity?"

Montblanc clutched at his groin as if making a desperate effort to contain his urine.

Tahir barked at Riyad, Ziya and Niyazi. "Let him go!"

Riyad reluctantly moved aside so that Montblanc could come out into the aisle.

Montblanc sidled forward, still clutching his groin, his urine trickling through his fingers.

Abruptly, Ferid and Said emerged from behind the curtain.

Ferid hissed. "What's going on?"

Tahir responded angrily. "He needs to piss!"

Ferid raised his gun. "That bastard again? He should be shot!"

Montblanc froze but let out more urine. "No . . . Please, no!"

Tahir rebuked Ferid. "He'll piss all over the plane—let him go!"

Ferid kept his gun trained on Montblanc for another moment, then signaled him on. "All right. I'll deal with you later!"

Montblanc nodded his head gratefully and staggered toward the tail section.

✗

The VC-10 progressed toward the runway. As it approached the monoslabs, Getachew nudged Wolde. Wolde waved at Abbas and Nazmi in the cockpit. Abbas raised his thumb in appreciation of their work.

Boaz howled dementedly. He had caught sight of Abu Ismail in the navigator's seat. He was near to his prey, and he felt invincible.

The wing of the plane coasted over their heads; then, slowly, the starboard tail with its twin engine pods roared past.

Boaz cast a look at the runway. The birds were clearing. He tapped Getachew and scrambled.

Getachew turned to Wolde. "Tewodoros! I won't keep my promise!"

Wolde did not have time to react. Getachew buried his knife in the base of Wolde's neck, killing him instantly.

He scrambled after Boaz.

They ran along the same path as the plane, invisible to all those inside.

✗

Montblanc opened the toilet door. As he staggered in, he glanced back. Ferid and Said had accompanied him and stood immediately behind. But they were cramped. The bomb, lying on its tracks, had blocked much of the aisle. The pulleys and jettison levers had further diminished space. The curtain partitioning the tail section from economy class was drawn. It had been partly opened when Ferid and Said had moved into the cabin; Montblanc assumed that Ferid, eager to vent his fury, had drawn it again.

He shut the toilet door behind him. Momentarily, his condition disgusted him. He wished he could wash.

He cast a quick glance at the toilet, found it fully equipped with paper handkerchiefs, toilet paper, even sanitary napkins. He grabbed a few tissues.

He tampered with the toilet lock and found the contact switch that lit the "Toilet Engaged" sign. He tore off the strip of plaster from his thumb. The strip had lost some of its elasticity after Riyad had pulled it off while searching him to verify that it covered a genuine cut.

He stuffed the tissues against the contact switch, taping the strip across to keep them secure and pressing.

He checked his watch: 3:31 P.M.

He opened the door casually. Ferid, grinning maliciously, turned to face him. Montblanc, too quick for Ferid's eyes, struck him hard on the neck. Said, whose view of Montblanc had been blocked by Ferid, caught the movement and veered around. Montblanc, barely disengaging himself from Ferid's crumpling body, punched Said in the gullet. Said, his esophagus smashed, gargled blood. Montblanc struck him on the temple and caught him before he collapsed.

Dragging the two with him, Montblanc squeezed back into the toilet. He sat Ferid on the toilet seat and laid Said on top of him. He checked their condition. Both were dead.

He removed their guns and hauled himself out of the tiny compartment. He moved cautiously to the curtain. Parting it slightly, he observed the four commandos in economy class. They were sitting in their seats. Niyazi was half listening to Habyarwanda who was thanking the commandos on Montblanc's behalf. The jammed "Toilet Engaged" sign remained lit up above the bulkheads.

He moved to the rear servicing and emergency exit door. He lifted the lock arm and made sure the lock teeth had disengaged. He waited for the plane to reach takeoff position and stop. His bladder, partially emptied, continued to protest.

�

Boaz and Getachew scurried to the VC-10's starboard side just as the plane straightened to face the runway at takeoff point. They took position immediately underneath the rear servicing and emergency exit door and waited, ready with their ropes and suction clamps.

✗

Abbas surveyed the runway. The birds had cleared. Another minute and he would be safe for takeoff.

He ran through the takeoff position checklist with Nazmi. "Booster pumps?"

"On."

"Compasses?"

"Checked."

"Controls and engines?"

"Checked."

✗

Montblanc pushed the door, praying the warning light's doctored bulb would self-destruct as it was meant to. The plug door swung out and slid along the fuselage on its parallel links.

Boaz and Getachew, waiting below, threw him their suction clamps. Montblanc secured them to the floor.

As Boaz and Getachew climbed the ropes, Montblanc gauged the engine noise, still at idling power but horrendously loud because of the open door.

He scrambled back to the curtain, ready for any of the commandos who might come to investigate the increased noise or, if the doctored bulb had failed to self-destruct, to check the door.

Boaz and Getachew scrambled in together and hauled in their ropes. Getachew pulled at the door and slammed it into position; Boaz snapped the lock arm shut.

Montblanc's face expressed his relief. Boaz and Getachew had taken mere seconds. If any of the commandos had reacted to the noise, none had left his seat. Now, with the engine sound back to normal, they were likely to assume Abbas had been testing the engines. He gave Boaz and Getachew the thumbs-up sign.

Boaz paused momentarily to inspect the bomb.

Getachew offered Montblanc his spare .38. Montblanc dropped the guns he had wrested from Ferid and Said and took the one from Getachew. He could trust that not to jam.

Boaz located the crew call light and pointed it out. Getachew and Montblanc nodded acknowledgment. The call light would serve as signal between them at drop altitude.

✗

Abbas scanned the runway. The bird-scaring jeep had driven the length of it and had turned toward the M-41 tank at the southern perimeter. The runway was clear of birds.

He called Fisseha. "Addis Control . . . Speedbird 054 ready to take off."

Fisseha's voice crackled. "Speedbird 054. Clear to take off."

Abbas checked his watch: 3:33 P.M. He turned to Abu Ismail. "We're three minutes late, Al-Mahdi. But I can make up for that in the air. We'll still be able to dovetail with KLM 320."

Abu Ismail nodded. He had been displeased by the delay but had accepted Abbas's caution. There had been occasions when the Prophet, too, had been delayed.

Abbas called Fisseha again. "Addis Control. Speedbird 054. Taking off."

Fisseha's voice sounded less strained. "Roger, 054."

Abbas put his left hand on the nosewheel steering; with his right hand he worked the throttles. Nazmi held the control column.

The Super VC-10 moved forward.

✗

Boaz, Getachew and Montblanc, guns ready, stood behind the curtain, observing the WOJ commandos through the slight opening. One of them, Tahir, had been casting anxious looks from the "Toilet Engaged" sign to the tail section. A moment earlier he had risen to check, but had sat down again as the plane started taking off. The other commandos were all seated, though they, too, had been casting looks behind them.

Boaz nudged Montblanc and pointed to Mohammed and Shamseddin, seated on the floor by the cockpit. They were the main problem. They were too far from the twenty meters effective range of the special bullets. They could only be hit from about halfway down the economy-class cabin. A move down the aisle would destroy the element of surprise. The stun grenades Boaz and Getachew had brought had to be ruled out. Though they would be effective, paralyzing both commandos and hostages for six seconds, the deafening noise would alert the flight deck. "It'll have to be you, Montblanc."

"Sure. I can take them."

Getachew looked uncertain. "How?"

Montblanc checked his gun. "They'll be expecting me to return to my seat. If I walk past it, they'll think I'm befuddled. They'll move to stop me. But I should have time to edge farther forward."

Boaz interjected. "The plane's picking up speed. Keep lurching forward as if you can't keep your balance."

Montblanc nodded. "I'll hit the floor as the nose lifts up. When you see me fall, move in—hit the rest. . . . "

Getachew still looked uncertain. "What about your gun?"

Montblanc smiled, wrapped his arms around himself and hid his gun under his armpit. "They'll think I'm about to collapse."

Boaz tapped him on the shoulder. "Right. Go—now!"

Montblanc took a deep breath and staggered into the cabin.

Tahir and Riyad turned around immediately. Tahir motioned he should hurry and sit down. Montblanc, arms crossed as if shivering, scurried forward.

He passed Niyazi in the seventeenth row; then his own row, and as far down as Ziya in the twelfth. He noted the plane was accelerating. Lift-off would be within seconds. He edged farther forward.

Riyad gesticulated with his gun from the eighth row. "Hey, get back to your seat."

Montblanc, whimpering, continued moving. He reached the tenth row. Riyad rose from his seat. Montblanc fixed his eyes on Mohammed and Shamseddin by the cockpit. They were standing up, too, watching him. Not threatened—just annoyed.

Montblanc, feeling the nose of the plane rise, lurched forward with a tormented yell.

As he fell, he straightened his gun and fired twice.

Simultaneously, behind him, he heard Boaz and Getachew fire.

He kept his eyes on Mohammed and Shamseddin. They toppled forward, chests torn open. He had timed his shots well. The plane's lift-off had compensated for the impact of the bullets, throwing the WOJ commandos forward instead of backward toward the cockpit door.

He turned around.

Boaz and Getachew were moving down the aisle. Niyazi, Ziya, Riyad and Tahir had collapsed in their seats, their heads blown apart. Blood had splashed all over the cabin and the hostages.

The plane lifted off. The hostages, who had sat through the brief action too stunned to react, started screaming.

✗

Abbas maintained a nine-degree climb. "Undercarriage up!"

Nazmi operated the controls.

The landing gear retracted, wheels thumping into their nacelles.

Abbas ordered again. "Flaps up!"

Nazmi selected the flaps. "Flaps up!"

Behind Abbas, Abu Ismail, hearing the shrieks of the hostages, interrupted his prayers. For a moment he wondered whether there had been a foolhardy attempt at resistance. Perhaps his commandos had had to shoot somebody. Then he reminded himself of the hostages' state of mind and judged the shrieks as hysteria. He smiled, full of self-rebuke for having had doubts again. "Listen to them. You would think they were going to Jehennem."

Hilmi smiled as he eased the throttles. "That's where they are going, Al-Mahdi, aren't they?"

"Oh, yes."

Abbas flicked the stabilizer trim as the aircraft reached climb-out speed of 280 knots.

✗

Boaz had moved into first class and had silenced the hostages by threatening them with his gun. But the cabin heaved with suppressed emotion.

The pulse of the economy class was even more erratic. Frenzy wrestled with fear; panic with hope. The emotions had created a stalemate—but only just.

Montblanc and Getachew concentrated on two of the women. Sitting in the same three-seat unit, they had infected each other with their screams. Montblanc slapped the more hysterical one.

Habyarwanda intervened, uncertainly. "My friend—don't hurt them. . . ."

Montblanc turned around apologetically. "Julius, if they're heard in the cockpit . . ."

"I will quiet them."

"Thank you."

Habyarwanda slipped between the two women and cradled them both. The women stopped screaming and started crying on his shoulders. Montblanc watched the Rwandan in amazement.

Habyarwanda looked up and smiled.

Montblanc grunted. "Julius, we'll need your help. We want the dead in the front . . . when you've comforted the ladies."

"Of course. . . ."

✴

Abbas, signing off, had informed Fisseha that he was at cruising level.

The controller, thinking he could at last flee from the nightmare, jumped up.

Emmanuel trained his gun on him. "Not yet."

Fisseha retreated uncomprehendingly. "But—they've gone."

"They'll be coming back."

Fisseha slumped into his seat in horror.

"Coming back? They have a bomb. . . ."

"Without the bomb—we hope."

"You hope?"

"We have men in the plane."

Fisseha shook his head in disbelief.

Emmanuel checked his watch: 3:38 P.M. He looked out of the windows and observed Amnon's men deploy toward the apron for the mop-up.

Fisseha reached for the radio.

Emmanuel veered toward him. "What are you doing?"

Fisseha mumbled dementedly. "If your men fail, WOJ will be angry. There'll be retribution. They'll blow up Addis. I must warn them." He flicked the transmitter. "Speedbird . . ."

Emmanuel shot him in the arm.

Fisseha tumbled out of his seat.

Emmanuel stared in agitation at the radio console, uncertain what to do if Abbas acknowledged the signal.

✴

At the top of the climb, Abbas selected the autopilot to altitude hold. The VC-10's nose sank gently to the horizon. The Machmeter registered acceleration. Abbas throttled back and turned to Nazmi. "Was that Addis trying to get through?"

"I think so. . . . "

"What could they want?"

✴

Emmanuel, cursing Fisseha who had fainted from his wound, listened to the radio. Abbas's voice was barely audible over the static. That meant the U.S. Air Force had started jamming the frequencies.

He glanced at the note Fisseha had last conveyed to Abbas. A request from KLM 320, overflying the region, to warn BA 054 of its flight path. It would have to serve as the reason for Fisseha's urgent call.

"Addis . . . This is Speedbird 054 . . ."

Emmanuel switched on to transmit. He prayed his voice would be unrecognizable in the static. "Speedbird 054 . . . This is Addis. Confirm clear of KLM 320."

✗

Abbas blared at his microphone. "054. Confirmed. Out."

He turned to Abu Ismail and smiled. "Warning us not to get too near KLM 320."

Abu Ismail nodded, scarcely pausing in his silent prayers.

✗

Boaz, positioned by the forward toilets, listened for signs of alarm in the cockpit. There were none.

He scrutinized the first-class cabin. The dead commandos had been strapped to the window seats of the first four rows. The fifth row had been left empty. Getachew had amassed the commandos' weapons and was transferring them to economy class.

In economy class, Montblanc and Habyarwanda—the Rwandan revitalized by the counteraction against WOJ—were supervising the hostages, including those moved from first class, as they settled down and secured their seat belts.

Boaz checked his watch: 3:45 P.M. They had been airborne twelve minutes. Soon they would be flying over the Awash River valley, south of the Danakil. They had decided to attempt to ditch the bomb in a volcanic depression eighty kilometers east of Gewani. April being the most arid month, the region's nomadic tribes were likely to have moved north or south along the river. The U.S. Air Force had confirmed that the vicinity of the depression appeared uninhabited. The jettisoning had been timed for 3:58 P.M. In thirteen minutes.

Boaz stiffened as he heard a shout from the cockpit. He steadied his gun. His stomach churned. He was not yet ready for Abu Ismail.

Laughter followed. The shout had been one of exultation. The plane had changed direction and entered the corridor for the Red Sea. Abu Ismail was now on course for Mecca.

Boaz composed himself. The assumption around which they had built their plan had been that once cocooned inside the plane, Abu Ismail would feel totally secure. The calm in the cockpit corroborated that. Furthermore, since takeoff there had been no communications from the flight deck to the commandos in the cabin—a possibility that had daunted them.

Since the piezoelectric crystal implanted in Abu Ismail's tooth had invalidated the option of a physical struggle, the only course open to them, despite the heavy burden of unpredictability it imposed, had been a psychological assault. It had taken Boaz most of the previous night's deliberations to wrest the Memouneh's agreement. And only because the Memouneh's intuition that the congruence of Boaz's and Abu Ismail's mysticism created a dimension where the Divine Will might uphold Right against Wrong had not waned.

Boaz inspected the carnage behind him.

The plan had unfolded in his mind during the long communion with Osman on the journey back from Gambela. He had reasoned that Abu Ismail would be as bereft by Allah's abandonment as he himself was by Osman's death.

The setting was macabre enough.

It had been devised to disorient Abu Ismail and to transfix him in a world outside reality. The WOJ leader, anchored in supramundane plains by the imminence of his objective and confident that his aircraft was inviolate, would resist adversity. But for an irrational explanation that the enemy had infiltrated the plane in midair, he would be unable to formulate a reason for the reversal of his position and the death of his warriors. Like most monomaniacs, he would reject brutal reality. He would scour his mysticism in search of an acceptable reason. And he would confront The Doubter.

How long this suspension of reality would last, Boaz did not know. Long enough, he hoped, to balance the odds. Then, as Abu Ismail crumbled before the relentless physicality of his warriors' corpses, they could struggle as two frail men governed by mortal fears.

The first imperative was that Abu Ismail should come out of the cockpit. Boaz would then have the wisp of a chance to engage him while Getachew secured the flight deck, took charge of the controls—and, hopefully without Abu Ismail's awareness—dropped speed and altitude to 250 knots and 2,000 feet, so that the rear passenger door could be opened without the risk of depressurization.

Montblanc and Getachew signaled readiness. Boaz waited for Getachew to relieve him by the cockpit corridor. He moved to first class and started putting on his black drapes which, but for their ominous color, looked identical to the ihram worn by pilgrims to Mecca.

Montblanc gave him an encouraging tap on the shoulder, then moved into economy class and closed the folding door behind him. Hereafter, he would remain in the tail section. If Boaz succeeded, he would jettison the bomb when Getachew dropped altitude to 2,000 feet.

Boaz examined his black drapes. He remembered Mecca. Simply by putting on the ihram he had felt clothed by Faith. On this occasion, too, the donning of a vestment transformed him. He felt he and The Doubter were one.

He checked that Getachew was in position inside the starboard forward toilet, then moved to the telephone that linked the cabin crew with the cockpit. Suddenly he felt crushed by exhaustion. He fought it, goading himself with his purest thought. To redeem Osman it was essential that Abu Ismail perish as an aberration of Islam.

He picked up the telephone and punched the captain's line.

Abbas answered. "Yes?"

Boaz spoke away from the mouthpiece. "Shamseddin here. May I speak to Al-Mahdi?"

"What's the matter with your voice?"

Boaz colored his tone with rebuke. "I am hoarse with exultation."

He heard Abbas chuckle. "Who isn't? Can I help, Shamseddin? Al-Mahdi's meditating."

"One of the hostages—calling himself a brother—wants to talk to him."

"I doubt whether Al-Mahdi would want to interrupt his meditation. What would a politician have to say to the Savior?"

Boaz tried to remain calm. "I don't know. But a word of reassurance might keep the hostages quiet."

"I'll see."

Boaz heard Abbas relay the message.

A moment later, Abu Ismail's voice thundered. "Yes?"

Boaz held his breath, then declaimed sonorously. "I am a humble Faithful, Abu Ismail. I have lived blessed by the fact that in every chapter, except the ninth—the one entitled 'Repentance'—the Koran stipulates that Allah is Compassionate and Merciful. I have believed that Al-Mahdi, when he comes, would have been suckled at Allah's bosom and consequently also be vested with compassion and mercy. I have observed you possess neither. I accuse you, therefore, before Allah! Of exploiting His Glorious Name for personal gain! Of killing in defiance of His Compassion and Mercy! Of plotting to destroy His Holy Abode! Of betraying His beloved Faithful!"

Boaz paused, casting a desperate glance at Getachew. The latter was trembling, bracing himself for the bomb's detonation. Boaz counted the seconds, unsure whether the silence indicated shock or fury.

Abu Ismail's voice hissed. "Who are you?"

Boaz heard fear in the voice. It assuaged briefly his exhaustion, his fear, his doubts. "Al-Munafiq!"

✗

Abu Ismail stared at the telephone. The voice puzzled him. In his previous encounters with The Doubter, the abomination had spoken in sulfurous tones, singed by the fire of infernal abodes. This voice was a man's. Though, of course, Al-Munafiq could assume any shape, any voice, any sin. What was unusual in this instance was that It should choose the commonplace guide of a puny mortal.

But The Doubter was dead! He, Al-Mahdi, had killed him. That explained the voice. A spirit, like the Jew's dybbuk, speaking through a medium. A last try from one who had been vanquished, but who could not accept death.

His course of action was obvious. He had to exorcise The Doubter's wraith. It would be easy. Manifestation of his divine self. In full glory. Haloed at the gates of eternal triumph. That would be enough. He spoke into the telephone. "Wait there!"

✗

Boaz replaced the telephone and noted that he was shaking.

Getachew whispered hoarsely. "Is he . . . ?"

Boaz managed a nod.

Compulsively, Getachew checked that the silencer was firmly screwed to his gun, then shut himself in the toilet.

Boaz retrieved his sense of urgency, moved out of the corridor, closed the folding door separating it from first class and scrambled to the starboard window seat of the fifth row.

✗

Abu Ismail had risen from his seat and was staring at the horizon, preparing himself for the confrontation with The Doubter's shadow.

Nazmi looked up, concerned. "Is anything the matter, Al-Mahdi?"

Abu Ismail smiled. "A specter who doubts, my son."

Nazmi signaled Abbas to take charge of the controls.

Abu Ismail turned sharply toward Nazmi. "No, stay! I have my warriors out there."

Nazmi looked anxious. "But—"

Abu Ismail's voice turned gentle. "Stay. This is something only I can do. Something I want to do. Must do."

Nazmi, Abbas and Hilmi exchanged looks.

Abu Ismail smiled, gesticulated at the controls. "You have your duties—perform them. Keep me on course for Mecca."

Nazmi, Abbas and Hilmi nodded.

Abu Ismail stopped by the supernumerary seat, then, as an afterthought, picked up one of the crew's .38s and walked out.

Nazmi remained anxious.

Abbas whispered to comfort him. "Let him be. He's roaming the heavens."

✗

At 3:50 P.M. Gentleman Jim informed the Memouneh that following lengthy deliberations on the hot line, the U.S. president had succeeded in securing the Soviet premier's collaboration against the crisis at hand.

This development, however, had not neutralized the Russian involvement in its entirety.

Whereas the Soviet premier, rushing back from his vacation in the Crimea, had had the time and the unimpaired executive authority to deactivate both Marshal Yeliseev's land forces and Air Force General Larinchev's Iraq-based bomber squadron, he had been unable to neutralize the strike capacity of the Soviet Indian Ocean fleet, based at Mukalla, South Yemen, under Admiral Tiblyashin. Despite every effort or threat from the Soviet premier, Mukalla had refused to acknowledge signals from Moscow. The Soviet premier could only conclude that Admiral Tiblyashin was being personally manipulated by KGB General Volkov, whom it had been impossible to locate.

It had to be assumed, therefore, that the six Soviet MiG-25 squadrons, each comprising twenty aircraft, would proceed to provide umbrella cover for the WOJ aircraft. In effect, as verified both by U.S. and Soviet ELINT, these squadrons had already taken off.

Though the U.S. president had wrenched from the Soviet premier the sanction to engage and destroy the Soviet squadrons, the premier, concerned with saving face both with his people and the world, had stipulated that such a course of action should be taken only when all other possible measures had failed. To this effect, he had insisted that the U.S. squadrons in the area should make every effort to shoot down the WOJ VC-10 before she entered the

MiG-25 umbrella. The fact that the WOJ plane contained OAU hostages was of no consequence to the premier. Soviet honor, once desecrated, could not be reconsecrated except by a trial in a theater of war.

✗

Abu Ismail paused, surprised that the folding door separating the cockpit and first class was closed and that neither Mohammed nor Shamseddin, assigned to guard the flight deck, was at his station.

Abu Ismail's anger flared. His warriors had never failed him. Then he realized that they must be watching over The Doubter. They were neophytes on the first rung of the mystic ladder. They would not yet know they need not have bothered. There was no escape for The Doubter.

He yanked the folding door open and entered the first-class section.

He stared uncomprehendingly at the vision facing him.

✗

The moment Abu Ismail crossed into first class, Getachew darted out of the toilet and into the cockpit.

He eased the door shut and in the same movement shot both Hilmi and Nazmi through the head.

As Abbas twisted around, more in surprise than alarm, Getachew glanced at the switch in front of the control column and confirmed that the autopilot was on. Then he shot Abbas through the neck.

He pulled Abbas out of the captain's seat, maneuvered him around the throttles and dropped him into the navigator's seat. He moved across to Nazmi, hauled him out of his seat, dragged him around to the back and pushed him on top of Hilmi. He paused for a moment to check that none of the corpses interfered with the controls. He ignored the blood that had spattered everywhere.

He sat in the captain's seat and reset the pressure altimeter to the regional setting to give him an indication of his height in the drop area. He paused another moment and composed himself. Then he switched off the autopilot, took control of the aircraft and commenced the descent.

✗

What he saw was a false vision. Abu Ismail realized that. An infernal mirage conjured by The Doubter.

But an effective one. Kaleidoscopic. His warriors, torn and bleeding, some with heads partially blown off, contorted in the colors of death, while a black spirit in black drapes, seated behind them all, remained constant. If *sir'at*, the hairline bridge that every soul had to cross for final judgment, had a gate, it must look like this. With the black spirit in black drapes as toll collector.

He touched the blue-eye talisman pinned to the underside of his clothes. Al-Mahdi knew how to confront mirages. The Blue Eye would ward off the Evil Eye, illumine the way, take him into the real cabin where his warriors, sturdy in flesh, guarded The Doubter.

✗

Boaz sat transfixed. He had checked his watch when the WOJ leader had opened the folding door. 3:51 P.M. Seven minutes to jettison. Since then, an eon had passed. But he knew: for him and for Abu Ismail the dimension of time had stopped. How long it would stay suspended he did not know. Nor what would follow. But time, for others, was progressing normally. None of the WOJ crew had stormed out of the cockpit. That meant Getachew had gained control of the aircraft.

He studied Abu Ismail as Abu Ismail gaped at him.

This was the moment for which he had toiled and wasted. This was the moment, he had believed, that would redeem the death of his sister, Perla, of his brother, Osman, the deaths of all the innocents. At this moment, he had presumed, the empty skies would have engorged with a compassionate Divinity and would invest his life and death with sanctity.

But the moment was barren. The confrontation, irrespective of the occult trimmings, was banal. Like the chance meeting of two rabid dogs on a dung heap. No intimations of predestiny. Nothing like the inevitable contest between Achilles and Hector on Ilium's plains.

Only comprehensive fear. And fatigue, sucking at him. But also Osman's spirit watching over him.

Abu Ismail was a disappointment. An aging man who had tempered sickness with the opium of grandiose delusions. Not the towering Son of Darkness who spewed destruction and before whom the Jew and the world trembled; certainly not the Savior of the True Faith his followers worshiped. A decomposing mutation of bones, flesh and blood. A bubonic mind that decorated plague with logic and rendered it respectable for all who could not accept chance mortality.

Only in one respect did Abu Ismail justify his reputation. He was the perfect harbinger of the Last of Days. If such a frail germ could so denaturalize human aspirations, who could doubt mankind's certain doom? Abu Ismail was as Hitler and Stalin must have been. And though he would be destroyed, there would be others. And the others would succeed. They would kill off the Perlas, the Osmans. They would push the world to its last day; feed sanctity to chaos.

Mercifully, he would not see that day.

But even that certainty did not banish the fear.

✗

Abu Ismail walked resolutely toward the folding door separating first class from economy. As he reached it, the spirit in black drapes beckoned him.

"Amin . . ."

Abu Ismail paused, surprised that the dark spirit should know his real name, discarded since he had taken up arms against the Jew. He himself had almost forgotten it.

He responded valiantly, like a fedayeen summoned to battle. "Yes?"

The black-draped spirit pointed at the seat next to him. "Sit down."

Abu Ismail hissed. "Al-Munafiq?"

The black spirit smiled. "Yes."

Abu Ismail felt disconcerted that The Doubter had evaded his warriors. Then he realized: The Doubter was his personal persecutor. His warriors, as foot soldiers of Al-Mahdi, were immune to doubts.

He raised his gun. A bullet would be sufficient to destroy the demon's earthly receptacle. "I have killed you, Al-Munafiq. Drowned you in the Sudd. Now I shall destroy your malign phantom."

The Doubter had extended a spectral clot. The clot had petrified as a granite hand.

The granite hand wrenched the gun. "You know bullets can't kill me. . . ."

Abu Ismail trembled, perturbed that The Doubter's shade should manifest such strength. He retreated and tore open his ihram. He clutched the blue-eye talisman, the bulb of garlic and the tiny horseshoe attached to it. The garlic would protect him; the horseshoe would repel Evil. "These will!"

Boaz forced himself to remain seated and glanced at his watch: 3:52. Six minutes. He peered out of the window. They were flying over the Awash River valley, gently banking toward the east. They were nose down. The spoilers on the wings were raised to reduce speed. Getachew was dropping altitude. It was vital Abu Ismail did not realize they had abandoned their allocated airway, and were descending. The charade had to continue. "Amin, why don't you surrender?"

Abu Ismail continued shaking his talismans.

"Look around you, Amin. . . . Your warriors . . . Dead. And not in the Paradise you promised them, but in the jaws of maggots and worms."

Abu Ismail surveyed the cabin defiantly. The grotesque images of his brave warriors, strewn mutilated by the windows, gouged his eyes. Too real. "Lifelike, Al-Munafiq. But I am not deceived. Nor frightened. I am immune to illusions."

"Your claim—the Savior of Allah and of the True Faith—that is an illusion."

"Is that why Allah lets me rest my face on His bosom?"

"It is not Allah who lets you do that. It is Shaytan. Allah hates you, Amin. *You* are The Deceiver! The half-priest who is a threat to the Faith!"

Abu Ismail let his eyes erupt so that his Savior's wrath should engulf The Doubter's phantom together with the pain in his limbs that had suddenly crept upon him. "Allah is here! With me! Allah will destroy you!"

Boaz gave him a pitiless look, dropped his eyes to his watch: 3:53. Five minutes. He wondered if the WOJ leader had overstepped reality. If he could stretch the condition for another five minutes. . . . Then, with the bomb jettisoned, the sick old man could be put down.

Boaz's hopes had been premature. One of the corpses had shifted with the plane's banking and had touched Abu Ismail.

Boaz rose from his seat.

Abu Ismail forced himself to touch another corpse, then looked up in horror. "My sons . . . My warriors . . ."

Boaz edged toward the aisle.

Abu Ismail wailed. "Dead? All of them?"

Boaz reached the aisle. "They followed a false savior!"

Abu Ismail spread his arms, directing himself to the heavens, to unsheath the sword of retribution that Allah had honed for him.

He found the celestial paths barricaded.

Boaz took a step forward.

Abu Ismail faced him and screamed. "Stay!"

Boaz froze in his tracks.

Abu Ismail wagged a finger at him. "You are not Al-Munafiq!"

ADDIS ABABA, ETHIOPIA

At 3:54 P.M. Amnon and MacDonald relieved Emmanuel at the control tower.

MacDonald proceeded to assign the men to defensive positions, summoning Tripps, Underwood and Bayyu to provide support.

Amnon signaled the Memouneh that the mop-up had been accomplished without further bloodshed subsequent to the surrender of Wolde's forces, that the British Airways passengers, crew and ground staff and the airport's skeleton staff had been freed unharmed, that his forces would keep the airport secure until the return or the destruction of the VC-10, and that the emperor should assemble a unit of Imperial Bodyguards to take charge of the airport thereafter.

THE AWASH RIVER VALLEY, ETHIOPIA

Abu Ismail waved his hands. They ached venomously. This was the mystic's worst ordeal. A wilderness where the elements clashed against each other. This was the chaos that had confronted Allah before Creation. Only this time, Allah was not present and everywhere.

He screamed at Boaz. "Who are you?"

Boaz hesitated a moment, then threw off his black drapes and rubbed at the black makeup on his face. "Boaz Ben Ya'ir. Jew. Colonel in the Israeli defense forces. And—ironically—the defender of Islam."

Fear formed a dome above Abu Ismail. If this was reality, it was even more illusory than The Doubter's witchcraft. He waved painful hands wildly. "How could a Jew—infiltrate—?"

"He did. With Allah's help."

Abu Ismail held his head. The chaos was beckoning him as irresistibly as the void beckoned a man on the edge of a precipice. He screamed. "You are Al-Munafiq! You must be!"

Boaz edged forward. "It doesn't matter what I am. I am here to stop you, Amin!"

Abu Ismail edged backward. "Stop me? When Allah has ordained I should destroy Mecca?"

Boaz continued forward. "Why should He? Mecca is His abode."

"Idols reside in Mecca!"

"Have you been to Mecca?"

"To contaminate my pure soul?"

"I have."

"You see . . . If Al-Munafiq—or Jew—can enter Mecca . . . Allah's abode is Al-Quds!"

Boaz gauged the distance between Abu Ismail and himself. A

few steps. "One of His abodes, Amin. Al-Quds is where the Single God embraces all His children—Jew, Christian and Muslim."

Abu Ismail shrieked. "The Jew will be wiped out. Like pestilence. When I incite the Faithful—tell them the Jew destroyed their precious Mecca—there will be jihad. And Allah's shrine will be cleansed."

Boaz shrugged in disgust and edged closer.

Abu Ismail jumped back and bellowed. "Stay! Stay! Or else!"

Boaz stopped—just out of reach. His body shook. Another step and he could crush Abu Ismail.

Abu Ismail retreated farther and wailed, partly in fear, partly in fury. "You cannot touch me!"

"I've killed better men than you. Look—your warriors . . ."

"I have more warriors in the cockpit!"

"I intend to kill them, too!"

Abu Ismail stood his ground. He gesticulated wildly, trying to anchor himself to a sensible reality. He realized one thing: unless warned, Nazmi, Abbas and Hilmi would be defenseless against the man-specter. Therefore, it was necessary to protect them. "Do you think I, Al-Mahdi, would be anything but invincible? I have a fuse —in my tooth. You cannot get past me. If you try, I will detonate my bomb!"

Boaz stood still. Exhaustion assailed him. His spirit protested. Perla, my sister, Osman, my brother, is it so important that you be redeemed?

Abu Ismail seized on Boaz's hesitation to mold chaos into order. Confidence would spin the spirit into a thread and snake it through the labyrinth. He reminded himself. As long as Nazmi, Abbas and Hilmi remained inviolate, Operation Dragons was attainable. All he, Al-Mahdi, had to do was distract the man-specter and edge back to the flight deck. When the demon dropped his guard, he could summon Nazmi. The boy, an incomparable warrior, would slay him. "What have you to say to that, Jew—or whatever you are?"

Boaz sat on an armrest as if deep in thought. He glanced at his watch: 3:55. Three minutes. Abu Ismail wanted to distract him. That was fine. He breathed deeply so that Osman's spirit, hovering around him, should enter his body and seal the cracks. "How can I lose, Amin? Allah hates you. He has forsaken you."

Abu Ismail thundered. "He cannot forsake me! I have the True Faith!"

"Your faith feeds on vengeance and murder! It glorifies death! How can it be true?"

"My Faith defies the Infidel's civilization. Mocks secular states, false concepts of liberalism, the utopia of a harmonious world forever trading comfort and money! My Islam is an ideology! Faith as well as discipline! Love and fear combined! For without them, there can be no heaven or hell!"

"Your Islam is a cult of power, Amin! You cannot bear that the Faithful want to humanize the Faith, worship a Compassionate and Merciful Allah, as it is ordained! You want them to worship *you!* You know you can only make them do so by contaminating the world. That is why you embrace the Russian."

Abu Ismail spluttered. "I use the Russian as I would a hoe. To weed out the Jew and the Infidel!"

"While the Russian uses you as his whore!"

Abu Ismail glared. It was time to destroy the evil presence—man or specter. He spat at Boaz and whirled the hand with which he would wield the True Faith. To his surprise, the man-specter's clotted hand once again turned into granite and enveloped his. Abu Ismail bared his teeth as the man-specter rose and moved to strike him. "Stop! Or we all die!"

Boaz held his blow but kept his hold on Abu Ismail's hand. He willed himself to remain standing; then, losing control, spat back at Abu Ismail. "Do you think I would care?"

Abu Ismail shook his head, confused. Pain seared through him. "What?"

Boaz sneered. "If I die, it would be deliverance. But if you die, that would be proof you're not Al-Mahdi!"

Abu Ismail continued shaking his head. What the man-specter said was meaningless. Jew or The Doubter, it was always afraid of death. Soon it would cease talking. It would try to bargain for its life.

"I'd be satisfied with that, Amin."

Abu Ismail pulled himself to his full stature, bared his teeth defiantly. "Try it, Jew!"

Boaz hesitated. One blow would break Abu Ismail's jaw. But if it did not? He dropped his eyes to his watch: 3:56. Two minutes.

Montblanc kept his eyes on the crew call light. Getachew would flash it at 2,500 feet to signal readiness. In a minute or so. Judging by the pressure in his ears, Getachew was descending fast.

He checked the bomb yet again. Clamped on wheels, it stood on two parallel tracks laid on boards in a downward incline toward the rear passenger door. A pulley, fixed by a ring to the ceiling, weighted at one end with a lead plate and attached at the other to the bomb's parachute, served both as the release mechanism and the parachute static line. All that was required was to open the rear passenger door and disconnect the weighted end of the rope from its moorings. The incline of the tracks would roll the bomb slowly out of the door. The rope would open the parachute when the bomb was well clear of the aircraft, then disengage.

They would take further care. As soon as the rear passenger door warning light indicated that Montblanc had opened the door, Getachew would bank the plane a few degrees to port. That would ensure clearance from the lower fuselage and prevent possible triggering of the booby-traps.

He checked his watch: 3:56. He took up position by the rear passenger door, pinning his eyes on the crew call light.

✗

Abu Ismail snarled. "You are afraid to try, Jew?"

Boaz held his breath and clung to Abu Ismail's hand. Abu Ismail had retreated to the cockpit corridor. Boaz was aware that Abu Ismail intended to rush into the cockpit and summon his men. He had to prevent that. The revelation that his men were dead, that the enemy, in force, had gained control of the aircraft, would compel him to detonate the bomb. He tightened his grip on Abu Ismail's hand. "You don't believe that, Amin!"

Abu Ismail shrieked. "Allah! Allah! Allah! Allah! Allah! Allah! Allah!" He tried to wrench his hand free. Boaz held on. With a strength that surprised Boaz, Abu Ismail pulled him to the cockpit door. "Nazmi! Nazmi!" He kicked the door open.

This time he could not reject reality. He stared at the corpses of Nazmi, Abbas and Hilmi. He saw Truth. The blood-smeared black man in Ethiopian Army uniform flying the plane. The ground approaching. The sky and the KLM plane out of his grasp. The weight of the man grappling with him. He saw the black pilot turn sharply and shout.

"Boaz!"

He spun around and thundered. "Jew—I am not afraid! We shall perish together!"

Boaz clawed frantically at Abu Ismail's face and bore down on his jaw. Abu Ismail's mouth opened slightly. Boaz tore at the lips, wedging his hand through the clenching teeth. "Getachew! Dive! Dive!"

Getachew pushed the control column.

Boaz and Abu Ismail toppled forward. Boaz clung to Abu Ismail's mouth. Abu Ismail bit hard on Boaz's fingers. They fell. The fall winded Abu Ismail. Boaz pulled violently at Abu Ismail's jaw. The dive of the plane buffeted them against the cockpit door, then against the corpses of Nazmi, Abbas and Hilmi that were now pitching forward. Blood coated them.

⚜

Montblanc held on to the bulkhead, and kept his eyes pinned on the crew call light. It had not flashed. They were in a dive. The hostages were screaming. Something had gone wrong.

⚜

Abu Ismail thrashed and flailed. Boaz pulled Abu Ismail's jaw once again, felt it tear from its socket. At last wrestling with Evil, vested with Osman's strength and goodness, he screeched in Abu Ismail's ear. "You deserve it. . . . The contaminated world . . . you're seeking to create! Gladly give it to you . . . Allah would . . . except . . . Allah is Compassionate and Merciful!"

Getachew held his dive. Finally, the needle of the radio altimeter flicked and started moving counterclockwise. He shouted. "Twenty-five hundred feet . . . Almost there!"

He punched the crew call light on the intercom-selector-box to alert Montblanc.

Abu Ismail, Getachew's call hammering in his head, gurgled blood.

Boaz, his fingers tearing at Abu Ismail's gullet, thundered. "You have forgotten . . . Amin . . . that . . . each time . . . an innocent dies . . . Allah dies with him! He . . . Allah . . . resides . . . in the pure souls of . . . my brother Osman . . . my sister Perla! You've forgotten . . . if you tarnish . . . the Glorious Name . . . there will be nothing . . . but . . . nothingness!"

Boaz became aware of his own tears. The struggle had pierced his armor. Indicting Abu Ismail, he had liberated his own love of God, buried during the years of vacuum, not irretrievably in darkness, as he had thought, but no farther than skin deep. A love of God as ardent as Osman's. A revelation.

⚜

Montblanc's eyes stood riveted on the crew call light. It had flashed once to signal that Getachew had reached 2,500 feet. It had to flash again to indicate the completion of descent to 2,000 feet, when the rear passenger door could be opened with no risk of depressurization.

His hands sweated on the handle of the door. The hostages were still screaming. He checked his watch: 3:57:05. Fifty-five seconds. He estimated the altitude as about 2,200 feet. Surely, a few seconds, a couple of hundred feet, were irrelevant.

The plane began to pull out of its dive.

He heaved on the handle and pushed against the door. It would not budge. He repositioned himself, trying to secure a better leverage in the tiny space on the side of the bomb. Heaved again. Put all his strength into his shoulders. Held his breath. Strained. Channeled all his energy into his muscles. Against the plug in the door structure that would yield, lift, disengage teeth, push the door and the air behind it. He felt the plug move. The air outside whistled shrilly. His lungs ached. He took another breath, deep and hurried. Heaved again. The door moved a fraction. The air outside pushed it back. He arched his shoulders. The veins in his throat and forehead thudded. Suddenly, his shoulders met with no further resistance. He clung to the edge of the opening as the rear passenger door eased out on its parallel link mechanism and slid along the fuselage. The fury of the air shocked him; the noise of the engines deafened him.

He scrambled to the weighted end of the pulley. Held on to the rope. Checked his watch: 3:57:55.

He muttered anxiously. "Come on, Getachew . . . Bank! Bank!"

✗

Getachew realized Boaz and Abu Ismail had ceased struggling. He checked the radio altimeter: 2,050 feet. The warning light of the rear passenger door had already lit up.

He punched the intercom-selector-box to signal drop, then banked to port. He kept his eyes on the airspeed indicator: 250 knots. His hand steadied on the throttles. Sweat ran down his back.

Behind him, Boaz stared at Abu Ismail in horror. "I've killed him!"

Getachew froze. "His heart monitor, Boaz! We've only got forty seconds!"

Boaz jumped up, streaked through the first-class cabin, pulled the folding door open and pushed past the outstretched hands of the hysterical hostages.

✗

Montblanc waited until the plane was settled in its turn, then disconnected the weighted end of the pulley from its moorings.

The bomb rolled toward the opening. Slowly. In its own time. It would contaminate the blast area for years to come.

A moment before it plunged into the void, the curtains parted and Boaz rushed in. "Let it go, Montblanc—let it go!"

✗

Getachew imagined the plane had lurched. Seconds later, he saw the parachute open.

He pushed the throttles. The plane gathered speed.

The gesture had been futile. They would not escape the blast. The bomb, parachute-retarded, would fall at about twenty-five feet per second. Its time of fall would have permitted the plane to attain a separation distance of more than eight miles. That would have been ample.

Except that now, with Abu Ismail dead, they did not have the margin. The bomb would detonate in midair. The fireball, mushrooming in milliseconds, would engulf them.

Despairingly, Getachew glanced back at the flight engineer's console. The rear passenger door's warning light was still on. He could not even take the plane up.

✗

Boaz stood still, regulating his breath. He stared at the void beckoning him. His inner voice prompted him. Now. Go. It is all over. You have finished.

He shook his head. The voice persisted. Go. A man has the right to end his life. Go.

He shook his head again. Not because the bomb's detonation was imminent, but because he had to live. As Osman had asked him.

Montblanc pushed past him to shut the door. "Don't look at the blast, pal! It could blind you!"

Boaz nodded, squatting on his haunches.

Montblanc heaved the door in, shut it and locked it. Then he squatted next to Boaz. And started laughing.

Boaz checked his watch: 4:00. He turned to Montblanc, puzzled.

"No explosion!"

EPILOGUE

Waters Spilt on the Ground and Lost.

2 Samuel, 14:14

April 25, 1974

ADDIS ABABA, ETHIOPIA

Quinn watched the troops outside the embassy change guard with vociferous barking of orders. But the discipline was mere glitter—the Dergue's anodyne to the emperor and the U.S.A. Another palliative had been the remains of the CIA-SO agents shot down in Gambela, recovered and returned in coffins draped with the Stars and Stripes.

He envied the Memouneh and his men who had returned to Israel, early that morning, in a U.S. Air Force transporter. They had escaped the realities of Ethiopia, leaving no trace of their sojourn—not even a cigarette butt in the abandoned safe house. They had taken fingerprints and dental records of the WOJ dead for their files; and Montblanc, MacDonald and the rest of the CIA-SO agents for the debriefing with Gentleman Jim. And they had taken their dead, Osman and Yitzhaq.

Quinn realized the envy was misplaced. The Israelis were returning to a different reality. For them the battle with Abu Ismail had been just another last-ditch stand. There would be others. He remembered the Memouneh's anxiety to return while the Jewish State still celebrated its twenty-sixth anniversary—as though afraid there might not be another one.

"Charlie . . ."

He turned around. "Getachew . . . I was hoping you'd come by. The experts have just returned from the Danakil."

"A dud bomb?"

"More than that. There had been no radioactive leak. Not a

crack in the plutonium shield—despite the detonations of the primary charges. A perfectly sabotaged bomb."

"Incredible."

"Not if you are Talat Fawzi."

"The WOJ complement in Abu Ismail's executive jet?"

"They were shot down over Lake Afrera. They must have provided quite a feast for the hyenas. No corpses."

"Any repercussions?"

"None. The pilot did not report he'd come under U.S. attack. The Ethiopian Air Authority's verdict should hold: a tragic air crash."

"That's it, then?"

"And the dead."

Getachew nodded.

Quinn handed him a cigarette. "What's it like out there, Getachew?"

"The British Airways passengers have been repatriated. The OAU hostages have been pacified. The WOJ dead—and Abu Ismail—have been buried in a common grave. The troops are out with pledges of support for the emperor. But . . . the crisis continues, Charlie."

"How does it look?"

"The Dergue is anxious to maintain the momentum of the creeping coup. So conflict is still the order of the day. Conversely, it's trying to dissociate itself from Wolde's treachery. There's much regrouping, jostling for positions, even the odd purge. Everybody wants to prove he's not somebody's puppet—like Wolde was."

"It could turn into a bloody mess, Getachew. . . . "

"And it could be the end of the monarchy. Yes, I know."

"What will you do?"

"What can I do? I won't run. But there's a ray of light. Some good men are coming to the fore. Abu Ismail's blackmail has shocked them into action. Now they see Ethiopia needs strong hands. To support the throne. For national unity. Men like General Aman Andom. Truly good men. Good patriots . . . I'm going to join them."

Quinn looked at him with surprise. "You—the emperor's most loyal subject?"

"I've been disloyal to the emperor before—by joining you. I'll be disloyal again, for Ethiopia's sake. It's the only thing I can do, Charlie. . . . This country needs both an emperor and a body of men who'll act as reformers and watchdogs. We might succeed."

"I hope you do."

Getachew's resolve succumbed to weariness. "When do you leave, Charlie?"

"Soon."

"How is Fawzi?"

Quinn checked his watch. "I'd better look in on him. . . . "

They shook hands. Without a word—as if they had no more to say to each other.

Getachew watched Quinn leave the room. Another man burned out by the fall of his immediate brother. He without Jameson; Boaz without Osman.

✗

Quinn tiptoed into Fawzi's room. He had drawn the blinds to ward off the midday sun. The dark offended him. He felt he had buried his friend prematurely. He heard the rustle of sheets and approached the bed.

Fawzi looked up, proffered a weak smile. "You're still here, Charlie. . . ."

Quinn examined the emaciated face for signs of strength. He saw none. "You won't get rid of me easily, Talat. . . . "

Fawzi closed his eyes, smiling.

Quinn moved to a chair and reached for the whiskey bottle on the table.

Yonatan had stated that Fawzi's heart might last another week. Quinn drank hurriedly, then poured himself another.

"*I sabotaged the bomb*"—that was all Fawzi had said, last night, at the end of his megatrip. Nothing about the conditions and pressures that defied imagination. Nothing about his self-sacrifice. Nothing even about the mechanism of the sabotage. Inconceivable bravery. From a man who had wanted simply to marvel at the design of the universe.

"Charlie . . ."

Quinn gulped down his drink. "Yes, Talat . . . "

Fawzi spoke faintly, his breath chasing his words. "I ought to tell you. You're not responsible for my condition. I planned it— long before you thought of sending the Dallapiccola code. . . . I planned it—when I found out what they wanted me to do. . . . First—I contaminated the base. . . . Then . . . I sabotaged the bomb casing. . . . Then . . . when that didn't work . . . I sabotaged the bomb. . . . "

Quinn, fighting off tears, lowered his eyes.

"Wouldn't you have, Charlie?"

"I—I guess so, Talat. . . . "

"Of course, it's easy to sabotage a bomb. A slight miscalculation of the weight of the warhead . . . and you arrest the chain reaction. But I—I tried to do more, Charlie. . . . I tried to nullify the nuclear option to the terrorist. You see, I could have escaped perhaps. I chose not to. I behaved as one of them . . . as if indoctrinated. . . . Because they could have found another physicist. . . . A man without scruples . . . It had to be me, Charlie. . . . I wanted them to think . . . if I failed, nobody else could succeed. . . . End of the nuclear option . . . That was the idea. . . ."

"That's what you've achieved, Talat. . . ."

Fawzi smiled. "My best work, Charlie . . . A circular maze. Chain reaction cut short at every corner. Something to surprise both Allah and *Shaytan*. . . ."

"Allah and *Shaytan*, Talat?"

Fawzi smiled again. "I wanted to show Allah that one man cared for his brothers. There's hope in that. And reason for Him to forgive us all. As for *Shaytan*—as long as one man defies him . . ."

Quinn nodded.

Fawzi's voice trembled. "Whether I've succeeded . . . whether another Abu Ismail . . . tomorrow . . ." He held Quinn's hand. "Charlie . . . take me home. . . ."

"Soon, Talat . . ."

"Soon will be too late. . . . I have a little strength . . . enough to get me home. . . . Today, Charlie . . . Please . . . I want nothing else. You and I—going home. . . ."

April 27, 1974

JERUSALEM, ISRAEL

The dawn prayers at Al-Aqsa Mosque served as Osman's last rites. In addition to Osman's wife, Samia, his daughters, Fatma and Hatijeh, and ten officers of King Hussein's Special Security Squad, invited to act as pallbearers, the mourners included Boaz, Sanbat, the Memouneh, Montblanc, the CIA-SO agents and Gentleman Jim. Gad Kidan, also invited, had declined on the pretext of observing the Sabbath.

After the prayers, the pallbearers carried Osman's bier through the gardens of Temple Mount toward Ghazali Square. They paused halfway on a level with the Golden Gate—also known as the Eternal Gate—sealed to mortals, from where, the Koran prescribed, souls should leave the body and ascend to Paradise.

Beyond Ghazali Square, they carried Osman's remains past an Israeli guard of honor, handpicked from every service, out through the Lion's Gate.

There, they placed the coffin in a catafalque.

The pallbearers and the Israeli guard of honor proceeded to their vehicles. The Israeli guard would escort the catafalque as far as the Abdallah Bridge. Thereafter, the Royal Jordanian Arab Legion would take Osman's remains to the National Cemetery, Amman. He would be buried with full military honors.

Boaz approached Samia. "May I ride with you?"

Samia forced herself to look at him. Since arriving in Jerusalem, she had refused to see him. She had talked only to Sanbat, briefly, for an account of her husband's death. "I would prefer to be alone, Boaz."

Boaz persisted. "We have not talked."

"What is there to say?"

"Much."

Samia glared bitterly at his ceremonial uniform. "Answer me this! Did you save Allah? You and Osman?"

Boaz glanced toward the Temple Mount as if the answer might lie there. "Allah does not need us to save Him, Samia. But we saved people. Many."

"Who will save me?"

Boaz met her eyes. "I don't know."

"And you? Who will save you?"

"I don't know that either."

"Will you live his life?"

"His life?"

"Isn't that what Osman gave you?"

"Yes."

"I'm to blame, too. I encouraged him to care for you."

"I know."

"What will you make of the life he gave you?"

"Something good, I hope."

"You'll fail." She turned and walked toward her car.

He kept pace with her. "Samia, I have a letter. . . ."

She stopped, faced him again. "For me?"

Boaz handed her Osman's letter. "To me. I know it by heart."

Samia took the letter. "Thank you."

"One other thing. I share your pain. I have lived with death all my life. It has taken my mother and father. Another father who adopted me. My sister. Countless friends. And now my brother. I want you to know. You are my only family—another sister. If you are ever in need. . . . Of anything. . . . Remember that."

Samia did not try to control her tears. "All I need is my Osman, Boaz. I accept I am your sister. But I shall want nothing. I died with him."

POSTSCRIPT

Talat Fawzi died on April 30, 1974, at his home in Beirut, Lebanon.

The Memouneh retired on July 31, 1974.

Charles Quinn took up a teaching post in Salt Lake City, Utah, in September 1974.

Getachew Iyessous was killed in Addis Ababa, Ethiopia, during the Dergue's "Night of the Long Knives," on November 23–24, 1974, while trying to defend General Aman Andom. With General Andom also killed, Major Mengistu Haile-Mariam emerged as the Dergue's strong man.

Hatijeh Nusseibi married Uwe Bjornson, a Swedish travel agent, on October 5, 1976, in Stockholm, Sweden.

Fatma Nusseibi married Captain Ibrahim Azzam of the Royal Jordanian Air Force on March 10, 1977, in Amman, Jordan.

Don Quixote Villon Beaumarchais de Vigny Combeau, known as Montblanc, was assigned to the CIA-SO training staff on June 27, 1977, the day the T.F.A.I. gained independence as the Republic of Djibouti.

Gad Kidan was promoted to a highly confidential post on July 3, 1977, by Israel's new government under Prime Minister Menachem Begin.

Sanbat Abraham married Bruno Perez, a Brazilian-born immigrant, on July 2, 1978, and settled in Moshav Ilaniya, Israel.

A self-acclaimed **Al-Mahdi,** one Mohammed Abdullah al-'Utaibah, and his supporters invaded the Great Mosque in Mecca on November 20, 1979, the eve of the Islamic year 1400, and held out against Saudi Arabian forces for two weeks. Some seven hundred people were reported dead at the end of the hostilities. The majority of the Islamic world accused Israel and the U.S.A. of perpetrating Mecca's desecration.

Samia Nusseibi died of cancer in Amman, Jordan, on February 18, 1980.

Boaz Ben-Ya'ir was presumed drowned off Caesarea, Israel, on February 22, 1980.

BIBLIOGRAPHICAL NOTES

page

1   Al-Hallaj, quoted by Phillip K. Hitti in *Islam: A Way of Life* (Minneapolis: University of Minnesota Press, 1970).

5   *The Jerusalem Bible* (Jerusalem: Koren Publishers, 1977), Gen. 49:1.

5   *The Koran*, translated by N. J. Dawood. 2d rev. ed. (London: Penguin Books Ltd., 1966), Sura 4:160.

5   *The Holy Bible: King James Version* (New York: American Bible Society), 2 Tim. 3:1.

6   Ethiopian proverb, quoted in *The International Thesaurus of Quotations*, compiled by Rhoda Thomas Tripp (New York: Harper & Row, 1970).

29   T. S. Eliot, "A Song for Simeon," in *Collected Poems, 1909–1962* (New York: Harcourt Brace Jovanovich, Inc., 1963).

31   *The Jerusalem Bible*, op. cit., 2 Sam. 11:15.

33   *The Holy Bible: King James version*, op. cit., Jer. 9:11.

57   Erwan Bergot, *The French Foreign Legion*, translated by Richard Barry (London: Tattoo Book, Wyndham Publications, 1976).

57   Ibid.

67   *The Holy Bible: King James Version*, op. cit., Eccles. 7:1.

71   e.e. cummings, *HIM: Three Plays and a Ballet*, edited by George Firmage (London: Peter Owen Ltd., 1968).

75   Samuel Ha-Nagid, "Wounded Lions," from *The Jewish Poets of Spain, 900–1250*, translated and with notes by David Goldstein (London: Penguin Books Ltd., 1971).

96   Antara, quoted by Morris S. Seale in *The Desert Bible: Nomadic Tribal Culture and Old Testament Interpretations* (London: Weidenfeld & Nicholson, 1974).

97   Cf. *The Holy Bible: King James Version*, op. cit., Ps. 137:5.

98   Edith Hamilton, *Mythology* (Boston: Little, Brown and Company, 1948).

110 *The Holy Bible: King James Version*, op. cit., Rev. 5:12.

110 *The Holy Bible: King James Version*, op. cit., Ps. 23:1.

125 Cf. *The Holy Bible: King James Version*, op. cit., Gen. 22:13.

129 *The Koran*, op. cit., Sura 2:187.

130 *The Koran*, op. cit., Sura 1:1.

150 *The Koran*, op. cit., Sura 2:187.

150 *The Koran*, op. cit., Sura 21:188.

165 Ibn Sa'd, quoted by Maxime Rodinson in *Mohammad*, translated by Anne Carter (London: Penguin Books Ltd., 1971).

184 Arab proverb, author's paraphrase.

196 *The Koran*, op. cit., Sura 47:16.

213 *The Jerusalem Bible*, op. cit., 1 Sam. 17:37.

537

217 Chia Tao, quoted by Alan Watts in *Cloud Hidden, Whereabouts Unknown* (London: Jonathan Cape Ltd., 1974).

244 *The Koran*, op. cit., Sura 63:12.

244 *The Koran*, op. cit., Sura 22:40.

247 Matthew Arnold, "Sohrab and Rustum" from *The Oxford Dictionary of Quotations* (Oxford, England: The Oxford University Press, 1979).

276 cf. *The Jerusalem Bible*, op. cit., Ezek. 37:3.

276 *The Koran*, op. cit., Sura 3:26.

277 *The Koran*, op. cit., Sura 16:34.

312 *The Jerusalem Bible*, op. cit., Ezek. 37:3.

313 Descriptions by Hiroshima survivors.

348 *The Iliad*, in *The Complete Works of Homer*, translated by Andrew Lang, Walter Leaf and Ernest Myers (New York: Modern Library, 1959).

349 Ibid.

352 Nikos Kazantzakis, *Report to Greco*, translated by P. A. Bien (New York: Touchstone Books, 1975).

424 Cf. Jean Rostand, "Pensées d'un biologiste," quoted in *The International Thesaurus of Quotations*, op cit.

529 *The Jerusalem Bible*, op. cit., 2 Sam. 14:14.

PERMISSIONS

The publisher wishes to acknowledge permission to use the following excerpted materials in this book:

Antara quoted by Morris S. Seale in *The Desert Bible: Nomadic Tribal Culture and Old Testament Interpretations.* Published by Weidenfeld & Nicolson. Reprinted by permission of Patrick Seale Books Limited. • Matthew Arnold. Quoted from *Sohrab and Rustum* by Matthew Arnold in *The Oxford Dictonary of Quotations.* Published by Oxford University Press. • Erwan Bergot. Quotation from *The French Foreign Legion* by Erwan Bergot, translated by Richard Barry. Reprinted by permission of Allen Wingate, Ltd., London. • e.e. cummings. Excerpt from *Him: Three Plays and a Ballet* by e. e. cummings. Reprinted by permission of Peter Owen Ltd., London. • T. S. Eliot. Line from "A Song for Simeon" by T. S. Eliot is reprinted by permission of Harcourt Brace Jovanovich, Inc., from *Collected Poems 1909–1962.* • Ethiopian proverb quoted from *The International Thesaurus of Quotations*, compiled by Rhoda Thomas Tripp. Published by Harper & Row, Publishers, Inc. • Al-Hallaj quoted in *Islam: A Way of Life* by Philip K. Hitti. University of Minnesota Press, Minneapolis. Copyright © 1973 by the University of Minnesota. • Edith Hamilton. Excerpt from *Mythology* by Edith Hamilton. Published by Little, Brown & Co. • Ibn Sa'd quoted by Maxime Rodinson in *Mohammed*, translated by Anne Carter. Reprinted by permission of Les Editions de Seuil, Paris. • *The Iliad* quoted from *The Complete Works of Homer*, translated by Andrew Lang, Walter Leaf and Ernest Myers. Published by Random House, Inc. • Nikos Kazantzakis, quoted from *Report to Greco* by Nikos Kazantzakis. Reprinted by permission of Simon & Schuster, Inc., New York. • The Koran. Excerpts from *The Koran*, translated by N. J. Dawood. Reprinted by permission of Penguin Books Ltd. • Lin Yutang. Grateful acknowledgment is made to Lin Yutang for permission to use his translation of Chia Tao's poem "Searching for the Hermit in Vain," from *My Country and My People*, published by John Day Co. • Samuel Ha-Nagid. Lines from "Wounded Lions" by Samuel Ha-Nagid are reprinted by permission of David Higham Associates Limited from *The Jewish Poets of Spain*, edited and translated by David Goldstein. Published by Penguin Books Ltd. • Jean Rostand. Excerpt from *Pensées d'un biologiste* by Jean Rostand, quoted in *The International Thesaurus of Quotations*, compiled by Rhoda Thomas Tripp. Published by Harper and Row, Publishers, Inc.

Moris Farhi was born in Ankara, Turkey, in 1935 to parents of Greek and
Turkish extraction. The Farhis were descendants of the Jews of Spain who
found refuge from the Inquisition in the Ottoman Empire. Mr. Farhi grew
up speaking Turkish, Greek, Ladino—the old Spanish of the Sephardic
Jews—and French. In 1954, at the age of nineteen, he left home for England where he attended the Royal Academy of Dramatic Art and subsequently worked for several years as an actor. In 1960 he began earning his
living by writing television screenplays, feature films and stage plays, as
well as poetry which has appeared in the anthology *Voices Within the Ark*
and the magazine *Modern Poetry in Translation*. Mr. Farhi has traveled
extensively in Europe, Iceland, Greenland, Ethiopia, the United States,
and South America and has lived in Israel. He lives today in London with
his wife, Nina, and his stepdaughter, Rachel, and is at work on a new novel
set in South America.

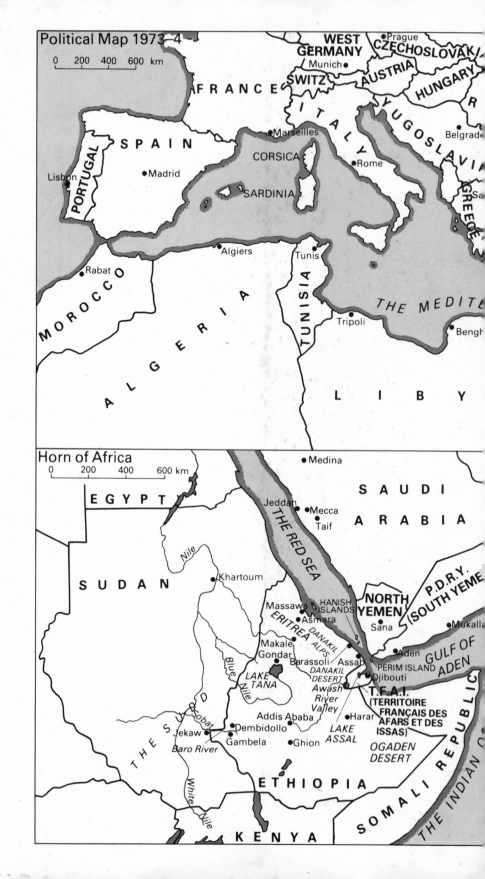

Political Map 1973–4

0 200 400 600 km

PORTUGAL

SPAIN

Lisbon

Madrid

FRANCE

SWITZ

WEST GERMANY

Munich

AUSTRIA

Prague

CZECHOSLOVAKIA

HUNGARY

ITALY

CORSICA

Marseilles

Rome

SARDINIA

YUGOSLAVIA

Belgrade

GREECE

MOROCCO

Rabat

Algiers

ALGERIA

TUNISIA

Tunis

Tripoli

THE MEDITE

Bengh

L   I   B   Y

Horn of Africa

0 200 400 600 km

EGYPT

SUDAN

Nile

Khartoum

Medina

Jeddah

Mecca

Taif

THE RED SEA

SAUDI

ARABIA

P.D.R.Y.

SOUTH YEMEN

NORTH YEMEN

Sana

Mukalla

Massawa

HANISH ISLANDS

Asmara

ERITREA

DANAKIL ALPS

Makale

Gondar

Barassoli

Assab

DANAKIL DESERT

Aden

GULF OF ADEN

PERIM ISLAND

Djibouti

T.F.A.I.
(TERRITOIRE FRANÇAIS DES AFARS ET DES ISSAS)

Blue Nile

LAKE TANA

Awash River Valley

Addis Ababa

Harar

Dembidollo

Ghion

LAKE ASSAL

OGADEN DESERT

Jekaw

Gambela

Baro River

THE SUDD

Sobat

ETHIOPIA

White Nile

KENYA

SOMALI REPUBLIC

THE INDIAN O

REPUBLIC